Praise for Dan and Robert Zangari

"Dan Zangari and Robert Zangari have crafted a superb opening epic to what promises to be a deeply involved and dedicated fantasy series."

—K.C. Finn, Readers' Favorite

"A solid story told in the tradition of older fantasy novels."

— 28th Annual Writer's Digest Self-Published Book Awards

"Absolutely fantastic! [In *A Prince's Errand*] you get those hints of the *Wheel of Time*—that huge epic scale Robert Jordan really tried to produce. You get that sense of majesty with the books that Brandon Sanderson writes. There is a gritty realism to it with something like Robert E. Howard, with threads of David Eddings... [*A Prince's Errand*] is a beautiful, beautiful piece of passion. If you're looking to pick up a book that will keep you hooked for a long, long time, make sure to get this book."

—Cameron Day, Comics, Clerics, & Controllers

"*A Prince's Errand* is an intricately crafted tale of high fantasy that is as rich in detail as it is in entertainment."

—Michael Cole, Design Wizard Blog: Top 50 Wattpad Books of 2018

BY **DAN ZANGARI & ROBERT ZANGARI**
PUBLISHED BY LOK PUBLISHING

TALES OF THE AMULET
A Prince's Errand · I

TALES OF THE AMULET: COMPANION STORIES
A Thief's Way

PREQUEL NOVELS
The Prisoner of Tardalim

Coming Soon...
TALES OF THE AMULET
The Dark Necromancer · II
Elven Secrets · III
The Mages' Agenda · IV
Treachery in the Kingdom · V
The Red Ruby · VI

PREQUEL NOVELS
Fall of the Elves
Extinction of the Lish'sha

TALES OF THE AMULET: COMPANION STORIES
The Last Barsionist
Mysterious Assassin
Return of the Elves
A Forgotten Hero
Guardians of Kalda

DAN ZANGARI & ROBERT ZANGARI

THE PRISONER OF TARDALIM

Prequel Novel One of TALES OF THE AMULET

PUBLISHING

A LOK PUBLISHING BOOK • SALT LAKE CITY

LEGENDS OF KALDA®

Tales of the Amulet

THE PRISONER OF TARDALIM

Hardcover Edition

Made in the U.S.A.

Cover Art by Kerem Beyit
Chapter Heading Illustrations by Suleyman Temiz
Cartography by Robert Zangari

Edited by Linda Branam

First Printing: June 1st,2021
First Paperback Edition: November 30th, 2021

ISBN 10-digit: 1-947673-14-9

ISBN 13- digit: 978-1-947673-14-4

Visit our web site at www.legendsofkalda.com

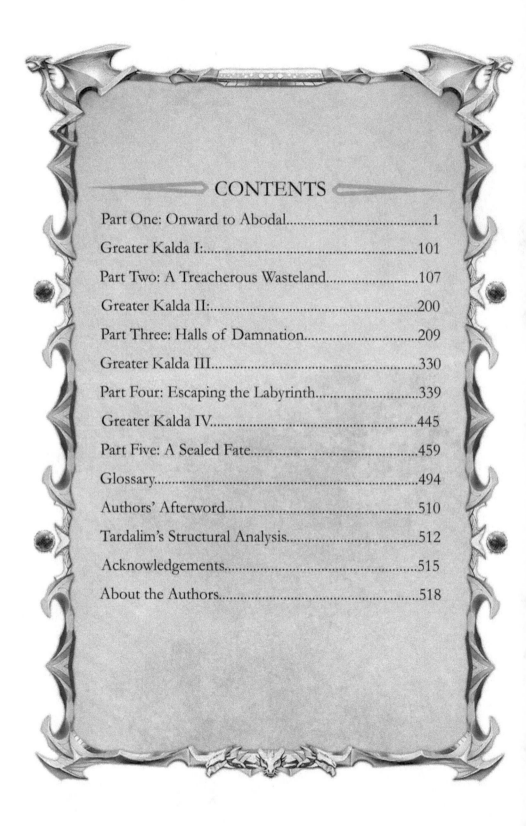

CONTENTS

For Dave,

Who helped us

Hone our craft.

Thank you for imparting your wisdom

And knowledge.

You've truly been

A wonderful mentor.

Bradisar

CARDA WASTES
(Terrain Unknown)

THE BLACK MOUNTAINS

Duras

COMDOLITH
Crimdor
HIGH VALLEY

Kardorth

Cordan
Karthar
MALTIN

THE ELVEN REALM
(Topography Estimated)
Merath

CORDATH
New Sorjin
Mitorn

LITOR
Litlim

KILDATH
Kildath

SEA OF
KORATH

TILSANA GULF

LOSIAN GULF

TURBULANT SEA

KALADORN
Estrom

KERINDOR
Kerlaris

Alath

Los

GASTRIM
Gastrim

KINGDOM OF LOS
Arbath

WESTERN SOVEREIGNTY

HENDEN
Henden

MELAR FOREST

Tor
Monddar

MINDOLARN EMPIRE
Mindolarn

KLIS
Klis

Klath

ALGIN GULF
Hilarn

Korum

HOLORUM

DENDRIM ISLES

KALISHIR OCEAN

ISLE OF
MERDAN

Keth

CARTH

CANTIR ISLES

NEMDAR ISLANDS

PRINCIPALITY OF SOROTH

Soroth

UNITED ISLES OF DAMNIR

The Worl
(ANOMALO

ISLE OF KENDA

ABODINE
WASTELAND

KALDA

CIRCA 6,793 C.D.

10 20 30 40 50 60 70 80 90 100
Length in Hundred Grand Phineals

Nyesil

THE FORSAKEN LANDS OF
AZRIN'II

Xilarim
DALISIN
CONFEDERACY   Osivir   DESERT OF
                                      ASH
Dalistim

SILRLAIN OCEAN   OCEAN OF TEMPESTS

Veir   Bithar
ACHEYLON
Arithan   IGEACEAN SEA

RUINED KINGDOMS OF
KRESH'DAL

THE FORBIDDEN LANDS
                              DESOLATE LANDS

                              SEA OF SAND

Rignuian Peninsula

              PEGALIC SEA

ABODAL

CIRCA 6,437 C.D.

10 20 30 40 50 60 70 80

Length in Hundred Grand Pliineals

The World's Frown
(Anaxandrus Corridor)

RUINED KINGDOMS OF KRESH'DAL
(The Forsaken Lands)

Abna Gulf

Voaganu

ESHARIAN COLLECTIVE

Arkh'ongr

Mainkar

Varquaha

Ulares

Wira'anim

Tirabai'acul

Lake Vaslizan

Dazali

Lake Nallian

Darmalna

Talchten

Talgossa Ice Shelf

Talatain'ashaar

R'omvinl

Vandaxa

NARSHAR PLAINS

Qanachcia

Terran Mountains

Parim'luz

Shari Forest

Yubinvdel

Tirdalim

Lake Cauleda

Ignalist

Calnassora

Bal'afdear

Fariubin'val

PLAINS OF VAGON

Paxebin'luz

Kaluxia

Valhla

PACIFIC OCEAN

PICALIC SEA

KALSHER

Tafchin's Fingers

Gallowrid Gulf

Lake Colkisan

OCEAN

PRINCIPALITY OF SOROTH

Bathirul
(The Desolate Lands)

MAP KEY

- Ice Shelf Coastline
- Arctic Land Coastline
- Ocean
- Ice Shelf
- Ice Lakes and Shores
- Ice Rivers
- Arctic Land
- Non-arctic Coastline
- Mountains
- Gorges & Canyons
- Non-arctic Land
- ⊙ Capitols
- ○ Cities
- □ Fortresses
- ▣ Ruined or Deserted Cities

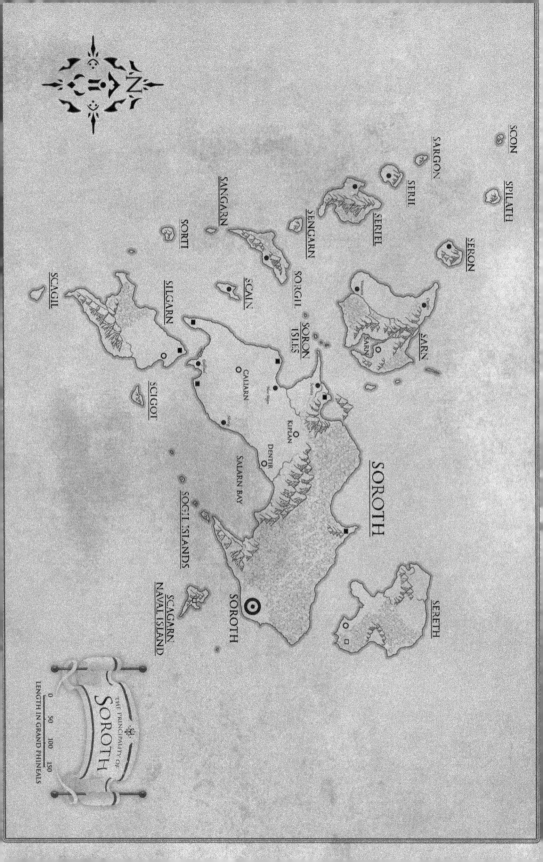

Once reserved for mortal men, gods were banished in their stead.
Held within a cage of gold, in shifting halls of gleaming stone.
Bound with burning in their bones, in Tardalim deep below.

Hellish things watch the gate, ne'er to let the righteous through.
Try they might for all delight, but none shall make it to the halls.
Blood and death will welcome them, in Tardalim deep below.

For none escape its wretched grasp, no god nor man nor thing between.
All who enter never leave, forever chained in misery.
Held for all eternity, in Tardalim deep below.

—From Niza Hiram's *Realm of Sorrow*

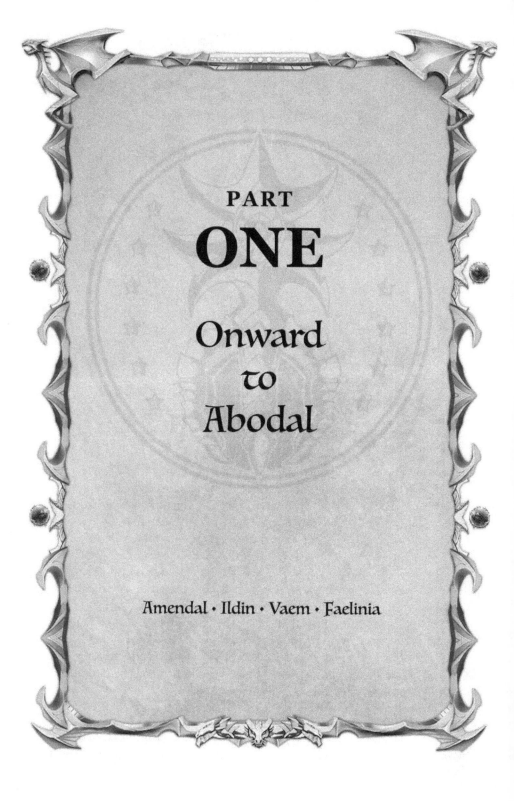

PART
ONE

Onward to Abodal

Amendal · Ildin · Vaem · Faelinia

1

A HOMECOMING
OF SORTS

"If I were to pick the most practical of conjurations, I would have to choose the quinta'shal. Some of you might recognize them by their layman's name, mages' parasite."

- From *Colvinar Vrium's Bestiary for Conjurers*, page 9

6,437 C.D.

The familiar sight of Soroth lifted a weight from Amendal Aramien. He slumped against the portside rail of the *White Duchess,* breathing deeply. Waves crashed against the hull, spraying the rail and wetting the sleeves of his charcoal-colored robe, but he didn't care. The waves were soothing. His nine-month trip to and from the Kingdom of Los had been exhausting. *Trip* was probably not the best word to describe the Aramien Test of Valor, his family's deadly trial deep within the perilous Melar Forest.

"Home at last," he whispered, running a hand through his wavy light-brown hair. It hung past his ears. *Completely unacceptable*, he thought. Amendal liked his hair short, neatly cropped. His scraggly beard also needed trimming.

When properly groomed, Amendal often turned heads when walking through crowds or taverns. When his beard was trimmed, it highlighted his strong jawline. His lips were a perfect balance between thick and thin, and women *loved* to kiss them. Like most Sorothians, Amendal's skin was a light olive—a great backdrop for his brilliant green eyes.

If Amendal had one flaw it was the divot beneath the bridge of his nose. It looked as if it had been broken, though Amendal never recalled breaking it in all his twenty-one years. He didn't mind the nose. No man could be *perfect*. He would rather have a slightly misshapen nose than be short and fat.

Sailors shouted across the main deck, giving orders to adjust the ship's heading. Three deckhands brushed past Amendal, running to the three-masted rigging of the ship. Sails were furled. Lines were tightened. But Amendal paid little attention to their adjustments. He was home, and that was all that mattered.

He shaded his eyes as he gazed to the sun, now descending toward the eastern horizon. Then he turned back to the city of Soroth, which spread across the western horizon.

The *White Duchess* would probably moor in an hour. *Three hours past noon.* He smiled, pleased with the timing. He looked forward to celebrating his survival at one of the most notorious taverns in Soroth, the Sea Vistonia. Normally, the Sea Vistonia was crowded, but midafternoon was one of the less crowded times to dine.

Amendal took another deep breath, recalling the savory taste of the serinian served at the Sea Vistonia. The yellow-fleshed fish was exquisite, especially when seasoned properly. The thought of it made him grin. *I can't wait!*

Finally, the *White Duchess* docked along Pier Twenty-Three, the second northernmost pier of the city.

Once the vessel came to a halt, Amendal grabbed his only belongings—a brown pack and a thick coat. Both were made from the fur of a sloglien, a beast that lived in the northern reaches of Kalda. The rarest, highest quality fabrics woven from sloglien strands could slow a piercing blow from a dagger. Amendal's coat and pack were made of a moderate weave, but the coat kept him plenty warm, and the pack had held many a sharp object without the slightest hint of fraying.

Amendal slung his pack over his shoulder as he crossed the main deck. The early fall weather was far too warm for the coat. He had needed it in Melar, since the woodland was in Kalda's northern hemisphere.

As Amendal neared the gangway, someone behind him shouted his name. He turned as the first mate, Alberous Kenard, jogged toward him. "I'm glad I caught you, Mister Aramien. My father and I wanted to wish you well."

"Thank you," Amendal said, his tone cordial. "I appreciate your hospitality. You and your father have a fine ship." Indeed, the *White Duchess* was probably the most luxurious vessel Amendal had ever traveled upon. And it was incredibly fast. The voyage from Klath to Soroth had only taken fifteen days instead of the usual twenty-seven.

Alberous smiled, nodding once. "If you ever find yourself in need of travel arrangements, feel free to charter us again."

"I'll remember that," Amendal said. "There are more parts of this world I'd like to explore."

"Do you fancy yourself an adventurer, then?"

The first mate undoubtedly suspected Amendal was like other young Sorothians who scoured the far reaches of Kalda in search of ancient wonders: rare gems and metals, relics, and tevisrals. It was a recent fad many had taken to. Tevisrals could manifest magic at a single touch or at a verbal command. Some of them constantly emitted magic. Men and women sold kingdoms for tevisrals, especially those who had no magical talent.

Amendal shook his head. "No, my interests don't concern relics, or gold, or rumored tevisrals. I am a conjurer, and I find the creatures of our world a far grander prize to obtain."

Alberous cocked his head, taken aback, but grinned with approval. "Well, I hope our paths cross again. Good day, Mister Aramien."

"Safe sailing," Amendal said, and descended the gangway.

Pier Twenty-Three was crowded, and Amendal pushed his way toward land. The pier was six blocks south of the Sea Vistonia, but he had to go inland a bit before turning north. He passed an assortment of merchants peddling their wares from fancy carts.

Amendal ignored their blandishments and hurried through the street leading from the docks. The crowd of merchants lessened, but there was still plenty of traffic on the street.

After traveling a few blocks from the pier, Amendal turned down an alleyway. His stomach grumbled, and he increased his gait to nearly a run. He was almost through the alley when a barrel ahead of him shifted.

An ambush? Muggings weren't uncommon in Soroth. *Perhaps I shouldn't have taken a shortcut...*

He halted abruptly and dropped into a wide stance, preparing to summon a conjuration. A frail boy rose from behind the barrel. "Oh sir," the boy said, his voice timid. "Please, do you have anything to eat?"

Amendal sighed with relief, eyeing the urchin. The boy was clothed in rags, his dark hair in tangles, his face dirty. *What an unfortunate sight...*

"I don't have any food," Amendal said, reaching into his pack. "But I can give you some money." He found his coin purse and rummaged through the few dozen coins. He had only taken Losian currency with him on the trip, since any Sorothian coin wouldn't have exchanged well.

Nothing smaller than a dorin... Amendal turned to the urchin, who was now standing a few paces away. "All I have are dorins," he said, his face stern. "From Los."

The boy frowned, undoubtedly knowing the coin's worth. Dorins were the standard coin of the Kingdom of Los, the denomination by which the other coins were measured. Typically, one could buy a month's-worth of food with a dorin.

"I see..." the boy said, despondent, then turned to his barrel.

"Wait!" Amendal shouted, extending a hand. "I didn't say I wouldn't give it to you."

The ragged boy staggered. "You... you can't give me that. If anyone found out, I—"

Amendal pulled a dorin from his purse and approached the boy. "Just be smart about it," he said, grabbing the boy's hand. He pressed the coin into the urchin's palm, then closed the youth's fingers around it. "If any merchant asks you about where you got it, tell them the son of Arenil Aramien gave it to you."

Tears welled in the boy's eyes, and his lips quivered. "Thank you," he murmured. "Thank you!"

Smiling, Amendal continued through the alleyway.

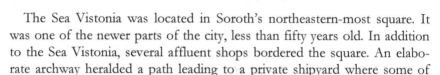

The Sea Vistonia was located in Soroth's northeastern-most square. It was one of the newer parts of the city, less than fifty years old. In addition to the Sea Vistonia, several affluent shops bordered the square. An elaborate archway heralded a path leading to a private shipyard where some of the city's upper crust moored their vessels.

Amendal hurried through the square, passing ornate horse-drawn carriages. Despite the time of day, the square was still crowded.

I hope the wait isn't long, he thought, and a pang of hunger struck him.

Amendal mounted the short flight of steps that led to a covered porch along the northern side of the building. The porch was built as an overflow for waiting patrons. Several dozen people could stand there and admire the beautiful seaside view.

Amendal, however, paid little attention to the view. Once at the double doors, he nearly threw them open.

Alarmed gasps filled the foyer, coming from the patrons seated beside the door. The host—standing at a podium several paces ahead—gave Amendal a disdainful glare. He and several patrons studied Amendal disapprovingly.

Probably don't like my beard, Amendal thought, sauntering toward the podium. "A table for one," he said, grinning. "Or a seat at the bar."

The host drew his lips to a line, and his eyes narrowed. "You don't look like the type of person who frequents our establishment."

"Oh, you think I'm too scraggily-looking?" Amendal chuckled.

The Sea Vistonia was a prestigious place, and Amendal knew that. He had made sure he and his clothes were clean before leaving the *White Duchess.* One of the luxuries of the Kenards' vessel was a fully functional bathing area. But he hadn't thought his overgrown appearance would be a problem.

"Nothing?" Amendal asked, but the host didn't reply. "Very well..." He sighed and pulled out his coin purse, opening it for the host to see its contents. "As you can see, I *can* pay. I'm not some vagrant. Now will you please put me down for one seat?" He tapped the ledger on the podium. "The name is Amendal Aramien."

The host started, blinking rapidly as his eyes widened.

That got you... Amendal grinned.

Several of the patrons in the foyer whispered to one another, though Amendal couldn't quite hear what they were saying.

"You…" the host muttered, "you're Master Arenil's son?"

Amendal nodded, and the host scribbled on the ledger.

Pleased with himself, Amendal stepped away from the podium. There was no place to sit in the foyer. As Amendal turned to the doors, a familiar voice called his name. It belonged to none other than his dearest friend, Ildin Cetarin.

Amendal spun from the doors, searching the tavern's dining area for his friend.

Ildin was lanky, standing slightly shorter than Amendal. His dark-blonde hair was combed over, hanging over his right ear—Amendal could never style his hair like that. A silver lock ran through Ildin's hair, aligned with his left eye. He also wore a goatee and mustache. His facial hair, however, did not completely surround his thin lips.

"It *is* you!" Ildin cried, weaving around tables full of patrons, his sapphire eyes gleaming with excitement.

A throaty laugh left Amendal's mouth, and he threw his hands into the air. "Ildin, my friend!"

Ildin hurried past the podium, and the two friends embraced, pounding each other's backs. Ildin pulled away, and clasped Amendal's arms.

"Look at you!" he exclaimed, smiling. "You look like a vagabond!" He studied Amendal for a moment, then his expression became somber. "I almost thought I wouldn't see you again… We were all worried. I mean, it only took your brother six months to complete your father's Test."

Amendal waggled his finger at his friend. "Come now, Ildin. Did you really think that forest could claim me?"

Ildin shrugged, and Amendal laughed again.

"Why don't we move outside," Ildin suggested, nodding toward the door.

Several of the patrons were whispering and eyeing Amendal with annoyance. "Fine with me," he said, then spun and threw one of the doors open.

The hushed chatter trailed behind Amendal and Ildin but ceased once the doors were closed.

Ildin leaned against the railing opposite the doors, staring at the view split between the forest and the ocean. Amendal joined his friend at the rail.

"You know," Ildin said, "I've been coming here every day for the last three months. Each day I sit at the bar and have a drink, asking the barman and the serving wenches if they've seen you." He glanced at Amendal. "I didn't start worrying till last month." Ildin turned back to the view, sighing.

"Every day, huh?" Amendal asked. "I thought you were assisting Master…" He fumbled for the name. "What's-his-name with those illusionist acolytes."

Ildin nodded. "Master Vigarian. Yes, I am assisting him, but he has a small class in the afternoon. So I have a few free hours before dinner."

"Aha!" Amendal nodded. "That's his name… Vigarian." He said the name slowly, which made Ildin laugh for some reason.

"Have you been home yet?" Ildin asked.

Amendal shook his head. "I literally just stepped off a ship less than half an hour ago."

"So I had good timing," Ildin said, patting Amendal on the shoulder. "I suppose you haven't heard much of what's going on in the world?"

Amendal shook his head. "Not really. Once I was out of Melar, I headed straight for Klath. The day I arrived, I was lucky enough to find a ship bound for Soroth. And the only news I heard was that the rebels in Tor had regained more territory."

Tor—the capitol of the Western Sovereignty—had once been part of the Mindolarn Empire, annexed some fifty years ago. Its citizens had not been happy about their forced fealty. Who would? Insurrection had brewed ever since. Eventually, the rebels regained their capitol city and began reclaiming their lands.

"That's it?" Ildin asked. "And here I thought the Losians would be celebrating..."

"Celebrating what?"

"The death of Emperor Mentas," Ildin said, his voice grim. "He was slain three months ago."

Amendal's eyes widened. Emperor Mentas was the supreme ruler of the Mindolarn Empire—one of the most powerful nations on Kalda. Mentas had been crowned emperor after his brother's demise eleven years before, since in the Mindolarn Empire the monarchy passed from brother to brother.

"Who is responsible for the emperor's death?" Amendal asked.

Ildin didn't answer.

"Was it the rebels?"

Ildin nodded, but didn't speak. He looked around for a moment, then glanced toward the doors. Amendal followed his gaze, but no one was around. Was Ildin worried that someone might overhear their conversation?

"They're calling him the Hero of the West," Ildin said. "I wouldn't be surprised if they started calling him Emperor Slayer."

Huh? Amendal wondered. *Emperor Slayer?* "Who are you talking about?"

Ildin gave Amendal a hard look.

After considering the identity of this Hero of the West, it came to him. "You're not talking about your sister's *husband*, are you?" He said the word *husband* with a hint of jealousy.

Ildin nodded curtly.

For the longest time, Amendal had yearned for Ildin's beautiful sister, Gwenyth, whose unmatched finesse when mustering illusory magic added to her allure. She was one of the most masterful illusionists in all of Soroth. Unfortunately for Amendal, Gwenyth was also ten years his senior.

By the time Amendal was old enough to consider a relationship with her, Gwenyth had relocated to Tor when the rebels took back the city. Not the typical Sorothian, she thought the Mindolarnian oppression of Tor's people was an atrocity. Gwenyth joined the rebels, working to take back the rest of their former country. It was then that she met her husband, a grand mage from Alath.

They had married nearly a year ago.

"And that's not the worst of it." Ildin sighed. "Emperor Medis has proclaimed retribution against Mentas's murderers, and their families."

Amendal frowned.

Ildin sighed again. "There's more… Shortly after you left, my parents received a letter from Gwenyth." He took a deep breath. "She was pregnant."

Amendal's eyes bulged.

Ildin stared at Amendal for a moment before continuing. "Throughout her pregnancy we received more letters. Last week she wrote us and included a sketched likeness of my newborn nephew." He blinked several times. "I'm an uncle, Amendal"—his voice quivered—"and I'll probably never meet my nephew…"

How horrible, Amendal thought, studying his friend. Ildin looked devastated, his eyes filling with tears, and Amendal wrapped an arm around his friend.

"What's his name?" Amendal asked.

Ildin wiped his eyes. "They decided to use the familial 'il.' I'm sure my sister insisted," Ildin said. "They named him Iltar."

Amendal nodded approvingly. "A good name."

They continued staring at the picturesque scenery for a while, not speaking at all. The silence was eventually interrupted by a squeaky hinge.

"Your table is ready, Mister Aramien," the host said.

Amendal turned to Ildin. "Care to join me? It will be my treat."

Ildin shook his head. "I better get back to the Order. We have a lot of things we're… dealing with. And we don't have a lot of time."

"Oh, you can't leave on that note," Amendal said. "What is the Order *dealing* with?"

Ildin forced a smile. "That's probably something you should discuss with your father. I'll see you tomorrow."

With that, Ildin strode across the porch and soon disappeared into the square.

Uneasy, Amendal set his jaw. *Something I should discuss with my father—?*

"Are you still coming, Mister Aramien?"

Amendal nodded and headed inside.

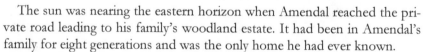

The sun was nearing the eastern horizon when Amendal reached the private road leading to his family's woodland estate. It had been in Amendal's family for eight generations and was the only home he had ever known.

Home at last! Amendal smiled, quickening his gait.

Insects chirped all along the path. Lightstone-lit lampposts lined the paved road, dispelling shadows cast by vast trees. The road wound back and forth before emptying into a large, oblong grove nearly twenty phedans in size, an area equal to five city blocks.

At the heart of the grove sat the Aramien estate house.

The estate house was more than just a home. Some people might have considered it a small palace. Dark-brown stone covered much of the lavish abode, and several walls were covered with fine beige plaster. Windows lined much of the estate house, with lightstone-lit candelabras on their sills. The house was wider than it was deep, with east and west wings. It rose three stories in some places, with steep, peaked roofs. There was a fourth floor, but most of it was contained within the roof. The only windows on those floors were dormers. Several turrets rose from the rooftops, each topped with golden statues depicting menacing creatures.

Amendal became giddy upon seeing his family's home. He dashed down the private road and whooped triumphantly as he neared the seven-tiered fountain in front of the house, throwing a fist into the air.

Hopefully that gets someone's attention, he thought, rounding the fountain.

A horse let out a sudden whinny.

Not what I intended... He glanced to his right, where a horse-drawn carriage was parked within the coach gateway leading to the stables. The horse whinnied again, stamping its hooves.

"Whoa!" Amendal cried, attempting to sooth the horse. "It's all right. I'm just excited to be home, that's all."

Amendal examined the carriage from afar, trying to glean a clue as to his family's guests. A red emblem was painted on the carriage door, but it was partially obscured. *Are those tentacles, or snakes?* He couldn't recall which nobles of the Principality had a red emblem for a crest.

The horse quieted, and Amendal continued toward the home's main entrance. The path leading to the large portico was lined with golden statues of the great serpentine creatures from various myths and legends, dragons.

Shadows danced across the parlor's windows. His father must be entertaining in there.

Amendal expected someone to open the ornate double doors before he reached them, but they were still shut when he grabbed the knob.

"Odd," he muttered, twisting the right knob—his father always kept the left one locked. The door clicked open, and Amendal stepped inside.

A hushed conversation carried from the parlor, the words indistinguishable. He recognized his father's strong voice but not the other, a woman's sultry tones.

Amendal closed the door behind him, expecting his father to step out of the parlor. *Did he not hear the door?* Confused, Amendal opened the door again and shut it louder than before, turning expectantly to the parlor's archway.

The conversation ceased and was replaced by footsteps.

Then Amendal's father stepped into the archway. If Amendal had ever wondered what he would look like in his old age, he needed to look no farther than his father.

Arenil Aramien stood in the archway, dumbfounded by the sight of his son. It was as if Amendal had stepped through a portal directly into the foyer.

"Did you think I was dead, too?" Amendal asked.

The surprise on Arenil's face was replaced with delight. "You... you made it!" Arenil exclaimed, hurrying across the foyer. He nearly tackled Amendal and held him tight. Amendal felt something trickle down his neck. *Were those tears?*

Arenil pulled back, but held onto Amendal. "Oh, my son...You're alive! A little scraggily, but alive nonetheless. Tell me, did you succeed?"

Amendal nodded and was about to elaborate when the visitor entered the foyer, a tall and slender woman. She wore a crimson blouse and tight pants of the same color, with matching boots. On her right hand was a single blood-red glove adorned with silver rivets, with a silver band rimming its cuff. Her hair was the deepest black and cascaded almost to her waist, framing her thin face. She had a sharp nose and tiny lips. Her face was made up, with eye shadow that accented her striking violet eyes.

Violet eyes? He had never seen a Sorothian—or anyone else from the Principality—with violet eyes. In fact, the only people he knew with strangely colored eyes were Mindolarnians...

Ah! The emblem on the carriage., Amendal's eyes widened with enlightenment. *It was the Mindolarnian Crest, the seven-headed hydra.*

Arenil cleared his throat, and Amendal turned to his father.

"It is not polite to stare, Amendal," he said, and the woman chuckled at the rebuke.

Amendal, however, was annoyed. Did his father think him a child still?

"Why don't you join us," Arenil said, sauntering back to the parlor. "What we're discussing concerns you, now that you've returned."

What did his father mean by that?

"Oh, forgive me," Arenil said, gesturing to the woman. "This is Vaem Rudal."

Vaem inclined her head. "It is a pleasure to meet you, Amendal."

"Vaem is a senior member of the Hilinard," Arenil said. "She specializes in tevisral research."

The Hilinard? Amendal thought. *So she is a Mindolarnian.*

But why was a Mindolarnian visiting with his father? Had it something to do with what Ildin had mentioned concerning the Order? Strange, if so. Although the Principality of Soroth was allied with the Mindolarn Empire, the Hilinard and the Sorothian Magical Order rarely worked with each other.

"I don't know if you have heard," Arenil said, "but the Mindolarn Empire has suffered a devastating blow. About a week ago Vaem came to the Order's council, seeking our aid in a matter she and her superiors believe will turn the tide of this war with the Western Sovereignty."

"Oh?" Amendal asked. He hoped he could hide his contempt. After his conversation with Ildin, he wasn't the most sympathetic to the Mindolarnians and their plight.

Arenil pursed his lips and studied his son before continuing. "Vaem and several others are putting together an expedition to the Abodine Wasteland. They have learned of an ancient reliquary rumored to house tevisrals of mythical power. From what they've discovered, the place is called Tardalim."

Amendal stifled a laugh. *Tardalim?* Tardalim was supposed to be the realm of eternal suffering, though it had other names, too: the Halls of the Damned, the Never-ending Labyrinth. Many religions claimed the impenitent were sent there after death to endure eternal suffering, although Amendal didn't believe that.

But Tardalim? "Who in their right mind would name a reliquary after that hellish place?"

Arenil narrowed his eyes at Amendal, apparently not amused by his son's scoffing. "Those of us on the Order's council took a vote," Arenil said. "And we believe it is in the best interests of both Mindolarn and Soroth to embark on this venture. What Vaem and I were discussing tonight was a list of individuals who had not yet agreed to join the expedition, but who were otherwise available.

"You, my son," Arenil said, gazing into Amendal's eyes, "are now on that list."

"The quinta'shals are versatile creatures. Their strength is formidable against non-magic-wielding combatants. I once held two men with only one conjuration. I probably could have subdued a third if one were present, using my conjuration's mammoth tongue."

- From *Colvinar Vrium's Bestiary for Conjurers*, page 10

Amendal could not believe what he was hearing. *Conscription? Among the mages of the Sorothian Magical Order... How absurd!* He blinked in horror as his father explained the reasoning behind the council's decision.

"... is a time of war, my son," Arenil said. "As allies of the empire, Soroth has been at war since before you were born. The Principality has lent aid to the Mindolarnian war effort well before there was ever any need.

"But now times are different. Our allies are in need, and they require more than just soldiers. I'm sorry that you don't agree, but these are the circumstances in which we live. We cannot change them."

Amendal furrowed his brow. Now he understood why Gwenyth had left Soroth all those years ago.

"This really is not a dangerous task," Vaem chimed in. "Do not let the name of the reliquary frighten you. It will be a simple expedition."

Amendal shot her an annoyed glance. Her words did not sound sincere. "People die while exploring the world all the time," he said. "And why can't *you* people go yourselves?"

Vaem's lips twisted in an awkward smile. She studied Amendal, but Arenil was the one who spoke.

"Mindolarnian forces are already strained on the battlefield. The rebels of the Western Sovereignty have received reinforcements from the Losians, as well as from other nations on the Mainland. Our allies do not have the resources to commit to an expedition."

Amendal sighed. He would have been better off staying in the Melar Forest. Those wilds were more appealing.

"Besides, we are not helping them without gain," Arenil added.

"Really?" Amendal scoffed. "And what do *we* get out of it?"

His father studied him for a moment. Arenil looked as if he were biting his tongue. Though Amendal and his father loved each other, they often clashed when it came to matters aside from the magical arts. "Every member of the expedition will be well compensated for their time. Those who go will earn more than enough to live on for a few years."

"So money…" Amendal nodded and began pacing through the parlor. "I probably have more in my purse"—he patted his bag—"than what I'd earn for tagging along."

Arenil did not look amused. "My son, this is far greater than you. If you only look at what your immediate gain will be, you will lose out on the greater purpose of things. That is a lesson you should learn early in life."

Still treating me like a child, Amendal thought, shaking his head.

"I'm sorry, Father, but I have more important things to do than chase treasure."

Vaem laughed, and Amendal shot her another annoyed glance, but he started upon seeing those violet eyes. There was something eerie about them.

"Oh, you spoiled boy," Vaem said. "You really have no choice in the matter."

Amendal raised an eyebrow at her. He was about to open his mouth to rebuke her when footsteps echoed from the foyer. Amendal turned, waiting for the owner of those footsteps. They belonged to none other than his elder brother.

Arintil walked straight-backed, a paragon of propriety. He looked much like Amendal, but had their mother's coloring—fair skin and blonde hair. And his eyes were more hazel than green. Despite a four-year gap, some people thought the brothers were twins. Perhaps if they had been, they would have gotten along better.

"Well, well," Arintil said with a smile, eyeing Amendal. "I thought I heard whining, and here you are." He entered the parlor, spreading his arms in a mock greeting. "Welcome home, brother."

Arintil did not come any closer. He expected Amendal to come to him.

Typical. "Thank you, brother," Amendal said, biting back a bitter tone.

"You know, we all thought you were dead." Arintil ambled through the parlor toward Arenil. "It doesn't take nine months to travel to Arbath, stroll through the Melar Forest, and return home."

Amendal glanced to Vaem, who didn't look the least surprised. His father must have told her where he had been. *Odd,* Amendal thought. Though the Aramien Test of Valor was an old tradition that dated back generations, it was rarely discussed with non-family members.

"Did you even encounter a gangolin?" Arintil asked.

"Would I return if I hadn't?" Amendal demanded. He glimpsed Vaem nodding in approval.

"Avoiding the question?" Arintil smirked. "So typical, Amendal... Let me guess. You spent your time carousing with Losian women, and this unkempt look was *purposely* assumed to make it seem like you traversed that forbidden forest..."

Amendal shook his head, rolling his eyes. *You insolent twit...*

"I just want to hear you say it, brother. Did you or did you not—"

"That's enough, Arintil," said their father with a firm tone.

Arintil subsided with a petulant look at Amendal.

"Sometimes you two act like children." Arenil sighed and turned to Vaem. "I'm sorry you had to witness that."

Vaem grinned, nodding casually.

"Now back to the matter at hand," Arenil said, looking to Amendal. "I urge you to reconsider. The consequences for refusing are not to be taken lightly."

Amendal pursed his lips. He hated being forced into a situation, and this *conscription* was no exception.

"Let me explain it plainly, brother," Arintil said. "In the morning you will receive an official summons from Grandmaster Secarin. Its contents will notify you of your participation in this joint venture with the Mindolarn Empire. That document will outline your compensation, while also disclosing the possible punishments for evading or refusing the summons. *If* you refuse, you will be stricken from the Order. You will be forbidden to practice magic within the borders of the Principality and barred from teaching anyone, under punishment of the current laws. If it is deemed that your participation would be integral to the expedition's success, a fine will be levied against you, as well as a sentence to jail time."

Amendal could not believe what he was hearing. What had happened in his absence? This was not the Soroth he remembered.

Arintil continued with his trite discourse, but Amendal ignored him.

This was not what Amendal had planned for himself after he returned home. He had imagined devoting himself to the conjuration arts. With the Aramien Test of Valor complete, his father would acknowledge Amendal as a full-fledged Aramien Conjurer, and he would be granted access to the tomes kept by his family that detailed the greater aspects of the Conjuration Channel of Magic. In those tomes were kept the greater secrets of the Aldinal Plane and the Visirm Expanse.

When starting their training, young conjurers primarily accessed the Aldinal Plane, a plane of reality containing raw matter, to manifest objects and creatures. Certain incantations manifested certain things. In order to diversify those conjurations, conjurers needed only to expand their repertory of incantations. Though these conjurations were readily accessible, they were not as durable as objects inherent to Kalda. But if destroyed, those conjurations could be summoned again.

The Visirm Expanse was different. It was a timeless void used by conjurers to trap creatures and objects they wished to summon at a future time. When a conjurer opened a portal to the Visirm Expanse, they either pulled creatures or objects into it or out of it. Anything inside the Visirm Expanse was untouched by time. Creatures kept there did not age; objects did not decay. But, when they were removed from the Expanse, they were subject to the entropy of the world. Creatures released from the Expanse required an enthralling component, or they would run amok. If a conjurer's concentration was spread thin, their minions might break free. A conjurer also risked losing the creature or object permanently, due to death or destruction.

Some conjurers dedicated themselves to one plane or the other. But Aramien Conjurers followed the Taidactin Code, an ancient methodology that utilized both planes. The ideals of the Taidactin Code sought to overcome the inherent weaknesses of both disciplines. They enabled conjurers to access the creatures and objects they had trapped within the Visirm Expanse by using the replicating power of the Aldinal Plane.

A combined portal from both planes manifested conjurations that were durable and replaceable, within limits: Only one copy of the trapped object or creature could be manifested at a time.

"… he's not even listening," Arintil retorted.

Amendal snapped from his reverie, seeing the anger on his brother's face.

"Your diatribe was boring me," Amendal said.

Arintil shook his head in disgust. "My *diatribes* are for your benefit, brother. You have not learned to take responsibility for yourself. Father and Mother will not always be around to take care of you. And I certainly won't coddle you!"

"Arintil…" Arenil touched his son's arm.

"I've tried to tell you, brother," Arintil said harshly, "you need to take responsibility for your life. You can't always be dabbling in the arts while carousing with loose women.

"I hope this expedition teaches you something, brother. I'd hoped you might return from the Test a better man, but you're still a spoiled brat."

As Arenil opened his mouth to rebuke his eldest son, Amendal shook his head, balling his fists. "Why don't we settle this like men…? I'll show you *exactly* what my time in Melar taught—"

"That's enough!" Arenil shouted, his voice near shaking the room. "Arintil, leave us be."

Arintil glanced at his father, then strode from the parlor.

Oh, I'm not done with you yet, brother… Amendal growled, stomping after Arintil.

"No, Amendal," Arenil said sternly. "Our talk is not finished."

Amendal stopped at the archway leading to the foyer. He turned around, breathing raggedly. If he were to stay, he had to regain a somewhat calm demeanor.

"Vaem, will you leave us for a moment?" Arenil asked in a pleasant tone.

The Mindolarnian nodded and left the parlor, following the path Arintil had taken.

Once Vaem was gone, Arenil slumped into an oversized armchair. "I'm sorry, my son. I know you had other expectations, but they will have to be put aside for now." Arenil studied Amendal for a moment before continuing. "It is just one expedition. Think of it that way."

Amendal shook his head, pacing once again through the parlor. "Where there is one, there are two…"

"Then take an apprentice," Arenil said through clenched teeth. "Amendal, there is no way to get out of this situation short of assuming other obligations."

Amendal groaned inwardly. *I knew you would say that.*

"If you agree to that, perhaps there is something I can do. You could stay here and continue pursuing your passion. I know it's not exactly what you want. But, the sooner you learn that life is full of compromises, the better it'll be for you."

Amendal sighed. *More lectures… Thank you, Father.*

"There is a boy that I have in mind," Arenil said. "He's about ten, and studying to be a necromancer. But he has some aspirations of becoming a dualist mage. If you were to take him as an apprentice, I might be able to persuade the council to waive your participation in this expedition."

"*Might?*" Amendal asked tersely. "Where there is one apprentice there will be another, and another." If Amendal accepted an apprentice now, the Order would bog down his time with teaching. That would be worse than going out adventuring. Amendal had no intention of becoming a teacher, especially to children. He might consider taking an adult as *an* apprentice, but not for many years.

"Amendal, if you don't go, they *will* expel you from the Order. I do not want that for my son." Arenil sighed, glancing to the foyer.

Amendal continued pacing. What else was there to say? They would argue all night until one of them fainted. He shook his head at the thought, then felt a tug at his arm. His father was standing beside him, his face close.

"Amendal, you have great potential. Of my two sons, you are the greater skilled."

Amendal shook his head. "You're just saying that."

"No… Your passion will drive you to greatness. One day you will far surpass Arintil. Your brother only continues his training in the magical arts because he *must* do it, because he is an Aramien. You *want* to do it. Even if you weren't born an Aramien, I can see you striving to become the greatest conjurer to walk the face of Kalda."

Amendal was taken aback.

"If you go with the Mindolarnians now, I promise I will find a way for you to fulfill your dreams and ambitions."

"Just this once?" Amendal asked, though his position hadn't changed.

Arenil nodded. "And I'll let you take transcriptions and notes from the family tomes on the expedition."

That's unusual, Amendal thought. No one besides those deemed worthy were permitted to see the contents of those tomes. "And when is this expedition to *hell* set to leave?" he asked, though he was not truly interested.

"In three days."

Three days? Amendal thought. "I don't know, Father..."

Arenil put a hand on Amendal's shoulder. "Just think about it. You don't have to come to a decision right this moment. I will tell the council you'll make your decision before the expedition sets sail. You should get some rest." He squeezed Amendal's shoulder, and then left the parlor.

Amendal turned to the window. He stared at the lightstones' constant, unflickering light. "There has to be another way."

He paced around the parlor, trying to think of alternatives. But nothing came to him. Amid his pacing he noticed a rolled parchment on the end table where his father had been seated.

That must be the list, Amendal thought. He grabbed the parchment and unrolled it. *Are you on this list, Ildin?* The names were organized by classes: necromancers, wizards, illusionists, conjurers, barsionists, transmuters, and arpranists.

To Amendal's surprise, Ildin was not on the list of candidates who hadn't already volunteered. Arintil wasn't, either. He wrinkled his brow. Surely they hadn't volunteered to go.

Suddenly, he realized his father's suggestion made sense. Arintil had several apprentices and taught at the Sorothian Magical Order. And Ildin had teaching responsibilities. They were both exempt.

Footsteps echoed from the foyer, and Amendal quickly rerolled the parchment. He placed it back where he had found it, then hurried out of the parlor. He passed his father and the Mindolarnian visitor, whose eyes followed him as he moved toward the stairway to his private rooms.

What a strange woman, he thought. Glancing over his shoulder, he found Vaem still staring at him.

⎯⎯⎯◄•►⎯⎯⎯

Amendal could not rest. After an hour, hunger pangs forced him from his bed, so he snuck off to the kitchen. Their family's chef, Dudanil, was probably fast asleep, but that was no problem. Amendal had spent many a day in the kitchen.

As with the rest of the estate home, the kitchen was roomy. During his boyhood, Amendal had thought all kitchens were this size, until he visited Ildin's home. The kitchen in the estate house was four times larger. Throughout the generations, the Aramien family had often hosted banquets and parties, so a large kitchen was a necessity.

"I wonder what we have to eat…" Amendal wove around the kitchen's four rectangular islands, moving straight for the pantry. He was rummaging through the shelves when he heard his mother's voice. "Eating this late will bring nothing but trouble."

Amendal peeled from the pantry, turning to face Bilia Aramien.

Bilia was just as tall as the rest of the Aramiens. She was slender, with golden-blonde hair that brushed her shoulders. Many people called her elegant, but to Amendal, she was simply his mother.

"I'm so glad you're home," Bilia said, grinning broadly. She hurried across the kitchen and wrapped her arms around him. "A pity you couldn't have arrived a week later."

So she knows of the expedition to Tardalim, too. Of course she knew. Arenil Aramien was not one to keep things from his wife.

"I'm glad to see you too, Mother."

Bilia pulled back, running her long fingers through Amendal's unkempt beard. "This is unacceptable!" She grimaced. "You need some grooming. And your hair… you don't look like my son."

Amendal chuckled as she shook her head and rustled his overgrown hair. "How are you able to sleep like this? You look like a vagabond…"

"I've managed." Amendal grinned.

She scowled in disgust. "I can't stand looking at it. Come with me. I'm going to cut it."

"Mother!" Amendal protested. "I will have it taken care of in the morning."

Bilia shook her head. "Nope," she said and tugged Amendal through the kitchen.

Amendal threw his free arm into the air and rolled his eyes. She was the one person he did not fight. There was no one more stubborn than Bilia Aramien. Once she set her mind to something, nothing kept her from it.

———◦———

Bilia led Amendal to her private dressing room, a small room not far from the master suite of the Aramien Estate. The room was decorated in whites: white marble flooring and off-white woodwork. A large floor-to-ceiling mirror hung on the wall beside a countertop holding cases of makeup.

Bilia grabbed a chair and dragged it in front of the mirror. "Sit."

Amendal complied, but was not amused.

"Don't worry, I'm not going to mess it up," Bilia said, grabbing a comb. "Besides, I don't think it could look any worse."

I'm sure it could, Amendal thought, staring into the mirror. His mother was examining various pairs of scissors.

"Just pick one…" Amendal muttered.

"What did you say?" Bilia asked, still intently examining the scissors.

Amendal bit his lip but didn't reply.

After an excruciating moment, Bilia began trimming Amendal's overgrown hair. "So, tell me all about your illegal jaunt through the forest."

Amendal chuckled. True, the Aramien Test of Valor was illegal by Losian law. One of the Losian kings had made the Melar Forest prohibited land, on account of unimaginable horrors. *What nonsense*, Amendal thought, then recounted the journey to his mother.

"After a month of trekking through the forest, I found some gangolin tracks. They were massive. Larger than I remembered from the stories Father used to tell us."

Bilia nodded, trimming around Amendal's ears.

"I finally caught up to the beast after a week. The thing was massive." Amendal shook his head in bemused memory—

"Stop it!" Bilia scolded. "I'll cut your ear."

Amendal closed his lips in an exaggerated fashion and took a deep breath before continuing. "I waited till it fell asleep, then opened my portal to the Visirm Expanse. The beast never saw it coming."

"That's impressive," Bilia said. "Well done, son!" She stopped cutting. "Something doesn't add up… If it only took a month to capture a gangolin, why didn't you return home sooner?"

Amendal looked at his mother in the mirror. "Why have one gangolin when you can have two? Or five?"

His mother's eyes went wide. "Amendal!"

He replied with a throaty laugh. "It was a pain tracking the others," he said. "But the struggle was worth it. The last two were together. I had to summon one of my gangolins to distract one while I captured the other."

Bilia shook off her surprise and continued grooming her son. "I guess I should have expected that from you. After all, you're like that with your women."

Amendal fought the urge to nod. *Why be with one woman when you can be with two, or three?* Over the last few years Amendal had been with *many* women. Prior to leaving for the Aramien Test of Valor, Amendal had been romantically involved with three women, all a little older than he.

"I saw Elara the other day," Bilia said, eyes focused on the hair draped over Amendal's widow's peak.

"Oh?" Amendal asked.

Bilia nodded. "She's betrothed."

"Really?" he asked with disbelief. "To who?"

"Oh, some noble boy from Sarn," Bilia said. "He's studying to be a barsionist, I think."

"Huh…" Did he dare ask if his mother had seen the other two?

Bilia continued cutting, clearing the hair around Amendal's forehead. "Your father and I ran into Yvenna about a month ago. She had a short fling with a traveling merchant from Merdan. Yvenna almost left with him, but they had a fight, and she decided to stay in Soroth."

"Well… that's good, I suppose," Amendal said. *Now what is she going to say about Sildina?*

His mother began trimming his beard, but didn't speak.

"Uh, Mother," Amendal said, trying not to move his mouth, "you haven't heard anything about Sildina, have you?"

"Your *other* lover?" Bilia asked. "Her family relocated to Silgarn to tend to her grandparents' farm six months ago. She followed them out there."

"Hm," Amendal said, examining his hair in the mirror. *Well, one out of three isn't too bad.* He remained quiet until his mother finished trimming his beard.

"There," Bilia said, brushing off loose hairs. "*Now* you look like my son."

Amendal grinned, admiring his mother's handywork. His hair was cropped short along the sides and back. It tapered to a length not quite a thumb's length. The hairs atop his head stood on end, revealing his widow's peak. And his beard was short but full. To his surprise, he looked good. "Thank you, Mother."

Bilia looked pleased with her work. "You're welcome," she said, folding her arms. "Now throw on some nice clothes."

"Huh?"

"You can't go out looking like that." She pointed to his robe. "Well, I guess you could. It just doesn't show off your physique."

Amendal burst into laughter, then ceased his mirth when he saw his mother's face.

Bilia sighed and moved in front of Amendal, grabbing his hands. "Amendal, darling, I know what you're facing. You couldn't have returned home at a more precarious time. I just think you should go out tonight, find a nice girl, and…" She left the implication hanging. "It will clear your head, and you'll have a better perspective on this whole expedition business."

Amendal nodded and rose from the chair, shaking off the rest of the clippings.

"I'm going to say one thing," Bilia said, swallowing hard. "Your uncle— my brother—has been exploring the world for many years now. He loves it, but he hated it at first. Just don't discount something if you haven't tried it."

Amendal nodded. Uncle Krudin was fond of retelling stories of his adventures. But that was not a life Amendal wanted.

"Now get changed and ride into town," Bilia said, wrapping her arms around her son. "Have some fun, and we'll see you tomorrow."

With a brisk nod toward the door, Bilia grabbed a broom and began sweeping the floor.

Amendal wandered back to the kitchen, but stopped short of entering it. *Perhaps she's right,* he thought. Turning heads in a crowd would be refreshing. If things went well, he would have a pleasurable night. At the very least, he could get his mind off this expedition to Tardalim.

Who knows, I might find a way to get out of this mess…

3

UNEXPECTED SURPRISES

"Now as you undoubtedly know, a quinta'shal consumes magic. This makes them ideal for use against hostile mages. When under your control, their digestive process can be accelerated to the point that there is hardly any loss of energy for the re-purposed blast."

- From *Colvinar Vrium's Bestiary for Conjurers*, page 12

Clothed in a fancy garb of dark blue—a long-sleeved coat and matching trousers—Amendal rode toward Soroth, but not on a horse. He needed something that could run faster, so he conjured a yidoth: a large feral feline native to the southern forests of the Mainland.

Amendal had stumbled across this particular yidoth while in the Melar Forest. The beast was as long as a man was tall, and its back came up to Amendal's stomach. It was covered in green fur, with large dark-brown spots sparsely spread across its body.

He rode the conjuration bareback, using his belt as a makeshift halter. Since he was in full control of the yidoth, he could easily rest the belt in the conjuration's mouth without worrying about undesirable bite marks.

The yidoth drew the eyes of everyone Amendal passed. Its green fur and spots stood out against Soroth's gray stone buildings and roads. The conjuration startled several people, drawing alarmed screams.

Yidoths appeared in several cautionary tales. Those stories often involved yidoths pouncing on unsuspecting travelers. Those stories were not too far from the truth, as yidoths often slept on tree limbs.

After causing several fits of hysteria, Amendal neared one of his favorite nighttime establishments, Makivir's Lounge. It was not the fanciest of places to spend an evening, but its crowds were always diverse.

At Amendal's mental command, the yidoth slowed, stopping abruptly behind a parked carriage. Such a halt would have caused a horse to rear up on its hind legs, but the yidoth simply stopped. Amendal dismounted, swiftly drawing his belt from the conjuration's mouth.

Before Amendal could don his belt, a middle-aged man rounded the carriage with a stunning younger woman in tow.

The man screamed upon seeing the yidoth, and stumbled backward. The woman started, but not a sound left her painted lips.

Amendal grinned and turned to the woman, gesturing toward her companion. "You know, if he scares that easily, he's not worth your time."

The woman glanced to the man, then back to Amendal. "Is… is that a yidoth?"

"Yes, yes, it is," Amendal said. "He's perfectly tame… well, most of the time. He only tried to eat one person on the ride through the city."

The man took another step backward, falling against a neighboring carriage.

Amendal burst into laughter. Amid his mirth he uttered an incantation. Golden light swirled around his hands—particles of conjuration magic. The golden light shot beyond the wary couple, forming a portal to the Visirm Expanse.

At Amendal's command, the yidoth trotted toward the portal. The man jumped in alarm but the woman remained calm. Once the yidoth's nose touched the portal, the creature was immediately sucked through the golden vortex.

"It wasn't real!" the man declared, standing and straightening his clothes.

Amendal dismissed the portal with a wave of his hand. "It was plenty real, and it could have eaten you." He strode past the couple and toward the entrance to Makivir's Lounge.

He heard the man swallow hard, then mutter something to the woman.

That was fun, Amendal thought. *I should ride conjurations through the city more often. Perhaps I'll start racing yidoths…*

The familiar scents of strong liquor washed across Amendal as he entered the crowded tavern. He pushed his way through the crowd until he reached the heart of the establishment: an open floor large enough to accommodate a few hundred people. Patrons frequently danced there, but tonight they were mostly talking. A few couples were kissing, some a little too passionately.

If music were playing in Makivir's Lounge, it would come from the stage at the far end of the open floor. But tonight the stage was empty. *I probably missed the music*, Amendal thought. That was fine. He wasn't much of a dancer.

He scanned the crowd, looking for pretty faces. *I wonder if Yvenna is here.* Amendal had considered stopping by her home, but it was late, and she was most likely out having fun. *Or with another man.* He pursed his lips. *Best to not think of that…*

Amendal turned his gaze to the booths lining the wall. Many were occupied by couples or small groups. A familiar face caught his eye among a group of six sitting in a booth. *Fendar?*

He stepped closer, recognizing four of the others. The sixth was concealed behind Jaekim—who was rowdily pounding on the table. Each had studied at the Sorothian Magical Order with Amendal. They were his acquaintances, not quite his friends. None were conjurers, but they had all graduated together, though three were older than Amendal. Those three had begun their studies at an older age. It had been a few years since Amendal had seen any of them.

"Fancy that," he muttered, pushing through the crowd toward them.

Fendar Callis sat in the corner, speaking animatedly—he was probably telling a story. Fendar had a flair for the dramatic. A dramatic flair was a good trait for an illusionist. He was an average-looking man with black hair and a short nose.

Beside Fendar sat Scialas Jeroid. She was an arpranist—a mage who specialized in healing. Arpranists could do other things, such as preventing injury or expelling diseases. Some even claimed their magics could extend one's life.

Scialas wasn't the most attractive woman—definitely not someone Amendal would bed. She was kind, though. When they were no more than ten years old, Amendal had climbed a tree on a dare from Ildin. He'd fallen and broken his arm. Scialas had quickly run to him as she mustered arpran magic. It took her a few tries, but she'd been able to mend the bone.

On the other side of Scialas was Morgidian Shival. Morgidian was a tough-looking fellow. If Amendal had been born that ugly he would have become an illusionist to improve his appearance. Morgidian obviously didn't feel that way, as he had trained to become a barsionist.

He was pretty good, too. During one of the Order's semiannual tournaments, Morgidian had climbed through the ranks and nearly won the competition. Usually, barsion magic was used for defense, but he managed to use it offensively. Barsionists mustered impenetrable barriers and shields. But, barsion barriers could be inverted, and that's what Morgidian had done. He had trapped his opponents and forced them to the ground.

Opposite Morgidian sat Dugal Vintris. He was a transmuter and a trickster. Dugal was a short and skinny man with a face like a weasel. During their final year at the Sorothian Magical Order, Dugal decided to play a prank on the younger acolytes. He had noticed the boys frequently practicing beneath a tree outside the Order's Main Hall.

Early one morning, Dugal took Fendar and snuck onto the Order's grounds. Dugal transmuted the grass to quicksand, and Fendar masked it with an illusion. They went about their day, waiting for the acolytes. Dugal said it had taken the acolytes a while to realize what was happening—he could sense them through the quicksand. Needless to say, those acolytes never practiced beneath that tree again.

Jaekim Nordim sat beside Dugal, laughing raucously at Fendar's tale. Jaekim was a necromancer. He specialized in mustering acidic magic.

Jaekim was tall and lanky, with light-blonde hair that looked almost white in the sun.

Amendal craned his neck, trying to see who sat beside Jaekim. A pretty hand reached for a tall glass on the table, but that was all Amendal could see.

Who is that? he wondered, maneuvering through the open floor.

A rowdy crowd of patrons blocked his path, and Amendal was forced to walk around them. While nearing the table, Amendal ran her possible identity through his head. There were at least twelve women who might mingle with those five. Amendal had bedded over half of them, and each hated him, to say the least.

Amendal was a few paces from the table when Morgidian spotted him.

"Amendal Aramien!" Morgidian shouted, rising from the booth, his hulking frame standing taller than Amendal.

"Morgi!" Amendal exclaimed, and the two of them embraced, slapping each other on the back.

The others at the booth stirred, turning toward Amendal.

"Hey now!" Morgidian said, stepping back. "Don't call me Morgi. I'm not a kid anymore."

"I know." Amendal grabbed Morgidian's shoulder. "It just makes me feel better to call you that. With your overwhelming masculinity"—he waved his hand up and down—"I have to do something to feel less intimidated."

Jaekim burst into laughter.

The others greeted Amendal, and then he saw *her.*

Faelinia Tusara, three years his senior, sat in the corner beside Jaekim, her hands resting atop her tall glass. Lush golden-blonde hair curled halfway down her back, partially covering her long face. She studied Amendal with her sea-gray eyes, and a teasing smile formed upon her full lips, revealing her dimples.

She was not one of the twelve women Amendal had considered. Aside from Ildin's sister, Gwenyth, Faelinia was the most stunning woman Amendal had ever seen. Unfortunately, Faelinia had resisted his advances over the years.

Faelinia's beauty was not her only attractive feature. During her studies at the Sorothian Magical Order she had studied both the Elemental and Arcane Channels of Magic—two subsets of the wizardry discipline. Not only was she an accomplished wizard, she was also an illusionist. Faelinia was considered a dualist mage, though she had mastered the combined knowledge of three disciplines.

"Well, fancy seeing you here," Amendal said to Faelinia. He let his gaze linger before he began talking to the others. "So what brings all of you out tonight?"

"Just enjoying the nightlife of Soroth," Fendar said. "You?"

"I needed to clear my head," Amendal said. "Riding a yidoth through the streets was refreshing."

Jaekim burst into laughter, slamming a fist on the table. He was obviously drunk.

"You did what?" Scialas asked.

"Rode atop a yidoth," Amendal said. "Oh, those things can run fast!" He grinned, focusing on Faelinia. He directed what he hoped was a smoldering gaze at her, filled with a lustful passion.

Faelinia, however, returned to her drink. She took a sip, then looked past Amendal.

What am I going to have to do? Amendal wondered.

Dugal slapped Amendal's side, distracting him from his quandary. "Say, I haven't seen you at any of the meetings. You're coming with us, right?"

"What meetings?"

"Where have you been?" Fendar asked incredulously. "The meetings for the expedition to the Abodine Wasteland. We're going to Tardalim!"

"Oh, *those* meetings." Amendal waggled a finger at Fendar. "Yeah, I'm not going to the Halls of the Damned."

Jaekim laughed, once more slamming his hand on the table.

"You do know we're not actually going to a hell, don't you?" Fendar asked. "It's a reliquary. Someone probably decided to name it after the place in the religious texts."

"Shouldn't that scare you?" Amendal asked, examining his friends.

Morgidian raised an eyebrow. "Why?" he asked. "It's a bunch of old ruins in an antarctic wasteland. I doubt there are even monsters inside it."

Amendal pointed a finger to Morgidian. "And another reason I'm not interested."

"Because there are no monsters?" Dugal asked. "What about the tevisrals, Amendal?"

"I'm not interested in tevisrals."

His friends stared at him in shock. Jaekim chuckled awkwardly, but Morgidian was the first to speak.

"Why not?"

Amendal shrugged. "Like I said, I have more important things to do."

"There couldn't be *anything* more important than unearthing tevisrals," Scialas said flatly.

"I could give you a whole list," Amendal said. "One." He raised his forefinger. "I have a lot of reading to catch up on. Two." He raised the next finger. "I haven't seen my family in nine months, and I'd like to spend some time with them. Three." He raised his third finger, "I have some practicing to do with my conjurations—more nighttime yidoth racing and such. Four." He extended his pinky. "My brother needs some help adjusting his attitude. And five." He extended his thumb. "I, I just don't want to go. Why should I waste my time adventuring when I can hone my art?"

Scialas blinked in disbelief.

"Those are the stupidest excuses I've ever heard." Faelinia said, shaking her head.

"Well, I have five other fingers," Amendal said, holding up his other hand. "I'm sure I can list something to your liking."

Jaekim snorted.

"I doubt they'd be any better." Faelinia sighed, then nudged Jaekim. "Let me out."

Dugal slid out of the booth, followed by Jaekim, who lost his footing and fell toward Amendal.

Amendal caught him and set him on his feet as Faelinia slid out of the booth, standing nearly as tall as Amendal in her heeled boots. She slapped some coins on the table, then spun toward the door. "I'll see you tomorrow," she said. "Good night, everyone."

"You're leaving already?" Amendal asked. "The fun is just starting."

Faelinia glanced over her shoulder as she moved away. "Good night, Amendal."

"Don't you want to see a yidoth race?" he called after her. "I'll let you ride mine. It's bigger than most!"

Faelinia waggled a finger over her head and disappeared into the crowd.

"Wow, what a rejection," Fendar said.

Morgidian chuckled. "I think you should have left the *riding* bit out. Tacky innuendo."

Amendal shot Morgidian an annoyed glance. "That wasn't an innuendo…"

"Sounded like one to me," Scialas said, shrugging.

Fendar gestured at Scialas. "I think *she* wants to ride your yidoth."

Face flushed, Scialas slapped Fendar, knocking him against the wall, evoking laughter all around the table. As he joined in their mirth, Amendal felt a hand on his shoulder. He turned to see Yvenna. She stood much shorter than him, with black hair and dark olive skin. Her brown eyes stared at Amendal with a lustful yearning.

"And here I thought you'd look more scraggily," Yvenna said, stroking Amendal's arm. "When did you return home?"

"Today," Amendal said. "I was hoping to find you here."

Yvenna's small lips twisted into a devious smile. "Care to walk me home?" she asked, her eyes inviting. "I was just about to leave."

Amendal studied her for a moment, then glanced quickly throughout the lounge. Where had Yvenna been hiding?

"Naturally," Amendal said, taking her hand.

He turned back to his friends at the booth. Their laughter had died, but Fendar was still rubbing his cheek. "It was good seeing you all," Amendal said, waving to his friends. "Don't die while exploring the Halls of the Damned."

As he and Yvenna walked toward the door, Jaekim laughed raucously and pounded a fist on the table. *That man can sure get drunk,* Amendal thought, shaking his head.

"I'm glad you made it home," Yvenna said, one hand in Amendal's and the other stroking his arm. "I thought you'd return sooner."

"Well, I got carried away."

Yvenna nodded, leaning her head against Amendal's arm.

She's surprisingly affectionate, he thought, *considering she almost ran off with another man.*

Once outside, Yvenna pulled Amendal in the direction of her home.

"Wait," Amendal said, stopping her. "How'd you like to ride a yidoth instead?"

Yvenna eyed him up and down, unsure of what he meant. Her eyes, however, lingered *elsewhere.*

Amendal threw his hands into the air. "It's not an innuendo!"

Confused, Yvenna furrowed her brow.

"I mean a conjuration," Amendal said. "So we can get to your home faster."

"Oh!" Yvenna laughed, bringing a hand to her mouth. "Of course! Why not?"

Amendal rolled his eyes, then strode into the street to summon his yidoth. As he had foreseen, tonight *would* be pleasurable.

———◦•◦———

A biting chill stung Amendal's hands, and he felt snow beneath his fingertips. *Snow?* He opened his eyes.

To his surprise, the ceiling of Yvenna's bedroom was not above him. Instead, he saw a clear sky. A yellow sky.

Amendal shot upright. "Where am I?!" he demanded, his gaze frantically darting about the frozen plain that extended away from him in all directions. Amendal rose to his feet and spun about. There were no footprints in the snow. All that marred the ground was an indentation where he had been lying.

A freezing gust blew over Amendal, causing him to shiver. He grabbed his arms, rubbing his hands on the sleeves of his charcoal robe. *My robe?* But that was back in his quarters at the Aramien Estate... And he had fallen asleep completely undressed.

What was going on? Wary, Amendal turned, crunching the snow beneath his boots.

A mountain rose above the frozen plain, taller than any he had ever beheld. There were other mountains farther away, but they barely peeked over the horizon. Snowdrifts surrounded him on all sides, spreading as far as he could see.

How did I get here? He recalled drifting to sleep not long after his and Yvenna's throes of passion. Her wild nature was refreshing. She was the ideal distraction. Well... almost.

Another gust washed over him, and he shivered, teeth chattering.

"This can't be a dream," he said, groaning. "It's too real..."

But the sky was all wrong. And the sun—it was blue!

"No... no, this can't be real!" he shouted.

"Why not?" a deep voice asked from behind him.

Startled, Amendal spun.

A man stood several paces away, his chest-length white hair and full white beard whipping in the wind. He wore a blood-red robe with odd symbols woven into it. Amendal had never seen anything like it. The stranger's sapphire eyes stared intently at Amendal, as if demanding an answer to the question. Those eyes looked like Ildin's... *They're the same shade.* But unlike Ildin, the stranger looked old, his face a mass of wrinkles.

"Why can't this be real, Amendal?" the stranger asked, stepping closer.

Amendal balked at the question. "Uh, because the sky is yellow...? The sky is never yellow."

"Not on Kalda," the stranger said with a shrug, stopping beside Amendal.

Unsettled by the answer, Amendal studied the stranger. Had he abducted Amendal somehow? That didn't seem likely.

I have to be dreaming.

"Not necessarily," the stranger replied, although Amendal hadn't spoken. Then he stepped ahead of Amendal. "Come. Follow me. There is something you *need* to see."

Amendal didn't move. He watched the stranger walk away, approaching the nearest snowdrift.

Before he reached the drift's crest, the stranger turned. "Well, are you coming? Or are you going to stand there and freeze to death?"

All right! Amendal grumbled to himself, rubbing his arms as he chased after the stranger. Snow crept into his boots with each step. The flakes melted, dampening his feet.

"Where are we going?" Amendal demanded through chattering teeth.

The stranger pointed toward the mountain. "To behold your destiny."

Crazed fool, Amendal thought. The stranger glanced over his shoulder, glaring at Amendal with disgust. *He can't hear me, can he?*

They walked for a time, cresting snowdrift after snowdrift. More snow filled Amendal's boots. Sharp pain—like pricking needles—shot through his toes with each step.

"Are we close?" Amendal growled between drifts.

The stranger grinned wryly. "Just over this next drift, my friend."

I'm not your friend...

The stranger cocked an eyebrow and pursed his lips, apparently not amused.

They ascended the snowdrift in silence, and Amendal started.

A gorge at least a grand phineal wide spread as far as he could see, surrounding that towering mountain. A grand phineal was the sum of a thousand phineals, each of which was about the length of a man's forearm.

"Behold, the reliquary your fellow mages are seeking," the stranger said, pointing across the gorge.

"Huh?!" Amendal blurted. "We're in the Abodine Wasteland?"

The stranger lowered his hand and grinned.

But the sky is all wrong... Amendal gazed skyward. Clouds approached from his right, but they were red. "This is so strange," he muttered, shaking his head. He turned away, his eyes focused on the snow drift. There was a purple sheen to the snow. *That's not natural, either.*

"Amendal," the stranger said, a hint of annoyance in his voice. "Pay attention..." He turned, staring at Amendal with a soul-piercing gaze. "It is your destiny to unearth the wonders of this reliquary."

Amendal burst into laughter. "What are you, my conscience?" he chuckled. "I *must* be dreaming..."

The stranger ignored the question and continued talking. "When you enter the *reliquary*"—he pointed to the mountain—"you must seek this." The stranger held out his other hand. A shallow, black, domed disk sat in the stranger's palm. It was polished, with a perfect reflection like a mirror.

Amendal hadn't seen the stranger reach into any pockets—not that the stranger's robe had pockets. "Was that up your sleeve?" he asked, pointing to the dome.

The stranger did not reply.

"Looks like something my mother might have in her private dressing room."

The stranger shook his head. "No matter what you do, Amendal, you must find this," he insisted. "It is of the utmost importance."

Amendal frowned. "Could you be any more vague?"

"Go to Tardalim, Amendal," the stranger said, his tone urgent. "Seek the shan'ak"—he gestured to the dome—"and fulfill your destiny. It is of the utmost importance. Heed this *conscription*, as you call it. Now go."

Amendal opened his mouth to speak, but the stranger flicked a finger at him.

The snowy plain distorted. The yellow sky vanished. Snow flew every direction, melting into violet droplets. The ground shook, forming an ever-spreading chasm between Amendal and the stranger.

Amendal shouted a slew of curses as the snow beneath his feet flew away. The ground gave way, and Amendal felt himself falling. Colors shot past him, forming streaks of zipping light.

Frantic, Amendal reached for something to grab, but there was nothing but light around him. "Damn you!" Amendal cried, "Damn you!"

A burst of brilliant light erupted in front of Amendal, blinding him.

"Damn you!" he cursed, feeling something soft against his bare back. Was that silk? He no longer felt himself falling. In fact, he was lying on his back.

Amendal blinked several times, finding himself staring at the ceiling of Yvenna's bedchamber. Slowly he sat up, breathing deeply.

Yvenna stirred beside him, shifting the silky sheets.

"It had to be a nightmare," he muttered. *And a crazy one at that...*

Yvenna stirred again, pulling the sheets off Amendal's feet. Prickling pain shot through his toes, surging to his ankles.

"Ow!" Amendal cried, reaching for his feet. To his surprise, they were as cold as ice.

4

THE DECISION

"The quinta'shals can often be used as shields against magical assaults. Depending on your skill, you might be able to effectively defend yourself without the use of a barsion barrier. Although... I would not recommend it."

- From *Colvinar Vrium's Bestiary for Conjurers*, page 13

A mendal gasped. He could not feel his feet. They were frozen, as if frostbitten. *How...? But it was a dream!* There was no way his feet could have frozen during the night, not at this time of year. Besides, the windows were closed.

"Yvenna!" he shouted. "Yvenna, wake up!"

A groan left Yvenna's lips, and she turned away, taking the sheets with her.

"You're no help," Amendal growled, then rolled out of bed. He snatched a blanket and wrapped himself in it.

The fireplace, he thought, eyeing the beige stone hearth across the room.

Amendal stumbled as he tried to walk. He couldn't feel the floor beneath his feet. The blanket sagged, and Amendal tripped over it, falling face-first.

"Great..." *Probably better if I crawl,* he thought, pulling himself across the floor.

The embers in the fireplace had died completely. Yvenna must have put them out before she fell asleep.

Amendal crawled to a stack of logs beside the hearth and began tossing one log at a time into the fireplace. He looked for the flint and the steel striker but didn't see them. *Must be atop the hearth.* Amendal struggled to stand, using his arms to pull himself upright.

"There," he said triumphantly, dropping back to the floor. He added kindling and began working with the flint.

When the flames had spread to the logs, Amendal propped his feet against the hearth.

The stinging was intolerable.

"I'm going to need an arpranist," he said with a groan. *Frostbite in bed... and during warm weather. How embarrassing.* His predicament struck him as ironic. He had been so careful while trekking through the Melar Forest. Snow had fallen several times, but Amendal had managed to keep himself warm—using the remains of inert earthen conjurations to make a shelter.

The fire grew hotter, and the stinging intensified.

Amendal lay beside the fire for hours. His feet had finally thawed when the sun peeked over the western horizon. But they still ached. He tried wiggling his toes, but they barely moved.

"I *really* need an arpranist."

"Wha...?" Yvenna moaned.

Amendal glanced back to the bed, seeing Yvenna patting the spot where he had slept.

"Why aren't you in bed?"

"I needed to warm my feet," Amendal said. "They *froze* overnight."

"Huh?" she muttered, sitting up and holding the sheet to her chest. Amendal didn't know why—it wasn't like he hadn't seen that part of her before.

"How, how did that happen?" she asked, a dumbfounded expression on her face.

"I don't know," Amendal said with a shrug. "I had a strange dream—no, a nightmare. I was stuck in the Abodine Wasteland with some crazed codger. My feet got wet, and they felt frozen in the dream."

Yvenna cocked her head. "You *really* don't want to go on that expedition, do you?" She rose from the bed, sheet still wrapped around her, and sat beside Amendal. "What would really happen if you refused to go?"

"Father says I'll be expelled from the Order. I wouldn't be able to practice my magic anywhere in the Principality."

Yvenna studied him for a moment, then ran a hand through his hair. "So, would you leave Soroth?"

Amendal shrugged. The image of the stranger holding that black dome came to him. He tried to shake it off, but it persisted. *Why am I thinking of that?* he wondered.

Go to Tardalim, he heard the stranger's voice in his mind. *Seek the shan'ak, and fulfill your destiny.* Amendal closed his eyes, trying to think of something else. But the words repeated in his mind.

"Get out of my head!" he snarled through clenched teeth.

"What's wrong?" Yvenna asked, wrapping an arm around him.

"That codger," Amendal said, grabbing his hair. "He's in my head!"

Yvenna pulled back, eyeing him warily.

I'm not mad.

"You're different, Amendal... Your family's foolish Test has changed you."

Amendal started. He didn't feel any different. It wasn't the trek through Melar that disturbed him—it was the dream.

"I think you need to talk to someone…" Yvenna said, sounding confused.

"It was just a nightmare," Amendal insisted. *At least I hope so,* he thought. If it wasn't a dream, it was something he couldn't explain, and that frightened him.

Yvenna sighed, looking out the window. "I think you should leave. Go rest at your parents' estate. And talk to someone… You don't see it, but I know that forest changed you. You're not *my* Amendal anymore."

"Not *your* Amendal?"

Yvenna stood, looking down at him. "I don't want to be with someone who is mad. I've dealt with enough insanity in my life, and I don't need a crazed lover."

Amendal shook his head. He *wasn't* crazed.

"Fine," he snapped, struggling to stand. He braced himself on a nearby chair and hobbled toward his clothes, which were strewn beside the bed. Amendal dressed in silence, then limped to the door.

Yvenna didn't mutter so much as a goodbye as he left.

Fickle woman, Amendal thought, shutting the door behind him. He stumbled through the hall, struggling to make his way to the stairs. He had to find an arpranist.

That meeting. There will be plenty of arpranists there.

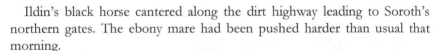

Ildin's black horse cantered along the dirt highway leading to Soroth's northern gates. The ebony mare had been pushed harder than usual that morning.

He had visited the Aramien Estate shortly after sunrise, hoping to find Amendal. But Mistress Bilia told him that Amendal had left late the previous night. Poor Amendal was struggling with his conscription for the Order's expedition to the Abodine Wasteland, she told him. So to ease her son's mind, Mistress Bilia had encouraged him to go into town and have some *fun* so as to clear his head.

That was probably the worst thing he could have done, Ildin thought. Clarity never came to Amendal during his erotic affairs.

Oh, Amendal…

While Ildin was at the Aramien Estate, Master Arenil told him of Amendal's homecoming and his poor reaction to news of the expedition. "Maybe he'll change his mind when I tell him I'm going." Hopefully Amendal would see reason.

The council was not taking any chances. Beside the hundred or so mages that were going, the council had enlisted the aid of nearly two hundred retired soldiers and mercenaries. This expedition was no band of would-be treasure hunters.

Sighing deeply, Ildin kicked the sides of his mare, and she quickened into a gallop.

After leaving that fickle woman's home, Amendal conjured his yidoth. The green feline now padded casually through Soroth's streets, drawing much less attention than it had the previous night, probably due to its less hasty pace. Amendal had decided on the more sedate gait because when the yidoth ran, Amendal's feet nearly touched the ground, and he didn't want to damage them any further.

The sun was rising above the mountains west of the city when Amendal neared Soroth's northern gates. A steady flow of traffic was already moving to and from the city.

The influx of traffic consisted mostly of horse-drawn carriages or single riders on horseback. Empty wagons were the only things leaving the city. Many farmers lived over the mountains to the west, cultivating the vast plains of fertile land. On the eastern side of the mountains, dense forest covered the island.

As Amendal passed the northern gate his eyes fell upon the buildings of the Sorothian Magical Order. They stood higher than the surrounding buildings, rising four stories, and were made from polished pale-gray galstra—a stone accented with colored flecks and streaks. Galstra was similar to granite, but it possessed a silky sheen rather than granite's hard brilliance.

While Amendal focused on the buildings, the clip-clop of a horse's hooves neared him.

"Well, well, look what the cat is carrying."

Amendal turned as Ildin rode up beside him. "Ildin! Fancy seeing you here."

"Heading to the Order?" Ildin asked.

Amendal nodded. "I need to find an arpranist."

Ildin sighed, shaking his head slowly. "What did you do now, Amendal?"

"What did I do?" Amendal snorted. "*I* didn't do anything."

The illusionist didn't look convinced. "Then who did?"

"Oh, I don't know…" he trailed off. *How do I explain this without sounding mad?* Ildin wouldn't judge him, would he? No. Ildin was Amendal's closest friend. Amendal could tell him anything.

"I think I have frostbite. I can barely move my toes, and my feet ache."

"Frostbite?"

Amendal nodded. "I was wandering through the Abodine Wasteland with some deranged lunatic. He had your eyes, Ildin."

"My eyes, huh?"

They turned south, Ildin's mount matching Amendal's pace.

"Yeah… and when I awoke my feet were frozen."

"That's strange," Ildin said. "Do you think it was something you drank last night?"

"That's just it—I didn't drink anything," Amendal said, shaking his head. "I was at Makivir's Lounge, but then *she* took me home with her before I could order a single drink."

"She?"

"Yvenna!" Amendal spat the name.

"I take it things didn't end well?" Ildin asked, giving Amendal a sympathetic smile.

"No…"

"That's probably for the best," Ildin said reassuringly. "She was one of your most ill-tempered lovers."

Silence hung between them as they turned east, toward the Sorothian Magical Order. The Order's gates were down the street a few grand phineals.

After a moment, Ildin broke the silence. "So, dreaming about the Abodine Wasteland, were you?"

Amendal nodded. "I suppose you know a great deal about the expedition?"

"Yes," Ildin said. "I was one of the first volunteers."

Amendal started, nearly falling off his yidoth. "You… what?" Ildin was the last person Amendal expected to willingly join the expedition. "But the empire and your sister…"

Ildin shrugged. "If I refused to go, I'd look suspicious. Say, why don't you want to go? I'm sure there will be some interesting creatures in those icy wastes. You could snatch a few while we're there."

You too, huh? Amendal thought and snorted. It seemed everyone in his life was pushing or pulling him toward that expedition. *Maybe it really is my destiny,* he thought. That word evoked vivid imagery from his dream.

That black disk, he mused, feeling an unnatural draw to it. Though the stranger's words weren't repeating in his head, the impression they carried filled Amendal's mind. If he did not go, would he be forever plagued by the stranger's imperative?

Dreadful thought.

"Well," Ildin continued, his tone sly, "if you're not interested in any of the wildlife, maybe a fellow adventurer will pique your interest. Faelinia Tusara is going."

Amendal had assumed that was the case. Her farewell at Makivir's Lounge implied as much.

"And I hear she is available," Ildin added. "At least that's what she told me. This might be your one shot to win her over."

Amendal raised an eyebrow.

"Intrigued now?" Ildin chuckled. "She just recently ended a relationship.

Claimed he was too *weak* for her." He paused, studying Amendal.

You sly illusionist, you. Amendal grinned at Ildin. *Baiting me with a woman.* Ildin understood Amendal all too well.

"Faelinia is hoping to find someone else less cowardly. I think she's hoping this expedition will bring out the bravery in some of us. Or at least reveal the cowards. We are going to a place named after the realm of eternal suffering, after all."

Amendal grinned. *A courageous man? If she only knew the ordeals I went through in Melar.* He could be courageous. Facing not one but five gangolins steeled a man. *Prove myself to Faelinia?* He nodded. *I could do that…*

Ildin kept talking, but Amendal didn't pay attention.

Would it really be that bad if I went? He wanted to expand his knowledge and abilities through the tomes his family kept sacred—and his father had granted him permission to take transcriptions of them. It would take time to gain greater levels of mastery, and the trip to the Abodine Wasteland *would* be long. His mind returned to Faelinia. Amendal could compromise for her.

And then there was that dream…

"…The way I see it, she—"

"You can stop, Ildin," Amendal said.

Ildin started, his brow furrowed. "You know, I'm not going to give up trying to get you to come along. I'd hate to see you expelled."

Amendal chuckled. "It won't come to that."

"Oh?"

"I'm going," Amendal said. "You've *convinced* me. I mean, I can't pass up a challenge like winning over Faelinia Tusara, can I?"

Ildin beamed. "Really? You're really going to come on the expedition?"

Amendal nodded.

They were near the entrance of the Order now. The wrought-iron gates were pulled open, and a steady flow of acolytes, apprentices, and full-fledged mages jostled one another into the Order's grounds.

"Now let's find me an arpranist before this meeting starts. I'll need my feet to walk across that godforsaken wasteland."

◦•◦

The diplomatic carriage of the Mindolarn Embassy moved slowly through the city streets of Soroth. Inside, Vaem Rudal sat sketching a tevisral design that had come to her shortly after she left the Aramien Estate. The tevisral's sole purpose was to receive and deliver audible messages. It would utilize a sub-branch within the Illusory Channel of Magic.

Illusionists were able to project their voices through their illusions, even across great distances. They could also hear through their magic. Vaem had known of several spies who utilized such methods to communicate with each other.

Ul'thirls operated on a similar principle—but the workings of those ancient tevisrals were far beyond the knowledge of the scholars at the Hilinard. Ul'thirls could *perfectly* reproduce anything in their presence and project it across the world. Often, one could not tell if they were speaking with someone through an Ul'thirl unless they saw the tevisral or knew of its presence.

What Vaem visualized was far simpler than that.

The rod on her sketch pad consisted of two parts that channeled magic—one to capture sound and another to emit it. There would need to be a deliberate delay, in case the recipient was not near the tevisral when a message was sent.

These tevisrals would be crafted in pairs because one receiving component would need to be bonded to the other rod's emitter. Rods thus crafted would work only with each other.

Unfortunately, she saw no way to overcome that limitation as—

"What are you sketching now?" The disgruntled voice belonged to General Vidaer, an elderly veteran of war sitting on the seat across from her. He wore a formal garb: black trousers and a red coat with golden tassels and buttons. Only the collar of his white ruffled shirt was visible.

Vaem looked up from her sketch pad and lifted her quill from the parchment. "Hopefully something that will make communication easier for the empire."

"Oh?" the general asked, leaning forward. The wrinkles around his violet eyes deepened.

"I would like to finish the design before we set sail," Vaem said, turning again to her sketch pad.

The general chuckled. "Are you afraid you won't be able to finish it?"

Vaem again stopped sketching, but did not look up from the pad. *No*, she told herself sternly. She would not fail like Meradis or Coridician.

"There is no shame in acknowledging your fears, Vaem. Fear prepares you for the inevitable."

I do not want to think about that, she thought. Vaem stared at the sketch, looking at her handwriting beside the rod's diagram. She lowered her quill to the unfinished sentence, but the carriage jolted, and the ink blotted beneath her quill. *Now look what you've done, you old reptile.* she thought spitefully, watching the ink soak into the parchment.

General Vidaer cleared his throat. "Your fears wouldn't be unjustified. Even I feel some trepidation at the thought of going to Tardalim." He eased back while settling his gaze on Vaem's satchel. He flinched, and his eyes widened in a mixture of shock and anger. "You're keeping *that* in plain sight?"

Vaem glanced to her open satchel. In one of its interior pockets lay an off-white tevisral that had been entrusted to her by the emperor. Cylindrical, with a rounded cone on one end, it was about twice the length of a finger. Much of its surface was smooth and did not emit light like most tevisrals. It was by far the most complex tevisral she had ever seen, a remnant from an ancient world where Ul'thirls were commonplace.

"I am keeping it close," she said, turning back to her sketch pad. "As the emperor instructed. Besides, it's not as if anyone in this backwater nation would know what it is."

General Vidaer snorted. "The nullifier is not something to be handled lightly."

Vaem looked up from her pad, raising an eyebrow at the general. If he hadn't known it was a tevisral, would he have even noticed it? She took in a calming breath and began sketching once again. The general droned on and on about the tevisral and her responsibility regarding it, but Vaem did her best to ignore him.

If only I could shut him up without consequence, she thought, glancing to her gloved hand. Her eyes fell upon the rivet near her thumb and she fought the urge to touch it. The glove in fact was a tevisral, one Vaem had made herself for her own... pleasures.

Eventually, the carriage lurched to a stop, and Vaem glanced out the window. They had arrived at the Sorothian Magical Order.

General Vidaer, now frustrated, threw the carriage door open and stepped down in a rush. *Glad to be rid of you,* she thought, eyeing his retreating back.

Now alone, Vaem carefully placed the sketch pad on the seat opposite her, leaving the design exposed so the ink could dry. She secured her quill and the ink vial before she exited the carriage with her satchel over her shoulder.

A goodly throng of young mages had gathered near the carriage, and Vaem pushed her way through them. She hurried across the grassy lawn, passing the Main Hall, a rectangular four-story building with the blandest of architecture. She quickened her stride, heading toward the southern end of the campus.

While passing a fountain south of the Main Hall, Vaem glimpsed a well-dressed man lying on the grass. He wore a blue formal-looking garb with golden accents: buttons, tassels and stripes. His clothes looked wrinkled, as if he had slept in them.

The man was also barefoot. An ugly woman knelt beside him, guiding green particles to his feet—arpran magic.

The fool probably fell while in a drunken stupor, Vaem thought.

The arpran magic ceased flowing, and the man sat up.

Vaem started, her eyes widening with surprise.

The man was none other than Amendal Aramien. He looked different with his hair and beard groomed. And those clothes...

Oh my... Vaem thought, smiling. Master Arenil Aramien had claimed his son was a notorious libertine, and now she knew why. He was *very* attractive!

She watched Amendal wiggle his toes and then jump to his feet. He pulled on his boots, then hugged the arpranist. They were soon joined by another Sorothian mage, one who Vaem knew had enlisted in the expedition early on. Vaem had forgotten his name, though she knew he was an illusionist.

Amendal and the two other mages crossed the lawn, heading toward the sunken amphitheater where the meeting was to be held.

"So, Amendal, have you finally succumbed to the inevitable?" Vaem whispered. The more Sorothians she had at her disposal, the better her chances of success. She would not fail the emperor like Meradis or Coridician.

⟞•⟝

"I'm glad you changed your mind," Scialas said to Amendal, grinning giddily. "It wouldn't be the same without you."

"Well," Amendal said with a sigh, "after thinking about it, I decided I couldn't live with myself if I let the lot of you run off to your deaths."

"So now you're a hero?" Ildin asked sarcastically.

Amendal lifted his chin in mock arrogance. "When have I not been?"

Scialas giggled at the banter as they approached the Order's amphitheater. Sunken nearly two stories below ground, it contained twelve rows of benches that surrounded a circular platform fifty phineals in diameter. The platform was used as the dueling ring during the Order's semiannual tournaments. Eleven empty chairs sat on the platform. *For the council, and who else?* Amendal wondered.

The amphitheater could seat several thousand, but today only the first few rows were sparsely filled with men and women dressed in robes of a variety of colors: wizards wore their customary orange and red, illusionists their dull gray, transmuters a tacky brown, and conjurers vibrant yellow. Interspersed through the crowd were necromancers in black, arpranists in forest green, and barsionists in navy blue.

Scialas led the way into the amphitheater, guiding Amendal and Ildin toward the fourth row, where the others Amendal had encountered at Makivir's Lounge were seated.

Fendar's eyes bulged when he saw Amendal. Dugal shook his head, grinning broadly.

"So what changed your mind?" Morgidian bellowed.

"Frostbite," Amendal said.

His friends looked confused.

"I don't want any of you getting frostbite," he added, noticing Faelinia seated on the third row. She glanced toward Amendal, but quickly returned her focus to the stage.

What do I have to do to hold your attention? It had to be an act of bravery.

Amendal and Ildin sat together, Scialas on the other side of the illusionist.

More mages filed into the amphitheater. Some looked a little too young to be there. One pair of youngsters sat behind Amendal: a boy and a girl.

"I really wish I could go," the boy said. "If only they'd be leaving a few months from now."

"Don't worry, Vargos, you'll get your chance to go adventuring."

"But this is going to be historical, Verdin," the boy retorted. "It's the first joint venture between the Hilinard and the Sorothian Magical Order." He sighed noisily.

Amendal turned to look at the two youngsters, guessing their age as about sixteen. By their conversation, he deduced they were near the end of their training—at least Vargos was. From the color of their robes, he knew the boy was a barsionist, the girl a necromancer.

The prospective barsionist looked completely disheveled as if *he* had spent nine months in the forest. His dark-blue robes were dirty, as was his face. And his black hair stuck out at odd angles all over this head.

The young necromancer was the opposite. Her black robes were neatly pressed, and her long dark-blonde hair was pulled back in a neat ponytail.

"I mean, there is bound to be something of great importance in this reliquary," Vargos—the disheveled one—said. "I just hope I can get a glimpse of the discoveries when they get back."

"I doubt they'll let an apprentice near the loot," Amendal interjected. "But I could probably arrange something for you."

Vargos cocked his head at Amendal. "How?" he asked, running a hand through his disheveled hair.

"You don't know who I am?" he asked.

Vargos stared blankly at Amendal.

"He's the son of Master Aramien," Verdin said.

"Oh," Vargos muttered, not sounding impressed.

"His uncle's the one leading that group you want to join," Verdin added.

"Oh…" Vargos's eyes widened. "Say, could you put in a good word to Krudin about me?"

Amendal blinked once before answering. "I don't even know you, kid."

"Well, we could change that," Vargos said. "Why don't you buy me lunch, and I can tell you all about me?" He grinned hopefully, looking a tad crazy.

"Uh, I think you should buy *him* lunch, Vargos," Verdin said.

Vargos compressed his lips in annoyance.

"How about when I get back, we meet at the Sea Vistonia," Amendal suggested. "Since I'm joining this expedition last minute, I need some time to get my affairs in order."

Vargos nodded. "Shake on it?" he asked, extending a hand.

"Not with your grubby hands," Amendal said. "And make sure you're cleaned up when we do meet. They won't let you into the Sea Vistonia looking as you do."

Amendal turned back to face the amphitheater's entrance.

More mages were filing in, and Amendal noticed the Mindolarnian, Vaem, in the crowd. As she descended toward the platform, her eyes found his and held them in a lustful gaze. She was so intent on him that she tripped on the bottom step but regained her footing gracefully.

Amendal felt Ildin nudge his arm. "Why is she looking at us?" he asked.

"Probably admiring my good looks," Amendal said. "I mean, the last time she saw me I looked worse than young Vargos." He thumbed back to the prospective barsionist.

"Was that a compliment?" the boy asked.

Amendal ignored him and continued talking to Ildin. "If I hadn't accepted your challenge, I'd probably bed her." He nodded to Vaem.

"Is that all you can think about?" Ildin asked.

"Yes," Scialas answered for Amendal. "That's why nothing ever works out for him. He's always looking for the *next* woman instead of focusing on the one right in front of him."

Ildin laughed, and Amendal shook his head. But maybe there was some truth to Scialas's observation. He looked at Faelinia, who was still looking at the platform. Was that why she had refused him over the years? Amendal's way with women was well-known.

Looking for the next *woman, huh?* Perhaps if he focused solely on Faelinia she would pay attention to him. So, he would do that... and something heroic.

More mages descended into the amphitheater, including the members of the Order's council. Amendal's father noticed him among the seated crowd, and his face beamed with excitement. He waved to Amendal and nodded approvingly.

Amendal returned the gesture with a mock salute. He'd been conscripted, after all, so why not salute like a good soldier?

5

A TRUE CONJURER

"When fighting alongside other mages—particularly elementalists, arcanists, and corusilists—quinta'shals make excellent close-quarter combatants. When soldiers and other allies are involved in a melee, those mages must exert an extra effort to not hit them—eruptions must be controlled and such. That is not the case with quinta'shals. A mage can indiscriminately unleash their might because any errant magic or explosions are simply absorbed by the quinta'shals and redirected by the conjurer. It is one of my favorite tactics."

- From *Colvinar Vrium's Bestiary for Conjurers*, page 14

Later that evening, Amendal walked the halls leading to his family's library in the estate house. He wore his formal yellow robes. This robe was more decorative than those worn by the Order's acolyte ranks. Golden threads lined the edges of the robe in thick lines and covered the various seams.

A sense of triumph filled Amendal as he neared the library. As a child he had often envisioned this moment. After every successful trek through Melar, each Aramien Conjurer was rewarded with the honor of greater knowledge in a ceremony held within their family's library.

The Aramien library was three stories tall, with ornate bookshelves lining the walls of each floor. Spiral staircases were placed in each of the corners, leading to the various levels. Three lightstone chandeliers hung from the ceiling, equally spaced between the walls. The only windows were three round dormers aligned with the chandeliers.

Arenil sat in a lounge chair in the center of the library. He wore robes similar to Amendal's, but a sigil adorned the front, denoting Arenil's position on the Order's council. Amendal's mother stood behind Arenil, wearing a beige gown adorned with diamonds and white opals. Amendal's brother, however, was not present.

Three books were stacked in Arenil's lap, each bound in leather. *Why only three?* Amendal wondered. The Aramien household possessed four tomes: *Battle Tactics of the Beastcallers, Greater Conjurations from the Aldinal Plane, The Laws of the Visirm,* and *Colvinar Vrium's Bestiary for Conjurers.*

The top volume was a dark brown with golden trim along its spine, and he could see it was *Battle Tactics of the Beastcallers.* The second tome was a dull red, and the third a dark emerald. Amendal couldn't read their spines.

"Good evening, my son," Arenil said, gesturing to the chair beside him. "Come sit for a moment."

Amendal complied, eyeing the tomes.

"Before I go into the ceremony," Arenil said, "I want to thank you for *willingly* joining the expedition."

"You're welcome, Father. Things became troublesome the more I resisted. Since accepting my *destiny*, life has been less frustrating. It seems I am being dragged to the Halls of Damnation regardless…"

Arenil laughed. "Troublesome, huh? Well, just because something is difficult doesn't mean it isn't worthwhile."

More lectures? Amendal thought. His father interjected his insights at every possible opportunity.

"Now, I am only presenting you with these three," Arenil continued, "because I am currently reviewing *Colvinar Vrium's Bestiary for Conjurers,* but these should keep you busy until I am finished."

"Thank you, Father." Amendal bowed his head. "I am very eager to begin studying."

"I'm sure you are, Amendal. I imagine you'll devour their contents." Arenil smiled. "There are great secrets held in these tomes. Armed with the knowledge contained within them, you'll be a powerful conjurer." He studied Amendal, his face stern. "If what you told your mother about the gangolins is true… then you will be far beyond formidable."

Amendal nodded, glancing to his mother, who was smiling broadly.

Arenil leaned back, taking a deep breath. "Five gangolins… I can't imagine a scenario where you'll need to conjure that many in the future. One would be enough to ravage a city…" He stared intently into Amendal's eyes. "I hope you are never in need of conjuring all of them. Such a predicament would be perilous indeed."

Arenil rose from his chair, holding the books face-up in his hands. "Amendal Aramien, arise."

Amendal complied, standing straight-backed.

"Place your hands atop these tomes," Arenil said, "and repeat the Oath."

Amendal placed his hands atop the dark-brown tome, his expression somber. He had memorized the Aramien Oath years ago. As his father spoke the Oath, Amendal repeated it with him:

"I, Amendal Aramien, vow to protect the knowledge kept in these sacred tomes. I will adhere to the standards set within them, magnifying my skills and abilities. To none will I reveal the incantations found within these pages, except to those who have proven themselves according to our family's Test of Valor. I take these responsibilities upon myself of my own accord and accept the consequences of breaking this Oath: banishment to the Visirm Expanse."

A pleased smile formed upon Arenil's face, and he handed the tomes to Amendal. "I now proclaim you an Aramien Conjurer."

Bilia walked around her husband's chair, holding a golden necklace with a mounted blue gem—a rogulin crystal, an exotic stone with innate magical properties.

Rogulin crystals were a component used by conjurers to catalyze teleportation across the world. Laymen often called them conjurer's stones, though some mages used that name, too.

Conjurers bound rogulin to themselves and gave the bonded crystals to another conjurer. The recipient would then be able to instantaneously teleport back to the first conjurer—if they were still living. Conjurers often exchanged bound rogulin with other conjurers.

There were tales of tevisrals that could bind rogulin. But such devices were the stuff of myth and legend.

"Congratulations, my son," Bilia said, lifting the necklace. "I bestow upon you this conjurer's stone, that you may always find your way back to us."

Amendal bowed his head, and his mother placed the necklace around his neck, then kissed him on both cheeks. "I am so proud of you," she said, running a hand down his beard.

"Thank you, Mother."

Amendal's parents beamed exultantly. Amendal found their pride deeply satisfying.

He tucked the tomes under an arm, then shot his other hand skyward, whooping triumphantly.

Amendal spent the rest of the evening perusing his family's precious tomes, selecting sections and chapters that were of most interest to him. He bounced back and forth among the three volumes for most of the night, noting which passages he wanted transcribed.

His father had volunteered Arintil to help with the transcription. Arintil was not amused. The previous night, after Amendal had left the estate to enjoy the night life of Soroth, Arenil and Arintil had a heated debate on the subject. But Arintil eventually relented. Their father had probably used Arintil's stuffy propriety against him. Arenil would lend a hand with the transcription the following evening. He had other responsibilities, having previously committed the Aramien Estate to hosting a banquet in honor of the expedition to Tardalim.

After Amendal selected the passages he wanted his father and brother to transcribe, he went to work poring over *Greater Conjurations from the Aldinal Plane*. The tome contained incantations for many objects and creatures not found in the curriculum of the Sorothian Magical Order.

For several hours, Amendal transcribed passage after passage, until exhaustion overcame him. He didn't sleep long, though. When he awoke the following morning, Amendal returned to his studies. He continued transcribing the passages and incantations from the tome. He even committed several incantations to memory.

Sometime in the midafternoon, the council members of the Order arrived at the Aramien Estate.

Though Amendal hadn't paid much attention, the staff his family kept on hand had prepared the grove for the expedition's farewell celebration. The Aramien Estate often hosted banquets and parties—particularly celebrations held after weddings, which were much more complex affairs than the festivities planned for the evening.

As more guests arrived, Amendal decided to move his studies elsewhere. There would soon be guests tromping in and out of the estate home, and he did not want prying eyes to peer at the sacred pages.

So Amendal retired to his private rooms late that afternoon. He sat on a large window seat in his bedroom with a view overlooking the lawn behind his family's home. Tables were set up in rows, enough of them to accommodate over three hundred guests.

He had learned from Ildin—and the meeting in the Order's amphitheater—that two hundred and eight non-mages were accompanying the expedition. They consisted of hired mercenaries, retired soldiers from the Sorothian Navy, and some hardy adventurers. They were all to be led by a retired commander from the navy named Calimir Sharn. He was a decorated officer who had spent many years fighting alongside the Mindolarnians.

If Amendal had known of their involvement to begin with, he probably wouldn't have been so apprehensive about joining the expedition.

A small contingent of scholars from the Order of Histories—Soroth's primary historical society—were also joining the expedition.

The scholars were some of the first to arrive at the Aramien Estate. Amendal watched them mill about the banquet tables, finding their seats.

Thereafter, Amendal only occasionally glanced out the window, focused mostly on the pages of *Greater Conjurations from the Aldinal Plane*. Throughout his transcriptions he memorized several intriguing incantations.

The sun was setting in the east when Amendal once again turned to the window. Most of the chairs were filled with men and women dressed in fancy attire.

The estate's staff was placing platters of food on a row of tables not far from the house. Hunger pangs struck Amendal's stomach as he eyed the food.

He scanned the banquet area, looking for familiar faces. There were several pretty women in that crowd, most of whom he didn't recognize. The variety was enticing.

No, that's not what I'm doing tonight… he scolded himself, fighting the urge to strut outside.

Then he noticed Ildin sitting at a table along the middle row, talking with Fendar and a few other illusionists. The rest of Amendal's friends were scattered across the tables. *Where is Faelinia?*

As he searched the crowd, a blood-red dress caught his eye.

The dress's owner was none other than Vaem. The Mindolarnian woman wove around the tables, studying each person she passed. Amendal hadn't remembered she was that curvaceous. Her black hair was twisted into a bun at the back of her head, and she wore a near excessive amount of makeup. She still wore only one glove, though… Odd, but it did match her dress.

She looked intriguing. If it had been several days earlier, Amendal would be swiftly making his way to the banquet to seduce her.

Not today. If he were to win over Faelinia, he would have to act differently from now on. *No more carousing with loose women or strutting through crowds,* he told himself. Hopefully, acting out of character would draw Faelinia's eye.

Amendal returned to his tome and marked it with a velvet strand. "Time to eat," he said, closing the tome and uttering an incantation. Golden light shot from his hands, gathering on the opposite side of the window seat. A portal soon formed, and Amendal focused on manifesting a gosset from the Aldinal Plane. Gossets were seabirds, mostly white, with yellow patches covering the crowns of their heads and with black feathers adorning their wingtips.

Soon, a winged silhouette appeared in the portal, and the gosset swooped from the mystical doorway.

Once the conjuration settled between his legs, Amendal reached for a blank sheet of parchment, tearing a piece from it. He quickly scribbled, "*Ildin, grab me a plate. I'm starving,*" signed his name, and rolled the note.

He commanded the bird to open its beak, then placed the rolled parchment in its mouth. Through his mental focus, Amendal put enough pressure on the parchment so the gosset wouldn't drop it.

Amendal chuckled as he opened the window and directed the bird straight for Ildin. Amendal closed the window just as the conjuration landed on Ildin's head.

The illusionist wasn't amused. He pulled the bird from atop his head and noticed the parchment. Amendal let the parchment drop from the conjuration's mouth, watching with gleeful anticipation.

Ildin shook his head as he read the message. He sighed and sent an annoyed look to Amendal's window, but soon rose from his seat.

"A good friend," Amendal said and returned to reading.

He flipped to a new chapter in the tome: "Giants and Gargantuans of the Elemental Realms."

Throughout his studies, Amendal had learned to conjure humanoid creatures made of ice, magma, dirt, and water. They were pure manifestations from the Aldinal Plane, as no such creature existed on Kalda—at least not anymore. Those conjurations were only slightly larger than he himself.

"*In the ancient days, conjurers needed larger conjurations to combat their foes, particularly during the fabled Dragon Wars*," the tome read. "*Many a conjurer went head-to-head with the dragons of Kalda. Those conjurers used elemental giants to waylay the majestic beings while their comrades assailed the dragons with ranged assaults…*"

Dragons? Amendal had never believed in the existence of dragons, but he didn't discount them, either. After all, gangolins resembled the descriptions of dragons—although gangolins lacked wings. They also had short tails, and every fictional depiction Amendal had ever seen of dragons showed them with long tails as well as wings.

Through the gosset now perched atop Ildin's shoulder, Amendal became aware of a conversation. All manifestations of the Aldinal Plane, even the inanimate objects, allowed conjurers to hear through their conjurations. They could even talk through them, if the conjuration had the capacity to verbalize speech.

Ildin was talking to a woman. *Vaem?* he wondered. Amendal glanced out the window, noticing Ildin at the serving table with the Mindolarnian woman. "Go for it, buddy," he said. If Amendal couldn't have a pleasurable evening, then Ildin should.

Grinning, Amendal returned to his reading and ignored the conversation.

The passage within the chapter about the elemental giants and gargantuans was rich in what the tome claimed as historical accounts. He was completely engrossed when a knock drew his attention.

"Thank you, Ildin," Amendal said, his eyes still on the page. "You can set it down somewhere over there." He gestured in the vague direction of his bed.

"You're not paying attention, are you?" That was not Ildin's voice.

Amendal abruptly turned to the door, where Vaem stood, holding two plates of food.

"It must be so lonely up here," she said, approaching the window seat. "Luckily, this seat is wide enough for two."

Amendal squinted at the woman, cautiously marking his place in the tome. He set the book upon his notes, not wanting Vaem to see the sacred contents in either form. Amendal did not want to be banished to the Visirm Expanse on his first day as an Aramien Conjurer.

"This is for you," she said, offering him one of the plates.

Amendal studied it, then glanced out the window. His conjuration was still atop Ildin's shoulder. *Guess I should have been listening.*

"Won't you take it?" Vaem asked.

"My apologies," Amendal said with mock solemnity, grabbing the plate. "I just get so engrossed sometimes. It can take a moment for me to get my bearings." That was not true.

"I can see that," Vaem said with a grin, staring at him intently. She grabbed a slice of cheese and placed it daintily in her mouth.

Does she intend to be provocative?

Vaem lingered beside Amendal for a moment before sitting next to him on the window seat.

"Tell me, why aren't you out there?" She gestured to the window.

"I have more important things to do," he said, nodding to the tome and the notes.

Vaem parted her lips, favoring him with a sultry gaze.

Even while I'm hiding, they still find me, he thought. How many other women were down there craning their necks for him?

"It must be an *interesting* read to keep you away from all those pretty women."

Clever minx...

Amendal waved his hand dismissively. "I've bedded half of them already."

"So, you need fresh blood?" she asked, grinning flirtatiously.

Amendal put more food in his mouth and studied her. Vaem definitely found him desirable. *Remember Faelinia...* "I'm turning over a new leaf."

Vaem set her plate on the window seat. "That's too bad." She sighed and leaned forward. "And here I thought we could have a *celebration* of our own." She slid her bare hand across her glove, then crawled toward him across the window seat.

He restrained a grin, taking another bite of his food. *Remember Faelinia—*

A faint buzz reached his ears, and a glint of pink shone from the window seat.

Is that—?

Vaem glided her gloved hand along his leg and leaned forward. "Perhaps I can persuade you," she said, easing her lips onto his. A sudden surge of euphoria filled him. He fought the urge to return the kiss, but oh, it was tantalizing. Her tongue pried his lips open, and the euphoria intensified.

He had kissed plenty of women in his life but rarely experienced such intense emotion during a single kiss. Especially one he did not willingly consent to.

Who is this woman—? But the question soon drowned in a sea of ecstasy. He struggled to focus on Faelinia, but the memory of her was fading. Unbridled passion consumed him.

After a moment, Vaem pulled back and rested her forehead against his. She gazed into his eyes with a primitive hunger.

What's happening...?

Studying Vaem, he noted that she had no wrinkles around her eyes. He had thought her to be well into middle-age, given her responsibilities regarding the expedition. But she looked no older than Amendal. *And... so beautiful.*

But those words instantly felt wrong. *Why?*

A faint memory flickered in the back of his mind, but it was just out of reach. He tried to recall the thought, but the more he reached for it, the farther it slipped away.

All he could do was stare at Vaem.

Vaem... She looked so young. But how? It defied reason...

"How old *are* you?" he murmured.

What a ridiculous thing to ask. One *never* asked a woman her age, especially not during lovemaking. Such probing always doused the flames of intimacy.

Vaem nestled her nose against his. "A hundred and seven," she said, kissing him passionately.

A hundred and seven? He instinctively returned her embrace. Why was he reciprocating? That faint memory returned, but still remained out of reach...

Vaem pulled back again. "Haven't you learned by now that you should never ask a woman *that* question?"

Without waiting for a reply, Vaem pressed herself against Amendal.

Ildin shook his head and rolled his eyes. "So typical," he muttered, averting his gaze from Amendal's window. The Seducer of Soroth didn't even have the decency to close the drapes.

And here I thought you'd hold out for Faelinia... Ildin sighed.

He took another bite of his food, and looked about the table. Fendar had noticed the debauchery, his eyes going wide. He nudged Jaekim, gesturing toward Amendal's window.

As usual, drunken Jaekim burst into laughter. His raucous mirth drew the attention of half the guests. Soon, everyone was staring at Amendal's window.

"If you can hear me"—Ildin turned to the gosset on his shoulder—"close the drapes. *Everyone* can see you."

Scialas stood nearby, looking dumbfounded. She turned to Ildin with a sigh and shook her head. "I suppose there's no hope for him after all."

Oh, Amendal, Ildin lamented, *when will you ever change?*

Amid the thought, Ildin saw Faelinia enter the banquet area and cross the lawn toward the tables laden with food. She looked lost in thought. Ildin groaned. *If he goes all the way with Vaem in plain sight, Faelinia will never have him.*

"Are you closing the drapes?" Ildin whispered to the conjuration. The bird stood motionless.

Ildin's eyes went back to Faelinia. She had not noticed the crowd gawking.

I have to do something, Ildin thought. Amendal was only kissing the Mindolarnian woman. If the rest could be left to the imaginations of the crowd, perhaps the damage would be mitigated.

Ildin whispered an incantation, moving both hands beneath the table. Even though everyone's attention was fixed on the window, they would see the magic fly from the crowd. And he did not want that. But putting his hands under the table wouldn't be discrete enough.

He looked at Amendal's window, then imagined that same window with draperies moving to veil the room. Such an illusion would be difficult to create. Most illusions manifested an immediate change. What Ildin wanted to accomplish was quite complex.

The gray magic gathered between Ildin's fingers, but before finishing the incantation, Ildin deliberately slowed his speech. The slow exhale of words sounded almost like a hum. The deliberate slowing was a technique used to delay a spell's complete manifestation but for Ildin, it would mask the formation of his illusion.

While focusing on maintaining the magic, Ildin guided the gray particles to the grass. His muscles tensed as the magic slithered across the ground. Both the guiding and the deliberate slowing were taxing. With all the mental focus at his command, Ildin maneuvered the magic toward a vine-covered trellis. The gray particles zipped partway up the wall, concealed behind the vines. Maintaining his strained focus, Ildin carefully maneuvered the magic along the mortar between the blocks of stone until it reached Amendal's window.

Ildin resumed whispering his incantation, and the magic immediately coalesced. The illusory window appeared, and then the draperies closed.

He let out a relieved sigh, slumping in his chair. No one seemed to notice him or the illusion.

Several sighs of disappointment echoed around Ildin, mostly from the younger men. They undoubtedly wanted a glimpse of Vaem undressing.

"You can thank me later," Ildin whispered to the conjuration. He glanced across the yard to Faelinia. Her back was turned to the crowd, and she was filling her plate with food. *Good, she didn't see it...*

The ecstasy was intoxicating.

"Oh, Vaem," Amendal moaned. She was all he could think of... He had heard voices, but he couldn't understand them. He didn't want to understand them.

All Amendal wanted was *her*.

Vaem...

"Let's move to the bed," Vaem said, rolling off Amendal.

Through blinding lust, Amendal stumbled after her. She whirled him to the bed, lifting his robe from him.

While she undressed him, that faint memory flickered at the back of his mind. *What was it...?* Did it really matter? It felt important somehow...

She pushed Amendal down onto the bed, then eased atop him, lifting her dress.

Another surge of ecstasy filled his mind.

Vaem…

Then, Amendal heard something. *Footsteps?*

Suddenly, Vaem was ripped from Amendal, screaming. Something gray was holding her, but he couldn't see exactly what.

A stern voice bellowed through the room, but Amendal couldn't understand it. Then another gray shape moved toward him. Through blurred vision, all he saw was a lumbering figure towering over him and reaching for his face.

Moist flesh spread across his cheek, and the euphoria vanished abruptly.

Amendal started. Vaem's muffled screams became clear demands while the blurred figure came into focus: a quinta'shal, a being most people called a mages' parasite. The quinta'shal towered above the bed, standing taller than any man. Its moist gray skin shimmered a pale-pink hue, but the aura soon vanished. The creature had consumed magic. Rows of enormous pores—larger than a man's thumb was round—pulsed along its arms and legs. The creature's featureless face stared at Amendal, its five-sided mouth pulled shut. Though the quinta'shal had no eyes, it *gazed* at Amendal.

"What were you doing?!" Arintil's voice bellowed.

He must have conjured the quinta'shal.

Amendal sat up, pushing the quinta'shal's tripod-fingered hand from his face. The slit on the creature's palm was closed tight, the skin around it wrinkled from excessive stretching. Quinta'shals expelled repurposed magic through those slits. Though the slit was closed, it stank of a faint, putrid odor.

The smell turned Amendal's stomach.

"I'll ask again," Arintil growled. "What were you doing?"

"What did it look like?!" Vaem retorted, dangling in the air.

Another quinta'shal stood at the foot of the bed, gripping Vaem around the chest with a pink tongue longer than a man's leg and thicker than an arm. More of those enormous pores pulsed all along the tongue. Quinta'shals absorbed magic primarily through their tongues.

"If you answer my questions with more questions," Arintil shouted, "I *will* hurl you into the void that is the Visirm Expanse! Now tell me, what were you doing here?"

Vaem struggled against that enormous pink tongue, but it tightened around her. She gasped for breath before muttering a reply. "Seducing… him…"

"For what purpose?" Arintil asked.

"Pleasure…" She struggled to breathe.

Arintil raised an eyebrow and looked to Amendal. "Did she see the contents of the tome?"

Amendal shook his head.

"Are you sure?" Arintil asked. "There was some kind of magic within you, although I couldn't tell what. It tasted similar to enthralling magic." Arintil had sensed the taste through his bond with the quinta'shal.

"Don't worry, brother," Amendal said. "I closed the tome and set it atop the notes before she got close enough to read anything." He glanced to the small table beside the window seat. The tome and pages were exactly where he had left them.

Arintil lessened the conjuration's grip, and Vaem gasped.

"You will leave my brother alone," Arintil said.

Hurried footfalls echoed outside Amendal's bedroom, and then Arenil appeared, looking flustered. He smoothed his formal yellow robes as he entered, scanning the room quizzically.

"What is going on here?" he demanded, looking to Vaem and Amendal. "*Everyone* could see you two."

Oh great… Amendal groaned. *This isn't going to help things with Faelinia.*

"She had enthralled him," Arintil said to his father.

"You what?!" Arenil cried, marching toward Vaem. She was still suspended in the air and didn't answer.

Arenil looked to the small table beside the window seat, then to Amendal. Though Arenil didn't speak, Amendal knew what his father was wondering.

"They're secure, Father," Amendal said.

"I have no interest in your pathetic tomes," Vaem spat. "Now put me down!"

Arenil nodded to Arintil, and the quinta'shal set Vaem on her feet. Its large pink tongue slid away from her, the forked end slithering across its strange lips. Then the quinta'shal closed its five-pointed mouth.

"This is outrageous, Arenil," Vaem shouted. "I demand—"

"You demand?" Arenil barked, his nostrils flaring with anger. "You are in *my* home, in *my* country. If there is any demanding it will be from *me!*"

Amendal had rarely seen his father so upset. Usually, Arenil was a patient man.

"You will leave my home at once," Arenil growled. "Arintil, escort her back to Soroth."

Vaem started. "You have no authority."

Arintil's conjuration opened its mouth once again and leaned toward Vaem. The Mindolarnian tensed.

"Go…" Arenil commanded.

Vaem looked at each of the Aramiens, then the conjurations. Her gaze lingered on Amendal, then she hurried out of the room. Arintil's conjurations were right behind her.

"Here," Arintil said, crossing the room to Amendal's bed. "I finished the transcriptions." He set a stack of pages on the bed, then followed after his conjurations.

"Thank you," Amendal said, but Arintil was already out of the room. He then looked to his father. "I told her I wasn't interested," he said. "That I was busy."

Arenil turned to the windows. "I wish you would have had the decency to close these drapes sooner."

"I didn't close the drapes," Amendal said. He looked to the window. There were drapes covering the window, but there was another set that was also drawn to the sides. The window, however, did not have two draperies.

"Well, someone had the decency of mind to veil your lewdness," Arenil said, shaking his head. He sighed, turning to Amendal. "This wouldn't have happened if your decadent reputation hadn't preceded you. I don't find it a coincidence that *this* happened only a day after you are granted these tomes." He gestured to the small table. "Despite her denial."

"I'm sorry, Father."

Arenil sucked in his breath. "You can't change the past, my son. Just be mindful of the future."

Amendal nodded.

"I'll place a conjuration to guard your door," Arenil said. "Now to attend to that rowdy crowd…"

6

SETTING SAIL

"There is another benefit to using a quinta'shal as a close-quarters combatant. When an unfed quinta'shal opens the secretion slits of its hands and sides, a putrid gas is expelled. Anyone near the conjuration will most likely go into a convulsive fit of vomiting."

- From *Colvinar Vrium's Bestiary for Conjurers*, page 14

That sensual encounter with Vaem preoccupied Amendal's mind throughout the night and into the following day, as he rode his yidoth toward Soroth. Vaem's seduction overshadowed him like the dark clouds brooding over the city. Whatever had affected him—that pink magic—couldn't have been the result of an incantation. She hadn't used one. Had Vaem used a tevisral? Perhaps that glove?

Troubled, Amendal commanded his yidoth to bolt into a gallop. Gusts of wind brushed past him as his pack bounced in time with the yidoth's stride. He was soon through the northern gates and racing through the city.

But what kind of magic was that? Pale-pink magics weren't typically associated with enthralling magic. Although, what he had experienced was not quite like an enthralling spell. *I wonder if Ildin knows anything about it.*

He considered the dilemma until he neared the city's southern piers, then pushed the thoughts aside as he guided his yidoth toward Pier Fifteen, where the expedition's vessel, the *Giboran,* was moored.

Amendal's yidoth sped around a sloping bend, and Soroth's docking district came into view. As usual, there were many vessels moored along the piers, the annual influx as crops across the various islands were imported.

Pier Fifteen extended from Soroth's southeast corner and was one of the longest piers in the city. Fifty vessels could comfortably moor along Pier Fifteen, while most other piers accommodated thirty-eight or so.

Once on the street bordering the piers, he noticed Ildin walking eastward. His friend wore a plain gray robe, like the one commonly worn by illusionist acolytes. Ildin claimed that robe fit better than the one denoting his mastery of the arts. Amendal felt the same way about his charcoal robes.

Amendal slowed the yidoth's stride, coming to a casual trot beside Ildin.

"You're not late," Ildin said, sounding surprised. "But you're wearing the wrong-colored robe."

"What does it matter what robe I'm wearing?" Amendal asked. "And why would you expect me to be late?" True, he had raced through Soroth, but it wasn't because he was rushing.

Ildin shook his head. "Are you trying to say she wasn't wild enough?"

"Do you mean Vaem?"

"Who else?" Ildin chuckled.

Amendal shook his head. "You won't believe what happened."

After Amendal related the entire incident, Ildin's jaw dropped. "It's my fault," he muttered. "I'm so sorry, Amendal."

"No use dwelling on it now."

"She insisted she needed to see you," Ildin said. "That it had to do with the expedition."

A crafty one she is, Amendal thought.

"And now I've fouled things up with the illusion." Ildin groaned.

"I do appreciate your intentions," Amendal said. "Too bad it went awry."

"You're telling me…" Ildin sighed, disappointed.

"Don't worry; I'm sure the truth will get around. Just mention it to Jaekim." Jaekim could spread rumors faster than a wildfire could consume a dried field.

"I'm sorry, Amendal. I was just trying to help…"

"Don't worry about it," Amendal said. "What are friends for but to help when you're in a bind… or when it looks like you're in a bind. Look, here we are." There was plenty of traffic on the pier. Amendal dismounted from the yidoth, opened a portal, and dismissed the conjuration. Then he and Ildin pressed their way through the shuffling throng.

The *Giboran* was moored not far from the shoreline. It was a large gray ship vaguely resembling the navy's Sarin-class warships. Five masts rose from the vessel's main deck, each adorned with plain beige sails. Amendal couldn't tell how many decks the ship had. At least three decks rose above the main deck over the vessel's stern, and there looked to be at least two decks within the gray hull. The *Giboran* probably needed a crew of a hundred. There were at least half that many sailors milling about the ship.

Two gangways connected the *Giboran* to Pier Fifteen. Sailors went up and down the one nearest the bow, delivering or fetching supplies from the pier, while members of the expedition ascended the gangway near the raised quarterdeck.

"Big ship," Amendal remarked.

"It needs to be, in order to fit all of us," Ildin said. "I've never been on a ship this big."

As they neared the gangways, a sailor waved them over. "Are you two embarking on the expedition?" The sailor held a ledger and quill.

"We are," Ildin said. "I'm Ildin Cetarin, and this is Amendal Aramien."

The sailor scanned the ledger, then flipped through several pages.

Amendal leaned forward, seeing a list of names with brief descriptions beside them. *Interesting manifest…*

The sailor made a tally mark beside Ildin's name, then continued flipping through the pages. "You will be staying in the barracks on the second deck below the main," the sailor said, marking the spot beside Amendal's name, one of the last on the list. "Select a bunk, then report to the galley. Commander Sharn wishes to speak with each of you privately. Now move along." The sailor waved to the gangway, and Amendal fought the urge to give a mock salute.

On the main deck, another sailor was directing the members of the expedition. "Go along the rail to the doors. You'll see the stairs on your left," he said, pointing aft. "Barracks are on the second deck below the main," the sailor continued as Amendal and Ildin passed him. "The galley is directly above the barracks. You get there by going along the rail…"

Amendal and Ildin followed the others down to the barracks, which seemed to take up the entire second deck below the main. Rows of two-tiered bunks ran from the port to starboard hulls. More sailors were repeating directions to the expedition members as they filed into the barracks. "Work your way toward the bow, and select the farthest available bunk," they told the newcomers.

Along the starboard hull, Morgidian and Dugal emptied their packs at a pair of bunks. Each wore robes representing their discipline in the magical arts. Morgidian easily climbed onto the top bunk, his large frame making the boards creak. Then he spread his thick coat over the bedding.

"I hope Morgi doesn't crush poor Dugal," Amendal said to Ildin, pointing at their two friends. Dugal was at least half the size of Morgidian.

"They really should swap bunks," Ildin said, chuckling.

Amendal and Ildin soon arrived at their bunks near the center of the barracks.

Ildin took off his pack and tossed it onto the top bunk, then joined Dugal and Morgidian, jovially gesturing back and forth between the bunks. Dugal pointed to the bottom bunk and said something Amendal couldn't hear.

Amendal set his sloglien pack on the bed. He took out his thick coat and laid it atop one end of the bed. There was no pillow, so Amendal would use his coat for padding.

He looked inside his pack, checking the lockbox containing his transcribed notes. Knowing that privacy wasn't a luxury on this trip, Amendal decided to keep the notes in the box. *Hopefully no one will try tampering with it.*

Though he had the only key, another mage would be able to open the box with magic. *Better leave something to guard it.* He closed the pack and contemplated his options as more expedition members filed into the barracks. He could see through the eyes of whatever he conjured. *So, nothing large,* he thought. *Just something to act as a deterrent.*

A spiked xileran should do, he thought, so he uttered the incantation to open a portal to the Aldinal Plane.

The golden vortex formed completely within the confines of his bunk, and the wavy silhouette of a snake appeared within the golden light, then the red-scaled xileran slithered from the portal.

Spiked xilerans were deadly in the wild. Rows of retractable spikes lined their backs, sharp enough that a mere prick from one would draw blood. The xileran slithered toward the pack and wrapped itself around it. Unlike most snakes, xilerans didn't coil on top of themselves. They often rested around boulders or tree trunks.

With his conjuration settled, Amendal strode over to his friends.

"…I'm not going to crush him," Morgidian retorted, climbing down from his bunk.

"I'm just saying…" Ildin raised his hands defensively.

"I like the bottom bunk," Dugal said in a stolid tone.

"It's not like *you're* sleeping beneath me," Morgidian said to Ildin. "Come on, let's go to the galley." He noticed Amendal and grinned widely. "Good morning, Amendal. Have a *pleasurable* night?"

"If by pleasurable you mean insightful, then yes," Amendal replied. "I spent the entire evening studying."

Morgidian squinted at Amendal, not convinced.

"There's no point lying," Dugal said, turning from his bunk. "We *all* saw you."

Amendal sighed, shaking his head. "What you saw was merely the advances of a desperate woman."

Morgidian raised an eyebrow and shook his head.

"Sure…" Dugal laughed. He crossed the barracks and Morgidian followed.

"What's it going to take…?" Amendal muttered.

"To convince everyone that you're not a womanizer?" Ildin asked.

Amendal gave his friend a sullen glare.

"Sorry," Ildin said with a sigh, "but I don't think you're going to change anyone's mind anytime soon."

⟫•⟪

The *Giboran's* galley was nearly as large as the barracks, and it was packed. Every table was occupied.

"Sure is crowded," Amendal remarked, moving through the crowd. "Maybe we should have arrived sooner."

"I don't think it would have made a difference," Ildin said. "Last night they announced that people could come aboard after the banquet. Let's go stand by Jaekim," he suggested.

Amendal nodded. Perhaps Jaekim would start spreading rumors about Amendal *not* sleeping with Vaem.

While crossing the galley, Amendal eyed Faelinia, who was at a table with several other women. His eyes lingered on her until he and Ildin reached Jaekim. She didn't look at him, though.

To Amendal's surprise, Jaekim did not have a drink in his hand. The necromancer looked remarkably sober. "You missed one incredible party, Amendal," Jaekim said, then snickered. "Or maybe you *didn't.*"

Amendal shrugged. "You all have it wrong."

Dugal laughed and shook his head.

"She was *that* bad?" Jaekim asked.

"I wouldn't know," Amendal said. "I didn't sleep with her." He didn't feel comfortable telling the entire truth to anyone but Ildin.

"But she looked so enticing in that dress..." Jaekim rubbed his chin.

"He didn't sleep with her," Ildin interjected. "Amendal is a full-fledged Aramien Conjurer now, and he spent the night studying his family's books."

Morgidian snorted with mirth.

"What...?" Jaekim looked to Amendal, confusion spreading across his face. "So you can't say whether she was good, or bad?"

"I said I don't know, Jaekim," Amendal said with impatience. "Why don't you sleep with her and find out."

Jaekim's eyes went wide. "You mean... you're *actually* leaving women for the rest of us?"

Amendal nodded. "You could say that. I'm turning over a new leaf."

Jaekim looked to Ildin, then Amendal, then back to Ildin. He went slack-jawed, scanning the galley. "You mean... you're not going to sleep with *any* of them?" He swept his hand across the crowd.

"Well, maybe one," Amendal said. He glanced in the direction of Faelinia, but she had her back turned to him.

"This is incredible!" Jaekim blurted. "You're serious?"

Morgidian's snorting turned into laughter and Amendal nodded.

"Listen up, everyone!" Jaekim shouted. "Amendal Aramien has officially renounced his promiscuous ways!" Several people turned to the shouting necromancer, but most ignored him. "No longer will we have to live under his shadow! The women of—"

The ship jolted. Amendal staggered into a wide stance, while Jaekim fell against a mage sitting at a nearby table.

"Looks like we're moving," Ildin said.

Jaekim pushed himself up and resumed shouting. Amendal ignored him. Some of the expedition paid attention to the necromancer, but not many.

Shortly after the ship began moving, several men wearing the black garb of naval officers entered the galley. One held the ledger the sailor had been marking when Amendal and Ildin came aboard.

"Good morning," the officer said in a booming voice. "I am Dardel Draile, first officer to Commander Calimir Sharn. Commander Sharn wishes to speak with each of you in order to most efficiently assemble our expedition. One by one you will go to his private quarters to be interviewed on your various skills and experience. If you need to leave the galley for any reason, please notify another expedition member and return promptly."

Dardel opened the ledger and called the first name on the list, Haedral Scurn. A middle-aged man with brown hair who wore the black robe of a necromancer rose from a table across the galley.

Scurn? Amendal wondered. The Scurns were a noble family from the isle of Sarn—the second largest island in the Principality of Soroth. They were a minor house, but Amendal had met plenty of Scurns during the lavish events held at the Aramien Estate.

A noble born necromancer? Amendal wondered, watching the other officer escort Haedral out of the galley.

"Guess we should get comfortable," Ildin said, plopping onto the decking. "Did anyone bring any cards?"

"I did," Dugal said, reaching into his robes and pulling out a deck of worn cards. "Who is up for a few games of Sharzen?"

Sharzen was an old card game that had originated on the Mainland. Amendal had heard that it started in Kildath, but a few people claimed it originated in the Kingdom of Los. The game consisted of seven suits, each with twelve cards. Each suit was named after a mythological creature.

The game was played by pairing cards in various combinations to earn points throughout a predetermined set of rounds. The number of rounds varied depending on the number of players and the number of decks involved. In one mode, cards were paired and then recycled after each round. At the end of the game the player with the most points won.

"I didn't bring any money," Morgidian said, dropping down beside Ildin.

"We'll use chips," Dugal said. "I brought a bunch with me."

Jaekim snorted. "As long as they're not those stupid spheres that they started using at Orchin's Tavern. Damn things roll all over the place."

"Are you playing, Amendal?" Ildin asked.

Amendal considered the question. He thought of his transcribed notes, but quickly decided it wouldn't be wise to read them in the galley. "Sure... I might as well."

It was late in the evening when First Officer Draile called Amendal to meet with Commander Sharn. He supposed the order in which people were called was based on when they volunteered or were "conscripted."

The other officer, named Nordis, escorted Amendal to the first deck above the main. They crossed the open-air bridge and strode into the portside corridor. Nordis knocked on the third door, then snapped to attention.

"Come in," a deep voice called, and Nordis opened the door for Amendal, gesturing for him to enter.

Calimir Sharn stood at the only window in the cabin, his eyes fixed on the darkened horizon. Though the commander was a thick-set man, he stood about average height—half a head shorter than Amendal. His thick, wavy hair was a mix of gray and black, and partially covered his large ears.

I thought he'd be taller, Amendal mused.

The retired commander turned from the window, facing Amendal. Calimir was a broad faced man with a bulbous nose. A deep scar ran along his left cheek to his chin. His brown eyes studied Amendal fiercely, his thin lips downturned in a grimace.

"Take a seat," he said, gesturing to a pair of armchairs along the bulkhead to the left of the door.

Amendal nodded, and seated himself, studying Calimir's quarters in a sweeping glance. *Not bad*, he thought. Compared to the barracks, it was luxurious. Opposite the chairs was a narrow bed. A crudely crafted lightstone lantern hung from the ceiling, swaying with the rocking of the ship and casting shadows across the cabin.

"You are Amendal Aramien?" Calimir asked.

"I am."

Calimir nodded. He sat in the other chair and grabbed a stack of parchments from the table between the chairs. "The son of Master Arenil." Calimir nodded again. "I've heard great things about you. You're quite talented, from what people say. Your friend, Ildin Cetarin, is quite enamored of your abilities."

"Oh, really?" Amendal asked, cocking his head.

Calimir narrowed his eyes. "You're not trying to jockey your way to notoriety, are you Mister Aramien?"

Mister Aramien...?

Amendal shook his head, leaning toward Calimir. "I didn't even want to come on this expedition. I was forced into it."

"I don't see a conscription mark in your notes," Calimir said, flipping through the parchment. "It says you volunteered."

"No, I was forced to come," Amendal said. "Just ask Vaem Rudal. She was present when I returned home to Soroth."

"Mistress Rudal, huh?" Calimir sat back, grinning. "Was she the reason you *conceded?*"

Amendal shook his head. "No, she's not. I have no interest in her."

"You changed your mind that fast?" Calimir asked with a displeased grunt. "There is a price to fickleness, son."

"So, you think I slept with her too, huh?"

"Everybody saw you," Calimir said. "And I've heard of your reputation.

There's no need to hide it. I'll give you no shame as long as your promiscuous behavior doesn't interfere with this expedition. In fact, I'd salute any man who can bed as many women as you."

With that broad face and bulbous nose, of course you would, Amendal thought.

"So, what do you really want out of this expedition, Mister Aramien?"

"I just want to be done with it," Amendal replied. "The sooner we finish, the sooner I can return to Soroth and focus on honing my abilities in the magical arts."

"Interesting..." Calimir nodded, glancing back to the parchment. "I see you're a conjurer. Have you ever used your conjurations in combat?"

"Besides duels?" Amendal asked. "No. But I have used them against other creatures."

"What kind of creatures?"

Did Amendal dare tell him more? Not many people knew of gangolins. Most men dismissed them as myth.

"Beasts bigger than this ship," Amendal said flatly. "Creatures that would haunt your dreams for a lifetime if you saw them."

Calimir raised his eyebrows, looking doubtful. "Cut the whimsical nonsense, Aramien. Tell me what you've *actually* fought."

He's not going to believe me, Amendal thought. "Gangolins, *sir*," he added the title with mock respect.

"And what on Kalda is a gango-what's-it?"

"Gangolin," Amendal corrected him. "Enormous reptilian creatures covered in scales. Many mistake them for dragons, but they don't have wings, and their tails and snouts are shorter. Some believe the gangolins are the basis for the dragon myths."

Calimir stifled a laugh, shaking his head. "And where did you encounter this... *gangolin?*"

I knew he wouldn't believe me, Amendal thought. "In the Melar Forest," he said.

Calimir burst into laughter. "So, you are an egocentric madman with delusions of grandeur?"

Angered, Amendal rose from his chair. *Why am I putting up with this?*

"Where are you going, son?" Calimir asked amid his mirth.

Amendal bit his tongue. *Stop calling me son,* he groaned, reaching for the doorknob. He pulled the door open before replying. "To my bunk. I'll not stand for your berating."

"Wait," Calimir said between chuckles. "Come back."

Hand still on the doorknob, Amendal turned to face the man.

"I haven't told you your assignment yet." The commander gestured to the chair. "I've divided the expedition into thirty squads, ten personnel each."

Amendal studied Calimir, then ambled back to the chair.

"Prior to our little meeting, I picked out your position. You didn't really help your case, but you didn't hurt it, either. I've heard the tales about the

Aramien Conjurers. If you're anything like your predecessors, you'll be valuable."

Anger simmering, Amendal studied Calimir.

"You are to be in squad one, along with your friend Mister Cetarin. I personally will be leading that squad with five other soldiers that have served under my command throughout my military career. Of course, Mistress Rudal will be with us, too."

"And who is the last member of our squad?" Amendal asked. The thought of being near Vaem for much of the expedition made him hate this trip even more. *It's going to be impossible staying away from that woman.* This assignment would only make it more difficult to attract Faelinia's attention.

"Two, actually," Calimir said. "Mistress Rudal doesn't count, nor does the other Mindolarnian. One of the two is a barsionist who served in the Sorothian Navy and has since become an adventurer. The other is a talented dualist mage named Faelinia Tusara."

Amendal felt conflicted as he left Calimir's cabin.

On the one hand, he was overjoyed to be in the same squad as Faelinia. They would undoubtedly spend the entire expedition together. That was remarkably convenient. But then there was the matter of Vaem.

From what Calimir said, Vaem had not refuted the rumors that Amendal had bedded her. He intended to confront her about it. That was not something he wanted coming between him and Faelinia.

"I should have kicked her out immediately," Amendal grumbled, striding toward the open-air bridge. Wind rustled the sails as he descended to the main deck. To his surprise, Faelinia stood near the forecastle, leaning on the portside rail and gazing at the stars.

"Fancy seeing you here," Amendal called.

Faelinia didn't look at him. "What do you want, Amendal?"

Arriving beside her, Amendal leaned against the rail. "Your hand in marriage," he said, trying to sound serious.

With an exasperated expression, Faelinia cocked her head toward him. "You? Seeking marriage?" She studied him briefly before looking back to the stars. "You're too promiscuous for marriage."

"Well, that's changing," Amendal said.

"I've heard," Faelinia scoffed. "Jaekim has been proclaiming you're a changed man."

"And you don't believe him?"

She looked back to Amendal, eyeing him up and down. "I don't think you could change if you tried with all your might. A man like you wouldn't be able to resist the temptation."

"A man like me?"

"You know what I mean," Faelinia said, returning her gaze to the stars.

"No… I don't," Amendal said innocently. "You're being *too* vague."

Faelinia chuckled, shaking her head. "A man with your looks…"

"Did you just call me attractive?" Amendal asked. Faelinia pursed her lips and closed her eyes. "I just want to be sure I heard right…"

She did not reply. After a moment, she opened her eyes and resumed staring at the stars. Amendal studied her briefly, then followed her gaze.

He stared at the sky for a while before pushing off the rails. "Well, squadmate, I'm going below deck for more studying."

Faelinia spun from the rail with a dumbfounded expression. "Squadmate?"

"Yes," Amendal said, grinning. "Did I not mention that earlier?" He shrugged innocently before turning away. "Good night, Faelinia."

Resisting the urge to look over his shoulder, Amendal waved his hand above his head just as she had when leaving Makivir's Lounge. Hopefully, Faelinia was staring at him.

Turnabout is fair play, after all.

7

THE SHORES OF ABODAL

"Quinta'shals do have their limits. If they consume too much magic, they can die from excessive ingestion. Luckily, the creatures' gray skin turns colors when they are full. Death can be abated by expelling the magic, but they can still perish from overexertion."

- From *Colvinar Vrium's Bestiary for Conjurers*, page 15

A frigid breeze washed across the *Giboran*. Wrapped in two thick blankets, Amendal sat against the ship's foremast, clutching a lightstone in one hand and the transcribed passages of his family's tomes in the other. His eyes, however, were not on the parchments.

Faelinia stood at the portside rail, gazing at the stars. A veil of flame surrounded her, shielding her from the cold.

Amendal had found her there at the rail each night these past two weeks. Although she gave him brief glances, she did not speak to him unless he spoke first. That suited Amendal just fine, for now.

After staring at Faelinia for a time, Amendal returned his gaze to the transcribed passages. He had read through everything twice and was currently committing incantations to memory from *Greater Conjurations from the Aldinal Plane*. Amendal mouthed the words to the incantation but did not focus his mind on summoning the conjuration.

In order to summon a creature or object from the Aldinal Plane, a conjurer needed to utter the incantation while also conjuring an image of the creature or object in their mind. From what Amendal understood, the process was similar to manifesting other forms of magic. Magic did not manifest unless both tongue and mind worked together.

The fiery glow lessened around Faelinia, drawing Amendal's attention.

Faelinia turned from the rail, hurrying across the main deck.

"I have an extra blanket," Amendal called to her.

Faelinia turned briefly, studying Amendal for a moment. Her eyes lingered longer than usual. "No, thank you," she said, then hurried below deck.

Well, that's different, Amendal thought, smiling.

Now alone—besides the crew manning the rigging—Amendal returned to his studies.

The clouds soon rolled across the sky above the *Giboran,* dropping flakes of snow.

"Snow?" Amendal muttered, watching the flakes land on the deck. One landed upon his nose, but soon melted. "We must be getting close to that godforsaken wasteland."

More snowflakes fell but melted soon after landing on the ship.

Better get below deck, he thought, pushing away from the foremast.

The following morning, Amendal awoke to Ildin shaking him.

"They've spotted land," Ildin said cheerily, his breath visible.

"Finally!" Amendal shot upright and looked around the barracks.

Others were milling among the various bunks, waking those that were sleeping.

"Let's go topside," Ildin said and darted away.

Amendal wrapped his blanket around himself and followed Ildin out of the barracks.

The main deck was crowded. Amendal and Ildin pushed their way toward the raised forecastle, but didn't make it past the ship's third mast. Ildin stood on his toes, but sighed at his futile attempt to catch a glimpse of the distant shoreline.

"You do realize we can get a better view, don't you?" Amendal asked.

Ildin turned with a quizzical expression on his face, then his eyes widened with enlightenment.

The two of them uttered their own incantations. White light gathered around Ildin's hands while a golden hue formed above Amendal.

Amendal focused on conjuring his gosset, and the bird soon flew from the golden portal. A biting chill stung the conjuration, but Amendal pushed through the pain and circled the bird toward the rigging. He guided the conjuration to the foremast just as a white silhouette of a man appeared on the mast's highest yardarm. The image of Ildin coalesced just as Amendal perched his conjuration.

"Good idea, Amendal," Ildin said, the words coming from both his mouth and his illusion.

Amendal nodded and closed his eyes, focusing his vision through the gosset.

A streak of white spread across the horizon as far as he could see, undoubtedly the snow-covered coastline of the Abodine Wasteland. Spires of white rose from the water around the distant shore. There were dozens of those spires scattered throughout the water. Both the spires and the shore were dotted with glinting specks.

"I think those are chunks of floating ice," Ildin said, his illusion pointing to the spires. "Icebergs, they're called. I've heard they are much larger than they look."

Both illusion and conjuration sat atop the rigging for a while, silently admiring the beauty of the exotic shoreline.

⬦•⬦

Vaem leaned over her map of Abodal. The detailed cartography showed the actual coastline of the continent, as well as the ice shelves that spread far into the ocean. Earlier that morning, a sailor had notified her that the icy continent had been spotted. But Vaem found it too cold to step outside for a glimpse of what was undoubtedly a streak of white between two shades of blue. Why leave the comfort of her cabin for something so lackluster?

A heavy knock rattled her cabin's door, and Vaem turned from the map.

"Vaem, are you in there?" asked the muffled voice of Kydol Virain through the door. She was a lieutenant under General Vidaer's command. Vidaer had dispatched her as the *Giboran* prepared to set sail, undoubtedly to ensure that *everything* about the expedition was reported to him.

"Yes," Vaem replied, opening the door.

Kydol—wrapped in several blankets—hurried into Vaem's cabin. She stood slightly shorter than Vaem, and her brown hair was braided and tucked beneath her blankets.

"It's frigid out there." Kydol shivered as she shut the door.

"Exactly why I didn't care to leave my cabin," Vaem said and returned to her map.

Kydol snorted and moved to Vaem's side. "I told Captain Edara to sail eastward. They will note each significant landmark we pass."

"Good." Vaem nodded.

The lieutenant leaned past Vaem, tracing her finger along the depicted coastline. "I would guess Crisyan Bay is perhaps a day or so away." She tapped on a divot in the coastline almost entirely enclosed by ice shelves. From the cartography, the bay looked more like a river.

We should hold a council tonight, Vaem thought. She turned to Kydol, who was tracing her finger from the bay toward a lone mountain. "Why don't you inform Calimir that I want to hold a meeting with the squad leaders?"

"As you wish," Kydol said and spun to the door. A chilled draft washed past Vaem as she continued staring at the map. *Soon, I will fulfill your mandate, my emperor.*

⬦•⬦

The *Giboran* traveled eastward for most of the day, sailing alongside the towering spires of ice. The crowd on the main deck lessened as the day drew on.

Amendal had since dismissed his conjured gosset, but Ildin kept his illusion atop the rigging. It had startled some of the crew as they adjusted the sails, nearly causing one of the men to fall. Luckily, another sailor caught him.

After dinner, Amendal sat in the galley watching his friends play a game of Sharzen. From where he sat, Amendal could tell Morgidian had a winning hand. Both Ildin and Scialas had horrible cards, and Amendal couldn't tell which was worse. The round ended, and Morgidian triumphantly threw his hands into the air.

Ildin sighed and leaned back in his chair, looking at Amendal. "Are you sure you don't want to play?"

Amendal shook his head. "I think I might go topside soon."

Ildin raised an eyebrow. "Uh, I don't think your *tactic* is working," the illusionist said, glancing over his shoulder. He was probably checking to see if Faelinia was nearby.

"Of course it is," Amendal replied, rising from his seat. "I'll see you later." As he neared the doorway leading to the stairs, one of Calimir's officers hurried into the galley, almost colliding with him. The officer apologized and hurried around Amendal.

As Amendal reached the stairs, the officer addressed those in the galley. "Commander Calimir is calling a council. Every squad leader is to report to the war room as soon as possible."

Intrigued, Amendal stopped short of the stairs. *A council?* Since setting sail from Soroth there hadn't been one meeting concerning the expedition, nor a single utterance of the name Tardalim.

The officer hurried back through the door, nearly bumping into Amendal again.

"Pardon me again," the officer said, darting to the stairs.

"Excuse me," Amendal called after him, "but what's this council about?"

"The topic concerns squad leaders only," the officer said, then descended the stairs.

Squad leaders only? Amendal was intrigued. He looked to the ceiling, thinking about Faelinia. *I could let one night slide...* he thought, turning back to the galley. He eyed Ildin, who was collecting a set of cards dealt out by Jaekim.

"Ildin," Amendal shouted, beckoning to Ildin, who reluctantly left the table.

"What?" he asked as he reached Amendal.

"Do you want to eavesdrop on that meeting?" Amendal whispered, a wry, anticipating smile curving his lips.

"I thought you were going to gawk at Faelinia?"

Amendal's expression turned sullen. "It's *not* gawking. Now, do you want to join me or not?"

Ildin glanced back to the table and shrugged. "I might as well. It isn't like I was winning anyway."

"Good. Follow me."

They descended past the barracks and arrived at the bottommost deck. Amendal led Ildin through several corridors, passing through the crew's quarters. Several sailors were snoring loudly.

"Uh, Amendal..." Ildin muttered, "the council is in the war room."

"Yes, I know that," Amendal replied. "Just stay close."

They left the crew's quarters and strode down a corridor leading to the cargo hold, where crates and barrels full of supplies were packed tightly, with narrow aisles separating the columns of supplies.

Amendal scanned each of the aisles, finding no one else in the cargo hold. "Perfect." Grinning, he made his way down the nearest aisle.

"So what now?" Ildin asked, still standing in the doorway.

"Just get over here," Amendal said, grabbing one of the barrels. He tried tipping it at an angle, but the barrel was too heavy. "Not that one," he muttered, moving to another barrel.

"Why are you trying to move stuff if we're just going to cast our invisibility?" Ildin asked. "That's what you want to do, right? Sneak inside the war room and listen?"

"It'll be too crowded," Amendal said with a grunt as he shifted one of the barrels, creating a small niche between the supplies. "Come help me make some room so we can sit."

Ildin complied and they soon hollowed out a niche wide enough for both of them to sit cross-legged.

"So what's your plan?" Ildin asked as he sat down on the decking.

"I'll conjure something, and you'll make an illusion of it."

Ildin raised an eyebrow and frowned, unconvinced.

"Just trust me," Amendal said. "I read about this tactic in one of my family's tomes."

Ildin chuckled. "I'm surprised. You *actually* managed to get some reading done amid your gawking."

Amendal rolled his eyes. "Now plug your ears. I don't want you hearing this incantation."

Ildin shook his head, but placed his hands over his ears.

The conjuration Amendal planned to use was from *Greater Conjurations from the Aldinal Plane*. Of all the knowledge kept within his family's tomes, the incantations were the most sacred.

Golden light coalesced between Amendal's hands, and the magic wisped together, forming a portal about the size of a child's fist. A winged outline appeared in the golden light, then a majestic insect-like creature—made completely of ice—emerged from the portal.

The six-winged conjuration fluttered through the air, landing on the decking between Amendal and Ildin. Jagged patterns of pale blues and whites adorned the crystal-like wings, complimented by the tiny shards arrayed around the creature's legs. An oblong abdomen shared the same jagged patterns with the wings and was tipped with a glistening stinger.

"Whoa!" Ildin blurted, hands still covering his ears. "What is that?"

"According to the sacred texts they are called seracius lepidors. I'm trying to come up with a better name, though. Seracius lepidor just seems too long."

"How about ice flyer?" Ildin suggested.

"Ice flyer?" Amendal asked incredulously. "That's just as bad as mages' parasite…"

"What's wrong with mages' parasite?" Ildin asked. "It's an accurate name."

Amendal stared at his friend in disbelief, blinking several times. "I can't believe you just said that."

Ildin laughed and leaned close to the tiny ice conjuration, studying it. After a moment, he straightened and uttered an illusory incantation. White light wrapped around the seracius lepidor. The conjuration glowed for a moment, but the luminescent hue faded as the illusory magic left the icy creature. The white magic clustered together, forming an outline resembling the conjuration.

Soon, an exact copy of the icy creature stood on the decking in front of Ildin.

"So do you plan to sit here while we eavesdrop?" Ildin asked.

"Yes," Amendal replied, commanding his conjuration to fly. "If we return to our bunks, we'll look suspicious."

Ildin frowned, but lifted his illusion from the ground. It fluttered, joining the real seracius lepidor in the air.

"Ready?" Amendal asked, and Ildin nodded.

Both illusion and conjuration zipped through the cargo hold. They flew through the ship, swiftly ascending to the main deck. In contrast to the sensation Amendal felt through his gosset, the icy insect was rather warm. Its vision was different, too. It was blurry, somewhat like looking through foggy glass. Amendal had conjured several insects throughout his life, and each time their vision was poor. Their hearing, however, was extremely keen, and the seracius lepidor's hearing was no less extraordinary.

Through his conjuration, Amendal could hear Ildin's illusion moving through air—not the fluttering of its illusory wings, but the sound of magic and air rubbing against each other. It was the oddest sound.

Normally, illusions were silent when they moved, unless sound was added to their movements. But Ildin had not added that component to his illusion.

As the illusion and conjuration ascended to the open-air bridge, a cacophony of noises assaulted Amendal's mind. Wind, rustling sails, footsteps, waves, conversations. It was nearly overwhelming.

Amendal struggled to focus on that strange sound caused by Ildin's illusion. It was somewhere ahead of him, flying above figures covered in dark brown. Those were probably the squad leaders in their thick coats. They were moving toward an opening that led to the ship's upper aft sections.

The strange sound shifted, as if contained.

His illusion must be inside, Amendal thought, zipping his conjuration through what he assumed was the corridor leading to the war room.

The conjuration flew above more dark-brown figures, and Amendal guided his icy insect through the door. Inside, he heard several familiar voices, one of which belonged to Vaem. She was talking to a woman unfamiliar to Amendal.

Amendal hadn't seen much of Vaem these last two weeks. He'd run into her twice, and both times he confronted her about the rumors concerning them. Vaem simply shrugged them off as fact, then attempted to lure him back to her cabin. During the first encounter, she had touched Amendal, and he felt the same irresistible yearning for her he had experienced back at the Aramien Estate. Luckily, Ildin was with him, and the illusionist cast a dispel that nullified the strange euphoria. At their second encounter, Amendal kept his distance.

"... do not come across it, we can resort to an aerial search," she said.

Amendal turned his conjuration's head toward Vaem's voice, but struggled to find her.

"We should near the bay's entrance soon," the unknown woman added. "Captain Edara told me they spotted a chain of islands to the northeast."

"Good," Vaem said. "According to my map, those islands are two hundred phineals west of the channel leading to the bay."

Amendal fluttered his conjuration to the ceiling, gripping the grain in the beams with the icy insect's frozen claws.

"Can you see anything, Ildin?" Amendal asked.

"Of course. Can't you?"

"Not really... do you see a map?"

"Yes," Ildin said, "it's on the table in the center of the room."

There's a table? Everything was so blurry, and he could barely see the individual squad leaders in the room.

"Close the doors, Braynar," Calimir's voice echoed through the war room.

"That was loud," Amendal muttered.

"Are the ears on that conjuration *that* sensitive?" Ildin asked. "Sure, he was a tad loud, but—"

"Quiet," Amendal interrupted Ildin. Calimir was saying something else.

"...good authority that we will reach our place of mooring within a day," the retired commander said. "Mistress Rudal has asked that we hold this council to discuss the particulars of our journey across the wastes."

As Calimir continued his opening remarks, Amendal saw a figure moving from the far side of the room. The person was tall, with dark hair. Vaem?

Perhaps this conjuration wasn't the right choice, he lamented.

"We will moor in Crisyan Bay." Vaem's voice trailed from the tall figure.

So it is her…

"Ice shelves cover much of the bay, but there is a narrow channel we can traverse," Vaem added. "The *Giboran* will moor at a dock at the far end of the channel, where it will wait for our return."

"There's a dock?" a man asked. "But no one lives in the Abodine Wasteland. Why would there be a dock in this Crisyan Bay?"

More questions filled the war room. Some wondered how Vaem had obtained her information, others asked about her map, and several asked why there was a dock.

"Hold your questions," Calimir said. "I'm sure Mistress Rudal will answer each of them."

Vaem began answering the questions, starting with the nature of Crisyan Bay.

"Well, this is interesting," Ildin said, sounding amused.

"Aren't you glad I pulled you away from those cards?" Amendal asked, but quickly returned his focus to Vaem's explanations.

"…built thousands of years ago, when the icy continent was still inhabited," Vaem said. Her answer was welcomed by snickering and laughter. But the scornful reactions were hushed by Calimir.

"Yes, there were ancient inhabitants, called the Eshari. Crisyan Bay was once home to one of their ports. From there we will make our trek across the wastes." She tapped on what Amendal assumed was the map, and the noise resounded throughout the war room.

Damned things are sensitive, Amendal lamented again.

Vaem continued answering each of the questions about the bay and the dock. Several of the squad leaders wondered how the dock could still be intact if it had been constructed thousands of years ago.

Vaem's counter to their skepticism was not what Amendal expected. "The dock—and most of the abandoned Eshari structures we'll encounter—was turned to crystal ages ago by a crysillac."

"A crysillac?" someone asked. "But those are only a myth…"

"Whoa," Ildin muttered. "Did you hear that?"

"No, I was sleeping," Amendal said sarcastically. "Of course I heard it."

Crysillacs *were* a myth. No one had ever seen a crysillac—at least not during Kalda's current era. Though their descriptions varied, the mythical crysillacs had one thing in common: they could turn whatever they touched into crystal.

A debate arose as some squad leaders heckled Vaem's claims. Another person—the one Vaem had spoken to before the meeting—defended the Mindolarnian's explanation.

Calimir settled the outburst, and Vaem continued speaking about the nature of an Eshari city near Crisyan Bay. It too had been turned to crystal.

"So, she claims crysillacs are real," Amendal mused aloud. "Now if I can catch one of those, this trip *will* be worthwhile."

"Didn't you tell me there were no creatures in the wastes that interested you?" Ildin asked.

"That was before I knew about the crysillac," Amendal said.

Vaem moved on to describing the trek across the wasteland. She spoke
as if she had been there.

Odd, Amendal thought, but then he recalled the nightmare during his first
night back in Soroth… The image of that enormous mountain flashed in
Amendal's mind, and he saw himself on the edge of the abysmal precipice
surrounding the towering peak.

Amendal shook the image from his mind and focused on Vaem's voice.

The Mindolarnian scholar went into detail about the various terrains they
would have to cross and the possible dangers of the Abodine Wasteland.
Amendal listened casually until she described the area near Tardalim.

"Once we are a few days away, we will find ourselves on an icy plain. The
plain will undoubtedly contain snowdrifts that we will have to traverse, but
they should be packed solid."

Snowdrifts? Amendal wondered, and that snowy plain of his nightmare returned to the forefront of his mind.

"…We'll know we are close when we can see the lone peak of the mountain housing Tardalim. It will rise above the southern horizon three or four
days before we'll reach the massive canyon at its foothills."

No… Amendal started, shaking his head. *That… that can't be right.*

Vaem continued describing the terrain around the reliquary. Her descriptions were exactly what Amendal had seen in his nightmare.

"Are you okay, Amendal?" Ildin asked. "You look pale…"

Amendal held up a finger to his friend, as Vaem was still explaining
about the chasm.

"… the actual entrance to the reliquary will be below the northern edge
of the vast precipice. So, we will need to descend into a network of caves in
order to access the bridge that spans the icy canyon."

"Can't we just go around this canyon?" a squad leader asked.

"No. It would take weeks to travel around the canyon. Besides, even if
we were on the other side, we wouldn't be able to reach the reliquary's entrance. I'm afraid the bridge is our only option."

Vaem began talking about the entrance to Tardalim, but Amendal didn't
pay attention.

Exactly like that nightmare. Was that a vision of the future? *It couldn't be…
no one can see the future. It must—*

Ildin's touch jarred Amendal from his confusion. "Are you all right? You
look as if you've seen a ghost."

"A ghost of the future, perhaps…"

The illusionist narrowed his eyes. "You're not making any sense."

Of course he wasn't making any sense. None of this expedition *made* any
sense.

A sick feeling formed in the pit of Amendal's stomach, and he suddenly
felt afraid.

Sleep did not lessen the fear that knotted Amendal's stomach. Nightmares consumed his slumber, but they fled after he awoke. He spent the entire morning belowdecks with Ildin, but he couldn't shake those foreboding feelings.

Prior to Amendal's waking, Ildin had made another illusion of himself and set it atop the foremast's highest yardarm. He was eager to spot the towering ice shelves that housed the entrance to Crisyan Bay.

As they ate their midday meal, Ildin suddenly leapt from his chair. "They've spotted the channel! Amendal, you have to see it! It's magnificent!"

The illusionist's declaration roused most of the men and women in the galley. Some darted toward the doorway leading to the stairs, eager for a look at the next leg of their voyage.

"Come on, Amendal," Ildin said, hurrying after them.

Amendal reluctantly rose. He did his best to push aside those frightful feelings, but they persisted at the back of his mind. Amendal walked slowly across the galley, joining the others moving toward the main deck.

Ildin waited at the portside rail for Amendal, gesturing for him to hurry.

The main deck was crowded by the time Amendal was topside, but not as crowded as it had been when land was first spotted.

Ildin grabbed Amendal's arm and guided him toward the raised forecastle. "Are you going to conjure something?"

"No," Amendal replied, staring at the towering sheets of ice south of the ship, beyond the starboard rail. The edge of the ice shelf rose far beyond the *Giboran*'s tallest mast. "Incredible…"

"Oh yes!" Ildin said, pulling at Amendal's arm. "Judging by the position of my illusion, the top of that shelf is probably three or four times higher than the ship."

Amendal and Ildin pushed through the crowd and climbed the stairs leading to the raised bow. The forecastle was crowded, but Ildin pushed his way forward. Amendal, however, remained by the rigging, grabbing a line and leaning over the starboard rail.

Less than a grand phineal ahead of the *Giboran*, an enormous archway of brilliant pale-blue ice marked the entrance of Crisyan Bay. He estimated that the archway was over a hundred phineals wide, and more than twice that in height. It was more than wide enough for the ship to sail through. The archway connected to another ice shelf just as tall as the one beyond the starboard rail.

Gasps of amazement echoed around Amendal as the ship neared the arch. The *Giboran* made a wide turn to port, but swung back to face the arch head on.

Awestruck remarks filled the air as the ship sailed through the archway and into a tunnel of glistening ice. The icy ceiling filtered the sunlight with a dark-blue tint, while tiny shards in the walls sparkled with turquoise light.

"How beautiful!"

Amendal started, then turned to see Faelinia standing beside him. She stared at the tunnel's icy ceiling, her sea-gray eyes sparkling. "Those shards almost look like stars."

"They do," Amendal agreed, settling back onto the forecastle. "Would you like a better view?"

Narrowing her eyes in what looked to be a playful expression, Faelinia nodded. She moved past him, grabbing the line and leaning over the rail.

"Not too far now," Amendal said in a flirtatious tone. He wrapped his arm around Faelinia's waist while grabbing the rail.

"What do you think you're doing?" she asked, sounding coy. She didn't turn, but kept her eyes on the icy tunnel.

"Making sure you don't fall in. The water is freezing, after all."

Faelinia gave him a sidelong glance, her lips forming a slight smile.

At least it's not a scowl.

After a moment, Faelinia returned her gaze to the icy tunnel, her lush golden curls hanging over the rail.

Amendal, however, kept his eyes on Faelinia, a more beautiful sight than the majestic scenery they were passing through.

Ahead of them, the tunnel broadened, and the ice that formed the ceiling thinned, allowing more sunlight to beam into the tunnel. Then the ceiling disappeared, and they sailed into an open channel. Walls of ice soared high, creating an icy canyon almost twice the width of the tunnel behind them.

Some of the crowd around them dissipated, and Faelinia pushed herself away from the rail. She turned to Amendal and ran a gloved hand across his chin. "Thanks for holding me when I didn't need it," she said with a teasing grin.

"Of course," Amendal said, "anything for a squadmate."

Faelinia shook her head and followed the others down the steps to the main deck. Amendal leaned back, one hand gripping a nearby line. He watched Faelinia cross the main deck and disappear into the ship's covered aft section.

Now that's progress, he told himself, leaning his back against the rail. He lazily stared at the icy walls while thinking of his next move to woo Faelinia.

His reverie was broken when the water beside the starboard rail darkened. *What is that?* he thought, peering into the channel's watery depths. He expected the *Giboran* to sail past it, but the shadowy spot moved with the ship. The object was about half the length of the *Giboran*, and dozens of dark lines rippled behind it.

"Ildin," Amendal called, his eyes still focused on the dark spot. "Ildin, come here!"

The shadow shrank, almost disappearing before Ildin reached the rail.

"What?" the illusionist asked.

Amendal pointed to the now tiny shadow. "*Something* is moving below the ship," he whispered.

Ildin shrugged. "Probably some kind of curious fish. I doubt it's anything to worry about. Look, it's gone."

Amendal searched the waters, but indeed, the dark spot had vanished. He swiftly crossed the forecastle, but there were no shadows beyond the portside rail. A hand gripped his shoulder, and Ildin whispered into his ear. "Are you sure you're doing all right? I mean, what with last night and those nightmares?"

"I'm not going crazy," Amendal retorted tersely. "I saw *something*, Ildin. And it was no fish." He lowered his voice. "The thing was half the length of this ship."

"Maybe it was a whale. Whatever it was, it's gone now."

"I don't think it was a whale," Amendal muttered, turning back to the water. "There were shadowy lines moving behind it, like tails or tentacles."

"What are you implying, Amendal?"

Amendal didn't answer. Whatever was following them *had* vanished. But was it truly gone? His mind began to race with possibilities of what could be swimming beneath them.

He had frequented many a tavern and heard sailors telling far-fetched tales of treacherous monsters from the deep—enormous creatures that could destroy a ship and consume its crew.

But those were just tales, myths, and fables. Weren't they?

"I doubt it's a sea monster," Ildin whispered. "Those things aren't real."

But that's what people think of gangolins... Amendal thought, searching the waters once again.

If the Abodine Wasteland was home to mythical creatures like the crysillac, could there be other monsters of myth lying in wait for unsuspecting travelers?

8

FROM THE DEPTHS OF THE SEA

"A common tactic mages use when confronted by a quinta'shal is to overload the creature with their magic. This can be difficult when dealing with a conjured or enthralled quinta'shal, as the mage controlling it is able to expel the consumed magic faster than those in the wild."

- From *Colvinar Vrium's Bestiary for Conjurers*, page 17

Amendal remained at the bow for several hours, searching for that dark spot in the water. Ildin humored him for a time by searching the waters off the starboard rail, but eventually he left to go belowdecks.

I wasn't seeing things, Amendal told himself, pacing back and forth between the forecastle's portside and starboard rails. There definitely had been *something* moving beside the ship. As he paced, Amendal mulled over the various myths and legends of monsters from the deep. Many seemed far-fetched. There was one monster, however, that lingered at the forefront of his mind.

The nactilious.

Despite the varied iterations of the tale, the monster's description was fairly consistent. The nactilious—an enormous cephalopod with dozens of tentacles and a hardened carapace around its oblong head—would attack unsuspecting ships.

Some variations of the myth claimed the monster feasted on men, devouring them whole. Other versions asserted that the nactilious sought the vessels for their hulls, as the beasts preferred eating wood. Some sailors believed that the metallic hull was invented because of the nactilious and its appetite for wood. Amendal found that reasoning silly.

"What are you doing?" someone called from above.

Amendal turned as a sailor swung toward him on one of the lines connecting the bowsprit to the foremast.

"Are you looking for something?" the sailor asked, landing on the decking beside Amendal.

Amendal nodded. "I saw something swimming in the water."

The sailor started, then hurried to the portside rail. He scanned the waters then turned back to Amendal. "Where?"

"Over there," he pointed to the opposite side of the ship. "But it's been several hours."

The sailor laughed. "Whatever it was, it's probably long gone by now." He ran a hand through his hair. "But I'll tell the captain. Never know what we might encounter on our way out of here."

The sailor descended to the main deck and headed toward the open-air bridge.

Soon, the channel of water emptied into Crisyan Bay. From what Amendal could see, the ice shelves surrounded most of the bay. The shelves were just as tall as those along the coast. Several icebergs dotted the bay, each nearly the size of a small island.

Sailor shouted reports, and Amendal noticed some members of the expedition coming topside.

I better get my things, he thought, then noticed Ildin in the group. The illusionist carried two packs, his and Amendal's. *What a friend.*

Ildin crossed the main deck, swiftly ascending the steps to the forecastle, holding out Amendal's sloglien pack. It bulged. "I threw in an extra blanket."

"Always thoughtful." Amendal took the pack, slinging it over his shoulder.

"Did you see the statues?" Ildin asked.

"What statues?"

Ildin looked beyond the ship's bowsprit, frowning. "They're not visible from here." His illusion was obviously still atop the highest yardarm. "They're at the far side of the bay, near the ice shelves. And they're huge!"

The *Giboran* sailed for another half hour before the other side of the bay came into view.

The statues Ildin had mentioned were colossal. There were seven of them, each made of glistening pale-blue crystal, depicting men and women in flowing robes. They towered high—not as high as the ice shelves but taller than the *Giboran*. Each stood atop a round pedestal a couple of stories above the waterline.

"Amazing," Ildin said, then leaned close to Amendal. "From what Vaem said in that meeting I didn't think the Eshari were human…"

"What did you think they were?"

Ildin shrugged, palms up. "I don't know. Something that could withstand the cold? I can't imagine living in a place as frigid as this. I mean, how could they grow anything?"

That was a valid point. There was no way a civilization could thrive in such a frigid wasteland.

Amendal continued eyeing the statues as the *Giboran* sailed through the bay. Ildin and those around him were making their own speculations about the statues and what their presence meant for the expedition.

"How incredible!" a burly man said, awestruck. "If they could make statues like that, just imagine what kind of tevisrals we'll find in the reliquary..."

"Wonders the world has never seen," a lanky woman murmured.

"They'll be incredible," someone else said. "Things beyond our wildest dreams."

Amendal cocked his head at those remarks. He didn't understand mages who sought tevisrals. Most people who sought tevisrals were inept at channeling magic.

"Hey!" Ildin nudged Amendal and pointed to the nearest statue. "Look up there."

Amendal followed Ildin's gloved finger to the statue's head. The ears on the statue were not round. They were long and pointed.

Ildin gasped. "They're elven." Others noticed the distinctive features, discussing the implication of what lay ahead. Though the elves of Kalda were a mysterious race, many men attributed the construction of tevisrals to them.

"Those ears look too long to be elven," Amendal said.

As the *Giboran* passed the statues, the crystallized dock came into view.

It protruded from an enormous cavern within the ice shelf lining the southern parts of the bay.

Ildin sighed. "Well, now the leisurely part is over."

———⊃•⊂———

The *Giboran* came to a halt within the mouth of the icy cavern, mooring so the crystalline dock was off the portside rail. Sailors furled the rigging, lowered the gangway, and dropped the anchors.

The members of the expedition who had come topside were filing toward the gangway. Amendal, however, remained near the starboard rail, searching the water.

You're being paranoid, he told himself. *Nothing is there.*

Amendal turned from the rail just as Jaekim and Morgidian came topside. Each beamed with excitement as they pushed their way toward Amendal and Ildin.

"Isn't this exhilarating?!" Jaekim said, sounding a tad drunk.

"Drinking already?" Ildin asked.

"Just one glass of halisium," Jaekim said, waving his hand airily.

Morgidian chuckled. "When isn't Jaekim drinking?"

Jaekim squinted thoughtfully. "When I'm sleeping." The remark drew laughter from all but Amendal.

Scialas and Faelinia soon came topside, but moved toward the disembarking crowd.

Amendal leaned back as his friends continued their banter. His eyes lingered on Faelinia, her golden hair pulled back into a ponytail. *What to do next...?*

Faelinia noticed Amendal and returned his gaze with a challenging one of her own.

Ah, the power struggle begins, Amendal thought. He compressed his lips, fighting the urge to blink.

The women moved closer to the gangway, but Faelinia continued staring. He knew all too well the games women played to guard their hearts. If Amendal looked away, Faelinia would perceive him as weak—although maybe not consciously. Such a simple defeat would ruin any chances he had with her.

His friends burst into laughter, but Amendal paid no attention.

An amused expression formed on Faelinia's face, and she glanced to Scialas. The arpranist was saying something, but Amendal couldn't hear.

That's one, Amendal mused. *Soon—*

The *Giboran* jolted, and Amendal staggered forward. Flashes of blue and silver raced overhead, straight for the vessel's masts. Freezing water splashed onto the main deck. Panicked screams, shouts of alarm, and cracking wood echoed through the air as Amendal struggled to turn around. He tripped and fell onto the deck, his pack slipping off his shoulder.

His eyes widened with shock and awe. "Whoa!"

Dozens of dark-blue tentacles—each as thick as a man—rose from the water, gripping various parts of the *Giboran*. Silver wavy patterns adorned each tentacle, with pulsing suckers arrayed along their length.

Those tentacles... that coloring. They looked like the limbs of a cephalopod. But no cephalopod Amendal recalled had those colors and odd sucker pattern, at least no *normal* cephalopod.

"Could it really be the nactilious...?" he muttered, attempting to regain his footing.

The *Giboran* tilted, and more water splashed over the starboard rail, dousing an armored mercenary beside Amendal. The man gasped and fell to the decking, his eyes wide.

Amendal scurried backward as the ship rocked. He managed to stand just as an enormous oblong shape broke the surface of the water, revealing an earthen-colored shell. Thick rivets lined the brown shell, along with wavy patterns of tan.

Deafening squawking echoed across the ship as more dark-blue tentacles shot through the air. The tentacles gripped the ship's masts, and the rest of the creature rose from the water. An enormous eye—twice the size of a man's head—gazed at Amendal, its filmy iris contracting.

The ship rocked again, and a glistening beak gaped wide above the rail, emitting another deafening squawk. The creature's orifice was lined with dozens of undulating bright orange feelers.

"What is that thing?!" Jaekim shouted.

Ignoring his friend, Amendal took in a sweeping glance of the ship. People crowded the gangway, pushing and shoving one another, while others jumped from the rails. He searched for Faelinia, but she wasn't aboard.

You'd better not die, woman, he thought, then turned to Morgidian. "Morgi, make a bridge!"

"Where?!" Morgidian demanded.

"The bow!" Amendal shouted, staggering toward his pack. He struggled against the rocking ship, but recovered his belongings.

With his pack in hand, Amendal darted to the forecastle. A cacophony of commotion resounded around him. Someone barked orders to attack the monster. Incantations were shouted, but each spell was indiscernible. Singing metal and clanking armor rang loud, followed by battle cries.

As Amendal ran, the ship rocked again and the enormous sea monster squawked as it climbed aboard. Tentacles whipped overhead, gripping the masts and yardarms.

A crack resounded above Amendal, and he looked up. A yardarm snapped in two, and the splintered beam fell directly toward him.

Amendal threw himself sideways as the yardarm struck the decking.

Morgidian dashed ahead of Amendal, blue light surrounding him. Jaekim and Ildin were right behind the barsionist.

Amendal recovered, bounding toward his friends. He swiftly ascended the steps, but was knocked forward by something that sent a freezing surge across his back. He gasped and fell to the steps, his back stung with excruciating pain.

A haze of agony filled Amendal's mind, and he struggled to move. The cacophony of battle turned to droning noise. *Am I going to die here?*

No. He couldn't die here. Not now.

With all his might, Amendal forced his arms forward. As he struggled to climb, hands clasped his arms. "Come on, Amendal!"

Amendal looked up as Ildin pulled him and his pack to the forecastle. Blue light shone behind him.

"...he's almost done," Ildin shouted. "Come on!"

Amendal pushed through the agony but struggled to climb the stairs. Ildin wrapped his arm around him, helping him toward the others.

"I thought it was going to eat you!" Jaekim declared.

"What?" Amendal gritted his teeth.

"One of those tentacles hit you," the necromancer said. "But then it slithered away."

Amendal blinked several times. He glanced over his shoulder, past Ildin. Mercenaries and soldiers were scattered across the main deck. Some were climbing the masts, swinging their weapons at the tentacles gripping the ship.

"Done!" Morgidian shouted, leaping over the railing. He landed on a transparent sheet of blue light—an inverted barrier of barsion magic, and dashed across it. The barsion spread from the ship, creating a bridge to the far side of the icy cavern.

"Go," Ildin told Jaekim. "I'll help Amendal."

The necromancer nodded, then followed Morgidian.

"You first," Ildin said, helping Amendal toward the rail.

Amendal struggled to climb, but Ildin pushed him onto the magical bridge. The illusionist was right beside him again and helped him to his feet. He wrapped an arm around Amendal once again and started across the bridge. Amendal struggled to move. Each step sent a surge of pain along his back.

"Are you going to be okay?" Ildin asked.

"I don't... know..." Amendal replied through clenched teeth. "This stinging is getting worse. Almost like it's going numb."

"You're going to need an arpranist."

***

Vaem fell against the bulkhead outside her cabin. The muffled noises of battle filtered through the corridor. "What on Kalda is happening?!" she growled and stumbled toward the doors leading to the open-air bridge, struggling against the rocking of the ship.

She staggered outside and gasped upon seeing the cause of all the commotion.

"A nactilious..." she muttered, gawking at the enormous sea creature. But only one? Nactili were rarely alone. They swam in small groups, hunting prey together. A nactilious never attacked alone, unless provoked. Was Crisyan Bay home to one of their nests? If so, there was little time before another nactilious joined the attack.

Vaem regained her composure, hurrying back inside as best she could.

Kydol staggered from the wall near Vaem's cabin, clad in her plated armor with the emblem of the empire emblazoned across her breastplate. "What's going on?!" the lieutenant demanded.

"The ship is under attack," Vaem replied, stumbling toward her cabin. "Now help me secure my things!" Once inside, she darted to the table where the map of Abodal was unfurled. Several of the weights used to secure it had fallen off the table, and a corner of the map was partly curled.

I can't lose this, she thought, sweeping the weights off the table. She swiftly rolled the map and dropped it into a tall cylindrical case holding other rolled sheets.

As Vaem turned from the table, a thud resounded against the outer bulkhead of her cabin. She started, backing away to the door.

"Who's attacking us?" Kydol demanded, pulling Vaem's satchel from under the bed. "Is it the Eshari?"

Vaem shook her head. As she opened her mouth, a resounding crack filled the cabin. Wooden splinters flew wildly. Vaem shielded her face, but a splinter struck her cheek, drawing blood.

A flash of teal and silver raced through the cabin, crushing the table where the map had lain. Was that one of the monster's tentacles?

No… Vaem's eyes widened. This tentacle didn't belong to the nactilious she had seen. That monster was on the other side of the ship. And its coloring was different.

The teal tentacle gripped the hole in the outer bulkhead, like a finger gripping a handhold.

"What is that thing?!" Kydol demanded, drawing her sword. She had since dropped Vaem's satchel, and the contents were strewn across the cabin—including the tevisral from the emperor. The off-white cylinder rolled across the decking and toward the door.

Idiot, Vaem growled, stumbling toward the rolling tevisral. It hit the door-frame and wobbled out of the cabin. She hurried after it and threw herself to the decking, landing atop the tevisral. *I can't lose you, either.* She pulled the ancient device from under her and turned back to her cabin. Kydol was swinging her sword at the teal-and-silver tentacle, but her blade didn't as much as dent the creature's limb. The nactilious swatted at Kydol, knocking her onto the bed, but the lieutenant rebounded and attacked again.

Vaem pushed herself from the decking and hurried back inside her cabin. She ducked, evading the flailing tentacle, and grabbed her satchel. It was mostly empty. Only her sketch pad was still inside. She shoved the case and tevisral into their pockets, but the tentacle smacked her against the inner bulkhead.

The freezing limb sapped her breath, and she slid to the decking. *Damned beast!*

Luckily, the satchel was between her and the bulkhead. Neither case nor tevisral had as much as shifted. Gasping, she crawled across the decking and scooped up her belongings. Though most weren't vital to the expedition, they were still precious. Her things secured, Vaem staggered to her feet and wobbled out of the cabin. She had to escape, especially now that a second nactili was attacking.

⊃•⊂

Amendal gritted his teeth as Ildin dragged him to the ledge where Jaekim and Morgidian stood. The stinging reminded him of the frostbite he had received during that nightmare.

"There's another one!" Jaekim shouted, clasping the sides of his head. "Oh boy, oh boy!"

"It doesn't look like our shipmates are having any success," Morgidian said with a groan. "They've been hacking at that thing's tentacles to no avail."

Ildin set Amendal and his pack down on the ledge. The ice beneath

Amendal was cold, but not as cold as his back.

"And no one's magic seems to be hurting it," Morgidian continued. "It's like the monster has its own barsion."

Amendal fought against the pain, gazing across the water to the crystallized dock. A set of teal-and-silvery tentacles rose from the water and wrapped around the ship's masts, revealing a teal-colored nactilious.

This second sea monster grabbed several mages and mercenaries and threw them into the water. Each of the men was abruptly stilled as they hit the choppy waves, undoubtedly debilitated by the water's frigid temperature.

All the while, the various members of the expedition attacked the sea monsters. But their attempts were futile. None of the destructive magics seemed to damage either nactilious.

"We have to retreat!" Jaekim screamed, shaking his head. "Those things are going to kill us all!"

More yardarms fell from the masts, and the foremast began to crack.

"Quit your sniveling," Morgidian snapped at Jaekim. "Start casting some magic."

"And draw the attention of those monsters?!" Jaekim blurted. "No way!"

Morgidian and Jaekim continued arguing while Ildin knelt beside Amendal.

"Can you summon *something* to stop them?" the illusionist whispered. "You know, *those* things?" He was probably referring to the gangolins.

"They... they hate cold..." Amendal said between grunts and groans. "Even... the conjured versions re-react adversely to frigid... temperatures."

Ildin frowned.

"Besides," Amendal continued, "there's not enough room."

The illusionist scanned the icy cavern in a sweeping glance. "Are they bigger than this cave?"

Amendal shook his head. "No, but... but there's no room for them to stand... not without going into the water. The stupid things would... probably just clam up before they could reach either sea monster."

"What are we going to do?" Ildin muttered, turning to face the awful scene of destruction.

Amid the pain, a moment of clarity came to Amendal. He saw the creatures for what they were—potentially destructive tools in the hands of a conjurer. *Capture them,* he thought. *Yes! That's it!* He grinned, then winced from the pain. They didn't have to defeat the monsters. Amendal could simply pull the sea creatures into the Visirm Expanse. *They'll make for powerful conjurations.*

Morgidian and Jaekim's debate became heated. Jaekim started slinging profane insults.

"You always want to run and hide, don't you?" Morgidian taunted. "Like a frightened child."

Jaekim gasped. "How dare you! I am not a—"

"I... I can stop them," Amendal said.

The mages ceased their bickering and turned to face Amendal. Jaekim looked dumbfounded.

"You can conjure something big enough to fight those?" the necromancer asked.

"I have a better idea," Amendal said, struggling to grin. "I'm going to need help, though. In order to... to subdue them, I need to focus. I can't do that with this." He gestured to his back.

Ildin's eyes widened with enlightenment. "I'll find Scialas," he said, directing his attention to the ship.

"What are you going to do, Amendal?" Morgidian asked.

A pained-but-mirthful chuckle left Amendal's lips as he glanced to Morgidian. "I'm going to add some exotic creatures to my menagerie."

"He's mad..." Jaekim muttered. "And we're all going to die!"

Faelinia had put considerable distance between herself and the battle. No, she was not a coward. Faelinia just preferred a distant vantage that allowed her to see the *entire* battle.

Once the first monster attacked, Faelinia and Scialas had leapt overboard. They bounded across the dock until reaching the cavern's icy banks. It was there that Faelinia decided to make her stand. Several others had fled in that direction, but the cowards were making their way through tunnels along the cavern wall.

Vibrant orange flame gathered around Faelinia as a second sea monster rose from the water. This creature, however, was a breath-taking mix of teal and silver. The teal-colored sea monster *climbed* over the crystallized dock, pulling itself toward the *Giboran*. Faelinia had heard of enormous monsters from the deep, but she never expected to find one during her adventures.

"This is horrible!" Scialas screamed.

Nearly a dozen flaming orbs coalesced around Faelinia, and she hurled the magic at the creature. "Make yourself useful," she told Scialas. "Start imbuing the mercenaries and soldiers with arpran auras."

If Scialas was pained by the remark, Faelinia didn't notice. She had more important things to worry about than her friend's feelings.

Through her mental control she rained several orbs down on the creature's hardened shell, but the blast didn't seem to faze the monster. Faelinia unleashed the rest of her orbs, but the magic had no effect.

A disintegrating blast might do the trick. It was times like this that she appreciated her knowledge of both the Elemental and Arcane disciplines of wizardry.

Faelinia uttered another incantation, and violet light gathered around her hands as she prepared a beam of disintegration. Such magic could evaporate whatever it touched. Dense objects or surfaces would take time to penetrate, but nothing short of barsion magic could withstand a disintegrating beam.

Amid her incantation, Faelinia noticed *something* flying toward her and Scialas. She turned, still uttering the words to muster her magic. A *man* approached, hovering through the air. As he neared, she saw it was none other than Ildin.

The disintegrating magic coalesced at that moment, a brilliant mass of violet light.

An illusion, she thought, aiming her hands toward the sea monster. Faelinia had sent many an illusion flying. It was fun.

Focus, she chided herself.

"Ildin!" Scialas gasped.

"Scialas, we need you," Ildin said. "Amendal was struck by that monster. He can't feel his back."

Faelinia turned from the exchange, unleashing her magic. The violet beam shot above those on the dock and collided with the sea monster's shell. She could feel the magic struggling to dissolve the hardened carapace.

"What is that thing made of?" she said between clenched teeth.

The blast faded, but before it dissipated completely Faelinia could sense what little damage she had inflicted upon the monster.

"Barely a dent..." She groaned, throwing her hands into the air. What was it going to take to kill these monsters?

Amid her despair, Faelinia turned back to the exchange between Scialas and Ildin's illusion.

"... a plan, but he can't focus through the pain," the illusion said. "Morgidian is going to make another barsion bridge so you can reach us."

The illusion gestured across the enormous icy cavern, toward a ledge protruding from the ice shelf. Three masculine figures stood along it, and another was sitting against the ice wall—undoubtedly Amendal Aramien.

What did you do to yourself now, you big oaf?

"Have you seen Fendar?" the illusion asked. "Or Dugal?"

Scialas shook her head.

A burst of blue light shot from the ledge, forming a ramp of barsion magic. *Clever,* Faelinia mused.

"Hurry across," Ildin's illusion said. "I'm going to look for the others." With that, the illusion soared through the air, searching the crowd on the crystallized dock.

What are you planning, Amendal? Faelinia wondered, watching Scialas dart up the barsion ramp, mustering arpran magic as she ran.

Faelinia took in a deep breath and returned her focus to the battle. A band of sword-bearing men and women dashed toward the teal-colored sea creature. The beast practically sat on the dock's crystal surface, swatting the advancing soldiers and mercenaries and hurling them into the frigid water.

"Let's try this again..." she muttered, eyeing the dent in the creature's brown shell. Once more, Faelinia uttered the disintegrating incantation.

The arpran magic surged through Amendal, vanquishing the pain in his back.

"That's better!" he declared, rising to his feet while glancing across the barsion bridge. Faelinia fired another disintegrating blast, and the sea monster squawked. It sounded more angry than pained.

She'll probably kill that one, he thought, glancing to the teal nactilious.

"You're really going to capture that thing?" Scialas asked, her tone full of awe. "Can you really do that? I mean, I-I'm not questioning your abilities. I… I just didn't know if something that big could be sucked into one of your portals."

"It's not going to work!" Jaekim shouted. "That'll only make it come after us."

"If you don't pipe down it'll *definitely* come after us," Morgidian said.

Scialas giggled at the banter. Jaekim shot back a snide remark.

Amendal ignored him, and shifted his focus to the dark-blue nactilious. Two of its tentacles had been hacked off by the men on the masts. He frowned upon seeing the maimed limbs. If he were to capture that nactilious it would always be conjured with those mangled tentacles.

Oh well. At least he would have a nactilious to conjure. He focused his mind and began the incantation to open a portal to the Visirm Expanse. Enthralling magic, part of the spell, would pull the creature into the portal.

The golden light appeared between his hands, then wisped across the water. Amendal directed the magic behind the dark-blue nactilious, but as the portal began to coalesce, a wave rose behind the *Giboran*. More dark-blue tentacles shot from the water, grappling the ship's aft hull.

"Do you see that?!" Jaekim screamed. "There's a third one!"

Perfect! Amendal cheered inwardly, redirecting the conjuration magic.

He focused on the third sea monster, guiding the rest of the golden particles toward the ship's crumbling stern. Though not as large as the other two, the nactilious was still colossal.

The golden magic wisped around the smaller nactilious, but the sea monster paid no attention to the portal forming behind it. It probably didn't understand what the golden light was doing.

Soon, the conjuration magic coalesced, forming a golden portal to the Visirm Expanse. The portal was too small, barely a quarter the size of the nactilious's colossal head. Portals to the Visirm Expanse always started small but grew as the conjurer funneled more magic into them.

Amendal repeated the first part of the incantation, mustering more of his conjuration magic and guiding the golden particles to the portal. The mystical vortex grew, spreading into the water.

Once the portal was large enough, Amendal continued with the incantation, mustering the enthralling component. Charcoal light shot from his hands, mingling with the golden portal.

"Aren't you finished yet?" Jaekim hollered.

Amendal ignored him, focused on finishing the incantation. Soon, a mass of dark gray magic shot from the portal, gripping the smaller nactilious.

The sea monster stilled as the enthralling magic merged Amendal's mind with the sea monster.

Back away, he commanded.

A resistance pulled at Amendal's thoughts and he felt the word "no." The nactilious couldn't be thinking the actual word, of course. The word was simply an interpretation by his mind.

Stunned, Amendal focused on moving the individual tentacles. They resisted his mental command, too. Gritting his teeth, Amendal mustered his might, but no matter how hard he tried, he could not move the nactilious.

"Why isn't the monster moving?" Scialas asked. "It should be moving, shouldn't it?"

"I told you it wasn't going to work!" Jaekim shouted.

"Amendal?" Ildin asked, blankly staring into space. He was undoubtedly focusing his vision through his illusion.

"It's resisting," Amendal said through clenched teeth.

"Here, let me help," Ildin said, turning from the ship. He uttered his own enthralling incantation. Charcoal light burst from his hands, beaming straight for the enthralled nactilious.

Amendal could feel Ildin's magic mingling with his. Ildin's thoughts were also present in Amendal's mind.

Release the ship, Ildin commanded.

Move! Amendal barked, focusing on the tentacles.

One of the dark-blue-limbs slithered down the hull, falling limp into the water.

"Ha!" Morgidian blurted, followed by a smacking noise. "It's working!"

"Don't hit me…" Jaekim complained.

Together, Amendal and Ildin managed to drop each of the dark-blue tentacles into the water, but they struggled to move the nactilious to the portal. The monster had an indomitable will.

Amendal had rarely encountered anything as stubborn as the nactilious. Not even the gangolins—with their colossal size and strength—had the mental fortitude to resist the pull into the Visirm Expanse. This ordeal, however, was a true battle of wills.

"Morgi," Amendal said through clenched teeth. "We need your help."

"What do you want me to do?" the barsionist asked.

"Push it!" Amendal replied, straining to keep his focus.

An incantation left Morgidian's lips, and blue light reflected off the icy ledge.

"Do you need another illusionist?" Scialas asked.

"That might help…" Ildin muttered. "I couldn't find Fendar."

Scialas darted down the barsion ramp without a word.

"You too, Jaekim," Amendal said, struggling to speak. "Try weakening it with a life-draining—"

The enthralled nactilious fought back, moving one of its tentacles toward the *Giboran.*

"Why not use my acid—?"

"No!" Amendal interrupted. "Siphon. Now!"

Amendal did not want Jaekim marring the nactilious. It had remained unscathed from the battle, and Amendal wanted the creature to remain that way. Besides, a life-draining spell would weaken the monster's resolve. Acid would only enrage it.

A flabbergasted sigh left Jaekim's lips, and then he began uttering his own incantation.

Morgidian's unformed barsion flew across the water as Jaekim mustered his life-draining magic. The orange hue lit the ledge as Scialas returned.

Another incantation sounded behind Amendal. He knew that alluring voice. It belonged to none other than Faelinia.

Soon, the barsion barrier formed between the smaller nactilious and the ship, pushing against the sea monster. Amendal could feel the pressure through his spell, but Morgidian struggled to move the colossal cephalopod.

A balled mass of orange strands flew from the ledge, followed by a dark gray cloud. Both magics struck the nactilious in unison.

Jaekim's life-draining magic weakened the monster, allowing Amendal and Ildin to move the nactilious closer to the portal.

You will move, Faelinia's command echoed through the shared enthralling bond within the sea creature.

Amendal could feel the nactilious's resistance waning. With their combined might, he, Ildin, and Faelinia managed to make the monster swim toward the portal. Morgidian's barrier helped prod the creature along, but not by much.

"We just have to make it touch the portal," Amendal said, his voice strained. He could feel Jaekim's magic weakening the nactilious again, making it easier for him, Ildin, and Faelinia to manipulate the monster.

An excruciating moment passed before the nactilious swam through the mystical doorway and disappeared into the Visirm Expanse.

Amendal could still feel the nactilious beyond the portal, frozen in defiance. The others' spells, however, had been nullified as the nactilious crossed the mystical threshold.

"You did it!" Scialas cried.

More joyous shouts erupted from the others as Amendal closed the portal. The golden vortex collapsed on itself, dissipating in the water.

Once the portal closed, a resounding crash echoed from the *Giboran.* Startled, Amendal spun. The top half of the ship's mainmast sank into the water. Limp mercenaries and soldiers floated around the yardarms and sails, but soon sank with the rest of the toppled rigging.

9

PREDICAMENTS

"Each type of magic exerts a different level of strain on quinta'shals. Annihilation and disintegration blasts are among the most taxing, followed by acid, and then fire."

- From *Colvinar Vrium's Bestiary for Conjurers*, page 18

Not a moment later, the foremast was snapped off the *Giboran* by the dark-blue nactilious and tossed into the water with a resounding crash. The monster squawked as it turned upon the men and women assailing it, swatting them with its tentacles. Arcane and elemental bolts struck the nactilious, but the magic seemed more an irritation than anything else.

"It's going to destroy the ship," Scialas muttered. "There has to be a swifter way to deal with those monsters than sucking them through your portals." She looked to Amendal apologetically.

You're not offending me, Amendal thought, giving the arpranist a sidelong glance.

"Scialas is right," Faelinia said. "We need to kill the other two." She turned to Amendal. "Your little stunt took too long."

"I didn't think it would resist like it did," Amendal said, turning back to the carnage. "Now we know that."

Faelinia began giving orders, but Amendal ran possible solutions through his mind. Magic was almost useless against the creatures. Summoning a gangolin wasn't feasible. But if he conjured something of similar size, he might just be able to rip the sea monsters from the ship. There was one solution, but it required summoning something he had never conjured—an earthen gargantuan from the Aldinal Plane.

Then there was the matter of something so massive hitting the water. He squinted at the *Giboran*. He could kill half the expedition with those frigid waves. But he had to do something. If he did nothing, they would lose the ship… But then, they might lose the ship anyway.

"… and Morgidian, start reinforcing the hull," Faelinia commanded, her voice stern. "The other monster was puncturing holes in the portside, so let's try to prevent any further damage."

Jaekim and Ildin were already mustering their magic. Morgidian immediately obeyed Faelinia, uttering an incantation.

"Scialas, come with me," Faelinia said, then she turned to Amendal. "Well, are you going to summon something, or not?"

Amendal gave her a flirtatious grin. "Of course! But you're all going to have to cover your ears."

Ildin glanced to Amendal, a smile forming upon his face. He undoubtedly knew what Amendal was planning.

"Cover our ears?" Scialas asked. "Why?"

Faelinia narrowed her eyes at Amendal. "I'm not doing that."

Amendal studied the women. There was no time for an explanation. "Fine, I'll stand out on the ramp," he said, gesturing to the barsion bridge leading to the cavern's icy banks.

"Not before we cross it," Faelinia said, swiftly dashing from the frozen ledge. She mustered violet disintegrating magic as she ran. Scialas was right behind her.

"Ladies first, I suppose…" Amendal sighed, then darted down the ramp while reciting the incantation in his mind. *I think that's it,* he thought, halting halfway across the barsion bridge. "I hope this works." He turned, facing the battle.

From this vantage, Amendal could see the teal-colored nactilious on the crystallized dock. Five of its thirty-some tentacles were inside the hull, while the rest of its teal limbs swatted at the expedition members assailing it. There were more holes in the ship's hull, and it looked as if the *Giboran* was taking on water. Morgidian's barsion had not yet surrounded the hull.

"Great," Amendal said with a sigh. "Just great…"

He scanned the dock, noticing that most of it between the ship and the icy banks was empty. "Good, hopefully the waves from my conjuration won't spill too far." *And hopefully that crystal won't crack.*

Golden light surrounded Amendal as he uttered the incantation from *Greater Conjurations from the Aldinal Plane.* Even his vision had a tinge of gold to it. He focused on a spot near the starboard bow. The golden light coalesced just above the water. He wanted to ensure that his conjuration wouldn't sink immediately. Since they were on an ice shelf, the ocean floor was probably a grand phineal beneath the water.

The portal to the Aldinal Plane spread wide, nearly reaching the cavern's icy ceiling. Part of it reached into the frigid water. All in all, the portal was over six stories tall.

Soon, the earthen hand of the elemental gargantuan emerged from the portal, followed by a foot. The other limbs appeared, and the entire conjuration leapt from the portal. The creature, an amalgamation of rock, dirt, and foliage, resembled an enormous man with a grossly thick body. Besides its vaguely humanoid appearance, it had no other features.

While the conjuration crashed into the water, Amendal reached out for the crystallized dock. *I hope it holds*—the enormous earthen conjuration sent waves in all directions. He expected the water to be frigid, but he felt neither shock nor chill when the conjuration hit the water. Waves washed across the dock, but stopped near those fighting the teal nactilious. Several waves rose over the bow, crashing upon the forecastle. Amendal could see several men struck by the water—they jolted, collapsing to the deck.

Amendal cursed under his breath, but focused on holding his conjuration above the water. To his surprise, the crystal was holding under the pressure of the conjuration's extreme weight. *Impressive,* he thought. *If that's the work of the crysillac, then I definitely want one. Imagine what it could be used for!*

Pushing aside his excitement, Amendal focused on maneuvering his conjuration. The creature gripped the dock, pulling itself above the water.

"Now to get closer," he muttered, gliding the earthen gargantuan toward the battle.

On the portside, magic, as well as dozens of mercenaries and soldiers, assailed the teal nactilious. Ildin's illusions were also flying through the air, attempting to distract the nactilious. *I think they can deal with that one.*

The earthen gargantuan reached the *Giboran* as the ship's hull was bathed in a bright-blue hue from Morgidian. But the bowsprit was not yet protected and barred the way to the dark-blue nactilious.

Still clutching the dock, Amendal's conjuration ducked beneath the bowsprit. Though its arm was extended, the conjuration had no problem keeping itself afloat. Once the gargantuan was in position, Amendal rested the bowsprit against its extended arm. "Impressive!"

Amendal reared the conjuration's free arm back, then arced the colossal fist around the *Giboran* and straight for the nactilious's shell.

The blow sent the ship reeling, immediately drawing the attention of the sea monster.

"What incredible strength!" Amendal cried, readying the colossal fist for another blow.

The dark-blue nactilious glared at the earthen gargantuan with its nearest eye, lashing several of its tentacles at the conjuration's fist. The tentacles wrapped around the colossal wrist just as Amendal unleashed another punch.

That blow was not as powerful as the first, but it forced the nactilious to focus on the conjuration. The sea monster climbed across the broken rigging and threw more of its dark-blue limbs at the earthen gargantuan.

"That's it!" Amendal shouted. "Hit me!"

Only half of the nactilious's limbs were attempting to restrain the earthen conjuration. The other half were either severed or swatting the soldiers and mercenaries still assailing it.

The gargantuan punched again, but the blow was a mere tap against the nactilious's shell.

Maybe the eye? Amendal thought, swiping an earthen finger across the shell. The rough boulders comprising the conjuration's fingertips scraped that filmy iris, drawing an enraged squawk from the nactilious.

The sea monster threw more of its limbs, wrapping the tentacles around the conjuration's mammoth arm.

Only two of the nactilious's tentacles were attached to the ship: one around the rear mast and another around the bowsprit.

"Good enough." Amendal grinned, glancing to the teal nactilious. The second sea monster had a firm grip on the ship and the crystallized dock.

That one should stop the ship from capsizing, Amendal thought, then relinquished his conjuration's grip on the dock.

Several resounding cracks echoed from the *Giboran* as the earthen gargantuan plunged into the water. Bowsprit and rear mast snapped from the combined force of the nactilious's grip and the conjuration's weight.

The nactilious attempted to flee, releasing its grip on the conjuration's arm, but Amendal swiftly grabbed the tentacles, and the earthen conjuration dragged the sea monster into the ocean.

Waves crashed against the *Giboran,* and the ship almost tipped onto its starboard side. Those on the main deck slid toward the rail. Some landed against it, while several fell overboard but were caught by Morgidian's barsion. Luckily, the grip of the last nactilious kept the *Giboran* from capsizing into the frigid bay.

Amendal averted his focus from the ship and closed his eyes. He concentrated wholly on the earthen gargantuan. The nactilious struggled to break free, but the gargantuan held on tight to the tentacles, dragging the sea monster into the depths of the ocean.

Faelinia unleashed another disintegrating blast, dissolving another part of the teal sea monster's shell. The blast evoked another enraged squawk.

Amendal had since ripped the other creature from the *Giboran,* seriously damaging the vessel in the attempt.

That clumsy oaf, she thought, gritting her teeth. With all her might she focused on burrowing a hole through that tough shell. As her spell faded, she pierced flesh.

"There!" she cried triumphantly.

With the shell breached, the other mages assailed the opening with their own magics.

The sea monster squawked, swiftly climbing the aft portside of the *Giboran.* Was the thing actually retreating?

Faelinia uttered another incantation as the sea monster scurried atop the highest deck, its teal tentacles flailing. The hull, however, gave way, and the monster fell inside the aft section. Bolts of acid, arcane, and disintegrating magic arced above the ship and struck the enormous creature.

Squawking in frustration, the colossal monster scurried through the damaged ship and dove into the water, sending waves that crashed against the *Giboran*. The vessel rocked back and forth, and Faelinia could tell it was taking on water. Though the damage was caused by the sea monster, Amendal's antics had done no favors to the *Giboran*.

They were going to lose the ship.

Ceasing her incantation, Faelinia dismissed her forming magic. She took in a deep breath and studied her surroundings. Several men and women emerged from the nearby tunnels, including Vaem.

Had she been hiding? Vaem had not struck her as a coward.

The scholar followed the others as they picked their way across the icy banks and back onto the crystal dock.

"Perhaps they were ferrying supplies." Faelinia glanced back to the dock where the provisions had been unloaded, but the crystal slab was empty. Hopefully Amendal had not knocked them off during his spectacular display of recklessness.

———◁•▷———

Vaem strode across the crystallized dock, marching toward the wreckage of the *Giboran*. The rigging was demolished, and the portside hull was pockmarked with gaping holes from the teal nactilious's assault. Only one of the masts was intact, but many of its yardarms were broken.

The ship would never sail again, if it even stayed afloat.

"How unfortunate," Vaem muttered, striding directly for Calimir.

The rugged veteran of war was angrily barking orders.

"... and secure the ship with some ensnaring magic," Calimir shouted. "Make sure the hull is reinforced with more barsion. I don't want this ship sinking before we can unload all our supplies." The commander shook his head and ran a gloved hand through his hair. He turned, noticing Vaem approaching with the others. "Oh good, you survived."

"Of course," Vaem replied, studying the mercenaries and soldiers who had fought on the dock.

"I'm ensuring that all our supplies are unloaded before the *Giboran* sinks," Calimir said. "Hopefully the mages can keep it afloat that long."

"Wonderful." Vaem feigned a smile. "We found some tunnels just beyond the shore. I suggest we start moving our supplies and provisions in there. There's no telling if the nactili will return."

"Nactili?" Calimir asked.

"Yes," Vaem said, tilting her chin slightly. "The plural for nactilious— those enormous cephalopods that terrorize the ocean."

"I know what they are," Calimir spat. "Don't be condescending, Mistress Rudal."

Vaem pursed her lips, watching as both crewmen and expedition members brought supplies to the broken main deck. "Go help them," she said to those who had followed her. They complied, hurrying aboard.

A moment later, Captain Edara—the owner and commander of the *Giboran*—stomped down the gangway. Edara was a lanky, dark-haired man with a gaunt face. His mustache and goatee extended almost to his chest. *Disgusting man...*

"You!" Edara pointed to Vaem, stomping toward her and Calimir. "Why didn't you say there were monsters lurking about?!"

"I didn't know," Vaem said tersely. *Don't you dare give me any attitude.*

"Calm down, Captain," Calimir said, waving his hand to placate Edara. "You're not the only one who has suffered losses because of those monsters."

Edara started, then spun on Calimir. "*Losses?*" he snarled. "We're stranded here, you fool! Look at *my* ship!" He gestured to the wreckage.

"Do not call me a fool, Captain," Calimir spat. "And do not blame this predicament on any of us! We had no way of knowing we would be attacked."

"Really?" Edara stepped closer to Calimir. "And what about the man who spotted the shadow in the water? Did none of your men take him seriously? Your mages could have protected my ship."

"I don't know who you're talking about," Calimir said.

The argument intensified, and Edara slung vulgar accusations at Calimir.

Exasperated, Vaem turned from the quarrel. Her eyes fell upon Amendal Aramien standing atop a bridge composed of barsion magic. He was focused intently on something. *You are quite impressive,* she thought. Vaem had watched him pull the smaller nactilious into the conjurer's void, an extraordinary feat, considering nactili had strong wills.

The expedition would have fared far worse without Amendal Aramien. *With you at my side, I will not fail,* she mused. *We will breech Tardalim and fulfill my emperor's mandate.*

———◦———

The depth where the earthen gargantuan dragged the nactilious was greater than Amendal had imagined. They had plummeted at least a grand phineal, maybe two. Darkness engulfed the watery depths, and Amendal struggled to discern anything through his conjuration besides tactile sensations.

The nactilious struggled against the gargantuan, but the strength of the earthen creature was far too great for the mythical sea monster.

As they descended, Amendal managed to climb his conjuration atop the nactilious. The earthen gargantuan wrapped its arms around the sea monster's shell.

A sudden jolt shot through the conjuration, and Amendal sensed they were on the ocean floor. The nactilious struggled to pull itself away, but the earthen behemoth pinned it in place.

"There!" he said, opening his eyes. He could sense the conjuration far below him. It was a staggering distance. Amendal ignored the commotion around him and uttered another incantation.

Why have one nactilious when you could have two? Of course, it was maimed a bit, but not as badly as the other one. At least this one had its shell intact.

Amendal grinned as the magic for the portal to the Visirm Expanse formed around him. He focused on that spot far below him, then hurled the magic into the frigid water.

Golden light illuminated the ocean floor as the magic wisped around his earthen gargantuan. The conjuration magic gathered beneath the pinned sea monster, but did not form a portal.

Forming a portal now would be fatal to the nactilious. Portals to the Visirm Expanse automatically pulled whatever touched them into that timeless void. If a portal was smaller than the object or creature the conjurer intended to trap, the portal would compress it. A living creature would certainly be maimed, if it survived at all. Most living things did not survive, and a dead creature in the Visirm Expanse was totally useless.

The technique for delaying the formation of a portal to the Visirm Expanse wasn't a simple thing. Most conjurers couldn't manage it, let alone maintain a conjuration while attempting it.

Luckily, Amendal was gifted.

Amendal sent more of his magic to the ocean floor, struggling to hold back the portal's formation.

Someone called his name, but Amendal ignored it. His focus was consumed by holding back the formation of the portal *and* controlling the earthen conjuration.

A hand grabbed his arm, but Amendal shook it off. This was not the time to be interrupted. He could not lose such a valuable creature. He did his best to ignore his would-be-detractor, sending more magic to the ocean floor.

"Amendal!"

He fought the urge to recognize the voice, spreading his magic across the ocean floor. With the portal unformed, it was hard to tell exactly *how* big it needed to be. He would have to err on the side of too large in order to safely trap this nactilious.

"Amendal!"

The magic spread beyond the earthen conjuration, but not the flailing limbs of the sea monster. The magic, however, definitely spread beyond the creature's head.

I hope this works, Amendal thought, and then released his restraint.

A golden wave rippled across the ocean floor as the portal coalesced. Once it opened, the magic pulled the nactilious into the Visirm Expanse—

the monster's dark-blue limbs flailed but soon vanished.

"Yes!" Amendal cheered, opening his eyes. But something unexpected happened. The portal also consumed the gargantuan, compressing the rocks and dirt of its body. The conjuration—now mangled a bit—floated in the void that was the Visirm Expanse. It was mostly intact, but it didn't quite resemble its original hulking form.

"Amendal!"

The shout finally drew him from his trance, and he turned to see Ildin beside him.

"I'm sorry," Ildin said, "but Morgidian is going to dismiss this ramp. He said it's too taxing, and he needs to dismiss it in order to maintain the barsion around the hull."

Amendal looked to the ruined ship, where men and women ferried supplies to the main deck. Others then dropped the supplies to the dock, where a third group carried them into the icy cavern. Jaekim was on the dock, waving both hands above his head. Was he trying to get their attention?

"It does look bad," Amendal muttered.

Ildin sighed. "I think we're stranded. Hopefully, when we haven't returned as planned, the Order's council will send a ship to inquire of us…"

"It won't come to that." Amendal gave his friend a wry smile. "Do you really think I'd leave home without a way back?"

Ildin's eyes widened.

"Come on," Amendal said, grabbing Ildin's arm. "It sounds like Jaekim is trying to get our attention."

———————⊂•⊃———————

Unloading the *Giboran* took several hours. Amendal had helped move supplies by conjuring several normal-sized earthen creatures from the Aldinal Plane. Some of the supplies were waterlogged. Luckily, most of the supplies weren't ruined, as they were frozen by the frigid water.

The *Giboran* had sustained excessive damage from the battle. The rigging was completely destroyed, and the hull was marred with far too many holes. If the rigging had been the only damage, the ship could have been salvaged.

Captain Edara had attempted to repair his vessel, ordering the cannibalization of the upper aft section, but the wood comprising the upper hull could not be fashioned appropriately without mooring the ship in a dry dock. But that did not stop him from attempting the makeshift repairs.

Once the ship was unloaded, Amendal left the crystallized dock and headed into the tunnels. The expedition's scouts had found another massive cavern, but this one contained the bases of crystallized buildings, each a semitranslucent pale blue. The cavern's floor was level, despite being covered in snow and ice. At one time it was probably a city square of sorts, as the entrances of several buildings were accessible.

Each of the crystal structures extended into the cavern's icy ceiling. The cavern was undoubtedly part of the ice shelf surrounding Crisyan Bay. Amendal supposed those buildings didn't reach too far into the ice shelf, unless they were comparable to the statues they had passed before mooring.

Members of the expedition were spread out within the cavern, their tents erected in little clusters. Probably organized by squad, Amendal thought, navigating the tents. He wandered the makeshift camp, searching for his friends.

He passed a group of sailors and mercenaries talking around a fire. "... so, what were those things?" a heavy-set fellow asked.

"I think that was a nactilious," a sailor replied.

"No..." a short mercenary said with mocking jest. "Do you really think so?"

"It fit all the stories I ever heard," the sailor said, not catching the sarcasm. "Some people say that Heleron created those monsters to plague the impenitent that sailed his seas."

"Are you calling us impotent?" a mercenary asked, and several of the other adventurers burst into laughter.

The sailor's expression indicated that he didn't find their twisting of words humorous.

Amendal continued through the camp and spotted several of his friends around a fire. Fendar had his arm around Scialas, and she leaned her head against his shoulder. *So, they are together,* he thought with approval. Jaekim sat across from them, downing a tankard. Morgidian was there too, recalling the events of the battle from his perspective.

"... I have never experienced anything that resistant," the barsionist said. "I can usually pin most things with my inverted barsion, but moving that monster was nigh impossible—" Morgidian cut himself short and looked at Amendal. "That Mindolarnian lady is looking for you. I guess Ildin mentioned you claimed to possess a way home?"

Fishing for an answer? Amendal thought, playfully narrowing his eyes at his friend. Then he nodded and took a seat beside Jaekim. "I do have a way off this icy rock."

Jaekim set his tankard down so forcefully that its contents sloshed. He turned to Amendal with bleary eyes. "And what's that?" the necromancer slurred the question.

Amendal didn't answer. "Where's Ildin?"

"With the other squad leaders and the Mindolarnian lady," Morgidian said. "They want you there at the meeting."

"Probably want to punish you for all the damage you caused," Jaekim slurred, then burst into raucous laughter.

The meeting was being held within one of the crystal structures. Despite the lack of natural light, lightstones, or open flames, the building was well lit. The light seemed to be coming from the walls, floors and ceilings, as if the crystal itself was glowing.

Amendal wandered the crystallized building for a time, until faint chatter carried down a hallway. He followed the sound to the room where Ildin and Faelinia were meeting with Vaem, Calimir, and the rest of the squad leaders. Several of them were lounging on crystallized furniture, while others stood around a large crystal table where Vaem's map was laid out.

"How good of you to join us," Calimir said in mock greeting.

"I was helping the poor captain."

"I see..." Calimir nodded. "And how go the repairs?" He did not sound convinced.

Amendal shrugged, fighting the urge to reply with his own contemptuous remark. "The sailors are working doggedly, but I doubt they'll be able to save her. Even if they stop up the leaks, the ship can't sail with one mast."

Calimir shook his head. "As much as I hate to admit it, I think Edara should consider his ship a lost cause."

"Would you leave him and his crew here?" Amendal asked.

"No," Faelinia replied. "We were just discussing ways to persuade him to come along."

Amendal raised an eyebrow. Would the sailors be willing to march across this godforsaken wasteland?

"It's better that we stay together," Vaem said. "We can better ration our provisions, and the sailors can fill in the gaps for those we lost in that battle with the nactili."

Nactili? Amendal mused. *So that's the plural for those creatures... Best I remember that.*

"Our best hope for survival is to reach the reliquary," Vaem continued, sounding determined. "That is still our utmost concern. We can focus on returning home later. Besides, if we leave the good captain and his men behind, there's a chance they won't survive."

Calimir nodded.

That sounds like a horrible strategy, Amendal thought. What was Vaem thinking? Would Vaem drive the expedition to the brink of death just to reach that storehouse of tevisrals? *I hope not...*

The commander cleared his throat. "Now, Mister Aramien, I hear you have an infallible way to return home. I don't really want to hope for a rescue from a vessel that might or might not come." He glanced to Ildin.

Here we go with that Mister nonsense. Amendal strained to keep a straight face.

"Tell me," Calimir continued. "What do you have up your sleeve?"

"It's actually beneath my tunic," Amendal replied, patting his chest. "I have a rogulin crystal bound to my father. It may not be large enough to carry the whole expedition back to Soroth, but it should be enough to send someone to inform the Order's council of our predicament and request a ship to rescue those left behind."

"Excellent!" Calimir exclaimed, extending an open hand.

Amendal leaned back. "Not so fast." He waggled his finger. "This is *my* crystal. If anyone is going to use it, it's going to be me."

Calimir dropped his hand, his expression turning grim.

"That's only fair," Vaem interjected. "Besides, Master Arenil might not be pleased if we return without his son." She said the words with a tone of bitterness. Vaem undoubtedly remembered the encounter with Arintil's quinta'shals. Amendal imagined his brother strangling the woman if she returned without him. *Poor Arintil really isn't that good with women...*

"Fine," Calimir said. "Once we are finished at Tardalim you can take some of us back to Soroth."

And here I was, hoping I could leave now...

Amendal stayed for the rest of the meeting but didn't participate. He sat with Ildin, and they both listened quietly. Vaem discussed a possible route to the surface, since the tunnels branching off from the cavern were all dead ends. Her plan required them to climb to the higher floors and look for an opening.

After doling out scouting assignments, Calimir closed the meeting.

Amendal lingered in the room with Ildin as the squad leaders left. Vaem eyed him, but he deliberately ignored her and kept his eyes on Faelinia. She was one of the last to leave the room.

"I'll see you back at camp," he whispered to Ildin.

"Do you even know where the tent is?" the illusionist asked.

"Just stand outside," Amendal said, hurrying after Faelinia.

The most beautiful woman of the expedition strode into the glistening hall, keeping her distance from the others.

Perfect, Amendal cheered inwardly. *Just the two of us.* He caught up to Faelinia, matching her stride. Amendal opened his mouth to speak, but Faelinia spoke first.

"You were rather heroic earlier today," she said, eyeing Amendal.

"Why, thank you, squadmate." Amendal grinned. "You were quite extraordinary yourself."

Faelinia grunted, rolling her eyes.

"You know, I couldn't have captured that nactilious without you."

"Modesty?" she asked with surprise. "From Amendal Aramien?"

"I can be modest," he said. "Among other things. You just need to get to know me better."

Faelinia's lips twitched with suppressed laughter.

"What do you say?" he asked, "We can spend the evening together. I know you're not seeing anyone. Ildin told me as much."

"Oh, he did?" she asked, narrowing her eyes. "And did he say *why* I wasn't seeing anyone?"

Amendal's grin broadened to a devious smile. "Because you want a courageous man. And you've admitted that I am. Heroism does imply bravery."

Faelinia shrugged. "Too bad your heroism was dim-witted. Otherwise…
I *might* be interested in you."

Amendal's jaw dropped. He had not expected a backhanded compliment.
What marvelous sarcasm.

Faelinia strode ahead of him, entering the cavern and disappearing
among the clusters of tents.

This is going to be more difficult than I thought. Amendal sighed. Not only
would he need to be heroic, he had to be smart about it. "Is that woman
really worth the trouble?"

Yes, she was.

A hand clasped Amendal's shoulder and he turned.

Ildin stood with his head cocked. "No luck?"

"Not yet." Amendal turned back to the cavern. "But by the end of this
expedition, Faelinia will be begging to marry me."

Ildin chuckled. "I'm starving. Why don't we eat? Then you can tell me all
about how you're going to woo her, from now until we leave Tardalim."

THE END OF
Part One

Fen'chalim'nidam flew through the massive halls of the only place he had ever called home. Every hall looked the same, made of white stone and lined with intricate stonework that glowed with coursing light. This particular corridor was untouched by the vile invaders.

A ping echoed through the hall, heralding the Shift.

I must hurry, he thought, pressing his arms against his sides while straightening his tail and quickening the flapping of his translucent wings. He flew faster, his wings alternating between flapping and folding.

The Shift happened all throughout his home, changing the hallways and blocking off certain rooms. This particular Shift would make the route back to the higher floors much longer, and Fen'chalim'nidam didn't want that.

Lines of orange light shone from the walls ahead of him, indicating the spot where the Shift would occur. After several wingbeats the hue began to redden.

Straight, straight, left, straight, right, he thought, recalling the new path that would lead to the next floor.

Two pings rang through the hall as Fen'chalim'nidam bounded through the air. The light became bright red. A hum resonated from the walls, floor, and ceiling just as Fen'chalim'nidam crossed the line of light.

"Phew!" he exclaimed, throwing his arms wide and relaxing his tail. He slowed his flight, fluttering in the air as the corridor changed behind him. It was fun racing against the Shift.

The race reminded him of happy times, times before the vile invaders. *Oh, Father*, he lamented, a frown forming at the end of his trunk. Fen'chalim'nidam missed his father. But he would have to cry later.

Saddened, Fen'chalim'nidam flew through the halls, following the new path that led to the next floor.

As he rounded the last bend, Fen'chalim'nidam saw part of a battlefield.

Though the stonework looked pristine, dead invaders littered the floor beneath the stairs. They were clad in red metal clothing that looked uncomfortable. Some of them had a weird picture on the metal covering their chests—a creepy creature with lots of heads.

Sadness turned to anger as Fen'chalim'nidam fluttered above the corpses. *Evil things!* He growled, his anger boiling.

The invaders were giants when compared to Fen'chalim'nidam. Granted, he was only half grown, but even if he were fully grown, they would still be almost twice his size.

"Ugly things," he spat. The invaders had flat faces, with a tiny stubby thing protruding between their eyes and mouth. And their skin was pinkish, and some had blemishes. *Weird skin.* Unlike the invaders, Fen'chalim'nidam's skin was a beautiful shade of gray with a hint of green. The invaders had arms, but instead of a tail below their waists they had things called legs. They didn't have wings, either. His mother had called them some name, but Fen'chalim'nidam couldn't remember what it was. He was content to call them invaders.

Fen'chalim'nidam flew up the stairs, passing more of the dead. He didn't know why there were stairs in his home. His people—the Tuladine—had no use for stairs. The invaders seemed accustomed to them.

More dead invaders lay beyond the stairs, but he saw fewer the farther he flew.

Twice the invaders had come. They were stopped the first time, but not before killing many of the Tuladine. The second time that they came was much worse. That was when Fen'chalim'nidam's father had gone missing, and all the full-growns he had ever known—besides his mother—had died. But Fen'chalim'nidam had not found his father among the dead Tuladine.

So, Fen'chalim'nidam began searching every hall and every room—well, as much as he could. The most recent invaders had let out a *monster*... The monster and the Shift made it difficult for Fen'chalim'nidam to search for his father. His mother insisted that his father was dead, but Fen'chalim'nidam didn't believe her. He couldn't believe her. But after checking almost every hall and every room he began to wonder if he was wrong...

Fen'chalim'nidam fluttered around a corner as faint scraping echoed from far down the hall. He gasped, but quickly closed the lips at the end of his trunk. The scraping grew louder and was accompanied by heavy breathing. Those were noises the monster made.

Not that way!

Swallowing hard, he spun and fluttered back toward the stairs. Fen'chalim'nidam had run into the monster several times, but each time the Shift had saved him.

The monster was big, much bigger than the invaders. It barely fit in the halls and could probably eat him in one bite. That made Fen'chalim'nidam shudder. He had seen the monster a long time ago, when helping his father check on all the rooms of their home. His father had said their people were watching the monster and others like it, making sure they stayed in their cylinders because they were dangerous. Fen'chalim'nidam thought it was stupid that they kept dangerous things in their home. It just didn't make sense.

Which way do I go now? Frantically looking about, he zipped around a corner, away from the stairs. But the scraping noises continued growing louder.

He had to find another way.

Fen'chalim'nidam fluttered past an open doorway, glancing through it. Could he hide inside there? It was a large room, with a really tall off-white cylinder at its center. The cylinder had a big ugly creature in it—but not quite like the monster behind him.

No, not in there… Fen'chalim'nidam thought, fluttering farther down the hall.

The scraping and the breaths grew louder. The monster was getting close!

Fen'chalim'nidam pressed his arms to his sides and straightened his tail. He had to fly faster!

The hall ahead of him was long, *really* long. *There are no other hallways!* he thought in desperation, fear tightening his stomach.

The scraping continued to grow louder, but then abruptly ceased. Fen'chalim'nidam swallowed hard, fighting the urge to look behind him.

But he couldn't resist for long.

The monster sighed heavily as Fen'chalim'nidam peeked over his shoulder. Only half of the black-and-orange-colored monster was in the hall. Its long head was turned away, looking toward the stairs. It leaned forward, bracing itself on four of its six arms. The thing liked to do that. When it moved, the monster used its legs *and* arms. Fen'chalim'nidam's mother had called it galloping. *Weird word.*

A ping resounded ahead of Fen'chalim'nidam and the monster spun, showing its hideous face and its frightening purple eyes. Fen'chalim'nidam screamed, flapping his wings faster. Rapid scraping noises echoed behind him as the monster darted through the hall.

Faster! Fen'chalim'nidam thought, searching for the Shift. Orange light shone down the hall. It was far away, but he might just make it…

A bellowing laugh echoed behind Fen'chalim'nidam as the scraping grew louder.

Two more pings filled the hall as Fen'chalim'nidam neared another doorway—the last door before the Shift. *Oh no!* He had been taught that if he hadn't reached the last doorway before a Shift that he should wait. But he couldn't wait, not with the monster chasing him.

A gust of hot air blew against Fen'chalim'nidam's tail, and he glanced over his shoulder. The monster was right behind him! The hideous thing cackled as two of its arms reached toward Fen'chalim'nidam, its claws ready to grab him.

Fen'chalim'nidam screamed and closed his eyes, flapping his wings with all his might. The hum resonated from the walls, floor, and ceiling, seeming to last forever.

Something brushed against Fen'chalim'nidam's tail as the hum ceased. But he kept flying forward. The scraping was gone, and so was the scary laugh.

Still flying furiously, Fen'chalim'nidam glanced over his shoulder. What was once a long hall was now a solid wall, and the monster was gone. It hadn't made it through the Shift. Heart racing, Fen'chalim'nidam ceased his hasty flight. He fluttered his wings, gently landing on the floor by curling his tail beneath him.

"I made it…" he said with a gasp.

Fen'chalim'nidam rested on the floor for a while, staring at the hall that was now a wall. "I should return to Mother," he whispered, looking around. "Now to figure out where I am…"

After regaining his composure, Fen'chalim'nidam made the long climb to the Roost. Unlike the rest of his home, the Roost was filled with all kinds of plants. He soared over teal grass and rustled the beautiful bushes. He zipped around the tall buildings that held the rooms for all the different families. Those used to be full of other Tuladine… but now they were empty.

He soon found his family's rooms and flew inside.

"Mother!" he called. "I'm back!" He flew through a tunnel to the room with her bed. His mother lay with her wings wrapped around her. Her black eyes were half open and she blinked slowly. The black spots on her reddish wings hid most of the wounds caused by the invaders.

"Fen'chalim," she called hoarsely, leaving off the last part of his name. "Come here."

Fen'chalim'nidam fluttered toward her, lowering himself beside her bed. "Yes, Mother?" He rested his hands on hers while coiling his tail and stilling his wings.

"I was calling for you," she said, not sounding amused. "Were you searching the halls again?"

"Yes, Mother. I still can't find Father."

His mother coughed and shook her head. "That is reckless! Orath'issian is still on the loose…" She coughed again. "Besides, you won't find your father. He's gone."

"But he's not with the other dead."

His mother shook her head. "You need to forget about him. Go, leave this place. Join the other younglings—" She coughed and gasped for breath. "Before they get too far away…"

Fen'chalim'nidam frowned. He was not going to abandon his father, not with the monster roaming the halls. His father was not among the dead, so that meant he was still alive, right? *I hope he wasn't eaten...* Fen'chalim'nidam quickly put that thought out of his mind. "He must be hiding... Yes, hiding from the monster!"

"No, Fen'chalim. Your father is gone. You would not understand his fate. Now please, obey me." His mother was trying to sound stern but her voice was weak. "Once I die, there will be no more Tuladine left in this place. Only our kind can escape this prison."

Fen'chalim'nidam frowned. His home *was not* a prison. Why did his mother insist on calling it that?

"If you do not leave, my son, you will endanger not only yourself, but the rest of this world. The prisoners here are some of the vilest to ever walk the face of Kalda. They cannot be allowed to escape."

She studied Fen'chalim'nidam for a moment and spoke again. "You must leave. These humans and qui'sha do not know the dangers they could release, and if they invade again, there will be no one to stop them."

"I'll stop them!" Fen'chalim'nidam declared. "I will fight them, Mother."

She shook her head. "You are too young, my son. If they come again, they will come with another army. Even if you were full-grown you would not stand a chance against—" She coughed again, more violently this time. His mother extended a hand, shakily reaching for his arm.

"Please, Fen'chalim.... Please leave."

Fen'chalim'nidam shook his head. "I will not leave without Father. He wouldn't leave without us, so I won't leave without him."

His mother's eyes closed, her hand sliding down Fen'chalim'nidam's arm.

"Mother?" he asked, shaking her hand.

She didn't respond.

"Mother?" he demanded. "Mother!"

Fen'chalim'nidam lifted his mother's hand, but her arm was heavy... and limp. "Mother?!"

She still did not respond.

"No..." he whispered, and tears trickled down his trunk to his lips. "No, Mother!" *Was she really gone?* He climbed atop his mother's bed and shook her, but she didn't move. She had told him many times that she would join the rest of their people in death. The invaders and the monster, that Orath-monster, had killed those of the Tuladine that could have healed her...

"Mother?!" he shouted, more tears streaming down his trunk. He wailed, burying his face in his mother's wings... wings that would never flap again.

⟞•⟝

Fen'chalim'nidam didn't know how long he wept over his mother. Eventually, he climbed down from her bed and fluttered from her room. His home suddenly felt very lonely.

He thought upon his mother's words, wiping the tears from his trunk. "I don't want to leave." This place was his home. He had never left it. But then he thought of that Orath-monster.

"My home isn't safe," he whispered. If his home was ever going to be the same, he would have to get rid of the monster. His mother's rod—a weapon that could fire purple blasts—caught his eye.

"I'll fight it!" Though he was small, he knew all the secrets of his home. The monster didn't seem to quite understand the Shift. "I'll use the Shift against it," he said, fluttering over to the rod. His mother's helmet and clothing lay near the weapon. The clothes would be too big on him, but he could use the helmet.

"I'll defend my home," he said resolutely. He grabbed the helmet and put it on. Its brim hung partway down his trunk and he could barely see. "And if those hooman and qui-qui invaders come back, I'll stop them, too!" When the first invaders had come, they were unaware of the Shift. Surely he could use the Shift against any new invaders, too.

Filled with determination Fen'chalim'nidam picked up his mother's weapon. The rod was awkward to hold, but he managed to grip it with both hands. Fen'chalim'nidam tilted his head back, adjusting his mother's helmet so he could see.

"All right, you evil invaders and scary monster, come and get me!" he declared, flying from his family's private rooms. He would defend his home, and he would find his father.

With a renewed resolve, Fen'chalim'nidam returned to searching the lower levels of the only place he had ever called home.

PART
TWO

A
Treacherous
Wasteland

Amendal · Ildin · Vaem · Faelinia
· Calimir · Morgidian · Edara ·

"One of the rarest creatures you could ever learn to conjure lurks in the depths of the sea, the fabled nactilious. Besides my master, I have met only one other conjurer who managed to tame one, and all my apprentices who have sought them have never returned."

- From *Colvinar Vrium's Bestiary for Conjurers*, page 45

Reoccurring nightmares plagued Amendal's mind. In each one, he found himself at the base of the towering mountain allegedly housing the reliquary. He tried to run from that godforsaken plain, but the tentacles of nactili burst from the snowdrifts. The flailing limbs—varied in colors—swarmed around him, striking him with a freezing debilitation. Helpless, Amendal watched in horror as the colorful limbs pulled him into frigid water that was once snow and ice.

But before he was drowned, the nightmare shifted. The watery grave became a towering corridor made of white stone with architecture unlike anything he had ever beheld. Other corridors branched off, but they were all the same no matter how far he traveled. He tried navigating the corridors to find a way out. But his efforts to escape were in vain.

Inevitably, scraping noises filled the labyrinth, as if they were the hurried footfalls of some creature. But no matter how fast he ran, he could never outrun his pursuer. As the scraping became deafening, an inky blackness flooded through the corridors. It enveloped a towering shadowy figure, a monstrous creature with an oblong head, a tail, and several arms and legs.

As the blackness and the monster overcame him, Amendal would find himself back at the base of that towering mountain, only to relive the nightmare again and again.

Amid one of the confrontations with the monster, Amendal gasped awake. He abruptly sat upright within the tent he and Ildin shared.

"By all that's magical…" He ran a hand through his hair, which was starting to get a little long. He tried focusing on his hair in hopes of distracting himself, but the nightmare remained at the forefront of his mind, particularly that monstrous creature shrouded in blackness. Unlike the nightmares he had had while aboard the *Giboran,* these were not fleeting.

A grunt and the rustling of blankets filled the tent. Exhaling deeply, Amendal turned toward Ildin. The illusionist shifted onto his side, wrapped in several blankets with only his nose exposed. Ildin grunted, then turned his back to Amendal.

Looks like I'm not the only one who is restless. A pang of hunger struck him. *It can't be morning already, can it?* Sighing, he reached for his sloglien coat, then wrapped a blanket around himself and exited the tent.

Silence hung over the icy cavern. Amendal expected it to be dark, but the glow from the crystallized buildings kept the cavern well lit. There was, however, one nearby tent that was lit by the faint glow of a lightstone. He didn't know to whom it belonged.

Everyone else is asleep, he thought, surveying the camp. Another hunger pang struck him. Now where did they put those provisions?

* * *

Inside his tent, Calimir took one last look at the list of casualties from the battle. They had lost thirty-two men and women of the expedition, not including those of Edara's sailors who had perished. Several of the dead had been mages from the Sorothian Magical Order, but the bulk of the casualties were soldiers—men and women Calimir had known intimately.

More than those thirty-two had fallen into the water, but the expedition's arpranists managed to save some by reversing the deadly effects of the ocean. Those that had died were some of the first to fall into the frigid water, and they were already dead by the time the battle was over.

The soldiers had managed to pull some of the corpses from the water, but most of the dead had sunk.

Damned beasts. Calimir shifted in the simple chair.

He wished at least one of the monsters had been slain. Vaem had tried to quell his vengeance by explaining the workings of the void that Mister Aramien used to trap the nactili, but Calimir didn't think existence in a timeless expanse was punishment.

"Their deaths seem like such a waste," he whispered, setting down the list. He rose from his chair and took three steps to his cot. He pulled aside his blankets, then simply stood in front of his cot, clutching them. Though he was no stranger to casualties, those he had lost to the nactili haunted him. He had expected casualties on this expedition—they were traversing the Abodine Wasteland, after all. But this many, this soon?

A foreboding fear crept into his mind.

No, we're not all doomed, he chided himself, still holding the blankets.

But despite his self-reinforcing thought, the fear remained. In fact, it grew.

No one really knew what inhabited the Abodine Wasteland. It was possible that leaving this cavern would only bring more death. How many more of this expedition would he lose—?

No!

But the fear remained, consuming his thoughts.

"Do not give in to fear." Calimir whispered the opening line of a recitation he had learned as a young soldier. "Fear will bring defeat. I will confront my fears and tear through them like a weak foe on the battlefield. Then shall my fears fear *me*. And I will remain, triumphant."

Foreboding images clouded Calimir's mind, and he fought to purge them by repeating the recitation.

It's not working...

Calimir repeated the recitation once more as he lowered himself to his cot. He pulled the blankets across himself as he finished the litany, but the fear remained.

If he could not sleep, he would have to find something to pummel.

After pilfering a snack, Amendal returned to his tent. He spent several hours tossing and turning. Every time he nestled into a comfortable position, the vivid images from his nightmare returned to the forefront of his mind. They knotted his stomach and squeezed his heart, preventing him from sleeping.

"None of that was real," he whispered.

The last time Amendal had experienced such vivid nightmares was after his first encounter with a gangolin. It was a precarious clash, but not as dangerous as the battle with the nactili.

Think of something else...

His mind raced, then fastened on the Aramien Estate, his parents, his family's sacred tomes. Nothing helped quell the disturbing nature of those nightmares—at least, until he thought of Faelinia.

Then the tension melted, replaced by a tranquility only produced by passion.

Yes, think of her, he told himself. *Think of the chase...* If Amendal was good at one thing, it was winning over women. He was an excellent conjurer, but he didn't want to spur his imagination in ways that would contribute to fearful dreams.

Amendal mused on the romantic struggle with Faelinia until he heard movement throughout the camp. Soon, faint chatter carried into the tent. He glanced to Ildin, but the illusionist was still asleep.

No point staying here, he thought, tossing aside his blankets. *I might as well get an early start.*

The previous night, during the meeting with the squad leaders, Amendal had received a scouting assignment from Calimir. The old soldier thought it pertinent that mages such as Amendal be the eyes and ears of the expedition. Illusions and conjurations were expendable, and sending them to scout uncharted territory didn't put anyone in immediate danger.

Once outside his tent, Amendal picked his way through the camp. He didn't recognize many of those who had awakened. Most were soldiers who were groggily tearing down their tents. A few mages were awake, but Amendal knew none of them. He deliberately made his way to where the provisions were kept and found a chef preparing a large pot of bubbling porridge.

Better than what I had last night, Amendal mused and hurried toward the chef. "Is that ready yet?"

The chef, a squat fellow dressed in black furs, glanced over his shoulder. "Not quite. It'll be a bit."

Amendal waited, tapping his foot and staring at the crystal structure he was to search. Part of the crystalline building was inside the cavern's icy wall, and it looked like only the southwest corner was accessible.

He glanced to the building next to it, the same where the meeting had been held. That building's nearest wall was almost the length of a city block. *I wonder if the northeast one is that long, too.* He had returned his gaze to the first building when the chef handed him a bowl.

"Here," the chef said with a grunt. "And don't leave your bowl and spoon lying about. Best you eat here."

Amendal shoveled a scoop into his mouth, impressed by the flavor. "Not bad," he said, and walked away.

"Hey, I said you should eat here!"

"I'll bring it back," Amendal said, his mouth half full. *Well, one of my conjurations will...*

Amendal was nearly finished eating when he arrived at the crystal structure he was to search. Intrigued, he attempted to peer through the translucent walls, but the space beyond the crystal was barely visible.

Now where is the door...? he wondered, scooping up the last of his porridge.

"My, you're up early," Faelinia said from behind him.

A smile spread across Amendal's face as he swallowed the last of his meal, then turned. Faelinia wore a pale-tan coat made of fur, its hood pulled up over her golden-blonde hair. Though she was completely covered, she still made his heart race.

"Well, we are in a hurry to find a way out of here," he said.

Faelinia rested a hand on her hip and glanced about. "It looks like we're the only ones here." She sighed, turning from Amendal.

Playing coy, huh? Restraining a chuckle, Amendal uttered an incantation. Golden light formed a conjuration portal between him and Faelinia, then Amendal summoned a hawk from the Visirm Expanse. A chill shot through the conjured bird as it flew from the portal.

Amendal made the hawk fly in a circle, then commanded it to pick up his bowl and spoon. The bird snatched the bowl with its talons while grabbing the spoon with its beak, all while flying. He guided the bird across the camp while turning back to the crystal structure.

"Showoff…" Faelinia muttered.

"I'm just being practical," Amendal said, his gaze fixed on the crystal building. "I don't see an entrance."

Faelinia strode past him, her eyes studying the crystal wall. "It's probably buried in the ice shelf. I'll start carving out a way to the north. Am I correct in assuming you can conjure something that can tear through the ice?"

"Of course," Amendal grinned. "Shall we have a race to see who uncovers the entrance first?"

Faelinia snorted in amusement. "A race?" she asked, chuckling. "Let me guess. You want a kiss if you win?"

Amendal shrugged. "If you say so," he said, then headed along the southern wall while uttering another incantation.

———⊃•⊂———

Ildin awoke to a commotion of shouted orders, clanging metal, and the flapping of thick canvas. He pushed the blankets down from his eyes but did not move them further. It was frigid.

"Amendal?" He glanced about the tent, but the conjurer was nowhere to be found. "Up already, huh?" Ildin sighed, sitting up. He pushed the blankets from his ears, hoping to better discern the noises outside.

While he strained his hearing, the tent flap opened, letting colder air inside.

"Hey!" he shouted, turning to the tent door. Morgidian stood at the open flap, Fendar and Scialas right behind him.

"You up yet?" Morgidian asked.

"No," Ildin muttered. "Close the flap."

Morgidian stepped inside, but left the tent door open. "They're scuttling the ship."

"I know…" Ildin grumbled and pulled his blankets across his face. "We discussed it last night."

"Don't you want to see it go down?" Morgidian asked.

"Not really," Ildin said, nestling back into his bedding. "I didn't sleep well." He grunted, turning his back to the tent flap.

"All right," Morgidian sighed. "I'll see you later." The barsionist's footsteps carried from the tent, but the draft remained.

Did he not close the flap? Ildin lifted the blankets from his face and turned to the door. The tent flap was still open.

"Morgi…" Ildin muttered under his breath, untangling the covers from around his feet so he could stand. Despite the blankets, a biting chill struck Ildin as he grabbed the open flap. He was about to close it when Vaem approached.

"He's not here," Ildin said, draping the flap across the opening.

Vaem stuck her hand forward, grabbing the flap beneath Ildin's gloved fingers. "I know. May I come in?"

Ildin held the flap in place. Was she planning to lie in wait for Amendal? *She couldn't possibly want to talk with me.* He considered her motives further before answering.

"I'm going back to sleep," he said, reaching for one of the tent door's ties. Ildin secured the flap to the tent wall before continuing. "And Amendal won't appreciate it if you're sitting here when he gets back."

"Amendal has already started his scouting assignment," Vaem retorted, her hand still in the door. "I have no intention of wasting my morning in his tent. It's you I want to talk to."

Ildin started. *Maybe I should have gone with Morgi.* There was still time to join them. He glanced back to his bed, eyeing the rest of his winter gear.

"It will only take a moment," Vaem said, her tone insistent.

Ildin stepped away from the door, removing his blankets. He had worn his coat to bed, but not his boots, scarves, or shawl. He quickly put on his accoutrements as Vaem stepped inside.

"Once we are aboveground we need some sort of an advanced scout," Vaem said. "But Calimir doesn't want to send a party ahead."

"Oh?" Ildin asked noncommittally, tying his boots.

"We've been debating, but I think an illusionist will suit us just fine," Vaem added. "You seem skilled enough. I mean, you effortlessly zipped those illusions back and forth during the battle."

Ildin silently wrapped a scarf around his neck, then grabbed another.

"All you have to do is keep an illusion ahead of the expedition. You'll be warning us of any potential threats, natural or otherwise."

Ildin tied his second scarf and studied Vaem. Was this assignment an attempt to keep him preoccupied so she could try to enthrall Amendal again? "Why me?"

"Because you're in squad one, of course," Vaem replied frankly. "You're already close to both me and Calimir. It makes perfect sense. What do you say? Will you accept?"

Ildin squinted at her, then moved toward the door, careful to keep his distance from her. "I'll think about it."

"If you refuse, we'll have to find another," Vaem said. "And we'll have to move that illusionist to squad one."

Ildin stopped partway through the tent door. Was she threatening him? If he wasn't around, who would protect Amendal from this woman and her intoxicating powers? He had to accept.

"Fine," Ildin said, turning to face her. "I'll do it."

"Good," Vaem smiled, stepping toward him. He backed through the tent door, keeping his distance as she exited the tent. "Aren't you going to secure this?" she asked, pointing to the flap.

"Once you're away…" he said, glancing at her right hand.

Vaem drew her lips into a line. She stared at him for a moment, then stomped away.

That was close… he thought, watching her disappear among the tents.

The notion of letting the *Giboran* sink to the bottom of the ocean enraged Captain Sauran Edara. How could Calimir and the other leaders of the expedition even consider such an atrocious act as a solution? True, the ship couldn't have suitable repairs, but with enough time he could mend the hull. He just needed three barsionists. Was that too much to ask?

Idiots… Edara grumbled, pacing along the crystallized dock. He yawned, rubbing his red-rimmed eyes. Neither Edara nor his crew had slept at all. Some had taken breaks and eaten with the expedition in the caves, but none had slept.

Three days, maybe four, he thought. *That would be enough time to complete the repairs.*

"It's not like that reliquary is going anywhere," he mumbled, examining the boarded-up parts of the portside hull. The ship glowed a pale blue, the result of the barsionists' magic. "They should just stay and help me."

During the night, Calimir and Vaem had come to Edara and informed him of their plan. Edara and his crew were to join them on the trek to Damnation. They told Edara that his ship was a lost cause, and they would be setting out in the morning. He had till then to stop up the hull, since the barsionists helping him would be leaving with the others.

The barsionists were keeping the *Giboran* afloat, since the ship was still taking on water. Despite all their repairs, there were still parts of the hull that leaked. Edara and his crew had tried to bow the wood, but the frigid climate prevented them from making suitable planks.

Lines from the rigging had been tied to the dock, but they would not hold the *Giboran* if the barsionists relinquished their magic. The weight of a waterlogged ship would be too much for those lines, and the *Giboran* would sink.

Noise carried from the cavern, and Edara turned. A crowd filed from the tunnels, Calimir Sharn at their head. The crowd marched straight for the crystallized dock.

"No!" he growled, running a hand down his long goatee. "I will not let you have her."

"Good morning, Captain," Calimir said, stopping a few paces away from Edara. The old soldier looked cautious.

You know I won't let you have her, Edara thought, noting Calimir's demeanor and the distance he kept.

"Are your repairs finished?" Calimir asked as Vaem stepped around him.

"You know they're not finished!" Edara spat, pursing his lips. His eyes went back to the crowd, which consisted of most of the expedition. *Did you bring them to restrain me if we resist?*

"That's unfortunate," Calimir said with a sigh. "It was a good ship. Luckily, we have another way to return home."

Edara started. "Is that all you think of *her*? Just a means to return home? Is that all I and my ship are to you?"

Vaem raised a painted eyebrow, but did not speak. Edara curled his lip. How could a woman even think of wearing makeup in this cold?

"There is a bigger picture here, Captain," Calimir said, his tone stern. "It is best for everyone that we commit your ship to a watery grave and press on. Otherwise, you and your crew will be left to fend for yourselves."

"You're taking the provisions?!" Edara shouted. *You're going to force your will upon me no matter what,* he thought, balling his fist. Calimir noticed the gesture and brought a hand to the hilt of his sword, but did not draw it.

"It is better this way, Edara," Calimir said. More soldiers gathered behind their commander, as well as a couple of mages.

"You can't force us to leave," Edara said. "Just give me three barsionists; they are all I need to keep the ship afloat. I'll send them ahead once we're finished."

"No," Vaem said, shaking her head.

"Fine." Edara glanced to the Mindolarnian. "Two."

"We cannot spare any of them," Vaem insisted. "Besides, you'll never be finished. Your ship is a lost cause."

"She's right, Edara," Calimir said. "Now have your crew vacate the vessel. We need to start moving."

Blinding rage filled Edara. He would not lose his home, his way of life. They would not take *her* away from him!

An enraged yell left his lips as he charged across the crystallized dock, fist poised to strike Calimir's face.

Calimir dropped back into a wide stance, raising his hands as Edara unleashed his fury, but Calimir dodged the blow.

Edara rebounded, but before he could ready another fist, soldiers surrounded him, grabbing his arms and legs.

"Let me go!" he shouted. "Let me go!"

"Clear the ship," Calimir ordered.

Edara screamed demands that he be allowed to finish the repairs. He could not lose his ship. She was everything to him. He could fix her. Edara struggled against the soldiers, but he couldn't free himself. He watched helplessly as soldiers climbed the gangway and boarded the *Giboran*.

The crew soon came topside and descended the gangway, looking sullen. The soldiers escorted them across the dock, past Edara.

"That's all of them, sir," a soldier reported to Calimir.

"Barsionists," Calimir shouted, "relinquish your magic!"

"No!" Edara scream, "Nooo!"

Calimir gave Edara a cold glance, then looked away.

Edara thrashed as the blue light enshrouding the hull vanished, and the *Giboran* rocked as she met the ocean. It was not obvious that the *Giboran* was taking on water, but Edara knew she was.

"Toss aside the gangway," Calimir ordered, and several soldiers obeyed, dropping it into the water.

"You…" Edara growled. "You bastard! You've killed her!"

Calimir turned, moving around the soldiers to face him. "You will thank me, Edara. It might not be now, but you will thank me for this act of mercy."

"Mercy?!" Edara wailed, still struggling. "How can you call this mercy?!"

Calimir ignored the question, and turned to the soldiers restraining Edara. "When he calms, you can release him. If he hasn't quieted by the time we're ready to march I'll send for you."

The soldiers nodded.

With that, Calimir and Vaem hurried away.

"Cowards," Edara growled. *You can't even face your victim as you murder her!* He struggled again, but the soldiers held him in place. "Murderers!" he shouted. "You've killed her! You've killed her!"

Shuffling footsteps echoed from the icy cavern, and Edara glanced over his shoulder. Though most of the crowd had dispersed, there were several who remained, watching the *Giboran* suffer.

"Won't you do something?!" he shouted to the onlookers. "She's dying!"

The onlookers looked despondent, undoubtedly afraid of defying their leader.

Calimir could have protected the ship when those monsters attacked, but he didn't. Calimir could have persuaded Vaem to wait, but he didn't. Calimir could have ordered repairs, but he didn't.

I'll have my vengeance on you, Edara vowed silently. *You've destroyed my life, and now I will destroy yours. You will not escape my wrath, Calimir Sharn.* The rage boiling within him simmered, becoming focused anger.

"Please, let him go. We'll watch him." That was Cluvis, Edara's first mate.

"I'm sorry," a soldier said, "but we have orders to restrain him."

Cluvis pled for them to reconsider. "Restraining the captain like this is only going to enrage him. Please, just let us be with him."

The soldiers discussed the matter for a moment, then one of them let go of Edara's arm. Soon, the rest of the soldiers relinquished their grips, and Edara fell to the crystallized dock. He landed on his hands and knees, watching his beloved slowly slip beneath the waterline.

Edara suddenly felt exhausted. The toils of the night, the lack of sleep, the waning of his rage—it all drained him. Hands clasped Edara's shoulders and back, as the loyal members of his crew surrounded him.

"I'm sorry, Captain," Cluvis said. "I'm so sorry."

Edara stared at his murdered beloved but did not speak.

His crew knelt beside him, offering their condolences while also making suggestions.

Edara didn't listen to any of it. An overwhelming sense of loss came over him. Hopeless, Edara watched his beloved settle into her watery grave, never to sail the oceans again.

"You can find nactili—their proper plural noun—in the colder wa-
ters of the world. Some sailors have even claimed sightings along the
edge of the World's Frown, but those waters are too warm to house
nests. Besides, the ever-persistent storms would only drive away the
nactili."

- From *Colvinar Vrium's Bestiary for Conjurers,* page 46

Steam rose around Amendal as his magma conjuration pounded at the ice encasing the building he was to search. The creature, a mixture of black-red rock and coursing lava, tossed aside chunks of ice as they came loose, leaving a trail of steaming shards. A head-and-a-half taller than Amendal, its molten muscles burst with flame as it moved.

The conjured hawk had returned not long after Amendal summoned the elemental, and he had since sent it back through the portal to the Visirm Expanse.

Over the course of several minutes, Amendal's conjuration managed to carve out a decent-sized tunnel along the crystal wall. It had repeatedly tried to cut into the crystal surface, but the building was just as resilient as the dock. Not so much as a scratch marred the pale-blue surface.

A trench started to form beneath the magma conjuration, and the fiery creature sank to where its head was almost even with Amendal's.

The conjuration had burrowed about fifty phineals through the ice when someone cleared their throat behind Amendal. Eyebrows raised, Amendal turned to find Faelinia standing behind him, her hands on her hips. "It looks like you lost," she said smugly.

"That's because there isn't a door on this side," Amendal said frankly, gesturing back to his conjuration.

Faelinia frowned in disapproval. "Come on, the others are waiting."

Amendal returned the magma creature to the Aldinal Plane, then followed Faelinia around the building and into the tunnel she had carved with her magic. Neither the tunnel's ceiling nor the walls were wet or dripping. *She must have used a disintegrating blast.*

They soon arrived at a wide opening a hundred phineals from the building's edge. *Had she burrowed through?* No, the opening was the building's entrance, but it lacked any doors. Why hadn't the ice shelf spread through an open door?

Perhaps a barsion barrier was once present, he mused, following Faelinia through a wide hallway. There was an odd lack of odor in the building, as if the air had been untouched for centuries. *Intriguing.*

Not far from the doors, the hallway emptied into an enormous circular room composed entirely of crystal. It looked like a tall foyer of sorts.

Several members of squads one and two stood in the foyer, their heads tilted back and their jaws slack. Each was dressed in winter gear. The soldiers looked like burly bears, as they had their armor on beneath their thick coats. Ildin, however, wasn't among them.

He can't still be sleeping, can he? And what are they looking at?

As Amendal entered the foyer, he followed the gawking gazes of his fellow explorers. He started with surprise as his eyes fell upon the room's vaulted ceiling that rose to a dizzying height.

He had never seen a ceiling that high in his life. Amendal was of course accustomed to vaulted rooms, but this crystal foyer exceeded anything in his experience. The ceiling was dozens of stories above the floor, and its crystalline nature allowed a view to a brilliant blue sky. If he had to guess, the foyer was forty or fifty stories tall.

Incredible, Amendal thought, glancing about the rest of the towering foyer. The base of a grand staircase stood opposite the hall he and Faelinia had traversed, its steps wrapped around the room in a counter-clockwise ascent, spiraling all the way to the top. Long landings marked each floor, with balconies that lined the entire circumference of the round room. Hallways branched off from those balconies, like the spokes of a wheel.

Faelinia called to the others, her voice echoing off the crystal walls. "We'll break up into pairs and search separate floors. As you can see"—she gestured to the crystal ceiling hundreds of phineals away—"this building *does* reach beyond the ice shelf. Since there will be six pairs, each pair will search every sixth floor. Mentil and Redogan will start with the tenth floor. Amendal and I will take the fifteenth. The rest of you split up however you wish. Once you're finished searching, come back to this foyer and we'll discuss our findings."

While the group split off into pairs, Faelinia turned to Amendal and beckoned to him with a gloved finger.

So, just the two of us...? He smiled and swaggered across the foyer. The others were nearing the stairs when he reached Faelinia. "It seems you *do* want to spend some time with me."

"Don't flatter yourself, Amendal." She turned, hurrying after the others. "Someone needs to watch out for you and your antics."

"Oh really?"

"Yes," Faelinia said, her tone insistent. "I don't trust that you won't try to conjure some colossal brute to rip through this building once we find this glacier's top. Someone needs to stop you from bringing this building down on us."

Ouch...

Faelinia turned away, swiftly heading for the crystal stairs.

"Well, this is getting more and more difficult," he muttered. *How am I going to win you over?* Whatever the feat, it had to be impressive.

※

Inspiration came to Vaem at the oddest times. This particular spark was spurred by watching the various members of the expedition tear down the camp. Several tents were quite wobbly, making it easy for them to be collapsed. Others, however, had been staked into ice that had melted and refrozen. Both situations were not optimal, and that is what evoked Vaem's creativity.

There is a better way, she mused, picking her way through the camp. Vaem found it best to record these insights when fresh in her mind, and so she hurried to her own tent. Hopefully, Kydol hadn't begun the process of taking it down.

Vaem sighed with relief as she saw her tent still standing, but she wondered what had delayed Kydol.

Their tent was larger than the others. It was of Mindolarnian design, and was tall enough that she could stand or walk without hunching. A simple desk stood opposite the tent door with a lone chair in front of it. Both pieces of furniture had been pulled from the *Giboran,* and Vaem intended to have them carried all the way to Tardalim.

Focus, she chided herself, crossing the tent to a trunk beside her cot. She removed her sketch pad and a rectangular box: a tevisral designed to keep its contents warm. This particular tevisral, a recent invention, kept Vaem's ink and quill from freezing. Unfortunately, Vaem had not been part of its design or construction.

She set the items on the desk, then opened the box. Visible warmth left the lid, and Vaem removed her quill and ink vial.

"Still wet," she mused, testing the vial. "Good."

Pleased with the condition of her writing utensil, Vaem sat and flipped through her sketch book. She briefly paused at the sketch of the communications rod and studied it. She had finished the drawing before setting sail. The morning the *Giboran* left Soroth, Vaem had a scribe from the Mindolarnian embassy make a copy to send to the Hilinard. The man barely finished it before the ship weighed anchor. If he hadn't done so, Vaem was fully prepared to keep him aboard and send him back in a longboat.

The thought of that possibility evoked a mirthful chuckle. "What a sight that would have been," she mused, finding a blank page. Vaem took a deep breath and swiftly began recording her inspiration.

"While sojourning in Abodal I had an epiphany, spurred by inadequate shelter. Tents are flimsy things, especially when pitted against nature. But we have the means through harnessing the Channels to produce something beyond the product of primitive man."

Vaem paused, eyeing her words with a sense of satisfaction.

"I propose the development of a tevisral that can be portable, yet sturdy enough to maintain a structure. Poles are commonly used to provide a tent's structure, and those poles require the use of stakes. But imagine a tent without stakes… No, it will not collapse."

She then drew a diagram of a simple A-frame tent, but with tent poles that were curved so that the flat ends were parallel to the ground. Vaem then sketched a magnified view of the pole, utilizing a cutaway method for diagramming tevisrals.

A thick disk sat at the bottom of the pole, where the pole and ground met. Within that disk she sketched various lines denoting the flows of magic needed to operate the proposed tevisral.

"Telekinetic magic can be used in two ways, and two ways only. To push or pull. This anchoring tevisral will utilize the pulling aspect of telekinetic magic."

Vaem drew lines to the points at both the bottom and top of the disk.

"Both ends will emit controlled telekinetic particles that will bind the pole in an upright position, or at least a position perpendicular to the surface it will rest on. Since not all surfaces are perfectly level—"

She paused, furrowing her brow. "Perhaps I can fix that…"

"Note: design a compensator for perfect uprightness," Vaem wrote to the side, and then resumed writing her notes.

She vigorously recorded her inspiration, detailing the various mechanisms that would need to be used to create such a tevisral.

"Now for an activation method…" The tevisral would have to be in place when activated. There were many ways to activate a tevisral: touch, sound, presence, movement. *Touch isn't an option. The tent would fall over at the first accidental bump.*

Vaem paused, leaning back in her chair. *Movement, perhaps? A combination?*

As she considered the dilemma, the tent flap opened behind her. Whoever was at the door didn't announce their presence. She glanced over her shoulder. Kydol stood within the tent door, holding its flap in one hand. "Yes?" Vaem asked.

"Am I intruding?"

Vaem pursed her lips. Well, she was experiencing a momentary block. *Thank Lord Cheserith,* she thought. If Kydol had been a moment sooner she would have interrupted the flow of creativity. Vaem hated interruptions.

Vaem shook her head. "What is it?"

"The *Giboran* is almost completely underwater," the lieutenant said. "And

Captain Edara seems calmer."

"Good." Vaem nodded and rose from her chair. "Any news from the scouts?"

"Nothing yet."

Vaem nodded, noticing she still had her quill in hand. She spun, placing it back in the heating box. No point in letting it freeze.

"Are you ready to tear down the tent?" Kydol asked.

"In a bit," Vaem said. "I am designing a new tevisral. If you would stay outside and keep watch it would be much appreciated. I'll emerge when I am finished."

Kydol bowed, then swiftly left the tent and secured the flap.

I like her, Vaem thought, smiling. She turned back to the desk, took her seat once again, and retrieved her quill.

"Hopefully those scouts will be awhile yet," she mused, returning her quill to the parchment.

⋯⊷•⊶⋯

Amendal and Faelinia's search of the fifteenth floor was quite tame, both in conversation and discovery. Amendal thought it best that he restrain his advances and focus on the task at hand.

He and Faelinia used their magic to scour the crystal tower. They stayed together, searching the halls near the landing, but Amendal's conjurations and Faelinia's illusions spread throughout the rest of the fifteenth floor.

Like every other part of the building, the fifteenth floor was made completely of crystal. Every room and every door was a translucent, pale blue. To Amendal's surprise, even the windows were crystal. But the windows looked out on nothing but thick sheets of ice.

There seemed to be varying types of crystal that comprised the towering structure. Certain walls lacked any transparency, while others were somewhat translucent. Their varying natures sparked dozens of questions in Amendal's mind. Were these walls always crystal? Or had the mythical crysillac—as mentioned by Vaem—turned the buildings into crystal? Were the nontransparent walls a part of the structural support? Were they dense stone that had been changed, or were they just thick crystal?

The crystal tower presented quite the conundrum that Amendal felt driven to solve. He didn't have the time, though, or the means.

They turned a corner, finding one of Faelinia's illusions down the hall. She had sent several of them flying through the fifteenth floor, finding the edges of the building. Faelinia had tried sending the illusions through the walls, as illusory magic could do that sort of thing, but something barred her illusions. So, she and Amendal searched half of the fifteenth floor with the illusions while the conjurations checked the other half.

"Well, this is the last section, I guess," Faelinia said, turning to Amendal. "How is your search coming along?"

"It's not," Amendal replied, focusing his vision through his earthen conjurations. Few of his creatures in the Visirm Expanse could resist the cold, so Amendal had resorted to conjurations from the Aldinal Plane. He had summoned thirteen of the earthen beings.

Faelinia sighed, stopping in the middle of the hall. "I can't believe this glacier is so tall."

"Well, we are in the coldest place on Kalda," Amendal said.

"Oh, stop…" Faelinia groaned, and proceeded down the hall.

They continued their search but found only ice beyond the windows.

With their search finished, Amendal commanded his conjurations to return to the towering foyer. He pushed aside his shared vision with them, focusing on Faelinia.

"You know, you don't have to stare," Faelinia said. "I know you're attracted to me."

"That's not why I'm staring," Amendal replied, his voice a monotone, since a great deal of concentration was needed to tune out the vision he shared with his conjurations. "I need to focus on something in order to not get dizzy."

Faelinia blushed, glancing away.

They didn't speak the rest of the way back to the foyer.

Several of the pairs were already waiting, gathered on the fifteenth floor.

"I didn't expect any of them to be finished," Faelinia whispered.

They continued toward the others, who were lounging on the floor.

"The lot of you finished quickly," Faelinia said, folding her arms and raising her eyebrows in inquiry. Amendal found the pose alluring.

"Ice sheets all over," a soldier said. "There's nothing down there."

"Oh, really?" Faelinia nodded, examining the other pairs. She focused in on two of the soldiers. "So the two of you searched every room on your floor?"

The soldiers glanced to one another, then turned back to Faelinia with defiant expressions.

"Look," another soldier said, rising from the crystal floor. He was as tall as Amendal, but with a thicker build. He didn't look like a Sorothian, as his skin was pale and spotted with freckles. "If you've seen one sheet of ice you've seen them all. There's no point in searching every room."

Faelinia narrowed her eyes, moving in front of the standing soldier. "There could be tunnels leading to the surface, Hevasir."

"From what, the windows?" a lounging soldier asked, laughing.

"There are balconies off some of the rooms," Faelinia said. "We encountered several"—she gestured between herself and Amendal—"and you would have known that if you searched the *entire* floor."

At that moment, Amendal's conjurations lumbered into the towering foyer. *To me,* he commanded each of them.

"Did you see anything *but* ice?" the standing soldier—Hevasir—asked Faelinia.

"No," she replied.

"See," Hevasir said with a grin. "You proved my point."

Faelinia looked ready to strike the man. Granted, she probably wouldn't use her fists. "All right then," she said, taking a deep breath. "Here's the new plan. The lot of you"—she gestured to each of the pairs—"will search the seventeenth floor while Amendal and I search the eighteenth."

Murmured complaints left the soldiers' lips.

"You're a spoilsport, Faelinia," Hevasir said.

"And you're a disgusting pig," she retorted.

Hevasir's lips twisted into a grimace. He and Faelinia looked as if they were about to come to blows.

Run, Amendal commanded his conjurations. Resounding footsteps echoed throughout the foyer as Amendal stepped between Faelinia and Hevasir. He was not about to let anyone bully her. Sure, she could take care of herself, but Amendal wanted to show Faelinia that he could be there for her.

The charging conjurations drew startled glances, and the soldiers all rose to their feet. Hevasir flinched, glancing briefly to the conjurations, but settled his gaze on Amendal.

"Why don't you move on up the stairs," Amendal said, waving a hand that said, "After you."

Hevasir glowered at Amendal, but backed away. The conjurations had arrived.

"Come on," one of the soldiers said, putting a hand on Hevasir's arm.

Amendal and Faelinia remained near the balcony as the soldiers climbed the stairs. Several of them were complaining, but their murmuring faded as they disappeared down one of the halls of the seventeenth floor.

"Well," Amendal said, putting his hands on his hips. "That's one guy I'd say isn't attracted to you."

Faelinia pursed her lips and turned to the railing.

"I'll send my conjurations ahead. I assume you want to wait for the other pairs?" Mentil and Redogan hadn't returned, nor had the pair who was searching the sixteenth floor.

"No," Faelinia said, pushing off the railing. "I'll leave an illusion."

Amendal and Faelinia climbed the stairs to the eighteenth floor with the illusions and conjurations trailing behind them, Faelinia quiet.

"I'll take that half," Amendal said, pointing to his left.

Faelinia nodded, then sent her illusions flying. They twirled through the air, zipping into the various halls.

"Now who's showing off?" Amendal said, grinning at Faelinia. But she ignored the flirtatious banter.

Her lips were drawn to a line, and her eyes were narrowed. She strode to one of the halls near the landing, but didn't gesture or call to Amendal as she had when beginning their search on the fifteenth floor.

Who was that guy? Amendal wondered. He kept his pace even with

Faelinia's stride. *That was no mere bickering. Former lovers, perhaps?* Hevasir couldn't be the coward Ildin had mentioned, could he?

"So, what's the story between you two?" Amendal asked.

"Who?"

"Hevasir and you. What's the story?"

Faelinia looked as if she were holding back a frown.

"All right then," Amendal sighed, "if you don't want to talk about it, let's choose a different subject. Crystal."

Faelinia scrunched her face in an exaggerated fashion. "Crystal?" she asked, averting her eyes from Amendal.

"Yes," Amendal said, cocking his chin toward the wall. "We're surrounded by it… so why not talk about it?"

Faelinia laughed awkwardly. "You're crazy."

"And you're not talkative," he shot back.

"I can be."

"Okay, then let's talk about crystal."

A weak smile spread across Faelinia's face. "What about it?"

"Anything," Amendal said. "What comes to your mind when I say the word crystal?" He gestured to the hall.

"Well, I would definitely not want to live in a house made of it."

Amendal nodded. "Privacy is preferable. I can agree with that. What else?"

They soon found the edge of the eighteenth floor. Their discussion on crystal had turned into speculation. Faelinia's mood had also lightened. The conversation was evidently a sufficient distraction.

"What kind of tevisral could turn this entire building into crystal?" Faelinia asked.

"Tevisral?" Amendal scoffed as they approached a pair of closed doors. "These buildings were turned to crystal by a crysillac."

Faelinia's laughter echoed down the hall as she opened the doors. "A crysillac?" she managed to ask between bursts of merriment. "You, you can't be serious?"

Amendal frowned at her skepticism. He shook his head while entering a rectangular anteroom with two corridors branching off along the far wall.

"How on Kalda did you even come up with that notion?" Faelinia asked, following him into the room. "A crysillac? What are you, a child?"

Do I dare tell her? he wondered. Faelinia had not been at the council held on the *Giboran. Perhaps I shouldn't,* he mused. If he mentioned Vaem, Faelinia might get the wrong impression.

Once at the left corridor, Amendal knocked on the wall. "Indestructible crystal. Isn't that what the crysillac makes? That dock didn't so much as crack under the weight of my conjuration."

Faelinia conceded with an amused grunt.

You're a difficult one, aren't you, Amendal thought, grinning at her.

They proceeded through the hall until it emptied into a large room filled with crystal furniture. Floor-to-ceiling windows lined the far wall, not blocked by ice. What lay beyond them was a sight grander than anything Amendal had ever seen. Several enormous crystalline structures rose from the ice shelf. There were at least a dozen crystal towers to the right and left, arrayed in a curving pattern.

Faelinia gasped. "I... I can't believe it."

Amendal sauntered to the window, getting a better look at what lay outside. The ice shelf was about one floor below them. Shadows spread over the snowy ground, cast by the buildings. Even at this height, the crystal buildings towered still higher.

Maybe fifty stories wasn't *an accurate assumption.*

The colossal structures were a magnificent sight. And there were more of them than he had initially seen. It looked as if there were rows of crystal towers, arrayed in a curve.

"There must be hundreds of them," Faelinia marveled, coming to Amendal's side.

"An entire city," Amendal said. "Imagine how many Eshari lived here. If this place is even a quarter the size of Soroth's footprint..." He left the assumption hanging. Soroth, the city, had a population of nearly two hundred thousand, but its buildings didn't soar into the sky.

"Millions," Faelinia whispered. "Millions of Eshari... but where did they all go?"

Where had they gone? Did the Eshari abandon this city? They must have. *Or a plague wiped them out,* Amendal thought. But there were no remains. Wouldn't this frigid climate preserve something? *They couldn't have perished from war,* he mused, studying the crystal towers. The structures would show signs of battle, wouldn't they? But then he recalled the resilience of the dock. So maybe not.

"Look," Faelinia blurted, pointing at the crystal tower across from them. "A balcony!"

Amendal followed the direction of her finger. "Isn't that the building to the south? Where we held the meeting last night?"

Faelinia nodded, then squeezed Amendal's arm. "Come on, let's go tell someone!"

Amendal glanced down at Faelinia's hand. She flinched and pulled back, looking surprised at what she had done. *That's progress,* he thought, intently studying Faelinia. She bit her lip, then hurried out of the room.

She's warming up to me, he thought, taking one last look out the window.

"But sailing frigid waters is not enough. If you truly want to add a nactilious to your corner of the Visirm Expanse, then you need to find their nests. But they are territorial. Nactili will attack in swarms."

- From *Colvinar Vrium's Bestiary for Conjurers*, page 47

A frigid breeze whipped across Ildin's face as he reached the balcony found by Amendal and Faelinia. He shielded his eyes from bright sunlight as the barsionists finished their incantations. Dark-blue magic wisped beside him, forming a transparent ramp leading to the icy surface below.

No sooner was the spell finished than Commander Calimir hurried down the ramp with several soldiers in tow.

Waiting to descend, Ildin studied his illusory replication of the map Vaem had brought. The Mindolarnian didn't want the real map damaged, so she had insisted that Ildin replicate it for his long-range scouting assignment. Unfortunately, he would have to recast the illusion each day.

I don't know why she just doesn't have it transcribed, he thought, stepping onto the thick-packed snow.

Calimir shouted orders, but Ildin ignored him. He closed his eyes, uttering an incantation. He could feel the illusory magic swirling around him, penetrating his flesh. His hair stood on end as a tingling surge spread across his entire body.

Still uttering the incantation, Ildin opened his eyes, watching as the white light coalesced into a humanoid form. Soon, the illusion of himself took shape.

Fly!

The illusion shot into the air, zipping along the crystal structure that the expedition had exited. Within seconds, the illusion reached the tower's pointed dome rooftop.

Stop...

Ildin spun the illusion in the air, taking in the view of the vast crystalline metropolis. The expedition was gathered at the city's northern end. Those crystal towers spread to the south and looked to be arranged in a circle. He sent the illusion higher until the city's layout became clear. If there were streets beneath the ice, then they would probably look like a flowery design on a map.

He turned the illusion back to the north, and saw Crisyan Bay, three grand phineals from the city's edge. While in the bay, Ildin had not seen the tips of the crystal towers, despite his illusion resting on the ship's highest yardarm.

The ice shelf was just high enough to hide the city. That can't be a coincidence.

Keeping his illusion in the air, Ildin studied the map, noting the direction they needed to take to reach the reliquary. He commanded the illusory map to hover while removing a compass from his coat pocket. Ildin oriented the map so it was aligned with due north, then shuffled around it to find the heading.

"There it is," he whispered, aligning his illusion on the line between the bay and Tardalim.

He sent it flying, and the illusion zipped over the tops of the crystal towers. It cleared the city—a length of several dozen grand phineals—in a matter of minutes, and sped across a snowy plain.

Time to find a suitable campsite.

———————⊃•⊂———————

Amendal didn't see any point in carrying his belongings. *Why do it yourself when you can have a conjuration do it for you?* He had dismissed all but two of his earthen conjurations. The walking clumps of dirt carried both his and Ildin's belongings.

When Amendal returned to camp he found Scialas sitting on a pack where Amendal's tent had been. Ildin was not around, and Scialas informed Amendal of the illusionist's scouting assignment. Amendal wasn't the least bit pleased when he heard Vaem had threatened Ildin.

I don't know about that woman, he thought, stepping across the ice.

The expedition had gathered outside between the crystal towers. Squads were crowded together, all carrying their winter gear. Amendal passed Hevasir, who was glaring at Faelinia. They definitely had a history between them.

Amendal quickened his pace, moving toward the rest of squad one. Calimir and Ildin, however, were not present. Vaem and Kydol stood together, pointing to the crystal towers and whispering to each other.

He counted the members of squad one. *Nine, including Vaem and Kydol.*

Two of the soldiers were missing, a man and a woman. Amendal didn't know if they had been killed or transferred to another squad.

Faelinia grinned when she saw Amendal and his conjurations approaching. "Well, that's a smart use of your talents," she said, chuckling. "Why carry your things yourself?"

"Want me to conjure one for you?" he asked.

Faelinia cocked her head questioningly.

"I'm just being a gentleman."

Faelinia snorted. "Amendal Aramien, a gentleman?"

Vaem glanced over her shoulder at that remark. She eyed Faelinia with what seemed to Amendal a jealous gaze.

"You'll find that I am many things," Amendal said, stopping beside Faelinia. "I know you're more than capable. But this way if we run into anything hostile you won't be impeded by your pack."

Faelinia rolled her eyes and shook her head. "Thanks for the offer, but I can manage."

Amendal leaned closer. "If you change your mind, I—"

"I won't," Faelinia interrupted, gently pushing Amendal away.

"Your loss," Amendal whispered. He noticed a pleasant expression forming upon Vaem's face. She probably thought Faelinia was resisting one of Amendal's advances. *Don't you dare get any ideas...*

A knowing smile spread across Vaem's lips, but she returned to her conversation with Kydol.

Before long, the entire expedition was gathered. Each of the squads was clumped together. Several conjurations stood within the ranks of the expedition, carrying the bulk of the provisions. The sailors from the *Giboran* had mingled with most of the higher-numbered squads. Captain Edara, however, stood alone and kept his distance. The captain looked scorned. His eyes glared across the expedition to Calimir, who stood with Ildin by a hovering map.

Calimir and Ildin were talking, probably discussing the route they should take out of the crystal city. Once they finished, Calimir turned to face the expedition.

"Squad leaders, line formation!" Calimir shouted. A rumble of commands echoed off the crystal towers, and the expedition filed behind Amendal and the rest of squad one.

Dardel, the man second in command to Calimir, stepped away from the others. "Company ready?" Dardel shouted the question.

A resounding affirmative echoed off the crystal towers.

While Calimir shouted another command, Amendal turned to Faelinia. "Do you think he even considered the noise might alert nearby creatures?"

Faelinia shrugged.

"Seems counterintuitive," Amendal muttered. If Amendal were in charge he would have made it a point for everyone to be as quiet as possible. Sure, they probably scouted the surrounding area before gathering the expedition, but what if *something* wandered close?

Ildin jogged across the densely packed snow, arriving beside Amendal. "Thanks," the illusionist said, gesturing to the conjuration holding his pack.

"Of course."

Ildin reached for his pack, but Amendal stopped him. "My conjuration can handle it. Just focus on your scouting."

"Well the scouting is all done," Ildin said with a chuckle. "I have my illusion sitting at our campsite. But I'll welcome an unladen stroll."

"You men…" Faelinia muttered.

"What?" Ildin asked, shrugging. "Why burden yourself unnecessarily?"

Amendal chuckled. "Work smarter not harder, I say."

Faelinia fought back a smile, her gaze lingering on Amendal.

Ildin started, looking back and forth between Amendal and Faelinia. The illusionist looked as if he wanted to ask a question, but he didn't. He was probably wondering if something had changed between them that morning.

Amid Ildin's perplexity, Calimir came to the head of squad one with Vaem and Kydol. They talked briefly, and then began the march through the crystal city.

"Miss Tusara, Mister Aramien," Calimir called. "Muster your minions to walk ahead of us. I want to be apprised of any impending ambush from creatures or natives."

Now you're cautious? Amendal wondered. Calimir shouldn't have issued all of that militaristic shouting.

Faelinia immediately began uttering an incantation. Arcane magic wisped around her, followed by illusory magic. Her magic took on the shape of various creatures, each with a cluster of deadly magic within them.

"That's clever," Amendal mused, watching as Faelinia mustered more of her illusions.

"Mister Aramien…" Calimir shouted.

Hold your horses, old man… he grumbled. *Now what should I conjure?*

———————⊙•⊂———————

Earthen conjurations seemed the safest things to summon. Amendal begrudgingly conjured ten more of the creatures. If the old soldier had made his intentions known earlier, Amendal wouldn't have just dismissed his conjurations.

The route the expedition took through the Eshari city was uneventful. From what Amendal could tell, the city had not been traversed for some time. Of course, there was fresh snow on the ground, so that could have covered any tracks. But if there were creatures lurking about, they didn't occupy this side of the city.

The expedition traveled for several hours, until they reached the edge of the crystal towers. The ice shelf continued beyond the crystal city, with occasional snowdrifts rising from the icy plain.

As the expedition passed the last crystal tower, Amendal eyed a colossal archway to his left. It resembled a pointed oval, and was made entirely of pale-blue crystal.

A pointed archway? He had heard that elves marked the entrances to their cities with towering archways. Elves liked pointed shapes, probably because of their ears.

Could the Eshari be a faction of elves? Those statues in the bay *did* have pointed ears. If they were elves, perhaps they had fled to the Mainland ages ago.

Elvenkind in Kalda were very secluded, but they had not always been like that—at least, not according to legend. Long ago, the elves spread across Kalda, mingling with humankind.

But now, most elves confined themselves to the northwest parts of the Mainland. Nearly every elf lived in the cities of Merath or Kardorth, though there were some nomadic elves, and there was a small settlement on the Isle of Merdan. Those on Merdan, however, were the remnants of those who had first settled the island, but had been driven from their homeland several hundred years ago.

"Ildin," Amendal said, nudging his friend and pointing to the arch. "What do you make of that?"

The illusionist glanced to the towering archway. "I don't know..."

"It looks elven, doesn't it?"

Ildin laughed. "How should I know?"

Amendal sighed, keeping his eyes on the enormous arch. He was intrigued by this Eshari city. His mind raced with possibilities.

What's happening to me? Amendal asked himself. *This... this feeling*—"Oh no," he said in consternation.

"What's wrong?" Ildin asked.

Amendal turned to his friend, his eyes wide with realization. "I think I'm succumbing to the lure of adventuring."

The illusionist burst into laughter.

Amendal ignored his friend, glancing back to the Eshari city, now several hundred phineals behind them. If that city were left over from ages past, what else lay hidden in the far reaches of the world?

That question spurred a tantalizing sense of curiosity Amendal had never felt.

Though it was well into the evening, the sun had not quite set. It had lingered on the horizon for several hours, leaving the frozen plain in a state between sunset and twilight.

"We're not too far from the campsite," Ildin said, frowning in concentration. "Do you see my illusion?" he asked, pointing into the sky.

Amendal narrowed his eyes. "Nope..."

"Whoa!" Ildin blurted. "There's something to the west, like a pack of creatures."

Calimir spun at the remark, throwing a fist in the air to signal a halt. "Where?" the old soldier demanded. "A pack of what?"

Ildin shrugged. "I don't know."

"You didn't move your illusion, did you?" Calimir asked.

"Just into the air..."

"Keep it there," Calimir barked. "You two!" He turned to Amendal and Faelinia. "Go find out what is crossing the plain. We need to know if they're hostile."

Faelinia nodded, sending one of her illusory birds to the west. It circled a nearby snowdrift, waiting for Amendal's conjuration.

"Ildin," Amendal said, turning to his friend. "I need—"

The illusionist, however, was already uttering an incantation to muster enhancing magic. Once he finished, white particles beamed from his hands, striking one of the conjurations. Amendal felt a quickening surge course through the earthen body, and he sent it running.

"Are you ready?" Faelinia asked.

Amendal nodded.

Despite Ildin's enhancement, the earthen creature struggled to keep up with Faelinia's illusion.

"Guide us, Ildin," Faelinia said, staring off to the west.

"Veer to the south," Ildin said.

Through his conjuration, Amendal watched Faelinia's bird turning to the left.

"I see the conjuration," Ildin said. "You're maybe five hundred phineals away. And you're moving faster than the pack. They're slow..."

"How many are there?" Calimir demanded.

Ildin tensed. "A lot... Hundreds, if I had to guess."

Calimir swore vehemently, then shouted orders for the expedition to prepare for battle. Incantations rang through the air, but Amendal kept his focus on the conjuration.

Faelinia's bird disappeared beyond one of the snowdrifts. She was flying it low to the ground, probably to keep it out of sight.

Faint trumpeting filled the air as the enhanced conjuration dashed up the snowdrift. Once atop the crest the pack became visible, though Amendal couldn't quite make out its individual members. They looked like a black mass moving south across the snow.

Suddenly, Faelinia burst into laughter.

"What?!" Calimir barked.

The conjuration bounded down the snowdrift. With each step, the creatures in the rear became more discernible. They looked rather squat, and each walked oddly. They were waddling. And they had fins, long fins.

Faelinia's illusion circled above the mass of creatures, drawing their attention. The trumpeting grew louder. The noises sounded more curious than hostile. Several looked up, revealing long black beaks with orange streaks. Bright orange feathers adorned their cheeks, accented by a splash of blue.

Some kind of bird? Amendal wondered. They looked too big to be birds. Besides, those fins didn't look like they could be used for flying. Certainly, there were bird-like creatures that didn't fly. Perhaps these were a cousin of sorts to those birds.

"They"—Faelinia struggled to speak through her mirth—"they're penguins!"

"A what?" asked one of the soldiers.

Ildin let out a confused sigh. "Penguins? What's a penguin?"

Amendal hadn't the slightest idea. His conjuration reached the rear of the pack. *Or is it flock?* he wondered. These penguins did look like birds.

Several of the penguins turned, but only gave the conjuration a momentary glance. They kept waddling across the snow, marching to the south.

"Are they hostile?" Calimir demanded.

Faelinia shook her head, still laughing.

Calimir ordered the expedition to stand down, and the mages mustering their magic cut their incantations short. The old soldier shouted some orders, and the expedition continued forward. Faelinia, however, couldn't stop laughing. The squads filed past her, but Amendal and Ildin remained near Faelinia.

"Do we need to carry you?" Amendal asked.

Faelinia shook her head, struggling to quell her mirth by taking deep breaths. "I can't," she said between breaths, "I can't believe we almost attacked penguins!"

Calimir shouted for the three mages, but Amendal ignored him. Hevasir passed by, staring sullenly at the stragglers from squad one.

Nearly half the expedition passed by before Faelinia stopped laughing.

"We should hurry," Ildin suggested.

Faelinia glanced at the head of the expedition, then to the southwest. "How far away is the camp?"

"Maybe a grand phineal," Ildin replied.

"We can meet them there," Faelinia said, turning away from the expedition. "Let's go after that waddle."

"A what?" Amendal said as Faelinia darted away. Was she referring to that group of penguins?

"What's she doing?" Ildin asked.

"I don't know." Amendal shook his head. "But I'm not letting her go alone." He concentrated on the enhanced conjuration, commanding it to follow the penguins. The creatures probably wouldn't get too far ahead, but the conjuration would leave tracks for Faelinia to follow. "Come get us when you arrive at the campsite. I'm sure Old Cali won't be pleased if you run off with me."

"Old Cali?"

Amendal winked, then took off after Faelinia, Ildin yelling after him to come back.

When Amendal was halfway between the expedition and the penguins, Faelinia passed the conjuration. *Damn, she's fast,* he thought, *and she's wearing her pack, too.* Faelinia had probably enhanced herself after darting away.

The most beautiful woman of the expedition caught up to the rearmost penguin, and the creature simply glanced at her. The penguin stood as high as her chest. It studied Faelinia briefly, but kept on waddling. Amendal kept his conjuration close to Faelinia, fearful that the animals might turn hostile.

Before long, Amendal caught up to the waddle and shouted to Faelinia. "And here I thought you were one of the smarter ones."

Faelinia glanced over her shoulder, but returned her focus to the penguin. She was *talking* to it. Did she honestly think she could have a conversation with it?

"Does it understand Common?" Amendal asked.

Faelinia shrugged, but kept on talking to the penguin. The creature occasionally glanced at her. It replied once with that trumpeting noise.

Amendal followed them, but kept his distance.

After a while, movement caught Amendal's eye over one of the snowdrifts. Ildin bounded toward them, running at an enhanced pace. Why hadn't he sent an illusion? *Probably wants to see the things in person.*

"Whoa!" Ildin blurted, coming beside Amendal. "Those things are big."

"I know!" Faelinia exclaimed. "I had no clue there was a breed this large. Usually they're half this size."

"So, what are they doing?" the illusionist asked.

"Returning to the colony," Faelinia said. "See, he's engorged." She pointed to the penguin's stomach. "He's bringing food back for his baby."

"Really?" Ildin asked, not sounding convinced. "And how do *you* know about these things? Exotic creatures fall into Amendal's realm of expertise."

Faelinia barked a short laugh. "My grandmother had a book that talked about rare creatures. The penguin was one of them."

"Huh?" Ildin said. "Are they worthwhile to use as conjurations?"

Faelinia's eyes widened in shock.

"He asked," Amendal said, rearing back. "Not me."

Ildin raised his hands in an attempt to placate Faelinia. "I'm just curious!"

"No!" Faelinia shouted, shaking her head.

The outburst drew a glance from the penguin, but nothing more.

Ildin glanced to Amendal and whispered, "You can cross those off the list."

"They were never on my list," Amendal replied.

"Good!" Faelinia said emphatically. "If you scooped one of these into your conjurer's void, you'd be killing a chick. And I won't allow that."

"Fine by me," Amendal said.

They walked with the penguins for a time, and Faelinia dispensed all she knew about the creatures. The birds migrated back and forth across the Abodine Wasteland, breeding on a particular spot and traveling back and forth to the ocean for food for both them and their young.

All in all, the penguins were interesting creatures, but they didn't seem like they would make useful conjurations. *Unless a person needed help catching fish,* Amendal mused.

"We should head to camp," Ildin suggested. "Calimir is barking."

Through his conjurations, Amendal could hear Calimir shouting orders. The old soldier wanted the camp erected and the barsionists to start casting their magic to shield the camp. The barsionists were to take shifts in the night maintaining a barrier to protect the camp and create a dome of sorts to trap the warmth of the fires.

"All right," Faelinia sighed. "Goodbye." She waved to the penguin and stepped away. "Be safe as you return to your colony."

The creature didn't really seem to care that he was losing his traveling companion. The bird kept waddling across the icy plain, trumpeting occasionally.

"They're so adorable," Faelinia said, glancing over her shoulder. "I wish I could keep one."

Ildin shook his head and glanced to Amendal with a questioning gaze.

"You really like those penguins, don't you?" Amendal asked.

"Of course!" Faelinia exclaimed. "Who wouldn't?"

*"Be prepared to spend a fortune rallying a fleet to help you. A single
ship will rarely survive an onslaught from a nactili swarm. Most sea
captains are well aware of that fact—well, the myths imply as much.
I suggest a well-armed fleet no smaller than twelve vessels."*

- From *Colvinar Vrium's Bestiary for Conjurers*, page 48

Over the course of several days the expedition pressed south across
the icy wasteland, passing mountain ranges and traversing ice-
capped canyons and frigid plains. The landscape was so foreign
that it could have been the product of some whimsical story. Day after day,
the sun's movement lessened, but despite its constant beaming, the cold
persisted.

Other than the penguins, the expedition didn't encounter any inhabitants
of the icy continent. But despite the uneventful nature of the trek, the unusual scenery kept the expedition's morale high and evoked a sense of wonder.

As they had on the first day, both Amendal and Faelinia let their conjurations and illusions lead the way. Faelinia had become bored staring at
Amendal's earthen conjurations, so she clothed them in illusions.

At first, Faelinia made them into armored men dressed like the Guardians of Soroth—an elite guard responsible for protecting the Principality's
state officials. They even wielded the guardians' weapon of choice, fanisars.
Fanisars were a staved weapon with a blade on one end and a spiked ball on
the other.

The next day, she changed the illusions, making them take on the appearance of menacing monsters, beastly beings with obsidian horns and
black leathery skin. Flame danced along their sharp fingertips, and their eyes

glowed like burning embers. Fangs protruded from their mouths, hanging below their lips. The illusion was an invention of Faelinia's imagination, as Amendal had never seen or heard of such a creature.

She claimed such illusions would scare off any beast that might think of ambushing them. They certainly frightened some of the soldiers.

It wasn't until the ninth day, when traversing an icy canyon, that the expedition spotted the first signs of life. They were only footprints, but these footprints were unusual.

Calimir called a halt. Those in the lead studied the tracks. Ildin and Faelinia sent their illusions flying, while Amendal kept his conjurations near, each clothed in the illusion of a green-scaled creature.

While the expedition prepared for a possible attack, Amendal knelt at one of the indentations in the snow. The footprint was about twice the length of a man's foot and nearly four times as wide. Six claw marks protruded from the print, each the length of a man's finger. The distance between the prints was considerable, too—about the height of a man.

What a stride, Amendal mused. "This couldn't be a troll, could it?"

Calimir heard the question, then relayed combat orders to the other squads.

Trolls were dangerous creatures, found only in the mountains of the world, as far as anyone knew. They stood several times taller than an average man, with huge snake-like snouts that could swallow their prey whole. Their victims were often eaten alive, their struggling forms visible as shifting bulges along the beast's sleek-skinned belly. Amendal had seen it happen when hunting one to trap in the Visirm Expanse. The troll had attacked a pack of wolves and consumed them all. It then proceeded to pound its chest and belly, beating the wolves until they stilled. Amendal had waited until the last of the wolves stopped moving before capturing the troll.

As Calimir finished his orders, Amendal moved ahead, studying another, more detailed footprint. A ridge of snow divided the six claw marks from a thin oblong pad. The rest of the print consisted of four more pads, each different in size.

Not like a troll, Amendal thought, pausing. A troll's feet were mostly flat.

Suddenly, Ildin spoke, rousing Amendal from his reverie. "I found a cave a few hundred phineals down the canyon. It looks empty, though."

"Let's continue forward," Calimir called. "But be wary."

They followed the footprints until they stopped along the canyon wall. Indentations in the ice veiling the canyon led to the cave, which was several stories above the expedition.

"I don't see any other tracks," Faelinia said.

"It probably climbed the canyon." Amendal pointed above the cave. The ice was not as thick up there, and any trace of the monster was probably indiscernible.

"Well, let's press on," Calimir said warily. "If the creature is not here, I don't want to stick around if it decides to come back."

Faelinia and Ildin continued to search the rest of the canyon with their illusions, but didn't find any more tracks. Ildin had set his scouting illusion at the end of the canyon, but Calimir decided to push the camp farther away in case the monster decided to feed on the expedition.

As they pressed on, Vaem mentioned that the tracks most likely belonged to a yaeltis—hulking two-legged beasts that roamed the Abodine Wasteland. She claimed the creatures had tusks encrusted with venom more poisonous than the deadliest snakes found elsewhere on Kalda.

Those yaeltis sound impressive, Amendal mused. I wonder if the family tomes mention them…

On the twelfth day after leaving the crystal Eshari city, a lone peak rose above the horizon. The sun had stopped moving and hovered directly over the mountain. According to Vaem's explanation on the *Giboran,* the expedition was four days from their destination. That evening, Vaem made that news known to everyone.

A growing excitement spurred the expedition as they continued their trek. Whimsical fancies were whispered by mage and soldier alike, speculating on the wonders that lay awaiting discovery.

The day before the expedition was to reach the reliquary, the expedition made camp on a plain that was all too familiar to Amendal.

Stomach knotted, Amendal swiftly retired to his tent once it was erected. He couldn't help thinking of the nightmares he had experienced during the journey to this godforsaken wasteland. Luckily, he hadn't experienced any of those nightmares these past few times he slept.

Amendal nestled onto his cot and wrapped himself in his blankets. He had hoped the warmth might quell his anxieties, but it didn't.

Amid his struggling, light raps pelted the tent door. "Who is it?" he asked, turning in his cot.

The tent door opened, and Faelinia stuck her head inside. Her hood was pulled back and her curly golden-blonde hair cascaded over one shoulder. The barsionists had since erected a dome around the camp, and the wizards were keeping the air warm.

"What are you doing in here?" she asked.

Do I dare answer that question? he wondered. "Just resting."

Faelinia furrowed her brow, then stepped inside, closing the tent flap behind her. "What's wrong?" she asked, sitting beside Amendal's cot. "You look spooked."

Is it that apparent? Amendal wondered. If he only had a mirror…

He stared at her for a moment, then answered reluctantly. "This place just looks familiar. And not in a good way."

Faelinia studied him intently. Was that concern on her face?

"You'd probably think me mad if I told you," he added with a weak chuckle.

She shook her head, placing a hand on Amendal's blanket-covered arm. "You can tell me." Her voice was gentle and concerned.

Amendal studied her questioningly. Did he dare tell her? *She might think of me as a coward,* he thought. *What kind of man is afraid of his dreams?* But if he didn't confide in her, she might think of him a bigger coward.

Faelinia stroked Amendal's arm, patiently waiting for him to speak.

Since leaving the crystal Eshari city, Amendal and Faelinia had spent a considerable amount of time together. Their joint scouting had created a bond between them. That bond was apparent in their conversations, which had turned from casual chatter to discussions about serious matters and even intimate talks about each other's pasts and future dreams.

To the outside observer, one might consider them old friends reunited. *Old friends confide in each other,* Amendal thought.

Swallowing hard, Amendal finally spoke. "Nightmares... I've had nightmares of *this* place—this plain, that mountain, and some strange halls of white stone. They started that first night I returned to Soroth..." He didn't dare mention the frostbite. She would definitely think him mad.

Faelinia nodded and moved closer to Amendal. What was she doing?

She pressed herself against him and wrapped him in her arms. Despite all the trekking, her scent was alluring.

Amendal was stunned for a moment, but then slid his arms from his blankets and returned the embrace. They didn't speak at all.

No woman Amendal had ever been with held him as Faelinia did. Of course, Amendal rarely unveiled his vulnerable side.

A rustling at the tent door interrupted the embrace. Faelinia pulled back gently, running a hand through his hair.

Ildin stepped inside, and his eyes widened with surprise.

Faelinia gave the illusionist a brief smile, then turned back to Amendal, leaning close. "That was a brave thing you did," she whispered, her tone sounding almost flirtatious. She winked at Amendal and stood.

"Good night, Ildin," Faelinia said with a wave, then left the tent.

Ildin's jaw went slack, but he swiftly tied the tent door. "What was that?!"

Amendal gazed past his friend. "I'm not sure... But I think I've reached a turning point with her." Perhaps there was hope for the two of them, after all.

Amendal awoke to an unusual amount of warmth. Why was it so warm? Was there a fire?

"Ildin?!" Amendal shouted, throwing aside his blankets and shooting upright. To his surprise, neither Ildin nor his belongings were in the tent. *Where is he?* Amendal wondered, hurrying to the door. The floor felt flat, too flat.

He swiftly untied the tent door, throwing the flap aside. "What on Kalda?!" The tent was no longer on the icy plain. It stood within a white four-story corridor of ornate design like Amendal had seen only in those nightmares of his. Pillars were recessed into the wall every couple hundred phineals or so, with glowing spheres—probably some kind of lightstone— protruding from them. Thick stonework lined the edges of the room, with intricate carved symbols adorning its surface. Amendal didn't recognize any of them.

I must be dreaming, he thought. But no, he was too lucid for a dream. He was about to pinch his arm when he noticed the sleeve of his charcoal robe. Where had his winter gear gone? He'd been wearing it when he fell asleep.

Still at the tent door, Amendal glanced to his cot, but the winter gear wasn't there.

There were no other tents or anyone else in the ornate corridor. He took several steps, noting that the floor wasn't level. Puzzled, he glanced at the floor, then the corridor. Both the floor and the ceiling were slightly curved, like a shallow bowl. He had never noticed that detail from his nightmares.

"Is this... Tardalim?" he muttered, turning around.

Amendal braced himself for that blackness that always flooded through these halls. He swallowed hard, cautiously stepping away from the tent.

Faint scraping, like claws against stone, carried through the hall behind him.

Amendal spun, uttering an incantation. If he *wasn't* dreaming, then he'd best defend himself. He was partway through the incantation, but no conjuration magic was forming. Not even a single golden particle.

Impossible!

He uttered the incantation again, but the magic didn't form.

The scraping grew louder, coming from a large doorway down the hall. It was an odd opening, an oval shape that reached almost to the ceiling.

The Aldinal Plane, he thought, uttering an incantation to conjure a magma elemental. The conjuration magic, however, did not form.

A shadow spread from the doorway, oozing into the corridor.

Amendal gritted his teeth, then glanced back to his tent. Without his conjurations, he was defenseless.

The poles, he thought. He dashed back to the tent, ripping one of the poles free.

Now armed with a makeshift cudgel, Amendal spun back to the doorway and saw the source of the shadow. It was not like the monster from his nightmares, but it was still a frightening sight.

Clothed in white fur that glistened, a hulking four-legged creature lumbered into the corridor, its pale-blue claws clicking against the stone floor. Its form resembled a wolf, but it was twice the size of any wolf Amendal had ever seen. A pair of transparent horns arced behind the creature's head, glistening in the light of the spheres.

Unnatural eyes glared at Amendal—the whites of the creature's eyes were not *white* at all. Instead, they were a dark blue, like the color of lapis lazuli. Irises as white as snow contracted, stretching orange and yellow flecks around the creature's pupils.

The monstrous canine growled, baring its teeth. Like its horns, they were a transparent pale blue. An azure tongue arched as the monster opened its jaws.

Amendal settled into a wide stance, gripping the tent pole like a broadsword. His heart pounded, a sense of dread welling inside him. Without his conjurations, could he survive an attack from such a creature?

A twisted grin formed upon the monster's muzzle. It lumbered toward Amendal, studying him with those unnatural eyes.

"I don't know what's worse," he said through clenched teeth. "You, or that blackness."

The wolf-like creature stopped several paces away. Its strange eyes studied Amendal's face, then the tent pole.

Amendal's heart beat faster. A conflict was inevitable. There was no way a predator like this would leave him alone.

I probably look like a tasty meal... he thought, scanning the wolf-like monster for any weaknesses. *If I can get on its back, perhaps I can use the horns—*

The creature lunged, and Amendal threw his hands forward, holding the tent pole horizontally. The monstrous animal collided with Amendal, knocking him backward. Amendal shoved the pole into the creature's mouth, barely keeping its teeth from clamping down on him.

As they hit the stone floor, a claw pierced Amendal's shoulder.

He screamed, but did not let go of the pole. He dare not let go.

Amendal fought with all his might to push the monster away, but the beast was too strong. It clawed at Amendal's side, tearing through his clothing and ripping through flesh.

Another scream left Amendal's lips, but he still struggled against the beast.

The creature mauled him again, drawing more blood from Amendal's left arm.

Amendal's grip buckled, and the monster managed to toss aside the tent pole.

No!

Defenseless, Amendal watched in horror as the wolf-like creature's jaws gaped open, ready to devour him.

"That's enough," commanded a deep, resounding voice, followed by a snap.

The creature froze, the tips of its crystal teeth against Amendal's face.

Heart racing, Amendal stared at the stilled monster. It was not breathing.

Something red flashed along Amendal's peripheral vision. He struggled to turn his head. To his right were the skirts of a red robe hanging to the floor.

"I hope you learned a lesson," that same voice said. "Cisthyrn are formidable foes." Amendal knew that voice. It belonged to none other than that crazed codger from Amendal's first nightmare.

Suddenly, Amendal saw the man standing above him, grimacing. "Why don't I fix that," he said, leaning down and touching Amendal's forehead.

A surge of rejuvenation—like an arpran spell—filled Amendal's body, and the pain abruptly ceased. But no incantation had left the old man's lips.

"Much better," the codger said.

Amendal blinked in disbelief, then felt at his wounds. They weren't there. *This* is *a dream,* he thought.

The old man raised a white eyebrow disapprovingly.

"Where am I?" Amendal demanded, still on his back.

"Why in Tardalim, of course," the codger said. "Well, sort of…"

Amendal rolled over onto his shoulder, then stood.

The man eyed Amendal with an amused grin. "I can't believe you had the guts to face a cisthyrn with only a flimsy tent pole. And here I thought your dim-witted bravery would come after you left Tardalim…"

What did that last bit mean? And what was a cisthyrn?

The crazed codger pointed to the white wolf-like creature. "Cisthyrn were native to Abodine some seven thousand years. They didn't always look like that, you know. It's amazing what Kalda's ancient peoples could accomplish…"

Amendal shook his head, not following the man's words.

"Come with me," the old man said, striding away from the stilled cisthyrn.

Wary, Amendal glanced back to the creature, then hurried after the stranger.

"Who are you?" Amendal asked.

The codger chuckled. "You don't need to know who I am. Not yet, at least."

Amendal didn't like that answer. He hurried after the old man, and the two of them continued down the strange halls.

"Why don't you try casting a spell again," the codger suggested.

Amendal felt at his chest, hoping to find the necklace that held the rogulin crystal bound to his father. It wasn't around his neck.

"Trying to escape?" The man laughed. "Oh, my friend… you still have unfinished business here. Lessons to learn, creatures to seize, mysteries to uncover… Now, cast a spell."

"Any spell?" Amendal asked.

The codger nodded.

Conjuration magic didn't work, Amendal thought. *Could something else?* After a moment of consideration, he uttered an incantation to muster a veil of invisibility. It was a fairly simple spell.

White-blue light appeared around Amendal's fingertips, then wisped around him. He watched as the magic bathed him in a veil of invisibility.

Okay… now what?

"Isn't it obvious?" the codger asked, chuckling.

Amendal dismissed his concealing magic, considering the purpose of the exercise. "Magic can still manifest here," he guessed, "just not conjuration magic."

The old man nodded again. "Now what does that tell you?"

If conjuration magic can't be used in—

A resounding clap, louder than thunder, echoed through the corridor. It was followed by the bellowing of his name from someone that sounded like Faelinia.

"Amendal," Faelinia's voice boomed through the hall. "Amendal, wake up."

"Don't let her distract you," the codger said dismissively. "Make the connection. You—"

Suddenly, everything changed.

Amendal was no longer in the four-story corridor with the stranger. He was back in his tent, lying on his cot. And his side felt wet.

"Are you all right?" Faelinia asked.

Amendal stirred, turning to face her sparkling eyes.

"I heard you screaming." She leaned close and whispered, "More nightmares?"

"Uhh, I don't know…" Amendal glanced beyond Faelinia. Ildin was not in his cot. He was probably scouting ahead with his illusions.

"You don't remember?" she asked incredulously.

Did he dare answer that question?

Amendal sat upright and the wetness trickled down his side. "What is that…?" he mumbled, gently poking at his ribs. His shoulder was also wet. And there was an iron-like scent in the air. *Blood?*

"Are you hurt?" Faelinia asked.

"I don't think so," he replied. "There's just something wet on my side, and my shoulder." He removed his blankets, then his coat. They were untouched by the wetness. His charcoal robe and undergarments were another matter.

"Is that blood?" Faelinia asked, sniffing the air. She touched Amendal's side briefly, then examined the fingertips of her gloved hand. "It *is* blood!" She gasped. "What happened?"

What had happened? *Was this like the frostbite?* he wondered, feeling where the wounds had been from that beast, the cisthyrn. But there were no wounds.

"I'm getting an arpranist," Faelinia said, leaving the tent.

"I don't think that's necessary," Amendal replied, but Faelinia was already gone.

14

A DIVERGENCE

"And be sure to enlist the aid of mages well-versed in the Manipulation Channel of Power. Nactili minds are extremely resilient. The enthralling component used when opening the portal to the Visirm Expanse will not sway a nactilious's will."

- From *Colvinar Vrium's Bestiary for Conjurers*, page 49

Ildin saw that the mountain housing Tardalim was exactly as Vaem had described during that meeting aboard the *Giboran*. It towered higher, higher than anything he had ever seen. His illusion—a perfect replica of himself—stood at the precipice of the gorge surrounding the mountain.

The mountainside was five or six city blocks away. Amendal had claimed the gorge was two grand phineals wide, and that estimate was no exaggeration. The gorge also seemed to spread eternally to the right and left, with no way around it. Even the bottom of the gorge appeared to stretch on forever. If there were a floor to that massive canyon, it lay beyond an abysmal blackness.

But wouldn't sunlight reach the bottom?

Unnerved, Ildin glided his illusion into the air, searching the canyon wall for a structure within it. Vaem claimed that the only way across the gorge was to extend a bridge from a gatehouse nestled within the canyon wall. But according to her, the gatehouse could only be accessed from a network of caves.

Calimir had asked how deep the gatehouse was situated, but Vaem didn't know. Ildin had passed a cave halfway between the camp and the gorge, but there were tracks leading to it, tracks like those they had seen in the canyon seven days before.

Upon hearing Ildin's report of the tracks, Calimir devised an alternate plan. Why meander through a maze when they could simply search along the gorge to find the gatehouse? Then, they could descend to the gatehouse by use of magic. Ildin thought his argument sound, but Vaem didn't.

Mindolarnian idiocy… He was careful not to mutter his thoughts, as he stood within Vaem's tent where the expedition's leaders had gathered.

Ildin's illusion glided along the canyon wall for a while, but he didn't see the gatehouse, or anything else for that matter. He expected to see a grand palisade rising from the mountain side, with towers and other fortifications befitting a place named after the Halls of Damnation. But there was nothing besides rock, snow, and ice.

"Do we even know what this gatehouse looks like?" he asked. His voice echoed within both the gorge and the tent.

"I told you this won't work!" Vaem spat, the fury in her voice apparent.

"Keep searching," Calimir ordered.

Ildin nodded, sending his illusion farther west. He had plenty of time to search for the gatehouse. The expedition was at least half a day's journey from the gorge.

"You won't find it," Vaem insisted. "Now let's settle this foolishness." Her voice was firm. "Do you see anything that is made of the same crystal as the Eshari city?"

That question sparked an argument between Vaem and Calimir. Ildin pushed their bickering aside, focusing on the gorge. He closed his eyes, and brought his hands to his ears. It was a common practice used by illusionists to immerse themselves within their illusions.

I don't… Ildin thought in reply to Vaem's question. His illusion shot toward the towering mountain, allowing him to see more of the gorge's northern wall. He saw nothing but shadows. If there were a crystal structure like those in the Eshari city, then there would be a blue light shining amid the darkness.

But there wasn't.

Ildin strained his focus, searching farther westward, but there was no light along the canyon wall.

The illusion spun, searching to the east. The gorge turned, wrapping around the mountain. But of what little he saw, the eastern side of the northern wall was also devoid of any crystal structures.

"Where could it be?" he muttered.

The illusion hovered as Ildin puzzled out the predicament in his mind. All the while, Vaem and Calimir continued arguing.

Ildin turned his illusion toward the abysmal blackness veiling the bottom of the gorge.

Could that be an illusion of some kind? If Tardalim were home to ancient tevisrals, wouldn't it make sense to hide those tevisrals with a tevisral of some kind? That notion was something only heard of in fanciful tales, but the expedition thus far had been filled with things most thought were myth or legend.

Fly! Ildin commanded, and the illusion darted into the gorge, diving toward the blackness.

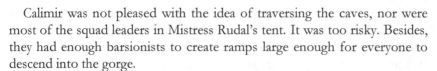

Calimir was not pleased with the idea of traversing the caves, nor were most of the squad leaders in Mistress Rudal's tent. It was too risky. Besides, they had enough barsionists to create ramps large enough for everyone to descend into the gorge.

"We must travel through the caves," insisted Mistress Rudal. She leaned over the table, glowering at Calimir. "There's no telling where the gatehouse is located, or how deep it is within the gorge."

Calimir wanted to snap at her, but he bit his tongue. *Insolent woman,* he thought.

"*He* said there were only three pairs of tracks," she said, gesturing to Mister Cetarin. The young illusionist had his eyes closed and his hands over his ears. He was obviously ignoring the argument. "If there are yaeltis in the caves they will be hibernating. *If* we run into them, we will have the element of surprise on our side."

Calimir shook his head. "I've heard the tales of yaeltis. They are dangerous creatures. And I will not risk the lives of any more of my men. We use the ramps."

Mistress Rudal bowed her head in frustration, grumbling to herself.

"But then we risk an attack while searching Tardalim," Lieutenant Virain said decisively. "The yaeltis will soon awaken from their hibernation, probably before we finish our search."

"I don't see the problem," Calimir replied. "From what you've said, the bridge across the gorge isn't always extended. As I see it, we simply retract the bridge once we reach the reliquary. And when we're finished, we'll have the barsionists block off the gatehouse from the caves while we make our ascent."

"But what if we can't retract the bridge?" Dardel asked. "Perhaps we should go after these yae...?"

"Yaeltis," the lieutenant said.

"We can keep a watch on the bridge," Calimir replied, "with at least one barsionist blocking it. If these monsters decide to attack, the barsionist can waylay them until we can get—"

"No!" Mistress Rudal shouted, slamming a fist on the table. "You're being bullheaded, Calimir! The caves are the only way to reach the gatehouse! The texts we have at the Hilinard claim as much."

So insistent, Calimir thought. Certainly, they might have to descend a considerable distance into the gorge. But descending a shallow ramp—even one that might be several grand phineals long—was better than meandering through a dark cave filled with monsters.

He took a deep breath and turned, staring out the open tent doors. As he quelled his frustrations, he saw Miss Tusara running through the camp. She was calling for someone named Scialas. *Wasn't she an arpranist?* he wondered. Had someone been injured—?

"I don't think your plan is going to work, Commander," Mister Cetarin said, his tone wary.

Calimir abruptly turned toward the illusionist. "Why?"

"There's something barring me from the canyon floor," said Mister Cetarin. "I can't even tell if my illusion is moving. It's like I'm stuck in this blackness…"

"Blackness?" Dardel asked.

"At the bottom of the gorge," Mister Cetarin answered. "Well, maybe not at the bottom. Do you think there could be some type of tevisral shielding the canyon floor?"

Several squad leaders laughed in amusement. Lieutenant Virain looked to Mistress Rudal for an answer, but the Mindolarnian scholar simply narrowed her eyes.

"Are you sure you can't breech this blackness?" Calimir asked.

"I've been trying for a while now…"

"If an illusion can't get through, I doubt we can," said a squad leader named Miraden.

Suddenly, Mister Cetarin stumbled backward, blinking and struggling to regain his footing. Miraden caught the young illusionist, helping him balance.

"What happened?" Dardel asked.

"My illusion's gone," Mister Cetarin said, bewildered. "As if it were dispelled…"

Each of the squad leaders looked warily at Calimir.

This doesn't bode well… Calimir thought. If an illusion could be dispelled by this blackness, then they might face the same problem with the barsion ramps. They could cast the ramps in sections, so only part of the ramp would vanish, but what about those on the dispelled barsion?

Calimir set his hands on the table, considering their dilemma. He did not want to venture into those caves. The squad leaders voiced their opinions and argued with one another, but Calimir ignored them, closing his eyes to ponder the situation.

He considered both options, weighing them by how he felt. Fear crept into his mind as his thoughts lingered on the cave. But an even greater fear accompanied the descent into the blackness.

"The caves it is…" Calimir muttered, opening his eyes.

A pleased grin spread across Mistress Rudal's face. She didn't even try to conceal the joy of her triumph.

"But we need to find the yaeltis before we get too far into the caves," Calimir said. "Mister Cetarin, start scouting the caves. I want to know where those monsters are hibernating. Report your findings to Eloras so he can sketch a preliminary map."

The young illusionist nodded and stepped outside the tent, uttering an incantation.

"Dardel," Calimir turned to his second-in-command, "start taking down the camp—"

"Why not send Amendal Aramien?" Mistress Rudal asked frankly. "I'm sure he would love the chance to add those yaeltis to his menagerie. If you don't send him, he might hold it against you."

Calimir narrowed his eyes at the Mindolarnian scholar. *So you want to send Mister Aramien into harm's way?* Calimir had witnessed her advances while traversing the Wasteland. But Mister Aramien didn't seem interested. Instead, he seemed enthralled by Miss Tusara. That had apparently sparked an unrestrained jealousy on the scholar's part.

The young mages had grown closer during their shared tasks of defending the expedition. Calimir had even seen Miss Tusara visiting the conjurer's tent the past night. Had Mistress Rudal noticed that as well?

"I'm sure he can take care of the yaeltis on his own," she said matter-of-factly. "They are hibernating, after all... He simply has to trap them in the Visirm Expanse, that conjurer's void." The last bit sounded quite demeaning.

I don't like your tone, Calimir thought.

"We might even get away without any fighting," said Lieutenant Virain. "He is quite skilled."

"Shall I send Mister Aramien ahead, sir?" Dardel asked.

Calimir shook his head. "No, we all stay together. I'm not losing another man to the dangers of these wastes. Now let's get this camp packed up. We can break for a midday meal once the caves are cleared."

The squad leaders left the tent, Calimir following.

But Mistress Rudal called to him before he could reach the tent door. "You made the right choice, Commander. There are powerful tevisrals guarding Tardalim. Tell me, have you ever heard of the Fate of Mirdrys?"

Calimir stopped and turned around, shaking his head.

"A pity," Vaem sighed, turning to face her desk. "Legend says that the men and women of Mirdrys used powerful tevisrals to protect themselves and their cities, veiling them in impenetrable barriers—not barsion, mind you. They were effectively hidden from the rest of the world."

Calimir narrowed his eyes.

"I think this blackness Ildin found was something like those barriers. We wouldn't be able to pass through it, no matter how hard we tried."

Oh really? Calimir thought. Was she not telling him everything she knew? When the argument about the barsion ramps first arose, she hadn't mentioned the information at the Hilinard. *She only brought it up to cement her position.*

"Are you holding anything back?" he asked, his eyes fixed on her.

"Of course not," she said, still facing her desk.

I don't believe you... he thought. Setting his jaw, he exited the tent. As Calimir crossed the camp, he noticed Miss Tusara again, this time with an unfortunate-looking young woman. Both were running. *What's their hurry?*

⊂•⊃

Faelinia dashed through the camp, Scialas trailing behind her. "Over here," she said, pointing to a cluster of tents to their right. They darted into the clearing between the tents, finding Ildin and Amendal talking at the tent door, both wearing their thick brown coats.

"… weirdest thing," Ildin said, shaking his head. "It was just gone."

Amendal narrowed his eyes and set his jaw, a thoughtful expression on his face. Her heart did a strange flip.

Stop that… Faelinia chided herself.

"You don't look hurt," Scialas said, eyeing Amendal.

"I'm not." His eyes settled on Faelinia. "I'm fine, really." Amendal's thoughtful expression turned wolfish.

Faelinia's face warmed. *No,* she told herself, *he'll have his way with you, then leave.* She knew Amendal's reputation all too well, but he wasn't that bad a man. If she only had their interactions while crossing the wastes to judge by, then falling for him would be easy.

"Well, uh, Faelinia said you were bleeding," Scialas said, stepping toward Amendal. She inspected his side and shoulder.

"I told you, I'm fine," Amendal said, his voice tainted with annoyance.

Faelinia shook herself from her stupor. "But you were bleeding! And not a little. You *can't* be fine."

"Bleeding?" Commander Calimir demanded.

Faelinia spun.

The expedition's commander came within arm's reach, then gestured between Faelinia and the others. "What's going on here?"

"When I found Amendal this morning, he was bleeding," Faelinia said.

"It happened in my sleep," Amendal said with a shrug.

Ugh… why can't you take this seriously, you big oaf? Faelinia thought. Ildin was trying to hide his surprise, but he wasn't good at concealing his emotions. After all, Faelinia had known him for many years, having studied the illusory arts with him.

"Just let me cast a spell to be sure," Scialas said.

"I'm fine, Scialas," Amendal insisted. "I checked it out after Faelinia left to fetch you and it's all healed up."

That's impossible, Faelinia thought. But how *had* Amendal received those wounds? His sloglien coat showed no signs of foul play. Everyone, including Faelinia, slept with their coats on. If someone had attacked Amendal, how had they stabbed him without piercing his coat? Besides, wouldn't receiving the wound awake him? *This is all so strange…*

"That blood was wet," Faelinia said, extending the blood-stained finger of her glove. At that moment, a breeze wisped around the tents, wafting the unmistakable iron scent.

"What happened, son?" Commander Calimir asked firmly, stepping past Faelinia.

"I don't know," Amendal said, his tone contemptuous.

"Well *something* happened." Calimir folded his arms. "How else do you explain the blood?"

Amendal didn't answer.

"Fine," Calimir said. "You best begin packing your things. We're break-ing camp." He turned to Ildin. "Have you reached that cave?"

"Not yet," Ildin said. "My illusion might be halfway there."

Calimir nodded. "Good. You'll most definitely find those yaeltis before we reach the cave."

"Yaeltis?" Amendal asked, intrigued.

He takes everything as a challenge, doesn't he? When they first encountered the tracks, there was speculation about them belonging to the fabled yaeltis. The thought of their poisonous tusks made her shudder.

"Yes, yaeltis," Calimir said. "Mistress Rudal suggested you go alone after them. I suppose she doesn't like you ignoring her advances," the com-mander added with a chuckle. "But I doubt you would want to venture into the caves alone."

"I've fared far worse," Amendal said with a wry smile.

What did he mean by that?

Calimir didn't look convinced. "If you say so..." He harrumphed and walked to his tent.

Once the commander was gone, Amendal turned to Ildin and backhand-ed the illusionist's arm. "Why didn't you tell me about the yaeltis?"

Ildin set his jaw, glanced toward Calimir's tent, then turned back to Amendal. "Because you might want to go after them... by yourself?"

Amendal laughed. "You know me all too well..."

"Well, shall I heal you or not?" Scialas asked.

"There's nothing to heal," Amendal said, and turned to Faelinia. "You're welcome to look," he added, his tone flirtatious.

Oh, please...

"So you were gored in your sleep?" Ildin asked, his voice low. He looked eager to change the conversation.

Amendal nodded curtly, and Faelinia's attention sharpened. What was he hiding?

"Like the frostbite—" Scialas asked.

"What frostbite?" Faelinia demanded.

Scialas turned to Faelinia. "The day before we left, Amendal came to me because his feet were frozen. He said it happened while he was sleeping."

"How do you get frostbite in your sleep?" Faelinia asked, confused. "It was practically summer in Soroth when we left."

Amendal simply shrugged.

Ildin glanced to Amendal, but attempted to look aloof.

You are hiding something. What could it be?

"I'll go ahead and pack our things," Amendal said to Ildin. "You should probably focus on the caves."

Ildin gave Amendal a sidelong glance, but his eyebrows arched in an enlightened expression. He nodded and hurried away.

"So am I needed, or not?" Scialas asked.

"I've already made myself clear," Amendal said, with an exasperated expression.

Scialas nodded and followed Ildin from the tent.

Faelinia studied Amendal. *Unexplainable frostbite and cuts...* she thought. What was going on with the big oaf? Whatever it was, she was going to find out. "You know"—she stepped close to Amendal—"you can tell me about the frostbite."

Amendal grinned. "One day. Have you eaten yet?"

Does he take everything as a sexual challenge? Faelinia pursed her lips before shaking her head. "No, I packed my things and came to roust you."

"Then let's eat breakfast."

<hr />

Even in his thick coat Captain Edara shivered. He stood at the edge of the camp, watching the barsionists dismiss their shielding dome. *They could have left me two barsionists,* he thought, grimacing. *I could have saved her.* This damned expedition hadn't run into *anything* these past few weeks. Who needed twelve barsionists when freezing temperatures were the only danger?

Once the dome collapsed, the members of the expedition gathered into their squads and formed a line. As usual, Edara moved to the rear. He and his sailors had stayed in the rear for most of the trek. The farther away he was from Calimir and Vaem the better.

Distance was his only method for suppressing his anger.

I will avenge you, Edara vowed to the vanished *Giboran.* He had not been able to shake the image of his ship sinking to her watery grave. Even in his sleep her death haunted him. Anger again began to simmer, but Edara managed to prevent his vengeance from contorting his face. *Hold it in,* he told himself.

They would reach Tardalim today, if the rumors in the camp were true.

Behind him, Cluvis and the other crewmen trudged through the snow toward Edara, carrying some of the expedition's supplies. The sailors had been demoted to pack mules. They murmured as they approached, each equally disenchanted by the arduous trek.

"Only a little longer, men," Edara said. "Only a little longer..." Cluvis set his jaw as he eyed Edara. The first mate knew of Edara's vow for vengeance. Cluvis had even volunteered to help aid the captain. "I'll have no qualms shoving a dagger into Vaem's pretty bosom," he had told Edara. But a dagger was not the method Edara wanted to use. Surely there was something in that reliquary that would be less conspicuous than a bloodied dagger.

As the sailors gathered around, several pointed to the lone mountain. They were arguing about the reliquary's name, Tardalim.

Halls of the Damned, Edara thought, *the realm of eternal suffering.* The murderous bastard called a command and the expedition began marching across the snow.

Weslis—one of Edara's most loyal crewmen—grunted, shifted his pack, and pointed to the looming mountain. "Do you think that's really the Halls of Damnation, Captain?"

Edara scowled. "If not, I will make it so."

"Nactili have several innate traits that make them formidable con-jurations. Not only are their wills resilient, but so are their bodies. The shells covering their heads, for instance, have one of the strongest naturally occurring tensile strengths on Kalda. Some scholars have speculated that they are more resilient than a dragon's scale."

- From *Colvinar Vrium's Bestiary for Conjurers*, page 50

D espite the uneventful nature of the trek, the expedition was armed to the teeth. Everyone was veiled in some sort of barsion. Mag-es—particularly elementalists and arcanists—were protected by barriers infused with their favored mediums of destruction, while the sol-diers, mercenaries, and sailors wore simple barsions. The weapons of the soldiers and mercenaries were imbued with a variety of deadly magics. Calimir was not taking any chances, and neither was Amendal.

He had summoned each of his quinta'shals in addition to the group of earthen elementals. Unfortunately, Amendal only had four of the gray-skinned creatures at his disposal. He needed more of them. Arintil had cap-tured seven quinta'shals, and Amendal's father possessed over a dozen.

Not wanting the quinta'shals to siphon the expedition's magics, Amendal had them march ten paces away from the party. Their long-forked tongues hung to their stomachs, ready to absorb whatever magic was thrust at them. Amendal expected the conjurations to react to the frozen ground, but the snow and ice didn't seem to faze the faceless creatures.

"We're getting close," Ildin said in a monotone, his blank stare directed ahead of the expedition where his illusion scouted out their route. He had discovered that the cave led to a vast network of winding tunnels intercon-necting enormous caverns. So Ildin sent more illusions to scour the frozen labyrinth, but those diverging branches were too much for one illusionist to scout alone. Faelinia and Fendar aided in the search, but their efforts were to no avail.

"Still no sign of the yaeltis?" Kydol asked.

Ildin shook his head.

Amendal held back a grunt. *Of course there's no sign of the beasts,* he thought. Who did these Mindolarnians think the expedition was, mindless children? *Imbeciles.* Amendal turned from Kydol and Vaem, who was eyeing him with a cold gaze.

"We should just press ahead," said a soldier from squad two.

Dardel shook his head. "I'm sure the illusionists will find the beasts soon."

As the expedition's leaders ascended a snowdrift, a debate arose among the soldiers.

Amendal shook his head. "Perhaps I should have gone ahead," he muttered. Surely, he could have found the yaeltis and pulled them into the Visirm Expanse. *There's still time to search on my own,* he thought.

"Don't even consider it, Mister Aramien," Calimir said, his tone harsh. "If you as much as disappear down a branching tunnel, I'll see to it that your compensation for this expedition is nullified."

Amendal gave the commander a sidelong glance. *Really, old man?* he thought. *Like I care about the measly coin from this venture...*

"I will not lose anyone else," Calimir added, cresting the snowdrift. The commander stopped atop the snowy mound and turned to the expedition. "The cave is just over this drift. The illusionists haven't found the dreaded yaeltis, so be on guard."

The commander continued his speech, but Amendal ignored the man and pushed past him.

A snowy plain lay beyond the drift. The tracks belonging to the yaeltis led to a cave housed within a rocky mound not more than two city blocks away. With the icicles hanging from the cave mouth, the rocky mound looked like the head of a creature rising from the snow with its maw gaping wide. From where he stood, Amendal estimated that the cave rose about three stories.

"Ildin," Amendal called, eyes still on the cave. "Are those tunnels as big as the cave's mouth?"

"Yes," the illusionist replied, stepping beside Amendal. "Each branch is almost identical in shape and size."

Amendal nodded, intrigued. The tunnels would be too small for an earthen gargantuan, but not for a giant from the Aldinal Plane... *Just about the right size,* he thought, grinning. "I'm stepping ahead to conjure something."

"Something you don't want us to hear?" Ildin asked.

Amendal nodded and descended the snowdrift, snow crunching beneath his feet. Calimir was still shouting his orders. *I'll probably be finished by the time he's done blabbing.*

He was a good ten paces from the bottom of the drift when Calimir yelled at him. "Mister Aramien!" Calimir shouted. "Get back here!" Amendal simply raised a hand and pointed to the left of the three pairs of yaeltis tracks.

Calimir continued shouting, but Amendal ignored him. Ildin translated, explaining that Amendal was moving aside to conjure something else.

Now how did that incantation start…? It had been several days since he had reviewed the transcribed pages from his family's tomes. He could pull the pages from his pack, but that would be cheating.

After bringing the desired incantation to mind, Amendal extended his hands and began mustering his magic. Golden light surrounded him but soon shot to a spot of crisp snow. The conjuration magic coalesced, forming an oval doorway four times taller than Amendal.

As he intoned the incantation, snow crunched behind him, as the expedition descended into the plain. He hoped no one would come close to investigate his summoning before he finished. The mystical doorway to the Aldinal Plane shone brighter and brighter until a hulking humanoid silhouette appeared within the golden light. *Step forward,* Amendal commanded.

The earthen giant emerged from the portal, landing on the snowy plain with a loud thud. Like the earthen gargantuan, the giant was made of clumps of dirt, grass, and rock. If one were to compare the two conjurations it would be like comparing a young child to their parent. *Would that make the regular-sized elementals comparable to infants?* He dismissed the portal and hurried across the plain. All the while, the giant's thunderous footfalls boomed behind him.

<hr />

Squad two and Amendal's squadmates in squad one had already entered the cave when Amendal rejoined the expedition. A faint breeze whipped across the cave mouth, creating a low-pitched howl. *Ominous…* he thought, falling in line beside Morgidian and the rest of squad three.

"Another impressive conjuration," Morgidian said.

"Do you want it to go ahead?" asked the leader of squad three, raising a fist to halt the expedition.

Amendal shrugged. "Sure, we'll let the big guy pass." He glanced to Morgidian and added, "Not you, my friend." Morgidian laughed, and Amendal sent a mental command to the earthen giant. The towering behemoth obediently strode to the cave. Icicles hung past the conjuration's shoulders, so Amendal commanded it to duck.

"You could rip some of those off to use as a weapon," said a mage from squad three, gesturing to the icicles.

"Are you kidding?" a soldier snorted. "They would break the moment he hit something."

"He could always stab the beasts with it," another soldier said, laughing.

"I'd rather have the yaeltis intact," Amendal said, following his earthen giant into the cave.

Ice covered the cavern walls, floor, and ceiling in thick sheets. But as the cave descended and bent to the right, patches of brilliant pale-blue crystal shone amid the ice. Amendal had expected the cave to darken as they moved farther from the entrance, but those patches made the cave glow like the crystal towers of the Eshari city.

"Amendal," Faelinia called from somewhere around the bend. Amendal couldn't see her, as his earthen giant blocked most of the tunnel. "Amendal, where are you?"

Amendal slowed his conjuration's gait and hurried around the earthen giant. Faelinia stood behind the squads in the lead, a bare hand on a patch of crystal that was glowing brighter than the rest. Why wasn't she wearing her gloves? Faelinia wasn't the only one who had halted. Those in the lead were also stopped, marveling at something on the cavern wall.

"Come here!" she exclaimed. "You have to feel this."

As Amendal neared, he saw that there was a distinct line around the crystal, as if it were repelling the ice. *Odd.* He stopped beside Faelinia.

"Touch it," she urged and grabbed Amendal's gloved hand. As he neared the crystal, a tingling sensation flowed through the glove and up his fingers.

"Whoa!" he blurted, pulling his hand back.

"You're fine, you big oaf," Faelinia said, grabbing his glove. She swiftly pulled it off, and a stinging chill pierced Amendal's hand. The chill, however, was soon replaced by a peculiar warmth that accompanied the tingling sensation.

"Come on, touch it!" Faelinia urged.

As flesh met crystal, the tingling intensified to a constant surge that negated the biting chill. "Incredible..."

"These other crystals don't do that." Faelinia said, moving farther into the cave and touching a patch that glowed dimly. "I think it has to do with those." She pointed to the ceiling.

Confused, Amendal looked up. Something white and blue fluttered across the cavern's ceiling, then another and another. *Those can't be bugs,* he thought, narrowing his eyes. The Abodine Wasteland was too cold for insects, wasn't it?

Amendal willed his conjuration forward and focused his vision through the earthen giant. Complaints sounded from those behind the conjuration, but Amendal ignored them. The others would soon discover that Calimir had called a halt.

One of the fluttering creatures landed on a patch of crystal, opening its white wings like a moth. In fact, it looked like a moth, except for four pale-blue tentacles dangling from the rear of its abdomen. Each tentacle was longer than the creature's wingspan and was covered in dark-blue follicles that pulsed with blue light.

"Do you know what that is?" Faelinia asked.

"Some kind of moth," Amendal said, tilting his head. "Is it feeding on the crystal?"

"What's going on?" Morgidian asked, stopping beside Amendal.

"We're looking at ice moths," Faelinia said, gesturing to the ceiling.

Ice moths? Amendal thought incredulously. That was almost as bad as calling a quinta'shal a mages' parasite...

"I see," Morgidian said, nodding.

Amendal pointed to the still moth. "They're doing something to those patches of crystal." The crystal where the creature hung glowed brighter and brighter. "Interesting..."

"If you say so," Morgidian said, stepping ahead of the others.

"We should keep going," a soldier said.

Several soldiers and mages pushed past Amendal and Faelinia, not at all interested in the crystal or the strange moths.

"Are you going to capture one?" Faelinia asked playfully.

Teasing me? Amendal thought, still eyeing the creatures on the ceiling. "Maybe," he said, his tone sly. "My brother hates moths—well, anything small that flutters, really."

Faelinia laughed, but quickly quelled her mirth as Calimir began shouting orders. "Let's keep moving!" the commander called.

"Are you going to rejoin us?" Faelinia asked.

Amendal nodded, and the two of them returned to the others in the lead. Several of the soldiers were speculating on the nature of the cave.

"...have been a crystal mine?" a soldier asked. "You know, a quarry those Eshari used to build their city."

"Seems too far away," Hevasir said.

"This is a crysillac den," Vaem said with annoyance. "They burrowed these caves."

Hevasir burst into laughter, as did several other soldiers.

A crysillac den...? Amendal raised an eyebrow, intrigued. No one really knew what a crysillac looked like, but if this was their den, then the beasts must be huge. *I definitely want one of them,* Amendal thought, *or maybe two, or three...*

One of the laughing soldiers managed to ask a question. "You mean those mythical creatures?"

"That's ridiculous," Hevasir said, still chuckling. "A crysillac? Are you serious?"

The soldiers continued laughing while Faelinia turned to Amendal, her eyes wide. "So, you were right," she said, undoubtedly remembering their conversation in the crystal towers.

"Settle down," Calimir said, gesturing to his men. He then turned to Vaem. "I thought you weren't holding anything back..."

Vaem sighed, shaking her head. "They *once* belonged to a crysillac," she said. "If these tunnels were currently occupied by a crysillac then every square phineal of this cave would be covered in dense crystal—not snow and ice. These patches are merely the dregs of their food, and those viliasim are simply eating the crysillac's scraps."

Viliasim. So that was the name of the moths.

"Very well," Calimir said, sounding wary. The old man obviously didn't believe Vaem. Well, if she was lying about the absence of crysillacs, then that would work out to Amendal's advantage. *Why capture one type of creature when you can have two, or three?* The notion made him smile.

"Trust me," Vaem said. "I would have said something if we were going to encounter a crysillac. They are formidable."

Faelinia glanced to Amendal, eyes wide with curiosity.

Hevasir snickered. "And how do you know so much about them?"

"The Hilinard is a vast storehouse of knowledge," Vaem replied haughtily. "It is home to knowledge that was taken from our world by those wretched Losians and their abominable king."

The icy tunnel continued descending the farther the expedition went. Icicles hung from the ceiling, some reaching to the cavern floor. The patches of crystal became more abundant, further illuminating the tunnel with a pale-blue glow.

Eventually, the tunnel's floor leveled. The crystal patches became more and more abundant, drawing wary speculation from the soldiers. Vaem, however, squashed their assumptions.

"We're getting close to that big chamber," Ildin said. "The one with all the branches."

Vaem nodded. "One of the old nesting grounds for the crysillac."

The tunnel wound back and forth twice before emptying into an enormous cavern. Awestruck remarks and adoring gasps echoed into the cavern as the leaders entered the vast chamber. The cavern's ceiling rose dozens of phineals, and Amendal estimated that it was six stories tall in some parts. Mammoth icicles hung from the ceiling, and some even reached to the icy floor, creating transparent walls. Most of the cavern's floor was uneven, with crude ramps leading to ledges and elevated sections. Three of those elevated areas were landings for other tunnels.

Calimir called for everyone to enter the cavern so the entire expedition could gather. Once everyone was inside the massive chamber, Calimir pulled the illusionists and squad leaders aside. Though they were a good twenty paces away, their conversation carried throughout the entire cavern.

"Are any of you near the end of those branches?" Calimir asked.

"They go on forever," Fendar said grumpily. "We'll never find their ends."

"Well, it might take days," Faelinia said. "But I've found no sign of any creatures."

"And you, Mister Cetarin?" Calimir asked Ildin.

Ildin shook his head.

"We should just press ahead," a squad leader suggested. "There are three other tunnels you haven't searched, correct?" he asked, pointing to the branches at the far end of the cavern. There were seven tunnels all in all; the one they had traversed that led to the surface and six others.

"I agree," another man said. "If these caves are so vast, we might not even encounter the yaeltis."

As the squad leaders voiced their opinions, Amendal stepped away with his conjurations. He sauntered toward the tunnels that had not been searched, looking for a place to sit. At the edge of a large but shallow bowled area near the center of the cavern, he plopped down. *Is this where the crysillacs nested?*

A debate arose among the squad leaders, but Amendal did his best to ignore it. He focused on the cavern floor, looking for possible clues as to which way the yaeltis had traveled. *Maybe worn spots in the floor?* he thought, his eyes sweeping across the frozen ground. But the ice was unmarred.

How thick was the ice?

Amendal glanced to the feet of his earthen giant. The ice beneath the conjuration showed no signs of stress, let alone cracking. *Well, that's no help...*

"Silence!" Calimir shouted, and the squad leaders quieted. "Illusionists, start searching those tunnels across the cavern. We'll break for a midday meal while the illusionists continue scouting. Mages, relinquish your magic on everyone but squads nine, ten, and eleven. Those of you still enhanced, stand watch at the tunnels."

Ildin's illusions of himself zipped into the tunnel due south of the party. Faelinia had taken the branch to the southeast while Fendar scouted the one to the southwest.

Oddly, the tunnel Ildin had chosen was *rising*. The crystal along the walls also became more and more abundant, almost to the point that there was no ice or snow. *That's scary,* Ildin thought. After the illusions had flown a grand phineal, the tunnel emptied into a vast chamber with a giant pit at its center.

"I found something different," Ildin said, his voice echoing in two places. He focused through only one of his illusions, studying the chamber. A near perfect circle, it was slightly smaller than the one where the expedition was resting. Three tunnels branched off from the circular cavern, two ascending and one descending. The pit must have been forty or fifty phineals in diameter and took up most of the floor. Walkways lined the cavern's walls, barely wide enough for three or four men to walk abreast.

Light shone from the pit, and Ildin glided his illusion forward to inspect it. Looking down, he saw a huge shaft plunging to a polished floor perhaps a hundred stories below him. Streaks of crystal lined the walls of the shaft in zigzagging patterns that looked like lightning. *How beautiful!*

He commanded the illusion to dive into the pit, and as it descended, he sent his other illusions into the three tunnels.

A dozen stories above the floor of the pit, the walls flared out to form a massive bulb-shaped chamber completely encased in crystal. When his illusion reached the floor, he saw strange crystallized formations that looked almost like vines were spread across the ceiling of the chamber. They continued into the shaft, becoming those zigzagging patterns.

Weird… The chamber was eerily silent around the illusion. There were two tunnels that emptied into the chamber; one halfway up the cavern wall to the east and another level with the floor directly to the south. The tunnel to the south, however, was not like the others in this labyrinth. It looked too smooth to have been hollowed by a creature. *Could that lead to the gate house?*

Calimir paced nervously, listening to the illusionist's reports. Miss Tusara had found some fresh corpses of wolf-like creatures down the branch she was searching. Unlike the other tunnels, the one she was investigating did not have any adjoining passageways.

"I think I found the gatehouse," Mister Cetarin said.

Miss Tusara sighed heavily. "And I found the yaeltis… But there's more than three."

"How many?" asked Mistress Rudal.

"Eight," Miss Tusara answered. "But some of them look small."

"Are they asleep?" Dardel asked.

Miss Tusara nodded. "A few are stirring, but they look like they're hibernating."

Calimir set his jaw. They could still sneak past the yaeltis. *No…* that was his fear trying to dictate his actions. *Do not give in to fear.* He recited the litany in his mind. *Fear will bring defeat. I will confront my fears and tear through them like a weak foe on the battlefield. Then—*

"I *have* found it!" Mister Cetarin exclaimed.

Calimir opened his eyes and quickly finished the recitation in his mind. "Good," he said curtly and surveyed the expedition. Most were busily eating a cold meal. "Finish your meals quickly," Calimir shouted. "Mages, cast your spells once again. Squads three and four, head down the southern tunnel and start preparing ramps so we can descend that shaft. Those of you standing watch can break for food after we slay the yaeltis."

Amendal was one of the first to enter the tunnel Faelinia had scouted.

The tunnel was not as brightly lit as the enormous cavern or the first tunnel the expedition had traversed. Only an occasional patch of crystal dotted the walls and ceiling. Icicles and other ice formations were prevalent in the tunnel, each glowing an aqua-blue hue.

As they turned a corner, a putrid odor invaded Amendal's nostrils. It smelled like death, but not quite.

"What's that smell?" a soldier asked.

"Probably those corpses," Hevasir said. "Dead things smell different in cold places."

Dardel shushed the soldiers, and the party continued in silence. Only their footfalls and clanking armor sounded within the tunnel. Amendal was especially careful with his earthen giant. With the creature's long stride it could easily keep pace with the expedition while remaining somewhat quiet.

The stench grew stronger as the expedition wound their way through the dim tunnel. They had walked no more than a half a grand phineal when Faelinia pointed to the left.

"The corpses are over there," she whispered, "in an alcove of sorts."

Amendal and several others rounded a bend in the tunnel, finding an icy room. The corpses mentioned by Faelinia were piled in the center, a heap of blood-stained white fur, pale-blue bones and translucent horns of the same coloring. Most of the creatures were mangled beyond recognition, but one was mostly intact, its snout pointed toward the party.

As Amendal's eyes met the dead creature's, he started, blinking in disbelief. *Impossible...* The creature's eyes were unnatural, with irises as white as snow and whites that were not white at all, but dark blue. The eyes were *exactly* like that creature in his dream, the cisthyrn. But how? That was just a dream, and...

A knot formed in Amendal's stomach. In his mind, he heard the behest from the mysterious old man. The words were as clear as if he were speaking them right beside Amendal: "Seek the shan'ak, and fulfill your destiny."

The corpses drew hushed speculation and wary comments from the expedition, but Amendal ignored them.

Destiny...? The realization of being fated to this dismal expedition was disheartening. But if those dreams were showing him the future, then he would be near useless in Tardalim. *Unless I go in with powerful conjurations.* The earthen giants would do, and maybe even a troll, but he could use more.

Amendal pulled himself from his reverie while the soldiers wondered about the yaeltis' strengths and capabilities. "Those yaeltis did this?" a soldier asked, poking his glowing sword at the corpses—the acidic magic eroded the end of a femur and some patches of fur.

"But those corpses look as big as a bear," another said, shuddering.

"Yaeltis are formidable," Vaem said. "As you can see, they took down an entire pack of cisthyrn. And cisthyrn are deadly."

Amendal flinched upon hearing the creature's name. Vaem's confirmation of the cisthyrn's identity only confirmed his assumptions. *I must be seeing the future. How else could I have dreamt about these creatures?*

"Is that what these beasts are called?" Hevasir asked, stepping toward one of the skulls and grabbing its horns. He pulled the head from the pile, examining it. The half-eaten skull was almost as large as Hevasir's torso. "This would make a nice trophy," he said with a chuckle.

"Let's keep moving," Calimir commanded.

"Sir!" a voice called from the middle of the expedition. "Sir, if I may."

Amendal glanced over his shoulder. A brown-haired man stepped forward, veiled in a putrid green bubble of barsion—a necromancer named Uldric. He wore a twisted smile. "Please, may I reanimate them?"

Calimir nodded. "You may, Uldric. We can use them as fodder."

"Much appreciated, Commander," Uldric said with an anticipating cackle. Uldric's eyes widened like a crazed fool as he uttered an incantation. Dark-purple light appeared, then surged into the pile of corpses.

Amendal turned from the pile as the bones began to shift. The skeletons creaked as the reanimating magic re-knit the creatures.

Eight yaeltis, Amendal mused, recalling Faelinia's report. He narrowed his eyes as he gazed farther down the tunnel. If he went ahead, he could catch at least one by surprise.

"Are you all right?" Faelinia asked, coming beside Amendal. "You look like you're off somewhere else."

"Yes," Amendal said, eyes fixated on the tunnel ahead. "Just planning—"

A sudden roar echoed from behind the expedition. Everyone spun. Soldiers readied themselves while mages began uttering incantations.

"Oh no!" Ildin exclaimed.

Amendal turned to his friend. Ildin groaned, then his face contorted. Had something attacked the other squads?

"What happened?" Calimir demanded.

"Those-those patterns of crystal along the pit," Ildin stammered. "They're limbs of some monster! And they just attacked squads three and four!"

Dardel's eyes widened. "One of those crysillacs?"

Vaem shook her head. "I doubt it. Crystal limbs, you say?"

Another deafening roar filled the tunnel, followed by bellowing grunts. The grunts, however, came from ahead of the expedition.

"The yaeltis are waking," Faelinia whispered.

Calimir swore furiously, then began shouting orders.

They should have sent me ahead, Amendal thought, pursing his lips. With the yaeltis awake, the party had lost their element of surprise. If those cisthyrn corpses were anything to judge by, then the yaeltis would probably wreak havoc on the expedition—despite the aid of magic.

More grunts echoed through the tunnel, followed by an enraged cry. That cry was not like the roar. Were the yaeltis angry at being awakened?

"How close are the yaeltis?" Calimir barked.

"Close," Faelinia whispered. "Three turns, maybe two hundred phineals, two hundred and fifty at most."

That doesn't give me enough time, Amendal thought. If he were going to capture a yaeltis he had to go now. "Faelinia, fill my quinta'shals with some disintegrating orbs." She gazed at him warily, but before she could reply, Amendal hurried toward the yaeltis with his conjurations. The earthen giant's footfalls drowned Calimir's orders, while more enraged cries echoed into the tunnel.

"Amendal," Faelinia called, her voice stern. "Don't do anything stupid!"

Looking over his shoulder, Amendal gave her a sly grin. "Is that concern I hear in your voice? Don't worry, I've faced far worse."

"Like other cephalopods of our world, nactili secrete an inky substance. Their ink, however, contains toxins capable of rendering a man blind. And if ingested, the ink will swell a man's throat until he dies of suffocation."

- From *Colvinar Vrium's Bestiary for Conjurers*, page 51

Morgidian's heart pounded as he darted up the barsion ramp, fleeing for his life. Though he was surrounded by a bubble of barsion, he was not safe. A dreadful cacophony of horrified screams echoed up through the pit. Those crystal vines whipped through the air, reaching for his squadmates. *Was this some sort of trap?* he wondered. *But why wasn't Ildin's illusion attacked?*

Shaking off the thought, Morgidian uttered an incantation. There had to be some way to keep these vines at bay. Blue light shone around his hands and he envisioned a curved barrier. The barsion particles flowed from his palms, persisting a few paces beside him. All the while, he and the others continued running up the ramp. Several members of squads three and four had already made it out of the pit and shouted for the others to run faster.

A crystal vine whipped toward Morgidian, passing through the forming barsion. The vine wrapped around his existing barrier as he finished the incantation. A shield of barsion magic formed, and Morgidian felt it penetrate the crystal vine. The barsion cut through the crystal, but not before the vine knocked him off balance.

Struggling to regain his footing, Morgidian nearly fell off the ramp but staggered to a halt. *That was close...* Then, heart pumping faster, he darted up the ramp.

Crystal vines flailed through the air as Morgidian cleared the pit and bounded toward the tunnel. *I should block it,* he thought. As he neared the tunnel, a vine swept across the ground and struck his barsion bubble. Tumbling, Morgidian commanded his shield to drop to the ground. The barsion shield struck the crystal vine, pinning it in place. Morgidian could feel a resistance as the shield struggled to cut through the vine.

"Hurry!" a soldier shouted. "Into the tunnel!"

Morgidian pushed himself up and stumbled after the others, uttering another incantation. He would need more barsion to bar those vines.

Once in the tunnel, Morgidian glanced over his shoulder. The last of the survivors had made it out of the pit, but two of the soldiers were snatched by the vines before they could reach the tunnel. More vines slithered past the barsion shield, racing toward Morgidian and the others.

Soldiers cursed while several other mages, including Dugal, uttered incantations.

Morgidian and the stragglers bounded around a bend but the vines continued their pursuit. One of the soldiers was snatched, and another tripped.

Blue light shone around Morgidian as he finished his incantation. He spun, spreading both hands wide. The unformed barsion shot through the tunnel, bathing it in a dark-blue hue.

The vines raced through the magic, grabbing more of Morgidian's squadmates.

End of the tunnel, Morgidian thought, envisioning the tunnel's mouth. If he were going to block the tunnel he might as well block it there.

A vine lashed toward Morgidian, wrapping around his barsion bubble. It lifted him from the icy floor, but he kept his focus on the forming barsion.

Brown light raced beside him, striking the icy wall. The ice liquefied, then shot toward the vine gripping him. Suddenly, the liquefied ice became steel that shackled the vine.

Morgidian jolted and finished his incantation. His barsion coalesced at the tunnel's mouth, becoming a complete barrier. Brilliant blue light flashed off the tunnel's walls as he and the vine holding him fell to the icy floor. The other vines fell limp, each shackled like the one that had held him.

"That was close," Dugal said with a sigh.

Morgidian nodded as he staggered to his feet. Frantic footfalls echoed through the tunnel, and then the man who had been snatched rounded a bend. "Thank you," the soldier said, rejoining the others.

Morgidian nodded. Then a sudden blow struck his barsion, and he focused his senses through his magic. More vines from the pit were striking his barrier. Though the magic was holding, he could feel it weakening.

Great... Morgidian shook his head, then glance to Dugal. "We should block this tunnel further."

"Are those vines weakening your barsion?" Dugal asked, his tone wary.

Morgidian nodded. "They're giving it a beating. There's maybe twenty striking it."

Dugal groaned. "Fine... how do you want to do this?"

"Let's alternate our barriers." Morgidian turned around. "I'll go first."

The enraged cries grew louder as Amendal rounded a bend in the icy tunnel. Most men would have run from those noises, but not him. The yaeltis were definitely not happy about being awakened. He recalled advice from his father: *Woe to the man who wakes a troll.* The same could probably be said of the yaeltis.

Amendal and his earthen conjurations rounded another bend, coming to another cavern. It was dim, like the tunnel, and he couldn't tell if it was as large as the first cavern. Four other tunnels branched from the cavern, each as large as the one where Amendal stood. The icy floor was uneven, with ledges of varying heights throughout the frozen chamber. Eight creatures covered in white fur were scattered across the cavern, each pushing itself up from the icy ledges.

Yaeltis… Amendal thought, eyeing the lumbering beasts. *Into the cavern,* he commanded his earthen conjurations. *And drop the gear,* he told the creature acting as his valet. At that moment he felt the last of his quinta'shals consume Faelinia's disintegrating magic. *Come to me,* he commanded and the quinta'shals obeyed. Through his mental bond with his conjurations he sensed Faelinia running beside them.

So, you can't bear to let me face them alone? Amendal grinned and returned his focus to the yaeltis. Five of them looked three times taller than Amendal. The other three were only maybe twice his size. Were the smaller ones perhaps the offspring of the larger beasts? Each of the creatures' faces was covered in bluish-purple, leathery skin. Their flat noses topped wide mouths that protruded in an inhuman manner. The larger yaeltis had curved tusks jutting from their thick jaws, each longer than Amendal's arms. An amber substance covered the tusks, and one beast's tusks were more encrusted with the substance than the others. The tusks of the smaller yaeltis were clear crystal and less than half the length of the larger beasts'.

As the earthen giant entered the cavern, each of the taller yaeltis glared at the conjuration with blazing yellow eyes. Their faces alight with fury, the five larger yaeltis unleashed bellowing roars that bounced off the icy walls. One of the yaeltis threw itself from its perch, landing on the frozen floor with a resounding thud that shook the icy chamber.

The lone yaeltis flexed its six-fingered hands. Its sharp crystalline claws looked like the tusks of the smaller yaeltis. *Six fingers,* Amendal mused. *Like a troll.* Well, the tracks they had found in the canyon did look like those of a troll. *I wonder if their cousins.* But trolls looked nothing like these yaeltis.

Settling into a wide stance, Amendal whispered an incantation to open a large portal to the Visirm Expanse. The words barely left his lips, but the golden light still manifested.

In a flash of movement, the advancing yaeltis lunged at the earthen giant. *Attack!* Amendal commanded. The break in his mental focus caused the golden light to flicker.

The earthen giant dashed forward, pulling its arm back to punch the yaeltis, but the beast was too fast. Creature and conjuration collided, and Amendal felt the blow. Amendal sucked in his breath as the conjuration crashed into the frozen ground with a resounding thud. Spider-web cracks spread across the icy floor and beneath Amendal's feet. *Impressive...* The yaeltis was stronger than he imagined.

He willed the other conjurations to attack as the giant recovered. The ten earthen elementals bounded toward the towering yaeltis—their heads barely reaching the beast's knees.

Roaring once again, the yaeltis grabbed the nearest elemental by the head and hurled it across the cavern. Although the earthen elementals weighed as much as five men, the yaeltis tossed it like a rag doll. The conjuration hit the icy wall with a resounding crack. Chunks of rock and clumps of dirt fell from its earthen body as it hit the icy floor. All the while, each of the other yaeltis—including the smaller ones—snarled, their mouths frothing.

Faelinia shouted for Amendal, and the quinta'shals darted by, each glowing a violet hue. The faceless creatures bounded into the cavern, forming a line between Amendal and the battle. Each quinta'shal had their three-pronged hands outstretched, ready to unleash the magic fed to them by Faelinia.

"I can't believe you," Faelinia growled, "dashing off alone *and* without a barsion!"

She began uttering an incantation but Amendal ignored her, focused on his own magic. His eyes settled on a spot toward the middle of the cavern. All the while, the melee between the lone yaeltis and the earthen elementals intensified. The yaeltis repulsed the smaller conjurations with ease while engaging in a fistfight with the earthen giant. The yaeltis managed to hold its own against the earthen behemoth.

A torrent of footfalls echoed from the tunnel. Calimir shouted a rebuke, but Amendal ignored him, too.

Finishing the first part of his incantation, Amendal unleashed his magic. The golden light zipped past his conjurations, coalescing into an oval portal behind the fighting yaeltis. Why weren't the other creatures attacking? They were just growling and flexing their hands.

Letting their rage build? he wondered. Perhaps they only attacked when their anger peaked.

Amendal finished the rest of the incantation, mustering the portal's enthralling component. Charcoal light wove through the air.

As the enthralling magic zipped over the battle, Calimir, Dardel, and several other soldiers bounded past Amendal. The soldiers darted around the quinta'shals, shouting battle cries. None of them wore their packs—they had probably dropped them in the tunnel. To Amendal's surprise, none of the quinta'shals siphoned the magic enhancing the soldiers. Faelinia had definitely filled them to the brim. Upon seeing the charging men, the other seven yaeltis bellowed deafening cries and leapt from their perches.

The charcoal magic mixed with the golden portal as the soldiers engaged the lone yaeltis. Unleashing an enraged bellow, the beast squatted and swatted Calimir away. As the commander soared toward the cavern wall, the lone yaeltis kicked another soldier, sending him flying back to the tunnel and toward Amendal.

Shocked, Amendal tripped over his incantation, causing his portal to flicker. He lunged sideways to evade, but was not fast enough. The soldier, and his barsion, collided with Amendal's right arm and the side of his torso with a resounding crack. The blow sent Amendal spinning through the air—being hit by barsion was akin to being hit by a stone wall.

Intense heat burned across Amendal's right side, and he struggled for breath. Severe pain shot through his arm and ribs, followed by a surge of cold. After an excruciating moment, he fell on his back, gasping. Amid the pain he felt his portal weakening.

No!

Amendal struggled to push himself upright as more soldiers ran from the tunnel into the cavern. *It has to hold!* he growled, fighting against the sharp pains. With all his might he focused on the portal, but the enthralling component dissipated.

Suddenly, violet light veiled his vision. Surprised, he glanced to his coat. It too had a purple tinge to it. *An infused barsion?*

"Next time, don't go running off," Faelinia said, fists planted on her hips. "At least not before I can protect you."

Recovering from his repulsion, Calimir staggered to his feet. That beast had swatted him away as if he were a common pest. If it weren't for his barsion, Calimir would be dead. Perhaps he was right to fear these monsters—*No*, he chided himself. *Do not give in to fear...*

Reciting the litany, Calimir quickly surveyed the battle. The other yaeltis, even the smaller ones, had engaged the expedition in a wild melee. Soldiers and mercenaries alike poured through the tunnel, charging toward the monsters. But the yaeltis near the tunnel's mouth kept repulsing soldier and conjuration alike. In one swift move, the beast grabbed one of Mister Aramien's conjurations by the legs and used it like a club. The conjuration struggled to break free, but the yaeltis had an iron grip.

Smart beast, Calimir thought, leaping from the ledge and charging toward the nearest yaeltis. His new foe grabbed a soldier and repeatedly slammed the man head-first into the icy floor. The blows caused the soldier's barsion to flicker.

He charged, raised his long-sword into the air and readied his shield—both imbued with destructive magics: fire and acid. The soldier in the monster's grasp continued struggling, his barsion fading.

Unleashing a battle cry, Calimir lunged at the yaeltis's right leg, ready to bash with his shield and stab with his blade. Fire sparked the yaeltis's white fur, but before the blade pierced flesh, Calimir was knocked away.

Within a heartbeat he crashed into the base of a ledge. His barsion flickered, but remained true.

Calimir swore as he regained his footing. Nothing short of ranged assaults would be effective on these monsters. At least he and the soldiers could waylay the beasts long enough for the mages to deal deathblows.

He readied to charge again as a faint roar—like the first they had heard—echoed from another tunnel across the cavern. *More monsters?* He pushed the thought aside and bounded toward his foe.

Before Calimir could reach the yaeltis, the monster slammed the soldier into the ground. The man's barsion vanished and a frantic cry left his lips. "Don't you dare!" Calimir shouted.

In one swift movement, the yaeltis lifted the barsion-less soldier and slammed the man against the tip of its amber tusk. "No!" Calimir cried. A resounding crack filled the air as the tusk pierced armor and impaled the soldier through his gut. Strangled gasps left the man's lips as he convulsed.

"Damned beast!" Calimir shouted. He lunged, ready to pierce the monster with his sword.

"That should do," Morgidian said, letting out a deep breath. He and Dugal had erected three sets of barriers, each composed of a layer of barsion and transmuted steel.

Dugal grunted. "It better do."

"Come on," Morgidian said, turning from the transmuted steel. "That first barsion is about to shatter."

Both Morgidian and Dugal hurried back through the tunnel. None of the other survivors of squads three or four were anywhere nearby. They had probably rejoined the rest of the expedition.

Upon nearing the cavern where the expedition had rested, snarling and grunting noises echoed into the tunnel.

"Do you hear that?" Dugal asked.

Morgidian nodded, slowing his stride to a creep. Dugal did the same, and the two of them skulked to a bend in the passage. The snarling and grunting grew louder, and Morgidian peered around the icy corner. Only part of the cavern was visible. White wolf-like creatures—how many he couldn't tell—sniffed the cavern floor. Each looked as big as a bear and had pale-blue horns.

"What are those things?" Dugal whispered.

Morgidian narrowed his eyes at the strange wolves. "I have no idea..." Had those strange wolves been tracking the expedition?

"Oh, this trip just keeps getting better and better," Dugal murmured.

Morgidian raised an eyebrow at his friend. Why did Dugal have to be such a pessimist? "Come on," he whispered and stepped around the corner.

"What are you doing?" Dugal demanded through clenched teeth.

The strange wolves quieted. The pack leaders turned toward Morgidian, undoubtedly hearing Dugal's outburst.

"Well, I wanted to sneak by," Morgidian said, settling into a wide stance. "But I don't think that's an option anymore." Hands raised, Morgidian began uttering an incantation to muster an inverted barsion.

Dugal cursed, and the nearest wolf edged across the icy floor. The strange wolf bared its teeth—teeth as pale-blue as its horns.

Is every creature in this wasteland so strange? Morgidian thought.

Brilliant blue light gathered beyond Morgidian's protective bubble as he stepped from the tunnel. He didn't want to be pinned down with no place to retreat. Dugal began uttering his own incantation, the ice and crystal reflecting the brown hue of his transmutative magic.

Morgidian edged into the cavern as he neared the end of his incantation. He hummed the last bit, holding the spell from completely forming. The strange wolf ascended the ramp, looking ready to pounce. The rest of the creature's pack—which numbered eleven—crept toward the ramp.

The strange wolf's snarl turned into a growl, and it lunged.

Morgidian exhaled the last of his incantation, unleashing his inverted barsion. The brilliant blue light struck the lunging wolf, knocking it backward. The wolf tumbled onto the ramp, and rolled over once before the barsion trapped it.

"Stay back," Morgidian warned, then began uttering another incantation.

Dugal's brown magic shot past Morgidian, striking the ground in front of the pack. The ice liquefied and burst toward the nearest wolf. The transmuted ice wrapped around the wolf's forepaws, becoming steel shackles. Frantic, the wolf struggled against its transmuted bonds.

Hopefully they'll back off, Morgidian thought.

The wolves continued snarling and baring their teeth. Several began to bark. The barking intensified, and those at the pack's head lunged at Morgidian.

Setting his jaw, he unleashed his inverted barsion and threw himself sideways. The magic struck one of the wolves as he fell over the side of the ramp. One of the wolves soared past him, bounding straight for Dugal.

"Into the center!" Morgidian shouted, crashing into the cavern's floor. As he regained his footing, another wolf lunged at him, knocking him backward. The creature's claws dug *into* the barsion, and Morgidian felt his barrier weakening. How was that possible? Could the creature's claws somehow negate magic?

Tumbling back onto his feet, Morgidian uttered another incantation, and the wolf lunged again. Morgidian threw himself sideways, landing on the ice, but his barsion took the brunt of the blow. The wolf spun and lunged again.

Great, Morgidian groaned, his spell flickering. The wolf clashed with his barsion once again, weakening the barrier further. Subduing these creatures wasn't going to be easy…

———⇒•⇐———

Despite the sharp pains in his arm and side, Amendal managed to manifest more conjuration magic. A cacophony of incantations, clanking armor, and thunderous footfalls echoed into the dim cavern. The reinforcing soldiers bounded past Amendal and Faelinia, joining the battle with the enraged beasts. The mages, however, took up positions around Amendal, each surrounded by their own kinds of magic.

Charcoal light, tinged with purple by the barsion cast by Faelinia, flowed from Amendal's hands and over the battle. As the enthralling component mingled with the portal, several of the mages finished manifesting their destructive spells.

An arcanist unleashed a disintegrating blast upon the yaeltis fighting Amendal's conjuration. The violet magic beamed above the soldiers, striking the yaeltis's chest before any of the other spells.

A defiant gasp filled the cavern as the yaeltis staggered, a hole burned through its chest. Bright pink orbs of arcane magic—unleashed by another mage—erupted in a blinding flash, veiling a volley of acidic javelins. Though Amendal couldn't see, he felt the earthen conjuration-turned-club hit the cavern floor.

Enraged cries boomed throughout the cavern, some higher pitched than others—undoubtedly from the young yaeltis. As the blinding flash faded, the enthralling component completely merged with the portal. Pushing the pain aside, Amendal focused on a yaeltis toward the back of the fray. The charcoal light oozed from the portal, a reflection of his mental struggle.

"Hold your magics!" Faelinia shouted, gray light clustering about her. Had she cast an enthralling spell? Amendal had been too consumed by the pain to keep track of her.

Battle cries reverberated throughout the cavern as the slain yaeltis collapsed in pieces on the icy floor. The enraged cries from the remaining yaeltis turned to lamenting wails. Had the beasts some semblance of a sense of loss? The yaeltis corpse was a mangled mess, acid eroding its fur. The beast was missing its head, and all that remained were bits and pieces of its tusks.

In response to Faelinia's command, several of the mages held their magics, humming their incantations.

"Attack the smaller ones!" Faelinia shouted. "Avoid that one in the back!" She had probably seen the enthralling trail oozing from the portal.

Amendal focused on the yaeltis farthest away, the one with the most-encrusted tusks. A small group of soldiers, including Dardel and Hevasir, were attacking that particular yaeltis. But none of the soldiers or mercenaries managed to land a blow against the beast. *Hopefully it stays unmarred,* Amendal thought, gritting his teeth against the pain in his side.

More soldiers were running to reinforce Dardel, but most were attacked by the smaller yaeltis—the juveniles, Amendal assumed. They were just as brutal as their parents.

Come on... Amendal strained against the pain. The charcoal magic was halfway between the portal and the battle. *Ignore the pain...*

An all too familiar scraping echoed from the tunnel—the reanimated claws of the cisthyrn scratching the icy floor. Out of the corner of his eye, Amendal saw the glistening wolf-like skeletons pouring into the cavern as well as more soldiers and mercenaries.

"Why are you waiting?!" Uldric demanded. "Oh..."

Faelinia shouted to the necromancer, "Focus on the smaller ones."

A surge of pain jarred Amendal's concentration. *Enthrall...* Amendal groaned, focusing on the gray magic. He couldn't lose the enthralling component again. But it took all his concentration just to maintain the portal.

Incantations sounded all around him, and the noise of battle rang through the cavern. *Focus,* Amendal chided himself. He strained to reach the yaeltis with the enthralling magic, but the gray particles hardly moved.

As he struggled, a gray cloud shot from Faelinia and raced through the cavern. Her enthralling magic struck the yaeltis, abruptly stilling the beast as it swung a fist toward Hevasir.

"Amendal!" Faelinia shouted, "Hurry! I can barely hold it in place."

Forget the pain, Amendal told himself. He did his best to focus on moving the portal's enthralling magic, but it merely crept through the air. Faelinia shouted to the soldiers, but Amendal ignored her cries. Amid the struggle, advice from his father entered his mind. *If you are ever struggling to capture a creature and your concentration is strained, relinquish control on your conjurations.*

Amendal strained to move the enthralling magic, but it hardly budged. If he was going to capture this yaeltis, he would have to sacrifice his conjurations. Gritting his teeth against the pain, Amendal released the earthen creatures and the quinta'shals, severing the mental bond to them.

With his concentration solely on the enthralling magic, Amendal managed to move it toward the yaeltis. After an excruciating moment, the yaeltis came under his control. A battle of wills entered Amendal's mind as the magic permeated the beast. He also felt the resistance Faelinia had mentioned, as well as her mental struggles.

Move! Faelinia's thoughts echoed in Amendal's mind. *To the portal,* he commanded, focused on moving the creature's legs. Deafening bellows echoed in Amendal's mind, but the yaeltis turned from the soldiers. As it lumbered to the portal a faint roar echoed from a tunnel to the right.

"Mages, watch those tunnels," Faelinia shouted.

Amendal closed his eyes, focusing on the yaeltis. He couldn't quite see the portal, but he could feel it. Each step was painstaking. "Reach for the portal," Amendal said through clenched teeth. He meant those words for

Faelinia and the yaeltis. He could feel the yaeltis raising its arms.

Rumbling reverberated beneath Amendal's feet as a deafening roar shook the cavern. Pained cries—from man and beast—echoed off the icy walls. *Focus!* Amendal gritted his teeth.

"Touch the portal!" Amendal shouted, straining his will. The yaeltis was almost there. Just another step—

The struggle abruptly ceased as the yaeltis was instantly transported to the Visirm Expanse.

"Finally," Amendal said with a groan and opened his eyes. The pain intensified, and he fell to his knees. Dreadful sounds reverberated throughout the cavern: battle cries, eruptions of magic, deafening roars, clanking armor. Amid the terrible cacophony, pained cries echoed off the icy walls, cries of dying men.

Amendal blinked several times, reorienting himself. His conjurations were running amok. The quinta'shals had expended most of their magic, attacking man and beast alike. Several of his earthen conjurations had been snatched by the yaeltis and used like clubs. Those elementals that hadn't been turned into cudgels were roaming aimlessly through the cavern. The earthen giant was the only one still attacking the yaeltis, though its punches were sloppy.

The six remaining yaeltis were injured in some way, but they still attacked the soldiers and mercenaries with relentless fury. The beasts repulsed the men and women while tearing apart the reanimated cisthyrns, but the necromancers' magic re-knit the skeletal creatures as soon as they were torn apart.

Barsions had faded from several of the soldiers, and two of them were on the ground, convulsing in a pool of blood. Each of those convulsing men had holes in their coats and armor. Had the yaeltis impaled them with their tusks?

Horrified screams echoed through the crystal cavern beneath the pit. Appalled, Ildin watched through his illusion as those vines—or tentacles or whatever they were—pulled the last remaining members of squads three and four toward the far side of the crystal cavern. Why hadn't the strange vines attacked his illusion?

A deafening roar shook the icy cavern, coming from the massive maw of the crystallized creature housed within the cavern wall. During his first descent into the pit, Ildin had mistaken the creature's mouth for a boulder or outcropping. He couldn't have been more wrong.

Those grasped by the vines struggled to break free. Soldiers sliced at the crystal limbs, but their magically enhanced weapons did little damage. The crystal maw gaped wide, large enough to swallow a house. Then the *thing* unleashed a second deafening roar, and in one swift motion it tossed the men and women into its crystal maw.

"No!" Ildin moaned. Though his illusion hovered within the cavern, Ildin slumped to his knees inside the dim tunnel, overcome with sorrow. Vaem and few others stood nearby. The sounds of battle with the yaeltis echoed into the tunnel, and Ildin set his jaw. How were they going to reach the gatehouse now?

From what he had seen, the expedition would have to pass that crystal monster. There were no other tunnels that connected to the chamber housing the doors to the gatehouse. If they descended the pit, then the expedition would suffer the same fate as squads three and four.

Another roar shook the cavern beneath the pit. Not a moment later, a fainter roar echoed into the dim tunnel where Ildin knelt. That roar, however, came from the cavern where the expedition was fighting the yaeltis.

"That can't be right..." Ildin whispered, spinning his illusion around. Through his magic, he eyed the only other tunnel in the cavern beneath the pit; the one to the east that was partway up the cavern wall. *Could they be connected?* What were the chances of that? A connection between the yaeltis den and the pit would be nothing short of miraculous.

Ildin closed his eyes, focusing his senses through his illusion. He strained to hear the sounds of battle, but the noises didn't reach the cavern beneath the pit.

"I might as well look," he said, and willed his illusion toward the tunnel.

THE PRICE OF VICTORY

*"The suckers on their many limbs are particularly retentive of cold.
Even after breaking the ocean's surface their suckers remain more
frigid than ice. Whatever a nactilious touches will convulse in shock."*

- From *Colvinar Vrium's Bestiary for Conjurers*, page 55

Flashes of blinding light and deafening eruptions filled the yaeltis den,
as Amendal propped himself up with his uninjured arm. If only I
could capture another, he thought, wincing against the pain. Unfortunately, he would have to be content with one yaeltis instead of two, or
five.

"Oh well," he muttered, eyeing his quinta'shals. The gray-skinned creatures had expended their magic and were trying to siphon the barsions and
the enhancing magic of the soldiers. "Now to regain control…"

Since his mental bond was severed, Amendal would have to cast another
spell to regain control of his conjurations. The spell resembled the enthralling magic used by illusionists.

As Amendal uttered the incantation, Scialas pushed through the ranks of
mages. "Amendal!" she called, arpran magic flowing from her hands. Scialas
was beside him in a heartbeat, the green light of the arpran magic nearly
surrounding her. "What happened to you?" she asked.

"He got hit by a flying soldier," Faelinia said. "Let me open his barsion."

While Amendal finished his incantation, the violet hue shifted—a result
of Faelinia reforming the barsion bubble into a shield. He sent the enthralling magic toward two quinta'shals, each siphoning the fiery barsions
from a soldier. The man spun on the conjurations, swinging his flaming
sword in an effort to ward them away. One of the quinta'shals swatted its
tongue at the sword, completely stripping the weapon of its magical fire.

The quinta'shal glowed a reddish-orange as Amendal regained control over it. Stop! Amendal commanded, and both gray-skinned creatures stilled. Attack the yaeltis, he commanded.

Both of the quinta'shals turned from the soldier. The man shook his head quizzically, but he too turned and rejoined the battle. Amendal winced as the conjurations bolted toward the nearest yaeltis, their three-pronged hands outstretched.

Unleash your magic, he commanded, and he felt the slits on each of the quinta'shals' hands violently open, blasting the fiery magic they had stolen.

Amendal began another incantation as the repurposed flame struck the yaeltis, igniting its fur. The yaeltis howled and reeled backward, settling its gaze upon the advancing quinta'shals.

A sudden surge of relief coursed through Amendal's injured side and arm, evoking a gasp that interrupted his incantation. The pain faded, and the broken bone in his arm realigned—that in and of itself was painful, but the pain was fleeting. Best not to resume until she's finished, he thought, breathing deeply. But perhaps I can now try capturing another…

"There," Scialas said. "That was worse than when you were a kid."

Amendal gave her a sidelong glance, and Scialas blushed. This was no time to be reminiscing on their childhood. He thanked her and turned back to the battle.

As Amendal uttered another incantation, a surge of piercing pain permeated his mind. Something had rammed one of his quinta'shals through the stomach. The pain was accompanied by a vile bitterness Amendal could taste in his mouth.

Amendal fought the urge to vomit while searching for his conjuration.

The quinta'shal, impaled on the yaeltis's tusk, involuntarily expelled the rest of the fire within it. The flaming particles seeped from the slits in its hands, chest, and thighs. Violet blood dripped along the impaling tusk, causing the amber encrusted substance to bubble.

"Are you all right?" Scialas blurted, coming to Amendal's side. She frantically swept her gloved hands across him.

"I'm fine." Amendal spat and resumed his incantation. The acrid taste was still in his mouth. Disgusting…

Now partially on fire, the yaeltis pulled the wounded quinta'shal from its tusk, tossing the dying conjuration to the icy floor. Enraged, the yaeltis swatted at the other quinta'shal, knocking the unmarred conjuration into a soldier, but not before the quinta'shal unleashed the rest of its magic. Fiery beams left the slit in the conjuration's palm, and a volley of deadly magic struck the yaeltis.

A blinding flash filled the cavern, accompanied by a scream of agony. As the light faded, the beast who had impaled the conjuration dropped to its knees. The yaeltis was drenched in acid and had several holes blown through its body.

Other screams, human screams, echoed throughout the cavern. Amendal turned as three soldiers—each lacking barsions—were hurled from the battle. They collided with the icy wall and fell limp on the cavern floor.

This battle has to end, Amendal thought and searched for his other quinta'shals. Each was by another yaeltis, siphoning more magic and glowing a pinkish gray. The yaeltis they were near held a soldier by his feet and repeatedly pounded the man's barsion. The soldier swung his acid-imbued blade to intercept the blows, but the yaeltis was unfazed by the acid.

While Amendal's enthralling magic took hold, the yaeltis shattered the barsion of the dangling soldier, and the man screamed with horror. Amendal aimed the conjurations' hands at the yaeltis's recoiling arm.

Both quinta'shals unleashed blasts of raw arcane magic while the yaeltis hurled its fist at the defenseless man. The repurposed magic struck the yaeltis's arm just as the beast's fist collided with the soldier, abruptly silencing his screams.

An explosion of pink light filled the cavern, accompanied by a bestial cry. Amid the flash, Amendal sent his conjurations dashing. Both quinta'shals raised their hands, discharging their siphoned magic in a deadly blast that struck the yaeltis's head.

———⊃•⊂———

Calimir threw himself sideways, evading the claws of a smaller yaeltis and narrowly avoiding collision with Vorsim—a mercenary from squad eleven. Only one of the smaller creatures remained. The other two had been slain by the mages, one corroding from an acidic javelin to the heart and another blown to bits by arcane bolts.

The yaeltis roared as it swung again, but Calimir lunged forward, keeping his shield raised above his head. The yaeltis's claws struck the shield's acidic barrier, and it screamed in pain. "Foul beast!" Calimir shouted and lunged, stabbing the yaeltis in the thigh. The yaeltis wailed and dropped to one knee.

Seizing the moment, Calimir lunged again, thrusting the sword through the yaeltis's chest.

Still wailing, the creature grabbed the sword, but screamed upon touching the flaming blade. The beast jolted backward, tearing Calimir from his weapon. The yaeltis staggered, then fell backward, collapsing with a pained groan.

The other soldiers and mercenaries who had fought the beast ran to it, stabbing the yaeltis repeatedly. The beast fell limp, but the soldiers continued stabbing it for good measure. One could not be too careful when dealing with treacherous monsters.

Calimir took one sweeping glance throughout the cavern. Only two of the wretched creatures were still alive. The yaeltis nearest them was missing an arm and struggled to repel the soldiers fighting it.

That one falls next. Calimir spun back to his most recent foe. "Commander!" shouted a soldier near the dead yaeltis. The man pried the flaming sword from the monster's chest and held the blade toward Calimir.

With thanks, Calimir reclaimed his weapon, then turned and pointed it at the maimed monster. "Charge!"

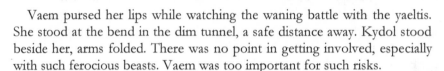

Vaem pursed her lips while watching the waning battle with the yaeltis. She stood at the bend in the dim tunnel, a safe distance away. Kydol stood beside her, arms folded. There was no point in getting involved, especially with such ferocious beasts. Vaem was too important for such risks.

A violet eruption veiled the cavern, and she turned away, shielding her eyes with the backside of her gloved hand.

"Impressive creatures," Kydol said.

Vaem nodded, pursing her lips. Her eyes lingered on Amendal, now made whole from his encounter with the flying soldier. He's lucky, she mused. If the soldier had been protected by a barsion imbued with destructive magic Amendal might not have survived. And that would be a pity in many ways.

I will have you, Vaem thought with a grin, watching as gray light shot from Amendal. The enthralling magic wrapped around his towering conjuration now attacking the soldiers. Though it had not killed anyone, Calimir would undoubtedly chide Amendal for losing control.

"A shame he only captured one," Kydol said. "I assume Mister Aramien views his conjurations as he does his women."

Vaem raised an eyebrow at Kydol, but turned back to the battle. The surviving yaeltis—now missing both its arms—howled as more soldiers converged on it. The beast struggled to kick the soldiers and mercenaries away, but its efforts were futile. Dardel and several other soldiers climbed a nearby ledge and launched themselves onto the creature's back. They repeatedly stabbed the yaeltis, and it staggered.

"Perhaps I was wrong," Kydol said, sounding amused. Vaem turned, following the lieutenant's gesture to the gathering of mages.

That irksome coquette, Faelinia, was shouting commands. Several mages were mustering enthralling magic while Amendal glowed a golden hue. *So, you're helping him get another of those creatures?* Vaem thought. She swallowed a twinge of jealousy and returned her focus to Amendal.

"He'll have two after all," Kydol said, grinning.

Vaem gazed farther into the cavern, toward the last yaeltis. The beast was fending off several soldiers and mercenaries. Its right tusk was broken, missing its tip.

"It seems Mister Aramien chose wisely," Kydol said with a snicker.

"What do you mean by that?" Vaem demanded.

Kydol shook her head and opened her mouth to speak, but before she could reply belabored footfalls echoed from the dim tunnel. Kydol spun, drawing her sword.

"Now what?" Vaem murmured. The footsteps grew louder. Scowling, she backed out of the tunnel. With the battle ending, it might be safer in the den than in the tunnel, if whatever owned those footfalls was hostile. Soon, faint conversation carried around the bend, hushed speculation of a creature within a pit.

Vaem relaxed. *The survivors of the other squads…*

Kydol, however, proceeded cautiously into the tunnel, her weapon still drawn. "Who's there?"

"Corasian," a tired voice replied. Vaem didn't recall the man. She found it unnecessary to familiarize herself with every member of the expedition.

Kydol continued into the tunnel and disappeared around the bend.

A pained cry filled the cavern, and Vaem spun back to the battle. The armless yaeltis staggered, stumbled, and then fell forward, crushing several soldiers. Lucky for them, they were still protected by their barsions.

Calimir shouted several orders, and the mass of soldiers and mercenaries turned on the remaining yaeltis. But the beast was stilled, and golden light was gathering behind it. That irksome coquette shouted for the soldiers to cease their advance.

Well, I suppose another of the creatures might be helpful, Vaem thought. The golden light erupted, forming an oval portal to the Visirm Expanse. As the beast lumbered toward the portal, the soldiers who had attacked it backed away. It soon disappeared into the portal, and cheers filled the yaeltis den. But soon those joyous outbursts were silenced by orders from Calimir, Dardel, and several other squad leaders.

Now that the den was cleared, Vaem stepped toward the mages and those guarding them. The guarding force consisted of Captain Edara, his sailors, and a few mercenaries. *Too cowardly to fight?* She eyed the scruffy-looking captain. Edara's scraggily beard looked even more unkempt than it had when they first set foot on this frigid wasteland.

Calimir and the others shouted more orders, calling for the expedition's arpranists to tend to the severely wounded. From what Vaem had seen, fifteen soldiers and mercenaries had been killed by the yaeltis. Over two dozen others had been wounded in some way, including the three convulsing men who had been impaled.

Poor fools, Vaem thought. An arpranist stood beside each of the convulsing men, mustering their magics. Unfortunately, their efforts would be futile. Vaem knew that an arpranist or two could certainly keep someone alive while the venom ran its course, but little was left of the mind after such an ordeal. If someone survived such poisoning, they were little more than mindless shells.

"And where have you been?" Faelinia demanded.

Vaem raised an eyebrow and turned. Faelinia stood beside Amendal, her eyes fixed on Vaem in a stern, cold gaze. The footsteps from the tunnel grew louder and were accompanied by the clanking noises of armor and hoisted weapons.

"I don't like your tone," Vaem said, narrowing her eyes.

Faelinia opened her mouth to speak but quickly averted her gaze to the dim tunnel.

"Vaem!" Kydol called.

Before turning around, Vaem glanced to Amendal, eyeing him up and down. *You won't relent as long as that irksome coquette is around*, she thought. *Perhaps I can separate you from her while in Tardalim...* The thought made her smile.

Kydol shouted for her again, and Vaem reluctantly turned from Amendal. Seven soldiers marched behind the lieutenant. *What happened to the mages?*

"You won't like this," Kydol said to her with a sigh. "We won't be going that way."

"Why?" Vaem asked.

"There's a beast guarding that pit," a soldier said, his voice shaky. "We barely escaped with our lives."

Vaem narrowed her eyes as the soldiers spewed frantic reports about the incident, about how they had fled from the vines Ildin had mentioned. They were crystal, but not crystal. *A creature with pliable crystal tentacles?* She had never heard of such a thing. Was it even physically possible?

"...they're behind us," a soldier said. "Dugal and Morgidian are making walls so those things don't come after us."

So two others survived, Vaem mused. That was still less than half that had ventured to the pit. And from the survivors' tale they hadn't even descended into the cavern. *Yes, best we not go that way...*

Amendal uttered an incantation to open a portal to the Aldinal Plane. His conjurations had sustained too much damage to be of any use. Bits and pieces of the earthen giant had been broken off, and several of the smaller elementals had been torn into pieces. He could still use three of the quinta'shals, though.

Faelinia and Fendar had helped him round up the conjurations, enthralling those Amendal hadn't regained control over. Together, they managed to subdue them.

As the portal to the Aldinal Plane formed, concerned chatter filled the icy cavern as well as incantations from the arpranists. Calimir was making his rounds, checking on each member of the expedition.

"Let the big guy go first," Amendal said.

"Are you dismissing all your conjurations?" Vaem asked, her tone haughty.

Amendal ignored the woman and focused on marching his conjurations toward the portal. *Best keep one of the quinta'shals nearby*, he thought and sent the command to the conjuration.

"Well, they were damaged," Faelinia said tersely.

One by one the conjurations entered the portal. The last earthen elemental was dragged by one of the quinta'shals, and together they vanished. No sooner had the conjurations departed than Calimir came stomping up, looking furious. He stopped an arm's length in front of Amendal, his bulbous nose scrunched and his nostrils flared.

"Mister Aramien..." he said through clenched teeth, "I told you—"

"Just wait a moment," Amendal interrupted, extending a hand. "Before you start reciting the 'consequences' of my actions, just know I don't care about the coin from this expedition. It means absolutely nothing to me."

Calimir narrowed his brown eyes and planted his gauntleted fists on his hips. "I despise your kind," he grumbled. "You think because of your privilege, you can do whatever you want. You endangered the rest of us with that ridiculous stunt of yours."

Amendal rolled his eyes as Calimir continued his tirade. The old soldier had the audacity to claim the yaeltis's awakening was Amendal's fault, when in reality the beasts had already awoken. *In fact, if it weren't for me, the battle would have probably taken place in the tunnel...*

"...and from now on you're to take up the rear, where you can't cause any more harm!" Calimir finished with a sigh and shook his head.

"Commander," Faelinia spoke up. "If I may—"

"No, you may not, Miss Tusara," Calimir spat.

Vaem cleared her throat. "That decision is unwise, Calimir. Especially with what lies ahead of us."

Calimir frowned, then glanced to the tunnel where the men from squads three and four were gathered. "Why are there only seven of you?" Calimir barked.

"We're all that made it, sir," a soldier said. "That creature snatched half of squad three before we were halfway down the pit."

Calimir growled.

"Traversing the pit is unwise," Vaem repeated.

"Well, is there another way?" Calimir snapped.

The commander and Vaem debated the matter while Amendal turned away. He studied Faelinia, who simply stood with her arms folded. "He's wrong," she whispered. "Though I thought you were being foolish, charging into the cave was probably for the best. Thank you."

"Of course," Amendal said, smiling graciously. "It's what I do."

Faelinia grinned and she let her gaze linger on Amendal.

While the debate between Calimir and Vaem intensified, Ildin shouted from the dim tunnel. "There's another way!" Ildin cried. The illusionist stumbled into the cavern, pushing aside his blonde hair. "Look!" He pointed across the yaeltis den to the nearest tunnel to the right. The argument between Calimir and Vaem immediately ceased. One of Ildin's illusions shot from the tunnel, then slowed to hover above the dead yaeltis.

Calimir cocked his head, then turned to Ildin. "Was that the illusion you sent into the pit, Mister Cetarin?"

"Yes," Ildin replied. "This cavern and the one beneath the pit are connected, although the path between them is quite the maze. I think it'll be better to go that way. The tunnel leading from the pit to the gatehouse is close to the one that empties into the pit."

Calimir set his jaw.

"So, make a mad dash to the other tunnel?" Vaem asked with a snicker.

Ildin shrugged. "I don't know, maybe we could use conjurations or those reanimated corpses as fodder."

"That could work," Kydol interjected, "and create a tunnel of barsion to protect us as we cross the pit."

Sounds risky, Amendal thought.

"That's something we'll have to discuss," Calimir said. He stalked off, shouting orders for the soldiers to fetch the expedition's supplies.

"What an idiot," Captain Edara said, stepping around a group of mages. There was still some bitterness in the sea captain's attitude and demeanor. Who could blame the man, what with all he had endured thus far. "The fool is going to get us all killed."

At least someone feels as I do...

"Where's Morgidian?" Ildin asked. "And Dugal?" He looked back to the soldiers who had survived the pit, but they shrugged.

"Maybe they're restin'," a soldier said.

"Probably waiting by everyone's packs," said another. "You all just left them there in the tunnel."

Ildin bit his lip, then glanced to the cavern's ceiling. Amendal followed his gaze. Ildin's illusion hovered in the air, then sped toward the dim tunnel they had traversed.

"I'm sure Morgi is fine," Amendal said, surveying the yaeltis den. The wounded had been gathered, and those that could be treated without magic were being tended to by unmarred soldiers. Amendal had expected to see the arpranists tending to those men, but the arpranists were still healing those who had been impaled by the yaeltis. Each convulsing man had three arpranists infusing them with rejuvenating magic, but the combined magic seemed to do nothing. Was yaeltis poison that deadly?

"Horrible way to die," Vaem said. "They really should just let them go."

"How heartless," Faelinia retorted.

"No, it's practical. Those men will be dead within a quarter of an hour. All those arpranists are doing is prolonging their suffering—"

"Oh no!" Ildin exclaimed. "Amendal, come on. Morgidian and Dugal are being attacked by those wolves!" The illusionist bolted toward the dim tunnel, as did Faelinia.

The cisthyrn? Amendal thought, intrigued. The more creatures to add to his menagerie the better. Grinning, he hurried after his friends.

Captain Edara watched as the arpranists struggled to mend the wounded soldiers. *It's that venom*, he thought. An arpranist could heal wounds, but if the source of the wound was still present, their magic could only do so much.

Edara had once seen a man impaled by a broken yardarm during a treacherous storm. Luckily an arpranist was aboard. The mage kept the man alive until the other sailors could remove the yardarm. But there were still parts of the man that couldn't be mended, because some of the splinters remained.

What interesting venom, Edara thought. He sauntered from the tunnel, nearing the wounded soldiers.

"Weldar!" Hevasir shouted, holding one of the convulsing men. "Weldar, can you hear me?!" The man, Weldar, didn't respond. His eyes were rolled back, and his tongue flailed.

"I'm doing all I can," said one of the arpranists. "But no matter how much arpran magic I fill them with, it doesn't seem enough. This venom is too powerful!"

"They should just let them die," Vaem said to Kydol, and both Mindolarnian women joined the others at the cavern's heart.

Heartless whore... Edara thought, fighting back a glare. He turned and continued through the icy cavern. The woman kept talking to her bodyguard, speaking of the effects of the yaeltis's venom.

So, the venom is incurable? Edara mused. The whore explained what occurred if one happened to survive an encounter with yaeltis venom—they would become a total invalid. *Perhaps I need not look any further...* he thought, grinning with anticipation. Besides, there might not be any inconspicuous tevisrals in the reliquary.

Determined, he sauntered throughout the cavern, eyeing each of the slain yaeltis. The larger beasts had an amber substance encrusted on their tusks while the smaller ones didn't. *That crusty stuff must be the venom...*

Edara studied one of the corpses, whose head was turned so the tusks were hidden from the majority of the expedition. Shaving off those tusks would draw too much attention. Setting his jaw, he glanced back toward the tunnel, to the first yaeltis that had been slain. The creature's head was missing. Could the mages have blown apart the tusks?

Shards of them would do nicely...

Edara immediately studied his surroundings. None of the soldiers were paying attention to him. Those that had not fetched the expedition's supplies were helping with the wounded. And Calimir... Well, the old fool was conversing with his squad leaders. The mages near the tunnel had spread out, mingling with the others in the cave.

Good... He grinned again and crossed the icy cavern. As he reached the headless beast, Cluvis joined him.

"What's going on, Captain?" the first mate whispered.

When Edara didn't reply, Cluvis appeared to take his captain's silence as an important answer.

Edara rounded the corpse, searching the ground. Nothing… This particular yaeltis was already dead when he had entered the cavern, but he did recall flashes of pink light in the tunnels—arcane magic. That kind of magic tended to make things explode.

Hopefully the tusks weren't disintegrated, Edara thought. He did recall those mages' parasites unleashing an arcane blast. If he couldn't find—

"Ah-ha…" he whispered. No more than five paces away lay a finger-length sliver of crystal, partly covered in that amber substance.

Ever cautious, Edara sauntered toward the shard and nonchalantly knelt as if inspecting his boot. The amber substance was layered quite thick on the shard, about the thickness of a small book. *Best I don't touch it,* Edara thought and reached into his coat.

He tugged at a pocket, gauging the strength of the seam holding it together. *Not strong at all…* He glanced up, noting those around him. All were preoccupied with other matters.

Pleased, Edara tore the pocket from the inside of his coat. He lowered his head, swiftly inverted the pocket, and claimed the shard.

You will be the instrument of my revenge… Edara mused, tucking the torn fabric back beneath his coat.

"With the proper practice, a lone conjurer controlling a single nactilious can inflict considerable damage on an enemy fleet. The fictional account of the Sortie of Hectilis is not that much of an exaggeration, though I have yet to meet a conjurer capable of maintaining control over five nactili."

- From *Colvinar Vrium's Bestiary for Conjurers*, page 57

Clutching his left shoulder, Morgidian warily eyed the two strange wolves circling him. Blood seeped through his fingers as he uttered an incantation to muster an inverted barsion. The forming magic, however, wasn't for the strange wolves.

Amid his attempts to subdue the last members of the pack, one wolf had breached Morgidian's barsion and pierced his shoulder. The other wolves were bound by Dugal's transmuted shackles. Several had been able to break free of Morgidian's inverted barsions, but luckily Dugal was able to seize them.

The last of the incantation left Morgidian's lips, and a band of inverted barsion formed around his shoulder, wrapping around his arm. Inverted barsions were good for more than trapping a foe—they made excellent bandages.

"There," Morgidian said with a grunt, settling into a wide stance.

One of the wolves lunged, and Morgidian threw himself sideways. As he rolled on the ground, the other wolf snarled and leapt into the air. Before Morgidian could regain his feet, the strange wolf pinned him to the ground and clawed at his barsion bubble.

Morgidian swiftly uttered another incantation. He would need to replace his barsion, especially if the other wolf decided to pounce. The creature's claws caused the barsion to flicker, and Morgidian felt the beast weakening the barrier.

As Morgidian struggled to renew his barsion, he heard Dugal recite an incantation from above. The transmuter was standing atop a tall pillar of stone he had crafted from the cavern floor.

Excellent, Morgidian thought. Dugal had put himself in a place where the wolves couldn't reach him.

Brilliant blue light shone within Morgidian's flickering barsion. Heart pounding, he hurried through his incantation. A hole formed in the barrier and the strange wolf shoved one of its claws straight for Morgidian's face. Uttering the last of his incantation, Morgidian threw his head back as the claw scraped along his chin, up his cheek and across his right eye.

His vision shifted as a wave of barsion erupted, immediately repulsing the strange wolf. Stinging pain washed across his face, and Morgidian fought the urge to scream. But by the Powers, it hurt!

A streak of brown light shot through the air like lightening, grappling with the wolf that had been repulsed. Liquefied stone wrapped around the vicious creature, instantly forming shackles. The transmuted steel left the strange wolf dangling a phineal off the ground.

"Morgi, are you okay?!" Dugal shouted.

Morgidian pushed himself up, but didn't answer. They still had one more wolf to contend with.

"No," he replied through clenched teeth, then began uttering another incantation. He would pin this beast, and hopefully Dugal would have the shackles ready before the strange wolf could break free.

Both of them uttered their incantations as the last wolf began circling Morgidian. Though focused on mustering his magic, he also sidestepped in time with the beast. He and the wolf danced the dance of a duel.

The strange creature kept its bizarre eyes on Morgidian, its disturbing white pupils constricting.

As the two of them circled, a flash of gray light zipped into the cavern. Morgidian started, turning to the light. It was one of Ildin's illusions.

"Oh no!" the illusion cried.

Morgidian turned back to his foe just as the strange wolf lunged. The beast had undoubtedly taken advantage of the distraction. Morgidian threw himself out of the way as Ildin's illusion shouted something else. Was he talking to Amendal?

The wolf soared past Morgidian, growling as it landed.

Still uttering his incantation, Morgidian staggered to his feet. His face and shoulder ached.

Creeping forward, the wolf lowered its head. Ildin's illusion, however, struck the cavern floor and stood between Morgidian and the wolf.

"Over here!" Ildin shouted, his illusion waving its arms.

The strange wolf glanced to the illusion, sniffing loudly. The beast cocked its head, and then stepped *through* the illusion and toward Morgidian.

"Wait!" Ildin shouted, his illusion spinning about. "Don't you want to eat me?!" The wolf ignored him, eyes fixed on Morgidian.

A worthy attempt, Morgidian thought as he finished his incantation. He stretched out his hands as the wolf charged, and the barsion magic struck the beast before it could get within a leap of him.

"That should hold you," Morgidian said with a grunt, turning from the pinned beast. Dugal was almost finished with his incantation.

"Are you all right?" Ildin asked, his illusion hovering beside Morgidian.

"Do I look all right?" Morgidian retorted, turning to show Ildin his face.

The illusion flinched.

"That bad, huh?"

"It adds... character?" Ildin muttered.

Liquefied stone shot from the ceiling like lightning and shackled the last wolf. The transmuted shackles, however, kept the beast on the ground.

"Those cisthyrn are really vicious," Ildin said.

"Cisthyrn?"

"Oh yeah, you weren't with us." Ildin pointed to one of the wolves. "That there is a cisthyrn. We found a bunch of dead ones near the yaeltis."

"Ildin!" Dugal called from his pillar. "Does Amendal want these beasts?"

Ildin laughed. "Oh, I'm sure he does! When does Amendal *not* want some exotic creature?"

It wasn't long before Ildin, Faelinia, and Amendal dashed into the cavern. Dugal had dismissed his pillar and was standing beside Morgidian.

"Twelve!" Amendal exclaimed, his eyes wide. He looked like a boy who had just discovered his family lived next to a candy shop. Amendal cackled, rubbing his hands together in anticipation. "Who needs money when one can have all these creatures?"

"Me," Dugal said, raising a finger. "I'll take your payment, if you don't mind."

Amendal laughed and began uttering an incantation to open one of those portals of his.

"He's not getting any payment," Faelinia said, picking her way around the shackled wolves—or rather, cisthyrns. She made her way to Morgidian and studied him. "You don't look so good."

"I'll be fine," Morgidian said. *Hopefully someone can fix my eye...*

Faelinia sighed, then studied the pinned creatures. Most were growling and snarling, though there were some who had accepted their captivity. "Ildin, let's enthrall these while Amendal opens his portal."

Golden light shone around Amendal, then shot to a space in front of him, swirling into an oval shape. Morgidian enjoyed watching conjuration magic form. There was something entrancing about portals.

Ildin and Faelinia uttered their own incantations, and the entire pack was soon enthralled. Morgidian dismissed his inverted barsions while Dugal released his shackles.

One by one, each of the strange wolves lumbered toward the portal and disappeared into the conjurer's void.

The arpranists hadn't succeeded in expunging the poison plaguing Weldar, Faziac, and Umardin. The thought of losing more men sickened Calimir. With this most recent encounter they had lost fifteen good men and women to the perilous waste. And according to the survivors of squads three and four, another eleven had been lost.

Twenty-six more, dead... Calimir shook his head, turning from the squad leaders. They had been discussing their next course of action. Many felt that they should find another way to Tardalim, one that was safer. But Mister Cetarin had said there was no other way into the cavern that contained the gatehouse.

I can't lose any more. Calimir glanced to Weldar. Though the hole in Weldar's torso had been mended, the poor man was still foaming at the mouth. The three arpranists were mustering more of their magic, but their efforts seemed fruitless. *Perhaps we should have descended into the gorge.*

"You're only prolonging their suffering," said Mistress Rudal.

Calimir glanced over his shoulder, but didn't respond. The Mindolarnian women stopped beside him. Lieutenant Virain eyed the dying men with a cold gaze. Had she engaged the yaeltis at all? Calimir didn't recall seeing her during the battle.

"Just let them die." Mistress Rudal sighed. "The arpranists will have to continuously tend to them for days, maybe even weeks."

"I'm not going to lose them," Calimir said, his tone firm. Weldar and Umardin had fought alongside Calimir for many years. And Faziac... Well, Calimir had known Faziac since the man enlisted in the Sorothian Navy.

A grunt left Mistress Rudal's lips. "You won't be doing them any favors. Letting them live would be cruel."

Cruel? Calimir fought the urge to snap at the woman. Allowing them to succumb to the poison would be cruel. No, he would not do that. "Surely we can heal them. Perhaps something in Tardalim can cure them."

"I doubt that," she said. "I only know of one ancient tevisral that *might* allow them to survive—but I seriously doubt those rings are kept in Tardalim."

Calimir raised an eyebrow at the Mindolarnian scholar. *Surely she's not telling me all she knows.*

"So stubborn." Mistress Rudal sighed. "I suppose there is a way to save them—or at least stop them from dying."

Calimir rounded on the woman. "Well, spit it out!"

Her lips twisted in a wry smile. "I doubt you'll like it."

"Tell me!"

"Very well," she said, haughtily averting her gaze. "You could always place them in the Visirm Expanse. Time does not touch that plane. They will remain frozen in that agonized state until they are removed."

That conjurer's void? Calimir set his jaw.

"Too arrogant to ask *him?*" Mistress Rudal snickered, undoubtedly referring to Mister Aramien. "Are the lives of your men worth swallowing your pride?"

Calimir glared at the woman. *What audacity...* No, there were other conjurers he could call upon. He would not involve Mister Aramien in such a crucial task. Turning from the Mindolarnians, Calimir faced the squad leaders. "Selicas, fetch your conjurer. I would have a word with him."

Selicas, a black-haired burly man and the leader of squad fourteen, nodded and stepped away.

"Are you sure that's wise?" Dardel asked, squinting his right eye in a mannerism that indicated he was considering a matter of great importance.

"Yes," Calimir said. "We'll place Weldar and the others inside the conjurer's void until we can cure them. Now, let's reorganize the squads. At least one of you is going to lose their command. If any of you are willing to volunteer, please do so now."

After adding those twelve cisthyrn to his menagerie, Amendal and the others returned to the yaeltis den. Calimir was loudly explaining his plan for dealing with the creature beneath the pit. It was a convoluted mess involving the use of conjurations and corpses as bait while the barsionists created a tunnel for the expedition to run through. The plan was remarkably stupid.

I should just go on ahead, Amendal thought, stopping short of leaving the tunnel. *I can take care of that* thing *all by myself.*

"Ildin," Amendal called in a hushed whisper. "Ildin!"

The illusionist spun. "What?"

Amendal gestured for his friend to come near while he kept an eye on the expedition. No one seemed to notice their return.

"I've got a better idea than that old fool," Amendal whispered. "But I need your help."

"*My* help?" Ildin asked, swallowing hard. He looked rather sheepish. "Uh, what do you want me to do?"

"Two things," Amendal said, taking a step back. "I need you to make an illusion of me and keep it with the party, and—"

"What?!" Ildin's eyes went wide.

Amendal waved his hand in a placating manner. "Just listen. I need an illusion of myself, and I need you to make another of you to guide me to that pit."

Ildin groaned and shook his head. "I have a bad feeling about this..."

"There isn't much time," Amendal whispered. "Come on, let's go back into the tunnel and make a copy of me. I'll sneak by invisibly. Once I'm in the other tunnel you can send your illusion to guide me."

Sighing, Ildin glanced over his shoulder.

"If you're worried about losing your commission, I'll pay you when we get home."

Ildin turned back to Amendal, giving him a frank smile. "Coin is not what I'm worried about. I saw that monster make short work of two squads."

"It'll kill more than that if I don't take care of it."

Ildin studied Amendal for a moment, then hurried back into the tunnel.

Perfect, Amendal thought, grinning. He followed Ildin around a bend, where the illusionist began whispering an incantation. White light flowed from Ildin's hands and wrapped around Amendal. A peculiar pricking sensation surged across his skin, then abruptly ceased. The illusory magic shot from him and coalesced beside Ildin in a white silhouette resembling a man.

Footsteps sounded into the tunnel, coming from the yaeltis den.

Uh-oh... Amendal swiftly whispered an incantation to muster a veil of invisibility. Whitish-blue particles flowed from Amendal's hands and up his arms. Meanwhile, Ildin's magic vaguely resembled Amendal's silhouette, becoming more refined by the second.

Amendal finished his spell first and vanished. He held his breath as the footsteps grew louder. *Hurry, Ildin...*

The white light of the illusory magic faded and a perfect copy of Amendal stood beside Ildin.

At that moment, Faelinia turned the corner, followed by Dugal. "And what are you two doing back here?" she asked.

Ildin shook his head, looking baffled. The illusion of Amendal did something similar and shrugged.

Faelinia narrowed her eyes at both illusion and illusionist. "Well, whatever you're doing will have to wait. Everyone's ready." Shaking her head, Faelinia spun and marched back to the icy cavern. Dugal, however, lingered in the tunnel. The transmuter was just staring at Ildin with an eyebrow raised.

Amid the awkward silence, Amendal crept to Ildin, then leaned close to his friend's ear. "That was close. Now which tunnel do I take?"

"First to the left," Ildin whispered.

"What was that?" Dugal asked.

Ildin's jaw tensed. "Nothing," he said and stepped away from Amendal. The illusion followed, and soon Amendal was alone in the tunnel.

He focused on his lone quinta'shal and commanded it to grab his pack—the soldiers had ferried all the supplies into the center of the yaeltis den. *Best one of them carry it,* he thought. If his pack were to suddenly disappear that would definitely arouse suspicion. *Now to get going...*

⸺⊃•⊂⸺

Creeping past the expedition was easier than raiding the kitchen of the Aramien estate house. Amendal had done his fair share of sneaking about over the years, especially during the parties his family hosted. Many a time he had managed to steal a slice of cake, or two, without being seen.

The tunnel beyond the yaeltis den was just as dimly lit as the one leading to it. As with the other tunnels, this one was three stories tall and nearly a perfect semi-circle. Amendal wished he had gotten more information from Ildin before leaving. Luckily, there were not any branching pathways. Hopefully, one of Ildin's illusions would be coming to show him the way.

After several twists and turns, the tunnel descended a shallow slope. Amendal focused through his quinta'shal still with the expedition. But none of the squads had begun moving. *Well, I don't need to hide anymore,* he thought, dismissing his invisibility and quickening his pace to a jog.

The tunnel's shallow slope steepened, forcing Amendal to run so as to not trip over himself.

"Great..." Amendal said grumpily between breaths.

Amendal bolted around a bend, then slipped on a patch of ice. He landed on his side and slid to the next bend, but caught himself on an outcropping. "Ildin didn't say anything about ice..." Well, this was an ice cavern, after all.

Pushing himself up, Amendal continued through the tunnel with caution. The expedition still hadn't begun moving.

He rounded several more bends, and then the tunnel opened onto a ledge within a massive cavern. Wary, Amendal crept to the edge and peered over. The icy stalagmites on the cavern floor looked about eight or nine stories away.

"I'd hate to slip and land on those..."

Setting his jaw, Amendal turned from the edge. A roar—not unlike those he had heard before—echoed into the cavern, coming from another tunnel across the icy chamber, two stories above the cavern floor. A rocky ramp along the cavern's wall connected that second tunnel and the ledge where Amendal was standing.

"I assume it's safe to say that's the correct path..." At that moment, the expedition began moving. "Well, no time to waste."

Amendal was partway down the rocky ramp when Ildin's illusion zipped into the cavern. The illusion settled beside Amendal, hovering in the air.

"Is it safe for me to run?" Amendal asked.

Ildin's illusion shrugged then flew into the tunnel ahead. It returned a moment later, nodding.

At first this second tunnel was dimly lit like the others, but it soon brightened. Patches of crystal shone from the ceiling, and then the walls.

"How far away is that *thing?*" Amendal asked, glancing to the illusion.

Since Ildin was surrounded by the others he didn't answer verbally. The illusion spelled out the words in the air. "You'll have to pass through two more caverns, then navigate a maze of tunnels."

As Amendal descended into the caves, the ice lessened, and crystal became more abundant. The second cavern he traversed was almost as bright as the tunnels near the surface. Each of the tunnels after that was made mostly of crystal. Ildin kept his illusion ahead of Amendal and pointed to the various branches he needed to take. All the while, more roars echoed throughout the winding labyrinth.

After rounding who knew how many bends, Ildin's illusion gestured for Amendal to halt. "This is the last tunnel. Let me scout ahead."

"Your spelling is growing tiresome," Amendal complained. "There's got to be a better way for us to communicate. Maybe some sort of sign language?" There were a few different types of sign languages used on the Mainland. But neither Amendal nor Ildin knew them.

Ildin's illusion shook its head and zipped away.

"Now where are the others?" Amendal closed his eyes and focused on sensing his quinta'shals. They and the expedition had just entered that first cavern. "I'll be finished long before they get here."

The illusion returned not a moment later, spelling words in the air. "After two bends there is a mostly straight section, and then the tunnel's mouth. The monster is still reaching its limbs into the pit."

Amendal nodded impatiently. "How soon did that *thing* react to the other squads?"

"When they got close to those limbs."

"And there aren't any of those limbs near *this* tunnel's mouth?"

The illusion shook its head.

"Good, then that's where I'll make my stand."

"Be care—" Amendal hurried past the illusion before Ildin finished spelling. They had to come up with a more effective means of communication in situations like this.

It didn't take long for Amendal to reach the tunnel's straight section. Another roar echoed into the tunnel, followed by faint but repeated thuds, undoubtedly the limbs of that *thing* flailing about. Amendal immediately began uttering the incantation to open a portal to the Visirm Expanse. If this *thing* was as powerful as Ildin claimed, there was no point fighting it head on.

Golden particles shot from Amendal's hands, weaving together at the tunnel's mouth. Amendal was halfway to the opening when the conjuration magic coalesced, forming a circular portal to the Visirm Expanse.

"You did it!" Ildin whispered through his illusion.

Amendal winked at his friend and gave him a wry smile. "Of course, I'm Amendal Aramien!"

The illusion looked as if he were going to burst with mirth.

Amendal and the illusion reached the tunnel's mouth, but nothing happened. Due to the size of the portal, Amendal couldn't see into the cavern.

"Well… I thought this *thing* was going to attack."

"Maybe the magic is preventing the monster from sensing you?" Ildin whispered.

Amendal furrowed his brow. Perhaps he had to draw the *thing*'s attention some other way. He cupped his hands to his mouth and shouted incoherent

noises. The thudding in the cavern ceased, but was soon replaced by a deafening roar.

"Hopefully that worked," Amendal said, glancing to the illusion.

Another deafening roar echoed into the tunnel. Then something hit the
portal.

In an instant, Amendal sensed a crushed cylindrical mass—longer than
any creature he had ever beheld—floating within the Visirm Expanse. It
dwarfed each of the other denizens of his menagerie. And, it wasn't made
of crystal. *Perhaps that was some sort of camouflage?* Red tentacles half a grand
phineal long protruded from a crushed orange mass, as well as... roots? *But
this thing couldn't be a plant...?*

Whatever it was, the *thing* had clearly not survived the teleportation into
the Visirm Expanse.

"Well?" Ildin asked, no longer whispering.

"It's dead," Amendal said. "Whatever it was..." He waved his hands in a
wide arc and dismissed the portal. The golden light collapsed upon itself,
revealing an empty crystal chamber.

Ildin's illusion flew ahead of Amendal, spinning around. "You did do it!"
the illusionist exclaimed. "Calimir!"

Amendal chuckled as Ildin reported the triumph. He paid little attention
to his friend and entered the crystal chamber. It was dome-shaped, as Ildin
had described, but there were two tunnels instead of one. *Perhaps that second
one was where that* thing *was lodged.*

As Amendal hurried down the ramp Ildin's illusion zipped in front of
him. "Are you going to wait for us?"

"No," Amendal said, then pointed to the tunnel that was much smoother
than the others. "Is that the right way?"

Ildin's illusion nodded, then fell in line beside Amendal.

They entered a strangely smooth tunnel, which looked as if it were part
of some man-made, or rather Eshari-made, structure. It was about the size
of the others within the caves, but it was perfectly straight. It was made of
crystal and stretched on for at least a grand phineal, its end obscured by a
kind of mist.

"This definitely isn't natural," Amendal said. "Someone made this."

The illusion nodded.

They were partway down the tunnel when a wave of moist warmth wafted past Amendal's face. *Steam?*

19

THE GATEHOUSE

"A few years past, a ship I chartered was chased by pirates. We managed to escape, but only because I conjured a nactilious and ripped their ship's masts from its hull. I could have done more damage, but I thought the mast-ripping a sufficient message."

- From *Colvinar Vrium's Bestiary for Conjurers*, page 58

The smooth tunnel was warm, but not intolerably so. Since it was three stories tall, the heat was well distributed. "What's causing this warmth?" Amendal said, fidgeting with his coat and undoing the buttons.

"Probably the steam vents," Ildin said.

"Huh?" Amendal asked.

"Hold on." The illusion held up a hand. "Calimir is shouting."

Amendal continued through the tunnel in silence, nearing that veil of steam. He fanned his hand in front of his face, but that didn't disrupt the thick vapor. *This is annoying...*

After a moment, the steam dissipated, and Amendal entered a vast chamber hollowed from dark-brown rock. The cavern rose at least a dozen stories, maybe more. Strange and colorful plants—like nothing Amendal had ever seen—grew all across the cavern floor, along the walls, and on the stalagmites and stalactites. Some dwarfed him, and many had colorful flowers and vines. Columns of steam rose from small craters scattered across the chamber. Two of those craters were beside Amendal, their steam wafting into the tunnel.

"Incredible..." Amendal murmured, stepping onto an earthen ramp, overgrown with the exotic plants.

"See," Ildin said, his illusion zipping ahead of Amendal. "And there's the gatehouse."

While Amendal picked his way down the ramp, he followed the illusion with his eyes. Across the cavern and imbedded within the earthen wall stood a pair of pale-blue crystal doors, seven—maybe even eight—stories tall. They were not transparent or translucent like the thick walls in the crystal towers. Strange symbols were chiseled into the doors, markings unlike anything Amendal had ever seen. Those symbols had sharp edges and looked as if they were made with sweeping motions. "A long-lost language?" he mused. Perhaps the language of the Eshari...

·Once down the ramp Amendal continued across the cavern floor. An elevated path—wider than the tunnel—led from the ramp and to the doors. It too was covered in those colorful plants. He was halfway across the cavern when he sensed the expedition quickening their pace. Soldiers pushed past his quinta'shal, and some were jogging.

"Calimir called for a quicker pace," Ildin's illusion shouted. "And it looks like I'll be joining you in the back."

Amendal laughed, rounding an orange plant whose colorful stems reached to his chest. The plant's flowered ends swayed as Amendal stepped around it, as if it were following him.

Odd....

He continued across the elevated path, careful not to step on any of the plants. He also commanded his conjuration to quicken its pace.

Amendal tugged at his coat, undid the top button, and shouted to Ildin. "Sure is warm in here!"

"I'll welcome the warmth," the illusion shouted back. "I don't care much for the cold."

The cavern floor beneath the doors was covered in just as many plants as the rest of the elevated path. Now beside the doors, Amendal could see that the strange symbols were glowing, their hue slightly darker than the crystal. "Coursing magic?" Amendal said.

"It looks like it," Ildin said. "Do you want to open these doors or wait for the others?"

Amendal paused, considering the consequences—not the consequences from Calimir, though. No, he was more concerned about what might lie beyond those doors. "Can you go through them?" He gestured to the crystal slabs.

The illusion shook its head. "I tried when I first found this place. It's like those walls of the buildings in the Eshari city."

"Faelinia had that same problem," Amendal said with a sigh. "What a pity..." Well, they needed to open the doors regardless. "We're going to need something big to open these..."

"One of your gangolins?" Ildin asked. He sounded eager.

"No, a gargantuan will do," Amendal said, stepping back and looking along the doors. There were no knobs or handles. No hinges, either. *Probably opens inward.* "All right, let's step back—Well, I guess you don't need to."

Ildin's illusion simply grinned.

After retreating back across the plant-covered path, Amendal opened a portal to the Aldinal Plane. The golden magic swirled in front of the doors, reaching nearly as tall as the crystal slabs. Soon, the silhouette of an earthen gargantuan appeared in the golden light, then the conjuration stepped into the massive cavern. The earthen gargantuan crushed several plants beneath its feet, sending glowing puffs of colorful pollen—red, blue, orange, and black—into the air. But as the colorful puffs settled on the ground they lost their glow.

"Was that some sort of magic?" Ildin asked, his illusion gliding toward Amendal.

"Magical plants?" Amendal asked. "I just hope they're not poisonous."

"If so, then you'll die a hero."

Amendal gave the illusion a sidelong glance, then guided the conjuration to the doors. With arms extended, the earthen gargantuan slammed its palms against the crystal slabs. The doors, however, didn't budge.

Setting his jaw, Amendal willed the conjuration to press on the doors. With its earthen hands on each slab, the conjuration pushed with all its might. But the doors still didn't move.

"Maybe you need another one?" Ildin asked.

To the right, Amendal commanded, and the earthen gargantuan positioned itself squarely with the right slab. It pushed with all its might, digging its feet into the ground and uprooting the exotic plants. Unfortunately, the doors still did not budge.

Amendal let out a heavy sigh and shook his head. "Maybe I do need another…"

⸻

Even with a second earthen gargantuan, the doors remained closed. They didn't move at all. Amendal had since removed his coat and continued pushing on the doors until he sensed the expedition drawing near. The others had entered the cavern beneath the pit and were proceeding to the smooth tunnel.

"I don't know what's going to budge these," Amendal said grumpily. He turned from the doors, moving to the edge of the raised path. Defeated, he plopped down on the path's edge, his feet dangling. The rest of the cavern's floor was a good half story lower than the path.

There has to be something locking the doors, he thought. Throughout his efforts, Amendal had examined the crystal slabs, looking for a lock. *They're probably locked by magic.* Perhaps whatever held the doors together needed to be dispelled… Unfortunately, Amendal didn't know how to cast such magic.

He contemplated the dilemma until his name was shouted across the cavern.

"Mister Aramien!" Calimir barked. "What in the nine seas do you think you're doing?!"

Amendal groaned and closed his eyes. He needed a moment before he dealt with the old fool. Calimir kept shouting, but Amendal ignored him.

"Mister Aramien!" His name was practically shouted in his ear.

"What?" Amendal asked, looking over his shoulder.

Calimir—despite his short stature—towered over Amendal. That bulbous nose of his was scrunched again and his nostrils flared. His eyes were alight with fury. "You insolent bastard! How *dare* you ignore me?"

Amendal sighed, redirecting his gaze across the cavern. "So, this is the thanks I get... shouting. Berating. I saved us all from another senseless battle, and this is how you repay me?"

Calimir growled, shaking his head. "You're our only sure way home. If that monster had swallowed you, you could have doomed us."

"But I survived," Amendal said. "Besides, the only way that creature could reach me was through the tunnel, and I had that blocked by a portal. I wasn't in any danger."

"He has a point," Vaem said, her voice sultry. "And we did avoid another battle."

Calimir glared at the Mindolarnian, then stalked away.

"Clever what you did," Vaem said, stepping to Amendal's side.

Wary, Amendal eyed her gloved hand, then scooted away, evoking a laugh from her.

Faelinia called his name, and Amendal glanced toward her. She pushed around the others, moving between Amendal and Vaem. "Are you all right?" she asked, kneeling beside him.

He nodded, then pointed to the door. "Damned thing won't open."

"That's because you have to speak the right words," Vaem said. She turned away, looking rather annoyed. "Brute force isn't the solution for everything," she said over her shoulder as she followed Calimir.

Words? Amendal wondered. Were those doors some sort of a tevisral?

Faelinia ran her gloved hand through Amendal's hair. "Ildin told us what you did. I don't know if you're brave, insane, or incredibly stupid, but thank you for preventing another fight."

Well, I suppose that negates the rebuke, Amendal thought, staring into Faelinia's sea-gray eyes. He longed to lose himself in their depths. But instead he said, "Of course. It's what I do."

Faelinia grinned, shaking her head. "Who are you...?" she murmured, then caught her full lower lip between her teeth. She looked intrigued—hungry, even.

I'll have you yet, Amendal thought, smiling. With the progress he was making, Faelinia would be begging to be with him before they left that godforsaken reliquary.

"You know," Faelinia said, straightening up. "*He's* quite mad at you." She nodded toward Calimir's retreating back.

"That's what Ildin said." Amendal thumbed toward the doors.

"I'm actually over here," Ildin said with a chuckle. The illusionist was beside Dugal, Jaekim, and Morgidian. The gash on Morgidian's face had been healed, though his eye didn't look quite right.

"Well, you look a tad better, Morgi," Amendal said.

Morgidian grunted. "I thought I told you to stop calling me that."

Amendal grinned and pushed himself to his feet. "Just keeping my masculinity in check... You did hold your own against those cisthyrn, after all. What kind of a man fights a pack of ice wolves by himself?"

Looking annoyed, Dugal raised a hand. "Uh, I was there too!"

"Ah-ha!" Faelinia snapped her fingers. "So that's why you went after that monster—trying to one-up Morgidian." She shook her head. "Men..."

Jaekim burst into raucous laughter.

"No," Dugal said with a sigh. "Just Amendal... Most men are not *that* stupid."

"What did you do with it anyway?" Morgidian asked, folding his arms. "I can't imagine you had time to make a sufficient portal to claim it alive."

"I didn't," Amendal said. "That's why it's a grand phineal–long husk."

Jaekim snorted, Morgidian raised an eyebrow, Dugal's eyes bulged, and Faelinia shook her head, muttering about men. The look in her eyes said she did not quite believe what she was saying.

"You... killed it...?" Jaekim muttered.

"Shocking, isn't it?" Ildin said, stepping to Amendal. He pointed to the crystal doors. "Looks like she's going to open them."

Amendal turned back to the crystal slabs. Vaem was speaking in a language Amendal didn't understand, the words sharp and staccato. The glow of the etched symbols on the doors grew brighter until they beamed a brilliant white. A streak of light shot through the seam between the doors, and Amendal thought he saw the crystal slabs move *away* from the expedition. Were they—?

In a flash of movement the doors slid open soundlessly.

Alarmed gasps and awestruck comments filled the cavern. Even Amendal found himself amazed at the occurrence.

"So that's why you couldn't get them open," Ildin said, his tone just as fascinated as the expressions on the others' faces.

Though the space beyond the doors was made of crystal like the Eshari city, it looked nothing like the abandoned metropolis. The architecture of what had been referred to as "the gatehouse" consisted of sharp designs, claw-like protrusions, and other aspects that made it look almost draconic—at least, what Amendal assumed was draconic.

Pillars spaced at least a hundred phineals apart lined the walls of the gatehouse, each divided into seven sections. The same strange symbols adorned those pillars in rows and columns. Towering humanoid statues of crystal—not unlike those in Crisyan Bay—stood between the pillars. Each was unique and tucked within a curved alcove.

From what Amendal could see, the gatehouse stretched on for over a grand phineal. The space was wide enough to fit an entire Soroth city block—in fact, if one were to lay three city blocks one after another inside the gatehouse, there would still be room to spare at either end.

Calimir shouted orders that echoed through the cavern, and then the old soldier began the march into Tardalim.

THE END OF
Part Two

GK–II

AES'SHIVAR
THE WARDER

Though the snowy plains surrounding Lake Vasliran were not as cold as Aes'shivar would have liked, she still found them pleasant. At least the snow she lay upon wasn't melting. Luckily, snow rarely melted in Abodal.

Once, she had seen snow melt while ranging near the northern shores, during the warmest times of the year. When she was a child her father had told her that there were places elsewhere in the world where snow vanished completely.

I would abhor such a place, Aes'shivar thought, digging her fingers into the lightly packed snow. "No, a place without snow would be no good." She raised her hands into the air. The white snow was stark against her smooth blue skin, a beautiful shade that matched the sky during the days where night was rare. Aes'shivar did have good skin, if she did say so herself. Others of the Eshari had lighter skin tones, and some where nearly a whitish-blue.

Still on her back, Aes'shivar returned her hands to the snow and closed her eyes. Playful grunts and growls carried up the snowdrift where she lay. Her pet cisthyrns were below her, playing with each other. Burlai, the younger of the pair, always riled up Ran'disan. Though he was old, Ran'disan did enjoy chasing Burlai around.

She had raised both since they were pups. It was common for a Warder of the Plains to raise young cisthyrn, and over the last ninety years Aes'shivar had raised five pups to maturity.

Burlai yipped with glee, his paws crunching the snow as he leapt back and forth. Ran'disan sounded as if he were lumbering toward the younger cisthyrn, then a resounding thwack filled the air, followed by a yelp. A whine was accented by tumbling and crunching snow, followed by a snarl.

"That's enough, you two!" Aes'shivar shouted, then whistled a command that stilled both cisthyrns. "Come!" Though her eyes were still closed, she felt the two of them plop down beside her.

"You two need to behave yourselves," she said, reaching toward the cisthyrns and stroking their snow-covered manes. After brushing her hands through their thick coats, Aes'shivar opened her eyes and sat up.

"And learn how to play nice." She turned to Burlai. The young cisthyrn had his snout to the ground, his lips downturned. "I know you get excited and want to play all the time, but you need to respect Ran'disan." Aes'shivar patted Burlai once then turned on the elder cisthyrn. "And you... you need to be more patient. Lighten up a bit."

Ran'disan gave Aes'shivar a look that said, "I'm too old to be scolded."

"No, you're not." Aes'shivar rose to her feet and stretched her arms while taking in a sweeping glance of Lake Vasliran. It was one of the smaller lakes on Abodal, but its farthest shores were still beyond the horizon. The ice-covered lake was a mix between clear blue and white patches. Those white patches were the weakest spots on the ice and would be the first to melt if the weather became too warm. But Aes'shivar had never seen water rise above the ice sheet.

"We would all melt if that ever occurred," she said, chuckling. The thought of Lake Vasliran becoming pure water was unfathomable. She hoped to never see such a sight.

Burlai rose from the snow and nudged his muzzle against Aes'shivar's hand. She glanced to the cisthyrn. "What?" Burlai had an apologetic look in his eye. "Don't apologize to me."

As she turned to Ran'disan, the older cisthyrn shot up on all fours, nose pointed to the lake. The cisthyrn's white irises contracted, and his tail stiffened.

Aes'shivar spun, scanning the lake.

Something gray—like a low cloud—hovered near the horizon, moving across the lake toward her. *Too small to be a cloud...* What could it be? Nothing crossed the lakes of Abodal, at least nothing that wanted to live.

Lake Vasliran, like every other body of water on Abodal, was inhabited by swarms of vaerym, a ferocious breed of amphibious horned serpents. Sometimes growing as long as twenty Eshari standing one on top of one another, vaerym often kept below the ice sheets, only breaking through if a creature dared traverse the lake's frozen surface.

Parting her lips, Aes'shivar hurried to her nearby pack. She rummaged through it, eventually removing her magnifier—a round domed object that was as large as her palm.

Aes'shivar raised the magnifier to her left eye, placing the flat side against her eyebrow and cheek. A faint tingle shot through her skin as the magnifier conformed to her face.

Closing her other eye, Aes'shivar touched the magnifier's domed side in a triangular pattern. The entire lakeside became visible through the magnifier.

"Now, what are you...?" She focused on the gray cloud and slid a finger down the magnifier's right side. The details of the lake enlarged, and the gray cloud became individual forms, winged forms. Again, she slid her finger down the magnifier.

Hundreds of the winged creatures flew across the frozen lake, their dark wings beating so quickly they were a blur. Each had a tail but no legs. Their torsos were like those of an Esharian, with a chest and arms. But their faces...Those trunks were unmistakable!

Though she had never seen one, Aes'shivar knew they were Tuladine, the only other sentient beings that inhabited Abodal. "But why are they crossing the lake?" The Tuladine had always kept to themselves, secluded in their lone mountain at the heart of Abodal.

Had something driven them from their home? *Surely, their charges couldn't have broken free...* But what else would have caused them to flee? No outlander had dared cross the frozen plains in over a thousand years.

A breeze carried up the snowdrift, and Ran'disan began to snarl, undoubtedly in response to the Tuladines' scent blown from across the lake. Burlai also reacted to the breeze, rumbling a displeased growl.

Aes'shivar chuckled and continued studying the approaching Tuladine. Of the several hundred creatures, four were larger than most. Though many varied in size they were all small by comparison to the other four. *Their young, perhaps?*

Several of the small Tuladine playfully fluttered toward the ice sheet, skimmed its surface, then twirled into the air in a carefree dance.

"Do they not know what's beneath them...?" Her heart quickened, and Aes'shivar scanned the frozen lake ahead of the Tuladine, searching for the darkened silhouettes of vaeryms.

But the lake was clear.

She swiped her finger up along the magnifier, reducing its enlargement. Nothing moved beneath the ice.

At least, nothing yet.

Aes'shivar resumed her magnification and focused on the Tuladine. The young ones continued to play dangerously close to the lake's frozen surface.

"Stay off the ice..."

Her heartbeat quickened as the Tuladines' playful flight became more and more precarious. Two of the tiniest creatures collided with each other and tumbled onto the ice. *They really are ignorant of the vaeryms...*

Innocently unaware, the two Tuladine remained on the ice and shoved each other, then fluttered into the air.

Heart pounding, Aes'shivar searched the lake again. A dark spot appeared in the ice, near where the pair had fallen. It was small, but it was growing.

"Oh no..."

The flock of Tuladine continued their approach at a casual pace, oblivious to the danger beneath them. *This will not end well...* Aes'shivar reduced the magnifier's view, noting the distance between her and the Tuladine. They weren't within earshot. Not even if she shouted.

But she couldn't let them become food for the vaerym. If the Tuladine were fleeing their home then the Eshari elders needed to know why, even if that meant sacrificing herself.

Aes'shivar twisted the magnifier, and it detached from her face. She grabbed her pack and shoved the magnifier inside while drawing a forearm-length rod—the dormant form of her favored weapon, a saniuri.

She tossed the bag aside as a curved blade—the length of her forearm—materialized at one end of the saniuri while a chain wove into existence from the other. Both blade and chain were made of tirlatium, a pale-blue transparent metal the Eshari elders claimed was only found on Abodal. The chain clanged as it coiled on the ground. The weapon finished its transformation as an elongated tetrahedron materialized at the chain's end. Its four points were sharp spikes the length of a finger.

Are you really doing this? she asked herself, loosely coiling the chain so the spiked end wouldn't drag. If she went out on that ice, she might not return.

But what other choice was there? Could she really stand by and watch *children* be consumed by a ravenous beast?

Aes'shivar took in a deep breath and bolted down the snowdrift. Her cisthyrns joined her charge, loping beside her. They were trained to follow her, protect her from danger. Burlai whimpered, knowing the terror brewing beneath the frozen lake.

As she neared the shore, Aes'shivar slid a finger along the bracelet containing her armor. Pale-blue light shot from the white jewelry and up her arm. It spread across her chest, up her neck, along her other arm, and down her legs and around her feet. In an instant, the light changed, becoming thin translucent plates of tirlatium armor that covered her entire body.

Hopefully I can draw the vaerym's attention, she thought. But vaerym rarely deviated from their prey.

Once near the frozen banks, she leapt into the air. The cisthyrn followed her lead and the three of them landed on the ice with a thud. Aes'shivar steadied herself, waiting for her armor to react to the slippery ground. Thickly riveted crisscrossed patterns would form beneath a Warder's sabatons, enabling them to run on packed snow or even ice. Aes'shivar swept one foot back and forth until she heard the sabaton scraping.

"Let's go!" Aes'shivar darted across the frozen lake. As she ran, she pressed the side of her helmet, causing the bottom of the faceguard to retract. Through the rest of the guard she could see the indistinct shapes of the fluttering Tuladine.

"Fly higher!" she shouted. "There is a monster below you!"

But the Tuladine did not change their flight.

Aes'shivar kept shouting as she ran. She scanned the lake, but there were no dark spots around her.

As she advanced, the flock of Tuladine halted. *No...* she gritted her teeth. "Don't stop!" she cried. "Fly away from the ice!"

One of the Tuladine zipped toward her, flying at a furious pace. In one

of its hands it held an ornate rod with three prongs on its end. The
Tuladine leveled the rod at Aes'shivar and her cisthyrn, violet light surrounding the rod's three prongs.

We're not the threat! Aes'shivar growled. "Get away from the ice!"

The zipping Tuladine halted, then lowered the rod. It ceased glowing,
then the creature continued forward.

A nasally noise carried across the lake, as if they were words. *Was that
Elarin?* Aes'shivar rarely spoke that tongue.

"Get away from the—"

Violent cracking erupted from beneath the flock of Tuladine, then massive slabs of ice heaved into the air, followed by a flood of white water.

Oh no—

Aes'shivar kept running, passing the nearest Tuladine as a deafening
shriek pierced the air. The vaerym shot through the breaking ice, its enormous dark-blue scaled body rising several stories, its black-shelled maw
opened wide as it shot toward the flock. Panicked shrieks and nasal cries
filled the air as the Tuladine scattered. The vaerym caught two of the
winged creatures in its glistening black beak, then fell toward the ice.

No! She had to draw the vaerym's attention from those children.

Ran'disan began to bark as the vaerym slithered from the hole in the ice.
The beast was as long as thirty stories were tall—larger than any other
vaerym Aes'shivar had seen. It was as thick as six Eshari standing upon one
another's shoulders. The vaerym's black shell covered the top of its head,
fanning backward at a shallow angle. The shell's edge was lined with seven
sharp spikes that looked taller than Aes'shivar.

Yelling as loudly as she could, Aes'shivar bounded toward the beast, un-
coiling her weapon's chain wrapped around the translucent vambrace. Once
the chain was free, Aes'shivar swung the saniuri's spiked end, slamming it
into the ice. She repeatedly swung the chain as she ran, hoping the noise
would lure the beast away from the young Tuladines.

A violet beam shot over her head and toward the vaerym, striking the
creature's shell. The blast eroded the shell's outer layer, but nothing more.

More beams shot from the dispersing flock, drawing enraged cries from
the vaerym. The beast ignored the young and sped across the ice and toward one of the larger Tuladine. It reared its head to strike but the winged
creature soared into the sky.

Shrieking, the vaerym turned, moving straight for the Tuladine near
Aes'shivar.

"Come to me!" she shouted, slamming the spiked tetrahedron into the
ice. Both her cisthyrns barked repeatedly. There was hesitation in Burlai's
bark, but Ran'disan's tone was fierce.

The vaerym glanced to Aes'shivar and her cisthyrns, but veered toward
the Tuladine behind her. Yelling with fury, Aes'shivar turned, and her
cisthyrn followed. She ran in a path ready to intercept the vaerym.

If she were to stop the beast she would have to climb atop its back.

Closer... she thought, counting the distance between her and the approaching vaerym. They were thirty paces away when Aes'shivar threw the chain. The spiked end of her saniuri sailed through the air. The vaerym shot past Aes'shivar, but the spiked tetrahedron struck the creature's dark-blue scales. The chain jerked, yanking her across the ice.

She lost her footing and fell forward, but held tight to the chain. More violet beams shot overhead, some striking the vaerym while others blasted the ice.

The vaerym raced toward the Tuladine, but the winged creature flew into the air like the other. At least the adults knew how to keep their distance...

Aes'shivar struggled to her feet as the vaerym spun. The beast stopped slithering and glared at her.

"Finally!" She sighed and pressed the side of her helmet, causing the faceguard to reform. Aes'shivar yanked the chain from the end of her saniuri, and the spiked tetrahedron liquefied. Its matter zipped along the chain, reforming on the end nearest her hand.

The vaerym shrieked as it dove toward her, beak gaping.

Aes'shivar bolted toward her foe, blade ready and chain swinging.

Violet beams zipped overhead, striking the vaerym. The beast squealed and jerked as the beams partially disintegrated its scales and shell. *Don't turn,* she thought, eyeing the monster's palate. She had to get close, close enough to anchor her chain in the vaerym's mouth. Only then could she swing up behind the shell and strike the deathblow.

"Eat me!" she cried, leaping to meet the vaerym's approaching maw. A pained squeal surrounded Aes'shivar as she landed in the beast's mouth.

The vaerym clamped down, but Aes'shivar slammed her spiked tetrahedron into the beast's palate while slicing her blade across its tongue. Another pained cry washed around her as the vaerym opened its mouth. Both Aes'shivar and the chain fell from the creature's maw.

With ease, Aes'shivar grabbed the chain's end, wrapping it around her vambrace. She swayed as the vaerym reeled. More violet blasts struck the beast and it writhed. Aes'shivar kicked her feet in time with the creature's pained sways. Soon, she arced through the air and landed on the vaerym's black shell. But before she could regain her footing she was knocked off.

The vaerym sped across the ice as Aes'shivar swung back and forth. Her cisthyrns tried to attack the vaerym, but the beast was too fast for Burlai and Ran'disan.

Aes'shivar threw herself sideways, hoping to redirect her sway. The vaerym turned, negating her efforts.

Great...

More blasts struck the vaerym, causing it to halt. It violently reared back and shook its head. The jolt sent Aes'shivar spinning down and around the spikes of the vaerym's shell.

"Yes!" she cheered, aiming to anchor her blade in the beast's neck. Metal struck scale, and Aes'shivar jolted. The vaerym screamed, and Aes'shivar dangled for a moment, then landed against the back of the beast's neck.

The vaerym writhed as Aes'shivar stabbed her way to the base of the shell. Soon, she reached the vulnerable spot and shoved her saniuri's blade through the scales.

An anguished howl shot across the frozen lake, followed by a thud that knocked Aes'shivar from the monster's back. The vaerym twitched as Aes'shivar fell upon the ice. The howl faded into a waning groan, and the vaerym stilled.

Taking a deep breath, Aes'shivar pushed herself up and scanned the sky. Only three of the large Tuladine were in the air. The rest of the flock hovered not far from where Aes'shivar had been lounging.

Those nasal sounds filled the air again and Aes'shivar spun toward them. One of the Tuladine fluttered toward her, its rod lowered. The winged creature raised its trunk, aiming its strange lips at Aes'shivar. It said something that she didn't understand.

Aes'shivar touched the side of her helmet and the bottom of her faceguard retracted. "My Elarin is... lacking."

The Tuladine nodded as the other two hovered beside Aes'shivar.

"I wish to thank you," the Tuladine said in Aes'shivar's native tongue, in that nasally voice. "I am Os'icasa'nidas."

"You're welcome," Aes'shivar said, then gestured across the lake. "But we really should move."

The three Tuladine eyed one another, then sped toward the shore. Once they left, Burlai and Ran'disan loped around the dead vaerym.

"Go back to the snowdrift," Aes'shivar said, pointing after the Tuladine. Burlai didn't hesitate, but Ran'disan bowed his head. Aes'shivar had trained him to bow whenever she wanted to ride him.

"I have to get the rest of my saniuri." She pointed to the corpse.

Ran'disan kept his head bowed.

"Stay here, then."

After retrieving her blade, Aes'shivar climbed atop her faithful cisthyrn. She held tight to Ran'disan's coat as he bolted across the frozen lake, watching for any dark spots lurking beneath them.

Crying and murmuring filled the air as Aes'shivar and Ran'disan cleared the ice.

Os'icasa'nidas fluttered to Aes'shivar as she dismounted. "Again I wish to thank you. We are in your debt."

"I don't believe in debts," Aes'shivar said, and the three other large Tuladine fluttered to a halt beside her.

"Strange," said one of the Tuladine.

Os'icasa'nidas nodded, trunk bouncing. "I do not want to seem as if I am taking advantage of your philosophy, but do you know the quickest route to Varquilus?"

Varquilus? Aes'shivar raised an eyebrow. Why would a flock of Tuladine head for the Esharian capital?

"I don't remember the way very well," Os'icasa'nidas said. "It has been too long."

"The capital is to the north," Aes'shivar said, pointing in the direction of the city. Varquilus was a two-week journey on foot.

"Could you show us?" another Tuladine asked, voice higher pitched than Os'icasa'nidas. Did that mean Os'icasa'nidas was male?

Aes'shivar nodded. "Of course. But why are you going to Varquilus?"

Each of the larger Tuladine bowed their heads and clasped their hands. Eventually, Os'icasa'nidas spoke. "Invaders came. Human. And lish qui'sha."

She started. *Outlanders? Penetrating the heart of Abodal?* The notion sickened her.

"They came twice," Os'icasa'nidas continued. "At first, we repulsed them. But this time… this time they managed to decimate us. Amid the battle we fled our Roost, taking as many young as we could. The others… Well… we are the last of the Tuladine."

Aes'shivar blinked in disbelief. It could not be a coincidence that the invaders came twice. No, they had deliberately sought the Tuladine and their charges… But to what end? The possibilities sent a shiver down her spine.

Another Tuladine spoke, in a voice deeper than Os'icasa'nidas. "We must inform the Guardians of what transpired."

Aes'shivar nodded. "I will take you to Varquilus."

With that, Aes'shivar pushed past the Tuladine and marched up the snowdrift. As a Warder of the Plains it was her duty to prevent outlanders from penetrating the heart of Abodal. Had she and her fellow Warders become too lax in their duties? No human had stepped foot on Abodal snow in over a thousand years. Now they had come twice, and with the most abominable creatures…

Never again, she vowed. *I will live my life on the plains if I must, but never will I permit an outlander access to this blessed land.*

PART
THREE

Halls
of
Damnation

Amendal · Ildin · Vaem · Faelinia
· Calimir · Morgidian · Edara ·

20

THE RELIQUARY

"Another of my favorite conjurations is the yaeltis. Not only are they fierce, but they are incredibly strong and tower above most creatures wielded by the lesser conjurers of our world."

- From *Colvinar Vrium's Bestiary for Conjurers*, page 97

Despite the vastness of Tardalim's gatehouse, the many footfalls of the expedition did *not* echo off its walls. *They must absorb sound,* Calimir thought, eyeing the ornate architecture. The detailed work on the crystal was beyond impressive. Though he had seen many ancient structures across Kalda, none were as grand as this gatehouse.

And it's just as warm as that cave... He had expected the gatehouse to be just as cold as those Eshári buildings.

. "I wonder who these statues depict," Dardel said.

The crystal statues, dressed in strange clothing, stood as high as the doors. Were they the architects of this place? *Or perhaps the original caretakers of this reliquary...?*

Intrigued, Calimir glanced to Mistress Rudal. She looked as if she wanted to answer Dardel's question.

She is *hiding something from us,* Calimir thought. But why? What was there to hide? *Perhaps the Mindolarnians know more of this place than they let on—* A sudden sense of apprehension knotted Calimir's stomach.

He fought to suppress the worry as the expedition crossed the gatehouse. Another set of towering closed doors stood before them, looking identical to the others, though their engraved markings did not glow.

Mistress Rudal quickened her pace, moving ·ahead of Calimir. She clutched an open scroll, undoubtedly containing those strange words she had spoken. He had only glimpsed the scroll, but the writing upon it was not the Common Tongue. She stopped a few paces from the door and began speaking those strange, sharp words. Calimir reached her as she finished.

As before, the engraved markings on this second set of doors glowed brightly. The doors themselves seemed to shift away, then fly apart. Light—sunlight—flooded into the gatehouse. But how was that possible? They were deep underground.

Shielding his eyes, Calimir studied the colossal doorframe, but there was no sign that there had ever been a door within it—or anything else for that matter. "How is that even possible?"

Mistress Rudal raised a painted eyebrow. "Baffled by the doors?"

Calimir gave the Mindolarnian scholar a hard look. He was about to rebuke the woman when Lieutenant Virain chimed in. "It's a form of transmutative magic," she said, her tone matter-of-fact. "The doors compress upon themselves, then compress within the wall."

Calimir couldn't believe what he was hearing. And, the lieutenant spoke as if it were a common occurrence. "*Within* the walls?"

Mistress Rudal chuckled and stepped forward through the colossal opening. Intrigued chatter rippled through the expedition's ranks: If the structure was this impressive, then the tevisrals were bound to be incredible. Many speculated on the value of such things, and the murmurs rose to a roar of excitement.

Blinking so his eyes would adjust, Calimir followed the Mindolarnian scholar, stepping onto a balcony the width of the gatehouse. He expected to find a chill in the air, but the balcony was just as warm as the gatehouse *and* the steamy grotto. Odd, since the balcony hung along a cliff wall, the northern wall of the gorge.

The balcony was wider than it was deep. Fifty phineals from the doorway, a solid railing—made with those same intricate and sharp designs—rose to shoulder height.

More statues—much smaller than those in the gatehouse—lined the balcony, standing atop thick columns as tall as the railing. But these statues were not humanoid. They were winged creatures of myth and legend.

"Dragons." Calimir's jaw went slack.

"Not quite," said Lieutenant Virain. She joined Calimir, and they walked toward the railing. "These are lesser beings: drakes, wyverns, seracai, and such. I forget the Common names for the other three types…"

Calimir had no idea what any of those were. He studied each of the statues. There were twelve in all, six pairs of breeds, or types, as the lieutenant put it. One pair was unlike the others, having six wings, thinner than those of the other statues. The heads of each pair were different, and he supposed that was how one discerned the different species. Each statue faced the doorway with their mouths gaping, baring sharp crystalline teeth.

Vicious maws, he thought, averting his gaze from the statues. The walls of the gorge stretched high, reaching for a clear blue sky. The illusion that hid the bottom of the gorge must operate in only one direction.

He continued searching the gorge, scanning the far wall for the reliquary.

But there was nothing on the other cliff face.

"Where is it?" Calimir stomped to the railing. Mistress Rudal was speaking that language again, somewhere behind him and to his left. *She must have found a way to extend the bridge… but to where?*

Gripping the rail, Calimir scanned the far wall, then his eyes settled on the reliquary some ten stories below him.

Housed within the cliff face, the crystalline structure looked as tall as the gatehouse but was much, much wider. A sprawling balcony lined the bottommost parts of the reliquary. Most of the details were obscured by distance, but the colossal features were quite visible. A pair of doors—identical to those in the grotto—was aligned with the gatehouse. Fourteen tall alcoves lined the reliquary's sprawling balcony, seven on each side of the massive doors. Crystal statues filled those alcoves, depicting armor clad men and women wielding swords, staffs, and double-bladed fanisars.

Double-bladed fanisars? he mused, leaning on the rail. He had never seen a double-bladed fanisar. Was that a long-lost—?

The rail in his grasp liquefied.

Off balance, Calimir staggered forward. *No!* He struggled to regain his footing. As the liquefied crystal retreated beneath the balcony, he tipped over the edge and toward the gorge's stalagmite-studded floor.

———◦•◦———

Frantic cries for Calimir resounded through the air while a burst of white and pale-blue light filled the gatehouse. Amendal started, shielding his eyes. As the light faded, a frenzied commotion filled the gatehouse. Soldiers pushed their way forward while others kept shouting for Calimir.

"What's going on?" Dugal asked as Ildin's illusion zipped through the gatehouse, flying above the expedition.

"I don't know," Ildin said. Then the commotion ceased. "Calimir looks fine… he's partway down the bridge to the reliquary—hold on."

Amendal and his friends pressed forward, awaiting Ildin's explanation. "It seems Calimir fell. Uh, Vaem's saying something."

"So this is what it's like to be in the back," Amendal said. "Always kept in the dark."

Dugal gave Amendal a sidelong glance.

Faelinia chuckled, eyeing Amendal with a playful gaze. "I guess you should have kept your mages' parasite ahead."

Good, Amendal thought, *the teasing has begun…*

The friends were almost to the second set of doors when Ildin spoke up. "I guess Calimir fell through the balcony's railing. Vaem mentioned something about him falling onto the bridge as it formed. I guess he could have been crushed from the bridge's formation?" Ildin glanced to Dugal, looking for an explanation.

"Transmutative magic doesn't do that," Dugal said. "The bridge would have formed around him. Perhaps it formed another way."

"Magic beyond the Channels of Power?" Morgidian asked, not sounding convinced. "I doubt that."

Ildin cleared his throat. "Anyway, I guess Calimir tumbled down the bridge and everyone thought he had fallen to the gorge's bottom."

Too bad he hadn't, Amendal thought.

"It must have formed fast," Faelinia said. "Can transmutative magic even take shape that quickly?"

Dugal looked puzzled and shook his head.

As they stepped onto the balcony, hushed chatter carried from the few squads waiting to cross the bridge. From what Amendal could tell, the bridge descended at a shallow angle.

"Look at those statues," Morgidian said, pointing to the railing. "Are those dragons?"

Amendal followed the barsionist's point. *Not quite,* he thought, narrowing his eyes. True, the statues were serpentine creatures with wings, but these were other beings that had once roamed the sky—or so legend claimed. He only recognized the drakes and wyverns.

While his friends speculated about the statues, Amendal turned and examined the massive doorway. It was surrounded by reliefs depicting only the heads of the same creatures as the statues. Their mouths were open and led to a hollow space within the gatehouse's wall. *Odd,* he thought. *I wonder what those are for...*

Faelinia called his name, and Amendal spun back to the bridge. Ildin, Dugal, and Morgidian were already descending with the others.

"Beautiful, isn't it?" Faelinia asked, unbuttoning her coat. "Sure is warm in here."

Amendal nodded, glancing upward. "There must be a tevisral of some kind warming this place."

Faelinia stepped onto the bridge. "Are you coming, or are you just going to gawk?"

Chuckling, Amendal joined Faelinia, and they descended the bridge together. The entrance to the reliquary was not what he had expected—especially not with those dreams of his. For one thing, the structure was crystal, but in his dreams, the halls of Tardalim were made of white stone.

So this isn't Tardalim, he thought, narrowing his eyes.

"What's on your mind?" Faelinia asked.

Amendal set his jaw. Did he dare tell her? Yes, she already knew about the dreams. "I don't think this is Tardalim."

"Then what is it?"

"I don't know," Amendal said, sighing. "But whatever this is, it's not what we're looking for."

The crystalline doors beyond the bridge flew apart, revealing a massive corridor that matched the gatehouse in breadth and grandeur. This corridor, however, was much longer—over three times the gatehouse's length. *We're almost there,* Vaem thought, clutching the scroll which contained the words of the Divine Tongue, the same used to unlock the doors of Tardalim. Singing metal filled the air as the expedition drew their weapons. Calimir—the fool—called for the mages to enhance the party once again.

Incantations roared in a discombobulated commotion as Vaem stepped toward the doors. *At last, I will fulfill the emperor's mandate,* she thought, a pleased smile on her lips. Kydol immediately fell in line beside Vaem, matching her stride.

"Mistress Rudal!" Calimir called. "Lieutenant Virain! Wait."

Her smile fading, Vaem glanced over her shoulder to the commander. "We're not in any danger," she said and stepped away.

The incantations grew softer as Vaem proceeded into the crystal corridor. From what she could see, the massive hall emptied into an even larger space. *The entrance must be in there,* she thought.

Behind her, Calimir continued shouting orders for the expedition to begin their search.

"Perhaps you should have told him," Kydol whispered. "I don't see any harm explaining what this place"—she waved her hand—"truly is."

"That would only provoke more questions," Vaem said, glancing to the lieutenant.

Kydol shook her head. "Those questions are inevitable."

I know what I'm doing, Vaem thought, eyeing Kydol. If she revealed the truth to Calimir, he would undoubtedly want to flee. No, it was better this way. All that mattered was breaching Tardalim and fulfilling the emperor's mandate.

Determined, Vaem hurried through the corridor with Kydol a step behind her. Eventually, they entered that vast space. It was a massive ten-story room, with two rows of crystal pillars dividing the space into thirds. Its architecture was not unlike the gatehouse, sharp designs reminiscent of architecture made by the wretched platinum beasts of the Kaldean Alliance. The characters of the Divine Tongue were etched upon the walls, reciting the history of Tardalim and giving a warning for what it held.

"*To be forever entombed,*" Kydol said with a laugh. Those words were part of the warning. "That ends today."

"It better," Vaem muttered. No, she wouldn't fail as Meradis or Coridician had. She settled her gaze, across the vast room, on a large circular dome of glistening white metal—no more than five stories in diameter—protruding from the crystal wall.

Not Tardalim…? Faelinia wondered, studying Amendal. While descending the bridge he had explained the dream from that morning. He had fought a cisthyrn within a white stone hallway, a hallway like the hallways he claimed to have seen in other dreams. Were those dreams of his somehow a glimpse of the future? The possibility worried her.

They reached the end of the bridge, where the stragglers were entering the towering doorway.

"Still crystal," Amendal said, his green eyes fiercely fixed on the corridor beyond the doors, a determined expression on his face. Despite those nightmares he had spoken of, he was still willing to enter Tardalim. Amendal was a brave man. *And quite attractive,* she thought, fighting back a smile.

Oh, what had she done? The thought made her jaw tense.

"I better start conjuring," Amendal said.

"What?" Faelinia spun, struggling to regain her composure.

"Are you all right?" he asked with an amused look in his eye.

What have you done to me? Faelinia took a deep breath before answering. "Yes, I'm fine." Amendal looked as if he didn't believe her. *He's too clever,* she thought. "Why do you need to start conjuring?"

Amendal studied her. "In those dreams I couldn't access either the Visirm Expanse or the Aldinal Plane. Something inside Tardalim prevents conjuration magic from manifesting, although other magics work."

A knot formed in Faelinia's stomach. Perhaps those dreams really were a warning. But if they were, what kinds of things lurked within Tardalim's halls?

An incantation left Amendal's lips, and he stopped short of the massive doorway. Golden light manifested around him, reflecting off the crystal walls. The golden particles wisped behind him, lingering near the bridge.

"Are you going to conjure your creatures here?" she asked.

He nodded and continued his incantation.

"I'll be back then," she said, hurrying down the hall. The rest of the expedition was a good fifty phineals ahead of them, and some were already in a massive room.

Orders from Commander Calimir and other squad leaders carried from the enormous chamber. She soon entered the space, taken aback at its grandeur. It was larger than any room or chamber she had ever seen. Dozens of corridors branched off along either side, each as large as the one leading to the gorge. *Why are these halls so big?*

"Miss Tusara!" the commander called. "Where have you been?"

Taking a deep breath, Faelinia pushed through the ranks and approached Commander Calimir. "Keeping track of Amendal. He's conjuring more creatures."

The commander raised an eyebrow, then looked back into the corridor leading to the entrance. "That man is more trouble than he's worth."

"Why don't I search with him?" Faelinia suggested.

Commander Calimir snorted. "Not like you can keep him on a leash." He looked as if he were considering the suggestion.

"Well?"

"Fine," the commander said, turning away. "Search the corridor to the immediate left of the doors—my left." With that, he spun and shouted more orders.

"Yes, sir," Faelinia muttered and turned away. The other squads had deposited their packs and supplies near the commander. Many were moving across the vast room to the various corridors. The remnants of squads three and four, however, were moving back to the entrance. They had since been combined.

Morgidian noticed Faelinia approaching and waved to her. "Did he put you on guard duty too?" the barsionist asked.

Faelinia shook her head. "No, I said I would keep track of Amendal."

One of the soldiers snorted.

She gave the man a peremptory glare, then turned back to Morgidian. "I figure if anyone is going to keep him reined in, it's me."

Morgidian grinned, nodding once. "Of course, he has his eye set on you."

Faelinia felt her cheeks reddening. What had come over her? *Oh, that big oaf...*

By the time Faelinia reached the entrance, Amendal had already conjured a yaeltis he had captured, as well as a troll—both creatures stood an equal height, over three times taller than Faelinia. Both had six claws on each hand and foot.

The troll, however, was not covered in fur. It looked more reptilian, with dark-green skin that had a moist sheen to it. Trolls were strange creatures, with peculiar snouts. Flabby gray-green skin hung at the sides of their long mouths. When a troll opened its mouth, that skin stretched so the creature could swallow its prey whole. Their gray-green underbellies were stretchy, too. Faelinia had never seen the dreadful feat, but the imagined sight had plagued her dreams as a child.

Another portal formed behind Amendal, barely taller than he. Within seconds, one of the cisthyrn emerged and stepped around the yaeltis.

"Amendal," Faelinia called. "We have an assignment." He didn't answer.

Each member of squad three except Morgidian filed past the conjurations. Three more cisthyrn emerged from the portal, then it collapsed. Amendal took a deep breath, then focused on Faelinia.

"Why don't you leave some of those," Morgidian called, gesturing to the cisthyrn. "I wouldn't mind those alongside me if some monster happens to come tearing from the gatehouse."

"Of course," Amendal said and approached Faelinia, his green eyes fixed on her.

Faelinia's heart fluttered, and her stomach tensed. She found herself biting her lower lip—she never did that!

"You don't have to stare," Amendal said, his lips forming a half-smile.

Morgidian burst into laughter—he sounded almost as raucous as Jaekim. That laugh brought Faelinia back to reality.

Focus, she told herself.

"Now, where are we going?" Amendal asked.

She eyed him from head to toe, then regained her composure. "Follow me."

⸺◦⸺

While Calimir doled out assignments, Vaem and Kydol strode through the enormous crystalline chamber. Vaem fixed her eyes on the white-metal dome nestled within the far wall—the true entrance to Tardalim. The dome was stark against the pale-blue crystal. It was situated an equal distance between the floor and ceiling, making its lowest point two-and-a-half stories above the floor.

The dome's center was plain and smooth until about halfway between the center and the edge. That outer half of the dome was divided into seven rings, each etched with random characters of the Divine Tongue. *Just like a dial,* Vaem thought, eyeing the rings. From what she had learned prior to departing Mindolarn, the rings must be properly aligned in order to access Tardalim.

"So how do we open this thing?" Kydol asked, pointing to the dome now a hundred phineals away.

"One must spin those," Vaem said, pointing to the dial-like rings, "and align them in the proper order."

"And you have the order?" Kydol asked, gesturing to the parchment Vaem held.

Vaem nodded and fixed her eyes on the metallic dome. The characters of the Divine Tongue were lightless, but Vaem supposed they would glow when properly aligned.

Kydol cleared her throat, and Vaem turned to face the lieutenant. "And how do you propose we spin those rings?" Kydol asked. "A conjuration, perhaps?"

"No," Vaem said, turning back to the metallic dome. A small speck of glistening white metal marked the wall below the dome. She knew that glint belonged to the mechanism which allowed one to interact with Tardalim's sealed entrance.

"I see," Kydol said, amused.

It wasn't long before Vaem and Kydol passed beneath the glistening metallic dome. Calimir's shouted orders barely carried to the far end of the massive room. Vaem couldn't tell if the commander was still doling out assignments or giving orders to erect the campsite. The commander had made mention of setting up camp somewhere within the reliquary.

Hopefully it won't take me that long to breach Tardalim, Vaem mused.

The massive metallic dome loomed above Vaem and Kydol, protruding a good twenty phineals from the wall. The metal speck Vaem had seen was actually a miniaturized replica of the dome, down to the minutest detail.

"Exquisite," Kydol said, reaching a gloved hand to the tiny replica.

"Indeed it is," Vaem said, studying the symbols. The characters were a jumbled mess that did not make any sense. When properly aligned they would form words in the Divine Tongue.

"Is it just a single word?" Kydol asked. "That seems too simple a lock for such a notorious place as Tardalim."

Vaem shook her head and unrolled the parchment in her hands. "It's a phrase: Nirda'mas ciralum mi'nias virak'na korshai'ma ma'niri, Vik'sha."

Kydol hummed with amusement, then spun the outer ring. The third, fourth, and seventh rings also spun, readjusting the characters on each of those lines. "A puzzle…" the lieutenant mused. She rotated the second ring and it adjusted the first and fifth rings as well. Kydol let out a growl and stepped back. "Well, that's frustrating!"

Vaem smiled at the remark. *It's just a pattern*, she thought, stifling a chuckle. "This is why I'm here," she said, stepping to the miniature dome. Only a brilliant mind could decipher such a puzzle. She eyed the rings, noting how the other rings had rotated. Of course, she would have to spin each ring to see how it affected the others.

Lips pursed, Vaem spun the third ring, causing the first, fifth, and seventh rings to spin. She continued spinning each of the other rings, memorizing the shift they caused among their counterparts.

"That's easy enough," she said, grinning.

Kydol snorted with derision. "Surely you couldn't have memorized the changes *that* quickly."

Vaem ignored the remark and began rotating the rings to make the first word, "Nirda'mas." She spun the outer ring and reached for the fourth. But before she could spin it each of the others spun on their own, readjusting in a manner that was unlike their original placement.

Did it reset? Vaem wondered.

"Not so easy after all," Kydol snickered.

Vaem gave the woman a cursory glance, then returned her focus to the mechanism. She studied each ring for a moment before spinning the second, third, and fifth rings. The characters for "Nirda'mas" aligned, and a faint hum resonated from the massive dome overhead. Part of a thin groove around the miniature dome became lit with pale-green light, about one-seventh of the mechanism's circumference.

"Good," Vaem said with a smile, then studied the order for the next word. She would have to move the first, fourth, and fifth rings, then the third, and then the seventh. She spun the first and fourth rings, but as she reached for the fifth every ring spun and the section of light around the circumference faded.

No… Vaem stifled a gasp. Had it reset completely?

"I stand vindicated," Kydol said.

Vaem glanced at the lieutenant. Kydol was grinning. *Oh, aren't you a smug one*, Vaem thought, narrowing her eyes. She returned her focus to the mechanism, contemplating its workings. Had it reset because she had taken too long to align the characters?

A timer would make sense, she thought. Taking a deep breath, Vaem spun the rings once again and formed the first word.

Captain Edara played the part of a good soldier, leading his men through the hallway that *murderous bastard* had assigned them to search. *These will be some of the last orders you give*, he vowed.

Footfalls faded as groups filed off, going down other hallways and corridors. Each hall was enormous, oversized far too much for an ordinary man. The hallways all looked the same, like the corridor within the gatehouse, their walls accented with intricately sharp designs and reliefs of serpentine heads. Those heads were all over, and all their mouths were hollow.

Strange, Edara thought. Another group veered off, leaving Edara alone with his sailors.

They had traveled no more than twenty paces when Cluvis leaned close to Edara. "Do you still want to find an inconspicuous weapon?"

The mention of vengeance made Edara's blood boil. *Not yet*, he told himself. Edara studied Cluvis for a moment before answering. "Perhaps. One can never have too many options."

"You know, Captain," Cluvis whispered, his eyes widening with anticipation, "we could find tevisrals that could kill them all. We can make them all pay for the *Giboran*, and claim the treasures of this place as our own."

Several of the sailors started, but settled their gazes on Edara. *Wondering if I'm as consumed by vengeance as Cluvis?* He fought back a grin. Edara liked the idea of claiming the finds of Tardalim for themselves. They would become rich beyond measure. With that wealth, Edara could commission a fleet to return to this godforsaken wasteland and pull the *Giboran* from her watery grave. He could have her back.

"Well, Captain?" Cluvis whispered, leaning in closer. His nose was practically touching Edara's cheek.

"Perhaps, Cluvis." He pulled back. "Perhaps…" He stared at his first mate with determination. Cluvis simply nodded.

Edara continued leading his sailors down the corridor until they reached a towering doorway that rose eight stories above them—like the doorway in the grotto, but only half as wide. *A single door as opposed to a double?*

An empty room lay beyond the doorway. Though the walls were translucent, Edara couldn't see beyond to any adjoining space.

"Nothing?" a sailor asked, confused.

"Let's keep going," another sailor suggested.

Edara pushed away from the doorway and continued down the hall.

They passed other doors much smaller than the last. In fact, they were about the right size for a man. *Odd,* he thought, approaching one of the doors. The crystalline slab was closed tight, lacking a knob and hinges.

"How does this open?" Cluvis asked, examining the door.

"Maybe those words?" a sailor speculated. "Does anyone remember what Vaem was saying?"

Murmured replies of not remembering filled the hall. Cluvis stepped forward, pushing on the slab. The crystalline door didn't move.

Edara set his jaw as Cluvis continued struggling. He looked farther down the hall at the other doors. Pale-blue light shone beside each of them, just above waist height. He glanced back to the door, settling his gaze on a rectangular outline beside it.

Raising an eyebrow, Edara touched the light, and the door vanished. Had it slid? Cluvis stumbled, falling into the room and landing face-first on the floor.

"You could have warned me," Cluvis grunted, pushing himself up.

Edara narrowed his eyes at his first mate. His gaze, however, was drawn back to the room. It looked like a suite of sorts, with elegant crystallized furniture throughout: sofas, chairs, and tables. There were other doorways, each with glowing patches beside them.

A suite? Edara wondered. *Within a reliquary?* That made no sense. He took in his surroundings with a sweeping glance before giving his orders. "Start looking," Edara said. "Bring me anything that could be a weapon." The sailors complied. Several searched the tables and beneath the furniture while others opened the doors. A bedchamber lay beyond one door, and a strange closet beyond another.

"What is this place, really?" He strode to one of the chairs and rested a hand on its back. But what should have been a plush cushion was firm rock. "Who would even sit in that?" he wondered aloud, disgusted.

Setting his jaw, Edara paced through the room. His sailors soon returned, reporting that they had found nothing. Edara and his companions left the suite and continued searching behind the other doors, finding more suites that were exactly like the first. Each was empty except for the crystallized furniture. They had searched twenty of the suites when Edara's frustration began to stoke his anger.

"Why aren't we finding anything?!" He stalked to a table and slammed his fist upon it. A resounding thud filled the room while sharp pain surged up his hand. "Damn it!"

"Perhaps we're not the first to come here," Cluvis said, sounding disappointed.

"Really?" a sailor asked. "How can you assume that, after all we've been through?"

Cluvis glared at the sailor, and the man drew back. Several others began speculating, but Edara ignored them.

Clutching his hand, Edara turned away. The pain only compounded his anger toward that *murderous bastard* and the *heartless whore*. Had this whole expedition been for naught? A complete and utter waste? They had killed *her* and for nothing!

Today is the last day you two draw breath.

Fury rose within Edara, a blinding rage that fueled visions of retribution. When the expedition camped for the night, he would exact his vengeance with that venomous tusk. With it, he would pierce the bastard's gut and slice his throat. Then, when the fool fell to the floor convulsing, Edara would find the heartless whore and slam the tusk between her breasts.

"Yaeltis prefer a cold climate, as their thick fur doesn't shed. You can find them in the far reaches of the world, like the Abodine Wasteland or the Carda Wastes."

- From *Colvinar Vrium's Bestiary for Conjurers*, page 102

The footfalls of conjurations large and small filled the crystal halls that *were not* Tardalim. Except for the conjurations, Amendal and Faelinia were alone. They had passed several other groups, who had gone their own ways, searching other corridors and chambers.

"So, what do you think this place is?" Faelinia asked, her tone playful.

More teasing, Amendal mused. He stared at her for a moment before answering. "A distraction." He glanced to a nearby doorway. It was like the others they had passed, enormous and open. "Something to deter the faint of heart."

"Faint of heart?" Faelinia asked, chuckling. "I don't think the *faint of heart* could make their way here."

Amendal shrugged. "You never know…" That evoked another mirthful outburst, and Faelinia studied him with yearning eyes. *I have you now*, he thought, pleased. What had turned the tide? Had it been the yaeltis, or that strange crystalline creature? *Perhaps both…*

"So, a distraction." Faelinia took in a deep breath. "From what, pray tell, *Mister* Aramien?"

"Who knows…?" Amendal glanced over his shoulder. His menagerie trailed behind him: seven cisthyrn, the two yaeltis, a troll—he wished he had more of those—the four quinta'shals, an earthen giant, and several other earthen conjurations.

What else should I conjure? Amendal wondered. His mind turned to his dreams, recalling the halls of Tardalim—or so the old codger had called them. *If only those corridors were larger.* Faelinia had voiced concern about Amendal's dreams, wondering if they were warnings. He considered the implications and wished he could summon a gangolin. If he were to face certain danger, then a gangolin would prove a fitting means of protection. One of the behemoths might fit in these crystal halls, but not the corridors Amendal had seen in his dreams.

"—you're no fun," Faelinia said.

"What?" Amendal asked, turning from his conjurations.

Faelinia smiled wryly. "You should have been paying attention." She winked and then turned to a nearby doorway. The opening was three stories tall—the only one of its size that Amendal had seen. They had passed other doorways that were seven or eight stories tall, as well as some of human size.

I suppose it won't hurt to look, Amendal thought, following Faelinia. "Wait," he commanded his conjurations, and the footfalls ceased.

The space beyond the doorway was large and empty, like the other exposed rooms he and Faelinia had passed. This room, however, was lined with crystallized racks and shelves, with rows of racks all throughout the room. *Weapon racks?* Amendal wondered. But where were the weapons?

"And what does this look like to you?" Faelinia asked, weaving around a row of empty racks. They looked tall enough to hold fanisars, or channeling staffs—weapons used by mages to focus their magic. A mage wielding a channeling staff could send an arcane orb flying faster than an arrow or a crossbow bolt.

"An armory," Amendal said. "But who knows if it ever held any weapons."

"And here I never pegged you as a skeptic." Faelinia chuckled, moving farther into the supposed armory.

Amendal smiled, pleased. The teasing *had* increased. *Good,* he thought and walked in the direction opposite of Faelinia. "Think about it," he said. "What use would a reliquary have for an armory?"

A laugh left Faelinia's lips. "To store weapons?"

"But *why?*"

Faelinia groaned. She was undoubtedly rolling her eyes.

Amendal let the silence hang, but Ildin's voice soon carried through the doorway. "There you are!"

Amendal peeled around a rack in search of his friend. One of Ildin's illusions hovered within the doorway, taking in the supposed armory in a sweeping glance.

"Have you found anything?" Ildin asked.

"No," Faelinia answered from across the room.

"Neither have we," Ildin said, sounding disappointed. "Nor has Jaekim's group or Fendar's. I wonder if someone else pillaged this place before us…"

"Amendal thinks this place is a distraction," Faelinia shouted.

The illusion perked up, intrigued.

Amendal simply nodded. "The tevisrals are not here," he said matter-of-factly. "What we're seeking lies within those white stone halls."

"White?" Ildin asked. "Like that circle in the far wall of the main room?"

Circle in the main room? Amendal wondered. He hadn't paid much attention to that grand space—he was too busy summoning his conjurations

"Wasn't that circle metallic?" Faelinia asked. "It looked too shiny to be stone."

That has to be it, Amendal thought. Whatever that circle was, it undoubtedly led to the *actual* Tardalim. "Let's go back," Amendal said, stepping toward the doorway.

Soon, Amendal was back in the hall with Ildin's illusion hovering beside him. Faelinia's hurried footfalls carried into the hallway, and soon she too was beside Amendal.

"Defying more orders?" Ildin asked. "At this rate you're going to be *owing* the expedition coin."

"I can pay it," Amendal said, glancing to the illusion, but was drawn to one of those reliefs protruding from the crystalline wall. Amendal and Faelinia had passed many of those reliefs. Each had its mouth open, mouths that were hollow.

But why hollow?

———————⋗•⋖———————

Calimir picked his way around the supplies deposited within the enormous welcoming room of Tardalim. At least, he supposed it was the welcoming room. *But what else could it be?* he wondered, studying the towering pillars. Why had the builders of this reliquary needed to craft a space so large? What purpose did it serve?

"The last of the squads is away," Dardel said, weaving around a cluster of packs.

"Good," Calimir said, still eyeing the pillars. "Have you seen Mistress Rudal or Lieutenant Virain?"

Dardel shook his head. "No, sir."

Calimir compressed his lips, not amused. Where had they gone? Both had kept a fair distance ahead of the expedition, but Calimir had lost track of them once he started doling out assignments.

"Have any of you seen them?" he asked the others—the members of squads one and two. None answered in the affirmative.

Damn you, women, where have you gone off to? First Mister Aramien and now the Mindolarnians. Who else was going to defy his command?

Setting his jaw, Calimir took the enormous room in with a sweeping glance. Light shone from the far end of the room, coming from that metallic dome. "When did that start glowing?"

"I don't know, sir," Hevasir said. "I don't recall it glowing when we first entered."

Neither did Calimir. He had noticed the starkness of the dome, but paid little attention to it. Perhaps that was a mistake. He had made too many of those on this godforsaken expedition.

"Dardel, come with me," Calimir said, stepping away from the supplies. "Hevasir, continue preparing the camp."

Both soldiers answered the command in unison, Dardel joining Calimir, and Hevasir barking his own orders.

Wary but intrigued, Calimir quickened his pace to a near jog. His long-sword clanked against his armor with each step. Dardel was no less noisy. The metal dome across the room had become more luminous than before. Strange symbols—like those he had seen in the gatehouse—glowed a pale-green. There was also a luminous ring around the dome, lining three-quarters of its circumference. Two feminine figures stood beneath the dome, facing the crystalline wall.

"The Mindolarnians," Dardel said.

Calimir nodded. What were they doing? *You* are *holding back,* he thought. But why? And what importance had this dome to the plundering of the reliquary? Calimir's displeasure quickened his stride.

Calimir and Dardel were no more than two hundred phineals away when the light on the metallic dome winked out, followed by an angry cry. *That sounds like Mistress Rudal…*

A moment later, the light shone once again from the symbols upon the dome. The ring of light, however, was only a fraction of what it was—no more than a seventh or eight of the dome's circumference. Why had the light changed?

Mistress Rudal and Lieutenant Virain were focused on a spot in the crystallized wall. The Mindolarnian scholar was fidgeting with something, but Calimir couldn't determine what it was.

He clenched his teeth, readying himself for a conflict with the Mindolarnians.

"Mistress Rudal!"

She answered with an angered grunt. The lieutenant, however, turned to face Calimir and Dardel. She looked rather surprised, perhaps even guilty.

What are you hiding? Calimir wondered, passing beneath the dome. It protruded a good twenty phineals from the wall. More light shone from the dome, and the ring of light around its circumference spread, though not as much as before. The scholar cocked her head toward the lieutenant, whispering something Calimir couldn't quite hear. Calimir glanced to Dardel, but the man shook his head.

"Commander," Lieutenant Virain said, stepping away from the wall. "What can I do for you?" She settled into a straight-backed stance, as if standing at attention.

Oh, don't pull that with me, Calimir thought. "What are you doing?" She glanced to the scholar, but raised her chin. Posturing? That was never a good sign.

"Opening the reliquary's vault," she said.

A vault? Calimir wondered, looking up to the dome. More of the symbols had become lit, and the ring had spread farther. That line of light around the dome was now the same distance as when he had first noticed it.

"Really?" Dardel asked. "A vault was never mentioned in any of our meetings."

Lieutenant Virain didn't reply to the passive accusation. She *was* hiding something.

A tenuous silence hung between them all. The only sounds in the air were the faint scraping of metal, like the churning of a cog, coming from near Mistress Rudal. What was she doing? Calimir sidestepped, narrowing his eyes. The Mindolarnian scholar was standing in front of a metal circle in the wall. Calimir sidestepped again to get a better look. The metal circle looked like a miniature version of the dome overhead.

"Don't interrupt her," the lieutenant warned, glancing up to the dome. "She's on the second-to-last sequence."

"Of what?" Dardel asked.

The Mindolarnian lieutenant didn't answer, but looked back to the dome overhead. A triumphant cheer left Mistress Rudal's lips, and more of those strange symbols became luminous. The ring of light was almost complete.

"Almost there," the scholar muttered, tension in her voice.

Brow raised, Calimir eyed the miniaturized dome in front of Mistress Rudal. Rings that she had not touched were spinning. Was she trying to align those strange symbols? "There!" she exclaimed, jubilant.

A click sounded from that miniature dome. The scholar turned from the crystal wall, smiling. "Do you really think they would keep the tevisrals lying about in plain sight?"

"Do you think omitting details was wise?" Dardel asked.

Mistress Rudal glanced at Dardel, her lips twisted in a snarl but then focused on Calimir. "I suggest you recall the others."

Calimir studied her for a moment, then focused on the dome. Each of the symbols upon its surface was glowing, and that ring of light now wrapped around its entire circumference. A low hum resonated from the glistening metal, and then grooves appeared within the dome's smooth sections, swirling from its apex to the circumference. In a flash of movement, the dome became a circular opening, wreathed only by that ring of light.

"Looks like we'll need barsion ramps," said Lieutenant Virain. "Best we—"

A high-pitched screech filled the room, followed by the rushing of water.

Startled by a high-pitch screech, Morgidian frantically searched the gorge. The roar of gushing water muffled the frazzled questions of squad three while a blinding white flash erupted from the gatehouse. Morgidian shielded his eyes while the gushing water sound grew louder. Something pressed against his boot—something wet and cold.

Flowing water? Morgidian wondered, blinking. But what happened to the barsion he had—*It's gone,* he thought. He could no longer sense any of the barriers he had put on himself or the rest of squad three.

Still blinking, Morgidian struggled to see through the spots plaguing his vision. From what little he could see, the ground was shifting. *How was that possible...?*

"Was that a dispel?" one of the soldiers asked.

"Where did those beasts go?" another asked, his question followed by splashing noises.

Morgidian spun, spraying water as he turned to where Amendal had left his conjured cisthyrns, but the wolf-like creatures were nowhere to be found. If that light had been a dispel the creatures would have been roaming aimlessly. A dispel wouldn't have caused them to vanish.

"What happened to the bridge?" a soldier cried.

A commotion filled the air as Morgidian glanced to where the bridge *should have* been. It, like the conjurations, was gone.

The last of the spots faded, and Morgidian focused on the floor. Flowing water covered the balcony, surging toward the empty spot in the railing where the bridge had stood. But where was the water coming from? Gushing water roared all around, even from the crystal hallway beyond the doors.

Water flowed down the walls in thick streams. Morgidian followed their course to the reliefs of those draconic heads. Every single relief on the balcony and within the hallway was spewing water.

Morgidian's eyes widened in horror. Had someone triggered a trap?

Shaking off his fears, Morgidian uttered an incantation to muster his inverted barsion. Hopefully he could stop up the holes before there was too much flooding. He was partway through the incantation, but no barsion was manifesting. A spike of dread pierced his heart, but Morgidian kept uttering the incantation. He finished, but no barsion formed.

"How...?" he muttered with a gasp. Had that white flash somehow prevented magic from manifesting within the gorge? Besides that prison castle in the Kingdom of Los, he had never heard of an area where one could not access the Channels of Power. *I should warn the others,* he thought. But what good would that do? Without the bridge, they would be trapped within this crystal tomb.

———◦———

Water splashed around Amendal, stirred by his conjurations' footsteps. The roar of falling water filled the crystalline hall from every direction. Each of those hollow-mouthed reliefs gushed water that flowed down the walls and pooled all across the enormous hallway. After only a matter of seconds the water had already reached above the soles of Amendal's boots.

Never a dull moment on this trip, he thought, shaking his head. First the nactili, then the perils of the crystal caverns, and now *this*. Ildin and Faelinia were debating the cause of the flooding, but Amendal ignored them. The flooding was the least of their concerns. What worried him more was the dismissal of his conjurations on the balcony. Amendal had sensed a flash of light, then nothing. Was it a dispel or something else?

YOU NEED TO HURRY, a voice said, as if whispered on the wind. FINISH CONJURING YOUR FORCES.

"What?" Amendal started, looking about.

"Not paying attention?" Ildin asked, a twinge of sarcasm in his voice.

Amendal glanced to his friend's illusion. "Didn't either of you hear that?" Ildin shook his head.

"A premonition, Amendal?" Faelinia asked, narrowing her eyes thoughtfully.

"I don't know…" Amendal said, setting his jaw. That voice sounded familiar. Like that of the old codger from his dreams. But he was only a figment of Amendal's imagination… wasn't he? *Perhaps I am going mad…*

"Well, I'm going ahead," Ildin said. The illusion zipped down the hall and disappeared.

"Where is he going?" Amendal asked.

"To see where the water is coming from," Faelinia replied, pointing to the ground.

Amendal glanced to his feet. Though there were constant ripples in the water a steady-but-slow current flowed toward the main room.

"It has to be going somewhere," Faelinia said warily. "Maybe the gorge…" She studied Amendal for a moment. "What did you hear?"

"A behest… To keep conjuring."

"Then you'd best obey." Then Faelinia began an incantation, mustering her own illusory magic.

Ildin's illusion zipped around a corner, entering the enormous space with the pillars and the metal dome. The dome, however, was gone and in its place a hole. *What happened?* Ildin turned his attention back to the water, which flowed toward the corridor leading to the gorge.

Why out there? he wondered, then sent the illusion flying toward the gatehouse. Waterfalls lined the corridor's walls, each flowing from those dragon-headed reliefs. It was a beautiful sight, but a treacherous one, too.

As the illusion approached the entrance, Ildin fixed his vision beyond the open doors. The water was flowing across the balcony and toward a hole where the bridge *should* have been.

"Where did it go?" he muttered.

"Where did *what* go?" asked a soldier from squad thirteen. Ildin had been reassigned to that squad for helping Amendal.

Ildin didn't reply but kept his illusion flying. The replica of himself flew through the doorway, but as it cleared the threshold, it… vanished.

Like that blackness… Ildin thought, recalling the abysmal veil barring them from accessing the gatehouse from atop the gorge. That blackness had simply dismissed Ildin's illusion, like a dispel.

"Care to enlighten us, Ildin?" asked the squad leader, a stout woman named Naedra.

Ildin spread his hands. "The bridge is gone," he said. "And the water is flowing toward the gorge."

"What does that mean?" a soldier asked.

Naedra gave the man an impatient glance. "That means we have time before we drown."

"We have to get out of here!" cried another soldier.

"I don't see how…" Ildin muttered, setting his jaw.

"What about those barsionists?" the first soldier asked. "Can't they make a ramp to the gatehouse?"

"Or stop up the water!" another cried.

Ildin glanced to the first man and pursed his lips. *I doubt that will work,* he thought. The others voiced their own concerns about the situation. If illusions were torn apart, barsion probably wouldn't last long either. And judging by the vastness of the halls and the number of reliefs, the barsionists would have quite the time stopping the water…

"Quit whining," Naedra barked. "Let's get back to Calimir. The commander will see us through this."

22

THE RISING FLOOD

"If you decide to hunt for yaeltis, I would suggest you search the Abodine Wasteland. Too many expeditions have gone missing in Carda. Although, I have heard rumors of conjurers finding yaeltis near the northern foothills of the Black Mountains."

- From *Colvinar Vrium's Bestiary for Conjurers*, page 103

The pooling water continued to rise in the crystal halls as Amendal uttered incantation after incantation. He had since conjured each of the cisthyrn he had lost. Whatever had washed across the gorge was not an ordinary dispel. It had sent the cisthyrns back to the Aldinal Plane, thus allowing Amendal to re-summon them.

"The water is flowing to the gorge," Faelinia said, her gaze fixed ahead. She had since created an illusion of herself and sent it to the vast room. "And that metal dome is gone…"

Amendal raised an eyebrow at Faelinia but continued with his incantation. Golden light wisped through the air, coalescing into a three-story portal several hundred phineals ahead of them.

"There's a hole in its place," she said, squinting. "I'm going to take a look."

The conjuration portal formed a moment later, and an earthen giant emerged from the mystical vortex, splashing water as it stepped into the corridor.

"Oh, Amendal…" Faelinia said with a gasp. "That hole… its walls are stone! *White* stone."

A knot formed in Amendal's stomach, though he didn't know why. After all, he *had* expected that metallic circle to lead to the actual Tardalim. *Perhaps it's the implications,* he thought, his mind turning to that shadowy figure that had chased him through Tardalim's halls. His stomach clenched at the thought. *Come on, Amendal,* he told himself, *you've faced gangolins and lived... surely this thing can't be worse.*

Hurried splashing filled the crystal corridor, drawing Amendal from his reverie. Two squads were struggling to run down an adjoining hall. Their leaders shouted at him and Faelinia, demanding answers from them.

"Vaem is at that hole in the wall," Faelinia said to Amendal, her jaw tensing.

"Are you deaf?!" a squad leader shouted, arriving beside the pack of conjured cisthyrn.

Amendal turned to the man. "We're in the dark just like you."

The squad leader swore and muttered to himself. Both squads hurried around the conjurations, passing Amendal and Faelinia.

"Calimir is shouting orders," Faelinia said, staring ahead.

Maybe I should conjure a gosset, Amendal thought.

A GOOD CHOICE, said that voice, the same from earlier. Was it really the voice from the nightmare?

Amendal glanced over his shoulder. Where was that voice coming from? *I'm losing it...* Grumbling, Amendal uttered an incantation, conjuring a gosset from the Aldinal Plane. Golden light wisped through the air, gathering near the earthen giant that was still ahead of him and Faelinia.

"He's recalling Morgidian's squad," Faelinia said. "And he wants the soldiers to find all the illusionists, so we can get everyone back to that room. It looks like we're going into that hole."

The portal formed and the conjured gosset sped through the air. "Of course we are," Amendal said matter-of-factly.

"I'm going to warn the others in this hall," she said, stopping. "Go on without me."

Amendal stopped as well, but kept his conjurations moving forward. "Then who's going to keep an eye on me?" he asked, grinning. "Someone has to rein in this reckless and dangerous conjurer."

Faelinia eyed Amendal with that yearning gaze. "Just go... I'll catch up." She spun and bounded back down the hall, white magic clustering about her.

What a woman, he thought, watching as Faelinia's enhancing magic surged within her, quickening her dash.

⊃•⊂

Calimir cursed furiously. The expedition's supplies were drenched. Small bags and loose items were floating away from the main cluster of supplies. Hevasir and several others were struggling to fetch the wandering items as they floated toward the entry corridor.

What was that woman thinking? He shook his head, stifling a growl. *She should have told me about that damned vault.*

Muttering another curse, Calimir grabbed his wet pack and hefted it onto his shoulders. Splashing footfalls and shouts carried into the enormous room from several corridors. Dardel ran from the hall leading to the gorge with squad three trailing behind him.

"Commander!" Dardel shouted. "The bridge is gone!"

"What?!" Calimir demanded. A bird—a gosset from what he glimpsed— flew from a nearby corridor. Calimir, however, paid little attention to it.

"It just vanished!" a soldier cried. "After that flash of light."

A dispel?

"And the gorge is partly full," said the squad's barsionist, Mister Shival. "I tried mustering my barsion, but I couldn't."

Calimir tensed. *That doesn't bode well,* he thought, turning to face the hole leading to the vault. It was only a few hundred phineals long. Vaem had claimed they would be safe within it. Calimir didn't see how, though, not with the water continuing to rise. Even if they could get everyone within the vault and shut its door, Tardalim would be flooded and they would have no way to escape.

"That's not the worst of it," Dardel said. "The doors to the gatehouse are closed, too. We're trapped."

"What about Amendal's crystal?" Mister Shival asked.

Calimir shook his head. Mister Aramien's rogulin was not large enough to whisk away the entire expedition. "No," he said, turning back to Dardel and the others. "We couldn't take everyone."

More splashing and hasty footfalls echoed into the enormous space. Squads seven and nine bounded from the corridor they had searched, followed by one of the earthen behemoths.

"Commander," Dardel asked. "What do you want to do?"

Calimir considered their predicament as the other squads approached. "We'll take refuge in the vault," Calimir said. "Mister Shival, make us a ramp. The rest of you, start ferrying as many supplies as you can."

⸻ ◦ ⸻

Amendal splashed his way into the enormous welcoming room. *So, we're trapped,* he thought. Well, not entirely. *I could still teleport away.* But then he would be dooming his friends. *And everyone else...* He shook his head. No, he couldn't do that.

The two squads that had passed Amendal were grabbing the expedition's supplies and carrying them across the enormous room. Hevasir and several others were following Morgidian, who was glowing with a brilliant blue aura.

Guess I better help, Amendal thought, then sent a command for his conjurations to move the supplies. All but the cisthyrns would be helpful. While the quinta'shals, yaeltis, troll, and elementals grabbed the supplies, several illusions flew into the massive space. Fendar's likeness was among them, zipping toward Calimir and the others.

Amendal set his jaw then uttered an incantation to conjure another earthen giant. The golden portal formed no more than a few paces ahead of him. Violent splashing echoed from the hall behind him as the conjuration emerged from the Aldinal Plane.

"How many more are you going to conjure?" Ildin shouted.

Amendal glanced over his shoulder. The illusionist darted from the rest of his squad, running toward Amendal.

"As many as I can," Amendal said. He could feel his concentration waning. He was near his limit.

"Do you want me to take control of any?" Ildin asked.

Take control? Amendal considered the offer. "That's a good idea," he said. "I'll have you enthrall a giant and some of those lesser elementals—once they get back from dropping off supplies."

Vaem smiled as the burly barsionist finished his incantation. His barsion ramp shot from the ground, bridging the flooded floor and connecting with Tardalim's circular gate.

At last, I will fulfill the emperor's mandate, she thought, sloshing her way to the base of the barsion ramp. Her trousers were drenched and her boots sodden. As she stepped onto the ramp, several illusions flew toward Calimir. The commander gave them orders to find the other squads. Each illusion flew off to different corridors, passing several squads that were sloshing through water.

Kydol joined Vaem, and the two of them ascended the ramp together.

"Shouldn't we wait for them?" Kydol whispered.

Vaem shook her head. "We'll be safe in the antechamber. The next set of doors can only be opened from the outside."

Kydol gazed warily at Vaem. What was her problem? Did she actually fear what lay waiting in Tardalim?

The water had risen halfway up Amendal's shins when he finished conjuring his fifth earthen giant. The flood seemed to be rising faster with each passing moment. Ildin had taken control of three giants, as well as eight of the smaller earthen conjurations.

"You know, you should have summoned magma elementals," Ildin said, a tinge of sarcasm in his voice. "Maybe we could turn all this water to steam."

"Do you really think that would work?" Amendal asked, not amused. The magma elementals could definitely evaporate some of the water, but that probably wouldn't slow the flooding.

Ildin chuckled, then uttered another enthralling incantation.

Amendal shook his head. The splashing and sloshing of footfalls filled the room as more of the expedition frantically returned from their searching. Some pressed toward the barsion ramp Morgidian had created, while others struggled toward the remaining supplies. Most of the packs were practically under water. Amendal had ferried quite a few supplies, dropping them off at the barsion ramp.

"Where is she?" Amendal muttered, searching for Faelinia among those that had returned. Nearly two-thirds of the expedition was in the enormous room. *She better not drown,* he thought. How cruel would it be to finally win her over, only to lose her to a flood? A pang of sorrow pierced Amendal's heart.

Sorrow? he wondered. Never before had he been sorrowful over a woman. *Well, isn't that interesting…* Pushing his worries aside, Amendal uttered an incantation to summon another earthen giant. As the portal formed, one of Fendar's illusions flew toward Amendal.

"That's smart!" shouted Fendar through his illusion. He had undoubtedly seen what Ildin was doing. "Do you want another to help?"

Amendal nodded amid his incantation—there was no time to reply verbally. Before the earthen giant emerged from its portal, Fendar and Scialas were beside Amendal.

"That's a great tactic," Scialas said. "Those giants can carry so much!"

Fendar turned to Scialas, his expression wary. "You better hurry into that vault."

"I'm staying," Scialas said, shaking her head and biting her lip. "I'm not leaving my friends."

"Is that all I am to you?" Fendar asked, his tone playful. He opened his mouth to speak, but before he could say more, Scialas leaned in and kissed him. She shot Amendal a glance, but returned her focus to Fendar.

Soon after, the earthen giant emerged, spraying water as it stepped onto the flooded floor.

"All yours, Fendar," Amendal said, searching the vast room once again. Several more squads had returned, but Faelinia was not among them. Fendar uttered an incantation amid Amendal's searching, mustering his enthralling magic. Amendal kept his hold on the conjuration until Fendar was nearly finished.

The earthen giant spun, but soon stilled under Fendar's enthralling grasp. The illusionist immediately sent the conjuration to the supplies, where it hefted the waterlogged packs and bags into one of its enormous earthen hands. There weren't many supplies left.

We should have them cleared in another trip, Amendal thought. He closed his eyes, focusing on his conjurations. The human-sized elementals were struggling to walk through the flood—the water had already risen to the creatures' knees. Amendal opened his eyes, glancing to his legs. The water was creeping up his thigh.

Best I send the smaller ones to the ramp, he thought. *Go!* he commanded the cisthyrns, quinta'shals and smaller elementals. The two yaeltis and the troll could still be useful. "We should ride them back," he whispered.

"Huh?" Ildin asked.

Amendal turned to his friend. "My larger conjurations can wade through this water faster than we can. Once the supplies are ferried, we should ride the elementals and the yaeltis to Morgi's ramp."

Ildin looked to his feet, lifting his right knee to his chest. His boot barely cleared the water. "Well, look at that..."

As the two illusionists ferried more supplies, Amendal scanned the flooding chamber once again. *Where are you, Faelinia?* Worry filled his heart once again as Amendal uttered another incantation.

Steam rose around Faelinia as she ran, a result of the flooding waters striking her flaming barsion. Her magic managed to push the waters aside, allowing her dry ground to run upon. "This way!" she shouted, glancing over her shoulder to the members of squad seventeen. Each was shielded with flaming barsions like Faelinia.

Her barsion began to weaken as she rounded a corner, entering one of the halls connecting to that main room. *I'll have to recast it,* she thought, passing beneath an illusion of herself hovering in the air. She had set several illusions as markers for those stragglers who had explored the left corridors. Luckily, she managed to find most of the squads that had not reunited with the main group. Prior to her searching, Faelinia had sent an illusion to Commander Calimir to discover where he had sent each of the squads.

"We're almost there!" The flames around her flickered, a result of the barsion weakening from the water's pressure. The flood had risen to her upper thigh. *I waited too long,* she thought, then swiftly uttered an incantation to muster more of her flaming barrier.

Red and orange magic swirled around her hands while her barsion continued to flicker. Faelinia was nearly finished with the incantation when her flaming barsion shattered. She tried to stop but the water surged through the void that had been her barsion, crashing around her and tripping her. Still uttering her incantation, Faelinia fell face-first into the flood. She instinctively shut her mouth as water surrounded her, the involuntary act interrupting her incantation.

No! she groaned inwardly, throwing her arms forward. Water seeped into her nostrils, choking her. Now completely submerged, Faelinia struggled to break the surface. Her hands eventually met crystal, and she swung her legs forward. Once her feet met the floor, she managed to stand.

The members of squad seventeen passed her as she broke the water's surface.

"Are you all right?" the squad leader asked.

Faelinia nodded. "Go!" She pointed down the hall. "The main room is straight ahead."

Squad seventeen continued down the hall as Faelinia steadied herself. *That was reckless,* she thought. *I probably should have erected two barriers instead of one.* Wringing out her hair, Faelinia began mustering her flaming barsion once again.

The last of the supplies were placed on Morgidian's barsion ramp as Amendal's eighth earthen giant emerged from its portal. *One more,* he thought. Fendar had laid claim on another conjuration while Ildin maintained control over the three he had initially enthralled.

"Let's go!" Ildin called, swimming to the lowered hand of an earthen giant. The water had since risen above waist height. Like Ildin, those that had more recently returned were swimming through the enormous room rather than wading through it.

Amendal turned about while Fendar and Scialas followed Ildin to the conjuration.

Where are you? Amendal wondered, searching once more for Faelinia.

Ildin shouted for him to hurry, but Amendal kept looking. "Amendal, come on!"

Only a few groups were still left in the enormous room. Most had already ascended Morgidian's ramp and entered Tardalim's actual entrance. The entrance, however, was not natural. Those who entered the five-story circular hole were forced to walk along its side and then its ceiling in a path that was like a corkscrew. *So bizarre,* Amendal thought. It was as if those who traversed the entrance were *pulled* to the walls and ceiling.

"Amendal!" Scialas cried. "Hurry!"

Shaking off his quandary, Amendal turned to his friends. "I'm going to find Faelinia."

Ildin's face tensed.

"We'll use illusions to find her," Fendar called. "Come on!"

With that, the earthen giant carrying Amendal's friends stepped away.

I'm not going to leave her, Amendal thought.

A NOBLE NOTION, the familiar voice said.

"You again…" Amendal grunted and narrowed his eyes, but was drawn to several men swimming from a corridor opposite him. They looked like the sailors from the *Giboran.* "I better get to higher ground."

Amendal sent a mental command to his nearest earthen giant, and the conjuration lowered its hand in front of its master. He waded toward the lowered hand and climbed atop it. At Amendal's mental command, the conjuration lifted him. Water dripped from Amendal's robes, pattering against the clumps of dirt and rock.

Ildin and the others were halfway across the vast room, as were the swimming sailors. There were, however, two men wading through the corridor from which the sailors had come.

Why aren't they swimming? Amendal wondered. He narrowed his eyes, straining to identify the two stragglers. They were none other than Captain Edara and his first mate. The captain was clutching his coat and holding it above the water.

"He doesn't want to get his coat wet?" Amendal wondered aloud, chuckling. *Go,* he commanded an earthen giant and the conjuration stepped toward the wading captain.

"Now to find Faelinia," he whispered. He could use gossets to fly through the corridors. There were twenty-one halls on each side of the enormous room. In addition to the one he had already conjured, Amendal would have to summon at least—

FOCUS ON THE ELEMENTALS, that voice said with a rebuking tone. That did sound like the codger... *SHE IS COMING.*

"Huh?"

A sudden urge pulled Amendal's gaze to a corridor across the vast welcoming room. Steam billowed from the hallway, filling the air between the pillars and the crystal walls. A moment later, several spheres of red and orange sped through the water.

Flaming barsion bubbles...?

The steam filled the top half of the room, partially obscuring Tardalim's entrance. A total of ten flaming spheres sped from the corridor toward the ramp. But why just ten? If Faelinia were with that squad there should have been eleven.

HURRY! that voice urged.

"Oh, shut up!" Amendal snapped. He reached out to his conjured gosset, which was resting on Morgidian's ramp. *Fly!*

The conjured bird obeyed, flapping through the steam. Amendal forced it to fly lower, and the bird skimmed above the water before disappearing into the corridor.

Through the conjuration's eyes, Amendal saw more steam nearly a grand phineal down the hall. *Is that her?* A lone sphere of flame was beneath the steam, speeding toward the gosset.

YES! NOW CONJURE! That voice shouted. YOU'RE RUNNING OUT OF TIME!

Amendal set his jaw and ignored the voice. The gap between the conjuration and sphere closed. A feminine silhouette appeared within the flaming barsion, her features obscured.

"Amendal!" Faelinia's voice reached the conjuration's ears. "Is that you?!"

A whoop left Amendal's lips and he threw a fist into the air. She *was* okay.

HURRY, YOU FOOL!

"Geeze... what's your problem?" he asked, then started. *Am I really arguing with a voice in my head?*

The conjured bird passed Faelinia, then flew around her. *Stay with her,* Amendal commanded, then shifted his focus. The earthen giant he sent after the captain had since rescued both Edara and his first mate and was halfway to Morgidian's ramp.

"All right..." Amendal eyed the flooded floor at the base of the ramp. "Time to appease the madness..." Before uttering the incantation to open a portal to the Aldinal Plane, Amendal commanded each of his remaining conjurations—the giants, the two yaeltis, and the troll—to move up the ramp and follow the rest of the expedition.

Golden light coalesced around Amendal, then shot across the room. As the portal grew in size, Faelinia ran around it, dismissing her flaming barrier once she was clear of the water. She ran to Tardalim's entrance, but spun. She lifted a hand toward the conjured gosset and Amendal directed the bird to perch upon her arm.

"Hurry, Amendal," she whispered to the conjuration.

The two yaeltis and the troll ascended the ramp next, then bounded past Faelinia. One of the earthen giants was right behind them.

Amid his conjuring, Amendal could sense the strange redirection of *down* as the conjurations moved through Tardalim's circular entrance. The portal coalesced just as the earthen giant carrying Edara reached the ramp.

Run! Amendal commanded, and the earthen giant bolted around the portal, narrowly evading the emerging conjuration.

Go! Amendal urged the emerging earthen giant. The conjuration lumbered from the portal, stepping on Morgidian's barsion. As the earthen giant took another step, the barsion flickered.

"Great..." Amendal shook his head.

NOW FOR YOU TO RUN! The voice shouted. *GO, AMENDAL!*

"No arguing with that," he said, then commanded his conjuration to cradle him while it bolted into a run. He lay on its palm, his feet against the earthen fingers. The ramp was a good two hundred phineals away.

Faelinia had noticed the flicker and spun, running after the conjuration carrying the captain.

"Come on, Morgi..." Amendal groaned. "Hold it a little longer."

The recently summoned conjuration bounded up the flickering ramp, reaching Tardalim's entrance within seconds. But that dash had weakened the barsion further, and some spots looked thin.

It's not going to hold, Amendal thought. If he ran his last conjuration atop the ramp it would undoubtedly shatter. *To the right,* he commanded, focusing on the flooded floor beside the circular entrance.

The conjuration carrying Amendal obeyed, narrowly missing the flickering barsion. It bounded alongside the ramp, running straight for the crystal wall. Through his mental bond, Amendal maneuvered the conjuration's arm, tightening the cradling grip while positioning the earthen limb above the ramp.

THAT'S RECKLESS, the voice said, snickering.

Amendal adjusted the conjuration's palm to face the entrance while bracing himself. *Run into the wall,* he commanded, leaning against the conjuration's palm. Just as the earthen giant collided with the crystal wall, Amendal splayed the conjuration's fingers. The collision sent Amendal flying through the circular entrance.

He felt the pull of *down* to his left, then fell *sideways.* Amendal landed on his left shoulder, tumbled, but soon came to a stop.

"Amendal!" Faelinia called, her tone wary.

Well, that was fun... Amendal pushed himself to his feet. He turned back to the vast crystalline room and started. That enormous welcoming room was *sideways,* with the flooding floor to his left and the ceiling to his right. But how was that possible? But he had fallen to his left...

Amendal shook his head in disbelief.

"Are you all right?" Faelinia asked, joining Amendal.

Still confused, Amendal turned to Faelinia, then pointed back to the sideways room.

"I don't know," Faelinia said, shaking her head. "I can't explain it. Come on." She tugged at Amendal and he reluctantly followed her. He kept looking back to the enormous room. With each step it looked as if that vast space was *rotating.*

YOUR CONJURATION! the voice cried.

"Oh... right," Amendal muttered. He had nearly forgotten about his earthen giant. *Get in here,* he sent the command. The earthen giant pulled itself atop the barsion ramp, then climbed into Tardalim's circular entrance. For a moment, the conjuration looked as if it were walking on the ceiling, then the wall, all while Tardalim's crystalline entry was *rotating.*

Amendal and Faelinia walked almost half a grand phineal before the corkscrew path became an abrupt curve. The path ended on a landing, where a wide but shallow flight of steps descended into a white rectangular chamber.

It was made of polished white stone identical to that in Amendal's dreams, rising four stories and as wide as it was tall—twenty men could walk abreast from wall to wall. From what Amendal could tell, the chamber was about two hundred phineals long, ending at a pair of double doors. Ornate stonework lined the edges of the space, along the floor and ceiling, crafted with intricately sharp designs similar to what was in the gatehouse. Pillars were recessed partway into the walls, equally spaced a hundred phineals throughout the chamber. Glowing spheres lined each pillar, brightly illuminating the large space.

The entire expedition—and Amendal's conjurations—were cramped together, not far from the lowest step of the wide staircase. Almost everyone was sorting through the supplies and wringing out what they could.

"Come on," Faelinia said, descending the shallow staircase.

Amendal, however, stopped at the highest step. *Perhaps I am seeing the future...* Swallowing hard, he looked around. The part of the chamber behind him was semicircular and wide enough to fit thirty men abreast. A hole marked its floor about the same size as Tardalim's entrance. A narrow walkway lined the hole, connected to the shallow staircase.

He reached out to the earthen giant behind him. But the conjuration was actually *below* him.

Confused, Amendal crept to the edge of the hole and looked down. The hole *was* the circular entrance. What was horizontal in the crystalline halls was now vertical. From his perspective, the vast crystalline entry room was a deep shaft beneath his feet.

"That doesn't make any sense..." He stared down into the hole, watching as the water level moved *across* the circular opening. The sight made his head hurt.

Soon, the last earthen giant emerged from the corkscrew path and marched ahead of Amendal, skipping the staircase entirely.

A chaotic commotion carried through the air, but Amendal ignored it. He was too preoccupied by the abrupt shift in perspective.

YOU SHOULDN'T FRET ABOUT SOMETHING SO TRIVIAL, the voice said.

"You call *that* trivial?" Amendal pointed past his feet, blinking in disbelief.

Ildin called for Amendal, repeating his name over and over. Amendal, however, didn't reply. "What are you staring at?" Ildin demanded.

Amendal pointed to the hole as Ildin came beside him.

"By all that's magical!" the illusionist swore with a gasp. "How is that possible?"

He and Ildin watched the water spread across the hole beneath them. Before long the waters completely covered the hole. Did that mean those crystal halls were submerged? If so, how would they escape Tardalim? According to his dreams he couldn't use conjuration magic...

"Now what?" Ildin whispered.

Amendal turned from the hole, eyeing the white stone walls. *Here goes nothing,* he thought, and began uttering a simple incantation to access the Aldinal Plane. Amendal was partway through the incantation, but no conjuration magic had manifested. The last of the incantation left his lips, but a portal did not form.

Ildin's face contorted with fear. "That doesn't bode well..."

23

LIMBO

"Yaeltis undergo a hibernation period in the warmer months, so the best time to begin your search is around late spring or early summer. And be wary of a yaeltis who awakens early from its hibernation."

- From *Colvinar Vrium's Bestiary for Conjurers*, page 108

Amendal pursed his lips and eyed his hands. The utter lack of conjuration magic shouldn't have surprised him, but it did. *So, we really are in Tardalim,* he thought.

"Are you okay?" Ildin asked.

Setting his jaw, Amendal turned to his friend. "Cast a spell. Anything."

Ildin ran a hand through his blonde hair, then after a moment, he uttered an illusory incantation. White light coalesced in front of him, becoming a hawk. "Well, that worked," he said. "Why didn't your portal open?"

"I don't know." Sighing, Amendal stepped away from the hole. "Something about this place prevents conjuration magic from working. But not other magics."

"Strange…" Ildin murmured.

The two of them stood on the top step of the shallow-but-wide staircase. *My resources are limited,* Amendal thought. He had only the conjurations he had brought with him. He would have to be careful. He couldn't sacrifice any of them, as he had in the battle with the yaeltis.

"I have a bad feeling about this," Ildin said.

Amendal nodded and stared at the enormous double doors across the chamber. Only some of the symbols on the door were glowing. *What is it with these enormous doors?* Amendal wondered. Why would the Eshari—or whoever built this place—need such colossal doors?

"Conjurer!"

Drawn from his reverie, Amendal turned to the long-bearded Captain

Edara and his first mate, who walked up the steps and stopped an arm's length away from Amendal. "Thank you," the captain said. "I appreciate your aid back there." He gestured to the hole from which they'd emerged after escaping the flooding chamber.

"Of course." Amendal bowed his head respectfully. "But why weren't you swimming?"

Captain Edara stared at Amendal with stony eyes. The first mate was equally unresponsive.

What's their problem?

"I just wanted to thank you," Captain Edara said, then turned around. He and his first mate descended the steps, mingling with the other sailors.

"Well then…" Ildin said. "That's the most awkward show of gratitude I've ever seen."

Amendal grunted. "No kidding…"

"Come on." Ildin rested a hand on Amendal's shoulder. "Why don't we see if you can join my squad?"

———————⊃•⊂———————

Faelinia spun, searching for Amendal. *Where are—?* Amendal was still at the hole, talking with Ildin. Captain Edara and his first mate, Cluvis, were descending the stairs. *Undoubtedly thanking Amendal.*

Despite what Faelinia had assumed, Edara looked rather perturbed, probably still upset about his ship. Edara and his crew had been rather distant the entire trek across the wasteland, which wasn't surprising, she supposed.

Turning back around, Faelinia picked her way through the crowded chamber. She searched among the squads and found every one of her friends. *I'm glad they made it,* she thought, sighing in relief. Had everyone managed to escape the flood?

She continued toward squads one and two, who were gathered near the doors. Commander Calimir stood beside Vaem, who was kneeling on the floor. The Mindolarnian scholar was looking at something on the ground.

"And how long will this take?" Calimir asked, his lips compressed into a thin line.

"Patience…" Vaem said beneath her breath.

Now that she was closer, Faelinia could see what Vaem was doing. The Mindolarnian scholar was touching several strange symbols atop a shallow dome. Each of the symbols was arranged in a seven-tiered diagram the likes of which Faelinia had never seen. *Is that some kind of ancient language?*

"Miss Tusara!" Faelinia looked up and quickened her pace to Commander Calimir.

"Yes, Commander?" she asked.

"You did well out there," Calimir said, pointing across the hall. "I'm impressed. If only every other mage were like you." Was that a jab at

Amendal?

A twinge of anger forced Faelinia's lips to purse, but she shook aside the emotion. *What have you done to me, Amendal?* she wondered, struggling to regain her composure. "I'm not the only one who was helpful, sir."

Calimir set his jaw then glanced across the hallway. "Just because Mister Aramien helped ferry supplies doesn't negate the fact that he disobeyed my orders on two counts. I will not tolerate disobedience in my ranks, and especially not in my personal squad."

Faelinia nodded once. *Best to put the matter aside,* she thought. "How many made it?"

"Everyone," the commander said, "thanks to you and the other illusionists. If we had lost any more..." He trailed off, then turned to Dardel. "Check in with the squad leaders. I want a report of what was found."

"Yes, sir." Dardel saluted the commander then hurriedly moved to the nearest squad.

"What are we doing now, Commander?" Faelinia asked.

"Waiting for Mistress Rudal to open these doors," he said, gesturing over his shoulder. "She claims there are tevisrals beyond it."

Faelinia turned to Vaem. The woman was muttering in a language Faelinia didn't understand. A sheet of parchment was unrolled beside her, lying on the floor next to Kydol's boot. There was a diagram written on the parchment, a diagram that looked similar to the symbols on the shallow dome.

Intrigued, Faelinia studied Vaem. Did the Mindolarnian scholar know that those crystal halls were *not* Tardalim?

⸻⊷•⊶⸻

"So, what do you think?" Ildin asked Naedra, the leader of the illusionist's squad. Naedra, a not so attractive woman frowned—Amendal would never have bedded her. She eyed Amendal up and down as if eyeing a garbage heap.

"I don't like him," Naedra said. "So, no." She turned away and resumed talking to the other soldiers of her squad.

That figures, Amendal thought.

Ildin sighed, slouching in defeat, but quickly scanned the enormous hall.

"It's fine," Amendal said. "I can practically be a squad all on my own. After all, I have more than enough conjurations." The illusionist gave him an exasperated look.

"You can't be alone, Amendal."

"Why not?" Amendal asked, but the illusionist didn't answer.

Ildin turned around, searching the crowded chamber. "Maybe we can try Jaekim's squad," the illusionist said, picking his way around his squadmates.

YOU DON'T NEED THESE FOOLS, that voice said. *BESIDES, THEY DON'T KNOW WHAT THEY'RE DOING.*

And you do? Amendal thought with derision, glancing to the ceiling. A faint chuckle, as if carried on the wind, wrapped around him. *I better not be losing my mind,* he thought, following Ildin to Jaekim's squad.

Jaekim and four other men were huddled against the wall to the left of the towering double doors. The men looked more like mercenaries than soldiers. Each held a single hand of cards. *Playing Sharzen at a time like this?* He shook his head as raucous laughter erupted from the group, coming from Jaekim. The necromancer had undoubtedly won.

"Who's in for another round?" Jaekim asked, smiling. Two of the men nodded.

"Not me," said one of the them, his armor rattling as he stood. He was nearly as tall as Amendal, but brawnier. He also had a more refined demeanor than the others of the squad. "It sounds like Dardel's collecting reports, so I'll sit out this round." He picked his way past Jaekim and the others, heading toward the doors.

"Excuse me," Ildin called to the brawny soldier. "Are you the squad leader?"

The man turned, eyeing Ildin. "I am. Miraden is my name." He glanced to Amendal then back to Ildin. "What do you want?"

"Are you willing to take him?" Ildin thumbed back to Amendal.

"Sure," Miraden said. "I'll gladly take an Aramien Conjurer." With a wave of his hand, Miraden turned and hurriedly picked his way across the hall.

"That was easy," Ildin said, turning to Amendal.

"At least *someone* appreciates my talents."

Ildin gave Amendal a weak smile.

"Amendal!" Jaekim called, waving excitedly. "Ildin! Come play!"

Cocking his head, Amendal turned toward Ildin. "Are you in for a game?"

"Maybe," Ildin said. "I want to get my pack, though." The illusionist stepped around Amendal, moving back through the cramped chamber.

"Are you coming?" Jaekim hollered.

⸺ ❖ ⸺

Soon after Amendal joined the game of Sharzen, Faelinia arrived. She told Amendal that the old soldier wanted her to try to pry the rogulin from him. Of course, Faelinia did not intend to obey the order. She was indignant about Calimir and his attitude toward Amendal. She was also to relay his banishment to the back of the expedition.

Banishment, huh? Amendal mused. Well, at least he would be away from Vaem.

"Are you going to stay back here?" Amendal asked Faelinia, taking his new hand of cards from one of the hired mercenaries of squad twenty-four.

Faelinia sighed, then glanced back to the doors. "I probably shouldn't…"

she said, her gaze wandering from his eyes to his lips.

Looks like she's ready for a kiss, he thought, holding back a smile. If anything good were to come out of this expedition it would be this change in Faelinia.

The most beautiful woman of the expedition bit her lower lip, then turned away, glancing across the crowded hallway.

Best act now. Amendal quickly stood. "Faelinia," he said, reaching out and brushing her arm. She spun at his touch, but as Amendal leaned forward to kiss her, a blinding flash filled the room. Startled, he lost his balance and fell into her. He thrust out his hand as she fell away from him, but he grasped only air.

The light faded, and Amendal found her on squad twenty-four's soaked packs. He extended his hand to help her up, but Faelinia got to her feet unaided. A commotion of speculation filled the chamber, a roar of questions concerning what lay beyond the doors. Faelinia immediately spun, looking toward the doorway.

There goes that moment.

The noises of perplexity continued to fill the chamber, and Amendal looked toward the doors. Neither of the white stone slabs were present, and what lay beyond was a hallway that seemed to stretch on forever. *Just like those in my dreams.*

"Whoa…" Jaekim said with a gasp. "Won't you look at that…?"

"I thought that was supposed to be a vault," a mercenary said. "Not another hallway."

Faelinia turned back to face Amendal, looking concerned. "Is *that* accurate?"

Amendal nodded.

Calimir called an order for the squads to assemble. The murmur of questions and perplexity ceased and was replaced by rattling armor, sloshing packs, and hefting grunts.

"I'd better go," Faelinia said. She bit her lip once again, shyly eyeing his lips.

"Wait," Amendal said. He was not going to pass up this opportunity. Focused on Faelinia's eyes, Amendal slid a hand around her waist. He pulled her close, causing her to lean back. Faelinia's eyelashes fluttered as Amendal wrapped his other hand behind her shoulder and pulled her closer. Her breathing quickened as he touched his lips to hers. She returned the embrace, running her fingers through his hair.

Their kiss drew rowdy cheers and crass remarks. Amendal ignored them, focusing entirely on Faelinia.

After a long moment, Faelinia pulled her lips away, but kept her forehead against his. Her fingers were still tangled in his hair. "Is that supposed to convince me to stay?" she asked, her voice like velvet.

Amendal grinned. "It's supposed to tell you how I feel."

Faelinia's eyes widened, and she parted her lips with a soft "Oh."

If only we weren't in these god-forsaken halls... he thought.

Faelinia pressed herself once more against Amendal and rested her cheek against his. "Come to my tent tonight," she whispered, then stepped back.

Amendal simply smiled at her, letting her slide from his arms. He straightened, watching Faelinia pick her way around the other squads.

"So, she's your only interest, right?" Jaekim asked.

With his eyes still on Faelinia, Amendal nodded. "I'm leaving the rest for you, Jaekim."

Soon after, the expedition was ready to proceed. Calimir called out the order to march, and the squads moved out one after another. Ildin and Fendar retained control over the earthen giants they had enthralled, keeping the lumbering behemoths beside their squads.

"Come on, men," Miraden called, stepping behind those of squad twenty-three. "Time to move."

"Can't we just hitch a ride?" Jaekim asked, pointing to Amendal's earthen giants.

Several of the mercenaries gave the necromancer a hard time, while Miraden shook his head, then waved them forward.

Amendal was among the first of squad twenty-four to follow Miraden, who was the only soldier in the squad. Amendal and Miraden walked side-by-side, passing Edara and his crew. The sailors were still sitting in the same place where Amendal had first seen them. Were they going to follow or just sit there?

"I don't care what the commander thinks," Miraden said, glancing to Amendal. "I'll gladly have you in my squad."

Amendal smiled. "I appreciate that. Your group seems a lot more relaxed."

Miraden chuckled. "Of course. We're mercenaries."

"I thought you were a soldier," Amendal said.

"Once I was." Miraden sighed. "But that was a long time ago."

Amendal raised an eyebrow as he studied Miraden. The man didn't look more than thirty. Perhaps he looked young for his age.

"You know," Miraden said, "I've heard stories of your family."

"Rumors, no doubt," Amendal said. "Far-fetched tales."

Miraden shook his head. "Your uncle is not one to exaggerate."

Amendal started. "You know my uncle?"

"I've embarked on several adventures with Krudin," Miraden said. "I had thought he would be joining us here... but he and those thieves of his already had something else lined up. They're exploring some ruins on the Kaladorn Frontier."

"Several adventures, huh?" Amendal asked, intrigued.

"That's right," Miraden said. "I much prefer adventuring over war. Of course, it can be just as deadly, but at least you're not constantly pitted against men who want to ram a blade through your gut."

I suppose that's one way to look at it...

The hallway beyond the massive doors was exactly like those in Amendal's dreams, though the floor was not quite as bowed. In fact, Amendal couldn't tell if there was a curve to the floor at all. More ornate stonework lined the hall's edges, and Amendal thought he saw strange symbols etched within the designs, like those in the gatehouse.

Pillars lined the walls on both sides of the hall, spaced about two hundred phineals apart. Like those in the other chamber, each was lined with glowing spheres. Amendal expected to find oval doors—like the one through which the cisthyrn had emerged in his dream—but none were present.

All in all, the hallway was quite boring.

The mercenaries of squad twenty-four rowdily conversed as the expedition pressed forward. Jaekim had suggested more games of Sharzen. The men laughed him to scorn, until Jaekim suggested they have one of Amendal's conjurations carry them while they played.

"I don't see why it won't work," Jaekim reasoned. "If Amendal puts the hands of that big creature together, then five or six of us can sit in its palms."

Teyvarn—one of the mercenaries—laughed and shook his head. "You think Calimir won't yell at us for that?"

Jaekim shrugged. "Does it really matter?"

As they continued debating the gambling proposition, Calimir called for a halt. Amendal strained to hear him, but couldn't quite make out what he was saying.

"Will you five shut up?" Miraden barked. "We can't hear."

Amendal craned his neck, attempting to peer above those ahead of him, but he couldn't quite see around the elemental giants Ildin and Fendar had enthralled. He glanced to his gosset, who was perched upon the shoulder of the nearest yaeltis. *Go,* he commanded, and the gosset soared through the hall.

While the bird flew to the expedition's head, Captain Edara and his first mate joined Amendal from behind.

"What's going on?" asked the sea captain.

"No idea," Miraden said. "I couldn't hear above those idiots." He jerked his thumb toward Jaekim and the mercenaries.

The captain chuckled and folded his arms.

Amendal, however, closed his eyes and focused his vision through the conjured gosset. The bird swooped around Fendar's enthralled elementals, soaring to the expedition's head.

Calimir and the others were stopped not far from an opening in the left wall that led to a squared landing and the base of an ascending stairwell paralleling the hallway. The side of the stairwell nearest the expedition was exposed, with an intricately crafted stone railing that was four times taller than it should have been. *Odd...* Amendal thought. Both landing and stairwell were just as wide as the hall the expedition had traversed. One of Faelinia's illusions zipped to the staircase and swiftly ascended.

Follow her, Amendal commanded, and the gosset flew into the stairwell. "Looks like we found some stairs," he told Miraden and Edara.

"Going where?" Edara asked.

"Up," Amendal said. From what he could tell, the stairs ascended eight stories—twice the height of the hallway where they stood.

The walls of the stairwell were adorned with exquisitely chiseled white stone bearing curved designs that ended in sharp points similar to those in the crystallized walls of the gatehouse.

Faelinia's illusion slowed as it neared the top step. Amendal's gosset circled her, evoking a smile from the illusion. Conjuration and illusion crossed a landing and entered a hallway nearly identical to the one where the expedition waited. This new hall's only difference was the odd oval doorways. They were like those in Amendal's dream, though not as large. But each doorway was blocked by white stone.

Why are they barred...? Amendal wondered. He guided the bird to rest on a normal-sized railing on the second floor, running the length of the stairwell.

"What's going on?" Miraden asked.

"Faelinia is scouting," Amendal said, focusing his hearing through his conjuration's ears. Calimir's voice carried up the stairwell, as did Vaem's.

"We need to go up," Vaem insisted. "And we need to hurry."

"I don't suppose you'll tell us why?" the old soldier demanded.

Vaem sighed with exasperation. "Just order everyone to follow me."

Two sets of footsteps carried up the stairwell, and Amendal turned his gosset's head. Kydol and Vaem marched up the stairs, the scholar's face wearing a scowl.

"Do you think it wise we move ahead?" Kydol whispered, her tone wary.

"We have time..." Vaem muttered. "After all, we're only on the first floor. I doubt *they* will attack any time soon. If there are any left..."

They?

Vaem continued talking but cut herself short upon noticing Amendal's gosset. A sultry grin formed upon Vaem's lips, and she waggled her finger at the bird. The Mindolarnians ascended the rest of the steps in silence, then waited on the landing.

So, Vaem did *know about these halls,* he thought. Had entering them always been the true purpose of this expedition? But why wouldn't she mention it? And who was this hostile group she alluded to? As Amendal pondered, Calimir ordered the expedition up the stairs.

"Amendal!" Jaekim called. "Hey, Amendal."

Opening his eyes, he turned to the necromancer. "What?"

"Weren't you listening?"

Not to you... he thought.

"Lower your conjuration's hands," Jaekim said. "We're gonna play some Sharzen."

Miraden sighed and shook his head in resignation.

Amendal sent the command to the earthen giant, and the conjuration obeyed. Jaekim, three of the mercenaries, and two of the sailors climbed upon the earthen hands. They made themselves comfortable as the conjuration raised its palms to its chest.

Soon, Amendal and the rest of squad twenty-four were moving toward the stairs. The conjured gosset was still on the railing, watching the expedition file onto the second floor. Faelinia had since sent her illusions zipping down either end of the second-story hall.

"That side has a dead end," she said, pointing in the direction of Tardalim's entrance.

"So we go that way," Calimir said, nodding in the direction they'd been headed on the first floor.

Before squad twenty-four reached the stairs, the rest of the expedition was already moving. Amendal, Miraden, and Edara led those in the rear up the stairs while Amendal's conjurations trailed behind the sailors.

Everyone was on the second floor when a ping echoed throughout the hall. The noise sounded as if it came from both behind and in front of the expedition.

"What's that?" Miraden asked.

Amendal set his jaw and glanced about. Floor-to-ceiling orange light shone from a narrow groove in the wall alongside the recessed pillar to his right. The line of light connected to another luminous line that ran along the ceiling to another lit groove on the opposite wall.

Farther down the hall, two hundred phineals away, at the next set of pillars, more of those orange lines shone along the walls and ceiling.

"This doesn't bode well," a mercenary said.

Wary chatter filled the hall, and Amendal spun. More orange lines ran along the pillars behind the expedition, connecting to lit lines running across the ceiling. From where he stood, the sets of lines looked like a series of squared archways stretching as far as he could see.

The lines of light, however, darkened to a mix between orange and red.

CAREFUL... that voice said.

"Huh?" Amendal blurted, drawing confused remarks from those around him. He glanced to the walls, noting his position in the hall. Amendal and the rest of squad twenty-four were twenty paces ahead of the reddening lines behind them. But some of the conjurations were behind the line, particularly the troll and the smaller earthen elementals.

To me! Amendal commanded, looking to the expedition's head. The middle squads were nearing the reddening lines ahead of Amendal while the leaders were not quite to the next set.

Two pings resounded through the hall, and the lit lines in the walls and ceiling shone a vibrant red. A hum resonated from all around—then a flash of white swept across the hall, along the red lines. Behind him, Amendal felt one of his earthen elementals struck by something massive.

The bond with the conjuration abruptly ceased and Amendal gasped. A roar of confusion erupted within the hall and Amendal settled his wide-eyed gaze on a slab of white stone that now blocked the hallway ahead of him and half the expedition.

"Faelinia!" he screamed. Others also shouted for their comrades, their cries frantic.

Heart pounding, Amendal staggered. Had they triggered another trap? Was that stone blocking the path or had the others been crushed beneath it?

TURN AROUND, that voice said.

Struggling to regain his composure, Amendal glanced over his shoulder. The conjuration he no longer sensed lay face-down on the floor, its entire back side missing. It was as if something had cut the conjuration in half, from top to bottom. And that cut was the cleanest Amendal had ever seen.

"How...?" he muttered, staring in disbelief at the earthen husk.

Had something similar happened to Faelinia and the others?

Ildin stared at the white stone barring the hallway ahead of him. Half of his squad had stepped past that line of light, including Naedra. *Is she dead?* And what about the others? Morgidian? Dugal? Faelinia?

Those squad leaders still in the hall called for everyone to calm themselves. But how could they? *The others are probably dead...* he thought, struggling to maintain his composure. Taking a deep breath, Ildin turned around, searching the hall. Amendal's conjurations were in the rear, but Ildin couldn't see Amendal. Ildin pushed his way past the other squads, moving straight for the conjurations. "Amendal!"

As Ildin neared the expedition's rear he found the conjurer turned away from the others, staring at something brown on the floor. Ildin darted toward his friend. "What are you looking at—?" he began. Then with a jolt, Ildin recognized an earthen conjuration, cut in half. But where was the other half?

"Huh?" Amendal muttered, glancing to the ceiling.

Is he hearing something? Amendal had mentioned hearing a voice while in the crystalline halls. Perhaps that voice was somehow connected to those strange dreams... But *how* was Amendal hearing voices?

Amendal shook his head, sighing. He turned, finally noticing Ildin. "Do you see that?" he asked, pointing to the maimed conjuration.

"Yes... What did that?"

Amendal shrugged and turned around, searching among the expedition. His face twisted in an utter sense of loss.

Ildin grabbed his friend's shoulder, gripping it tightly. "Maybe she's not dead. Maybe that slab is just a wall."

Amendal looked as unconvinced as Ildin felt.

The wary commotion died down in the hall, and several of the squad leaders called for a council.

At first glance, Ildin counted ten complete squads, plus the sailors. *Not quite half….* The leaders gathered near the stone wall blocking the hallway, while everyone else spread across the floor. Two-thirds of the squads were made up of mercenaries. Only five of the scholars were present.

Ildin was about to sit down on the floor when his eyes fell upon those strange not-quite-oval doorways. The stones that had once barred them was gone.

"Look!" he said, swatting Amendal's arm and pointing to one of the openings. "Come on, let's go check that out." Without waiting for a reply, Ildin hurried across the hall, weaving around those who were sitting. Several others had also noticed the unbarred doorway and were picking their way toward it.

Four soldiers had already stepped inside when Ildin reached the opening. Awestruck remarks reached Ildin's ears as he peered through the doorway. From what little he could see, the space beyond the door was four stories high and made of the same white stone as the hall. Throughout the space hung beige cylindrical crystals encased by golden framing—each barely taller than a man and with darkened silhouettes at their centers. The crystal cylinders lined every wall and were also arrayed in rows throughout the room, stacked on top of one another four times over.

The soldiers approached the nearest of the cylinders, gasped, and then eyed one another in distress.

"Oh no…" a female soldier muttered, staggering backward.

"Someone find a arpranist!" another soldier cried.

One of the soldiers darted from the cylinder and bolted to the door.

Ildin reeled away as the man ran past him and into the hall, shouting to the squad leaders that someone was trapped.

Someone trapped? Ildin wondered, turning back to the door. But only the four of them had entered the room… Confused, Ildin stepped inside, moving straight for the cylinder. As he neared the beige crystal, the darkened silhouette became clearer. Trapped within the crystal was an unclothed man with a frozen expression of horror smeared across his face.

Ildin gasped. "By all that's magical…"

"Now, as you're hunting for yaeltis, be mindful of the tracks. Their footprints look very similar to a troll's, since both creatures have six claws. Trolls don't inhabit the Abodine Wasteland, so if you find tracks similar to a troll down there, then you're in luck. Yaeltis like to climb, so watch for any claw marks on the walls of canyons or along a mountainside."

- From *Colvinar Vrium's Bestiary for Conjurers*, page 109

The sight of those beige crystals sent Amendal's mind spinning. He walked through the strange room, eyeing them. Each cylindrical crystal held a man or a woman trapped within it, frozen in a moment of utter dread. Hundreds of those crystals filled the chamber, perhaps even a thousand.

Who were they? Amendal wondered, passing a woman whose hands were raised as if attempting to shield herself.

Sharp tangs rang through the air—the repeated blows of soldiers striking the crystals nearest the door, attempting to free those trapped within the crystals.

Amendal passed another crystal, which held a man who looked as if he were screaming.

"Amendal!" Ildin called, weaving around a row of crystal cylinders. "Amendal, there's another room like this across the hall."

"Another room...?"

"It's like a prison," Ildin said, tapping on the nearest crystal. "And these are the cells."

HE'S SMART, that voice said. *BUT I WOULDN'T EXPECT ANYTHING LESS OF SOMEONE FROM HIS FAMILY.* Amendal set his jaw and glanced to the ceiling. Was this voice ever going to leave him alone?

Ildin raised an eyebrow and stepped closer to Amendal. "Did you hear something?" he whispered.

"Just that nagging voice," Amendal said. "So, a prison you say?" He eyed the nearest crystal. The golden framing around the crystal did look like a cage.

Ildin nodded. "I wonder if they're still alive. That would be a fate worse than death."

Amendal brushed his hand along the nearest of the supposed crystal cells. "It's warm," he said in surprise. No crystal he had ever touched gave off warmth.

The illusionist raised an eyebrow and pressed his hand on the crystal. "Strange," he muttered. "But don't most religious texts claim Damnation is where the wicked will forever embrace their sins, frozen in their horror amidst the flames of Tardalim?"

Amendal shrugged. "So I've heard. Never made much sense to me." Like most Sorothians, Amendal was not religious.

Ildin nodded. "Even the names coincide with what we've seen—Halls of the Damned, the Never-ending Labyrinth. This place *is* Damnation—the *actual* Tardalim!"

Amendal glanced to his friend, raising an eyebrow skeptically. Ildin didn't seem to notice and kept talking. "What if this is a prison left over from eons ago, built by a civilization far more sophisticated than our own? Perhaps once this place and its prisoners—trapped in this crystallized state— were common knowledge. Then over time it became distorted, and the details of the prison became a legend, and then made their way into myths and religions?"

Ildin's reasoning sounded very similar to that of those scholars at the Order of Histories back in Soroth. Prior to leaving for the Aramien Test of Valor, Amendal had heard his father and brother discussing a theory recently published at the Order of Histories. Several scholars proposed that the religions of Kalda's current era were the result of twisting the past with superstition. The scholars were bold enough to suggest that religious histories were simply fictional, and that the gods did not exist—at least, not in a way that they were portrayed in their current religious dogmas.

"Interesting theory," Amendal said, stroking the crystal once again.

Ildin tapped the crystal, then the golden casing. "I wonder if this casing is a tevisral of some kind…" He gestured back to the soldiers trying to breach the crystal casing. "They aren't even scratching the surface of the crystal, so whatever this is, it's definitely not natural."

"I can agree with that," Amendal said. The ringing of metal ceased and was replaced by sighs of defeat. "Why don't we go back," Amendal said. "We don't know how long that doorway will stay open."

"Good point." Ildin spun from the crystal. "I'd hate to be trapped in here."

Amendal and Ildin returned to the hallway. Most members of the expedition were quietly conversing about their predicament, and some were talking about the missing staircase.

Missing staircase? Amendal looked down the hall. The staircase, the landing, and the railing were gone. Where they should have been was a solid wall with one of those oval doorways. *What is wrong with this place?*

Shaking his head, Amendal nudged Ildin and pointed down the hall.

"What?" Ildin asked, then his eyes bulged. "Where's the stairs?! We didn't walk *that* far. They should be just past that pillar!" He hurried through the hall, passing the conjurations.

Amendal ran after his friend, shaking his head. *We only passed one set of pillars.* He passed another open door and glanced inside. From what he could tell, the room beyond the doorway was packed with hundreds of those crystal cells. *How many people are trapped in this place?* If all these doorways had similar rooms, then there must be thousands within this hall alone. *Maybe tens of thousands...*

"This doesn't make any sense!" Ildin shouted, throwing his hands into the air.

Amendal came to a halt beside his friend, studying the wall. *That's about the right distance,* he thought, recounting the time it took for him and squad twenty-three to walk from the stairs to where they had been stopped.

"Where did this wall come from?" Ildin asked. He continued spewing confused questions while Amendal glanced back to the stone wall barring their path.

This hall is uniform looking, he thought. The ornate pillars were recessed into the wall at equal intervals. Each oval doorway was centered between pillars, too. *Those lines of light were also the same distance apart...*

Intrigued, Amendal glanced back and forth down the hall. The direction opposite of where they were heading stretched on for quite a way, perhaps a grand phineal or so. *But hadn't Faelinia said it was blocked?* Confused, Amendal reached out to his gosset. "Fly..."

The gosset soared through the hall while Ildin mustered a dispel. White light gathered around Ildin's hands, and once the magic formed, he slammed it against the wall. The white particles permeated the stone, but soon vanished.

"Nothing..." Ildin said with a sigh. "Not even a flicker. And here I thought it might have been transmuted."

Amendal closed his eyes, focusing his vision through the conjuration while Ildin speculated about their predicament. He expected to see a blocked path at the hall's end but instead he found an intersecting hallway. "It's not blocked anymore..."

"You mean the end of the hall?" Ildin asked.

Amendal nodded, opening his eyes. *Back to me,* he commanded the bird. "Faelinia said it was blocked. That's why we went left instead of right."

Ildin rubbed his chin in thought.

"There's an intersection down there now," Amendal said.

"How is that possible?" Ildin asked.

Amendal watched the conjuration fly back through the hall. *Have the halls shifted somehow?*

EXACTLY! that voice cheered. *WELL DONE!*

Raising an eyebrow, Amendal glanced to the ceiling. But if the halls had shifted, wouldn't they have felt a jolt?

"Is that voice speaking to you again?" Ildin asked.

Amendal nodded. "How crazy would you call me if I said the halls were shifting?"

Ildin's eyes widened in surprise. He looked as if his mind was churning with ideas he had not considered. "That's why this all looks the same," he mused, a smile breaking across his face. "Look! The hall is divided into uniform segments! And those lines of light mark where the shifting occurs." The illusionist burst into triumphant laughter. "Amendal, you figured it out! Come on, we have to tell the others!"

Still laughing, Ildin hurried back through the hall to the rest of the expedition.

Shifting hallways, Amendal thought, studying the hall once again. If that were true, then Faelinia and the others were probably still alive. *But how would we get back to them?*

Considering the dilemma, Amendal followed Ildin. The illusionist was already at the cluster of squad leaders, explaining their supposition.

IT'S NOT A SUPPOSITION, that voice said. *LOOK AT YOUR CONJURATION.*

Amendal slowed his gait and eyed the severed elemental. It had been sheered in half. A clean cut. *If these halls are shifting, then that occurrence can be lethal.*

Applause rang in Amendal's mind, but he shook it off and hurried toward Ildin.

"...only way *this* makes sense," Ildin said, pointing to the wall barring the hall. "These hallways move."

Several squad leaders snorted. "And how does this work?" one of them asked, his tone mocking.

"I don't know," Ildin said. "But look." He pointed down the hall. "That end isn't blocked anymore."

Miraden narrowed his eyes. Was he considering Ildin's explanation? He looked at Amendal, worried. "Is he right?" the retired soldier asked.

"Yes," Amendal said.

"Why didn't we feel anything?" a squad leader asked. "If what you're saying is true, then we should have all been knocked about."

"Maybe," Ildin said with a shrug. "Maybe not... What if there was a tevisral that stopped us from feeling forces like spinning?" Several of the squad leaders laughed.

"It's better than what you've come up with," Miraden said, glaring at those mocking Ildin.

Another squad leader sighed and shook his head. "Miraden, you're not believing this, are you?"

Miraden glared at the squad leader. "How else do you explain the missing stairs? I vote we go the other way."

"We need proof," another said.

"Amendal's conjuration is proof!" Ildin blurted. "Just look at it. It's cut in half."

An argument ensued, but Amendal did not participate. He eyed the remnants of the expedition, then took note of the distance between the pillars. *We all have to stay between those glowing lines,* he thought. *Those are the safe spots...*

WONDERFUL! that voice cheered. *I KNEW YOU'D UNDERSTAND.*

Amendal set his jaw and glanced to the ceiling, not amused.

"Come on," Ildin said, tugging Amendal's arm. "I've had enough of this."

The argument intensified among the squad leaders. Several wanted to stay put, but the majority thought they should keep moving.

He turned from the arguing squad leaders and followed Ildin toward Fendar and Scialas. Once Ildin reached them, he began relating the theories about the halls.

"Shifting halls?" Fendar asked skeptically. "But that's not possible."

"Why not?" Scialas asked. "Everything on this trip has been nothing but the impossible."

Fendar shrugged, but noticed Amendal approaching. "Do you believe Ildin?" he called to Amendal.

"He's the one who came up with it," Ildin said.

"Came up with what?" Jaekim asked from behind Amendal. The necromancer swiftly rounded a soldier lying on the ground and joined Fendar and Scialas.

"The idea of shifting hallways," Scialas said.

Jaekim burst into laughter, but soon bit his tongue. "You're serious about this..."

"They are," Fendar said.

"Bilanus and Orin want to stay put," Ildin said. "I think that's just asking to be trapped. Who knows, another wall might show up over there." He pointed back toward the stairs. "At least, where they should have been."

"What do you think, Amendal?" Scialas asked.

Amendal clasped his hands behind his head. "I don't think we should stay put."

"You think it's safer moving?" Jaekim asked. "I'd much rather stay here."

"No," Amendal said, shaking his head. "Moving about will be just as dangerous. If we stay, we risk dying of starvation. If we keep moving, we risk getting squashed or attacked."

"Attacked?" Ildin asked, surprised.

Jaekim's face scrunched into wrinkles. "Squashed? How do you suppose that?"

"The shifting walls," Amendal said. "Just take a look at my conjuration."

He pointed back to the severed elemental. "It must have been on those lines of light. The other half is probably in another hallway."

Ildin lowered his voice. "What did you mean by attacked?"

Amendal related what he had overheard Vaem telling Kydol. The Mindolarnians knew of *something* inhabiting the white-stoned halls of Tardalim. But Vaem had mentioned the threat in the plural. Was there more than one of those creatures from his nightmares?

"Do you know what *they* are?" Scialas asked.

Amendal nodded. "I saw one of them in my dreams, my nightmares."

"Like the frostbite dream?" she asked.

"Yes…" Amendal looked about. "And if it's as terrifying as in my nightmare, we shouldn't stay put."

"Amendal!" Miraden called. "Jaekim!"

Now what…? Amendal turned, his jaw tensing. Miraden approached, picking his way around lounging soldiers.

"Let's get moving," Miraden said. "Our squad is taking the lead."

"We're leaving?" Fendar asked.

Miraden nodded. "We took a vote, and we're not waiting around for a rescue. A note is being left behind, in case Calimir manages to find this space again. We'll leave breadcrumbs, so to speak."

"I doubt anyone will come rescue us," Amendal said. "Vaem wanted to keep moving. From what I heard, she intends to reach this place's higher floors as fast as possible. We have a better chance of running into them than being found."

Miraden nodded. The look on his face told Amendal that Miraden knew that information had been obtained through the gosset. "I'll tell the others we need to keep going up. Hopefully we'll find the commander."

Miraden turned around and hurried to the squad leaders.

"Well, let's get packing," Fendar said with a sigh.

Ildin decided to join squad twenty-three, since most of his squad was missing. Miraden didn't seem to have a problem with him joining their ranks. Jaekim had been the only other mage, beside Amendal.

"Are you ready?" Ildin asked.

"Ready as I'll ever be," Amendal said. He commanded his conjurations to move forward. Ildin sent his enthralled earthen giants next.

"That's a good buffer," the illusionist said, then leaned close to Amendal. "Hopefully they can take care of whatever is out there."

I hope so, Amendal thought, his stomach knotting. *It will be fine. It has to be fine.*

Once the conjurations were twenty or so paces away, Amendal began his march. Ildin kept an even pace with him while Jaekim, Fendar, and Scialas trailed behind them. The five friends broke formation, forming their own squad of sorts.

When they passed the wall that should have been the stairs, Scialas spoke. "I'll put a regenerative imbuing upon each of you." She uttered an incantation, mustering arpran magic.

"Too bad Morgidian isn't here," Fendar said.

Jaekim grunted. "Are acidic barsions not good enough for you?"

"Are you actually going to cast them?" Fendar asked.

A snicker left Jaekim's lips, followed by an incantation.

The five friends had walked a good four hundred phineals or so before the other squads began moving. Amendal's group was halfway to the intersection down the hall when Miraden and the mercenaries caught up to them.

"Which way are we going?" Miraden asked.

"I don't know," Amendal said. "Let's get everyone to that intersection, and then Fendar and Ildin can start scouting."

"Fair enough," Miraden said. "Let's duck into the left side first, between the pillars like you said." Prior to leaving, Amendal had shared all his observations with Miraden.

Amendal's conjurations were the first to reach the intersection, and he guided them to the left. As they rounded the corner, a high-pitched nasally voice screamed, "Foul invaders!"

A flash of violet filled the hall, and Amendal felt a hole punched through his earthen giant's chest, while a purple beam sped overhead. *A disintegrating blast?* Amendal immediately shifted his focus to his conjurations while Miraden shouted a command to prepare for battle.

A strange gray-colored creature, no larger than Amendal's torso, hovered in front of the wounded earthen giant, its wings fluttering in a blur. The winged creature had a strange amalgamation of features unlike anything Amendal had ever seen.

A gray tail dotted with charcoal spots was the only body part below the creature's waist. Its midsection was human-like, with a torso and arms that looked like that of a toddler, a gray-skinned toddler. The creature's wings— which spanned from head to tail—fluttered so quickly that Amendal couldn't tell what color they were.

In its tiny hands, the creature hefted a rod-like object, aiming the three prongs on its end at the head of Amendal's conjuration. "For my mother!" the creature shouted. The words came from bizarre lips at the end of a trunk that protruded from beneath an oversized helmet of strange design.

A nasally cry filled the hall as the prongs of the rod-like object glowed, then fired a violet beam that disintegrated the earthen giant's head.

"It is important to note that yaeltis are solitary creatures. Once they are born, the mothers leave the children to fend for themselves. Oddly enough, the young are the fiercest. Sometimes siblings stick together, hunting other creatures like cisthyrn and colina."

\- From *Colvinar Vrium's Bestiary for Conjurers*, page 113

Amendal threw himself sideways, attempting to take cover behind his conjured yaeltis. Battle cries filled the hall, as well as incantations. The winged creature's nasally screams bounced off the walls while beams of violet pierced the maimed conjuration in an erratic manner. What was that winged-thing doing?

Fendar and Ildin's enthralled earthen giants advanced on the flying creature. The illusionists attempted to swat it, but it moved too quickly, weaving in and around the earthen hands. All the while, the creature kept firing disintegrating blasts with its bizarre rod-like weapon.

To me! Amendal sent the command to his quinta'shals. Jaekim had not yet cast an acidic barsion upon Amendal, so the conjurations' protection would have to do. All four quinta'shals gathered around Amendal, raising their hands while extending their long, forked tongues. They were ready to intercept the disintegrating blasts if the creature decided to fire in Amendal's direction.

A roaring charge filled the air behind Amendal, as well as clanking armor and singing metal. The mages continued uttering a cacophony of incantations that produced barsions, enhancements, elemental imbuings, and destructive blasts.

DON'T LET THEM KILL HIM, that voice said. Amendal frowned, pushing himself upright. *Why?* he asked. Was this creature some denizen of Tardalim?

Then, focusing on the melee, he sent a command for his other giants to attack. He closed his eyes and concentrated on his two yaeltis. Of all his conjurations, they were the most mobile. The earthen giants were lumbering brutes in comparison.

Go, Amendal commanded. *Run!*

Both conjurations bolted toward the chaotic battle. The soldiers and mercenaries were practically useless, as the winged creature kept itself near the ceiling. It wildly unleashed those disintegrating blasts, narrowly missing the men and women. *Can the creature not aim?* Why was it so sloppy?

Both yaeltis passed Fendar and Ildin. The two illusionists were uttering their enthralling incantations while gray light gathered about them.

Good idea, Amendal thought. If this creature was a denizen of Tardalim, then they'd best keep it alive and pry whatever it knew from its mind. He didn't need a voice in his head to tell him that.

Miraden and several other squad leaders called for a change in tactics. Nearly half the soldiers sheathed their weapons and drew bows or crossbows. The mercenaries, however, were only armed with melee weapons.

Through their swatting, the earthen giants managed to repulse the winged creature back through the hall. Violet light flashed off the walls, and more disintegrating beams struck another earthen giant. The blast went through the conjuration's arm at the elbow. If it had been anything other than an elemental, its arm would have been rendered useless.

Amid the winged creature's destructive volley, the two conjured yaeltis joined the fray. Both yaeltis dodged several beams as they bounded into the hall, but an errant blast struck one of them in the knee.

Pain shot through Amendal's knee, and he buckled. Though he was not hurt, he could feel the pain shared through his conjuration's bond. *Focus on one,* he thought, clenching his teeth. It would be easier to control a single yaeltis.

With his mind focused completely on the unmarred yaeltis, Amendal forced it into a dash. *Crouch,* he commanded an earthen giant, and the conjuration obeyed. The yaeltis leapt atop the crouched earthen giant, then launched itself toward the ceiling and the winged creature.

A high-pitched scream left the winged thing's long trunk as it spun to face the yaeltis. Violet light shot from the creature's weapon just as the yaeltis's paw smacked it. Amendal cringed in the shared pain, but forced the conjuration to follow through.

The blow sent the winged creature spinning. It plummeted beside the yaeltis, weaponless. *Where's that rod?*

In less than a heartbeat, the winged creature regained its flight. Amendal's conjured yaeltis fell, turning to swat at the fluttering creature.

"No!" the creature screamed, its oversized helmet bobbing back and forth. "Where did it go?!"

Arrows and crossbow bolts whizzed through the air, but the creature evaded and flew to the ceiling.

As the yaeltis landed on the floor, two gray clouds—the illusionists' enthralling magic—shot through the air and directly toward the winged creature. The creature dove, evading both the magic and the volley of bolts and arrows. It wove around the earthen giants, dodging their swatting blows. All the while, the enthralling magic sought the winged thing.

"Mother's rod!" the creature shouted, zipping along the floor.

Mother...? Amendal thought, pushing the yaeltis upright as the winged creature zipped by, the magic closing in. Could this creature be a child? When it had engaged the earthen giant it had yelled something about its mother...

Destructive orbs from the mages—made of arcane, flaming, and acidic magic—zipped around the conjurations and toward the creature. But as with the arrows and crossbow bolts, the winged thing evaded the deadly orbs.

"Where is it?!" the creature screamed, and the enthralling clouds engulfed it. No sooner was the winged creature shrouded, than it flew from the magic, wings still fluttering. It continued screaming while zipping around the yaeltis. Had the magic not taken effect?

Perhaps it's immune...? Creatures like the nactilious were resistant but still showed some signs of subjugation. This creature, however, wasn't impeded in the slightest.

Regaining his composure, Amendal swatted at the creature again. It turned tightly, and the yaeltis missed, slamming its hand against the white stone wall.

Another volley of arrows and bolts flew between the conjurations. The creature evaded the projectiles once again. For all its clumsiness with the rod, it was graceful in flight.

One of the arrows struck the yaeltis in the face, then another in the neck, and a third in the shoulder. Amendal gasped with the pain but continued reaching for the winged creature.

An enthralled earthen giant lunged, barreling into the yaeltis. Both conjurations tumbled to the floor, but before the earthen giant hit the ground, it reached into the air. The earthen hands surrounded the winged creature as it made a tight turn.

Screeching with that nasally pitch, the creature dove, but not before the giant clamped its earthen hands around it. At that moment, an acidic orb struck the earthen hand, dripping acid down its rocky fingers.

The giant landed on the yaeltis with a resounding crash that Amendal felt in his chest. The blow knocked the wind out of him, and he struggled for breath.

Triumphant cheers filled the hall, and the squad leaders called for the mages to cease their destructive incantations.

Still struggling for breath, Amendal pushed his quinta'shals aside and fell to the floor. The cool stone was a welcome embrace.

DON'T LET HIM DIE, the voice said. HE IS ESSENTIAL TO ESCAPING TARDALIM. Amendal furrowed his brow. Why was that voice so cryptic?

You're so annoying…

"Amendal!" Scialas called, "Amendal, were you hit?"

Amendal pushed himself up, sucking in a deep breath. "No," he said with a gasp. "My conjurations were wounded. That's all. Both yaeltis will need your help."

Scialas arrived beside him and gripped his arm. "Let me help you."

With the arpranist's aid, Amendal regained his feet. Whimpering and crying reached his conjurations' ears. Those baleful noises sounded nasally. *Is the creature hurt?*

"Come with me," Amendal said, grabbing Scialas's wrist. "My conjurations can wait."

Together, Amendal and Scialas hurried into the intersection, passing the crowd of mercenaries and soldiers. None seemed to be wounded. *Well, that's lucky…* Due to the creature's horrible aim, Amendal expected to find the hallway riddled with holes from the disintegrating magic, but the white stone on the floor and walls was completely unmarred.

How was that possible? The thought of Tardalim's walls being impervious to magic made his stomach knot. Was the stone laced with barsion somehow, or a continuous transmutation? Was the wall's impervious nature the reason conjuration magic could not be manifested here?

Ildin called for Amendal, moving from the others with Fendar in tow. "I'm sorry about the yaeltis. But I saw an opportunity and had to take it." So Ildin had been the one to capture the winged thing.

Amendal waved a hand in dismissal. "How is the creature?"

"Still trapped," Ildin said. "I figured I wouldn't crush it in case it had anything useful to share."

Fendar grunted. "I don't see how we'll extract that information. Our enthralling spells trickled right off it as if we had splashed it with water."

So it is immune… What kind of creature is this? Setting his jaw, he continued toward the towering conjurations. Clanking armor and hurried footfalls heralded the squad leaders' approach. They dashed ahead, heading for the toppled conjurations.

Amendal and the others quickened their pace. The faint nasally cries grew louder with each footstep, despite being muffled by the conjuration's earthen hands. Soon, he was at the feet of the toppled yaeltis. Ildin's enthralled earthen giant was still atop the furry beast. The elemental's arms, however, were resting on the floor beyond the yaeltis, partially out of view. The squad leaders rounded the yaeltis's head, disappearing behind the two conjurations.

Best get over there, Amendal thought, quickening his pace. Several squad leaders began shouting demanding questions at the winged creature. Their harsh interrogation only made the nasally crying worse. *Like a berated child…* he thought.

Amendal pushed his way past Miraden and joined Bilanus, who was doing the bulk of the shouting. He ignored the burly man and stepped up to the conjuration's acid scarred fingers. The crying grew louder with each of Bilanus's questions. Though it was dark between the earthen hands, there was enough light to see the winged creature. The gray tail shook, as did the tiny hands. The oversized helmet atop its head wobbled above the trunk.

"Stop that," Amendal snapped. "Can't you see it's frightened?"

"It attacked us!" Bilanus shouted. "It *should* be afraid." The towering squad leader turned from Amendal and continued railing at the winged creature. Amendal glanced to the other squad leaders. Several continued yelling, augmenting Bilanus's shouts. Others, including Miraden, had stopped and were straining to peer inside the earthen hands-turned-prison.

"Bilanus, shut up," Amendal said.

The burly squad leader turned. "You're not in charge. In fact, you're far from it!" He began hurling accusations at Amendal, blaming him for the death of several soldiers from the battle with the nactili.

So annoying. Amendal closed his eyes, reaching out to his yaeltis. Though it was pinned, one of its arms was free. *Pick him up,* Amendal commanded. He opened his eyes as the yaeltis's white-furred arm swept across the floor toward Bilanus. The yaeltis snatched the squad leader and lifted him into the air, and Bilanus's shouts became frantic cries for help.

"Shut up, or I'll *make* you shut up!" Amendal shouted, then turned to the other squad leaders. "Let me handle this."

Miraden nodded. "Let's get to scouting," he said to the squad leaders. He stepped away, followed by Orin. Soon, only the mages remained with Amendal and the winged creature.

Taking in a deep breath to calm himself, Amendal moved toward the earthen hands. "It's okay," he said, leaning toward an opening between the rocky fingers. The space was barely large enough for Amendal's hands to fit through. "The mean men are gone," he said. *Best talk to this thing like a child...*

The creature inside continued crying, but its shaking had lessened. From this angle, Amendal could see more of the creature. Part of its tail was covered in white boils. There were also black marks that Amendal did not recall seeing earlier.

"Are you hurt?" Amendal asked. "Did the green stuff burn you?"

Scialas knelt at another opening between the stony fingers, peering inside. "I can help you," she said, assuming a motherly tone. "I'm an arpranist. Do you know what that is?"

The winged creature shook, and its trunk flailed.

"You don't?" Scialas asked. "That's okay. I'm a mage that heals people. Here, let me show you." She turned to the others. "Do any of you have something sharp?"

Fendar pulled a knife from his boot. "Why do you want it?"

Scialas stood, took the knife and went back to the earthen hand. "Watch," she said, then sliced the blade across her palm. Blood dripped from the wound as Scialas uttered an incantation. Arpran magic swirled

around her hands, then seeped into the self-inflicted wound. Amid her incantation, the other mages gathered around. Ildin stood beside Amendal
while Fendar and Jaekim sat beside Scialas.

"See?" she asked. "It's all better. Now can I cast the same magic on
you?"

"Why?" the creature asked.

"So you don't hurt," Scialas said. "Those boils look painful."

"It will be fine," Amendal said, putting his hand to the opening. "I promise it won't hurt. You can take my hand if you want."

The creature didn't budge. Its crying had lessened, but it still whimpered.
Arpran magic shot into the earthen prison, illuminating the conjuration's
hands with a vibrant green hue. The winged thing had its back pressed
against the rocky palm, its wings stilled. They were a semitranslucent gray,
with charcoal-colored spots. And it had four wings, its lower pair half the
size of the upper two.

"Those are pretty wings you have," Amendal said as the magic surged
toward the creature. "I wish I had wings."

The creature turned its head toward Amendal, but due to the helmet's
oversized nature Amendal still could not see the winged thing's face.
Arpran light surged across the wounded tail, reducing the boils from the
acidic orb. The magic surged up the creature's torso and to its wings.

As the arpran light faded, the creature quieted. It lifted its tail, then eased
forward. Each of its wings fluttered for a moment, then the creature settled
back against the earthen hands.

"That's better," Amendal said, smiling. "My name is Amendal. What is
yours?" The creature turned, and he assumed it was studying him.

"I'm Scialas," the arpranist said.

The creature sat still for a moment, then reached its tiny hands to its
helmet. It hefted the oversized headgear and dropped it on the earthen
palm beside its tail. The creature's face was quite bizarre. The sides and top
of its head were rounded, similar to a human's, but where a man's nose and
mouth should have been was the base of that trunk. Two completely black
eyes stared directly at Amendal. There were no hairs on the creature's head,
and it lacked eyebrows and eyelashes. There were creases above the creature's eyes, where eyebrows should have been. Two slits lined the trunk
near its base, which Amendal assumed were the winged thing's nostrils. The
lips on the creature's snout downturned into a grimace. Never had
Amendal seen such a wondrous creature.

"Exquisite," Amendal said, his smile widening.

Scialas stifled an alarmed gasp, but the creature didn't seem to notice.

"You are a beautiful thing, you know that?" Amendal said.

"And you're ugly," it said in that nasally voice.

Amendal burst into mirthful laughter. "Oh my... I like you."

"Wow," Ildin said. "I think that's the first time anyone has called you ugly."

Jaekim snorted. "If Amendal's ugly, then what are we?"

The creature blinked several times, but didn't turn from Amendal. "Ugly invaders…"

"Invaders?" Amendal asked, cocking his head. "Are these halls yours?"

The creature nodded. "This is my home."

"I'm sorry for intruding," Amendal said. "We didn't know anyone lived here."

"I live here…" the creature said, annoyed.

"Does anyone else?" Scialas asked. "Do you have family?"

The creature turned to her but didn't answer. It studied the arpranist for a moment, then turned back to Amendal.

"It mentioned a mother," Fendar said. "And it sounded like it wanted revenge when it attacked."

The creature's eyes narrowed, and that line where the eyebrows should have been became exaggerated. "Don't talk about my mother!"

"Okay," Fendar said, raising his hands defensively. "I didn't mean to hit a sore spot…"

"Dumb invader," the creature said with a grumble. It settled back and folded its arms. That line above its eyes was still quite prominent.

Foul invaders, Amendal thought. *That's what it called us when it attacked.* He recalled what the creature had said. *For my mother.* Had she died to others exploring Tardalim? If so, when had that occurred? Weren't they the first to set foot in these halls?

"I'm sorry about your mother," Amendal said. "I can't imagine losing a parent."

The creature fidgeted.

Amendal eyed the winged thing for a moment. "You know, you still haven't told me your name."

"Why do you want to know?" the creature asked.

"Well," Amendal said with a sigh, "that's what people of my homeland do when they meet strangers."

"Your people sound stupid," the creature said.

Amendal chuckled. "Sometimes they can be. But I think it's polite to introduce yourself. Besides, what am I going to call you? Winged creature? Pretty gray thing? Those aren't good names…"

The creature straightened, then leaned toward Amendal. It lifted its trunk, pointing its lips toward Amendal's face. "Fen'chalim'nidam."

"That's a mouthful," Jaekim said with a snort.

Scialas slapped the necromancer and shot him an exasperated glare.

"Fen'chalim," Amendal said. "Nidam? Is that your full name?"

"What is *full name?*" the creature asked.

He blinked before asking another question. "Is Nidam your surname? My full name is Amendal Aramien. Aramien is my surname."

Fen'chalim'nidam mouthed the name. "Amendal'aramien," the creature slurred the names.

"No." Amendal shook his head, then said his full name with a deliberate pause between both names. "For short, people call me Amendal."

"Weird name," Fen'chalim'nidam said. "My name is Fen'chalim'nidam... but Mother calls me Fen'chalim, sometimes."

"That's still kinda long," Jaekim said, and Scialas slapped him again.

"So, she gave you a nickname?" Amendal asked. "Can I call you that? Or is that special to your mother?"

Fen'chalim'nidam shrank back. The creature obviously didn't like being called by that particular nickname.

Probably reminds it of losing its mother, Amendal thought. "What if I gave you another nickname?" he asked. Fen'chalim'nidam stirred. "I like nicknames. Helps people bond, I think. We have a friend whose name is Morgidian, but I always call him Morgi."

"Why?" Fen'chalim'nidam asked.

"Because it's what friends do," Amendal answered. "And it's something he and I share. No one else calls him that. It makes our friendship special." Fen'chalim'nidam blinked. "So, if we're to be friends," Amendal continued, "then I should come up with a nickname for you. One only I use."

Fen'chalim'nidam blinked several times. Was it not amused?

Hopefully it's considering the offer of friendship... he thought, mulling over possible variations of the creature's name. *How about Fench?* The name used the same sounds, just with different emphasis.

"How about Fench?" Amendal asked.

A smile formed upon the end of Fen'chalim'nidam's trunk. "I like that."

"Fench it is," Amendal said. "Now that we're friends, why don't we see if we can help each other out? After all, that's what friends do."

------———◇•◇———------

While the others began scouting both directions of this new hall, Amendal spent time conversing with Fench. He discovered that Fench was actually a male of his kind, the Tuladine. He was also the last of his kind.

Ildin had since freed Fench of his prison, allowing the winged creature to flutter about. Prior to releasing him, Amendal promised to feed Fench if he did not run away or try to kill any of the expedition with his rod-like weapon—which Ildin had returned to the creature.

Food was quite the motivator.

Fluttering in the air, Fench held a variety of dried meats and cheeses in his tiny hands. "I like this one," he said, waving his trunk over a slice of blue-speckled cheese called hevanisa.

"It is good," Amendal said. "Our chef back home makes several dishes with it."

"What is *chef?*" Fench asked.

"Someone who makes food," Amendal said. "Don't your people have chefs?"

"No." Fench shook his head, sliding his trunk across the slice of hevanisa.

"Who prepares your food, then?"

"The Roost does," Fench said, pointing to the ceiling. He had mentioned the Roost several times, but did not explain what he meant by the term.

"I still don't understand what this *Roost* is."

"It's safe," Fench said. "Only the Tuladine go there."

"Can you take us to the Roost?"

Fench lifted his trunk from the cheese. He studied Amendal, blinking several times. "Why?"

"So we can be safe," Amendal said. "Our friends don't know how to find us, but I know they're going up." He pointed to the ceiling. "Perhaps if we can make it to the Roost, we can meet back up with them."

Fench returned to his cheese. He didn't speak until after he had eaten all his hevanisa. "Why did you come to my home, Amendal'aramien?"

Amendal harrumphed. "I didn't have a choice," he said. "I was forced to come here, or be punished."

Fench gasped. "That's bad!"

"I agree," Amendal said. "I just want to go home, but I can't do that until the others find the tevisrals rumored to be in this place."

Fench blinked several times, hovering close to Amendal. "And you want to go home?"

"Yes. There are important things at home."

"And you can't go home if you don't find those tevissss...."

"Tevisrals," Amendal said. "And yes..."

"What are tevisss... ralls?" Fench asked.

"Objects that manifest magic," Amendal answered, gesturing to Fench's weapon lying on the floor. "Like that rod you were using. But tevisrals are not just weapons. There are lots of different kinds of tevisrals."

"Is that why invaders come?" Fench asked. "They want the tevisss... ralls?"

Amendal shrugged. "It's why we're here—well, not me."

"What about the... the *prisoners?*" Fench asked, contempt in his nasally voice.

So, this is *a prison,* Amendal thought. Perhaps Ildin's theories were right. "No, just tevisrals."

Fench returned to eating his meats and cheeses in silence. Was he considering the request? Amendal sat, watching the winged creature eat while hovering. It wasn't long before he finished his food.

"Okay," Fench said, fluttering in front of Amendal. "If your friends only want tevisss... ralls, I will take them to the Roost. But you will not touch the *prisoners.* Promise?"

Amendal nodded. "You have my word."

"Word?" Fench asked, blinking.

"It's what you say when you make a promise," Amendal said, chuckling.

"Now which way do we go?"

Fench turned and pointed back in the direction he had come from, down the left branch of the intersecting hallway.

*"I wouldn't recommend hunting juvenile yaeltis. For one thing, they
are only the size of a taller-than-average man, and their tusks have
not yet formed. The ideal specimens are those in their prime. You can
tell a yaeltis's age by its white, crystal-like tusks."*

- From *Colvinar Vrium's Bestiary for Conjurers*, page 114

Faelinia sighed in defeat, shaking her head. For nearly half an hour—
perhaps more—she and several other mages had tried to breech the
stone wall that had divided the expedition. Faelinia and several other
arcanists had unleashed disintegrating blasts, but the magic had simply dissipated before reaching the stone. Dugal and several others had tried
transmuting the stone, but their magic was nullified as well.

Grunts and groans filled the air, coming from soldiers pushing against
the wall. Despite all their efforts, the wall didn't move.

"This is hopeless," Dugal said from beside Faelinia. Morgidian stood beyond the complaining transmuter, his arms folded, looking studious as always.

Incantations sounded from around Faelinia, heralding the formation of
disintegrating blasts. Violet beams shot from the nearby arcanists, but their
magic halted at the wall. To an observer it looked as if the magic were making contact. The point where the magic was nullified was so miniscule that
it was practically undetectable.

"We're wasting time," Faelinia muttered. If they were going to reunite
with the others, they would have to go about it another way… *That big oaf
better be all right.*

"Are you giving up?" Dugal asked.

"No," Faelinia said and turned away from the immovable wall.

Those who were not helping breech the wall were lying about. Many
looked exhausted.

Faelinia picked her way around the resting men and women, moving straight for Commander Calimir. The leader of the expedition stood a little way off from the others, arguing with Vaem and Kydol. Though Faelinia couldn't hear the commander, his anger was smeared across his face. When they had first become separated from the others, Calimir had grabbed Vaem and slammed her against the wall, demanding answers. At least now he acted more civilized.

"...expect me to just trust you?" Calimir demanded.

"We're wasting time," Vaem said. "We need to move, now."

"Why?" Calimir asked, his tone firm and indomitable.

"It will take too much time to explain," Vaem said, then glanced toward Faelinia. "These efforts are futile, and I'm sure *she'll* agree with me."

Calimir turned to Faelinia, then looked beyond her, undoubtedly studying the others' futile efforts. "Miss Tusara?" he asked.

"We can't penetrate the wall," Faelinia said. "Our magic isn't even reaching the stone. I think we should keep moving."

"Finally, we agree on something," Vaem said, giving Faelinia a weak smile. "These halls will change again, but they won't be how they were."

Calimir spun on the Mindolarnian scholar. "What?" he barked.

Vaem sighed with exasperation. "As I said before. The halls of Tardalim are in constant flux. No one pathway remains the same for long. Now follow me. We need to ascend to the higher floors."

"And abandon the others?" Calimir asked. "Have you forgotten that Mister Aramien is our only way home?" He shot a glare to Faelinia. "We wouldn't be in this dilemma if you had taken that rogulin as I asked."

Faelinia pursed her lips and averted her gaze from the commander.

"So how do *you* propose we rectify this mess?" Calimir asked Vaem.

The scholar raised a painted eyebrow before answering. "We ascend to the higher floors. As *I* said before, I'm sure the others will follow. Amendal's gosset was eavesdropping while I spoke to Kydol here about our course of action." Vaem paused, taking in a deep breath. "So I'm sure he heard every word. If the others don't follow, we'll at least run into Amendal. I doubt he'll wait around if the others in his party decide to stay put."

Silence hung among the leaders while incantations and struggling noises sounded in the distance. Faelinia turned back to the wall, considering Vaem's reasoning. If what she'd said was true, then Amendal would most assuredly try to meet up with them on a higher floor. But how many floors were in this place?

"Fine..." Calimir sucked in his breath. "Miss Tusara, start searching for another staircase."

"Yes, Commander," Faelinia said, turning back around. She swiftly uttered an incantation, a slight variation of what she used to muster her usual illusions. This particular illusion was not completely cohesive. With this illusion she could leave bits and pieces in the air as markers.

White light formed beside Faelinia, taking a shape that resembled her. While the magic formed, Kydol and Vaem turned away from the commander and proceeded down the hallway.

Once the illusion was finished, Faelinia sent it flying. Before uttering another incantation, she focused on the two Mindolarnians, dropping a piece of the illusion behind them. *What else aren't you telling us?* Though this was supposed to be an expedition of discovery, Faelinia felt there was more to it than unearthing long-lost tevisrals. *What else is in here that you want, Vaem?* Whatever it was, Faelinia was determined to find out.

Fench led Amendal and the others through the halls of Tardalim's second floor, despite the objections from Bilanus and a few others. They assumed Fench was leading them to their deaths.

Amendal didn't agree with them. *He's too innocent,* he had thought. Fench was definitely a young child, and his actions and intentions were rather transparent.

Amid a lengthy debate, Fench flew off, saying they needed to beat something called "the Shift" which Amendal assumed was the shifting of Tardalim's halls. Not wanting to lose the little guy, Amendal bolted after Fench. The rest of his squad, his friends, and the sailors all bounded after him. From what Amendal could hear through his conjurations, the winged creature's abrupt actions made short work of the argument between the squad leaders.

They had run nearly two grand phineals when Fench called back to Amendal and the others. "The stairs are over here! Hurry! Before the next Shift!"

Fench sped around a corner, through a hallway that looked more like a corner segment. Unlike the straight parts of the halls, it lacked any doorways along its walls.

That's three types of halls we've seen. He rounded the corner and darted into another straight corridor. Fench fluttered two hundred phineals away, at the base of a staircase identical to the one leading to the second floor.

"Hurry!" Fench waved. "We need to beat the Shift on the third floor."

With that, the winged creature flew up the stairs, disappearing from sight.

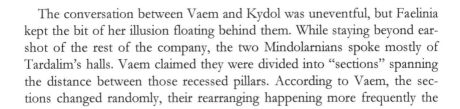

The conversation between Vaem and Kydol was uneventful, but Faelinia kept the bit of her illusion floating behind them. While staying beyond earshot of the rest of the company, the two Mindolarnians spoke mostly of Tardalim's halls. Vaem claimed they were divided into "sections" spanning the distance between those recessed pillars. According to Vaem, the sections changed randomly, their rearranging happening more frequently the higher one climbed.

After searching for nearly three grand phineals, Faelinia finally found a staircase to the upper floors. Her illusion had zigzagged back and forth, leaving pieces of itself at every turn. To her surprise, the "illusory bread-crumbs" ascended in a curving manner. From her perspective the stairs were actually above her and to the left, rising at a slanted angle. But how was that possible?

It took half an hour for the expedition to reach the stairs. Oddly enough, this staircase was identical to the last one they had ascended. She studied the stairs, but they did not ascend at a slant, as she had observed earlier. *What's going on?*

Calimir called for everyone to continue up the steps, but Vaem and Kydol had already ventured ahead. The Mindolarnians were already atop the next floor's landing when the rest of squad one started climbing.

As she ascended the stairs, Faelinia reached out to the illusory bread-crumbs she had left behind. To her surprise, they too ascended in a curved manner but rose the opposite direction, behind her right shoulder. *Wouldn't they have been below us?* Shaking off her confusion, she kept her thoughts on the illusory particles while climbing the stairs. Though those illusory bread-crumbs nearest Faelinia were below her, the ones farthest away were still above her.

"So strange…" she muttered, stopping atop the third-floor landing. This place—Tardalim, or whatever it was—made absolutely no sense…

"Miss Tusara!" Calimir called. "What's wrong?"

Faelinia shook off her puzzled musing and strode from the landing. The hallways of the third floor were identical to those of the first and second stories. "Sorry, Commander. I was a little distracted…" she said, and then relayed her observations to Calimir.

"We should all gather here," Vaem said. "Between these pillars." The scholar turned to the commander. "I suggest we wait here until another staircase is found."

"Agreed," Calimir said. "Miss Tusara, take the left branch."

Faelinia nodded and sent her illusion flying. Calimir called for another illusionist, instructing them to search the other direction.

While everyone crowded into the third-story hallway, Faelinia's illusion sped around an abrupt bend not more than five hundred phineals away. From what she had seen of the second floor, some sections of Tardalim's halls were straight, others were bent at right-angles, and some were intersections. Occasionally, hallways were blocked off, like the hall where they had been separated from the others.

Tardalim was apparently a never-ending labyrinth.

Faelinia's illusion had flown no more than a grand phineal when she found another staircase leading to the fourth floor.

"I found it," she said.

Vaem smiled, looking pleased. Calimir immediately began shouting orders for everyone to move forward. He wanted the expedition traveling side-by-side rather than single file. The commander did not want the expedition separated again.

"We'll know when a change occurs," Vaem said. "When the walls become lit, that's when we have to move, or stay put. But whatever we do, we need to stay within the glowing lines."

With Fench's help, navigating the halls of Tardalim was easy. And, they had not yet encountered the Shift, as Fench called it.

Once on the seventh floor, Fench stopped atop the landing. "Wait... the Shift is going to happen soon."

Amendal came to a halt beside Fench and studied the adjoining hallway. The lines in the wall were not lit. "How do you know?"

Fench shrugged. "I just do."

The others ascended the stairs, and soon everyone was atop the landing with the conjurations on the steps.

"What are we waiting for?" Miraden asked.

"A Shift is coming," Amendal said.

Ildin raised an eyebrow. "Shouldn't the walls be glowing?"

"Let's move into the hall," Miraden suggested. "Hurry!"

Clanking armor, heavy footfalls, and jingling weapons echoed around Amendal as the expedition ran. Amid the commotion, Amendal turned to the winged creature. "Fench?"

"I guess we can go that way," Fench said. "It's not as fast though." He fluttered from the landing, hovering only a few paces away from the railing.

While following Fench, Amendal rubbed his chin, pondering the Shift. Had it a pattern to it? How else could Fench know where the various routes led?

"Fench, is there a pattern to the Shift?" Amendal asked.

The winged creature rubbed his trunk. Fench had done that several times during their conversations. Amendal assumed it was like stroking a chin in contemplation.

"Not really," Fench replied. "It's always different. My father said no two pathways are the same. And the times between Shifts are different on each floor."

"How different?" Ildin asked.

"Long and short," Fench said. "Longer at the bottom."

Miraden nodded. "So, Shifts are more frequent the higher we climb?"

"Yup!" Fench said, sounding proud of himself. "At the top it's really fast, about every—" A ping echoed throughout the hall, coming from all sides. "It's here!" Fench cried with excitement.

Orange light shone along the recessed pillars, creating lines along the walls and ceiling. There was even a line on the floor—*How had I missed that?*

Amendal wondered. Each set of the orange lines was spaced two hundred phineals apart, as they had been on the second floor.

"Get close together!" Miraden called. The expedition clustered near the wall, with Amendal's conjurations closest to the railing.

While the orange hue gradually darkened, Amendal glanced down both ends of the hall. To the right of the stairs, a long hallway stretched on for quite a way. On the other side, not more than six segments away—a little over a grand phineal—was an intersection like where they had met Fench.

Faint pounding reached the ears of Amendal's cisthyrns, coming from the left branch of that intersecting hallway. *Are those footsteps…?* A knot formed in Amendal's stomach, and images from his nightmares flashed in his mind.

"Does anyone else hear that?" Amendal asked warily.

"Hear what?" Ildin asked, his face contorting with fear.

Miraden spun to Amendal, hand on his sword hilt. "Where?"

Amendal pointed toward the intersecting hall. The pounding grew louder but Amendal could only hear it through the cisthyrns. He glanced to the light on the walls. The luminous lines were a shade between orange and red. Would the Shift happen before the owner of those footsteps appeared?

The orange light darkened as Amendal heard the pounding with his own ears. Low hissing and reverberating growling carried from around the corner and into the hall. Every member of the expedition spun. Armor clanked. Metal sang. Soldiers and mercenaries settled into battle stances while squad leaders gave commands to the mages.

Fench's trunk and tail stiffened. Was that an instinctive reaction of utter dread?

Amid the cacophony of incantations, the lumbering footfalls grew louder, as did the hissing and growling. An orange haze misted from around the left branch of the intersecting hallway. Halfway up the wall, a black oblong head—as long as four men were tall—peered around the corner. The haze dissipated, revealing the abhorrent facial features of that monster Amendal had seen in his nightmares.

Frozen, Amendal stared in horror. The hissing grew louder as the monster opened its vicious maw, revealing rows of sharp obsidian teeth. The light from the walls glistened off the four black horns protruding from its long jaw: two jutting from near the center of its chin and two others near the jaw-joint. Each horn ended in glistening points that curved downward.

Violet eyes narrowed at the expedition, and the gill-like rivets along the sides and crown of its oblong head flexed. The monster had twelve of those strange gills, arrayed in rows of four on either side of its head and along its crown. Each of the rivets opened toward the creature's snout, allowing a view to their vibrant orange gill filaments. Every gill filament pulsed, misting an orange haze.

A deep guttural growl left the monster's mouth as it stepped around the corner. As in the dream, the monster had eight limbs—six arms and two legs—with sharp horn-like protrusions jutting from its joints. The thing advanced on its legs and foremost set of arms, its riveted tail arcing and scraping against the ceiling. Though the creature was crouched, it struggled to fit in the hallway. Amendal had only glimpsed its length—perhaps fifty to seventy phineals long, not including the tail.

The monster's violet eyes shifted, looking directly at Amendal—or was it Fench?

Amendal fought the urge to use his conjurations as a shield. Moving them would crush his companions.

The monster unleashed a deafening bellow and bolted straight for the expedition.

"Hold your ground!" Miraden shouted.

Two pings resonated through the hall as the monster bounded past one set of pillars. It bared its teeth and passed another segment as the light on the walls and ceiling became a vibrant red.

A hum resonated from the walls, floor, and ceiling as the monster passed a third set of pillars. The monster was two segments away when a flash of white swept across the hall.

Before Amendal could blink the monster had vanished—well, not vanished but rather the segment of the hall where it had been Shifted to another part of the seventh floor.

A wave of gasps and sighs filled the hall, and the tension melted. Mages abruptly cut their incantations short while soldiers sheathed their weapons.

"What was that thing?!" Bilanus demanded.

"Do you know what that is?" Orin shouted to Fench.

Startled, Fench fluttered behind Amendal. Tiny hands squeezed his shoulder *He knows*, Amendal thought.

Miraden stepped up to the two squad leaders. "Let's keep moving," he said. "Fench, which way do we go?"

⬦ • ⬦

It had been several hours, but Faelinia and the others managed to reach a flight of stairs leading to the eighth floor. The halls had changed once while they were on the fifth floor, forcing them to find another route. She and the other illusionists found a staircase to the sixth floor, but it was more than five grand phineals from where it should have been. That led her to believe there was more than one staircase on each floor. Vaem had implied as much during their initial conversation about Amendal and the other half of the expedition.

It was now probably well past nightfall. Soldier and mage alike plodded up the stairs, exhausted from the ordeals of the day. The battles in the caves, the flooding of the crystal ruins, and the arduous trek through Tardalim had not made the day any easier.

"When are we going to rest, sir?" Hevasir called to the commander. Several other soldiers voiced the same question.

Partway up the stairs, Vaem turned and shot a perturbed glanced back to the weary men.

What is her problem? Faelinia wondered. They had to rest at some point.

Calimir slowed his ascent but did not stop. "Let's set camp in the halls up ahead."

"We should keep going," Vaem insisted.

The commander shook his head. "I'm calling a break. We need to rest."

"We should've rested after the flood," a soldier complained. Others voiced similar sentiments.

Faelinia could not help but sympathize with the men. Now atop the stairs, Vaem grumbled and quickened her pace across the landing, disappearing behind the railing.

"This place is so monotonous," a soldier complained. The man had a point. Every hall and every staircase had been identical in every way.

Once the expedition was on the eight floor, Calimir doled out his orders concerning the camp. The commander had selected their campsite two sections away from the stairs. "Supplies along the walls," the commander shouted. "Squads will sleep in rows, from wall to wall. We have no need for tents."

While everyone settled in, Faelinia and her squadmates picked their way toward the recessed pillar that marked the camp's edge. Several of the soldiers complained about the day, but she remained silent. *No point griping,* she thought. Once near the pillar, hurried pounding echoed up the staircase and into the eighth floor.

Is that Amendal? Intrigued, Faelinia spun to face the stairs. Confused questions filled the hall, drowning out the pounding. Those who had already begun unpacking stood upright, partly obscuring the railing and the landing.

She reached out to her illusion, sending it to the stairs. Through it she could hear the pounding clearer than before. The noise sounded more like galloping than footsteps. *Strange...* she thought. But Amendal had not conjured anything that could gallop—unless two conjurations ran in a way that sounded like galloping.

As Faelinia sent her illusion down the stairs, an enormous black figure leapt from the seventh-floor hallway, over the railing, and onto the stairs. An orange mist trailed behind the black creature as it bolted up the staircase in a single stride.

Shocked, Faelinia instinctively uttered an incantation, mustering a disintegrating barsion. Other mages did the same while soldiers scurried about and drew their weapons.

Violet light surrounded Faelinia as the hulking black beast bounded into the hallway. The creature was unlike anything she had ever seen—with an oblong head, eight limbs, and a wicked tail that ended in three sharp pincers. The creature was so tall that it had to crouch on its legs and foremost arms to fit in the four-story hall.

The monster halted upon seeing the expedition, its violet eyes studying them with a sweeping gaze. "WHERE IS THE TULADINE?" the monster bellowed. A reverberating growl left the terrifying maw, and more orange haze misted from those strange gills atop its head. Another growl filled the hall as it lowered its snout, scraping its tail across the ceiling.

A bubble of barsion, infused with disintegrating magic, surrounded Faelinia as the monster spoke again. "NO... YOU ARE NOT THE SAME FOOLS." Had this monster ran into Amendal and the others?

Barsions coalesced all across the expedition's ranks, shielding mage and soldier alike. Destructive orbs formed around several mages while others restrained deadly blasts, humming their incantations.

"ATTACKING ME IS AN EXERCISE IN FUTILITY," the monster bellowed, the orange mist streaming down its body.

"We will defend ourselves!" Calimir shouted from behind a form-fitting barrier of barsion. He turned to speak to Vaem, but Faelinia could not hear what he said.

The monster eased back while extending one of its fore limbs. *It's going to pounce*—Wary, she swiftly began an incantation to muster a disintegrating blast. But before a speck of the violet magic could manifest, the monster sprang toward the expedition, unleashing a deafening cry.

FURY OF
THE DAMNED

"There are several important aspects to watch for when studying a yaeltis's tusks. First is size. They should be longer than your arm. The ones I keep in the Visirm Expanse have tusks nearly as long as my legs. The second is the sheen. If the tusk is too bright, then the yaeltis has not matured enough. You want to find one with a decent balance between shiny and dull. Too dull means the yaeltis is fairly old."

- From *Colvinar Vrium's Bestiary for Conjurers*, page 114

Calimir cursed furiously as the horrifying beast landed amid the party, crushing several soldiers. *No!* He drew his sword from its sheath. His shield, however, was across the camp. *I'll have to do without it,* he thought as he dashed toward the monster, hoping that the barsion encasing him would be sufficient protection.

The beast whipped its tail while swatting away the nearby soldiers and mages with its six arms. Never in all his years had he seen anything like this creature, especially not something intelligent enough to speak. Amid the monster's movements, that orange mist settled into the hallway, veiling everything in an orange hue.

Steeling himself, Calimir lunged with his sword ready to strike. Behind him, frantic screams intensified into sounds of utter dread.

That black tail swept toward Calimir as it flung a soldier and mage across the hall. Throwing himself forward, Calimir narrowly evaded the tail. As he fell, he glimpsed those near the monster not shielded by barsion. The men and women screamed, clutching their heads. Had their panic been a result of the mist?

Calimir continued his dash and leapt over a pair of packs. The creature had grabbed several mages who were mustering deadly blasts. Several soldiers swung at the monster's forelimbs, but the beast didn't seem to care. It was too busy trying to crush the mages.

What was this creature? Was it a protector of this never-ending labyrinth? Calimir shot a fierce glance to Vaem—the scholar was running away from the battle. *A coward and a liar...* he thought, coming within weapon's reach of the monster.

Incantations sounded all around Calimir, laced in a dreadful cacophony with those horrified screams.

Calimir lunged to pierce the monster's hind leg, but the blade bounced off the black flesh. *If it is flesh at all...* Calimir thought, regaining control of his sword. He swung the blade with all his might, but the sharp edge barely broke the surface of the monster's flesh.

Stunned, Calimir readied his weapon, but the monster spun. Its hind leg struck him and sent him tumbling backward.

As Calimir recovered, the barsions of those in the monster's grip shattered. Incantations were replaced with pained cries and desperate screams.

A wave of barsion shot from Morgidian's hands, toward those of the expedition who were screaming. Those who had not been initially protected were rolling on the floor, clutching their heads. *Is it that haze?* he wondered. He had heard tales and myths about monsters that could make a person go mad. Creatures with strange innate abilities didn't seem uncommon for the Abodine Wasteland...

Destructive incantations sounded amid the wailing. Those in the monster's clutches—now without their barsions—wailed in dying agony. Several wails were cut short, followed by thuds.

Morgidian spun. Those who had been swept up by the monster lay on the floor, frozen in their final moments of terror.

He gasped as the monster snatched four more mages, including Faelinia. Despite its captives' destructive barsions, the monster continued to squeeze each of them. An enraged growl left the monster's terrifying mouth—undoubtedly a result of clutching those deadly barsions. But the magic laced within those protective barriers didn't seem to be damaging the beast.

The captive mages immediately ceased mustering their destructive spells and began uttering incantations to bolster their barsions—but not Faelinia.

She's trying to kill it, he thought. But Faelinia's barsion might shatter before she had a chance to unleash her destructive blast.

Morgidian could not let that happen. He began uttering an incantation, blue light surging about him. If Faelinia wasn't going to reinforce her barsion, then he would.

Faelinia felt her barsion flickering. The disintegrating magic between her hands intensified, but the spell was not quite finished. Her barsion had to hold long enough for her to deal the deathblow.

Bluish-purple particles danced across her destructive bubble. Was one of the barsionists attempting to protect her?

"CLEVER," the monster bellowed. It spun once again, lowering Faelinia near its face. "BUT YOUR HUMAN MIND IS TOO SLOW TO PROTECT THEM, HEDGETRANCER."

A crack spread along Faelinia's barsion as she finished her incantation. *Yes!* she cheered inwardly, unleashing the blast toward the monster's head. Part of the beam struck the enormous hand gripping her, but the disintegrating magic barely eroded the monster's flesh.

Faelinia started, but focused to condense the beam. The violet blast struck the monster's cheek just below the eye. But the monster's cheek was as resilient as the flesh of its hand.

"IMPRESSIVE!" the monster cackled, then jerked its head away. Before Faelinia could redirect her magic, the disintegrating blast sped to the monster's neck, striking a white-metal cord thicker than a man's thigh. The cord—made from three woven strands of glistening metal—broke apart particle by particle. Bits of the blast seeped between the cords, striking the monster's neck, where the flesh seemed to be considerably weaker.

If she couldn't pierce the monster's skull, then she would sever its head.

The pressure on her barsion lessened as blue light surged across the weakened barrier. *Odd...* she thought. Had the monster eased its grip? A heartbeat later, the blue light completely enclosed her in a fresh bubble of barsion magic.

As she pondered, her violet beam tore through the metal and struck the monster's neck, boring a hole through its dark flesh. A triumphant cackle left the monster's maw as the metal fell to the floor. *Had it wanted me to strike there?* But why? No matter, her disintegrating blast was tearing through the monster's flesh. She would sever its head in no time.

While her magic bored a hole, several other mages finished their incantations. Acidic javelins struck the monster's black flesh while arcane eruptions veiled the hallway in a blinding flash.

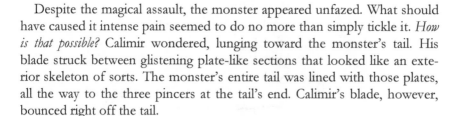

Despite the magical assault, the monster appeared unfazed. What should have caused it intense pain seemed to do no more than simply tickle it. *How is that possible?* Calimir wondered, lunging toward the monster's tail. His blade struck between glistening plate-like sections that looked like an exterior skeleton of sorts. The monster's entire tail was lined with those plates, all the way to the three pincers at the tail's end. Calimir's blade, however, bounced right off the tail.

"Impossible!" he cried.

The monster whipped its tail, striking Calimir's barsion. He flew backward, hitting the white stone wall. As he recovered, the monster hurled the four mages that it had clutched in its claws—each was surrounded by a fresh layer of barsion cast by Mister Shival.

Miss Tusara was among those mages, unleashing her fury in a destructive beam. The monster sidestepped, evading the violet blast, but Miss Tusara redirected it in a beautiful display. Curving through the air, the disintegrating magic struck the monster's neck.

Was the beast weaker there?

The violet blast faded, revealing a deep divot below the monster's jaw. "Focus on the neck!" Calimir shouted.

Arrows imbued with flaming magic flew from several soldiers, and one struck the spot eroded by Miss Tusara. Others struck the monster's flesh, but did not pierce the beast. The flaming shafts fell to the stone, one igniting a full pack of supplies.

The monster bellowed an amused chuckle. It turned its head to Calimir, its violet eyes glowing. The eyes made Calimir start with panic.

Do not give in to fear, he told himself, reciting the litany.

More arcane bolts, flaming orbs, and acidic javelins struck the monster's neck. Amid a blinding flash the monster bellowed, "FOOLISH HUMANS." Was that mirth in its voice? "YOU CANNOT SLAY ME—"

A ping resounded throughout the hallway.

Calimir blinked away the blinding flash, finding an orange line of light running between his legs and across the floor. The hall was about to change.

We don't have time to kill this thing, he thought, his stomach wrenching. Men and women—those who had been afflicted by the mist—were still screaming. Most were incased in barsion. Several were thrashing about among the expedition's supplies. As a result of the battle, the expedition was separated across three sections of hallway.

With everyone scattered, Calimir couldn't see everybody to safety, and especially not with the battle raging. Even if they could escape, they would have to do so without their supplies. They would be cut off—*But what if the beast followed?*

More deadly magic assailed the creature, but had little if any effect on it.

No, we have to run. If they could time it right, perhaps they could lose the monster. Or better yet, get it to cross the line as the hall changed. *That would kill it.*

"Retreat!"

———◦•◦———

Faelinia finished mustering a dozen disintegrating orbs as the orange lines appeared in the walls, floor and ceiling. Soldiers and mages bounded past her, heeding Calimir's command to flee.

Though most of the expedition was running past her, there was a small group darting back to the stairs. Uldric, the necromancer who had reani-mated the cisthyrns, was among them. Several dozen men and women were still thrashing on the floor amid the expedition's supplies, wailing and screaming.

They're going to be trapped, she thought.

"THIS ONLY DELAYS THE INEVITABLE," the monster bellowed, swatting a fleeing soldier into the wall. The blow made the man's barsion flicker. Before the soldier could resume his flight, the monster snatched him with its tail. "I WILL CONSUME YOU ALL."

With her eyes fixed on the monster's neck, Faelinia unleashed her orbs. The violet bolts whizzed above her fleeing comrades. Several struck the hole in the monster's neck while others circled the vile beast. Its head cocked, the monster swatted at the orbs.

Two more pings echoed through the hall, and the monster shot a glance to the reddening lines between it and Faelinia. "A PITY..." the monster growled, settling its gaze on Faelinia. As their eyes locked, a flash of white veiled the space between them. Before Faelinia could blink, the monster and the screaming men and women were gone.

Besides Uldric, five others managed to escape to the stairs. All six of them collapsed atop the landing. The sounds of battle had ceased and no one was screaming. *Thank the Channels...*

"What was that thing?" a soldier asked.

Kaerune—one of the squad leaders—shook her head. "I don't know, but I never want to see it again."

"What do we do now?" another soldier asked.

Taking in a deep breath, Uldric glanced to the hallway beyond the land-ing. It looked much like the other hall—well, without the monster.

"We find a staircase," Kaerune said. "And hope that thing doesn't come back to eat us."

"What are we waiting for?" Uldric asked, shakily rising to his feet. "We should get going." He stepped out of the landing and studied the hallway. Both ends went on for quite a way. *Great... which way do we go?* If only he had kept his reanimated ice wolves... Once the danger in the crystal cav-erns had been dealt with, Uldric had dismissed the necrotic bond.

The soldiers soon gathered around him, looking as perplexed as he felt.

"I say we toss a coin," the first soldier said.

"That's stupid," another spat. "What if we go the wrong way?"

"We only have two choices," Kaerune said. She sighed and looked down the hall both ways. She pointed to the left of the landing, what would have been the same direction as the expedition's original heading. "Let's go that way."

"Why not the other way?" another soldier asked. "Since these halls change wouldn't we be going in a different direction than the others?"

"Exactly why I want to head that way," Kaerune said. "That puts us as far away from the monster as possible."

With that, the squad leader led the way down the hall.

Hopefully not to our deaths.

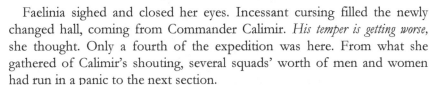

Faelinia sighed and closed her eyes. Incessant cursing filled the newly changed hall, coming from Commander Calimir. *His temper is getting worse,* she thought. Only a fourth of the expedition was here. From what she gathered of Calimir's shouting, several squads' worth of men and women had run in a panic to the next section.

That meant that the expedition had been spread across four sections of hallway.

Those with the supplies, and the beast, are probably dead, Faelinia thought. She ignored the commander's rant and studied the hallway. A solid wall barred the way to where the monster had been. On the opposite side, the hallway emptied into an intersecting corridor.

Faelinia set her jaw and glanced about. There were no other illusionists nearby. *I'll have to do all the scouting myself.*

After Faelinia mustered her illusions, Morgidian and Dugal approached her. They tried speaking to her, but Faelinia was too focused on finding a staircase to the ninth floor. Both illusions ran into dead ends, and Faelinia was forced to backtrack to other branches in the halls.

Eventually, she found the stairs and Vaem. Both Mindolarnians were together, sitting atop the stairs. Faelinia found it odd that they were just sitting there, until she noticed that walls blocked the first hall atop the ninth floor.

In response to Faelinia's report, Calimir spewed even more vehement curses. "How dare she...?" the commander growled.

"Calm yourself, sir," Dardel said.

The commander shook his head. "I want you to enthrall her," he told Faelinia. "Pry everything she knows out of her!"

Faelinia tensed—she did not like the idea of forcing Vaem to tell them everything she knew. But then again, what other dangers were lurking in this place?

After shouting several commands, Calimir began his march.

Leading the survivors, Calimir stomped onto the landing beneath the stairs to the ninth floor, the rest of the expedition trailing behind him. *You're going to tell me everything,* he thought, eyeing Mistress Rudal. The Mindolarnian scholar sat smugly atop the highest step, quietly conversing with the lieutenant. Had she known about the monster? She had insisted they keep moving…

You killed my men… Calimir spent no effort to hide his fury.

"Commander," Dardel said. "Don't be hasty. Watch your tongue."

Calimir stifled a curse, his upper lip quivering. He had had enough of Mistress Rudal and her omissions.

Once he was halfway up the staircase, the scholar noticed him. *Stare at me*, he thought. *I want you to see me coming.*

Mistress Rudal eased forward, arching an eyebrow. She set her pack on the landing, touched her right glove below the thumb, and then descended the stairs.

"What audacity," Calimir whispered. He quickened his pace, moving ahead of Dardel and the others. His second-in-command pled for him to reconsider, but Calimir was not going to back down.

He was ten steps away from Mistress Rudal when she spoke. "Oh, Calimir, Calimir… You should have listened."

Now nearly within arm's reach, Calimir raised a fist. He swung at her while shouting, "Why you deceptive—"

Mistress Rudal grabbed his wrist with her gloved hand, and his fury dissipated. He studied her, confused, and glanced to the cuff of her glove, which had a pinkish tint to it… His fleeing anger left a void in his heart. But it was soon filled with a burning passion. A desire for *her*… for Vaem. Though he had wanted to strike her, now all he wanted to do was embrace her.

Her beauty… why hadn't he noticed it before? *Oh, Vaem…*

She eased her grip and lowered his arm. What had he been doing? That didn't matter. His only concern was for her, to please her.

Calimir stepped closer, drinking in her beauty. He *yearned* to please her. He would take her, here and now on these steps. Passion swelling, Calimir reached for Vaem, but she stepped back.

"Later…" she whispered, pressing her free hand to his chest. "Not here."

Calimir's heart raced.

"Once we're safe," she whispered. "I *promise.*"

The word tamed his lust—how, he did not know.

"We need to keep moving," Vaem said. The soldiers and mages groaned. They sounded tired, but that didn't matter. It's not what she wanted. He would give her what she wanted.

"We keep climbing," Calimir said, his eyes trained on Vaem's lush figure.

Someone spoke to him, but he didn't know who, nor cared. All that mattered was Vaem.

"Come," Vaem said, turning around. "We have a long way yet."

"Act swiftly when trapping a yaeltis. Begin by luring the beast from its cave with a conjuration, like a yidoth. Yaeltis can't tell the difference between actual creatures and those conjured from the Aldinal Plane."

- From *Colvinar Vrium's Bestiary for Conjurers*, page 115

After encountering that strange monster, Fench led Amendal and the others at a furious pace. The illusionists had to enhance everyone to keep up with the winged creature's headlong flight.

After several hours, they reached the twenty-fifth floor. Fench finally slowed and turned to Amendal and the others. "The next staircase is not far," he said, sounding out of breath.

Soldiers muttered phrases of relief. Though they had been enhanced, the hurried climb through Tardalim had been exhausting. Even Amendal was tired. *I should have ridden atop a cisthyrn.*

Weary, the party continued through the halls of the twenty-fifth floor. As they walked through a short maze of corridors, a putrid scent filled the hall. Amendal gagged, the noxious fumes assaulting both his and his conjurations' noses. It was more pungent through the cisthyrns' nostrils. Soldiers and mage alike coughed, and several wondered aloud at the cause.

"It smells like death," Jaekim said, sounding intrigued.

Fench nodded, rubbing his trunk. "The invaders," he said.

Amendal raised his sleeve to his face. He hadn't put much thought into Fench's claims about invaders, but now he was curious.

They continued through the corridors, eventually entering a hallway that ended at a dead end five sections away. Partly liquefied corpses littered the hallway and the nearby stairwell. Much of the floor around the corpses was stained a dark reddish-brown. Most of the dead were armor clad, though some wore the battle garbs of mages—robes with metal plates fused into them.

Had Fench's people done this? *Or was it that monster from my nightmares...?* Amendal tightened his jaw and glanced to the winged creature. Fench flitted above the corpses, moving straight for the stairs.

"Wait!" Miraden called.

Fench spun, hovering in place. He lifted his helmet to reveal his hairless eyebrows. "Why?"

"We need to clear a path," Miraden said. "I don't want to step through *that.*" He pointed to the rotting corpses. Fench blinked at the retired soldier, looking confused—at least, what Amendal assumed was confusion.

"I'll move them," Amendal said. Ildin and Fendar chimed in as well. *Perhaps I should let them handle it,* Amendal thought. Illusionists couldn't smell through creatures or conjurations they enthralled.

Miraden called for everyone to step aside, and Amendal commanded his earthen giants to move ahead of the party. Ildin and Fendar did the same with the conjurations under their control. All the while, the soldiers and mercenaries crept back toward the maze of corridors. Amendal did the same with his other conjurations, especially the cisthyrn.

While the non-elemental conjurations retreated, the first of the earthen giants reached the corpses. Amendal focused his vision through the stony creature while dropping it to one knee. Among the dead, Amendal caught sight of an armored man turned on his side. The front of his breastplate was partially exposed and two crimson serpentine heads were emblazoned upon it. The heads looked similar to those of Mindolarn's seven-headed hydra...

Intrigued, Amendal commanded the earthen giant to turn the man over, revealing the entire emblem on the breastplate. It *was* the seven-headed hydra of Mindolarn.

"Oh no..." Amendal gasped.

"What is it?" Miraden shouted warily.

Amendal took full control of the earthen giant, turning over armored corpse after armored corpse. Each bore the symbol of the Mindolarn Empire on their breastplates.

She lied to us... Amendal's anger boiled. He had suspected Vaem was hiding something from them, but not something like this.

"By all that's magical!" Ildin gasped. His conjurations had also turned over several corpses.

A hand gripped Amendal's shoulder. Opening his eyes, Amendal turned around. Miraden stood beside him, his face twisted with worry.

"Well?" Miraden demanded.

"They're Mindolarnians," Amendal said. "They're all Mindolarnians!"

Miraden flinched and turned to the corpses. The man set his jaw, then cautiously moved toward the conjurations. An uproar of complaints surged among the soldiers, mercenaries, and mages. Several voiced Amendal's thoughts of betrayal. After all, everyone was under the impression that they would be the first to plunder Tardalim. Amid the outburst, Captain Edara stepped forward with a few of his sailors. There was a fury in the sea captain's eyes.

"That heartless whore..." Edara shook his head, mumbling to himself. Amendal thought it sounded like a vow of vengeance.

Amendal studied the sea captain for a moment, then returned his focus to the conjurations. Miraden was crouched beside the first earthen giant, inspecting the dead. Careful to not crush the retired soldier, Amendal began shoving the corpses to the wall. Some of the corpses dripped putrid liquid from their armor, leaving wet streaks on the stained ground. Ildin and Fendar's enthralled conjurations had already begun clearing the bodies and were partway to the stairs.

Soon, a wide path was cleared to the stairwell, though it was damp from the shifted bodies. Ildin moved to the landing and began clearing the steps by dropping the corpses over the railing. Collisions of metal rang through the air as the party approached the stairs.

Fench had since flown up and down the steps, reporting that the Shift had not yet occurred on the twenty-sixth floor. Both ends of the hallway above them were blocked.

Ildin soon finished clearing the stairs and moved his enthralled conjurations ahead while Miraden ordered everyone to wait on the stairs. The mercenaries complained loudly, but Miraden spurred them with insults and threats of being left behind as fodder for that monster. That compelled most to enter the stench-filled stairwell.

There were some who had obeyed immediately, particularly the soldiers and squad leaders. They had begun sifting through the corpses, some voicing hopes of discovering any sort of plunder: coins, trinkets, and tevisrals.

Disgusting, Amendal thought, carefully picking his way around the damp spots in the cleared path. The idea of rummaging through liquefied bodies made him shudder. He stopped at the bottom step, behind Edara and his sailors. He considered pushing his way to the top, but several of the men complained the stench was just as bad if not worse on the twenty-sixth floor.

Great...

Fighting the urge to vomit, Amendal returned his focus to his conjurations and took note of their positions. Most were in the cleared path, except a yaeltis and most of the cisthyrn. *Better clear some more room...* He sent a command to his earthen conjurations and they shoved more corpses out of the way. Soon, there was enough space for all his minions.

KEEP CLEARING, that voice said in Amendal's mind. IT IS CLOSE.

Amendal raised an eyebrow and shook his head. Was that voice referring to the polished dome the codger had shown him? According to that dream of his, finding it was the whole reason for coming to Tardalim... But why would he need to go to an ancient reliquary to find something among dead

Mindolarnians? Besides, he had no intention of touching those rotting corpses. Moving them with his conjurations was bad enough.

An irritated rumble echoed in Amendal's mind. *THERE IS A SHAN'AK AMONG THE MINDOLARNIANS. FIND IT!*

Amendal buried his face further into his sleeve. *There's no way I'm digging through those corpses,* he thought, eyeing the men sifting through the dead Mindolarnians. Several were inspecting weapons from fallen soldiers while others were studying an object that looked like a tevisral.

DON'T LET THEM DISCOVER IT! the voice said vehemently.

Amendal shook his head, his nose rubbing against his sleeve. There was no way he was going to move those corpses. But if he didn't comply, would the voice haunt him for the rest of his days? That thought made him reconsider.

"Fine," he muttered. *You win...*

"Are you all right?" Ildin whispered from beside Amendal. When had the illusionist moved? *Hadn't he been at the head of the party?*

Amendal studied his friend, his face still in his sleeve. "Do you remember the 'request' during the frostbite incident?"

Ildin nodded and moved closer. "What about it?"

"The old codger wants me to dig," Amendal said, then wiggled his eyebrows and his head toward the corpses. "He says it's in there."

The illusionist's eyes widened. "Really? In *that* heap?"

Amendal nodded and another rumble echoed in his mind. *THE SHIFT IS COMING...* the voice said. *HURRY!*

Growling into his sleeve, Amendal sent a command to the earthen conjurations and they began sifting through the corpses. *You know, you could tell me where it is.* The voice didn't reply. Amendal sighed and closed his eyes. He saw through each of the conjurations, but focused on the smaller earthen elementals. He let the earthen giants do the heavy lifting while the others did the sorting.

Many of the faces were sunken, lacking eyes. Their ajar mouths were empty of teeth. The hands of those not in armor were shriveled, looking like bones draped with dried skin. Amendal shuddered.

Soon, one of Amendal's conjurations came to a corpse with an oddly shaped face that was anything but human. Amendal flinched, but regained his composure.

"What's wrong?" Ildin asked.

Amendal didn't answer. Through his conjuration he studied the odd corpse. The strange skull protruded like the snout of an animal, and the rotting skin was a dark pink instead of putrid beige. The rest of its form was human-like, except its hands, which seemed larger, its fingers longer than a man's and tipped with black. On the floor beneath the corpse were hundreds of tiny crimson diamond-shaped plates. Were those scales?

Something black lay beneath the crimson scales, lodged into the dark reddish-brown gunk covering the floor. Its surface was smooth and it looked rounded, like a dome. Whatever it was looked too small to be that shan'ak thing, unless it was partly buried—

GOOD... the voice oozed in Amendal's mind, sounding pleased. NOW DIG IT OUT!

Amendal opened his eyes and glanced toward the ceiling. *That was a confirmation if I ever heard one...*

He quickly returned his focus to the earthen elemental, commanding it to kneel. Its rocky fingers swept the crimson scales away, then picked at the gunk. Chunks of the putrid substance came loose around the black object. It soon came free, and Amendal commanded the conjuration to retrieve it. The object *was* the shan'ak from his dream: shallow, dome-shaped, and the size of a man's hand. But only part of it had a polished sheen, the rest was tinged by the putrid substance encrusting the floor.

Hold on to it, Amendal commanded the conjuration, and the earthen elemental obeyed, concealing the black disk in its rocky hand.

"Did you find it?" Ildin whispered.

Amendal opened his eyes and turned to his friend. He began to nod, but stopped. Captain Edara was staring intently at Amendal. Had the sea captain overheard their conversation? *Not that it matters*, Amendal thought. He had been cryptic.

Ildin glanced over his shoulder, noticing the captain. "Let's go back to Miraden," the illusionist suggested, pushing his way through the crowd of mercenaries and soldiers.

Amendal followed after Ildin. He passed Edara, who continued studying him with cold eyes. *What's his problem?*

Once Amendal was partway up the stairs, Miraden began shouting furiously. "No! I forbid it!"

"But we would have an entire army!" Jaekim shouted, sounding flabbergasted. "Why shouldn't we use them?"

Amendal raised an eyebrow as he picked his way up the stairs. The two men could only be arguing about one thing: reanimating the dead Mindolarnians.

"Because they stink!" Miraden shouted.

"Do you want us all to vomit?" Bilanus asked frankly. "Can you not smell them?"

Amendal stepped around a short mercenary, so he could see ahead to the top step. Jaekim threw his hands into the air and shook his head. "What if that *thing* comes back? We could use the dead as a front line!"

Fendar and Scialas stood beside Jaekim, appalled at the necromancer's suggestion. Scialas put a hand to her mouth, looking woozy.

"Perhaps if they were just skeletons," a soldier said, shrugging. "But not like this. Those bodies..." He couldn't seem to find the words.

"The answer is no, Jaekim!" Miraden shouted. "Do not reanimate them!"

Fench fluttered among the men, his tail swaying. "What is reanniemay...?"

"He wants to bring them back from the dead," Orin said. Fench gasped, and then squealed. He quickly grabbed the bottom of his trunk to stifle the noise.

Jaekim's eyes widened while his jaw slackened. "How dare you accuse me of being an arpranist! I don't *bring* anything back from the dead. I *use* the dead!" He spun on Miraden. "And if you don't let us"—he gestured to another mage beside him—"then we won't have a chance against that monster when it returns."

Miraden's eyes narrowed. "My answer is firm, Jaekim." The retired soldier spun from the steps, disappearing beyond the rail.

Jaekim threw his hands into the air again. "You let the conjurer use his pets! Why can't I use mine?!"

"Because his don't stink," Bilanus pointed to Amendal. "Well, except for those mages' parasites…"

Quinta'shals, Amendal thought, fighting the urge to correct the man. If there hadn't been tension among the party, he wouldn't have bit his tongue.

Jaekim muttered to himself as Amendal reached the highest step. Ildin hurried after Miraden, who was standing in the section of hallway beyond the stairwell. It too was littered with corpses. Among the dead Mindolarnians were winged creatures that resembled Fench, although they were twice his size. Those dead Tuladine were covered in thin armor that matched Fench's helmet.

Amendal turned to Fench, but the young creature didn't seem to notice its dead kin. *Or perhaps he's ignoring them*—

A sharp ping resounded from the walls, followed by the luminescent lines heralding a Shift.

"Be ready to move!" Miraden shouted. The light on the walls and ceiling darkened in color, followed by two more pings. The white stone blocking the hallways vanished, revealing long corridors.

Fench immediately fluttered to the left and Miraden chased after him. Amendal followed, sending a mental command for his conjurations to do the same. Beside him, Jaekim continued muttering complaints.

Amendal was glad Miraden had been firm in his orders. The thought of rotting corpses walking among the party was sickening.

"I do hope we can rest soon," said a mercenary beside Amendal.

Another mercenary snorted. "Not till after we get clear of the stench."

———◆———

Faelinia was perplexed at Commander Calimir's abrupt change in behavior. Vaem had done *something* to him. Whatever had happened abated the hostilities between the two of them, enabling the expedition to continue their ascent.

They managed to climb up to the fifteenth floor without any further incidents, but Morgidian and the other barsionists had kept everyone shielded with their magic. They encountered only one rearranging of the halls on the twelfth floor, which forced them to take a new route that was at least ten grand phineals out of the way.

Unlike the other floors, the staircase to the sixteenth was nowhere to be found. Faelinia had sent her illusions down every possible turn, but each corridor was blocked. The report drew complaints of fatigue.

"We'll rest here!" Vaem shouted. "Squad one will take first watch, then two and three."

Sighs of relief filled the corridor. They had been meandering through Tardalim's halls for quite some time. *Was it past midnight?* Perhaps they had marched all night...

While everyone settled down, Faelinia picked her way to a nearby doorway. They had passed many of those doorways, but most were blocked. The corridor's uniform nature spurred her curiosity. What lay behind each of those doors? She wished she'd had the time to investigate the rooms beyond them.

One benefit to first watch, she thought, sighing.

Faelinia peered through the door as she approached. Rows of cylindrical beige crystals—encased by golden framework—lined a large room, stacked on top of one another four times over. Each crystal contained a darkened silhouette, either masculine or feminine. Were men and women trapped inside them? *Or entombed?*

Intrigued, Faelinia entered the vast room, studying it with a sweeping glance. It looked to be as wide as the hallway sections were long. She glanced over her shoulder, noting the width of the hallway and the depth of the room. *That's the same length,* she thought. Faelinia put the measurements aside and approached the nearest crystal.

The feminine silhouette inside became clearer with each step. The woman looked bald, and her skin was a dark blue, and her face—Faelinia flinched and brought a hand to her mouth to muffle a scream, but no scream came. The woman trapped inside was not a woman at all, but a hairless creature covered in blue *scales*. And her face... it was an elongated snout that looked reptilian.

"What's wrong?" Dardel shouted from behind Faelinia.

She fought to turn, but every muscle felt frozen. Faelinia couldn't help but stare at the creature in the crystal. "They're not human," she muttered. "And it's unlike anything I've ever seen."

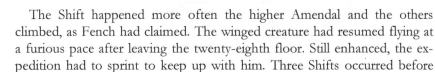

The Shift happened more often the higher Amendal and the others climbed, as Fench had claimed. The winged creature had resumed flying at a furious pace after leaving the twenty-eighth floor. Still enhanced, the expedition had to sprint to keep up with him. Three Shifts occurred before they ascended the next flight of stairs.

On Tardalim's thirty-first floor, the Shift happened every few minutes. Fench told the expedition to stop several times even before a Shift occurred. Bilanus contested Fench's claim that the Shifts had no pattern to them, but Fench ignored him.

Eventually, the expedition ran into the section housing the staircase leading to the thirty-second floor. Two faint pings resonated from up the stairs as they began their ascent. Fench fluttered halfway up the staircase and spun.

"The Shift is really fast up there," Fench said. "You have to be careful."

"How fast?" Miraden asked.

Fench shrugged. "Fast. You'll see. Just listen."

The rest of the party crammed into the landing while the conjurations waited in the section along the stairs.

Another ping resonated from the upper halls. The light indicating the Shift reflected off the walls of the stairwell, followed by two pings. By Amendal's estimate, the Shift occurred almost every minute.

"The stairs don't move up there," Fench said. "So it's not too hard to find your way to the Roost."

Several of the mercenaries and soldiers exchanged dumbfounded looks. "Well, that's good," one of the men said, sarcastically.

"Everyone bunch together on the landing," Miraden shouted. "And be ready to run."

"Why don't we use the conjurations?" Ildin asked. "We can ride atop them, so we're not so spread out."

Miraden studied Amendal, then the two illusionists.

"It's a good idea!" Fench said, a smile forming on the end of his trunk.

"Can you two handle that?" Miraden asked Ildin and Fendar. "I know Amendal can."

"Yes," Fendar said tersely. Ildin nodded, not seeming to take offense.

Miraden turned to the men and called out the squads that were to ride atop the conjurations. That left only three groups that would be running, including Amendal's. Another ping resonated as everyone got into position.

"Fench, how close are we to the Roost?" Miraden asked.

Fench stroked his trunk. "Uh, well this is the last floor. That's why the stairs don't move."

"That's not what I was asking. How far away are the stairs, in terms of grand phineals?"

"Grand what?" Fench asked.

Miraden narrowed his eyes at Fench but didn't speak. That drew mirthful chuckles from most of the squads, including Amendal. *He's so much like a child...*

Bilanus, however, wasn't laughing. "And what about the tevisrals?" he asked, his tone serious. "Where are they?"

Fench eyed the squad leader, then answered him. "The teviss... ralls are hidden beneath the Roost. I'll show you."

"If you don't lure the yaeltis with bait, they'll most likely charge and try to impale you on their tusks. Of course, such an impaling will kill you. But yaeltis tusks are poisonous—the older the yaeltis, the more potent the venom. Even the feeblest yaeltis can kill with a simple prick from their tusks."

- From *Colvinar Vrium's Bestiary for Conjurers*, page 115

A ping echoed throughout the halls of Tardalim's thirty-second floor. Amendal came to an abrupt halt, sweat beading on his forehead. *Stop!* he commanded his conjurations. They obeyed as the lines on the walls and ceiling became luminous.

"We're not far," Fench said. "Wait for two more Shifts, then on the third run backward." That was the fourth time that he had told them to turn around.

Without Fench the thirty-second floor would be an impossible maze to navigate. *I doubt the others will make it this far,* Amendal thought.

"Get into position," Miraden shouted between heavy breaths.

Amendal sent the command to his conjurations as he turned around. The second set of pings filled the hall before he reached the section's border they had just crossed. A solid white wall appeared in front of them. Amendal had tried to watch the Shift occur, but it all happened too quickly.

Everyone crept to the section's edge, forming a line. The conjurations took up position behind them in two rows.

A single ping filled the hall, and Amendal readied to dash. The others did the same while Fench fluttered above them.

Amendal wiped the sweat from his forehead as the double pings filled the hall. The wall in front of him vanished, and he darted forward. Fench sped overhead, crossing into the next section of hallway before Amendal and the others could get halfway across. The winged creature slowed his flight, stopping two more sections away.

"Hurry!" Fench called.

They were one section away from Fench when a single ping filled the corridor. *Faster...* Amendal chided himself, eyeing the color-shifting lines.

The hue darkened to vermillion as he crossed the line on the floor, but he kept running. So did the others. The double ping reverberated through the hall and Amendal felt something hard grazing the backs of the conjurations in the rear. *Too close...*

"Keep going!" Fench shouted, zipping overhead. Once again he flew ahead of the party, stopping two sections away. This dash would be only slightly shorter than the last. "The stairs will be in the next section!"

Amendal ran with all his might. When he was half a section away from Fench, the heralding ping filled the corridor.

The party neared the winged creature but kept running. They were halfway through that section when the Shift occurred, a single ping ringing through the hall.

In the blink of an eye, the hallway ahead of them changed. A staircase lined the left wall, identical to every other they had ascended in Tardalim. Fench flew into the new section and hovered over the bottom step, waiting for the group to join him.

"Stay straight!" Miraden shouted.

Amendal didn't dare turn toward the stairs, lest he bump into someone. He passed beneath Fench and stumbled as he stopped. Ildin did the same, as did Scialas. Fendar was more graceful. And Jaekim... well, he looked like a drunk with his arms flailing—but then Jaekim always appeared intoxicated.

The conjurations fell in line as the luminous lines darkened. Amendal bent over, hands on his knees, and the double pings filled the hall. The corridor in front of them changed into a corner section, bending to the right.

Lowering his head, Amendal breathed heavily. Those around him sighed with relief while others whooped and cheered.

"You two-legs did pretty well," Fench said. "And no one got squished!"

Miraden called for Amendal and the illusionists to allow the squads to dismount from the earthen giants. A wave of dizziness washed over Amendal as he commanded the conjurations to kneel, then he began pacing back and forth. It felt like he had run a dozen grand phineals. *Have to keep moving...*

"To the stairs," Miraden shouted. He didn't seem winded in the slightest.

Breathing heavily, Amendal trudged toward the stairs. Those who had ridden the conjurations hurried after Miraden, but Amendal and his friends lagged behind. Another Shift occurred as Miraden began climbing the stairs.

"That was... grueling..." Ildin said between breaths.

"No kidding!" Jaekim snorted.

Scialas just nodded and held her side as she walked.

"Shall we send the conjurations ahead of us?" Fendar asked.

Amendal nodded. He stopped short of the bottom landing and paced along the stairwell. Soon, another Shift occurred. He gestured to Ildin and Fendar. "You two go first."

The enthralled earthen giants moved toward the stairs, but waited for the last squad to begin their climb. Fendar sent the conjurations under his control first.

Another Shift occurred, and Amendal ceased pacing. He leaned against the wall beneath the railing, staring at the floor. Its concave curve was more pronounced than any of Tardalim's other levels. Amendal glanced to his left, where the Shift had formed a long corridor. The curve in the floor continued throughout each section, causing the floor to *rise* the farther it extended into the distance.

"Do you see that?" Amendal asked, pointing to his left. A lone ping heralded a coming Shift.

"See what?" Jaekim asked. He reached into his pack, removing a flask.

"The floor—"

The double ping filled the hall, then a wall of stone appeared in place of the long corridor.

"What about the floor?" Scialas asked.

"It's bowed," Amendal said. "I saw it before, but it looks more pronounced up here."

Fendar nodded. "I noticed that as well. The floor's curve seemed to gradually increase the higher we climbed."

"I don't see anything," Jaekim said.

Ildin folded his arms, raising an eyebrow at the necromancer. "That's because you're drunk..."

Jaekim shrugged, then plodded toward the stairs.

The last of Ildin's enthralled conjurations was partway up the stairs when Fench fluttered over the railing. He hovered beside Amendal, a grin forming on those strange lips of his.

"Are you coming?" Fench asked.

"Yes," Amendal said, pushing himself from the wall.

With his conjurations trailing behind him, Amendal and his friends followed Fench up the stairs.

"I'll be glad to rest," Ildin said, bracing himself against the railing.

"Are you sure that monster can't reach us?" Scialas asked.

Fench nodded, his trunk bouncing with each head bob. "No *prisoners* can enter the Roost. Only the Tuladine and friends."

"Are you sure we can enter?" Ildin asked.

"Pretty sure," Fench said. "I remember a two-leg came a long time ago. He entered and left the Roost. And when the first invaders came my father said no *prisoner* could get past these stairs, but the invaders could."

"How is that possible?" Fendar asked, raising an eyebrow.

Fench shrugged.

Amendal and the others soon reached the top of the stairs. But instead of emptying onto a landing, the stairs opened into an enormous oval space. It was four stories tall like the rest of Tardalim, but was over a hundred phineals wide and perhaps four or five hundred phineals deep. Elaborate stone reliefs adorned the walls from floor to ceiling, depicting a vicious battle between men, elves, and dragons. There were other creatures as well, some Amendal didn't recognize. The ceiling was also adorned with a continuation of the reliefs, depicting only winged creatures.

A battle from the Dragon Wars? The reliefs reminded him of passages from *Greater Conjurations from the Aldinal Plane.* He put the thoughts aside and glanced to the floor. It too was curved, like a shallow bowl. None of his friends seemed to notice the floor. They were too busy admiring the reliefs.

At the far end of the room, two enormous, polished, black stone statues, carved in the likeness of the Tuladine, hovered a phineal above the floor. The statues faced each other, their trunks arching to hold aloft a transparent sphere that was as round as a man was tall. The statues held golden spears, the tips pointed down and behind them.

Miraden stood beside the left statue with two squads' worth of men, mostly soldiers. *Where are the others?*

Beyond the statues, an ascending staircase led to an angled oval tunnel. From what Amendal could tell, the tunnel ceased at the highest step. On either side of the stairs were round doorways, like those throughout Tardalim.

"Where are the others?" Ildin asked.

"Getting teviss... ralls," Fench said, annoyed.

Miraden nodded and pointed to the doorways. "They'll be joining us shortly. Now Fench, will you show us where we can rest?"

"Yup!" The winged creature flew toward the stairs in a corkscrew, his arms stretched wide. As he passed between the statues the transparent sphere pulsed with gray light. Fench zipped through the oval tunnel and disappeared within a vast space beyond the steps.

Miraden and the others followed, and the sphere pulsed a yellow hue. *Why the different color?* Amendal wondered. He and his friends followed Miraden, with the conjurations trailing behind them. The larger conjurations barely fit between the two Tuladine statues.

Before climbing the stairs, Amendal turned around. As the conjurations passed beneath the sphere it pulsed with a pale golden light speckled with a variety of colors. *It has to be sensing different types of creatures. I wonder if—*

"Are you coming?" Ildin called.

Turning from the sphere, Amendal hurried up the steps.

⟞•⟝

Faelinia could not rest. She tossed and turned atop the hard floor, but she couldn't shake the image of that *thing* trapped within the crystal. Dardel had been equally perplexed. So were Morgidian and everyone else who saw it… except for Vaem and Kydol.

Why? Faelinia wondered, turning onto her back. *What does she know?* Vaem had simply raised an eyebrow at the strange being and then walked away.

Hoping to think of something else, Faelinia turned onto her side, facing the hallway behind them. The large corridor stretched for perhaps a grand phineal before turning left.

While staring at the bend, her thoughts turned to Amendal. Where was he? *I hope he didn't encounter that monster,* she thought. If he had, the big oaf wouldn't have had a barsion. The monster would have turned him mad, like the others. *He's too confident in his mages' parasites.* But a mages' parasite couldn't defend against the monster's maddening haze, could it?

Better to be protected by a barsion—

A hunched-over figure limped around the distant bend, wearing what appeared to be a black robe. Faelinia couldn't tell if the person was a man or a woman. Their hair looked dark. Whoever it was slumped against the wall and struggled with each step.

Faelinia leapt to her feet, spinning around. "Commander!"

But Calimir was nowhere to be found. Nor was Vaem. What had she done to the commander?

Dardel rose from the ground and hurried toward her while directing his gaze down the hall. "Who is that?" he demanded. Jaw set, he gripped his sword hilt, called for an arpranist, then ran.

One of the mages on second watch picked his way through the camp as Faelinia chased after Calimir's second-in-command.

Soon, Faelinia, Dardel and the arpranist were running together. Now closer, Faelinia knew the person was a man, but she didn't recognize him. Perhaps he was a necromancer, since he was wearing a black robe. Was he one of the mages who had run ahead in a panic, or had he been separated from Amendal? If the latter, where was Amendal? A knot formed in her stomach. *Oh, Amendal…*

The limping man staggered, then fell forward. He lay motionless on the ground. Dardel groaned, and the arpranist began uttering an incantation. Arpran light swirled around the mage, tingeing Tardalim's white walls with a green hue.

They were upon the man before the incantation was finished. Faelinia knelt beside him and gasped. His robe was tattered and stained with blood. Large gashes marred his back while deep gouges disfigured his neck. Had he been mauled by the monster?

"He's alive," Dardel said, pulling his hand from the man's neck. Dardel eased his hands around the man's head, turning the fellow's face toward his. "It's Uldric!"

Faelinia had seen this man flee with several soldiers during the battle with the monster. But where were the soldiers?

As she pondered, the arpran magic surged through Uldric. His wounds glowed green, then began to regenerate. He gasped and shook, but Dardel grabbed his shoulder, steadying him.

"You'll be all right," Dardel said.

Uldric sucked in a breath, then eased back onto the floor. Faelinia moved to his side, studying the necromancer. Uldric's face was haunted. He stared through Calimir's second-in-command, rarely blinking.

"What happened?" Dardel asked. "Where are the others?"

Uldric didn't answer.

Dardel rubbed his chin, then turned to Faelinia. "Can you make him talk?"

Faelinia was shocked at the suggestion. "Place a mind control spell upon him?" she asked, aghast. "After what he's been through?!" She fought the urge to spew a rebuke. Uldric had experienced enough trauma.

"We need to know." Dardel's tone was somber. "The monster could be upon us again."

Faelinia stepped back, folding her arms.

"Please," Dardel said, rising to his feet. "We have to know."

Lips pursed, Faelinia considered the request. "Fine... I'll do—"

"It came..." Uldric muttered, still lying on the floor. "I wanted to hide. But Kaerune pushed us forward."

Dardel spun and knelt beside Uldric once again. The necromancer wheezed, then continued speaking. "It charged at us... I tried to run, but it swiped me with its claws. I... I fell and the screams—oh, those screams!"

Uldric's eyes widened, his breath quickening.

"What happened next?" Dardel asked. "How did you survive?"

Uldric blinked. "I crawled to an open door. The monster was too busy with the soldiers. It ate them, one by one. The monster tore them in pieces, ripping them from their armor as if shelling nuts. When it came for me, I was already through the door. It tried to grab me, but clawed my leg. I scurried back, as far as I could. Eventually, it left. I was about to wait, but I heard moaning outside the room. I crawled back into the hall and found Kaerune—well, what was left of her. She begged me to kill her..."

Uldric paused as the last of his wounds became whole.

"And?" Dardel urged.

"Siphoning her life barely restored me," Uldric said, then fell silent.

How horrible... Faelinia turned away, shaking her head.

"Let's move him," Dardel said. He and the arpranist grunted, then walked past Faelinia with Uldric under their shoulders.

This expedition is all wrong, she thought. Faelinia took a deep breath and closed her eyes. While following the others, she settled her eyes on the tears in Uldric's robe. She had expected them to be jagged, with lots of fraying. But the tearing looked more like cuts. Had the monster's claws been *that* sharp?

Amendal staggered to a halt as he entered the Roost. The others did the same, and several gasped in awe.

The Roost was a gigantic spherical chamber. Its ceiling was perhaps two thousand phineals above the stairs. In contrast to the rest of Tardalim, the Roost was teeming with strange flora. None of the white stone was visible. The floor immediately around the steps was covered in lush dark-teal grass. Strange violet bushes with seven-pointed leaves lined the oval tunnel housing the stairs.

Structures that resembled auburn-colored tree trunks rose all throughout the Roost. They were even protruding from the sides of the chamber and hanging from the ceiling. Those nearby were over twice the height of the tallest buildings in Soroth. Many were covered in florescent yellow vines whose leaves had streaks of orange and red within them. Each of those tree-like structures had holes along their sides. Were those windows, or doorways? *Was that a difference Fench and his kind even considered?*

Miraden, the soldiers, and the mercenaries walked from the stairs, their heads tilted back.

Ildin's jaw went slack and his eyes widened. "This is incredible!"

"It's so beautiful," Scialas murmured, kneeling and running her hand through the dark-teal grass.

"A paradise," Fendar whispered.

Jaekim pushed past Miraden and flung himself on the ground, spreading his arms and legs wide. "I'll just sleep here," he said, flask still in hand.

Amendal stepped around his friends, searching for Fench. The winged creature fluttered down from one of those tree-trunk-like structures, minus his helmet and weapon. He zipped around Miraden and the other soldiers, stopping in front of Amendal.

"Welcome to my home!" Fench said, his arms stretched wide.

"It's a big home," one of the soldiers said.

"Well, it's not all mine." Fench turned and pointed the direction where he had flown from. "My rooms are over there."

"In one of those tree trunks?" Miraden asked.

"Tree... what?" Fench rubbed his trunk and then held it up. "This is a trunk."

"Do you not know what a tree is?" a soldier asked.

Fench just blinked at the man. Ildin gave a brief explanation, but Fench cocked his head.

"That tall structure," Miraden said. "The ones covered in the vines. They look like the trunk of a tree."

"You mean the houses?" Fench asked, gesturing to the structure beside him.

Miraden nodded, then looked at the other so-called houses all throughout the Roost. "There must have been so many of your kind."

Fench lowered his head and dropped his trunk. "There used to be... before the invaders."

Poor thing, Amendal thought.

"You're not alone any more, Fench," Ildin said

Fench shook his head. "No, I'm not. You're here now."

Miraden raised an eyebrow at Fench's statement. He studied the others before speaking. "Where can we set up camp?"

"Anywhere," Fench said.

Hefting their packs, the few soldiers and mercenaries followed Miraden around the oval tunnel housing the stairs. They marched toward an open space between several of those tree-trunk structures and began erecting tents. Amendal and the others, however, stayed with Fench.

"I'm exhausted," Ildin said.

Jaekim began to snore softly. Fench spun in the air, nearly tipping over sideways. "What is that?!"

"Does your kind not snore?" Fendar asked.

Fench stared at the illusionist, blinking several times.

Scialas giggled. "Sometimes we make those sounds when we sleep." She glanced to Fendar. "Jaekim isn't the only one who snores."

Fendar frowned and shook his head.

"Amendal, can you take the conjurations back?" Ildin asked. He ran a hand through his blond hair and struggled to stand straight. "At least for a little while?"

"I can try," Amendal said. Reclaiming a conjuration that had been severed from him was a fairly easy task, but there was the matter of conjuration magic not manifesting in Tardalim... That and staying awake himself.

IT WILL WORK, that voice said. *RECLAIM YOUR EARTHEN CREATURES.*

Eyebrows raised, Amendal glanced to the distant ceiling.

"What?" Ildin asked. "Did *he* say something?" ·

Amendal nodded. "Bring them up here."

Fendar turned to Amendal, confused. "Who is 'he'?"

"The voice in my head..."

Scialas and Fendar exchanged concerned glances.

"Wake me if you get too tired," Ildin said. "I... I just need to nap."

Amendal nodded and uttered an incantation. He and the others stepped away from the stairs, allowing enough room for the conjurations to enter the Roost. Charcoal light swirled around his hands as the enthralled conjurations ascended the stairs. Ildin would have to relinquish his control before Amendal could reclaim the earthen giants.

"One at a time," Ildin said.

The first conjuration stepped onto the dark-teal grass, standing perfectly still. As Amendal finished his spell, the earthen giant jolted and took an aimless step. But before it could roam free, the charcoal light struck it.

Stop! Amendal commanded, and the giant stilled. The reclaiming felt like a weight in his mind. Reclaiming all of them would be extremely taxing. "If I only had some messel…"

"I could check the supplies?" Scialas said.

Amendal nodded and commanded the conjuration to step aside. "That would help."

"What's messel?" Fench asked.

"A drink that helps you stay awake," Ildin said, and another conjuration ascended the steps. "It stops you from falling asleep."

"Like umviliums!" Fench said and zipped away.

"What?" Ildin asked, but Fench had already disappeared beyond the Tuladine houses.

Amendal began uttering another incantation. Before long, he finished reclaiming his conjurations from Ildin and Fendar. As he had assumed, reacquiring the additional conjurations was quite taxing. *Perhaps if I were rested, it wouldn't be so bad.*

Several groups of mercenaries had since entered the Roost and joined Miraden and the others in the camp. They carried full sacks, but Amendal hadn't seen their contents. Scialas and Fendar had also joined them and were helping organize a very late meal.

In an effort to combat his fatigue and mental exhaustion, Amendal lowered himself to sit cross-legged on the grass and stared at the camp. *Focus,* he told himself and exaggerated his breathing.

Fench soon returned, zipping around the conjurations. The winged creature circled once, then came to an abrupt halt. His tail came close to slapping Amendal in the face. "Here!" Fench said, extending his cupped hands toward Amendal. The umviliums looked like tiny maroon seeds. "Eat!"

Amendal furrowed his brow. "All of them?"

"Yes!" Fench said, moving his hands close to Amendal's lips. "Do you want me to feed you?"

Shaking his head, Amendal cupped a hand. After Fench meticulously moved each one, Amendal shoved them into his mouth.

A surge of heat—warmth, not spice—ignited in his mouth. It spread down his throat, across his cheeks, and around his head. The warmth brought a renewing clarity. The taxation of the extra conjurations faded. It was as if Amendal had awakened from a restful night's sleep.

The clarity, however, evoked an unquenchable thirst. "Fench," Amendal croaked, "I need water!"

"Yaeltis poison is secreted throughout hibernation and lingers on the tusks. The poison hardens as it dries, encrusting the tusks before the hibernation period ends."

- From *Colvinar Vrium's Bestiary for Conjurers*, page 116

Amendal's throat burned. "This way!" Fench cried, zipping around a tree-trunk-like building. Amendal, cradled by one of the yaeltis, commanded the conjuration to run after the winged creature. Fench flew past two more structures, then turned right. "It's here!"

The conjured yaeltis turned, bounding straight for a clearing that held a large pool of clear water. *Lower me!* Before the yaeltis's hand reached the ground, Amendal leapt toward the pool. He stumbled onto the dark-teal grass, tripped, then fell face-first. Pushing himself up, he staggered toward the water. Once near the pool he threw himself onto its bank.

Landing on his chest, Amendal shoved his hands into the water. A stinging chill pierced his fingers. He struggled to cup his hands as he raised them from the frigid pool. But before his hands reached his lips, the water drained completely.

No! Amendal shoved his hands back into the water, and the chill pierced his fingers once again. "Oh, it burns," he cried.

Amid Amendal's pain, he heard the fluttering of Fench's wings. The winged creature flittered over the pool, then dipped his tail into the water. His lower wings stopped fluttering, and only the upper two continued moving.

"Do you need help?" Fench asked. He lowered his tiny hands into the water, unfazed by the frigid temperature.

Hands shaking, Amendal pulled them from the freezing pool. He struggled to retain the water as he brought his hands to his lips. What little made it into his mouth sent a shiver down his spine. His mouth was a strange dichotomy of too hot and too cold. The frigid water sent a spike of pain through his nose and up his forehead.

Water splashed, and Fench dipped his tiny hands into the pool. "Here," he said, extending his cupped hands.

Amendal struggled to breathe as Fench pressed his clammy hands to Amendal's lips. Surprisingly, the water was not as cold. But how was that possible?

Fench dipped his hands back into the water, then proffered another drink. Amendal accepted it and the burning began to lessen. Fench continued helping, until Amendal was finally able to speak.

"That's better," he said. "Thank you, Fench."

A smile formed on the end of Fench's trunk. "I'm glad you feel better. I don't know why it was burning."

Sucking in a deep breath, Amendal stood and surveyed the Roost. They had run a considerable distance. *Where are we?* He reached out to his other conjurations, which were still at the stairs. He couldn't see them, but they were partway up the chamber's curved wall to his left. *Up the wall?*

Amendal started. How was that possible? The ground where Amendal stood felt like level ground. But according to where the conjurations were, *he* should be partly on the Roost's curved walls.

"This doesn't make any sense," he muttered, focusing on the conjurations, particularly their directional senses. To them, they too stood on level ground.

"What's wrong?" Fench asked.

Amendal turned toward the winged creature. "We're on the wall."

Fench rose from the pool, shaking his tail and flapping his lower wings. "No we're not. This is the ground. There are no walls in the Roost."

Confused, Amendal turned back to his conjurations. True, it felt as if he were standing on the ground, but so were the conjurations. Amendal set his jaw and looked about the Roost. He studied the structures hanging from the ceiling. They too were surrounded by the dark-teal grass.

"What about up there?" Amendal asked, pointing to the ceiling. "Isn't that this chamber's ceiling?"

Fench followed the gesture. "No... That's ground. Every place is the ground."

Impossible! Amendal thought. "That's absurd..."

"Ab-what?"

Amendal chuckled, then reached out to his conjured gosset. It was perched atop one of the earthen giants, as it had been for most of the trek through Tardalim. *Fly,* he commanded. He was going to discover the truth for himself. Amendal kept the conjured bird a few stories off the ground. He struggled to keep it flying in a straight line, but he didn't want to fly above the strange buildings.

He followed the conjuration with his mind, occasionally spotting it among the buildings protruding from the side of the Roost. It soon neared the ceiling, but to the conjuration the ceiling *was* the ground.

Amendal watched the bird fly between the hanging structures while sensing through the gosset that the buildings were not hanging at all. A strange sense of disorientation came over Amendal, and he fell forward. He closed his eyes, but couldn't shake the sensation.

The gosset continued its flight, nearly completing a full circle around the Roost. Once it was near, the disorientation abated. *To me,* he commanded. The gosset flew above the frigid pool, then fluttered to perch atop Amendal's shoulder.

"What is this place...?" he muttered.

"My home," Fench said.

Amendal raised an eyebrow at the winged creature. "This place isn't normal..."

"Yes, it is."

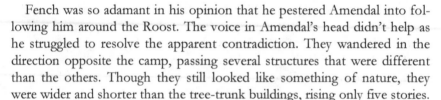

Fench was so adamant in his opinion that he pestered Amendal into following him around the Roost. The voice in Amendal's head didn't help as he struggled to resolve the apparent contradiction. They wandered in the direction opposite the camp, passing several structures that were different than the others. Though they still looked like something of nature, they were wider and shorter than the tree-trunk buildings, rising only five stories. They were arranged in an oval around a clearing that held another staircase. Fench explained that it was where the younglings learned.

They continued for a little while longer until they reached an open area about the same size as several Soroth city blocks. Four rivers, spaced equally apart, flowed toward a pit at the heart of the open area. Each river emptied into a perfect ring—two or so dozen phineals wide—that wrapped around the pit. From what Amendal could tell, the pit looked twice as large as the tunnel at Tardalim's entrance. It was hemmed by a stone walkway that seemed to prevent the rivers' overflow from entering it.

"What is that?" Amendal asked, pointing to the pit.

"It goes somewhere else," Fench said. "It's how we *leave*." He put a perturbed emphasis on the last word. "The others went that way."

"You're telling me that pit leads back to the entrance?"

Fench shook his head.

"So, there's another way out of Tardalim?" he asked. "Besides the entrance."

"That's the only way," Fench said, and fluttered away.

The only way? Amendal wondered, eyeing the water rimming the pit and the stone walkway. If the overflow was as frigid as the pool, then the expedition would need a way across. But there were no bridges to the pit, or across any of the rivers. *Why would the Tuladine need a bridge?* he thought. *They probably just fly into the pit—*

A call from Fench interrupted Amendal, and he turned to face the winged creature. Fench was on the other side of the river, waving for Amendal.

"How am I going to cross that?" he shouted, pointing to the river.

Fench pointed toward the nearby buildings, at the yaeltis lumbering into the open area.

They continued their tour of the Roost, eventually arriving back at the camp erected by Miraden. Many of the soldiers and mercenaries had returned from their plundering. A savory aroma filled the air with hints of tangy herbs. Near the camp's heart, one of the sailors stirred a stew within a cauldron that looked as if it had been transmuted. The fire pit beneath the cauldron was probably the source for the transmutation.

So the ground here is changeable, Amendal mused. *Maybe Dugal can make a bridge to the pit.*

Fench sniffed loudly beside Amendal. "What is that?!" he cried with excitement and sped toward the chef, his tail flailing. He zipped in front of a mercenary, accidently slapping his tail against the man's face.

"Careful, fairy!" the mercenary spat.

Amendal chuckled, watching Fench flutter to an abrupt halt in front of the boiling stew. The sailor glanced nervously at Fench, but then returned his attention to the stew.

"It smells so good!" Fench said.

Miraden emerged from between a pair of tents, smiling. "You're welcome to have some." Fench squealed with excitement, and the sailor poured him a bowl.

Amendal turned, eyeing Miraden as he approached. Once near, he leaned toward Amendal. "Are you tired?" Was he worried about the conjurations running amok?

"I'm fine," Amendal said. "When Ildin and Fendar wake up, I'll have them enthrall the conjurations."

"That might be awhile," Miraden said. He sucked in his breath and looked about the camp. "How do you feel about moving them? In case you accidently lose control."

Amendal shrugged. It wasn't a bad suggestion, but after eating those umviliums he hadn't felt the slightest bit of fatigue. "I think I'll be fine. Fench gave me something that has me wide awake. But I'll move them."

"Much appreciated," Miraden said, then stepped away. "Now if you'll excuse me, I want some rest."

———◦•◦———

Even after Ildin and Fendar awoke, Amendal had trouble sleeping. The effect of the umviliums had not worn off in the slightest. Prior to relinquishing control, Amendal had claimed the shan'ak from his earthen conjuration. He had also asked Fench to wash it in the pool of frigid water. There was no way he was going to carry it around with all that gunk on it.

In an attempt to relax, Amendal lay on his cot inside his and Ildin's tent, studying the strange black object. What was it? And why was it important? Amendal glanced to the tent's ceiling, hoping to hear an answer from the voice in his head.

Nothing? The voice had spoken only once after he discovered the shan'ak, and the remark wasn't even related to the strange object. *Perhaps I'm free of him...*

Sighing, Amendal twirled the shan'ak. Its entire surface was incredibly smooth. *For all I know, this could be a paperweight...* He glanced to the tent ceiling again, but there was still no reply. Well, whatever it was, Amendal was going to keep it for himself.

He leaned on his side and slipped the black object into his pack, shoving it down toward the handwritten copies of his family's tomes.

As Amendal nestled back into his bed, soldiers and mercenaries began moving through the camp, boasting of their discoveries. Some claimed to have found weapons that burst with magic, and armor that was more than mere metal. Others spoke of finding ancient tevisrals, things that were rumored to exist in only myths and legends.

Amendal closed his eyes and turned on his side. He breathed deeply, hoping to relax enough to fall asleep. But not even the slightest hint of fatigue overcame him.

This is a waste, he thought. Those umviliums seemed to have doomed him to perpetual sleeplessness.

He tossed on his cot, facing a tent wall where several mercenaries loudly conversed with Edara's sailors. The noise didn't help, either.

Amendal tossed again, pulled his blanket over his head, and plugged an ear. With the conversation muffled, Amendal's mind began to wander but soon settled on Faelinia. Where was she? How far had she and the others ascended through Tardalim? *Probably not very far,* he thought. Without Fench, navigating Tardalim's shifting halls would be near impossible. Of course, she was probably scouting ahead with her flying illusions and finding staircases, but there was no way that would work once they reached Tardalim's higher floors.

"They're not going to make it here..."

Well, unless Vaem had a solution. She knew the expedition needed to ascend to the higher floors. Perhaps she had a way of navigating Tardalim. Besides, those other Mindolarnians had made it to the twenty-fifth floor. Could they have had—?

Is that it? Amendal wondered, opening his eyes and staring at his pack. Was that shan'ak something that could navigate Tardalim?

Intrigued, Amendal tossed aside his covers and reached into his pack. He fished the shan'ak out and studied it once more. Was it a sort of mapping tevisral? Could it show the Shifts? But wouldn't Fench have recognized it?

"Well, he is a child..."

Turning the shan'ak over once more, Amendal returned it to his pack. He soon eased back onto his cot and closed his eyes.

There has to be a way to find them, he thought, turning on his side. The sailors were still boasting of their discoveries. "Treasure hunters..." he complained with a grunt. Amendal tossed again, plugging his exposed ear. Suddenly, horrific images flashed in his mind. He saw that monster chasing Faelinia and the others through Tardalim's halls. It consumed her companions, and then—

"No!" He sat upright, running a hand through his hair.

The tent door flapped open, and Ildin poked his head inside. He started as his sapphire eyes settled on Amendal. "You're still awake...?"

"I can't sleep." Amendal shook his head. "Those damned umviliums."

"Maybe I should eat some," Ildin said.

They stared at each other for a moment before the illusionist broke the silence. "Miraden is organizing a rescue party. Fench says he can show us how to find the others with some kind of map."

Amendal tossed aside his covers and leapt to his feet. "When do we leave?"

"In this encrusted state, the poison is dormant. But when it touches something moist, the poison activates. Blood seems to catalyze the poison faster than any other liquid."

- From *Colvinar Vrium's Bestiary for Conjurers*, page 117

Determined find Faelinia, Amendal hurried from his tent with Ildin in tow. The camp was teeming with excitement. The talk of tevisrals carried through the air as Amendal made his way to the meeting Ildin had mentioned.

Several dozen men and women were gathered not far from the tents. Miraden paced in front of the group, hands clasped behind his back, speaking of the predicament he supposed had befallen Calimir and the others. "That monster is still out there," he said. "If it were not on the loose, I might not be as concerned. In due time they could reach the higher floors, but time is not on their side."

Miraden continued as Amendal and Ildin stopped behind a pair of brawny mercenaries. "Why doesn't he just say that we're going?" Amendal whispered.

Ildin gave him a sidelong glance. "You don't make a good soldier."

Amendal rolled his eyes. A fluttering of wings buzzed around him, then Fench zipped past Ildin and over the heads of those listening to Miraden. Fench carried an assortment of dried meats and cheeses. *He must really like those,* Amendal thought, amused.

"...although, I am not going to force any of you to come," Miraden said. "I'm sure we'll only need a handful of us."

"Why not send an illusion?" a soldier asked frankly. He folded his arms, awaiting an answer.

"If there are wounded, they'll need help," Miraden said. "We could very well send an illusion, but if they require aid that'll only delay them getting to safety."

Several of the men scoffed at Miraden's reasoning and walked off.

Cowards.

Another soldier voiced concerns about the risk, followed by another. Miraden restated his opinion, and Orin seconded it. Soon, a debate ensued.

Well, if no one else went, Amendal could always take his conjurations with him. *Now wouldn't that be a heroic gesture,* he thought, grinning. Faelinia was undoubtedly already interested in being with him, but this would send her over the edge. *An assured victory.*

"I'll go!" Amendal said, pushing his way through the wary soldiers and mercenaries. Several started at his declaration. *They probably think me mad…* No matter. He would rescue the others, even the old soldier—unless the monster had already eaten him. *If I were only that lucky…*

"Thank you, Master Aramien," Miraden said and stopped pacing.

Master…? Amendal fought back a grin and glanced to Ildin. The illusionist was still in the back, shaking his head. Several more men and women jogged toward the group, including Fendar and Scialas. The arpranist's eyes widened as she saw Amendal.

"We will be leaving shortly," Miraden said. "Stay if you're brave enough."

Several more mercenaries departed. The newcomers ventured questions about the gathering. Most of them stayed, including Fendar and Scialas. All in all, there were twenty-three who were willing to go.

After taking a head count, Miraden leaned closed and whispered in Amendal's ear. "You're not too tired?"

"I couldn't sleep if I wanted to," Amendal said. "And I do."

Miraden chuckled, patting Amendal on the shoulder. "You remind me of your uncle."

"I didn't know old Krudin had trouble sleeping…"

Once the rescue party was ready, Fench led Amendal and the others through the Roost. Fench claimed there was a place that could show where the rest of the expedition was located within Tardalim. But he wasn't clear on how it worked. Fench was clueless when it came to the specifics of Tardalim's workings.

Amendal walked at the head of the party with Ildin and Miraden. Fench fluttered ahead, loudly licking the jerky he had taken from the provisions. Several of the women muttered about the winged creature's lack of manners, but Fench didn't seem to care about what they were saying.

Too busy enjoying his food, Amendal thought, chuckling.

Soon, they arrived at a clearing where a seven-tiered tower stood. It was quite different from the tree-like buildings. Not only was it twice as tall as the other structures, it was made of the same white stone as the rest of

Tardalim. Violet moss covered the lower tiers, while multicolored vines climbed its walls. The lowest tier was wider than the rest—perhaps the size of a Soroth city block. The other tiers tapered to a single spire that was perhaps thirty phineals across.

"It's up there," Fench said, pointing to a balcony protruding from the highest tier, twenty stories above the party.

"And how are we going to get up there?" Fendar asked.

Fench shrugged and continued licking his jerky.

"There's bound to be an entrance somewhere," Miraden said. "Let's clear that moss away."

The rescue party split up and moved around the tower. They peeled the moss from the walls and hacked at the vines. After several minutes of searching, Orin discovered an oval door, like those they had seen throughout the shifting halls.

"If only it had a doorknob…" Orin said with a sigh. He felt at the door, then tried to slide it open.

"Perhaps we need to say those words," a soldier suggested. "You know, the ones Vaem spoke at the gatehouse."

Miraden turned to the man, not amused. "And do you remember those words?"

The man flinched.

"There has to be a way to open this," Ildin said.

Green light shone from a groove in the center of the door. The door split open along the groove. Then its two halves disappeared into the walls.

Amendal chuckled and stepped forward. "Well, that worked."

"I don't see how," Orin said. Miraden, however, stepped inside without speaking a word. Amendal followed him, sending a mental command for his conjurations to stay put.

Despite the overgrowth outside, the hallway within the tower was pristine. Light seemed to radiate from the walls. Unlike the other hallways in Tardalim, this particular corridor was of normal size.

"Now to find a staircase…" Miraden said.

The buzz of Fench's wings filled the hall, and the winged creature flew over Amendal's shoulder. Amendal ducked, narrowly evading the creature's wildly flailing tail.

Someone's excited… He grinned, watching Fench zip around Miraden.

The retired soldier called after the winged creature, but Fench didn't stop. "He really is a child…" Miraden said with a groan. "Fench, get back here!"

Ildin caught up to Amendal as Fench returned. "I don't think there are stairs in here," Fench said.

"Then how do you get to the different floors?" Miraden asked, but quickly extended a hand. "Don't tell me. You fly."

"Yup!" Fench flipped in the air.

They passed several doors and other corridors that branched off. Eventually, the hallway emptied into a seven-sided room with doors adorning each wall. Each door glowed with a pale-green hue.

"Where to now?" Ildin asked. Amendal narrowed his eyes, taking in the room with a sweeping glance. Strange etchings adorned each door, like the symbols they had seen in the crystallized gatehouse.

"Start checking the doors," Miraden said, moving to the right.

Amendal went the opposite direction, and once within arm's reach of the nearest door, it slid open. He set his jaw, but continued forward. A cylindrical chamber lay beyond the opening, barely large enough to fit five or six men. Intricate stonework lined its floor and ceiling, with narrow columns recessed into the curved wall. A large symbol was etched into the floor, glowing a vibrant green.

NOT THAT ONE, the voice said. TWO MORE OVER.

Eyes narrowed, Amendal glanced to the ceiling. Now you're talking? He turned back to the cylindrical chamber, but a sigh of displeasure rumbled through his mind.

"Fine..." He harrumphed and hurried across the hall. The others had discovered similar cylindrical spaces beyond each of the other doors. What were they? Fench fluttered across the seven-sided space and straight for the door mentioned by the voice in Amendal's head. The door slid open as Fench neared it, revealing another cylindrical chamber. It was almost identical to the other, except the symbol on the floor was different.

Amendal stopped short of entering, resting a hand on the edge of the door. "Do you know what this is?"

Fench shook his head, his trunk swaying.

Taking a deep breath, Amendal stepped inside. Ever cautious, he studied the room. Truss-like stonework arced along the domed ceiling, culminating in something that looked like a stony chandelier with gems inlaid within it. Is that a tevisral?

Amendal turned, but stopped as he faced the wall to the left of the door. Four rows of those strange symbols were etched into the wall. The bottommost row pulsed with dark orange light while the other glowed a pale-blue hue.

TOUCH THE HIGHEST ROW, the voice urged.

"Why?" Amendal whispered.

"Why what?" Fench asked. He fluttered close, slowly edging through Amendal's vision with a cocked head and dangling trunk.

Amendal leaned back as Fench's face came within a fraction of a phineal from his. "That's a little too close, Fench."

"Sorry..." The winged creature pulled back in a flash of gray. By the Channels he was fast.

TOUCH IT!

"Fine," Amendal muttered, jabbing his finger against the highest row. The pale-blue hue darkened to orange, and the door slid shut. Fench squealed while Amendal tensed. A heartbeat later, the door slid open, but what lay beyond was not the seven-sided room.

"We're here!" Fench exclaimed, zipping through the open door.

How was that possible? The place where Fench had pointed was a good twenty stories above them. Perhaps the cylindrical room moved through a portal. *But I didn't feel the effects of a teleportation spell...*

Shaking his head, Amendal entered a large two-story room about the size of the tower's highest tier. Strange-looking desks protruded from the walls, each with glowing squares and rectangles arrayed across their tops. Across the room was an opened doorway leading to the balcony they had seen from below.

"Over here!" Fench exclaimed. He hovered above an elaborate oval table at the heart of the room. Made from the same white stone as Tardalim's halls, the tabletop was thicker than a hand span. A pyramid-like object—with its top half cut off—lay at the table's center.

"Is this it?" Amendal asked, gesturing to the table. "Where's the map?"

Fench grinned, then touched something behind the odd pyramid. Particles of white light shot from all around the table, coalescing in the air. *Illusory magic?* The particles formed a sphere as Amendal's name was shouted from behind.

He turned as Ildin, Scialas, and Miraden exited the cylindrical room. The three of them stopped after only a few paces from the opened door, staring past Amendal with wide eyes.

"Is that the map?!" Ildin demanded.

Guess I should look, Amendal thought and turned around.

The illusory sphere was much larger now, taking up most of the space between the table and the ceiling. It had turned a transparent blue, with dozens of layers divided into hundreds, if not thousands of tiny cubes. He couldn't quite tell how many layers were in the sphere, but they only took up half of it. Orange lines zigzagged throughout each of the sphere's layers. Those lines near the outer layers were static, while those closest to the center kept changing. The sphere's center was hollowed out, with short fiber-like strands pointing to its heart.

"Incredible..." Miraden murmured.

Amendal leaned closer. Since he couldn't quite discern the inner layers, he did the only reasonable thing. He hopped onto the table and stuck his head into the sphere. He expected his skin to tingle, but it didn't. Perhaps the sphere wasn't made of illusory magic after all. Then he realized that the various cubes were actually tiny representations of the individual sections of Tardalim's halls. They were oriented with the floor toward the sphere's outer edge while the ceilings were closer to the hollowed center.

That's why the floors are curved... he thought. Each section's floor was not part of a bowl, as he had supposed. The floor was actually the inside curve of a sphere. Eyes widening, he shifted his gaze to the hollowed center. Those fiber-like strands were not strands at all, but miniature representations of the Tuladine homes...

"By all the Channels of Power!" he gasped, searching the various layers. The orange lines passed over each of Tardalim's staircases, which were placed at various angles throughout the sphere. During their trek they had clearly walked on what should have been the sphere's sides and top. But at no time had Amendal, or anyone else for that matter, felt like they were on anything but the floor. *But how, how was that possible?*

A wave of disorientation washed over him. He staggered backward, lost his footing, and tumbled off the table, hitting the ground with a thud. The pain, however, was nothing compared to the shocking realization that Tardalim and its shifting halls defied the laws of nature.

Ildin could not believe his eyes. How was Tardalim's structure even possible? *A sphere buried within a mountain,* he thought. *And an enormous sphere at that.* Two tubes spread from the sphere, one parallel to the tabletop and another pointing to the room's ceiling.

Well, we did enter through that odd tunnel. Ildin stepped closer, eyeing the tube level with the table. Where it connected to the sphere looked like a room tipped on its side with a pair of doors facing what was *down* to Ildin. *So, what we thought was* up *was actually going to the center.* That meant some force was pulling them to the sphere's exterior. *How bizarre!*

Chatter carried into the room from behind Ildin, undoubtedly more of the rescue party entering from that cylindrical room. How it brought them from the lower level to the highest baffled him. It was not by means of teleportation. *Perhaps a lift,* he mused. Ildin had heard tales of such contraptions.

The newcomers gasped in awe as they realized what hovered above the table.

Ildin, however, walked toward Fench to get a better view. He focused on the orange lines along the sphere's exterior layers. Each had strange symbols within them, symbols that changed. *Curious,* he thought, tracing the line to a stairwell with his finger.

"So the lines are routes," Ildin said to no one in particular.

"That's right!" Fench exclaimed.

Ildin turned to the winged thing. "But how do we find our friends?" he asked, glancing to Amendal, who was rounding the table.

"The dots," Fench said matter-of-factly.

"I see no dots…"

"Oh," Fench said, those strange lips at the end of his trunk turning down.

"Is there a way to make it bigger?" Amendal asked.

Fench beamed with excitement. "Yes! Go out there!" he pointed to the balcony. The winged thing pressed on some lit squares recessed into the table, then something hummed outside.

Amendal immediately spun, hurrying to the balcony.

Before Ildin could catch up to Amendal, the balcony shifted. The railing *liquefied,* then a ramp extended over those tree-buildings. It spread at a slight angle, toward the center of the Roost. The ramp ceased moving about a hundred phineals away. White light shone at its end, then burst in a brilliant flash.

Rubbing his eyes, Ildin stepped onto the balcony and blinked several times. He started as another representation of Tardalim filled the air, much larger than the one atop the table.

Ildin found himself smiling broadly. "How beautiful!"

Fench fluttered into the balcony through the illusion of Tardalim. "Look, over here!"

Amendal and Ildin hurried toward Fench, stopping at what Ildin counted as the nineteenth layer from the sphere's outer edge. Dozens of yellow dots filled one of the cubed parts of that layer. There were also two yellow dots with red in their centers, and another that had orange at its heart. *Why are they different?*

"There are your friends," Fench said.

"So, they're on the nineteenth floor?" Amendal asked. "But there should be more of them…"

Ildin quickly counted the dots. *Seventy-six.* He bit his lip.

"Could there be more elsewhere?" Amendal asked, his tone urgent. He was probably worried for Faelinia.

Fench flew through the illusion, making several sweeping passes. "I don't see any."

Perhaps that monster had attacked them, as it had tried with Ildin and the others. *The monster—!* Ildin thought. "Fench, where is the monster? Do you see it?"

Fench shook his head, his trunk swaying.

"What color is it?" Amendal asked.

"Black and orange," Fench said. He fluttered off again. Fench made more passes than he had before. "It's gone! But… but it can't be gone!"

"Perhaps it can hide itself," Amendal said. "No matter, we need to get down there and fast."

Miraden hurried up the ramp, stopping beside Ildin. "What did you find?" the squad leader asked.

"They're on the nineteenth floor," Amendal said. "And we need to hurry before that monster returns."

⟞•⟝

Miraden decided that Fendar would remain at the odd map of Tardalim. That suited the illusionist just fine. Fendar made two illusions: one to fly through the shifting map to discern the right course, and another to accompany the rescue party.

While Miraden led everyone from the tower, Amendal reclaimed his conjurations from his friends. They divided the creatures amongst themselves as they had before, but Fendar left his enthralled earthen giants to guard the camp.

Along the way, Miraden had ordered the mages to cast various spells upon the party, in case they ran across the monster. Once they left the Roost, Fench led the way. Though Fench claimed to know how to find the others on his own, Miraden still wanted Fendar to relay directions.

Their descent from the thirty-second to the thirty-first floor was quite swift. They had to backtrack only once. Though they were not trying to beat the Shift, Miraden pushed them to run through each level they descended.

Once on the twenty-eight floor, Fendar informed the party that the others had ascended to the twentieth floor and were moving toward a nearby staircase. The route from the twenty-first to the twenty-second, however, was considerably longer.

We can catch them there, Amendal thought.

After reaching the twenty-second floor, Miraden demanded a report from Fendar. "They're not even halfway to the stairs. It's a straight shot from where they're at, though."

"A Shift will happen soon on that floor," Fench said.

"How soon?" Miraden asked.

Fench shrugged. "Soon."

Miraden shook his head and sighed. "Fendar?"

"I have no way of telling," Fendar said through his illusion. "I assume it's these symbols in the routes, but I can't decipher them."

"Be prepared to redirect us," Miraden said.

Hold on, Faelinia. I'm coming. With renewed determination, Amendal bolted ahead of the others. He and his conjurations had to be the first thing Faelinia saw.

Fendar's illusion zipped overhead, keeping pace with Amendal. "Take the third right, follow its zigzag. Then it's a straight shot."

Amendal nodded as Fench fluttered beside him.

"Why are you running so fast?" the winged creature asked.

"I intend to save someone, Fench. And I need her to see me before anyone else."

Amendal soon reached the stairs. A feminine figure, more divine than anything else in the world, floated in the air. *She's alive!* he thought, his heart taking courage.

Faelinia's illusion spun toward Amendal. The expression on her illusory features became overjoyed. "Amendal!" she cried through her illusion. "You're safe!"

Though Faelinia's illusion sped toward him, Amendal did not slow his dash. Once he had joined the illusion, it kept pace with him, studying him with wide eyes. "What happened to you?"

"It's a long story," Amendal said. "But I'm here to rescue you."

"Rescue me?" Faelinia cocked her illusion's head, then noticed Fench. She looked surprised. "What kind of creature is that?"

"I'm Fench!" the winged creature declared.

She blinked once, then looked behind Amendal.

Darting to the steps, Amendal led his conjurations down to the twenty-first floor. The larger conjurations cleared the stairs in several leaps while the smaller ones skipped only a few steps at a time.

"Why are there so few of you?" Faelinia asked.

"The others are safely waiting in the Roost," Amendal said, leaping from the bottommost step and bounding into the hallway. "Once we found out where you were, Miraden and I put together a small group to bring you and the others to safety."

The illusion furrowed her brow. "The Roost?"

"My home," Fench said.

"It's the highest floor," Amendal added. "Undoubtedly where Vaem wants to go."

"How many of you are left?" Faelinia asked warily.

"All of us," Amendal said.

The illusion looked taken aback. "You're lucky..." Her words were haunted.

"I take it you fought that monster?" Amendal asked.

"You encountered it, too?!"

Amendal shook his head. "Only saw it. Is that old soldier still alive?"

Faelinia's illusion nodded. "But he's strange... something happened to him."

That's it? Amendal wondered. "You're not going to say more?"

"Not now," she said. "Oh, I see you!"

Amendal shifted his focus down the hall. Several hundred phineals away, a wide row of men and women—shielded in barsion bubbles—stretched from wall to wall. They approached at a belabored gait. One of the women, enveloped in a violet bubble of magic, broke formation and ran toward him. Faelinia.

I do have you now, he thought, grinning. Why else would a woman run so enthusiastically toward a man?

Faelinia's disintegrating barsion dissipated amid her dash. Once near, she spread her arms.

Perfect! Amendal slowed, but continued his advance, readying to catch her. They met, and he wrapped his arms around her, twirling to break their momentum. Before coming to a stop, Amendal commanded his conjurations to halt.

"Oh, Amendal!" Faelinia's eyes widened with relief. She pulled herself close, resting her forehead against his.

"We need to hurry," Amendal whispered. "There is no—"

Faelinia pressed her lips against his in a passionate kiss. For a moment,

Amendal forgot they were in such a perilous place. She pulled back, raising her eyes to his. "I've missed you, you big oaf," she whispered, then pressed her lips to his once again.

Amid their embrace, Fench fluttered around them. "Why can *she* get that close?"

Amendal stifled a laugh, interrupting the kiss. He and Faelinia turned to Fench, but before Amendal could answer, orange light erupted within the hall in a blinding flash.

With one arm around Faelinia, Amendal spun. Alarmed gasps echoed throughout the hall, followed by hurried incantations. Behind the frantic survivors of the expedition, that enormous black monster settled into a wide stance, an orange haze misting from its body.

Amendal started and Fench squealed. Where had the monster come from? Had it been invisible? And what was that blinding flash?

"GIVE ME THE TULADINE!" the monster bellowed. "AND PERHAPS I WILL LET YOU LIVE."

"The average time of death from yaeltis venom is roughly a quarter of an hour. The venom can paralyze a man within moments of contacting the victim's blood. Once paralysis sets in, other bodily functions fail. Delusions will be the last thing the victim experiences. What a horrid way to die."

- From *Colvinar Vrium's Bestiary for Conjurers*, page 118

Faelinia could not believe her eyes. Where had the monster come from? When it attacked before, she had heard it galloping from several hundred phineals away. But now, it was as if the monster had just *appeared* behind the expedition.

Many of the mages finished their incantations as the soldiers and mercenaries dashed toward the monster. Those still mustering their magic backed away, retreating toward Faelinia and Amendal. However, some of the soldiers were fleeing. Commander Calimir was among them, as were Vaem and Kydol. But why was the commander fleeing?

"Go!" Amendal cried, and heavy footfalls echoed all around. The towering conjurations bolted past Faelinia and into the fray.

"HOW AMUSING," the monster bellowed, swatting at the soldiers while turning toward the conjurations. It cocked its head toward Faelinia, its violet eyes staring directly at her—no, beside her. Was it looking at Amendal?

That winged creature squealed again, but its cry faded behind Faelinia.

In that moment, Amendal's mages' parasites arrived and encircled them. The gray-skinned creatures lowered into wide stances, their pink tongues hanging to their waists.

Faelinia shook her head. "You need a barsion, Amendal." She swiftly uttered an incantation to shield him. While her magic coalesced, the deserters ran by. Faelinia glared at Vaem, but neither the scholar nor the commander noticed.

Battle cries filled the hall from behind as violet particles shot from Faelinia to Amendal, but some of the magic wisped toward the mages' parasites. As the disintegrating barsion formed, Ildin's illusion zipped by, followed by an illusion of Fendar. Both illusions flew straight for the monster's head.

A good distraction, Faelinia thought, and repeated the incantation to shield herself. In that moment, Amendal's towering conjurations reached the battle. One of the earthen giants lunged, poised to punch the monster's face.

Morgidian dodged the monster's deadly tail, mustering more barsion. One layer would not be enough to protect everyone, not with how quickly the monster had shattered the barriers in the last skirmish.

Battle cries, singing metal, incantations, and thunderous footfalls filled the air. The dreadful cacophony evoked a mirthful cackle from the monster.

A resounding smack rang through the air, and Morgidian spun. An earthen giant stumbled from the monster, falling upon several soldiers. He could feel their barsions weakening.

With annoyance tainting his incantation, he shifted his focus to those pinned beneath the conjuration. The earthen giant swiftly rejoined the battle, and those that had been pinned scurried around the hunk of rock.

Soon, a brilliant wave of blue barsion shot from Morgidian's hands, surging through the air and surrounding the scurrying soldiers. *Careful, Amendal—*

Blackness shot toward him, and he threw himself sideways. The monster's tail struck the floor where he had stood, the pincers bouncing off the stone.

"IT'S NO USE, HEDGETRANCER," the monster bellowed, then swung its tail once again. Morgidian tried to dodge, but the pincers wrapped around his barsion bubble. The monster lifted him, then hurled him down the hall whence Amendal had come.

"No!" he cried, spinning as he flew through the air. Bolts of lightning surged past, accompanied by acidic orbs and flaming bolts.

Something struck his barsion—rather, *he* hit something. It was soft, yet firm.

"Morgi," a voice bellowed beside his barsion. *Amendal?* he wondered, struggling to reorient himself. Purple leathery palms clutched his barsion. One of Amendal's yaeltis. "Keep some distance," Amendal's voice bellowed from the conjuration. It lowered Morgidian, gently setting him on the floor.

"Nice catch," Morgidian said, taking in his surroundings. The monster had repulsed him a good eighty or so phineals. Soldiers filed past him, running at magically enhanced speeds. But they charged without barsion.

"Wait!" Morgidian called, but they didn't stop.

How foolish… he grumbled, then swiftly uttered an incantation.

———————⊃•⊂———————

Explosions of light clouded the battlefield, but Amendal could still sense his foe through his conjurations. The monster attacked with incredible precision. Despite being severely outnumbered, the monster held its ground against the conjurations and soldiers.

What is this beast? Amendal wondered. It was no ordinary creature. *And it spoke…*

The yaeltis who had caught Morgidian joined the battle, followed by the cisthyrns. The wolf-like conjurations galloped around the soldiers, leaping toward the monster, ready to sink their claws and teeth into the beast. But the monster swatted them away before any could land a blow.

Now surrounded by Amendal's conjurations, the monster shifted its focus. Its six arms alternated between striking the towering conjurations and bracing itself. That orange haze filled the air around it, exhaled in large puffs from its gill filaments. Soon, the mist engulfed Amendal's conjured troll, and Amendal fought a maddening urge swelling within the creature.

Fight! Amendal commanded, but the troll did not obey. The fear grew in its mind, debilitating it. He adjusted his focus, taking total control of the conjuration. He leapt the troll into battle and swung its fists, but the monster intercepted the blows. Amendal punched again and again, but the monster deflected the troll's fists.

Meanwhile, each of the cisthyrns succumbed to that dreaded haze. They whimpered and backed away. Soldiers darted around the debilitated conjurations, advancing on the monster. But their weapons—despite being imbued with deadly magic—barely inflicted any harm.

Get up! Amendal commanded, but the cisthyrns didn't move.

More magic struck the monster, erupting in a blinding flash. Amendal managed a blow against the monster's head, but the beast was unaffected. The erupting light faded, revealing abrasions on the monster's neck. Amendal swung the troll's claws toward the open flesh, but the monster spun and punched the troll.

Amendal gasped, and the troll flew backward, hitting the wall.

"Those cowards!" Faelinia spat. Was she referring to Vaem and the old soldier—?

Breathing heavily, Amendal glanced to Faelinia. She was gazing down the hall toward the stairs. Ildin was now beside her, uttering an incantation. White light coalesced into an illusion of himself, and Ildin sent it flying into battle.

"We should try to pin it," Ildin said. "Use the Shift to cut it in half."

Amendal nodded. *Only if we can subdue it…*

"What's the Shift?" Faelinia asked.

As Ildin explained, Amendal returned his focus to the troll, pushing it forward. It took considerable effort to coerce the troll to fight. He sent the conjuration back into the fray, but the monster landed another blow to the troll's chest. Bones cracked, and Amendal dropped to his knees. As the troll struck the wall, one of the yaeltis succumbed to the terrorizing haze.

No... Amendal gritted his teeth, watching the battle through his conjurations' eyes. Ildin's illusions zipped in front of the monster while his enthralled earthen giants attacked. It was a clever strategy, but it didn't seem to faze the beast in the slightest.

"Amendal!" Scialas cried, skidding to a halt beside his barsion.

"The... troll..." he managed between gasps. As he stood, the other yaeltis succumbed to the mind-numbing fear. The monster punched the yaeltis in the face, sending it reeling into one of the earthen giants. The yaeltis's tusk struck the rock, cracking.

The monster spun on the earthen giants, but struggled to move them. *Probably too heavy,* Amendal thought, sucking in his breath.

"Shall we try some ensnaring tentacles?" Ildin asked. "Then the conjurations can help hold the monster in place."

"Good idea!" Faelinia shouted, then began uttering an incantation. Ildin also mustered his magic, and the two of them began to glow with green light.

"There's only one problem," Fendar said through his illusion, then pointed to the battle.

The monster was safely nestled within one of Tardalim's sections and showed no signs of budging. *Perhaps if we can weaken it, we can knock it back— that abrasion!* He immediately shifted his concentration to the yaeltis cowering nearby—the one with both tusks intact. "I have an idea."

His friends turned to him, intrigued.

"Yaeltis venom." If the monster's reaction was anything like the soldiers they had lost, then it could easily be maneuvered.

Ildin nodded approvingly.

"That might just work," Faelinia said.

It better, Amendal thought, then commanded the yaeltis to move. The furry creature rose from the stone floor. It was half a section away from the monster. Unfortunately, the monster would see the yaeltis coming.

Distract it, he commanded the earthen giants. He closed his eyes, putting all his mental effort into controlling the yaeltis. The fear within the conjuration was just as intense as with the troll.

Fighting the terror, Amendal charged the conjuration into battle. The yaeltis leapt over a band of soldiers and around an earthen giant. It lunged into the air, tusks poised to pierce the monster's neck.

Ildin's enthralled earthen giants attacked as one, drawing the monster away. Together, with Amendal's stony conjurations, they created an opening.

Venom encrusted tusk struck the abrasion, but barely pricked the monster. That immovable flesh jolted the yaeltis's head backward. Amendal struggled to regain the conjuration's footing, and the yaeltis landed atop several soldiers. The blow, however, was enough to evoke an enraged scream from the monster.

"CLEVER, BEASTCALLER!" the monster bellowed, turning to face Amendal. The name made him flinch. Beastcaller was an ancient term describing conjurers. According to his family's tomes, that was their earliest title—a title which some said originated during the Dragon Wars.

"YOU WILL REGRET THAT," the monster cried, its tail speeding through the air.

Amendal pushed the yaeltis upright, freeing the soldiers. But before the conjuration could evade, the monster's pincers pierced the yaeltis through the eyes. The blow sent pain surging through Amendal's head, dropping him to his knees. The bond to the yaeltis vanished, but the echoes of the pain lingered.

Another enraged cry filled the hall. Amendal struggled to shift his focus. His earthen conjurations were still attacking the monster. They tried grabbing its limbs, but the monster bolted, running straight for Amendal.

After it! he commanded. The conjurations obeyed, but the monster was too swift. Within a heartbeat, the monster snatched Amendal with one of its claws. Through his conjurations he could see himself raised into the air, his violet barsion flickering.

"OPEN YOUR EYES, BEASTCALLER!"

The earthen giants reached the monster, as did most of the soldiers. One of the conjurations gripped the monster's tail and the others wrangled its rearmost arms. But the monster didn't bother with them. It focused entirely on squeezing Amendal's barsion.

Green light burst from Ildin and Faelinia, sending a dozen ensnaring tentacles toward the monster. They wrapped around its foremost arms, including the one gripping Amendal.

More incantations sounded all around, but Amendal couldn't focus on them. The lingering pain was too distracting.

"LOOK AT ME, BEASTCALLER, AND I PROMISE I WILL KILL YOU SWIFT-LY!"

Ildin's enthralled conjurations joined the struggle, one grabbing the arm gripping Amendal. All the while, the lone yaeltis, the troll, and the cisthyrns continued writhing on the floor. That orange mist spread, engulfing each of the quinta'shals. They too succumbed to the maddening effects, aimlessly staggering through the hall and exhaling the magic each had consumed.

Ignoring his conjurations' dread, Amendal noted the monster's position within the hall. Its tail and legs were in one section, while the rest of it was in another—

A ping resounded through the hall, heralding the Shift.

"Hold it!" Miraden shouted. The command was echoed by Dardel, and several others. Morgidian and Ildin both called for everyone to fall back while Faelinia uttered another incantation.

Stay! Amendal clenched his teeth. Through his conjurations, he saw his barsion flickering. Hopefully it would hold. If not…

"YOUR EFFORTS ARE FUTILE!" the monster bellowed.

The barsion shattered. *No—!* Agonizing pain engulfed Amendal, piercing every part of his body.

The shared vision with his conjurations ceased. The air around him became hot. His skin itched, then burned. Amendal coughed, gasped, and opened his eyes. The orange haze engulfed him. Nightmarish figures formed in the mist, but the worst was a giant violet eye that evoked a terror that made him wail. Its horrific iris swirled around an abysmal pupil in an unnatural fashion.

Then, like a thousand daggers, the agony pierced his mind. He tried to scream, but couldn't. He could only stare at that terrifying eye. Something—a force or a will—reached inside him, prying vivid images from his mind, starting with his earliest memory.

———⊃•⊂———

Ildin started as Amendal's earthen giants jolted, then stilled, relinquishing their grips and partly freeing the monster. The conjurer looked paralyzed. He had been screaming, but the wails were abruptly cut short. The terrifying creature began to shake, but jerked back repeatedly. Was it succumbing to the yaeltis venom?

"CURSE YOU, BEASTCALLER!" The monster bellowed and thrashed about, weakening Ildin's ensnaring magic. *Hold—!* The monster's tail flew through the air, impaling one of the mages' parasites.

The lines on the wall darkened to red, and the ensnaring magic snapped. Cackling triumphantly, the monster lurched backward and Amendal resumed screaming. As it retreated, the monster swiped another mages' parasite, slamming it against the lit lines in the wall.

"Amendal!" Ildin cried.

A double ping resounded through the hall as the monster pulled Amendal toward the dividing line. Then, in an instant, the monster and all the earthen giants vanished. But the black hand clutching Amendal fell to the floor with a resounding thud. Amendal thrashed about, clutching his head and wailing in torment. The monster's severed hand twitched beside him.

Ildin darted from the others, dropping to his knees beside his friend. "Amendal!" he cried, reaching for the conjurer, but Amendal rolled away. He mumbled incoherent nonsense. He sounded mad, deranged.

Soon, their other friends came to a halt around them.

"What's wrong with him?" Fendar asked.

"That haze," Faelinia muttered. "Amendal!" She struggled to grab the conjurer. Ildin hurried to her, and together they stopped Amendal from rolling. All the while, Amendal continued spewing deranged nonsense.

"Hold him still," Scialas said, then uttered an arpran incantation.

Miraden and Dardel arrived beside Ildin and added their efforts to controlling Amendal.

The screaming conjurer fought them, kicking Ildin in the stomach. Gasping for breath, Ildin instinctively let go. The soldiers jumped onto Amendal, pinning him in place while Faelinia uttered an enthralling incantation.

That's smart… Ildin thought, rubbing his stomach.

"Oh, Amendal!" Morgidian blurted, running to join Ildin. The burly barsionist groaned and shook his head.

Ildin turned and opened his mouth to speak, but the severing of an enthralling spell jolted him. Taken aback, he reached out to his enthralled conjurations. They were close, beyond the wall ahead of him, within a section of the twenty-first floor turned a different direction. Through his mental bond, Ildin watched as the monster attacked the conjurations, wielding the limbs of several earthen conjurations like cudgels.

The appearance of green particles roused Ildin, and he watched them wisp around the soldiers, striking Amendal. The arpran magic surged across the conjurer, then disappeared. A moment later, Faelinia finished her incantation. Gray light zipped into Amendal's nose and mouth, abruptly stilling him.

"There," Faelinia said with a sigh, then turned to Scialas. "Well?"

Scialas narrowed her eyes and bit her lip. "I… I don't know. I can't tell what's wrong with him. There's something in his head…"

That haze? Ildin wondered.

"Can you remove it?" Faelinia asked.

Scialas shook her head, drawing a hushed murmur from Faelinia. Miraden and Dardel eased off Amendal, allowing Faelinia to stand him upright.

"What happened to him?" Miraden asked.

Dardel shrugged. "That orange mist seems to drive people mad." Dardel explained how in a previous engagement, the monster had afflicted those not protected by barsion, hurling them into a state of delirium. Unfortunately, the afflicted were separated from Dardel's group by a Shift.

Another severed bond jolted Ildin. Now, only one of his enthralled conjurations was left. In fact, it was now the monster's only foe. Seven cisthyrn lay limp on the floor, their white coats bloodied. Two mages' parasites were torn in half, their corpses atop pools of purple blood near the dead yaeltis. And the troll—

Ildin's stomach heaved, and he brought a hand to his lips. He severed the bond to the elemental and focused on his own surroundings.

The soldiers and mercenaries were all gathered together. Squad leaders took head counts. No one else seemed to be suffering like Amendal. Well, besides the conjurations not caught in the Shift. Five of the cisthyrns lay on the floor, whimpering. The lone yaeltis cowered against a wall, breathing heavily.

I should enthrall them, Ildin thought.

As he uttered an enthralling incantation, Miraden and Dardel discussed the situation, speaking of the Shift, the Roost, and the cache of tevisrals. But Miraden did not mention the Mindolarnian corpses. *Why?* Talk of tevisrals drew intrigued comments among the survivors.

"I'll get the yaeltis," Faelinia said, then began her own incantation.

Ildin's magic enthralled the cisthyrns, and he felt a resistance within the beasts. Amendal still had a hold on them, despite being under the influence of Faelinia's enthralling magic. *Follow me,* he commanded, but the creatures didn't obey. Struggling with the cisthyrns, Ildin turned around and joined Miraden and the others. They were talking to Fendar's illusion about the route back to the higher floors.

"...the other one has to be Fench," Fendar said through his illusion. "Those fifteen are only a few sections into the twenty-second floor."

Miraden set his jaw. "And the monster?"

"It's trapped," Fendar said. "There's no way for it to get to any of the staircases... well, ones that ascend. It can go down. Let me check the other floors..."

"Just keep an eye on it," Miraden said. "Hopefully it doesn't find a way to get ahead of us."

Dardel nodded. "Lead the way, Miraden. We'll follow."

Miraden nodded, then darted down the hall. Soldiers, mercenaries, and mages all ran after the retired soldier. Ildin, however, searched for his friends. Morgidian, Dugal, Faelinia, and Scialas all stood around Amendal. Faelinia was whispering to them, but Ildin couldn't make out what she said.

He sent one of his illusions after Miraden, then approached his friends.

"...something is wrong with him, but I don't know what." Faelinia shook her head, eyeing the soldiers as they ran. Ildin joined the group while keeping his illusion near Miraden.

"The commander did look strange," Scialas said.

Morgidian nodded. "He didn't seem himself this morning."

Not himself? Ildin wondered. He *had* seen Calimir fleeing and thought it odd. He hadn't thought the commander a coward.

"He changed after the last fight with Vaem," Faelinia said.

Ildin cocked his head. *Vaem?* "What happened? Did she touch him?"

Faelinia studied Ildin quizzically. "I believe so. I thought I saw him swing a fist at her, but I don't recall her being struck."

Great... Ildin sighed, running a hand through his hair.

"I take it you know what happened?" Dugal asked.

Oh, he did, all right. "Vaem..." How was he going to explain it? Amendal hadn't even explained it all to him. "I think Vaem has a tevisral. It... makes people extremely *susceptible* to her in... uh..." Ildin squeezed his eyes shut, scrunching his face. "In sexual ways..."

"Really?" Scialas blinked several times.

Morgidian folded his arms. "Is that what happened to Amendal during the banquet?"

Ildin nodded. "Do you really think Amendal wanted to sleep with her?"

"Yes," Dugal said flatly.

Morgidian playfully nudged Dugal.

"What?" the transmuter demanded, pointing to Amendal. "It's what he does."

"So, Amendal *didn't* want to sleep with her?" Scialas asked.

Jaw tensed, Ildin glanced to Faelinia. She grinned wryly. "Uh... no," he said. Did he dare bring up their bet? "He had decided to change his ways. In order to..." He trailed off. *Don't say any more,* he told himself.

Faelinia's smile broadened. She glanced to Amendal, biting her lower lip, but her expression soon saddened. Ildin looked past her, studying his closest friend. Though the conjurer seemed calm, there was terror in his eyes. *Oh, Amendal...*

"We should continue this later," Morgidian said, pointing down the hall. "We're going to lose them."

Ildin and the others spun while Faelinia uttered an enhancing incantation. The last squad turned a corner half a grand phineal away. Ildin focused on his illusion, zipping it back down a maze of corridors. "There's only one way to go."

"Then let's go!" Morgidian said. The barsionist led Ildin and the others down the hall at a reckless pace. Scialas and Ildin pulled ahead, but Faelinia finished her incantation, and soon all of them were running at magically enhanced speeds, following the zigzagging path that led to the stairs. To Ildin's surprise, the twenty-second floor hadn't shifted yet.

They were halfway to the stairs leading to the twenty-third floor when they caught sight of the others. Those who had fought the monster had since rejoined Calimir and Vaem.

Once Ildin and his friends were two sections away from the others, Fendar's illusion called for a halt, thinking the Shift was almost upon them. During the battle he had watched the changing symbols along the routes and believed them to be a timer of sorts.

As Ildin neared the back of the expedition, a ping resounded through the hall. *Looks like Fendar was right,* he thought. The lines of light on the walls darkened to red as Ildin and the others rejoined their companions. Before Ildin could breathe a sigh of relief, the double pings filled the hall.

"That was close," Dugal muttered.

Morgidian nodded, breathing heavily. "That's what we get... for socializing..."

Dugal snorted. "Gossiping is more like it."

While his friends bantered, Ildin focused his hearing through his illusion. Fendar relayed a new route, one that was actually shorter than the one they'd used for their descent. Dardel noted the directions while Miraden informed Vaem and Calimir about Fench and the Roost. The commander, however, wasn't paying attention to the report. He gazed at Vaem like a starved beggar staring through the windows of a bakery.

He is under her influence, Ildin thought, unnerved by the predicament. What would this mean for the expedition?

Miraden finished his report, but still made no mention of the dead Mindolarnians.

Confused, Ildin turned back to his friends, who were still bantering. "It seems Calimir is enthralled," Ildin said, glancing to Faelinia. "No, perhaps enthralled isn't the right word…"

"Enamored?" Dugal asked, his tone sarcastic.

"So what do we do about it?" Faelinia asked.

"A mages' parasite can suck the spell out of him," Ildin said. "But it can also be removed by a dispel." There was no time to explain the encounter Amendal had had with Vaem on the *Giboran*.

Dugal cleared his throat. Morgidian turned toward the transmuter, then Dugal repeated the noise, and all of them looked at him.

"Why is Calimir's predicament our problem?" he asked.

"Do you think Vaem can be trusted?" Faelinia asked, and the transmuter shrugged.

A high-pitched whistle carried through the hall, followed by shouted commands from Dardel. Hurried footfalls echoed throughout the hall. Soon, Ildin was once again alone with his friends.

"We should discuss this later," Morgidian said. "Once we reach that Tu-la-whatever Roost."

"I agree," Faelinia said. She turned to Amendal, and her face contorted with sorrow.

Of all people to go after, why did the monster have to attack Amendal? True, Amendal's conjurations would have proved devastating, but the monster seemed to have singled him out even from the beginning. Was it because Fench had been with Amendal?

Morgidian and Dugal darted after the others, followed by Scialas. Faelinia, however, remained beside Amendal.

"Oh, Amendal…" Faelinia murmured, stroking the conjurer's face.

"Do you want me to take over?" Ildin asked.

Faelinia took in a deep breath and shook her head. She turned from Amendal, tears in her eyes. "Let's go, Ildin. We need to get Amendal to safety."

Vaem had not stopped smiling since hearing the report from that squad leader, Miraden. *Oh, the praises I will receive!* She imagined herself entering the throne room of the Mindolarn Palace, bearing the wonders of the past—not tevisrals, but allies of Lord Cheserith from ages long forgotten.

Surely, our war with the Losians will be won. If the divine being the Sorothians

called a monster was anything to judge by, then the rest of those imprisoned here would be more than formidable. The world would bow once
again to Mindolarnian rule.

While ascending to the higher floors, Vaem considered the identity of the
so-called monster. But she was not well versed in the ancient pantheon of
the gods. Such an understanding was not required for devotees of
Cherisium, although perhaps if she were more devout... From what little
she understood, the pantheon was divided into various degrees of power
and glory. Of course, Lord Cheserith was over them all. She knew the
names of the gods who were considered closest in glory to the Father of
All—Ku'tharn, Heleron, Visalisan, Desidan, and Forcu'sia.

He must be one of the lesser gods, she thought. From what she remembered,
there were hundreds if not thousands of them. *How many are imprisoned in
Tardalim?* Throughout their hasty climb, Vaem had tried to open the various
doors lining Tardalim's halls, but had no success. *A pity.*

The higher Vaem and the others climbed, the quicker the halls changed.
Miraden called the occurrence the Shift, a name given to the change by that
lone Tuladine. *It's lucky one Tuladine managed to survive,* she thought. Speculation on the alternative almost sullied her joyous demeanor.

Once on the twenty-seventh floor the change occurred three times before they could reach the next staircase. *We could have been lost here.*

After reaching the stairs to the thirty-first floor, Miraden shouted to everyone that the next two floors would be the trickiest to navigate.

The expedition ran through the thirty-first floor, stopping several times
to wait for a Shift.

On their third stop, the expedition halted at an open door. Curious,
Vaem dashed toward it and peered inside. The room beyond the door was
small. A single golden cage was suspended in the air, barely large enough to
fit a man. But unlike the others she had seen, this cage was empty. No crystal. No prisoner.

But this couldn't be where that divine being was held. True, a god could
change their form, but Vaem had been told that the shackles placed upon
the prisoners of Tardalim prevented such things. This cage was too small.

Had Coridician freed more than the so-called monster? If so, why had he
failed to free the others? The thought twisted her stomach with worry.

The pings of the Shift rang through the hall as Vaem studied the cage.
The Divine Tongue was etched upon it. *"Prisoner number: thirty-nine million,
four hundred and ninety-seven thousand, and fifty-two. Sini'sha breed, captured and held
in human form. Warning: specimen capable of manipulating water, despite his bonds—"*

Vaem started as a pair of pings echoed behind her. Before she could read
any more, the door closed. *Capable of manipulating water?* There was only one
divine being who possessed such a trait.

Heleron...

But that so-called monster couldn't be Heleron.

Shouts from the squad leaders roused Vaem from her thoughts.

Hurried footfalls filled the hall as Vaem chased after the others. She was in the rear now, with Amendal's friends. The handsome conjurer was running beside Faelinia and Ildin, but there was something wrong with him. He moved like a puppet.

Soon, the expedition halted again. Another door was open on the opposite wall. Vaem hurried to it and peeked inside. This second room was much larger, with an enormous empty cage at its heart.

"Prisoner number: nine hundred and forty-one thousand, eight hundred and seven. Cafis'sha breed, captured and held in unknown form. Warning: specimen is capable of emitting a mist that causes irreparable mental debilitation. Believed to be named Orath'issian."

So, that's his name, she thought. She had heard that name before—

The double pings filled the hall and the expedition began running once again. Vaem dashed alongside the members of squad five, still pondering. *If Coridician had freed Heleron and Orath'issian, why had he not claimed Tardalim?* Her worries returned.

They soon ascended to the thirty-second floor. Unlike the other floors, there were no doors in any of the hallway sections. The expedition navigated the halls, led by that illusion, and eventually arrived at the stairs leading to the Tuladine Roost.

Finally! Vaem thought, her worries fading. With the prospect of freeing Tardalim's prisoners within her grasp, a surge of triumph filled her soul. *Now to get to that tower Miraden mentioned.* Surely it would contain mechanisms to make freeing Lord Cheserith's allies easier.

While Vaem climbed the stairs Kydol approached. "We've done it!" the lieutenant said, grinning. "We've finally succeeded!"

Vaem nodded. "The emperor will be pleased."

"We shall be reverenced," Kydol said. "Revered by the citizens of the empire."

Vaem gave the lieutenant a slight smile. *The gods will walk Kalda once again,* she thought. *And the world will be at peace.* Determined, Vaem ascended to the heart of Tardalim.

THE END OF
Part Three

Zulsthy'l moved like lightning. He dodged a sweeping kick to his head while parrying a punch aimed at his chest. In that same heartbeat, he sidestepped across the dueling ring, intercepting a fist aimed at his face. His knuckles collided with his foe's wrist, making a faint pop that evoked a yelp from his opponent.

Too hard, he thought, eyeing his four foes with a sweeping glance—the young potentials training to become usa'zin'sha.

He spun to intercept a kick aimed at his waist. He caught the potential by the ankle and spun him off balance. "Impressive," he said, evading another kick and throwing himself sideways to the floor. He quickly rolled onto his feet and said, "You almost had me."

Settling into a wide stance, he studied the four potentials now advancing as one. Two were male, and two were female. Each wore long-sleeved tunics and free-flowing pants—the traditional garb of those studying at the Dohaliem. The four of them looked no older than thirteen or fourteen, but they were at least fifty, perhaps sixty, years old. One of the males clutched his wrist and attempted to pop it back into place.

Beyond the dueling ring, other potentials watched with eager anticipation. Some whispered to one another, but Zulsthy'l couldn't quite discern the details of their conversations.

"Remember what I taught you," Zulsthy'l said. "Split your opponent's focus."

They immediately spread out, their footsteps echoing off the stone dueling ring. *Good,* he thought. If they approached him as one, he could easily lead them around the dueling ring like a child tugging a kite.

The four of them lunged, and a sense of exhilaration filled him.

As swiftly as before, Zulsthy'l advanced. The young male clutching his wrist kicked, but Zulsthy'l grabbed his leg and threw him toward the two potentials beside him. The wounded youth collided with his fellows, sending them to the stone floor.

A fist grazed Zulsthy'l's shoulder, rustling his black tunic. He spun toward the last standing potential, and the young female unleashed a flurry of punches. He blocked and parried, but she nearly landed several blows.

"Not bad!" Smiling, he sidestepped, but stayed within arm's reach. He eased back with each parry, block, or interception, carefully leading her away from the others.

"Remember, aggression won't always grant you control over a battle." He grabbed her wrist, pulled her forward and swept out her feet. But before she hit the ground, Zulsthy'l grabbed her collar with his free hand and yanked her upright. She tried to pull away, but he twisted her arm and maneuvered her to face her fellows.

He was about to throw her toward the other potentials when the doors of the dueling chamber opened. The creaking metal heralded two masculine figures carrying ornate staffs. Both wore thick brown coats, and their faces were obscured: one shrouded with a hood and the other masked beneath a form-fitting helm. Though their faces were hidden, Zulsthy'l knew exactly who they were: his son, Dorith, and his mentor, Ilnari.

His exhilaration fled, replaced by overwhelming anxiety. *What are* they *doing here?* he thought, releasing the young potential. She spun to strike, but stopped short of landing a blow. The others on and around the dueling ring also noticed Zulsthy'l's distraction and turned to the doors.

Hushed whispers of confusion filled the dueling chamber, coming from the potentials observing the match.

"I apologize for the intrusion, Father," Dorith said. He pulled back his hood, revealing his wrinkled face and short cropped white hair. "But we must *talk*."

Zulsthy'l's jaw tensed, and the murmuring grew louder.

Dorith's face was stern, his thin lips downturned and his hazel eyes somber. Ilnari probably had a similar expression on his face, but it was hard to tell with that metallic mask. Though it had had openings for Ilnari's eyes and lips, Zulsthy'l could not see those features from where he stood.

"We will continue these exercises later," Zulsthy'l said, waving a hand in dismissal. "Please leave us." The whispers faded as the potentials complied. His opponents hurried from the dueling ring while the onlookers pushed past Dorith and Ilnari.

The murmuring faded as the doors closed. Once they were alone, Zulsthy'l stepped across the dueling ring. "What's happened?"

"It's Tardalim, Father." Dorith stepped onto the ring, approaching at a somber gait. "The prison has been invaded thrice over the past six months."

Zulsthy'l started, blinking in disbelief. In the seven thousand years since Tardalim's creation, no one had as much as reached the lone mountain. Even though during the eve of the Thousand Years War, those of the Cheserithean Empire had attempted to find it, the Eshari had repulsed them. And after the war, all knowledge of Tardalim was destroyed. It lived on only in folktales and myth. *But three separate incursions...?* Zulsthy'l stroked his beard. "Are you sure?"

Dorith stopped a few paces from Zulsthy'l. "Would I lie, Father?" He planted his staff and leaned on it while Ilnari stepped to his side. "We only found out today. We've been in the Western Sovereignty, aiding the rebels of Tor."

He explained how over the last year he, Ilnari, and several others had secretly joined the rebels to insure the assassination of Emperor Mentas. After the emperor's death, Dorith and Ilnari stayed to help organize skirmishes along the borders of the empire. Some of the others stayed with them, but Dorith's granddaughter, Alnese, left.

"...and today, when Alnese returned to my home, she discovered the beacon to Tardalim active." Dorith paused, taking in a deep breath. "The first incursion was squelched. We can only speculate on the outcome of the second. But, I believe the Tuladine were overcome or forced to flee, as no message accompanied the alert of the third incursion."

Unsettled, Zulsthy'l paced around the dueling ring. "And do we know who these invaders are?"

"The Mindolarnians, I believe. At least, from what was described about the intruders in the message after the first incursion. Although I doubt they acted alone."

Zulsthy'l halted abruptly.

"A tevisral was found among the invaders," Ilnari said. "One the Tuladine believed capable of nullifying the prisoners' containment. From their description it sounds... elven in design."

An elven tevisral. Mindolarnian invaders. *Oh no—!*

"I believe Cheserith's disciples are behind this, Father," Dorith continued. "But why they acted now, I do not know."

"The Ma'lishas' intentions are irrelevant," Ilnari said. "Their involvement is conjecture at best. We must focus on maintaining Tardalim."

"Or retaking it," Dorith said, giving Ilnari a sidelong glance. "My posterity is rallying as we speak, and they plan to meet us on Abodal."

"And I intend to inform Shem'rinal," Ilnari said. "Hopefully he can persuade the Kardorthians to lend us aid..."

Zulsthy'l pressed his lips into a line. The elves of Kardorth had kept to themselves over the last few centuries, wanting to stay aloof from the affairs of the human realm. The rise of the Mindolarn Empire had only driven them further into isolation. *This is a matter we will have to take into our own hands,* Zulsthy'l thought, sighing. "I will rally what Guardians are here," he said. "Have you informed my father?"

Dorith nodded. "We sent word via a messenger when we arrived. Hopefully, he will meet us at the transportium."

"Good," Zulsthy'l said. "I should fetch my armor—"

Dorith waved his hand, and white-blue particles shimmered in the air beside him. They soon dispersed, revealing a form-fitting suit of platinum armor that hovered in the air. Unlike most suits commonly worn in the human realm, Zulsthy'l's armor was one solid mass, lacking seams and joints. It was also adorned with scaled patterns.

"We tried your home first," Dorith said. "When we didn't find you, I thought it prudent to bring your armor along."

"Always thoughtful." Zulsthy'l gave his son a weak smile, then touched the right gauntlet. The glistening metal liquefied—though not by transmutative magic. The suit's transformation was beyond the Channels of Power. The white liquid hummed as it moved beneath Zulsthy'l's black garb and across his skin, covering him within seconds. The armor solidified, but Zulsthy'l could still breathe, see, and feel through the scaled suit. In fact, the armor enhanced his senses.

"Es'umak." The armor reacted to the command, receding from his head, neck, and hands. He turned to Dorith and Ilnari, studying them. "I suppose the two of you are prepared with more than your fanisars?" He pointed to their ornate staffs.

"Of course, Father," Dorith responded.

"Good," Zulsthy'l said and stepped from the dueling ring.

Once outside the Dohaliem, Zulsthy'l led Dorith and Ilnari through Usazma'thirl, the underground city of the usa'zin'sha. Despite being set within a massive domed cavern maintained by tevisrals, Usazma'thirl looked like most cities in the human realm. The buildings were simple, yet beautiful, made from transmuted matter shaped to look as if they had been constructed from brick, stone, or wood.

Few citizens of Usazma'thirl walked the streets, which surprised Zulsthy'l. But those present paid their respects with a greeting and a bow. Some looked curious, undoubtedly a result of Dorith and Ilnari's presence. They were well-known among the usa'zin'sha.

Not far from the Dohaliem, Zulsthy'l hurried to a two-story home with decorative wood adorning its façade. Before he could knock on the door, it swung open.

Zulsthy'l's daughter, Nai'ul, stood in the doorway, her curly black hair bobbing as she cocked her head. Her pale-gray eyes darted from Zulsthy'l, to Dorith, then to Ilnari. "The lot of you look too serious for this to be a family reunion..."

Dorith chuckled. "It's good to see you too, sister."

Nai'ul waggled a finger at Dorith. "Half-sister."

"Enough," Zulsthy'l said. "I need you to help gather the Guardians here in Usazma'thirl."

Nai'ul arched an eyebrow. "What happened?"

Dorith reiterated what he had told Zulsthy'l, but in fewer words. Nai'ul hurried past them without a word.

"Meet us at the transportium," Zulsthy'l called after her, closing the door she'd neglected to shut. "Always eager, that one."

"If a tad overzealous," Dorith said, chuckling.

They continued through Usazma'thirl, and Zulsthy'l informed several others of the predicament with Tardalim, enlisting their aid as he had Nai'ul's.

Before long, Zulsthy'l, Dorith, and Ilnari reached the city's main thoroughfare. Traffic was sparse, and those on the street paid little attention to Zulsthy'l and his companions—most were young potentials practicing a variety of social interactions.

They soon passed through the city's main gate—a seven-sided archway made of glistening white stone—and crossed an ornate bridge. It spanned the magma river that was Usazma'thirl's moat. The bridge ended at a ledge where a switchback path ascended to a small cave leading to the surface.

Dimly lit by lightstone sconces, the tunnel wound upward at a steep grade. As Zulsthy'l and the others climbed, Dorith speculated about the Mindolarnians' motives for invading Tardalim. "I don't think it was in retaliation to our actions. The first incursion happened before Mentas's demise."

"It has to be part of a greater plan," Ilnari said. "Especially *if* the Ma'lishas are involved."

"How else do you explain their possession of this nullifying tevisral?" Dorith asked. "The Mindolarnians have been making advancements in tevisral manufacturing but they are not *that* advanced. And how else could they have known how to breech Tardalim?"

Ilnari didn't reply.

Dorith was most likely correct. The tevisral in question had undoubtedly been in the Ma'lishas' possession for nearly the past four centuries. But the Ma'lishas' involvement didn't explain how the Mindolarnians knew how to enter the prison—that knowledge was held only by Zulsthy'l and his fellow Guardians. This was the most disturbing aspect of the incursions.

A faint howl carried through the tunnel, the chilling song from the winds that swept across the tunnel's mouth. The tunnel turned once before opening to the surface of the Carda Wastes. Reddish and orange hues tinged the darkening sky beyond the tunnel.

They soon neared the exit of the winding tunnel, where a lookout sat, huddled just inside. She wore a thick sloglien coat, and her face was veiled in a mask made of the same fur. She glanced in their direction, but kept silent as they stepped onto the snow-covered plain. The freezing wind stung Zulsthy'l's face and hands, sending a chill down his spine. Shivering, he stopped to examine the woman while Dorith and Ilnari continued their march from the cave, their boots crunching the snow.

"Do you only *watch and observe?*" he asked, referring to the usa'zin'sha's code.

She cocked her head, looking at Zulsthy'l with familiar teal eyes. Ah, a formidable pupil of his from three centuries ago.

"No. Why do you ask?" she replied.

"It is time for us to fulfill an oath, Vai'kassia. Find someone to relieve you, and then join us at the transportium."

She nodded and stood. Zulsthy'l turned back to the others as her footsteps faded into the cave. Now several dozen paces away, Dorith and Ilnari had their hoods pulled over their heads.

Best I keep warm, too, Zulsthy'l thought, hurrying after them. "Es'umak." The white metal around his neck and wrists liquefied, swiftly covering his hands and head. Those parts of him once exposed to the winds warmed immediately, a result of his armor's regulating properties. He could feel the cold wind whipping against his armor, but he was warm.

The last rays of sunlight faded as Zulsthy'l and the others crossed snowdrift after snowdrift. Kistern and Kaelyrn shone bright in the night sky, their light illuminating the snowy plain. All the while, Zulsthy'l considered the dire situation before them. Perhaps the *Edicts of the Mage-King* were made in error... The world was a far different place than when the prisoners were first exiled to Tardalim. Now, Kalda was primitive by comparison. The human realm could not stand against the prisoners of Tardalim. If the captives were set free, they would swiftly subjugate humanity under a yoke of tyranny.

That was something he could not allow.

But would the Mindolarnians stop their attempts to free Tardalim's prisoners? They were a relentless people, led by relentless rulers. *If only Tardalim could be moved...*

Shifting hues of myriad colors danced atop the crest of a nearby snowdrift. Zulsthy'l and the others quickened their pace, kicking up snow as they hurried to the luminous crest.

Beyond the snowdrift lay the transportium—a teleporting tevisral built long ago. Carved from beige stone, it consisted of a seven-sided dais large enough to accommodate fifty men, its entire surface covered in a seven-spiral pattern of etched characters of the *true* magical tongue, all shifting in varying hues. Seven ornate pillars, one at each of the dais's points, rose a story-and-a-half above the spiral pattern. Each pillar was carved with intricate designs culminating at the top in scaled claws reaching toward hovering transparent globes, each the diameter of a man's torso.

Zulsthy'l scanned the area around the transportium. Only two pairs of footprints—partly covered by windswept snow—led away from the transportium, undoubtedly belonging to Dorith and Ilnari.

Dorith was the first to descend the drift, carefully walking in the old prints. Ilnari did the same, but Zulsthy'l remained on the crest. He looked eastward, waiting for his father's arrival. The distant horizon was shrouded in darkness.

The wind howled, spraying loose snow around Zulsthy'l. He felt the tiny flakes against his armor, but they soon wisped away. In many ways, his armor was a secondary skin—alive and connected to him in every way.

Eventually, two winged figures glistened in the eastern sky, their platinum scales reflecting the moonlight.

"He's coming!" Zulsthy'l called, glancing over his shoulder. Dorith and Ilnari were kneeling at the far side of the dais, near a podium that had risen from the dais's surface. *What are they doing?*

Curious, Zulsthy'l descended the snowdrift and stepped onto the transportium. The stone at the dais's heart—which was devoid of glowing emblems—liquefied. Dorith reached the liquefied stone as it receded into the dais, revealing a fist-sized chamber containing a polished black disk—an ancient tevisral used to bind rogulin, thus enabling instantaneous teleportation.

Dorith lifted the domed disk, which fit in his palm. "Do you approve?"

"It will definitely make transporting our forces easier," Zulsthy'l said. "Better than rebinding dozens of crystals to your anchor—"

White light flashed through the sky, and Zulsthy'l spun. One of the glistening figures—which was now a burst of light—sped through the air, surging like lightning toward the cave leading to Usazma'thirl.

The other, now just over two grand phineals away, turned toward the transportium—Zulsthy'l's father, Zu'mal'thisr'nsar. Enormous in size and majesty, he was one of the largest sha'kalda, with a wingspan of over two hundred and thirty phineals.

Zulsthy'l's father soon burst into a brilliant flash. By aid of his armor, Zulsthy'l watched as his father shrank and changed from his true form. His wings receded into his back, his tail shortened, his neck compressed, and his snout flattened. Claws smoothed and horns diminished to nothing. The transformation finished as Zulsthy'l's father—and the surging light around him—struck the snow, spraying it far and wide.

If Zulsthy'l had watched without his armor, his father's transformation would have looked like lightning striking the ground, persisting only for a moment to show the silhouette of a burly man within a ball of light.

Zu'mal'thisr'nsar's brilliance faded as the snow settled. He stood tall, almost a head taller than Zulsthy'l, and was of a brawnier build—a reflection of his true form. Like Zulsthy'l, he also wore white-scaled armor.

"Aren't you too old for dramatic entrances?" Ilnari shouted from across the dais.

Zu'mal'thisr'nsar grunted. "Never..." His voice was deep, yet gentle. "Besides, such *entrances* are swifter than simply landing and transforming. It's more... economical." His logic drew laughter from Dorith. "Now, what is this predicament that requires the assembly of our tetrad of leadership?"

Ilnari spoke first, relating their dilemma in succinct points. Then Dorith chimed in, elaborating details Ilnari had left out.

"Then we have no choice," said Zulsthy'l's father. "We must secure Tardalim, no matter the cost. And we should banish its inhabitants from

Kalda, as our ancestors did with the lish'sha."

That was a solution Zulsthy'l had dismissed. *It would be too grueling a task…* And they would need a shiz'nak to open a portal to another world.

Ilnari evidently held the same view. "That is a monumental undertaking," he said. "It will take decades and a force far greater than we currently possess."

"Then we enlist the Esharian Collective," Zu'mal'thisr'nsar said. "It is time they forsake their prejudice against the rest of Kalda's inhabitants."

"Are you volunteering to go to Varquilus, Grandfather?"

Zulsthy'l's father turned to Dorith, his face stern. "I fear no one, least of all the Eshari. Now, we've wasted enough time discussing this matter. I will retrieve a shiz'nak while the three of you travel to Tardalim."

"Why don't I accompany you?" Ilnari said. "I know the friction between you and the Ril'sha. Maybe I can—"

"I do not intend to request a shiz'nak from them. We don't have time for the Ril'sha's petty bureaucracy. I will retrieve a shiz'nak *elsewhere.* If any of the prisoners have been freed, they will need to be exiled at once."

Ilnari nodded. "Then I will head to Kardorth."

Zu'mal'thisr'nsar turned to Zulsthy'l and Dorith. "How soon can the two of you reach Tardalim?"

"That depends," Dorith said, turning to Zulsthy'l. "Do you want to fly from Merdan to Abodal?"

Zulsthy'l considered the question. Dorith most likely intended for them to teleport to Alath and travel the trans-tube line to the Isle of Merdan. *That would be faster than flying directly to Abodal,* he thought. *Not to mention less exhausting.* At one time, the trans-tube line ran from Merdan to Abodal, but the Eshari had collapsed the line halfway between the isle and the icy continent. "It will be faster for us to follow the trans-tube line to its end."

"Around thirty-two hours, then," Dorith said. "We should reach the northern shore in a little under a day. Hopefully we'll have some favorable winds."

"We should regroup once on Abodal," Zulsthy'l said, turning to his father. "Will that give you enough time to retrieve the shiz'nak?"

Zu'mal'thisr'nsar nodded. Then in a blinding flash, he transformed and took to flight, soaring southward.

"Best I leave, too," Ilnari said and turned to Zulsthy'l. "Do you have any rogulin spheres bound to *that?*" He pointed to the disk Dorith held.

"I do," Zulsthy'l said. "I'll make sure one is sent to Kardorth."

"Much appreciated," Ilnari said with a bow, then stepped to the dais's center. "Now if you'll excuse me."

Zulsthy'l stepped off the transportium, and Dorith soon joined him on the snow. "Good luck, old friend."

Ilnari nodded with a smile. Then he spoke the words to activate the transportium. The transparent spheres atop the pillars became lit with flowing strands of purple and blue particles. A hum resonated from the dais as the spheres began to flash, pulsing at an ever-increasing rate until indigo beams shot from them, encasing the dais in a dome.

The hum grew louder, and the dome levitated off the dais, with Ilnari inside it. A thunderous eruption filled the air, and the hovering dome shot skyward, disappearing within a heartbeat.

Setting his jaw, Zulsthy'l stared across the sky to the south. *If the Eshari hadn't destroyed all their transportiums we wouldn't need this convoluted travel route.*

Setting his jaw, Zulsthy'l turned and climbed the snowdrift. Dorith was right beside him, and the two of them looked back toward Usazma'thirl.

"What do you think of Grandfather's proposal?"

Zulsthy'l sucked in his breath. "I think we should discern what has actually transpired before committing to any action."

"Why did I know you'd say that?" Dorith chuckled. "You know, Tardalim should have been ripped from this world centuries ago. I've always wondered why it remained."

"It was safely hidden. I'm sure if Dusel had thought it a threat he would have pushed for its removal."

Dorith grunted. "Sometimes I think we give him too much credit."

"Perhaps… but we wouldn't be having this conversation if it weren't for him—"

Hundreds of figures in black crested the distant snowdrift, kicking up snow around themselves. Some leapt from drift to drift while others ran at incredible speed.

I hope they are enough, he thought. Many of those approaching were the strongest of the usa'zin'sha, and several rivaled even Zulsthy'l and his father.

Nai'ul was among the first to arrive, as well as many of Zulsthy'l's former pupils. Their faces were stern, their eyes fierce.

Once they were gathered, Zulsthy'l clasped his hands behind his back and whispered the word to retract his armor. It was best that they see his face as he spoke. "Guardians of Kalda! We have vowed to keep this world aright, to preserve the innocent and to shield the defenseless. A shadow creeps from the far reaches of the world, one that must be vanquished. It is time we live our oath and secure Tardalim."

PART

FOUR

Escaping
the
Labyrinth

Amendal · Ildin · Vaem · Faelinia · Calimir
· Morgidian · Fench · Edara ·

"At last we come to my favorite conjuration. No other beast can match them in strength or grandeur. Enter the gangolin."

- From *Colvinar Vrium's Bestiary for Conjurers*, page 247

Faelinia, her friends, and what remained of Amendal's conjurations were the last to cross the vast oval room on Tardalim's thirty-third floor. Those strange reliefs along the walls made her think of stories her father had told her as a child, *The Dragon Wars*. She turned from the reliefs, eyeing the strange obsidian statues hovering in the air. The clear sphere between them pulsed with yellow light as the expedition passed between the statues.

"The camp isn't too far," Ildin said, pointing to a staircase. "Miraden had us set up in a nearby field."

"A field?" Morgidian asked, raising his eyebrow.

Ildin nodded.

"The Roost isn't like the rest of Tardalim," Scialas said. "It's actually quite pretty."

Intrigued, Faelinia opened her mouth to speak, but a horrified cry echoed in her mind. *Amendal.* Since enthralling him she had pushed aside vivid and terrifying images, as well as deranged thoughts that would have been screamed aloud if Amendal were not enthralled.

It's okay, she sent the thought to Amendal. *You're safe.*

Though he was walking calmly, she could feel that Amendal wanted to run. He wanted to clutch his head and wail.

"Oh, Amendal…" Her whispered lament drew the attention of the others, and they all stopped short of the statues.

"I can take over," Ildin said, worry contorting his face. His thin lips quivered as tears filled his eyes.

Faelinia shook her head and pressed forward. "No." She wiped her eyes and headed for the staircase leading to the Roost.

Her friends trailed behind her, talking about the thirty-third floor. Morgidian asked about a pair of hallways beside the stairs, and Ildin said the tevisrals were hidden there. Dugal was intrigued.

None of that matters, Faelinia thought. She drew Amendal to her and grabbed his hand.

She was halfway up the stairs before she lifted her eyes to the vast space that was the Tuladine Roost.

"Oh my…" she murmured. The Roost was larger than any space or cavern she had ever beheld. It was beautiful, as Scialas had claimed, teeming with all sorts of strange and colorful flora. Morgidian and Dugal reacted with similar awe, speculating about its size.

Ildin chimed in, talking about how one could walk on the walls and ceiling.

On the walls and ceiling? Faelinia started, but immediately recalled her observations while ascending to the third floor. The bits of her illusion that she had placed throughout the second floor had been *above* her. Had the expedition been going into Tardalim's center when they thought they were actually ascending to higher levels? If so, this Roost would be at the very heart of Tardalim, its core.

The thought made her woozy. She staggered from the top step and stumbled onto lush dark-teal grass. She sucked in her breath while the others walked around her.

"It's this way," Ildin said.

The rapid beating of wings whirled around Faelinia. A flash of gray zipped by, and that winged creature came to a halt, hovering near Ildin. Its dark-colored wings were a blur, and its tail swayed. *What was its name?* Strange words echoed in her mind, coming from Amendal.

"There you are, Fench," Scialas said.

The winged thing nodded and fluttered toward Amendal, studying the conjurer.

"Why did you run?" Ildin asked.

Fench blinked several times and turned to the illusionist. "What is *run?*" The question was high-pitched and nasally.

Scialas giggled, and Ildin ran a hand through his blond hair.

"Well, it doesn't have any legs," Dugal said matter-of-factly.

Morgidian gave the transmuter a sidelong glance, but turned back to Fench. "It means to flee."

Fench blinked again and rubbed his trunk, looking back to Amendal as if expecting an answer.

What a strange looking creature, Faelinia thought.

Ildin cleared his throat. "Back to my question, why did you *flee?*"

"I was scared," Fench said. He hung his head and his trunk became limp. "I don't like the Orath-monster."

"You poor thing," Scialas said, reaching for the winged creature. "Now look what you did, Ildin. He's scared!"

Ildin shrugged.

"Come here, Fench." Scialas patted her shoulder. "You can sit here." Fench fluttered toward her and perched, draping his tail along Scialas's chest. The creature's wings stilled, revealing a beautiful pattern of spots.

"Orath-monster?" Morgidian asked. "Is that its name?"

Fench nodded. "Orath-something. I can't remember. My mother said its name only a few times. The invaders let it out."

Let it out? Had the monster been trapped, like those strange creatures in the crystal cylinders?

"Was it one of the prisoners?" Ildin asked, and Fench nodded. The winged creature leaned toward Scialas's head, and she reached up to comfort him.

The six friends stood in silence for a moment until Faelinia spoke. "We should get Amendal to the tent. I'm leaving the yaeltis here."

Ildin nodded and sent the cisthyrn to join the hulking beast. Once the conjurations were together, Ildin hurried around a stone railing enclosing the stairwell. Faelinia followed, with the others trailing behind. They soon neared a cluster of tents within a large field of that dark-teal grass. Many of the survivors from Faelinia's part of the expedition were gathered on the far side of the camp.

While they picked their way through the tents, a savory aroma—like that of a hearty stew—tingled in her nostrils. It made her stomach growl.

"Oh, I need to eat!" Dugal exclaimed and loped off toward the tantalizing aroma.

"Will you grab me some, too?" Morgidian called after him.

If Dugal replied, it wasn't with words.

Once at Amendal and Ildin's tent, Ildin rushed to open its canvas flap. Faelinia hurried inside with Amendal trailing behind her. "Which cot is his?" she asked, and Ildin pointed to one beside the door.

Through her enthralling bond, Faelinia guided Amendal into the tent. She eased him toward the cot.

"Lie down," she urged, and he obeyed. Though he lay calmly, the terror continued to rage in his mind. Faelinia closed her eyes and brought a hand to her forehead.

"Is it still bad?" Scialas asked as she entered the tent. Fench was still perched atop her shoulder.

Faelinia nodded. Ildin slipped past her and knelt beside Amendal. Morgidian entered the tent and Scialas edged toward the cot, making room for him. Looking frustrated, the burly barsionist set his jaw and folded his arms.

"There has to be something we can do," Ildin said, balling his hands into fists.

"What's wrong?" Fench asked.

Ildin cocked his head toward the winged creature. "He was engulfed by that monster's orange haze. Do you know anything about it?"

Fench shook his head so quickly his trunk swung back and forth, nearly slapping Scialas across the face.

Guarding against the flailing trunk, Scialas looked to Ildin. "I could try healing him again." Ildin nodded, then turned back to Amendal.

Faelinia watched as a green aura surrounded Scialas. The arpran light surged toward the conjurer, coalescing around his head. Faelinia could feel the rejuvenating magic coursing through Amendal. The arpran particles seeped through his skull, but something prevented them from moving farther.

"It's worse than before," Scialas muttered. She sighed, and the green aura faded from Amendal.

"Perhaps the sickness will run its course?" Morgidian asked.

Ildin shook his head, muttering something Faelinia couldn't hear.

They stood in silence for a while until Dugal arrived. The transmuter awkwardly carried three bowls. "I got some for you, too," he said to Faelinia.

She gave him a weak smile and accepted the stew.

"How is he?" Dugal asked.

"Not good," Morgidian said, shaking his head. "Not good..."

What do we do? Faelinia wondered, raising a spoonful to her lips. While she ate, Amendal continued to struggle against her enthralling bond. His terror stung her heart, and tears once again filled her eyes. She turned away, and a tear trickled down her cheek.

"What about the tevisrals?" Dugal asked. "Maybe there's something in that treasure trove that could cure him. On our descent through the caves, I overheard the soldiers discussing a conversation between the commander and Vaem, about a tevisral that could save those impaled by the yaeltis. If there are tevisrals that could do that, perhaps one can help Amendal."

"Hm," Morgidian said, "it's worth a shot. Do you know what it looks like?"

Dugal shook his head.

The talk of tevisrals made Scialas grunt. "What can a tevisral do that I can't?"

While they discussed their dilemma, Amendal's terror intensified. Faelinia flinched and nearly dropped her bowl, spilling part of the stew.

I need to do something, she thought. She couldn't bear Amendal's suffering any longer. "I'm putting him to sleep," she said, and began uttering an incantation. Pale-gray light coalesced around her, but soon zipped toward Amendal. Faelinia felt the magic penetrate his skin, but it stopped short of reaching his skull. It was blocked, like Scialas's magic.

"It didn't work," Ildin muttered and turned to Fench.

Defeated, Faelinia wobbled toward Ildin's cot. She struggled to hold a firm composure, but Amendal's terror had eroded whatever emotional resolve she'd once had.

Though his plans for vengeance were frustrated, Captain Edara was still determined to avenge his beloved. He sat upon his cot within the small tent he shared with Cluvis, scraping his knife across the small yaeltis tusk. *This better work...* he grumbled to himself. The encrusted venom turned to an amber powder that fell into a pouch barely the size of his fist.

Since ascending the labyrinth, Edara had reconsidered finding an inconspicuous tevisral. His sailors were among the first to enter the treasure trove beneath this Roost. But to his dismay, none of the tevisrals that had been found were deadly—well, besides the ones that transformed into weapons. Unfortunately, those remarkable tools of war were not inconspicuous.

And what weapons they did discover were confiscated for the damned mages' guild. "What do they need weapons for...?"

True, the weapons were magical in nature: swords and fanisars whose blades formed from light and burst with all sorts of magic, bows whose strings wove out of thin air, and arrows that appeared within quivers. But what use had a mage for such things?

To make matters worse, the other tevisrals that were discovered baffled the scholars who had come along. And the damned fools were reluctant to tinker with them. All they wanted to do was sort them by size and shape. *Idiots...*

Frustrated, Edara returned to the venom as his mode of vengeance.

After his first search of the treasure trove, Edara had a dream about serving warm tea to the murderous bastard and the heartless whore. As they took their first sips, both convulsed like those who were impaled by the yaeltis. Though it was not directly expressed in the dream, Edara knew the tea was laced with the venom.

So, after failing to find a suitable and discrete weapon a second time, he sent his crew to the farther reaches of the treasure trove while he retired to his tent. After all, ideas that came during one's dreams were inspired, weren't they?

Poisoning would not be as pleasurable as stabbing, but Edara could enjoy watching his enemies writhe on the ground—as long as they survived the labyrinth's perils. *Death best not cheat me of my vengeance—*

A loud commotion of triumphant shouts carried through the quiet camp, and Edara ceased whittling. He craned his neck toward the tent's walls, but couldn't make sense of what he heard.

He shoved his knife into the dark-teal grass, wrapped the broken tusk in the torn fabric from his pocket, and then tied the pouch holding the amber venom.

Once his things were tucked away, Edara hurried to the tent door. But before he could open it, Cluvis stumbled inside. His first mate's jaw was set, his eyes fierce. "Oh, Captain... they've returned."

Intrigued, Edara pushed past Cluvis and stepped outside. The noises of various conversations carried from the field that was the makeshift mess area. A crowd had gathered, made of mage and mercenary alike. They surrounded soldiers and Edara's enemies. But, the heartless whore led the murderous bastard from the crowd as if he were leashed. The Mindolarnian lieutenant was with them as well, and the three of them soon disappeared among the tents.

Where are you going...? Edara stroked his long beard.

"Seems they lost a lot of people," Cluvis said, coming beside Edara. "Only half of them survived, or so I heard."

Edara nodded and stepped back into the tent. Cluvis was quick to secure the tent flap. Together, they returned to Edara's cot and sat.

"Thinned ranks should make our revenge easier," Edara whispered.

Cluvis rubbed his hands together, nodding. "Now all that is left is for you to finish."

Edara chuckled, then pulled his knife from the grass, eyeing the amber residue sprinkling the blade. "Soon, our beloved will be avenged."

Ildin's frustration grew, stoked by Faelinia's sobs. *Oh my friend.* He fought back a scowl while turning to Fench. "Is there any food here that can put Amendal to sleep?"

The winged creature rubbed his trunk and then pushed off Scialas's shoulder. He flew out of the tent without a word.

Hopefully that's a yes... Ildin thought, turning back to his friend. Amendal lay motionless, staring at the tent's fabric ceiling.

"What about a dispel?" Dugal asked. "If we can dispel the haze, perhaps Scialas can heal him."

"That might work," Morgidian said. "I'll hold him down with a barsion." He began uttering an incantation and the tent walls glowed with blue light. Soon, an inverted layer of barsion spread across Amendal, wrapping around him and the cot.

Ildin sucked in his breath. *Here goes nothing...* White light shone around him as he uttered the incantation. Once the dispel formed he flung it at Amendal's face, focusing the magic to surge only through the conjurer's head. But it only dismissed part of Faelinia's bond. *How was that possible?*

"It didn't work?" Dugal asked.

Ildin shook his head.

"This is ridiculous..." Morgidian muttered.

Dugal and Scialas speculated on Amendal's condition while Ildin slumped in defeat. *I wonder if Faelinia can relinquish her hold...?* Faelinia was still sobbing. Amendal's terror was probably too much for her.

"I have him restrained," Morgidian said to Faelinia. "You can relinquish your magic."

"He'll just scream," she said between sobs. "It'll be worse."

Ildin sucked in his breath and studied the conjurer once again. *What happened to you, Amendal?* The others continued talking, but Ildin ignored them. *I wonder what that voice would say...* He looked to the tent's ceiling. *I don't suppose you'll talk to me, will you?*

He heard nothing besides his friends and their speculations. Dugal wanted to go search the tevisrals they had found. *Hopefully Fench will return soon.* If they couldn't free Amendal from his madness, perhaps they could at least help him sleep.

The conversations of the survivors faded as Vaem hurried through the odd structures of Tardalim's core. *Such strange things,* she thought. But tree-like dwellings did make sense for winged creatures.

Prior to leaving for Soroth, Vaem had tried researching the Tuladine, but the Hilinard was rather lacking in information about them. The creatures had once lived across Kalda but had vanished several millennia ago, after Lord Cheserith's exile. What knowledge remained of them was merely myth.

And now they will *be myth,* she thought, quickening her pace. *An extinct race...*

Kydol called for her, and Vaem glanced over her shoulder. "Do you know where you're going?" the lieutenant asked.

"The man claimed the tower was this direction," Vaem said, pointing between two tree-like buildings. "I'm sure we will see it." She increased her speed, jogging briskly.

"Why are we hurrying?" Calimir asked from beside her. "Isn't this far enough away? I *need* you, Vaem."

"Patience..." she said to him.

He kept pace with her, his eyes filled with lustful yearning. *I need to find a way to preoccupy him,* she thought. *Perhaps I was too hasty about enthralling him.* But what other choice had she? If she had not used the euphorinizer on Calimir, the commander would have beaten her—perhaps even killed her. Using the tevisral had proved convenient in avoiding further conflict, but Calimir's relentless attempts to bed her were growing tiresome. Normally, she enjoyed such attention—after all, that was the euphorinizer's sole purpose. But Calimir had been rather dull and unsatisfying...

"I've been meaning to ask," Kydol said, now running alongside Vaem. "How did you do it? Change him, I mean."

Vaem gave the lieutenant a sidelong glance as they rounded a building. Did she dare answer? Vaem had kept the euphorinizer a secret for many years. But now someone had witnessed its effects. "A tevisral," she said curtly.

"That's it?" Kydol laughed. "Nothing more?"

Vaem raised an eyebrow but kept her focus ahead. She did not want to say any more about it. The euphorinizer was one of a kind, a precious tevisral she had created and kept to herself.

"I've never heard of such a device," Kydol said. "Is it like the ancient mind-circlets?"

Vaem shook her head, hoping to deter the lieutenant with an unspoken lie. The euphorinizer *was* derived from a mind-circlet, although it was not as powerful—mind-circlets could destroy and rebuild one's identity, like the gaze of a god.

Several years ago, the scholars at the Hilinard had tried replicating an ancient mind-circlet, but failed. Their failure, however, inadvertently laid the groundwork for developing the euphorinizer's primary mechanism. Vaem had been among those who made the discovery. Then she secretly conducted her own research on it. When her colleagues abandoned the project, Vaem continued her work and eventually created the euphorinizer.

"So, did *you* make it?" Kydol asked.

Vaem didn't reply. *Why does she have to be so inquisitive?*

"Your secret is safe with me, Vaem—"

"Why not there?!" Calimir shouted, tugging at Vaem's arm and pointing to a seemingly private spot between two of the buildings. "It's quiet. No one will hear!"

She shook her arm loose and kept running. "I said be patient! Do not ask me again!"

The commander obeyed, but the strained expression on his face showed the struggle between his swelling urges and Vaem's command.

Kydol laughed again. "My, I would love to have one of those," she said amid her mirth. "Oh, to have a man fawning over you, obeying your every command. Tell me, how long does it last?"

"Long enough," Vaem said through clenched teeth.

"I see..." Kydol nodded, directing her gaze to Vaem's hand. "Is it the glove? Or are you hiding the tevisral in it?"

Vaem ignored the question, although the lieutenant continued pestering her. But no matter how hard Kydol pried, Vaem would never divulge anything about the euphorinizer. She had used it in secret for many years for her pleasures, and she was not about to change that.

Soon, a towering structure partly covered in fluorescent vines and violet moss appeared above the tree-like buildings. Its top was partially surrounded by a blue aura. *There it is,* Vaem thought, triumphant. She quickened her pace to a sprint, and the others followed.

After they rounded several of the tree-buildings, the rest of the tower came into view. It consisted of seven tiers, each covered in overgrowth, and rose twenty-one stories—a good number. The blue aura, however, was actually a glowing sphere hovering beside the tower's top.

The living diagram of Tardalim, Vaem thought, recalling the explanation

mentioned on their way to the Roost. The idea of seeing Tardalim's workings through a projection of light was intriguing.

Vaem led the others around the building until she spotted a clearing in
the vines and moss. The white stone within the cleared area consisted of
shallow grooves resembling the round doors all along Tardalim's halls.

"Well, I suppose this is the entrance," Kydol said. "How do we open it?"

Green light shone within the shallow grooves, and then the stone within
the light slid apart.

Voice activated, Vaem thought, smiling. *Keyed to the Common Tongue, no
doubt...* She stepped ahead of the others into a well-lit corridor whose architecture was very similar to the rest of Tardalim's halls.

As she continued down the hall, she removed a tall cylindrical case from
her pack—the same one that held the map of Abodal. Ever careful, she
twisted its lid and removed several rolled sheets of paper. "Hold these," she
said, handing the sheets to Kydol. The lieutenant obeyed, and Vaem returned the case to her pack.

With her hands free, Vaem turned back for the pages, but Kydol was not
beside her. The lieutenant stood a dozen paces away and was too busy reading to notice the gesture.

"I don't understand..." Kydol mumbled as Vaem approached. "How...
how could the emperor have known—?"

Vaem snatched the sheets, and Kydol flinched. "Come," she said, moving back down the hall. All the while, Kydol muttered to herself about the
pages' contents. *It seems Vidaer didn't inform her...* The thought made Vaem
smile.

Unlike Kydol, when Vaem first read those pages, she had been intrigued.
The sheets contained detailed information that she assumed was known
only to the Tuladine—specific instructions of how to operate and access
the various terminals inside Tardalim, including the sequences of characters
to access the prison's innermost workings. The emperor never explained
exactly how he had obtained the information, but Vaem assumed he had
received a manifestation of the *Will*—the means by which Lord Cheserith
communed with his most devout followers.

The hallway emptied into a seven-sided room with doors on each wall, all
lit with a pale-green hue. There were six doors total, numbered from two to
seven; even to the right and odd to the left. This particular chamber had
been documented in the pages Vaem carried. According to the instructions,
each door led to lift-like chambers that rose to the tower's various tiers.

Each doorway had the words in the Divine Tongue inscribed upon and
around them. They were labeled with their tier's number and purpose. To
the right: "Two: Structural Workings." "Four: Records and Manifests."
"Six: Offices and Communications." On the left: "Three: Defense Network." "Five: Containment." "Seven: Security and Surveillance."

"There," Vaem said, pointing to her immediate left. "We should disable
the Shift before we do anything else."

"A single gangolin has the capacity to topple a small army. I once had the pleasure of decimating a battalion of footmen. The battle was glorious! None survived."

- From *Colvinar Vrium's Bestiary for Conjurers*, page 247

After speculating about poor Amendal, Morgidian and the others spoke briefly about the situation with Calimir. Ildin insisted that they needed to dispel the hold Vaem had on the commander. Dugal, however, didn't care. In fact, he was adamant that they do nothing for the commander, as Calimir wouldn't sanction any action to help Amendal.

Faelinia was the only one who hadn't voiced her opinion on the matter. She was too busy crying.

Morgidian, however, came down on Ildin's side. If Vaem had gotten a hold on the commander, then the entire expedition would be subject to her whims—whatever they might be. The Mindolarnians had already come to Tardalim before and had obviously failed. Whatever Vaem wanted was probably not aligned with the expedition's mandate from the Order's council.

And that made Morgidian nervous.

With the commander wrapped around her finger, so to speak, there was no one preventing Vaem from doing as she pleased. She had to be stopped.

Once everyone finished their stew, Morgidian, Scialas, and Dugal left the tent. Dugal was insistent about finding a tevisral that could help Amendal. "I'm sure we'll find something," he said, running a hand through his hair. "As grand as this place is, there is bound to be some sort of tevisral that can heal him."

We can only hope, Morgidian thought.

The trio picked their way across the camp as lively conversations carried between the tents; talk of the monster, the tevisrals, and the strangeness of Tardalim. As they neared the camp's edge, Jaekim emerged from a tent.

"You're alive!" the necromancer exclaimed, hurrying toward Morgidian and the others.

"Of course we're alive," Dugal said. "And where have you been?"

Jaekim thumbed back to his tent. "I just woke up! Oh, I needed that nap! Not sure how I made it to my tent, though…"

"We had to carry you," Scialas muttered. "And that was no nap."

"It wasn't?" Jaekim scratched his head, then muttered to himself.

"It's probably around noon," Morgidian said in amused exasperation. Then he pointed to the camp's edge. "Why don't you come along with us? We're looking for a tevisral to help Amendal."

The necromancer jerked back. "Help Amendal? What happened to him?"

"It seems he's gone mad," Dugal said. "The monster got to him, engulfed him in that mist."

Jaekim looked utterly confused.

"The big black thing," Scialas added. "The one we saw briefly. Its mist makes people crazed."

Jaekim's eyes bulged.

"Come on," Morgidian said, walking past Jaekim. "We can talk while we search."

◦

Fench flew toward the field where the two-legs made their flimsy rooms. *Weird things…* He held tight to the kisalics, careful not to drop them. Zipping around the flimsy rooms, he soared toward the one where Amendal lay.

"That mean Orath-monster," Fench whispered.

He soon entered and fluttered to a halt. That female two-leg was still crying, and Ildin was kneeling beside Amendal. The sight reminded Fench of when he last spoke to his mother.

Mother… Sorrow filled Fench's heart.

"You're back!" Ildin said, rising from beside the weird bed-thing.

Fench nodded and held out his arms, dropping two of the kisalics. He had brought five. Usually, it only took eating one to fall asleep, but Amendal had eaten umviliums, and he was bigger than a Tuladine.

"What do we do with these?" Ildin asked, picking up the kisalics. Both easily fit in his palm.

"Eat them," Fench said. Why did two-legs always ask silly questions?

Ildin chuckled, examining the kisalics.

"Like this." Fench dropped all but one and held the kisalic by its ends. He dug his fingers into its skin, and broke it in half. Thick white juice oozed from the kisalic as Fench fluttered to Amendal. He held the broken food over the hooman's mouth, waiting for it to drip. But kisalic juice always took a long time to drip.

"Does he eat the whole thing?" Ildin asked.

"If he likes bitter things," Fench said. "I don't like the outsides. Yucky…" He shook his head and his trunk flapped back and forth.

Ildin shook his head, too. *He probably doesn't like bitter things, either…*

"Why don't I feed him?" Ildin said, kneeling by the weird bed-thing.

"If you want," Fench said. He waited for Ildin to grab the broken kisalic. The gooey juice had almost dripped onto Amendal's mouth.

Ildin took the food and turned around. "Faelinia, be ready to make him swallow."

The female two-leg didn't say anything. She just kept crying.

Fench studied her for a moment, then turned back to Ildin and Amendal. Ildin was ripping pieces off and putting them in Amendal's mouth. *Yucky…*

It took a long time for Ildin to feed Amendal all five of the kisalics. Fench had since coiled his tail on the ground and leaned against Amendal's big brown bag.

"He's asleep…" the female two-leg muttered. She had finally stopped crying.

"Good," Ildin said, sighing. He turned from Amendal, looking across the tent. "I can stay with him, if you want to rest."

She shook her head.

"Well, lie down on my cot," Ildin said, turning to Amendal again. His weird lips puckered and his forehead wrinkled. Sighing, Ildin reached for Amendal's neck. *Why was he doing that?* Ildin did something Fench couldn't quite see, then lifted a golden string that held a blue rock. "We should probably keep this safe," he said, moving toward Amendal's big brown bag. "Excuse me, Fench."

Ildin reached for the bag's top, and Fench leaned back. Once it was open, the two-leg dropped the rock inside. "I'm going to look for Vaem," Ildin said, walking to the door. "Why don't you let me take over the yaeltis?"

The other two-leg, Fae-something, muttered a reply but Fench was too preoccupied with Amendal's bag. The flimsy door flapped shut as Fench stuck his head into the bag—well, part of it. He let his trunk hang outside. If it were inside it would just get in the way. Curious, he grabbed the blue rock.

What is this? he wondered, raising the rock to his eyes. It had shiny yellow specks in it. Fench looked back inside and saw the black thing Amendal had him wash. Holding the rock by the gold string, Fench lifted the black dome from the bag. He looked back and forth between the two things, his trunk swaying.

I wonder what these are for?

Ever curious, he pushed the things together. As they touched, brown light surged from the black dome thing and wrapped around the blue rock.

As more brown light appeared, the two things pushed away from each other, forcing Fench's hands apart. The push only lasted a short while, stopping as the light faded.

Fench jerked, and rested his hands on the pack. "That was strange..." he muttered, looking back and forth between the two things.

———⊃•⊂———

Beyond the tents and the makeshift mess area lay the tevisrals. They were arranged in rows and columns on the dark-teal grass, organized by size. Five robed men, who Morgidian didn't know, were studying the various objects and taking notes.

"Excuse me!" Morgidian shouted to them.

The nearest fellow turned, raising a thick gray eyebrow. "Yes?"

"Have you catalogued any of these?" Dugal asked. "By what they do, I mean."

The man shook his head. "We're just sorting them by size and shape, pairing identical objects."

Another man at the end of the farthest row turned, and shouted. "We don't know what most of these do. They're unlike any other tevisrals we've seen."

Morgidian drew his lips to a line. *Great...* He sighed, studying the various rows. The objects glowed with different colors, though some were not lit. *Probably dormant.* None looked familiar in the slightest. These tevisrals were not like what he knew and understood.

"This could take a while," Dugal said.

It'll take too long... Morgidian turned back to the camp. If anyone knew anything about these tevisrals it would be Vaem. *But I doubt she'll help willingly.*

"So now what?" Jaekim asked.

"We start looking," Dugal said, stepping past Morgidian. The transmuter knelt beside the nearest row of tevisrals and began inspecting the objects one by one.

Jaekim groaned, but joined Dugal on the grass.

"What are you thinking, Morgi?" Scialas asked.

Morgi? He raised an eyebrow and turned to the short arpranist. "Is Amendal rubbing off on you?"

Scialas giggled. "I'm just trying to lighten the mood."

Morgidian gave her a weak smile. He studied her for a moment before answering. "If we find Vaem, she might be able to identify something that can help. She seems to know a lot more than she lets on."

Scialas nodded, parting her lips. "She did know about the yaeltis, and the cisthyrn. Maybe she knows something about that monster..."

If she did, why didn't she say anything? Morgidian wondered. But Vaem and Kydol had fled when the monster first appeared. Perhaps she did know.

"Well, we should find her."

Together, Morgidian and Scialas turned back to the camp. Most of those still eating were sitting on the grass in small circles. Several of the squad leaders were eating together, including Dardel. Morgidian, however, didn't see Vaem among them. In fact, he didn't see the commander or the Mindolarnian lieutenant.

"Perhaps Dardel knows where Vaem went."

Scialas snapped her fingers. "To the tower, I bet! This way!" She hurried off, running across the dark-teal grass and toward strange buildings that looked like trees.

Vaem, Kydol, and Calimir emerged from the cylindrical lift chamber and stepped onto the tower's eight floor; the middle level of the third tier. The space beyond the lift chamber was almost identical to the seven-sided room on the first floor. The only differences were that there were no other doors, and a short hallway was aligned with the lift chamber.

"This way," Vaem said and strode into the hallway. The clicking of her boots echoed off the stone as she entered a curved corridor with polished stone walls. Partway down the curved hall was a six-sided archway leading to a large space. According to the texts from the emperor, each level of the Tuladine Tower's third tier was divided into four large rooms.

"In there."

She hurried to the archway. The room beyond the arch was quite large and shaped like a fan. Inside, terminals used to access Tardalim's various defenses jutted from the walls. To an ordinary man of Kalda, the terminals probably looked like slanted desks. Fortunately for Vaem, such sophisticated things were not foreign to her.

"Does it matter which one we use?" Kydol asked.

Vaem shook her head and walked to the nearest terminal. Blue and green lines surrounded the slanted top, each glowing faintly. She touched the bottom corner, and blue lines shot from the terminal and into the air, forming a rectangular shape with rounded edges. Green light winked into existence within the rectangle, forming a basic greeting in the Divine Tongue. The greeting vanished and was replaced by the words, "Please enter the correct sequence."

More puzzles… Narrowing her eyes, Vaem thumbed through the pages in her hands. *There…* She re-ordered the sheets so the page about the tower's third tier was on top. It held specific instructions about how to use "black spheres" with inscriptions of the Divine Tongue etched into them. *But there are no bla—*

The slanted surface shifted, and seven black spheres appeared. Crisp symbols formed upon each one, the most basic characters of the Divine Tongue. Had they formed by transmutative magic? If so, it had been too quick for her to catch.

"That doesn't seem very efficient," Kydol said.

Vaem scowled at the lieutenant, then returned to the spheres. They had five symbols, arrayed so that when a sphere was gripped, one's fingers and thumb could easily touch each one. She looked to the sequence of characters used to access this particular part of Tardalim. They were an incoherent jumble, gibberish, really.

After committing the sequence to memory, Vaem studied the seven spheres. *That should be easy enough.* She placed her hands on the spheres containing the sequence's first few characters, gently pressing her fingers upon the corresponding symbols.

Once she completed the sequence, the spheres shone with white light and then vanished. The words also disappeared and were replaced by a directory of sorts for Tardalim's various defenses. But some of the words were surrounded by a black hue.

"How remarkable," Kydol said, stepping beside Vaem. "It's hard to imagine that all of Kalda was once this sophisticated."

Vaem raised an eyebrow. *No it's not...* She shifted her focus back to the directory. She touched the line of text labeled The Shift. The directory changed, becoming another directory with rows of numbers, from one to thirty-two. Wary, she touched the line with the number one. The words changed as they had before, now with a detailed list of descriptive functions that undoubtedly had to do with the shifting halls. *This won't be a simple task,* she thought. Would she have to disable each function within each floor? *Irritating safeguards!*

Kydol harrumphed, and Vaem turned to the lieutenant. "It looks like this will take some time."

A murmuring sigh left Calimir's lips and he edged closer, whispering Vaem's name in a seductive tone.

"Not now!" Vaem spat. *If I only had some way to bind him...*

"Why don't I activate another terminal," Kydol said. "I can help move things along."

Vaem raised her brow at the lieutenant. But Kydol had been helpful in the past. "Fine," she said, returning her focus to the words hovering in the air. "But be careful."

Scialas led Morgidian at a furious pace until they arrived at a towering seven-tiered structure whose white stone was barely visible beneath violet moss and multicolored vines. The tower looked like a rainbow. Morgidian's eyes were drawn to a gigantic sphere hovering beside the building's highest tier. *How odd...*

"Vaem is probably at the very top with Fendar," Scialas said, moving straight for a round door surrounded by the strange vines. She felt at the door, which had no knob. "I can't remember how to open this…"

No sooner than the words left her mouth than green light shone from a groove along the door's center. In an instant, the door split in two down the groove, then slid apart, disappearing into the wall.

Scialas shrugged and hurried inside, entering a corridor untouched by the wild overgrowth.

Morgidian edged to the door. Had it reacted to Scialas's voice? He studied the door, then whispered the word, "Close."

Both parts of the door slid from the wall, shining along the groove before becoming one solid mass.

Morgidian nodded. "Very interesting…" He studied the door for a moment then said, "Open."

The door complied, its slabs sliding into the wall.

"Morgi…" Scialas called, her voice distant.

Rousing himself, Morgidian stepped inside. "I'm coming!" To his surprise, Scialas stood a hundred phineals away, where the corridor emptied into a small room. He ran to join her, passing several doors and branching hallways. Together, they entered a seven-sided room. Doors, each etched with glowing symbols, adorned the walls.

"It's this way," Scialas said, moving to the farthest door on the left. "We go in here. I think it's a lift of some sort?" As she neared the door, it slid open, revealing a cylindrical chamber.

They hurried inside, and Scialas touched a row of strange symbols etched into the chamber's wall. The doors shut, but opened again before Morgidian could blink twice. He expected to hear conversation, but all was silent. Scialas hurried out of the chamber, calling for Fendar.

A large, two-story room with white stone walls lay beyond the doors. It was empty, except for a large transparent blue sphere hovering atop a white stone table. Strange-looking desks jutted from the walls, each glowing with varying colors. Across the room was a balcony, part of its railing missing. A narrow pathway jutted from the balcony, where a robed figure stood within blue light—*Is that Fendar? And is that a bridge?*

Scialas hurried through the room, still calling for Fendar.

Morgidian, however, returned his focus to the transparent sphere atop the table. It had many layers to it, but the center was mostly hollow. Orange lines were spread across the various layers, all leading to the center. And clustered within part of the center were yellow specks. *That can't be Tardalim, can it?*

He pushed the thought aside as a joyous reunion carried from the balcony. *Best I join them,* he thought, hurrying from the table. Fendar and Scialas stood upon the odd bridge, holding each other. They exchanged a brief kiss, Fendar seeming reluctant to step away.

"I'm so relieved you're safe," he said. "How is Amendal?"

Scialas shook her head. "Not good… I think he's getting worse. Have you seen Vaem?"

Fendar set his jaw, then glanced across the bridge. "Let me check the map."

The map? Morgidian raised an eyebrow and examined the light surrounding the bridge. It was the same color as the sphere atop the table.

"Incredible, isn't it?" Fendar said, chuckling. "Oh, the wonders of this place..."

Taken aback, Morgidian studied the blue light. It too had layers, like the sphere atop the table, as well as orange lines. One of Fendar's illusion zipped through the blue light, moving toward the center and into an area filled with tiny yellow specks.

"Where is the monster?" Scialas asked.

"On the twenty-fifth floor," Fendar said. "I'll show you after I find Vaem—oh! I think she's in this tower, somewhere in the middle... Yes, the middle level of the third tier."

Scialas looked confused. "How did you figure that out?"

"Remember those odd dots?" Fendar asked. "The ones that were yellow but with red centers?"

Scialas nodded.

"When Calimir and the others ran from the monster, those dots were among them. Once my illusion caught up with them after the battle, I compared the positions of the dots to where everyone stood in the hall. Vaem and Kydol were those dots with red in their centers."

Scialas flinched. "What does that mean?"

Fendar shrugged.

Different dots? Morgidian thought, confused. "I'm sorry, what dots?"

"The yellow ones," Fendar said, pointing toward the center of the transparent sphere. "Each of those yellow dots on the map represents one of us. Fench, if you've met him, is gray. Amendal's conjurations are also different colors."

Scialas let out a heavy sigh. "So, why are Vaem and Kydol different?"

Fendar shrugged again. "Come with me." He turned, walking across the bridge. Morgidian and Scialas followed, passing through layer after layer of blue light as Fendar continued his explanation. "Now the monster... he's black and orange, like Fench said. But there was no black-and-orange dot anywhere on the map, at least until you all caught up with Morgidian and the others."

"So it just appeared?" Scialas asked. "From where?"

The illusionist shook his head. "Remember the other dot, the yellow with an orange center?" Scialas nodded. "That dot is nowhere on the map," Fendar continued. "And from what I heard, no one died in the battle with the monster. It should still be on the map."

Uldric... Morgidian thought, eyes widening.

"But it's not," Fendar said. "That yellow-and-orange dot went missing after the black-and-orange one appeared..."

The illusionist continued speculating as the three of them entered the light representing the Tuladine Roost. While Morgidian eyed those yellow dots, he considered the problem with the monster, that Orath-something, as Fench called it. *Was that not Uldric that returned...?* But could this Orath-whatever really take on another form? He had heard of creatures that could mimic someone... Those creatures—phantasmal essences—were often the culprits behind most ghost stories. But the monster was no phantasmal essence.

"...wait," Scialas said, shaking an open hand. "*It* was with them?" She turned to Morgidian, looking confused.

Fendar nodded.

Morgidian set his jaw. *Uldric* had *to be that Orath-thing...*

"Morgi?" Scialas poked his shoulder.

"I think Orath-whatever-his-name can change shape," he muttered. Fendar looked confused. "The name Fench gave the monster. Now, last night, one of the necromancers came into camp, wounded. He claimed they were attacked, and that he was the only survivor."

Scialas paled as her eyes widened. "Oh no... If that thing can shape-shift, what are we going to do?"

"Watch it from here, of course." Fendar sucked in his breath. "It's the only way to be sure. But I doubt the monster will be able to navigate the thirty-second floor. As you can see, the lines change so fast it's almost impossible to navigate."

Morgidian turned and stepped into the light representing the thirty-second floor. The orange lines and arrows, however, weren't changing. Nor were the halls. *Why aren't they moving?* The Shift, as the others had called it, was swift on that floor.

"That's not right..." Fendar said, shaking his head. "Why isn't the Shift happening?"

Vaem... Morgidian thought. Clenching his teeth, he stepped into the layer representing the thirty-first floor. Its rearranging of halls should have also occurred, but the orange lines were as they had been when he first stepped through the giant illusion.

"She stopped the Shift," he said, fighting back a growl.

"Vaem?" Scialas asked, her tone wary. "Bu-but how could she stop the Shift?"

A sense of determination swelled within Morgidian as he crossed the bridge. "Come on. We need to find Vaem and stop her. Fendar, we're going to need your help."

*"I might tout the gangolin as the ultimate conjuration, but they do
have their weaknesses, particularly an inability to function in frigid
temperatures. Even while one is enthralled, a conjurer will have trouble maintaining control, not to mention the mental anguish shared
through the bond."*

- From *Colvinar Vrium's Bestiary for Conjurers*, page 248

After claiming the conjured yaeltis from Faelinia, Ildin created five
illusions of himself. Each contained a dense cluster of dispelling
magic. Such a tactic was used by illusionists to conceal destructive
blasts, but Ildin thought it just as useful for veiling a dispel.

Once the illusions were flying through the camp, Ildin commanded the
five cisthyrn and the lone yaeltis to follow him. If he were to confront
Vaem he would most definitely need them.

Focused through his illusions, Ildin hurried toward the camp. A jumble
of conversations assailed the illusions: men and women talked of tevisrals;
the survivors from the first half spoke of the monster, relaying details of the
battle that had occurred after the expedition was separated.

Unfortunately, he neither heard nor saw Vaem among those in the camp.
His illusions zipped about, flying above the tents and the congregation near
the mess area. Calimir and Kydol were also missing. Where else could they
be?

Ildin and the conjurations were near the camp when one of his illusions
zipped past the rows and columns of tevisrals. The scholars who had accompanied his part of the expedition were sorting them. Dugal and Jaekim
were among the scholars, hefting several large rectangular objects of intricate design. Those tevisrals were longer than a man's leg and were as thick
as one's thigh. But where were Morgidian and Scialas?

"Dugal!" Ildin called through his illusion. The transmuter jumped, dropped the odd tevisral, and looked up.

"Don't ever do that…" Dugal said, exhaling loudly.

Ildin fought back a smile. "Sorry, but have you seen Vaem?"

Dugal shook his head. "Morgidian was saying something about her before he and Scialas ran off." He pointed to the grassy plain beside the mess area. "They went that way."

Ildin turned the illusion, following Dugal's gesture. The vine-covered tower caught his eye. Had Scialas taken Morgidian to the tower? Could Vaem be there, too? Miraden had probably mentioned the three-dimensional map of Tardalim during their ascent. If he hadn't, Fendar would have said something about it.

He sent an illusion flying toward the tower. He set the other illusions to continue sweeping through the camp while he uttered an enhancing incantation. If Vaem and the others were in the tower, then he and the conjurations would need to get there quickly.

White particles soon appeared and seeped into his legs, quickening his gait.

<hr/>

After deactivating the Shift, Vaem and Kydol had moved on to disabling Tardalim's other defenses. Unfortunately, many of the functions could not be stopped. The most irritating of all was the barrier preventing conjuration magic from forming within Tardalim. Supposing that something might be wrong with their terminals, Vaem and Kydol checked the others throughout the room. To her dismay, none permitted access to the other functions.

"What do we do now?" Kydol asked.

Vaem took in a deep breath and closed her eyes. "We move on to the fourth tier. The emperor has requested we free certain gods. Their locations should be in the records portion of this tower."

The lieutenant nodded once before picking her way across the room. She wove around the terminals but stopped short of the seven-sided archway.

Vaem narrowed her eyes. *Why is she—?* Footsteps carried through the curved hallway and Vaem drew her lips to a line.

The footsteps grew louder. Then three mages appeared beyond the archway—some of Amendal's friends: the burly barsionist, that homely arpranist, and one of the illusionists.

"What are you doing here?" Kydol demanded, straightening her back.

The burly barsionist turned to her, a scowl on his face. "I could ask you the same." He sounded fierce and determined.

"What have you done to the Shift?" the illusionist asked.

Vaem raised an eyebrow. *How does he know what we've done?*

"I don't know what you're planning," the barsionist said, turning to Vaem. "But it can't be good. Now relinquish your hold on the commander, and come with us."

Vaem flinched.

"You have no authority over us," Kydol said, moving her hand to her sword's hilt. "Back away."

The three mages shook their heads almost in unison. "If you don't come peacefully"—the barsionist stepped toward Kydol—"we will bring you back by force."

Kydol lunged toward the barsionist, drawing her blade. As her sword sang through the air, the barsionist uttered an incantation. The illusionist also mustered his magic—the incantation sounded like a dispel.

"Stop him!" Vaem commanded, pointing to the mage now surrounded by white particles. "But don't kill him."

Calimir obeyed, bounding across the room while drawing his sword. He twirled his blade so its fuller rested along his forearm. The illusionist spun, but before he could finish his incantation Calimir bashed him with the flat side of his sword.

The blow sent the mage flying.

Yelling a battle cry, Calimir spun toward the arpranist. He swung the pommel toward the woman, striking her in the face. She screamed, and Calimir charged at the illusionist once again, yelling a battle cry.

Good, Vaem thought, *he can keep them preoccupied.* She touched a silver rivet below the thumb of her right glove, the euphorinizer's activating mechanism. A tingling sensation surged across her gloved hand, following the tevisral's emitter strands woven along the glove's fingers. Faint pink light shone from the silver band rimming the glove's cuff, manifesting without sound.

While the tevisral activated, Vaem picked her way across the room. Grunts, incantations, and screams carried from the hall. Several paces from the archway, Calimir loomed over the illusionist. The commander's sword was bloodied, and the mage lay on the ground, clutching his leg and screaming. Had the man tried to run?

She darted a glance to Kydol. The lieutenant swung her blade at the barsionist, but the burly man dodged her blows with ease. He tumbled sideways, still mustering his magic. Kydol swung as she charged, but bright-blue light burst from the barsionist, striking the lieutenant's legs. The blue magic instantly became a band of barsion that toppled Kydol.

The tingling ceased along Vaem's hand, indicating the tevisral was ready. Now several paces from the archway, she ran toward the barsionist. The man spun to face her and backed away, uttering another incantation.

"Oh no you don't!" she shouted, dashing into the curved hall. The barsionist eyed her glove, his face tensing. She was no more than a leap away when he turned to run. He had fled only partway down the hall before Vaem caught up to him, her fingers grazing the back of his robe.

The brief touch made the tevisral discharge, and a sudden surge squeezed her hand, as if the glove had tightened. Faint pink light shot from her fingertips and into the barsionist's robe, abruptly stilling him mid-motion. They collided and fell to the ground face-first. She landed atop his back, and the man groaned in ecstasy.

"Look at me," Vaem said, sliding off his back while reaching for his face. She grabbed his chiseled chin, forcing his eyes to hers.

"Oh, Vaem…" His face contorted into a yearning expression. If this were any other time, Vaem would gladly enjoy the man's company.

"Dismiss your barsion," she commanded. "And subdue your friends. Then, I'll give you pleasure."

The barsionist leapt to his feet, twisting his hand in a dismissal while uttering another incantation.

Vaem rose as blue light tinged her vision, and an enraged cry filled the hall, coming from Calimir. Kydol, now freed, pushed herself from the ground. The lieutenant ran to the ugly woman, who was attempting to pry Calimir from the illusionist.

While the barsion coalesced beside her, Vaem eyed her glove. Never had she needed to activate the euphorinizer so soon after using it, nor had she ever envisioned doing so. *Hopefully it isn't a problem*, she thought, pressing on the glove's silver rivet.

Ildin had finished enhancing the last cisthyrn when his illusion reached the top of the tower. To his surprise, Fendar was gone. Only his illusion remained, hovering in place within the layer representing Tardalim's twenty-fifth floor.

"Fendar!" Ildin called. "Have you seen Morgidian or Scialas?"

The illusion didn't move.

"Fendar!"

Finally, the illusion turned. "Help!" The word was laced with pain.

Ildin started. "Where?! Where are you?"

Fendar's illusion zipped from the bridge, plummeting along the tower. Ildin commanded his illusion to follow. Fendar's reflection stopped halfway up the third tier, pointing to the overgrown wall.

"Hang on," Ildin said through his illusion. "I'm coming!"

Running as fast as he could, Ildin bolted from the camp. *With me!* He sent the command to his illusions and his enthralled conjurations. The cisthyrns galloped ahead while the yaeltis bounded behind them, and the four illusions shot from the camp.

With the illusions now beside him, Ildin chased after his enthralled conjurations, darting around tree-like building after tree-like building. Soon, the tower came into view. He sent his illusions flying to the tower's entrance, but the door was closed.

"Oh great…" he grumbled between breaths, his voice echoing from his illusions. "Why can't you be open?!"

The door glowed, then slid apart.

Ildin blinked in disbelief, but quickly regained his composure. *Inside,* he commanded the illusions. They zipped into the pristine corridor, entering the seven-sided room before Ildin and the conjurations reached the tower. He commanded the cisthyrn to enter, but ordered the yaeltis to remain out-side—the beast was too big to fit inside the tower, anyway.

Though the tower's entrance was only a few dozen phineals away, it felt much farther. His heart pounded from exertion and worry. What had hap-pened to Fendar? He had sounded pained. Had something dangerous been lurking in the tower, or was Vaem responsible for Fendar's predicament? And were Morgidian and Scialas with him? If so, were they hurt, too?

Finally, he ran through the tower's entrance and the door shut, clipping his boot. Ildin stumbled and fell to the floor. *That was close...* He took in a deep breath, sprang to his feet, and then darted through the hall after the five cisthyrns.

As he ran, he considered the predicament ahead of him. He had only five dispels, barely enough to wash through a small room or part of a hallway. The cisthyrns could attack, but how many could he bring with him? The lifts were not large enough to fit them all. *Perhaps I should muster some ensnar-ing tentacles.* He could free his friends with the dispels if they were bound by magic, and the cisthyrns could attack or act as a barrier while he unleashed his ensnaring magic.

That'll do, he thought and began uttering an incantation. He brought his hands to his chest as green light swirled between his palms, forming tiny strands that wove together.

Ildin soon entered the seven-sided room and came to a halt, studying the glowing doors that led to the various lifts. But which lift went to the third tier? The farthest one on the left ascended to the top. And the middle on the right led to the fourth tier...

He glanced to his immediate left, then stepped toward the door. It opened at his presence, and he willed his illusions inside the lift. They flut-tered to the ceiling, making room for him and the cisthyrns. But only two of the beasts fit inside. Still mustering his magic, Ildin pressed himself against the wall, near those strange lines of symbols. Ever careful, he turned, extending a finger to the middle row. All the while, the ensnaring magic continued to form, becoming thicker strands.

The doors shut as Ildin neared the end of his incantation. He exhaled the last bit, humming the first sound of the last word. The doors sprang open. Pained screams and ferocious cries flooded into the lift.

Go! The command caused the magic to flicker, but Ildin quickly regained his focus.

His illusions zipped through the open doors and into a hallway aligned with the lift. Both cisthyrns galloped ahead, and Ildin darted after them, focused through his illusions.

He started in surprise as the illusions entered a curved hallway. Commander Calimir had Fendar pinned to the ground, his armored forearm pressed against the illusionist's mouth. Fendar held his left leg with bloodied hands. The illusionist tried to roll away, but the commander dug his knee into Fendar's chest.

Beside Fendar, Scialas lay on the ground, her entire body surrounded by a band of barsion. Vaem loomed over the arpranist, reaching a gloved hand to Scialas's face. And Morgidian... The barsionist was gazing at Vaem with lustful eyes.

Regaining his composure, Ildin redirected his illusions. They shot through the room, colliding with his friends, Calimir, and Vaem.

An enraged cry left Vaem's lips as the illusions exploded in a brilliant flash of white light. Ildin's shared vision with them ceased, but he felt the dispelling particles spreading throughout the commander and the others. The barsion around Scialas, however, was too thick to be dispelled and merely flickered.

Light faded as Ildin skidded to a halt. Both cisthyrns stopped beside him, snarling and baring their teeth. In a crystallized moment, he locked gazes with Vaem. She glared at him with a fury more intense than he'd ever seen. Her fierce violet eyes evoked a terrifying sensation that was akin to needles filling his stomach.

"You insolent fool—!"

Ildin exhaled the last of his ensnaring incantation, and the balled strands shot toward Vaem. He willed them to expand, and Vaem tried to dodge, but several green tendrils grabbed her.

She screamed as the magic jolted her backward, dragging her across the stone floor. Ildin turned to Kydol, who was now retreating. He willed the ensnaring tentacles toward the lieutenant, and several expanding strands soared through the air, sweeping her legs out from under her.

The ensnaring magic latched to the curved wall, and both Mindolarnians were pulled into the main mass, their arms and legs bound. They shouted threats, Vaem more vehement than Kydol, but he ignored them.

"Oh, Fendar!" Scialas cried, struggling against the barsion wrapped around her. She uttered an incantation, arpran light gathering beneath her bonds.

Morgidian staggered, raising a hand to his forehead. "What... what was that?" He looked about, then waved his hand toward Scialas, causing the barsion to dissipate.

"You ruined everything!" Vaem shouted. "Oh, you cannot fathom what you've done!"

Ildin hurried to his fellow illusionist, who was now freed from Calimir. Fendar groaned between coughs, his face swelling and his leg gushing blood. Eyeing the wounds, Ildin knelt beside Fendar, pressing his hands on his friend's leg. Fendar screamed, and Ildin's hands were soon covered in blood.

"You're going to be fine," Ildin said with reassurance. Pained groans carried over his shoulder, but Ildin ignored them.

Fendar thrashed as Scialas—glowing with green light—knelt beside him. As the rejuvenating magic surrounded Fendar, Ildin glanced to the source of the groaning. Commander Calimir was curled on the stone floor, clutching his head.

*"But I've theorized that a conjurer with sufficient mental fortitude—
and a complete disregard for pain—might be able to maintain a sufficient degree of control over a gangolin. Yet, how one might attain
such a mental state is beyond my understanding."*

- From *Colvinar Vrium's Bestiary for Conjurers*, page 249

Pain replaced Calimir's euphoria. It was as if spikes had been pounded into the back of his head, their sharp ends protruding from his eyes. Confused, he struggled to push himself upright.

Nearby, Mistress Rudal shouted at the top of her lungs, threatening Mister Cetarin. *What happened?* He struggled to open his eyes. Between rapid blinks, he glimpsed his sword lying beside him, bloodied and rocking ever so slightly.

Incantations carried through the air, but Calimir couldn't discern what magics were being mustered. Sharp pain shot through his head, and he struggled to recall the events of the past few moments. He had fallen, but everything before that was a blur. A blur tainted with lustful passion, a yearning for Mistress Rudal.

But why had he yearned for her—

A sudden sharpness surged through his head, and Calimir raised a hand to his face. He closed his eyes, but that did nothing to stave off the pain. The yelling intensified. Each shout evoked an excruciating ringing in his ears. It surged through his head, attempting to escape through his eyes.

"Commander," a feminine voice whispered. He didn't recall the voice, nor its owner.

Blinking against the pain, Calimir struggled to focus on the woman now kneeling beside him. She spoke again, but her words were that of an incantation. Soon, green light surrounded her—but its appearance evoked only more pain.

Calimir cried, clasping his eyes.

Why, why am I hurting? He searched his memory, but the last clear moment he could recall was the aftermath of the battle with the monster. Everything else was a blur... well, almost. Faint flashes of intense passion came to him, moments of ecstasy with a woman whose beauty was beyond measure. Lush dark hair. Violet eyes more stunning than twilight. And skin—Mistress Rudal's face flashed amid his memories.

Calimir groaned with disgust. Had, had he been with... with her?

A sudden surge of rejuvenation filled Calimir. It flowed through his head, clearing his foggy memories. He blinked in disbelief as he recalled—to some degree—the events of the past day: his lewd acts with Mistress Rudal, his bowing to her every whim, and his craven retreat from the monster.

She had made him spineless.

"You..." Calimir growled, grabbing his sword and pushing himself upright. "You harlot!" He spun, nearly slicing the woman who had healed him. Calimir readied his sword but halted.

Mistress Rudal was bound to the wall with green tentacles. Lieutenant Virain was beside her, equally shackled by the magic.

Cautious, Calimir took in his surroundings. He stood within a one-story curved hallway made of white stone. Four mages stood nearby, each friends of Mister Aramien. One of the mages, however, looked ragged, his robe soaked with blood. *Had... had I stabbed him?* He vaguely recalled a scuffle with the man.

"Are you all right, Commander?" asked Mister Cetarin. Two of those ice wolves stood beside him, baring their crystal-like teeth. Calimir nodded, then turned back to Mistress Rudal.

"You fools!" she spat. "Release us at once!"

"No," Mister Shival said, his tone contemptuous. "We know you are not telling us everything. You knew about the monster. Why else would you run? I won't ask a third time: tell us how to reverse the effects of its mist."

Calimir furrowed his brow. Had they found those that were debilitated by the monster's haze? *Perhaps we didn't lose them...*

"You can't!" she shouted. "It is beyond the Channels of Power. What your friend is experiencing is tantamount to a cursing—nothing can restore him. Nothing. Now release us!"

Calimir raised an eyebrow. *Who are they talking about?*

"Nothing?" Mister Shival did not sound convinced. "We heard what you told the commander in the yaeltis den," the barsionist added, stepping toward Mistress Rudal. "About a tevisral that could reverse the venom's effects. Surely, something comparable to that is here in Tardalim. You *will* identify it for us."

Mistress Rudal shook her head, her lips curled into a vindictive snarl.

"Fine..." Mister Shival sighed and uttered an incantation, blue light surging around his hands.

Someone tapped Calimir's arm, and he turned. Mister Cetarin leaned close, his face twisted with worry. "Commander, I know he's been trouble, but he needs help." Calimir eyed the illusionist and set his jaw. Was he talking about Mister Aramien? When had he been around the monster? *Horrible that I cannot remember.*

"Please, sir," Mister Cetarin said. "He doesn't deserve this fate. If there is a tevisral here that can help him, then we have to find it."

Taking in a deep breath, Calimir turned back to the barsionist. Blue light shot across the hall, wrapping around Mistress Rudal in a translucent band that extended from her shoulders to her knees. An inverted barsion?

"I will squeeze you until your bones turn to powder," the barsionist growled, his tone fierce. "Scialas will mend you. Then I'll squeeze you again, and we will repeat this cycle until you help us!"

Such anger... Calimir straightened his back and stomped to the man. Mistress Rudal was responsible for their predicaments, and she did deserve punishment, but not torture. "Mister Shival," Calimir barked. "Stop this at once! You're acting out of line!"

The barsionist turned, fury in his eyes. "Out of line? After what they've done? They knowingly brought us to this death trap. We're just as expendable as the other expeditions."

Calimir cocked his head. "What are you talking about?"

"The Mindolarnians have been here before," Mister Cetarin said. "Twice."

Calimir spun. "What?!"

"They've used us," the barsionist spat. "We're the third expedition to come here."

The words hit Calimir like a battering ram. *The third expedition?* But that contradicted what he and the Order had been told. Although, it did give one explanation to Mistress Rudal's actions and demeanor... Her knowledge of Tardalim, coupled with her secretive behavior, now made sense. But why lie? Was the Mindolarn Empire after more than just tevisrals...? What else was in Tardalim?

Fighting his own tangle of furious emotions, Calimir turned to face the Mindolarnian scholar. "Is this true?"

Mistress Rudal didn't answer.

Calimir glanced to the others and took in a deep breath. "I hope there is evidence to back up your claims?"

"There are corpses on the twenty-fifth floor," said Mister Cetarin. "Most were clad in Mindolarnian armor. And one of the residents of Tardalim told us about the other expeditions."

"Resident?" Calimir narrowed his eyes. "One of the Eshari?"

The mages shook their heads.

"His name is Fench," the arpranist said. "The Mindolarnians slaughtered his people, with the help of that monster."

Calimir flinched. "The Mindolarnians brought the monster with them?"

Was that why Mistress Rudal and Lieutenant Virain fled? *It must be...*

Mistress Rudal began chuckling, her mirth derisive.

The arpranist shook her head. "I think it was a prisoner here. The other Mindolarnians let it out. I think Vaem came here to free them *all.*" Mister Shival and Mister Cetarin looked surprised at the accusation, as did the other man.

Mister Cetarin paled. "That's why Fench wanted us to promise not to let out the prisoners." He turned to the still laughing scholar. "You never wanted the tevisrals at all, did you? Why, why do you want to free them? You can't unleash monsters like that upon the world!"

The only reply was condescending laughter.

Calimir turned away as the mages continued discussing the matter. There was still so much he didn't know—particularly what had transpired during his... well, his indisposed state. *I have to get back to the others.* He recalled a vague report from Miraden. He had mentioned strange tevisrals and a safe haven called the Roost, but the details of the conversation were jumbled with lustful desires. *Miraden hadn't mentioned corpses, had he?*

Troubled, Calimir paced toward Mistress Rudal. Her mirth had subsided, though she still looked amused. Lieutenant Virain, however, was downright disgusted. *I can't trust either of them...*

He wanted to ask their true intentions for coming to Tardalim, but he knew they wouldn't answer. He closed his eyes and recalled following them... to a tower? And something about Tardalim's halls and defenses... and, gods?

That doesn't matter, he thought, shaking his head. If they had found tevisrals, then his purpose here was complete. *The sooner we can leave this godforsaken place the better.*

Taking in a deep breath, Calimir turned to the conversing mages. "Mister Shival, please escort these women to the campsite. I want them restrained. And Mister Cetarin, gather the other squad leaders. It's time we hold this expedition's final council."

<hr />

The last of the encrusted venom fell into Captain Edara's pouch. *At last,* he thought, wiping his knife upon the dark-teal grass. Smiling, he tied the pouch shut and tucked it under his cot, nestling it beside his pack.

With the venom cleared away, the yaeltis tusk looked like a curved crystal. To his surprise, it was smooth to the touch. Edara had expected it to be marred with divots, as the encrusted venom had an uneven texture to it. *Perhaps the venom is secreted irregularly.*

He eased back onto his cot, stroking the tusk. Now that the venom was a powder all he had to do—

The flapping of canvas carried through the tent, startling Edara. He sat upright, moving the broken tusk toward his only pant pocket, but his visitors—Dardel and Miraden—stepped inside before he could conceal it.

The expedition's second-in-command raised his brow. "I didn't expect to find you here."

Edara snorted. "Is that why you didn't have the decency to announce yourself?"

The two squad leaders looked to each other, then Miraden spoke. "Calimir has returned from the tower. He's called a council and wants you present."

Edara narrowed his eyes at the two men. *So, he wants me to attend?* But why? What possible reason could the murderous bastard have, to want him at the meeting? True, he had been invited while aboard the *Giboran*, but he hadn't attended any of the meetings since the death of his beloved.

"Come now, Captain," Dardel said. "This is urgent."

"Really?" Edara eased the broken tusk to his pocket. He rose from his cot, standing so the two men couldn't see what he was doing. But by the looks on their faces that only aroused suspicion.

"What do you have there?" Miraden asked.

Edara froze. His jaw tightened, and his face flushed. *No! Damn it, no—*

LIE TO THEM, a deep voice said in his head. *SAY IT IS A CISTHYRN HORN.*

Slowly inhaling, Edara considered the suggestion. He had heard that name before... was it the name of those ice wolves? But where had that voice come from? "A memento," he said. "From one of those ice wolves."

Miraden nodded. "I didn't take you for a trophy man."

Dardel didn't reply and swiftly exited the tent.

It worked... Edara thought, fighting back a smile. He watched Miraden step outside before crossing the tent. *Surely Heleron smiles upon me... and my vengeance.*

Once outside, Edara secured his tent door. Miraden was nearly to the clearing but Dardel was gone. Those gathered in the mess area were being rousted by other squad leaders.

Edara caught up to Miraden and cleared his throat. "Do you know what this meeting is about?"

Miraden shook his head. "But the commander did sound angry."

Edara harrumphed, and Miraden chuckled. They soon met up with other squad leaders, all heading toward one of those strange tree-buildings a few dozen paces from the camp. Calimir, the murderous bastard, paced in front of the bizarre structure, hands clasped behind his back. The sight of him made Edara's blood boil.

Calm yourself...

He reached into his pocket and gripped the broken tusk. Its smooth texture eased his fury, reminding him of his plan.

They soon reached the group of other squad leaders. Miraden stepped around his fellows and moved to the head of the group. Edara, however, stayed in the back. Any closer and he might give in to the temptation to stab the *Giboran*'s murderer.

More squad leaders joined the group. Edara counted those in attendance. *Only twenty-one.* Edara's part of the expedition had not lost any squad leaders during their ascent.

Calimir had begun speaking, talking about some influence the heartless Mindolarnian whore had placed upon him. Edara returned his attention to the murderer's words.

"Since being freed from Mistress Rudal's unnatural influence," Calimir said, "it has come to my attention that she has lied to us. I am sure most of you now know that we were not the first expedition to venture here."

"You mean the Mindolarnian corpses?" asked a woman.

"Yes," the bastard said, nodding. "Unfortunately, despite our questioning, Mistress Rudal will not say a word about those other expeditions. She has been unrepentantly defiant."

Edara strained to hold onto his composure as Calimir continued talking about the so-called betrayal by the Mindolarnians. None of the squad leaders were surprised about anything the bastard said, until he spoke of the monster.

"According to Mister Shival, the monster is on its way here. Tardalim's halls no longer change. What caused them to do so was stopped by Mistress Rudal—at least, from what I can remember. My time under her influence is laced with... distraction."

"How do you know this then?" a squad leader demanded.

"Can we verify this?" another asked. "What about that map atop the tower?"

Amid more questions, Dardel approached, clutching something in his hands. Calimir glanced to his second-in-command, then turned back to the others.

"It was confirmed by Mister Shival. Though the details are unclear to me, I watched the two Mindolarnians tamper with Tardalim's workings. They stopped the change in the halls and altered several other things. Mister Shival and Mister Cetarin believe there is a barrier preventing the monster from entering this place, but I am not certain it still stands. I can't remember all of what Mistress Rudal said she stopped, but I think that barrier to be one of them. Which brings me to the purpose of this council; we must leave Tardalim at once."

Edara expected to hear a commotion of complaints, but the squad leaders were silent.

"We have what we came for, and that monster has killed too many of us. I will not lose another man or woman to it. As we speak, the barsionists are sealing off three of the four stairwells leading to the Roost. The stair nearest us is still open. Those of you with squad members still searching the treasure trove, go find them. Bring them back here. Once everyone has returned, the barsionists will seal off the last stairwell."

"But then how can we leave?" a woman asked.

"There is another way out of here. Well, the only way, according to Mister Cetarin. It's through a pit across this Roost. Those of you not gathering your squads will begin ferrying our supplies and the tevisrals there."

"Do we know where the monster is now?" a squad leader asked.

Calimir nodded. "Mister Callis is tracking it through that map atop the tower. Last I heard, it was on the twenty-ninth floor."

Taking a deep breath and pulling his shoulders back, Calimir said, "This is enough discussion, for now. If your squads are searching, go find them. If not, stay here for your assignments."

Men and women dashed away, but Edara stood still, his desire for vengeance swelling within him. *If only I could kill you now...* He fingered the broken tusk, stroking its sharp end. But he couldn't carry out his revenge now. There were too many witnesses.

Dardel leaned close to the murderous bastard, furtively extending a clenched fist. The commander took something blue his second-in-command handed him, and then whispered something Edara couldn't hear.

Curious, he craned his neck and stepped forward, but before he could take another, a hand gripped his shoulder.

"Your crew is still gathering tevisrals, aren't they?" Miraden asked.

Edara glanced over his shoulder, then to the squad leader. The mention of his crew made his anger simmer, and he began to worry. Of those still searching the treasury, his crew was the farthest away. "They are... best I get to them."

He turned and ran past Miraden, toward the camp.

Vaem struggled against her bonds as those fools prodded her through the camp. *It will not end like this,* she thought. *It can't! I cannot fail the emperor—!*

Shoved from behind, she stumbled forward, tripping and falling upon the teal grass.

"Get up!" the barsionist bellowed.

"If you hadn't pushed me..."

The man snorted with derision. "Perhaps if you weren't struggling, I wouldn't have to push you."

Fighting back a growl, Vaem eased onto her knees. She glanced to Kydol, who stood beside her. Like Vaem, the lieutenant's hands were pulled behind her back, tied with green cords woven from magic—the handiwork of Ildin.

"Get up!" Morgidian shouted, tugging on the cord binding Vaem.

Jerked to her feet, Vaem steadied herself and stepped forward. All around her, soldiers and mercenaries hurried in and out of tents with their belongings. *I hope you all die...*

Prodded once again, Vaem stumbled forward. They continued through the camp, and then her captors pulled her to a stop. Ildin stepped around Vaem and Kydol and opened a tent door to their left.

"Inside!" Morgidian barked.

Vaem held her ground. She tried to press the rivet to activate the euphorinizer, but it was not quite in reach of her fingers. *If the damned cords would only give!* But cords woven from magic never gave.

"Go!"

Kydol complied, stepping past Vaem and into the tent. *Idiot woman...*

"Stop that," the barsionist said. "Ildin, throw her inside."

Vaem continued to struggle, but not a heartbeat later the yaeltis grabbed her. Her feet now dangled, and the beast tossed her into the tent. She landed on her shoulder and gasped as intense pain flared down her arm and up her neck. She rolled onto her stomach, and part of her arm became numb. "You... you insolent vis'ack!"

She breathed through the pain as her captors' feet crunched the grass around her. Out of the corner of her eye, she saw the two mages dragging Kydol to a cot. They set her atop it, and Morgidian uttered an incantation. Blue light surrounded Kydol and the bedding—undoubtedly an inverted barsion.

Once they were done with the lieutenant, both men turned on Vaem.

"Get up!" the barsionist barked.

Vaem closed her eyes, fighting back the pain. She didn't dare move. Boots crunched on grass. A force jerked her upright, sending a dart of pain through her arm. Although she fought to remain silent, she still screamed and fell to her knees. They dragged her through the tent, and more pain surged across her arm. Parts of her shoulder went numb as they tossed her upon a cot. She fought to stay conscious.

Incantations sounded above her, followed by blue light. A force soon pressed against her, causing another wave of pain that evoked an involuntary gasp.

"It's a pity you didn't cooperate," Morgidian said. "But we still need to know about that tevisral. Why don't you pry it from her, Ildin?"

A reluctant sigh filled the tent, then the illusionist uttered an incantation. Soon, gray particles danced in the air above Vaem, then wisped into her nostrils. Tingling pricking crept through her skull, lingering behind her eyes.

Though she had never succumbed to enthralling magic she knew what it *should* feel like. The pricking intensified, then stopped.

"It didn't work!" Ildin gasped.

"What do you mean?"

Ildin stumbled over his words. "It... it didn't take hold. Like when we tried to enthrall Fench."

Morgidian stepped close, his brows raised. He opened his mouth to speak, but the tent door flapped open, followed by boots crunching crisp grass.

"Are they secured?" The voice belonged to the squad leader, Miraden.

"They are," Morgidian said, turning around. "But we haven't learned about that tevisral."

"Did you try enthralling them?" asked the squad leader.

"It didn't work," Ildin said, sounding confused. Despite her pain, Vaem smiled at the illusionist's perplexity.

"Well, leave them," Miraden said. "We need to erect a barricade. Fendar says the monster is on the thirtieth floor."

The barsionist sighed and turned away. He disappeared, three pairs of footsteps left the tent, and then the canvas door flapped shut.

"Perhaps we aren't doomed after all," Kydol whispered.

Vaem winced against the pain. "Perhaps..." She eased her head back, her shoulder throbbing.

"We must trust in Lord Cheserith," Kydol said, sounding hopeful. "We've prepared the way for the divine being to reach us. Once he defeats those fools and finds us, he'll grace our minds and know our purpose here. We will return triumphant, and with a host so powerful no kingdom on Kalda will defy our empire."

Those words should have invigorated Vaem, but they didn't. Her thoughts turned to the so-called monster, Orath'issian. Would he free them, as Kydol hoped? Or would he kill them in his rage?

A sudden sense of defeat overcame her. Though she had remained defiant, determined to fulfill the emperor's mandate, now she was no better than Meradis or Coridician: a failure.

Forever doomed within the Halls of Damnation.

"There are few places left in this world where one might find a gangolin. Most men believe them to be extinct—nothing more than the stuff of myth. Oh, are they wrong! I have heard rumors that packs roam the Desert of Ash in the Forsaken Lands. But I found my two in the heart of the Melar Woods."

- From *Colvinar Vrium's Bestiary for Conjurers*, page 251

Twigs and leaves crunched beneath Amendal's feet as he ran. Frantic, he leapt over a fallen branch as thick as his waist. He landed with a thud as a honking-shrill washed over the woodland: the call of a gangolin. *Have to get away...* Heart thumping, he ran down a dirt path between thick trees. The lowest branches hung three or four stories above him while their tops reached to incredible heights.

He had spent nearly six months among those trees. And now he had returned. *But when did I leave Tardalim...?*

Another honking-shrill shook the trees. Leaves rustled, and some fell while the branches swayed. The ground shook, and Amendal tripped and fell. He hit the ground as another cry filled the air.

He groaned. But before he could stand, the ground shook again, accompanied by a distant boom. Heart beating faster, he looked over his shoulder. The shaking and booming continued while the nearby branches bounced. Several trees fell, one crashing upon the path several hundred phineals away. In its place was a towering beige limb: the forearm of a gangolin.

"Have to get away," he muttered. Once the ground stilled, Amendal pushed himself up and ran.

The gangolin's deafening cry filled the air much closer than before. Leaves rustled again, some falling around him. *Have to run, have to run...*

Amendal dashed down the path, crunching more leaves. *Too loud, too loud…* The gangolin would hear the crunching; it would definitely hear the crunching.

Another cry shook the trees, but this time it was answered in kind. The second honking-shrill was distant, fainter.

Not another, not another…

"Amendal," a deep voice called from the trees.

Shaking his head, Amendal pushed himself to run faster. Faster. Faster. *Have to run faster…*

An annoyed sigh left the trees, but soon faded.

Amendal glanced over his shoulder, and something red passed between the trees to his left. Was it another beast? Someone else in the trees? *I hope the gangolins eat it first. Yes, eat it first!*

The path ahead of him curved to the right, ascending at a shallow grade. Soon, the trees thinned, and a large clearing appeared, partially surrounded by a cliff wall that rose three stories and spread as far as he could see through the trees.

"Where to go?" he muttered, turning back and forth. "Where to go?"

"You truly are deranged," that deep voice said, chuckling.

"Who's there?" Amendal spun.

Standing on the path was the old codger, running a hand through his long white hair. He wore his blood-red robe, remarkably free from dirt. *How did he stay clean?* Amendal's lips twisted in distaste.

The codger sighed. "Well now, it seems you have crafted yourself quite the nightmare."

Amendal clenched his jaw and his fists. *Nightmare? What nightmare?* He was in the forest, the Melar Forest. Catching gangolins. *Yes, catching gangolins.*

"Your repetitions are irritating," the codger said. "Come with me, Amendal."

"No!" Amendal spun and ran for the cliff. He had to climb and keep running. Before he could grab the earthen wall, the codger spoke again.

"You can escape this nightmare if you come with me. If not, the gangolins you've created will keep chasing you, no matter how far you run."

Finding a handhold, Amendal began his climb. The honking-shrills shook the forest and the cliff wall. Dirt fell, and Amendal raised his eyes. The blue sky was clear beyond the treetops. That was the first time he had been able to see the sky since entering the forest. *But when did I enter the forest…?*

"You didn't!" the codger called. "You're dreaming, Amendal. You are still in Tardalim."

Too real to be a dream, he thought, nearly halfway up the cliff. *Too real…*

Gangolin cries shook the trees again, knocking a rock loose from the cliff wall. It fell, nearly hitting Amendal's arm. *Faster. Faster.*

Another pair of calls filled the air as Amendal pulled himself atop the cliff. He clawed his way across the ground until his feet dangled no more. Now on solid ground, Amendal ran again. There was no path, so he leapt over tree roots and fallen branches. Ominous birdsong sounded in the trees. A flash of red appeared ahead of him, becoming the old codger.

"Get out of my way!" Amendal shouted through clenched teeth.

The codger shook his head, and Amendal darted to the right, tripping over an exposed root.

"Look at you," the codger said with a sigh. "You're so crazed that you can't even realize where you are…"

Not a dream, he thought, pushing himself up. *Not a dream*. A honking-shrill blew through the trees, followed by another. Both were close.

"You can't run from them forever, Amendal! Come with me."

More gangolin calls filled the air as Amendal ran deeper into the forest. Four calls. They were all around him. *What to do? What to do?*

He staggered over uneven ground and fell, landing upon the forest floor half a story below where he had come from.

"You're still in Tardalim!" the codger called, now ahead of Amendal. How could he move so quickly?

Amendal squinted at the white-haired man as the four gangolins cried again. One ahead, two behind, and one to the right. *I'm trapped!* The codger shook his head, an amused smile spreading across his face.

"Oh, if you could only see yourself," the codger said, chuckling. "Others will have no doubt about your madness now. Of course, some already thought that because of your eccentric behavior. But now you are truly mad."

Amendal parted his lips and raised his eyebrows. The gangolin calls grew louder. The ground shook behind him, followed by a boom. *It's coming!* He looked over his shoulder, but he couldn't see the creature. Only the trees and small patches of blue sky were behind him.

"Maybe I can let them pass…" he muttered, looking around. The ground behind him was hollowed out, a shallow cavity within the dirt. He could hide there. Dig a hole so he could cover himself. *Yes, yes, that would work!*

Determined, Amendal clawed at the dirt. Clumps of rock, grass, and dirt fell around him. The cavity grew. But it wasn't big enough yet.

"Perhaps I can dig a tunnel." He nodded. That's how he could escape. A tunnel, a tunnel out of the forest. *I could dig to the other side of the world.* He chuckled and nodded. *They wouldn't find me then!*

The ground shook repeatedly, and a deafening cacophony of booms filled the air. Both rustled the leaves, causing many to fall around him.

"Digging will not help you," the codger said, his voice over Amendal's right shoulder. "I don't know if I can put this more simply, but you are deranged, crazed by the qurasiphage that Orath'issian sprays from his gills."

Orath'issian? Amendal wondered, still clawing at the dirt. The vague memory of a black monster came to him. But it felt distant, as if *it* were a dream. *Yes, that's the dream, not this!*

"Oh, you're a stubborn one," the codger said with a sigh. "Typically, qurasiphage sends a person into a delusional frenzy that strips all their mental faculties, except the physiological urge to run. It overstimulates the mind, causing a cascade of overpowering stimuli that cannot be stopped— not even arpran magic can halt it."

The codger continued spewing nonsense as the shaking intensified. *Have to keep digging,* he thought, clawing at the dirt.

"If you had not consumed those umviliums you wouldn't be able to think. You would be no more than a terrified primitive animal." The codger chuckled, amused at his nonsense. "You wouldn't even be *here.* I imagine Orath'issian would have steered clear of you if he knew you had eaten the Tuladine fruit. Now you will be quite formidable." His chuckling grew to laughter so loud it carried through the trees.

The codger's mirth sent a shock of fright through Amendal. *He's drawing them to me!* Ever frantic, he clawed faster. He had to escape. He could go through the ground, he knew it!

"It is all far beyond your understanding," the codger said, pacing to Amendal's left. "But when the residue of the umviliums and qurasiphage met, they formed something different that spread through your veins. That new substance altered your mind, expanding some of your mental capacities while diminishing others."

The codger grabbed Amendal's shoulder, and the ground stilled. The gangolins' booming footsteps faded. All was silent within the forest.

Hands in the dirt, Amendal straightened and studied the forest. The leaves were still. Not even a breeze rustled them. Everything was quiet. Peaceful.

But he still had to run. He had to get away.

Pulling his hands from the dirt, Amendal spun. The codger stood in his way, but Amendal danced around him and bounded onto another dirt path. Had it been there before?

"Come now, Amendal. You're safe."

Amendal ran with all his might, but after a short dash the ground shook. The forest floor groaned as he tripped, falling on the dirt—no, something hard. Sharp pangs shot through his ribs and up his arms. The other falls in the forest hadn't been this painful. *They hadn't been painful at all...*

He gritted his teeth against the pain but started in surprise. Instead of dirt, a black surface—smooth and polished, as if it were stone—spread beneath him. Was it obsidian?

"What—?"

The polished ground heaved upward. A force pressed Amendal against the black surface as leaves and branches crashed all around him. Soon, the rising ground cleared the tree tops.

A yellow sky spread above the forest, spotted with crimson clouds partly obscuring a blue sun. The nearby tree tops disappeared and so did the horizon. But how and why did the sky change?

The upheaval settled and the force pinning Amendal dissipated. Panic flooded his mind, and he struggled to his feet. He staggered forward but something stopped him. He jolted, held in place at his arms and legs by something hard.

"Not so fast," the codger said, his footsteps echoing off the polished ground. "I'd hate for you to fall to your death."

Blinking quickly, Amendal darted a glance to his arms. They were encased within pillars of black stone rising from the strange ground. His feet were also wrapped in the stone. *How had that happened?*

It didn't matter. He had to run. He had to get free!

"Relax," the codger said, now standing in front of Amendal.

"I have to get out!" Amendal cried. "Let me go!"

The codger shook his head. "We have much to discuss, my friend."

He had called Amendal that before. This, this was no friend. He was a delusion! *Yes... conjured from my imagination.*

"Call me what you wish," the codger said, pacing to the left. Amendal followed him with his eyes. The polished ground was a large, jagged oval half the size of a Sorothian city block. And he was standing in the middle of it. Shaking his head, he glanced beyond the oval. The trees beyond the black ground looked tiny. How high had the ground risen?

The codger chuckled. "It is a staggering height." He returned to Amendal, stopping an arm's length away. "Now that you're out of that dream, your thoughts should become clearer."

But am I not still here in the forest? Besides the strange sky and sun, the forest was just as it had been—well, except for the lack of gangolins. But it felt different. He thought of his hasty flight, but the thought was fleeting, like trying to recall images from a dream after waking... *Why hadn't I used my magic?* He could have defended himself against the gangolins with his conjurations. *Or sucked them through a portal.* That thought evoked an involuntary cackle.

The codger smiled and nodded as if he were approving of something. "That is good. Your reasoning is returning."

Amendal set his jaw and squinted at the old codger. The urge to run lessened. If he weren't so high above the forest he would probably be struggling still.

"That's not to say your insanity will dissipate. Eventually the qurasiphage will leave your body, but its effects will remain. It is much like solistum—whatever it touches cannot be changed by any part of the Arpran Channel. Unfortunately, that is a price you'll have to pay."

"What price?" Amendal spat.

The codger's jovial demeanor waned, though he still looked somewhat amused. "Why, the price of fulfilling your destiny, of course. Yes, you retrieved the shan'ak, but *this*"—he gestured up and down—"was also a necessity. Once you are free from the qurasiphage, your thought processes will be sharper than anyone's. You will be able to see patterns where most see chaos. Take Tardalim, for example. A normal man might stare at that three-dimensional map for years and not learn the patterns. But you, you could probably perceive the entirety of Tardalim's functioning in a matter of days."

Amendal cocked his head and leaned back as far as he could.

"And, your abilities in the magical arts will improve tenfold. Combined with your natural talents, you will become an unstoppable force. You shall supersede the greatest conjurers who ever walked the face of Kalda."

It seems I have gone mad, Amendal thought.

The codger resumed pacing. "Of course, your mind is not as keen as the Ma'lishas—no mortal could ever hope to attain such grandeur."

Amendal blinked in confusion. What had happened to him? And how had he imagined all these strange words? He thought back before his hasty flight through the forest. Images were blurred to near incomprehension. But one stood out: a vibrant violet eye, unnatural in form and size. The mere thought of it sent a surge of terror through him.

"Good, you are remembering." The codger stopped pacing and studied Amendal. "And your heart is slowing."

Was it?

Amendal looked to his chest, turning his thoughts inward. His heart *was* beating slower.

The codger turned away, staring toward the horizon. Amendal followed his gaze. The blue sun had dipped below the clouds. After a while, the old codger finally spoke. "Now that you're calm, we can talk of other matters, particularly your impending flight from Tardalim."

Amendal chuckled, then let his mirth explode. *I really am crazy... how ironic.* Now that he wasn't running, the delusion wanted him to run.

"Escaping Tardalim is of the utmost importance," the codger said. "You must flee with Fench. After all, he's the only one you can trust."

That wasn't true. *I can trust Ildin, Morgi, and Faelinia. Faelinia...* Thinking of her, he smiled.

The codger raised an eyebrow. "No, you really can't trust them. You must depart, and only with Fench. Leave the others behind."

Amendal shook his head. "I'm not a coward!"

"Ah-h, there's that dim-witted bravery..."

The codger droned on and on, elaborating on the reasons Amendal must leave Tardalim, and why no one else could accompany him. But Amendal didn't care in the slightest. He would not leave his friends, or Faelinia. Annoyed, Amendal raised his chin and turned away from the codger. The old fool had nothing important to say.

"You are what matters here, Amendal. No one else. This expedition is expendable."

Amendal snorted and kept his nose in the air.

"You have done what was required of you," the codger said in a firm tone, as if he was scolding a child. "Now flee once you awake. There are powers beyond your understanding—powers other than Orath'issian—who are converging upon you, and though your mind has expanded, you are not a match for them."

"I'm not deserting my friends."

The old codger growled.

Amendal grinned. *Now look who's annoyed.*

"Fine," the codger said with a sigh. "Begone!"

Yellow and red streaks whirled past Amendal, and he felt himself falling. The light soon dispersed and became a terrifying black pit. But the blackness was fleeting.

Amendal blinked, finding himself within a tent. *Am I still dreaming?* Faint conversations carried through the canvas. They all spoke of danger and retreating. Was he back in the Roost? While sifting through his memories Amendal wiggled his fingers and toes. "Oo, they work..."

"You're awake," Fench said in his nasally voice. He hovered in front of Amendal, his trunk nearly touching Amendal's nose.

"Well, hello to you, too..." Amendal pushed Fench's trunk aside and sat upright.

Fench blinked, a smile forming upon the end of his trunk.

Amendal looked past the winged creature to Ildin's cot. To his surprise, Faelinia lay upon it, wrapped in a blanket.

"Faelinia!" he called, swiftly crossing the tent. Fench fluttered beside him, staying close. Amendal knelt beside the cot as she stirred, turning slowly to face him. Faelinia blinked several times, then violently sat upright. She murmured his name, then reached out and stroked his face.

He smiled at her touch.

"I must have drifted off..." she said. "Are you okay?"

Amendal nodded. "I suppose. I mean, I'm not wounded, am I?" He patted his arms, his stomach, and lastly his hips. "Nothing's missing!"

Faelinia narrowed her eyes, studying him up and down.

"The old codger says I'm crazy, but what does he know!" Amendal snickered. "He's just a delusion."

A wary expression formed on Faelinia's face. Why was she worried?

She cupped Amendal's face between her hands. "What's wrong with you...?"

"Nothing?" *She* didn't think he was crazy, did she? *Hopefully she's not like Miss Fickle Foots...*

Faelinia sucked in her breath. "We have to find Scialas... Fench, did she or the others return at all?"

Fench shook his head. "Just some two-leg."

"What 'some two-leg' would that be?" Amendal demanded, tilting his chin and squinting one eye. "What'd he look like? He wasn't wrinkly, was he?"

The winged creature blinked twice before shaking his head. "He didn't say his name." Fench fluttered across the tent, settling beside Amendal's pouch. "But he took the blue rock, from in here."

Blue rock?! He felt at his chest, but the rogulin necklace was gone. "The bastard stole my crystal!"

"As with the other creatures I have mentioned in this compendium, the gangolin will need a sufficiently large portal to enter the Visirm Expanse. On all fours, a typical gangolin will stand roughly forty phineals tall. I suggest creating a circular portal no less than seven stories in diameter."

- From *Colvinar Vrium's Bestiary for Conjurers*, page 252

Amendal stomped to the tent's door. He had to find Old Cali and take back his rogulin crystal. Faelinia called after him, but he ignored her, throwing the tent flap open. He stepped outside, then started with surprise.

All around him soldiers hurried about carrying full packs, while mercenaries and mages took down tents. The codger's admonition came to him: *Now flee once you're awake.* He considered the warning. But no, he couldn't leave his friends.

Faelinia called after him again as Fench fluttered out of the tent. The winged creature rested his tiny hands on Amendal's shoulder, as if propping himself up.

Amendal stepped away from his tent, nearly bumping into a soldier laden with packs. "Wait," he said, grabbing the man. "What's happening?"

The soldier reeled as he faced Amendal. "We're leaving… where have you been?"

"Sleeping," Amendal said.

The soldier pulled away. "Well, please excuse me, I'm in a hurry! That monster could be here any moment."

That monster? he thought. *Orath'issian…* The codger had said he was coming.

"The Orath-monster?" Fench asked. "But it can't get in here."

Amendal glanced to Fench as Faelinia emerged from the tent. "You mean Orath'issian?"

The winged creature nodded, his trunk bouncing. "How do you know its name?"

"From my dreams…"

Fench blinked as Faelinia came beside them.

"What is all this?" she asked. "Are we moving camp?"

Amendal shook his head. "Come on, let's go find Old Cali." Faelinia cocked her head, confused, but quickly regained her composure.

Together, the three of them hurried toward the clearing where the food had been prepared. But what was once a mess area was now a staging ground for war.

Soldiers and mercenaries were donning their armor and drawing their weapons. Once girded, they fell in line before a column of mages. One by one, each soldier or mercenary was enhanced, bathed with arpran auras, and enveloped in form-fitting barsion. Their weapons were imbued with destructive power, though some of the weapons looked as if they emitted magic on their own.

A soldier sheathed in armor marched by, hefting a sword whose blade was made of a translucent green substance that dripped acid. The weapon's hilt and handle were also of a strange design.

Amendal squinted at the sword, intrigued. *Is that some sort of tevisral?*

Putting the thought aside, he pushed his way through the staging area, searching for Calimir. But the commander was nowhere to be found. *Maybe he's run away again… like he did before that last bout with Orath'issian.*

"I'm going to ask around for the commander," Faelinia said, stepping toward a soldier waiting in line. Their conversation was too quiet for Amendal to hear, so he continued surveying the area. His gaze landed on Miraden, who darted from the camp, running toward the tree-trunk-like buildings.

I bet he knows. Amendal hurried after the squad leader, with Fench fluttering beside him, wings beating in an oscillating pattern that varied in pitch. Amendal hadn't paid attention to the sound before. Had he even heard it?

He returned his focus to Miraden. The squad leader approached a group of men and women gathered at the base of a building. Faint instructions carried through the air, spoken by none other than the old soldier. Calimir's voice made Amendal's heart quicken and his stomach tense. Old Cali's instructions, however, were soon interrupted by Miraden. "Sir, all but the sailors are accounted for."

Calimir grumbled as Amendal pushed his way into the crowd. "Those bilge rats are more trouble than they're—"

"You!" Amendal shouted, shoving a woman out of the way. She reeled and shouted a rebuke, but Amendal ignored her. A table stood between him and the commander, but that would not bar him. "You stole it!" Heart beating with fury, he flipped the table over. Polished stone weights flew into the air, followed by a large scroll that fluttered to the ground. Calimir's face contorted in surprise, but he regained his composure as Amendal lunged, fists balled. Yelling, Amendal swung, but before he could land the blow someone tackled him. He was forced onto his stomach as Fench squealed.

"Get off me!" Amendal shouted. He struggled to break free, but whoever was atop him was too heavy to shove off. All the while, hushed murmurs carried through the crowd, several speakers wondering what had come over Amendal, while others expressed surprise that he wasn't consumed by terror.

"My, what anger," Calimir said. "It seems you've lost control of yourself, Mister Aramien."

Amendal continued struggling as Faelinia shouted his name. He peered over his shoulder, but couldn't see her or the face of the man pinning him to the ground. "You have no right!" he shouted. "It's *my* crystal!"

The old soldier chuckled. "I'm sorry, but I don't trust you. And that rogulin is our only means of saving this expedition. I will not leave it in your care. Hevasir, release him."

Oh, you, Amendal thought. *It figures.*

Miraden added to his report as Hevasir eased off Amendal's back.

"Are you all right?" Faelinia asked, her voice above him.

Grumbling, Amendal eased onto his knees. "No... I'm not!" Once he was upright, Faelinia urged him away to the side and wrapped her arms around him. Fench fluttered beside her, his hands clasping the end of his trunk.

"As I was saying," Calimir said, "Dardel will lead those who do not teleport away. Once we are outside, you'll begin your trek back across the wasteland..."

The old soldier continued talking, but Amendal ignored him.

After moving a few paces from the others, Faelinia stopped Amendal, turning him toward her. She looked into his eyes, stern and determined. Her fierceness was... exhilarating. "That was reckless!" she whispered. "What were you thinking?"

"I'd like to know that answer as well," Miraden said. "I didn't peg you as a violent man."

Amendal glanced to Miraden and grumbled, "I'd like to see how you react when someone steals *your* property."

Miraden raised an eyebrow, but turned back to the crowd. Fendar said something. But had Fendar been among the squad leaders? Amendal spun, searching for his friend.

Fendar's illusion hovered near Calimir. "It's on the thirty-second floor now."

"Which way is the monster headed?" Calimir asked.

The illusion pointed behind the commander. "It's moving erratically. I can't tell if it's headed for that stairwell."

"Go warn the barsionists there," Calimir said. The illusion nodded and zipped away. "We'll resume this meeting once outside." The old soldier issued several orders, the last were for the men and women to prepare themselves for a possible battle.

AS I SAID BEFORE, that voice boomed in Amendal's mind, *TAKE FENCH AND FLEE. NOW!*

"I'm not leaving," Amendal whispered, shaking his head. "I'm not abandoning them. Besides, *he* still has my crystal!"

Miraden turned, warily eyeing Amendal. "Who are you talking to?"

Amendal shot the man a perturbed glance, but turned away, awaiting a response from the old codger. But he said nothing.

"What's wrong with him?" Miraden asked.

Faelinia sucked in her breath. "It's that orange haze… it… it's changed him."

"Disturbing…" Miraden shook his head, looking disappointed.

Faelinia elaborated on the matter, but Amendal ignored her. He turned back to Old Cali. *I need to retrieve my crystal,* he thought. But it would be difficult, especially without any conjurations. Had any survived? Fendar still had those two earthen giants, didn't he? But they weren't guarding the camp… "I guess they'll have to do…"

"What are you muttering about?" Miraden asked.

"Reclaiming my conjurations," Amendal said. "A pity there's only two left."

"Two?" Faelinia shook her head. "We saved more than that. Ildin has them."

"Really…?" Amendal widened his eyes. "Where are they?!"

Miraden pointed toward the camp. "One floor below us. Morgidian is helping with the barrier to the thirty-second floor, and Ildin is—" Calimir called for Miraden and the squad leader hurried away.

"Come on," Amendal said to Faelinia, turning back to the camp. "Let's go get my pretties!"

———·———

The grass crunched beneath Edara's boots as he darted around a tree-like structure. *That staircase has to be close,* he thought, panting. He rounded another building and darted into a clearing like the one where the camp was made. At its far end, a waist-high wall hemmed one of the stairwells. A tall man and a short woman stood at the wall, both dressed in dark-blue robes—the barsionists that murderous Calimir had mentioned.

Had they already sealed off the stairwell?

They'd better not…

As he approached, both barsionists turned toward him.

The woman furrowed her brow, wrinkles forming around her eyes. "What are you doing here?"

"My crew," Edara called through heavy breaths. "They're still down there."

The man glanced to the stairs then back to Edara. "I wasn't aware anyone was searching near here."

Now less than a hundred paces away, Edara saw a blue hue around the short wall. *No!*

"Take down the barsion!" he shouted. "I have to get to them!"

The barsionists looked at each other, then whispered something Edara couldn't hear. Anger welled within him. He couldn't abandon his men. He couldn't lose them like he had the *Giboran*. The murderous bastard would not take them as he had his beloved.

Edara clenched his fists as he neared the barsionists. If he had to, he would—

"Wait!" the woman said, extending an open hand. Edara skidded to a halt. "We'll let you pass if it's clear. But first we must prepare another barrier. Once we hold our incantations, we'll dismiss the barsion, and then you go."

Edara relaxed his fist as the two mages began uttering their incantations. They walked around the waist-high wall as blue light surged around them. Edara followed, stopping near the highest step.

The entire stairwell was covered in a layer of blue light that looked akin to the stilled waters of a secluded cove. Though the two hovering statues blocked most of the vast room below, what was visible was empty. Lifeless.

Soon, a ripple washed across the barsion, and then the magic vanished completely. Edara hurried down the stone steps. He had descended a third of the way when the barsionists exhaled the last of their incantations. Blue light tinged the stairwell, reflecting off the obsidian statues.

Now halfway down the stairs, faint pounding carried into the vast space. *Was that the monster approaching?* But the bastard said it was still two floors away...

He was near the bottom step when orange light flickered from the stairwell across the room, the same which led to the maze. *What was that?* He paused, glancing behind him, but the barsionists were turned away.

Edara continued down the stairs, leaping off the bottom step. As he landed, a pained cry carried across the vast space. "Please... help!"

Startled, Edara glanced to the far stairwell. A bare-chested man with short dark hair staggered up the stairs from the maze. Had someone been separated from the other half of the expedition?

"Help..."

Edara glanced back to the barsionists, but they still had their backs turned to him, looking at something above them. They were oblivious to the cry for aid. *Probably can't hear through the barsion.* He turned back to the man and started.

Standing completely naked, the man wobbled just beyond the steps, his head bobbing. Thick scars marred his chest. His right hand was missing, severed at the wrist.

Edara stepped forward and squinted. The man looked like one of the mages. *That necromancer with the ice wolves—*

A force, an overpowering will, penetrated Edara's mind and he became still.

COME CLOSER, a bellowing voice commanded. Edara felt his legs move, though not of his own volition. He tried to look away, but all he could do was stare at the naked man. He continued across the room, passing between the hovering statues.

Images flashed in his mind, memories of the past day; the search for tevisrals, the whittling of the dried venom, the meeting with the murderous bastard. He recalled all of it with perfect clarity. The memories ceased as Edara stopped two paces from the naked man.

The stranger's eyes were violet, but they were strange. Unnatural. Dark lines swirled around his pupils.

"You will do nicely," the man said and his face contorted, though not with emotion. His features changed, like a transmutation. His brow thickened, his cheeks sank, his jaw stretched. Dark hair grew from his chin and his upper lip while the hairs atop his head slithered to his chest. Wrinkles formed around his eyes, and his lips became thin.

Horrified, Edara stared at a mirror image of himself. He wanted to scream, but he couldn't. He could do nothing but stare into those violet eyes.

"How fortunate," the figure said, sounding exactly like Edara. The thin lips twisted into a wicked grin as cool fingers gripped Edara's throat. They squeezed, and Edara couldn't breathe—he couldn't even struggle for breath. He could only stare into the mimicry's eyes, which had become his own.

Darkness crept into Edara's vision, encroaching upon all but those mocking eyes. Eventually even they were consumed.

Hurrying down the stairs to the thirty-third floor, Amendal grinned upon seeing the towering yaeltis and the five cisthyrn. Ildin, Morgidian, and two others Amendal didn't recognize stood with the conjurations, near a wall of white stone where the stairs to the lower levels should have been. *You saved them,* he thought, eyeing Ildin. *What a wonderful friend you are!*

Leaping off the bottom step, Amendal ran toward his friends, leaving Faelinia and Fench behind. "Ildin! Morgi!"

The illusionist spun about, eyes wide and jaw agape. Morgidian also turned, brow furrowed. Ildin called out in surprise and ran toward Amendal. As they embraced at the room's center, Amendal saw tears in the illusionist's eyes.

"You're... you're all right," Ildin said, patting Amendal's back.

"Of course I'm all right," he said, chuckling. Why did everyone think he wasn't?

Ildin pulled back, but kept a hand on Amendal's shoulder. "I... I thought we'd lost you. And when Vaem wouldn't tell us about any tevisrals that could help, I..." His face contorted, and he turned away, wiping his cheek.

Morgidian soon approached, his arms folded. "Well, at least you're not screaming like a lunatic anymore."

Amendal raised an eyebrow and cocked his chin. *The squad leaders had thought the same...* But he couldn't recall doing such a thing.

"How are you feeling?" Morgidian asked.

"Fine," Amendal said, shrugging. "Why wouldn't I be?"

His friends exchanged wary gazes.

"Do you remember what happened?" Morgidian asked.

Amendal squinted at him while wings flapped around him. "Not really... why?" Fench fluttered to Amendal, settling on his shoulder as if it were a perch. Amendal glanced to the winged thing, eyeing him up and down.

"We thought you were going mad," Ildin said and pointed behind Amendal. "Faelinia had to restrain you. You wouldn't stop screaming."

"It was... disturbing." Faelinia stopped beside Amendal and took his hand.

"I don't remember any of that," he said. But then he recalled the dream in the forest. Running in fear. Total panic.

Before he could consider the matter further, Miraden shouted across the vast space. "We need to fall back! All but the sailors are accounted for." Amendal and the others turned to face the squad leader.

"Where are they?" Ildin asked.

Miraden threw his hands into the air.

"I'll look for them," Ildin said, then began uttering an illusory incantation. Faelinia did the same.

Amendal felt drawn to their words, noting the differences in their cadence and speed. *Faelinia will finish first,* he thought, playing both of their incantations in his mind. Never before had he heard incantations play out in his mind like that—especially ones not associated with conjuration magic. The words from the old codger came to him: "You will be able to see patterns where most men see chaos."

"We need to fall back," Miraden said. "The commander is calling for everyone to prepare for battle. The monster is getting closer, and only two-thirds of the supplies have been moved. Before Fendar's illusion flew away, he said the monster was on the thirty-second floor."

"It ascended fast without the Shift," Morgidian said. "Damn that woman."

Amendal gave the barsionist a sidelong glance. *What was wrong with the Shift?*

"The three of you"—Miraden pointed to the barsionists—"need to secure this access to the Roost." He then looked to Ildin and Faelinia. "If either of you finds the sailors, direct them here. We can let them into the Roost as long as the monster hasn't broken that barrier." He pointed to the stone wall barring the stairs to the lower floors.

Faelinia's illusion formed first, but Ildin's coalesced only a heartbeat later. Amendal smiled at seeing his prediction come true. The illusions zipped away, flying past the obsidian Tuladine statues and into the halls beside the stairs.

"I'll send another to the tower," Ildin said. "So we can track them." He turned to Amendal. "Shall we transfer the creatures once we're inside the Roost?"

Amendal nodded.

Ildin repeated his illusory incantation while Miraden called for everyone to follow him. The retired soldier ran across the room and up the stairs.

Before crossing the vast room, Amendal took one last look at the reliefs adorning the walls. In the scene to the right, a colossal battle was being waged between a dragon and another horned beast with a wide serpentine snout. *A gangolin...?* Its horns were unmistakable; covered in tines, they were curved up and around the creature's head, ending in a sharp point at its jaw. The dragon looked as if it were struggling against the gangolin. But were gangolins stronger than dragons? *Perhaps it was enthralled, or a conjuration,* Amendal thought, recalling a passage from his family's tomes.

As the party ascended, Morgidian and the other barsionists began mustering their magic, glowing with a blue aura. *They'll finish four steps from the top.* Amendal cocked his brow at the instinctive thought.

When they were partway up the stairs, Ildin finished his incantation, and the illusion sped ahead. "Which conjuration do you want first?"

"The yaeltis," Amendal said. "And I'll reclaim it now." He began the incantation to reclaim the beast, but the words felt slow. It did not match his will, so nothing manifested. One had to match both mental focus and incantation in order for magic to form.

He immediately stopped and restarted the incantation, now speaking the words over twice as fast. He slowed his will to match the words, and the charcoal light appeared around his hands. It formed quickly and shot toward the yaeltis in an instant.

Faelinia gasped while Ildin stared at Amendal with a blank expression across his face.

What's their problem? he thought, sensing Ildin's magic fading from the yaeltis. "Now the lead cisthyrn."

Amendal spoke the incantation once again, faster than before. The reclaiming magic formed within a heartbeat. The cisthyrn fell under his control as the barsionists held their incantations, exhaling the final sounds. Curious, Amendal looked ahead to Morgidian. The barsionist was on the fifth step from the top.

I was right again, he thought. If they had not begun holding their incantation, the barsion would have formed—

"How are you doing that?" Ildin demanded. "I've never heard anyone utter an incantation that quickly *and* muster magic."

Faelinia tightened her grip around Amendal's hand. "It's... not normal."

Amendal raised an eyebrow as he stepped onto the Roost's teal grass, then stepped aside, allowing the conjurations to ascend the stairs.

Ildin began speculating to himself.

I could tell him, Amendal thought, glancing to the conjurations. All five stood by the barsionists. Morgidian and the others unleashed their magic, covering the stairs in a transparent sheet of blue light. *Eh, it can wait till later.*

Repeating the incantation again, Amendal spoke only slightly faster than before. Each time he had to slow his mental focus to match his words. He repeated the process until the other three conjurations were under his control. "That's better... now for the earthen giants. Have any of you seen where Fendar put them?"

"Last I knew they were at the tower," Morgidian said, approaching with folded arms.

"They're there," Ildin said.

Amendal clapped his hands. "Great! Now let's ride these cisthyrns to the tower! Anyone for a race?"

Morgidian gave him a sidelong glance.

Focused through each of his conjurations, Amendal moved the cisthyrns to his friends. To his surprise, he felt no mental taxation. Six conjurations wouldn't exert much strain, but he should have felt *something*. The focus through each of his conjurations was clear and sharp, as if he were only controlling one.

"Oh no!" Ildin gasped and his eyes went wide. He spun, looking up the curving floor of the Roost.

"What is it?" Morgidian asked.

Amendal followed his friend's gaze. A faint blue light winked out followed by a fleeting flash of orange.

"The monster..." Ildin muttered. "Fendar said it just entered the Roost."

"From snout to tail-tip a gangolin is between ninety and a hundred-and-twenty phineals long. Although, I have heard that some have grown as large as a hundred-and-fifty phineals."

- From *Colvinar Vrium's Bestiary for Conjurers*, page 252

Calimir spun at the frantic voice that called his name. The illusion of Mister Callis sped toward him and the few squad leaders preparing for battle. They all turned, equally puzzled.

"Commander!" the illusionist cried. "The monster is inside the Roost!"

Calimir flinched. How had it breached the barsion? "Where is it?"

"It's approaching from the stairwell you dubbed number three." The illusion pointed across the camp, in the direction opposite the tower. "But, Commander, it... it looked like Captain Edara."

Mister Callis related how he had sent an illusion to stairwell three and informed the barsionists of the monster's approach. Upon his arrival, they told him that the sea captain had just descended to find his crew. As they talked, Mister Callis watched through the map as the dot representing the monster entered the thirty-third floor. The one he supposed belonged to Edara winked out, but then through his illusion he saw the sea captain banging on the barsion.

"... and they were confused. I told them not to let him in, but then the captain burst into orange light, and the monster was in his place. It shattered the barsion before they could reinforce it."

"We have to kill that thing," said a squad leader.

Calimir nodded and looked about the staging area. Most of the camp had been torn down. Only a few tents remained, including the one where the Mindolarnians were held. Besides himself, thirty soldiers were gathered in what had been the mess area. All were ready for battle, and many wielded the tevisral weapons found in the treasury. Nearly as many mages were also in the staging area. "Recall everyone," he said. "We will converge on this monster and kill it once and for all."

Several squad leaders darted away. Miraden and another dashed in the direction they had sent the supplies. Over half of the survivors had traveled to the pit Mister Cetarin had mentioned. Though they probably weren't prepared for battle, the trek from that side of the Roost would grant them ample time to ready themselves.

"Move to the tower!" Calimir shouted, reaching for one of the tevisral weapons that looked like only an ornate sword hilt. At first glance, one might think the blade had been broken at the curved guard, or that it never had a blade to begin with. Much of the handle was covered with etched scaled patterns, ending in a claw-like pommel that clutched a reddish-orange jewel.

Upon his touch, the hilt burst with flame and a blade formed, as if it were made of condensed fire.

<hr>

Incantations sounded around Amendal as he and his friends rode the cisthyrns. They galloped at a furious pace, weaving around the tree-trunk buildings of the Roost. When enhanced, cisthyrns were almost as fast as a yidoth... almost. Fench had since flown away, undoubtedly terrified by the prospect of Orath'issian entering his home.

Poor thing...

A veil of blue light surged around Amendal, and a form-fitting barsion washed across his robe. Soon, another wave of barsion wrapped around the cisthyrn he rode. "Don't forget the yaeltis!" he shouted to Morgidian. The barsionist raised a brow while mustering more of his magic.

They soon arrived at the clearing housing the Tuladine Tower. Both earthen giants stood outside the entrance as still as statues. Amendal rode up to them and leapt off the cisthyrn. Landing with a grin, he turned back to the others. "When we return home, we'll have to do some cisthyrn racing." He laughed giddily. "Can't you imagine the faces of patrons exiting Makivir's Lounge as we bolt past?"

"You really are mad," Morgidian said with a sigh.

Amendal mustered the magic to reclaim the conjurations. As the gray light surged into the earthen giants, thunderous footsteps echoed from beyond the nearby buildings.

"It's here..." Ildin muttered.

"Why would the monster come here?" Faelinia asked, then began mustering a disintegrating barsion.

As Amendal repeated the incantation, a flash of black and orange darted from the tree-trunk buildings, and Orath'issian bounded across the clearing. He leapt into the air and cleared the tower's second tier, slamming into the third with a resounding crash.

"Did it crack the stone?" Ildin blurted.

The others hurried away as Amendal finished the reclaiming incantation. His magic surged into another conjuration, and as before he didn't feel any additional mental strain by claiming the earthen giants. *How strange...*

He glanced to his friends, who were staring in horror at the tower, then hurried to them.

Orath'issian climbed swiftly, pushing himself from the sixth tier. He grabbed the bridge extending into the enormous map of Tardalim and swept his maimed arm across it. Two figures—one surrounded by green light and the other a gray hue—flew from the magical map. They cried in surprise as they plummeted toward the tree-trunk buildings, but soon disappeared.

"No..." Ildin wailed. "No. No!"

Morgidian bellowed a fierce growl, then uttered another incantation, mustering more barsion. Faelinia gasped, her face contorting in dismay.

Furious, Amendal returned his gaze to the monster.

Orath'issian threw a fist inside the room atop the tower's seventh tier. Was he trying to destroy the map? *Somehow he knows about it...* After several blows, the map surrounding the bridge flickered, then vanished. The bridge collapsed, and Orath'issian fell with it. His middle arms tried to grab onto the lower tiers, but he couldn't manage a grip and crashed into the nearby clearing.

Unfazed, the monster shook himself, rose to his feet, and turned toward Amendal and his friends.

"SO, YOU SALVAGED THE BEASTCALLER'S PUPPETS," Orath'issian snickered. "BUT THEY DO NOT STAND A—YOU...!" Orath'issian's violet eyes fell upon Amendal, his bizarre snout contorting in confusion. "HOW ARE YOU NOT A DRIVELING IDIOT?"

Faint commotion carried from the buildings behind Amendal. Incantations. Then, footsteps?

"Calimir's coming," Ildin said, and Morgidian finished his incantation. A wave of barsion surrounded one of the earthen giants as the monster shifted his attention to the noises.

"NO MATTER," Orath'issian bellowed. "THIS TIME I WILL CLAIM THE TULADINE." The monster charged as the commotion grew louder, and battle cries carried into the clearing. Faelinia and Ildin darted in opposite directions while Morgidian held his ground, uttering another incantation.

Focused through each conjuration, Amendal advanced them on Orath'issian. The yaeltis and the monster clashed, and they tumbled into the clearing.

Orath'issian pinned the yaeltis with his left foremost arm while his middle arms pummeled the conjuration's barsion. Amendal struggled, but couldn't move the yaeltis. The beast's barsion began to flicker.

He thrust the yaeltis's knee into Orath'issian's gut as the earthen giants converged upon the monster. Orath'issian swatted at them with his rear-most arms, but Amendal managed to dodge the blows. The monster swung its tail, and Amendal *knew* the precise moment to throw the conjurations out of the way.

Blue light shot past Orath'issian, surrounding the other earthen giant as it recovered.

The battle cries grew louder, and soldiers enhanced and protected by magic flooded around Orath'issian. Amid those charging were Dugal and Jaekim. The soldiers drew Orath'issian's attention, and he reared off the yaeltis.

With the conjuration freed, Amendal immediately scuttled the furry beast away.

"Wa-wha-what is that thing?" Jaekim gasped.

"You don't want to know," Dugal said and turned to Morgidian. "Shall we try to shackle it?"

Morgidian nodded, but he was mustering more barsion.

"Wait!" Amendal called. "Before you do that, make me some weapons. Big weapons."

To Calimir's surprise, the monster was quite agile. It moved through the clearing with incredible speed, snatching soldiers as it bounced from either side of the advancing force. The monster squeezed them with its middle and rear arms, not seeming to care about their destructive barsions.

Calimir and the others charged with impeccable speed and accuracy, but the monster managed to move before they could land many blows. To Calimir's dismay, not even the weapons from the treasury managed to penetrate the creature's ebony hide.

With an enraged growl, the monster swept its maimed arm toward Calimir, hurling away several soldiers. But Calimir managed to evade the blow. Rebounding, he dashed toward the monster and neared its legs, his magical weapon ready. Flame met that ebony hide, but the blade failed to pierce it.

How many times must we strike you? He landed another blow, but the monster kicked him away.

A scream filled the air as Calimir tumbled backward. He landed on his back, watching in horror as the monster crushed a squad leader and another soldier with its bare hands. Their dying wails faded as the creature hurled them away.

Growling, Calimir pushed himself up and darted back toward the monster. As he advanced, Mister Aramien's conjurations pulled away. The monster didn't seem to care. It crushed another soldier and tossed the dead man aside.

Once near its legs, Calimir lunged with his flaming blade raised high. He instinctively brought his shield arm across his chest, though he lacked a bulwark. The fiery blade sliced along the black hide. Flame persisted along the blade's path, but if it charred the monster, he couldn't tell.

Bursts of pink light flashed above him, accompanied by booming explosions.

The monster spun, and Calimir chased after it. Acidic orbs flew through the air, as well as orange cords—life-draining magic from the necromancers. The cords latched onto the monster's middle right arm, but they didn't seem to weaken it in the slightest. The woman in the clutches of that hand was still squeezed, her barsion flickering.

"YOUR DEFIANCE AMUSES ME," the monster bellowed, hurling two more corpses from its grasp.

———◦•◦———

Violet light tinged Faelinia's vision as she finished her incantation. A disintegrating beam shot above the battle, striking the Orath-monster's neck. As before, the blast barely eroded the monster's flesh. The beam persisted for barely a heartbeat before the monster spun away, and Faelinia's magic sailed over the distant buildings.

She groaned, redirecting the violet beam toward the center of the Roost. The Orath-monster was moving too fast for her to keep a steady blast on one particular spot. *Perhaps a beam is not the best choice.*

The monster skidded across the clearing, swatting a female soldier with its tail. She flew toward Faelinia, crashed to the ground beside her, and tumbled by.

Meanwhile, several other mages assaulted the Orath-monster with their magic. One of the necromancers had a life-draining cord latched around the monster's rearmost right arm. Arcane orbs erupted around the cord while acidic javelins struck the monster's elbow. An icy shard collided with that arm, but it shattered upon impact.

Why are they attacking the limbs? she wondered, redirecting her disintegrating beam. The violet magic struck the Orath-monster's neck again, but at a different point than the first. As it had before, the monster evaded, nearly colliding with one of the Tuladine buildings. Faelinia tried to redirect her magic, but the beam struck the ground. She dismissed the blast and took in the battle with a sweeping glance.

The mages continued assailing the Orath-monster with their magic, striking erratically. Soldiers swung their weapons, hitting the monster as best they could, but they rarely landed a second blow.

Amendal's conjurations had since pulled back. The yaeltis was kneeling, reaching for the ground. The conjured beast lifted a glistening double-edged sword surrounded by a faint blue aura. Brown light shone from the ground near the other conjurations, flowing from Dugal. *Transmuting weapons,* she thought. *And reinforcing them with barsion... good thinking, Amendal.* But those weapons wouldn't be enough to pierce the monster's flesh.

Focused on the transmuted blade, Faelinia began mustering a disintegrating enhancement. Violet light soon shot from her hands, zipping across the clearing and toward the yaeltis's weapon. It surged around the transmuted blade, persisting like a cloud.

Amendal, who was standing near Dugal and Morgidian, turned toward her and blew her a kiss, his arm moving in an exaggerated arc. The boyish gesture almost made her forget their predicament. She replied in kind as the earthen giant reached for the ground.

The elemental's blade had not yet formed. *Best I wait,* she thought, glancing back to the battle. The Orath-monster dodged a variety of bolts and orbs. Needing a better vantage, she glanced to the tower. There was an opening in the vines, not far from where she stood. She turned back to the earthen giants, and the conjuration had already lifted its blade.

Repeating the last incantation, Faelinia hurried to what she assumed was the tower's entrance. The clearing in the vines had a circular outline etched into its surface. If it were a door, she had no idea how to open it. She finished her second disintegrating enhancement and hurled it across the clearing.

As it wrapped around the transmuted weapon, she dismissed her disintegrating barsion and reached for the nearby vines. They were thin and brittle. Several crumbled at her touch.

Too weak to climb. She stepped back, gauging the height of the tower's lowest tier. It was about three stories above her. A tale from her youth came to her mind, of a mage climbing buildings with ensnaring tentacles.

Pleased with the idea, Faelinia uttered an incantation, and green light surged around her.

That's fifteen, Amendal thought, watching as another limp man was hurled toward the tower. Though all the soldiers were encased in multiple layers of barsion, Orath'issian was able to crush their protective barriers before the barsionists could reinforce them.

Though he was darting back and forth, Orath'issian was maneuvering the soldiers, pushing them closer to the mages.

What is he trying to do? Amendal glanced back to the tower, eyeing the seventh tier. *Does he know we could track him?* If so, Amendal hadn't the slightest idea how the monster knew. He began to return his gaze to the tower but stopped upon seeing Faelinia scaling the second tier. Green tendrils were wrapped around her waist, connecting her to the ledge of the third tier. *A higher vantage would be better.*

Dugal had nearly finished his incantation when Ildin approached with several illusions surrounding him.

"The last one's ready!" Dugal said, and began walking toward the battle, uttering another incantation.

Morgidian finished mustering another layer of protection for the yaeltis and turned to Ildin. "We could use your help."

"Doing what?" Ildin asked.

"Shackling Orath'issian," Amendal said and focused through his conjurations. "So we can kill him!" The earthen giant hefted the sword, and then Amendal sent all three conjurations running toward the monster. He glanced back to Faelinia, who was not quite halfway to the tower's third tier. *She can imbue the last one later.*

Morgidian grunted and briefly relayed his plan to Ildin. It was a variation of what they had tried on the twenty-first floor, but this time it would involve transmuted metal and barsion. He wanted the illusionist to coordinate with any other barsionists and transmuters. "If we can bind him all at once, we should be able to hold him long enough for Amendal and the mages to strike death blows."

Ildin nodded and sent his illusions flying.

Ignoring his friends, Amendal focused completely on his conjurations. The earthen giants reached the battle first and swung their weapons in unison.

Orath'issian spun, knocking several soldiers into the nearest Tuladine home. His tail sped through the air in an arc, straight for the yaeltis's face. Amendal turned the beast, blocking the tail with the conjuration's sword.

As in their last bout, Orath'issian ignored the soldiers. He still held several in his rear hands, squeezing them until their barsions shattered. But this time, instead of crushing them, he dropped them. They fell through that haze of his, screaming in terror as they hit the ground.

Orath'issian lunged at the conjurations, kicking one of the giants. The elemental tumbled toward the tower as the monster spun on the yaeltis, knocking the beast away. Before Amendal could recover either of them, Orath'issian unleashed a flurry of blows on the last earthen giant. Amendal reacted by dodging the first, blocking the second, and parrying the third, but Orath'issian's tail swept the conjuration's leg out from under it.

The earthen giant fell, crushing several soldiers. Luckily, their barsions held true.

Orath'issian spun back to the soldiers, snatching two more.

Well, that was worthless, Amendal thought. *Maybe I should learn more combat tactics...*

He pushed the three conjurations upright as his incantations turned to humming. Amendal held the conjurations back while glancing to his friends. Both Dugal and Morgidian were holding their incantations. The ground in front of them had been liquefied and Morgidian was nearly consumed by blue light.

"They're almost ready," Ildin said.

Orath'issian continued his rampage, crushing another soldier and tossing him aside.

"Now!"

The liquefied ground in front of Dugal arced into the air, changing from a dull brown to glistening gray. Three other columns of transmogrified ground sped through the air, racing toward Orath'issian.

An enraged growl filled the air as dirt transformed into metal and wrapped around the monster's arms and legs. Ensnaring tentacles shot from several other mages, also binding him in place.

Go, Amendal commanded and the conjurations charged. While they ran, Faelinia imbued the bare, transmuted sword.

Battle cries filled the air as the conjurations reached Orath'issian. The remaining soldiers had converged upon the monster, hacking at his legs and forearms. All but one of Orath'issian's arms was bound.

"A CLEVER TACTIC!" Orath'issian shouted. Destructive beams and deadly bolts struck him. The conjurations swung their blades after the magic, striking the monster's back. The blades recoiled, but Amendal swung them again as Orath'issian cackled. "A PITY IT WILL NOT WORK."

The conjurations swung again, and Orath'issian burst with an orange flash. Their weapons sailed *through* the light. Each transmuted shackle buckled as orange lightning surged past the crowd of soldiers. The man in the monster's clutches fell, his barsions shattering upon impact.

Calimir blinked in disbelief. The monster was gone, replaced by a streak of orange lightning that struck the ground, spraying dirt and grass. Earthen debris collided with Calimir's barsion as the light coalesced into a blazing orange ball that skidded across the ground. Within it was the silhouette of a man crouching.

Mister Shival and Mister Callis had speculated that the monster could change shape, but Calimir hadn't expected the transformation to be so... majestic.

Calimir spun as the light soon faded. A naked blonde-haired man—covered in fresh wounds and missing his right hand—tumbled through the clearing between the mages and soldiers. The others were equally shocked, but quickly regained their composure and charged.

The naked man rolled across the ground, grabbing one of the tevisral weapons dropped by a fallen soldier. He leapt to his feet as the blade burst with violet light. Not a heartbeat later, he charged at those advancing upon him. He swung his blade at a soldier without barsion, decapitating the man.

"Surround him!" a squad leader shouted.

The naked man pushed his way past several soldiers until he was surrounded. But instead of attacking, he burst with an orange flash. A surge of orange lightening shot from the crowd and exploded near a tree-like building.

The monster's silhouette appeared within the light, skidding like the na-

ked man. The light faded, and the monster collided with the tree-like building, splitting it in two.

What manner of monster was this? And transforming from something so
large to the size of a man... How was that even possible?

Shaking the conundrum aside, Calimir shouted for his soldiers to attack
once again.

"A gangolin's size is practically unrivaled among other beasts of our world. The only creature of comparable size would be the mythical dragons."

- From *Colvinar Vrium's Bestiary for Conjurers*, page 256

Now atop the tower's fourth tier, Faelinia whispered the words to a variation of a powerful incantation, one that would muster a swarm of disintegrating orbs. It was a spell that had taken a great deal of discipline to master. Even so, what she intended to do with it exceeded anything she had ever done.

Violet disintegrating light surged around her, coalescing into spherical clouds that colored her vision. Though it looked as if it were one expansive aura, there were over a hundred of those clouds hovering around her. She neared the end of the incantation, but repeated the words of an earlier segment.

Through her forming magic she watched as the Orath-monster recovered from its bizarre transformation. It turned on the mages and lifted several into the air, squeezing their barsions.

A squad leader called for the mages to pull back, and they ran between the tree-like buildings. "YOU CANNOT FLEE!" the Orath-monster bellowed, chasing after the mages and kicking several across the clearing. The soldiers hurried after the creature, joined by Amendal's conjurations.

As they ran, four robed figures dashed into the clearing, each shielded by barsion—undoubtedly the barsionists who had sealed off the other stairwells. They chased after the soldiers, mustering their magics.

Now, only a lone figure remained in the clearing, kneeling among the corpses. Was that Jaekim? A surge of magic—what color she couldn't tell—flowed to the corpses, and one of the dead soldiers rose from the ground, grabbing one of the tevisral weapons. Another dead man stood, followed by another.

Shifting her focus, Faelinia returned her concentration to her forming magic. She repeated the earlier segment several times, then continued with the rest of the incantation. Focused on the violet clouds immediately around her, she willed them to condense, forming fist-sized spheres. She repeated the final segment over and over, and each time more spheres took shape. As they coalesced, it became harder and harder to maintain their forms. It was a struggle to keep them from breaking apart and dissipating into oblivion.

Soon, the expansive aura was no more, and nearly two hundred destructive orbs had formed. Her hands quivered as she brought them together.

Focus... She sucked in her breath and glanced to the necromancer raising the dead soldiers. Twelve were standing, now. She exhaled and searched for the battle. The Orath-monster had reached the expedition's camp, gripping several mages. It shattered the barsion of one and hurled the limp victim toward what was the mess area.

"The neck..." she told herself, her voice shaky.

Taking another deep breath, she willed three of the orbs to fly from the tower. They zipped in an arc, moving one after the other.

Faelinia focused on the lead orb, guiding it toward the monster. The orbs wove around its rear limbs and struck the Orath-monster's neck. Her foe jerked as the other two orbs followed, but only one struck true. The third sped to the ground, but Faelinia managed to redirect it, sending it upward in a wide arc.

Go! She willed three others to speed across the Roost. They joined the third from the first volley. She rained them down upon the Orath-monster, but only half struck the wretched thing. The others plummeted into the grassy ground, eroding the teal blades and the dirt beneath them.

While readying a third volley, faint cries echoed across the Roost. Faelinia turned, watching a crowd charge toward the partly broken-down camp, all shielded in a variety of barsions.

"Good," she whispered, hurling the third volley. "Now we can end you."

——————⇨•⇦——————

Fench trembled as he flew from his family's rooms, carrying the things that were most precious to him. *Stupid two-legs,* he thought, clutching his family's gray bag that was stuffed full. His parents claimed the bag had been used by his father's father when he first came to the Roost. His mother's helm bobbed on his head, occasionally obscuring his vision. *I shouldn't have helped them!* His mother had warned him. She had been right. *Except... they aren't all bad.*

His thoughts turned to Amendal while he wove around the tall homes. *If Amendal had not been hurt by the Orath-monster, maybe none of this would have hap-*

pened.

Faint booms echoed softly above him while he zipped toward the river. Fench followed it to the pit. But the two-legs were gone. Only their sacks and packs lay about, gathered beside the water. Some things were piled atop one another, others were put in nice rows.

Fench fluttered to a stop, hovering in the air. *Where did they go?*

"To their deaths," a deep voice said.

Surprised, Fench flitted toward the voice. A two-leg sat atop a pile of packs, wearing what Amendal had called a robe. It was red with funny lines in it. The two-leg stroked the white hairs on his face, eyeing Fench.

"It seems one of you had the right idea," the two-leg said, sighing. "A pity Amendal isn't with you. That would have made this ordeal a lot simpler."

Fench blinked and his trunk stiffened. Looking at the two-leg made him feel sick. It was worse than seeing the Orath-monster.

"Frightened, Fench?" the two-leg asked, chuckling. He smiled, and the skin around his eyes made lines. "You have nothing to fear from me. In fact, I want to help you."

The fear grew, and Fench felt his wings beating slower and slower until his tail touched the grass.

"But first you'll have to find some courage," the two-leg said, rising from the packs. He jumped onto the grass without a sound. The other two-legs had made the grass crunch as they walked, but this one didn't. Still stroking those hairs on his face, the two-leg looked up, toward the distant booms. "Otherwise, you and Amendal will never make it to safety."

The two-leg knelt in front of Fench and leaned close. Fench wanted to fly away, but he couldn't.

"Come with me," the two-leg said, raising a finger toward Fench's face. "I have something important to show you."

Vaem struggled against the barsion pinning her to the cot. Each jolt caused the pain in her shoulder to flare, but she had to escape. Once the battle had started, the barsion pinning her had flickered several times. She supposed Morgidian was losing his focus. Mages tended to stretch themselves thin if they tried mustering too much magic. *That's why tevisrals are better.*

The explosions and cries were growing louder with each passing moment.

"I hope he dies," Kydol said amid grunts and groans. "Then we can be free." She too had started struggling when the barsion began flickering.

"We can only hope," Vaem said through clenched teeth. The pain intensified, and she gasped. She ceased thrashing and instinctively pressed herself against the cot. But even that was painful.

Vaem squeezed her eyes shut.

A growl left Kydol's lips as she continued struggling. The lieutenant swore under her breath and whispered a prayer.

The barsion flickered again, then lessened in vibrancy.

Pushing through her pain, Vaem struggled once again. A thunderous crash resounded from outside the tent, followed by another explosion. The barsion continued flickering as something struck the tent's ceiling. The tent poles snapped and fabric fell toward Vaem, veiling her face. A tremendous force struck her left leg, breaking bone and cot. Kydol's prayer was cut short.

Overcome by the excruciating pain, Vaem watched as the tent was ripped from her, pulled away by a towering figure. The fabric rippled in the air but soon fell, revealing one of those earthen conjurations. It dashed away, moving out of her vision.

A deafening roar rippled through the air amid more explosions.

She struggled to lift her head and called for the lieutenant, but Kydol didn't answer.

Gritting her teeth against the pain, Vaem struggled to turn toward her fellow captive. But where the lieutenant should have lain was a bloodied mess oozing from a flickering band of inverted barsion. The sight wrenched Vaem's stomach, and she squeezed her eyes shut.

I am doomed.

———◦•◦———

Amendal skidded to a halt as his earthen giant recovered. Though his conjurations landed only an occasional blow, he was learning the tells for each of Orath'issian's movements. Unfortunately, the monster had slain most of their forces, including three of the cisthyrn. To Amendal's surprise, their deaths hadn't been painful. The other two cisthyrn he kept beside him.

Roars from the monster and shouted incantations filled the air, accented by an occasional wail of agony. Disintegrating orbs plummeted toward Orath'issian, striking the back of his neck, his flailing arms, and the ground around him.

Only a handful of soldiers remained, but the monster ignored them. He also ignored the conjurations, using his tail or rear arms to swat their blows away. He focused on the mages Old Cali had brought with him, strategically slaying them. The arpranists had fallen first, then the barsionists—except Morgidian. For some reason, the monster hadn't turned on Amendal or his friends. *He's planning something*, Amendal thought.

"We need to try binding him again," Dugal cried as he joined Amendal and looked around, frantic. "Where is everyone else?"

Morgidian stumbled past the transmuter, mustering more of his magic. He had replenished the barsions of the remaining soldiers, but he was struggling to maintain all of them.

It's no use, Amendal thought. If they did manage to trap Orath'issian again, he would only free himself by transforming. *But if he transformed into a human, would he be more susceptible to Faelinia's orbs?*

Orath'issian snatched the last three of Old Cali's mages while grabbing one of the soldiers. Only four remained, including the old commander. Despite all their efforts, Orath'issian showed no signs of slowing his relentless assault.

Perhaps I should have fled... Amendal thought, but shook the cowardly notion aside. No, the old codger was not going to manipulate him. They could stop Orath'issian. He just knew it.

The mages' barsions flickered as they continued mustering their magics: flame, arcane, and lightning. All the while, faint noises carried through the camp.

Amendal craned his neck toward the sounds, and they soon rose to a clamor of incantations, armored footfalls, and battle cries. Miraden charged past, leading the rest of the expedition. But unlike Calimir's force, they hadn't any tevisral weapons. *Perhaps that's a good thing.*

Orath'issian spun on the reinforcements. "AH, MORE PLAYTHINGS," he cackled, shattering the barsions of those in his grasp.

Strangled screams interrupted the forming magic; flame evaporated, lightning flickered, and the arcane cloud dissipated.

Orath'issian crushed those mages as three of Faelinia's orbs struck his neck. The monster jerked away, dodging two more that disintegrated the ground. He glanced toward the tower, baring his obsidian teeth.

Don't you dare go after her, Amendal thought, watching the soldiers and mercenaries surround Orath'issian.

The reinforcing mages encircled Amendal, several unleashing destructive blasts. He scanned the newcomers, but couldn't discern their disciplines by their clothes. Several weren't mustering magic. "Everyone, listen to me!" he shouted, waving his hands in the air. "We need to coordinate if we want to kill him. We need to trap him so he transforms again." Amendal explained his plan, and many of the mages looked confused. But no one opposed him.

While he finished with the instructions, mangled soldiers approached from the tree-trunk buildings, each glowing with a dark-purple hue and wielding tevisral weapons. Jaekim ran beside them.

"... and hopefully that'll give her time to strike," Amendal finished, glancing to the necromancer.

Jaekim stumbled to a halt near Ildin, breathing deeply. "I... need you to.... enhance them... I want them... to jump... on the monster's back—"

Amendal flinched as a limp soldier flew between him and Jaekim, tumbling across the teal grass. The soldier stopped rolling, his face turned toward Amendal. It was Dardel. His jaw was slack and his eyes wide.

Ildin muttered a lament and sucked in his breath.

Incantations sounded from the other mages, and Amendal glanced back to the battle. Orath'issian swatted a soldier with his tail, hurling the woman past what remained of the camp. Six more of Faelinia's orbs rushed toward the monster, but only two struck. The other four nearly hit the ground, barely zipping above the grass. *Seems the more orbs she expends the better control she has...* he thought, then turned to Ildin. "Tell Faelinia what we plan to do."

The illusionist nodded and sent one of his illusions flying over the Tuladine homes.

Returning his focus to the incantations, Amendal parsed what should have been a jumble. *Two transmutations, and three ensnaring tentacles.* Dugal had already begun humming the last of his incantation. *Six should work,* he thought, waiting for the others to hold their spells.

"She's ready," Ildin said.

Amendal nodded, noting the six mages exhaling the last few sounds of their incantations. He raised his hand into the air, then swung it down, signaling the others to unleash their magic. Green tendrils shot from the crowd while brown and teal sludge arced into the air.

Orath'issian, however, noticed the approaching magic and burst with orange light. He shot like lightning, landing between Amendal and the soldiers. The ensnaring tentacles and the transmuted ground arced above the now-human Orath'issian.

The monster-turned-man eyed the mages as six disintegrating orbs swirled around the arcing transmutations. Orath'issian spun, undoubtedly hearing the approaching magic, and dove sideways. The orbs neared his left leg as he erupted in another orange flash.

Had they hit?

Orange lightning surged toward the camp, flashing once again. The monstrous silhouette staggered as the light faded. He bellowed a deafening roar, laced with pain and fury, and bared his obsidian teeth. A large hole marred his left leg, exposing partly eroded orange muscles and red sinews hanging from black bone.

So, it did work... Amendal smiled. *That's how we kill him!* He willed his conjurations to charge while considering a plan. But the monster had transformed upon seeing the danger. *What if he couldn't see—?*

"HOW CLEVER," Orath'issian growled, and more orbs arced toward him. He dodged, landing near a robed figure huddled in the wrecked camp. Green arpran light flowed from the mage and surged into someone Amendal couldn't see. Orath'issian's leg buckled and he snatched the arpranist with his tail, green light trailing through the air.

Focused through his conjurations, Amendal saw a dark-haired feminine figure crawling from the monster's hind leg. She wore a single red glove on her right hand. *Vaem.* Was the arpranist trying to mend her?

The monster ignored Vaem, steadying himself against the charging soldiers, mercenaries, and conjurations. "YOU HUMANS ARE PROVING TO BE MORE TROUBLESOME THAN I EXPECTED."

Orath'issian hurled the arpranist at the advancing yaeltis. Amendal made the conjuration dodge, but before he recovered, the monster burst with orange light. Orath'issian zipped past the charging soldiers and mercenaries, but no sooner had he became human than he erupted once again.

Orange lightning shot past the nearby buildings, and Orath'issian retook his monstrous form, charging toward the tower.

Amendal willed his earthen giants after the monster. They *had* to intercept Orath'issian before he reached Faelinia. Calimir called for everyone to turn, and the expedition ran after the conjurations, weaving around the tree-trunk buildings.

Come, he commanded the yaeltis, warily watching Orath'issian through the other conjurations. "I have a special task for you," he told the yaeltis. "You and I are going to kill that monster."

Faelinia launched another volley of orbs as the Orath-monster advanced. Its heavy footfalls echoed off the tree-like buildings as it approached. The others were chasing after it, but they were too slow.

She gritted her teeth, guiding the orbs to the monster's neck. The first two missed, but the third struck true. She redirected the volley as the monster galloped into the clearing.

"I'll try to distract it," Ildin said through his illusion.

"YOU ARE TROUBLESOME, FAELINIA!" the monster bellowed, leaping toward the tower.

She staggered at the sound of her name. How did it know who she was?

The monster landed atop the lowest tier, then swiftly ascended. Ildin's illusion flew toward the monster, but it ignored the magic. Before Faelinia could send more orbs to her foe, the Orath-monster towered in front of her. It reached for her, and Faelinia willed two dozen orbs toward the wretched thing. The violet spheres struck, but the disintegrating magic barely tore through the ebony hide. In that same instant, the monster snatched her with its left hand.

"SUCH SPIRIT," the Orath-monster cackled, lifting her toward those violet eyes. It growled as her disintegrating barsion began to tear through its hand. The monster squeezed harder, attempting to shatter her barsion.

No!

She willed a dozen more to fly and struck the monster's eye. The thing screamed. She willed more to strike, hoping to distract it and give the others a chance to converge.

An enraged growl washed around her as that violet eye met her gaze. She stilled as an overpowering will, far stronger than her own, penetrated her thoughts. It felt akin to an enthralling spell, but was much stronger. Images of her life flashed before her, and she felt her orbs dissipate. So did her disintegrating barsion. Only Morgidian's barrier remained. That orange haze wafted against the form-fitting barsion, but soon fell.

The images soon overtook her, and she relived the entirety of their trip across the Abodine Wasteland. The moments with Amendal became intense flashes of passion, and she yearned to be with him. The barsion from Morgidian flickered as she relived her ascent up the tower.

"PERFECT," the monster said.

A pink blast flashed behind the monster, and it jolted.

Faelinia gasped as her gaze no longer met those violet eyes. *What was that—?*

The Orath-monster leapt from the tower's fourth tier and hurled Faelinia away. She spun through the air, helplessly glimpsing the others as they converged upon the monster.

I have to redirect—the barsion shattered as she struck something hard. Her head hit that same surface, and she fell. But before she landed, everything went black.

Morgidian started as his barsion around Faelinia shattered. She had been hurled from the tower, but she had moved so quickly that he couldn't tell where she had been thrown. Soldiers darted past him, as did Amendal's earthen conjurations, but not the yaeltis. Neither of the massive weapons had a disintegrating imbuing. *Had the monster killed Faelinia?*

Frantic cries from Amendal carried over the advancing force. *He really is mad*, Morgidian thought.

He continued running, and mustered more of his magic. There was no point trying to trap the monster when it could simply free itself at any moment. Better to protect the soldiers and mercenaries.

They wove around the tree-like buildings and bounded into the clearing, where the Orath-monster stood, ready to pounce.

"YOUR EFFORTS ARE FUTILE," it shouted. "NOW GIVE ME THE TULADINE, AND I WILL END YOU SWIFTLY."

Barsions formed over those at the head, and the monster lunged. It tore through their ranks, snatching soldier and mage alike.

Morgidian threw himself out of the way, rolling over the teal grass. The Orath-monster charged past, but before Morgidian could recover, a black streak flew toward his barsion. A tremendous force struck the barrier, sending him tumbling through the air. He flew past several tree-like buildings. Then he hit one and fell.

"Great…" he grumbled and looked around. He could barely see the battle, which was almost a grand phineal away. Several of his barsion barriers shattered, followed by dying wails that filled the air. Eruptions flashed above the tree-like buildings, but no amount of deadly magic seemed to faze the monster. The others shackled the Orath-monster, but the wretched thing escaped in a blinding flash.

Will this ever end?

Sucking in his breath, Morgidian ran back to the battle, mustering more of his magic. The Orath-monster transformed again, resuming its relentless rampage.

Calimir struck the monster's maimed leg as the mages tried shackling the beast. But as before, once the monster was bound it became a ball of light.

The monster-turned-man landed among the reanimated soldiers, pried a tevisral-weapon from a walking corpse, and then darted toward Calimir and the others. How it moved with that wounded leg was beyond Calimir's understanding.

Miraden and many others converged, but the monster shattered a woman's barsion, spun around her and gleefully shoved his blade through her back. Magic raced toward the monster-turned-man, but the thing evaded and burst once again.

Shielding his eyes, Calimir took in the battle with a sweeping glance. To his dismay, the monster had killed ten more of his men and women.

Despite Ildin's efforts to coordinate with the mages, the monster continued freeing himself. *At this rate, none of us will survive this...* Eighteen more had died since the battle returned to the clearing.

Dugal grumbled beside him. "This isn't working. We have to try something else."

"I'm trying to climb my undead!" Jaekim blurted. "But he just keeps moving too fast!"

"I'm not talking about your *pets!*" Dugal snapped.

If only Faelinia hadn't been hurled away—

A call from Amendal rang over the pandemonium, and Ildin spun. The conjurer stood beside one of those strange buildings with his cisthyrns, waving for Ildin to come to him.

Wary, he glanced back to his friends. "Amendal wants us."

Dugal didn't move, but Jaekim stumbled beside Ildin. Another call came, and Ildin hurried to Amendal with Jaekim.

The conjurer's face was twisted in anger. "I have a plan to kill him. But I need a distraction."

"How?" Jaekim asked. "Your last plan isn't working..."

Ildin raised an eyebrow at the necromancer, but turned back to Amendal.

The conjurer shook his head and waved his hands dismissively. "You're doing it all wrong! You have to lure him to the right spot, then hit him!"

Set a trap...? But what would—Ildin snapped his fingers. "An illusion of Fench!"

"Precisely, and hidden transmutations. Like what Dugal did to those kids under the tree all those years ago."

Under the tree...? Ildin couldn't recall the incident.

"With Fendar," Amendal added. "Masking the ground. We just do that here! To him!" He pointed to the monster.

Him? Ildin turned, looking back to the battle. Others were now in the monster's grasp. Had they lost another four?

"We don't have much time," Amendal said. "Now, can you make an illusion of Fench?"

Ildin considered it. It was possible for illusionists to craft likenesses without having first copied the individual... *But it might take longer than we have—*

The beating of wings carried around the building, then Fench fluttered overhead, holding that rod of his. He dove toward Amendal, hovering beside him. *That's fortuitous,* Ildin thought.

"Perfect!" the conjurer cheered, then pointed to Jaekim. "That'll save us some time. Now haul Dugal over here."

<hr />

Amendal led his friends around the battle, moving in the direction he supposed Faelinia had been hurled. Though her imbuings on the swords had vanished, Amendal prayed she was still alive.

They stopped a grand phineal from the clearing, and Dugal began transmuting the ground. Amendal didn't want to take any chances, so he had the transmuter prepare a dozen spots. Unfortunately, that was rather taxing for poor Dugal.

While Ildin masked the ground, Amendal explained his plan to Fench. "I want you to lead him here." He pointed to the grass between him and the farthest spot of liquefied ground. "Can you do that?" Fench nodded. He didn't seem worried in the slightest that Amendal wanted to use him as bait. Perhaps that was because Amendal was risking himself as well. "And give me your rod."

He expected Fench to resist, but the winged creature willingly handed it over and explained how to use it. "I'll have Ildin and Dugal make a copy for you to hold."

Amendal reached out to his earthen giants to observe the battle. During their preparations another forty had been killed. Orath'issian, however, was not unscathed. They expedition had inflicted some harm, and the abrasion upon his neck was larger. *This better work...* he thought, hoping the codger would answer one way or the other. But he didn't. *Probably because he wants me to leave...*

"We're ready," Ildin called.

Amendal told his friends to replicate the Tuladine weapon, then rode his cisthyrn a few hundred phineals from the spot he had pointed out to Fench.

Turning back to the spot, Amendal hefted the rod, holding it up so he could look down it like a channeling staff.

Though he had never wielded a channeling staff, he had read plenty accounts of how they were used. As children, he and Arintil had often played games of make-believe and used branches as those fabled weapons.

Probably should practice, he thought, turning aside and aiming at a nearby Tuladine home. He pressed a small oval indent on the rod's end and a violet beam flew from the three-pronged tip. The magic struck the bark-like surface within a heartbeat, boring a hole through the building.

Odd that it works here, he thought, recalling how the weapon did not damage the shifting halls.

Putting the thought aside, he gauged the distance between him and the spot where he wanted Fench to fly to, then searched for a building an equal distance away.

There... He pressed the indent again, noting the time it took for the beam to strike.

Fench zipped away, and Amendal's friends concealed themselves under veils of invisibility. *Best I do the same.*

Whitish-blue particles surged around him and the cisthyrn, enveloping them in a veil of invisibility.

Time to move you, he thought, reaching out to the nearby yaeltis. It too was invisible, and Amendal willed it to climb a home behind him. Holding the transmuted blade in its mouth, the conjuration used those round openings to climb up the building.

As the yaeltis reached the top, Fench flew into the clearing. Amendal watched through his conjurations as the winged creature yelled to Orath'issian, demanding that he get out of his home.

The monster spun and bolted after Fench.

He took that rather easily, Amendal thought. *Perhaps too easily...* No, the monster had a single purpose, and catching Fench was central to it.

Soon, Fench flew between the buildings ahead of Amendal with Orath'issian bounding right behind him. No more than a heartbeat later, a dozen spires of earthen slush shot from the ground. But before they solidified, Orath'issian burst with orange light.

Amendal fought the urge to blink as the lightning zipped toward him. It struck the ground farther away than he expected, becoming that ball of orange light. Amendal took aim at the burly silhouette and instinctively recalculated the timing of his blast. *Now!* He fired a disintegrating beam. It sped toward the fading light as Orath'issian appeared.

Before the monster-turned-man could move, the violet magic struck Orath'issian's naked belly, eroding flesh and evoking a surprised growl. He staggered, and Amendal fired again and again. Orath'issian began to glow as the magic neared him. The beams were swallowed within the orange burst, and if they struck, Amendal could not tell.

The transformative lightning arced above Amendal and zipped past him.

Good, he thought, turning his cisthyrn.

Orath'issian burst once again, but farther away than Amendal expected. The monstrous silhouette staggered from the orange ball, a hundred phineals past the perched yaeltis. *He's too far,* Amendal thought. *I'll have to lure him back.* He dismissed his invisibility and readied his borrowed weapon.

"CLEVER…" Orath'issian bellowed, wobbling from the fading light. He turned about, undoubtedly looking for Fench. Amendal had lost track of him, too.

He'd begun firing the rod when a gray flash zipped from above. Fench fluttered past Amendal and toward the now advancing force.

Orath'issian ignored the blasts, fixed his gaze upon Fench, and lunged awkwardly. As he neared the perched conjuration, Amendal willed the yaeltis to jump. The invisible beast landed upon Orath'issian's back, slamming its transmuted weapon into the abrasion on the monster's neck. Though it was not imbued, the blade still pierced flesh.

Reeling, Orath'issian unleashed deafening screams. The monster staggered, and attempted to buck the yaeltis off, but Amendal willed the beast to grab one of Orath'issian's horns while holding tight to the transmuted sword.

The blade continued sinking through flesh as monster and conjuration neared. Orath'issian's tail whipped about, but instead of arcing for the yaeltis it sped toward Amendal.

Surprised, he reared the cisthyrn upon its hind legs and fell backward. Orath'issian's tail shattered the conjuration's barsion, impaling the cisthyrn. The dead conjuration was flung away before Amendal hit the ground.

The tail arced to strike again as the blade jerked in the yaeltis's grasp. It sank farther into Orath'issian's neck, and the monster jolted. His tail floundered as he tumbled forward. His screams ceased, and Orath'issian crashed into the ground.

The yaeltis, still invisible, leaned to twist the transmuted sword in Orath'issian's neck, but the blade didn't budge.

Amendal staggered to his feet and felt the monster twitching beneath the yaeltis. *Are you truly dead?* His friends gathered around, and Fench fluttered overhead. Soon, the rest of the expedition arrived, but halted upon seeing the twitching Orath'issian. The reanimated soldiers, however, climbed atop the convulsing monster.

"We did it!" Ildin shouted. "It's dead!"

More triumphant cries filled the air, but Amendal ignored them. He reached out to his last cisthyrn and willed it to him.

He dismissed the concealing veil around the yaeltis while commanding the elementals to surround the twitching monster. If Orath'issian wasn't dead, then he best keep the conjurations close.

Once the cisthyrn neared, Amendal climbed atop it, willing it into a gallop and shouting for Faelinia. He had to find her. He would rather rot in this miserable place than abandon her to it.

"But unlike a dragon, a gangolin is fairly unintelligent by comparison."

- From *Colvinar Vrium's Bestiary for Conjurers*, page 256

No longer shielded by barsion, Calimir dropped to his knees, exhausted from the battle with the monster. Others did the same, exhaling sighs of relief. Mister Aramien's shouts for Miss Tusara had faded as he moved away from the clearing. His tall conjurations stayed behind, standing around the now-dead monster. The yaeltis still had its sword in the monster's neck. Though it was dead, the monster twitched. Its tail bounced, and its limbs shook, while pale orange blood pooled beneath it.

Turning from the horrific sight, Calimir studied the survivors. Twenty-three soldiers and mercenaries were slumped on the ground between the tree-like buildings, some resting on their weapons, others on their knees. Among those slumping were Miraden and Hevasir. A dozen mages were also resting in the grass, but a few—the friends of Mister Aramien—were checking the survivors, accompanied by that winged creature.

Where is Dardel? Calimir wondered, eyeing each of the survivors. But his second-in-command was not present. "Oh, Dardel…" Calimir dropped his tevisral-weapon. Blade and flame vanished before the hilt landed on the grass.

I've lost too many, he lamented. They had left Soroth with three hundred men and women, and now not even a sixth remained. He must do all he could to see the rest to safety.

"Are you all right, Commander?"

Calimir looked at Mister Shival, the barsionist, and fought back a scowl. "I'm not wounded, if that's what you're wondering."

The barsionist nodded, and Calimir glanced back to the monster. *If only we had left sooner.* If it hadn't been for that Mindolarnian harlot, perhaps they could have departed before the monster arrived. "It's her fault..."

"Whose fault, sir?" Miraden asked.

Calimir turned toward the squad leader, who was standing beside Mister Shival. "Mistress Rudal," he replied, and reached for the weapon. It burst once again with flame, and the blade appeared as it had before. *That'll be troublesome to carry...*

"Speaking of Vaem," Morgidian said. "I lost control of the barsion binding her."

Miraden narrowed his eyes at the barsionist, then turned back to Calimir.

"It's fine," Calimir said, waving his hand in a dismissal. "She can rot in this prison." He glanced past Miraden, watching the soldiers and mercenaries now on their feet. "Get everyone back to the camp. We need to salvage anything we hadn't taken to the pit."

⊃•⊂

Amendal rode his cisthyrn around the Tuladine homes, shouting for Faelinia. He had ridden a considerable distance, but hadn't found her.

Though he continued shouting, he shifted his focus to his conjurations, which still stood around Orath'issian. The earthen giants held their weapons at the ready while the yaeltis kept its blade in the monster's neck. The monster had stopped convulsing, but Amendal didn't want to take any chances. Frustrated, he willed one of the earthen giants to kick the lifeless monster.

"Faelinia, where are you?!"

He continued weaving around the towering homes. How far had Orath'issian thrown her?

Through his conjurations he sensed the survivors stirring. The blades his conjurations wielded became dim, and then they lost cohesion, turning to piles of dirt that covered Orath'issian. He turned the yaeltis as Morgidian approached the conjurations.

"We're leaving, Amendal," the barsionist shouted, then related Old Cali's plan to return to camp and then head to the pit.

That still gives me time to find her, he thought.

Morgidian hurried away, and soon the conjurations were alone with the dead Orath'issian.

After he'd rounded several of the tree-like buildings, the fluttering of wings carried overhead. Fench descended in a dizzying dive, then zipped around Amendal. "You need to come with me," Fench said, his voice more nasally than usual.

"I haven't found her yet," Amendal said. "I have to find her!"

"But... bad things will happen!"

Amendal cocked his head at the winged creature, who kept pace with the cisthyrn. "What are you talking about? We're not in any danger."

Fench blinked several times before answering. "The wrinkly one will leave you behind."

"Then stay with me," Amendal said. "They others can't leave without you, right?"

"Yes, but..." Fench's trunk stiffened. "Scary things will happen if you don't leave now."

"What do you mean?" Amendal asked. *No*—the old codger had warned him of powerful forces converging upon Tardalim. But how would Fench know about that? And was it even true? Amendal squinted at Fench while raising his chin. "Did the codger speak to you? What did he say?"

Fench blinked again, looking unsure. "What is cod-jur?"

"An old man with a red robe," Amendal said, then shouted once more for Faelinia.

"The scary two-legs?" Fench asked. "Oh... he was scary. Made me feel sick. He showed me scary things. But he said they wouldn't happen if you left right now."

Amendal stopped his cisthyrn and turned to Fench. *Scary things?* Had the old man really visited Fench? "You saw him?"

Fench nodded, his trunk still stiff.

Sighing, Amendal looked about and shouted to the codger. "If you want me to leave, tell me where she is!"

He waited for a reply, but none came. *Figures...* Amendal grunted and willed his cisthyrn into a gallop. Fench kept pace beside him, muttering about the frightful scenes that would occur if they didn't flee at once.

As Amendal searched, one of Ildin's illusions descended and floated beside him. "We're headed to the pit," the illusion said. "I have your pack, and Calimir is determined to leave without you."

"I'm not leaving without her," Amendal said, and then shouted for Faelinia. "Besides, you need Fench to leave, and he's going to stay with me."

The winged creature trembled.

"He doesn't look so sure about that," Ildin said.

"We can't stay," Fench said. "Bad things will happen..."

The illusion's face tensed. "What bad things?"

Fench trembled, muttering incoherent babble.

"What's wrong with him?" Ildin asked.

"The scary two-legs," Fench said. "He... he..."

Amendal shook his head. "He's referring to the codger. Seems he's bothering Fench now." Ildin's illusion looked unsettled.

"I'll keep looking for her," Ildin said. "I can cover more ground than you, anyway. Just head to the pit."

Fench flew away, disappearing around one of the tree-like buildings.

Amendal grumbled to himself. *Damned codger...*

"It doesn't look like Fench will stay," Ildin said. "I don't think you want to be trapped in here. And I don't want to have to tell your parents that their son is stuck in Damnation."

LISTEN TO HIM, the codger's voice boomed. *LEAVE. NOW!*

Amendal sucked in his breath. No, he didn't want to be trapped in this place, but he couldn't abandon Faelinia… *If only I could conjure in here.*

"Let me guide you to the pit," Ildin said. "And I'll send some illusions to search for Faelinia."

Amendal shook his head. "I can find it with my conjurations." He willed the earthen giants and the yaeltis to run back toward the tower. With any luck he could catch up to the others at the camp.

"Fine," Ildin said. "But let me help you get the right heading."

"You're awfully stubborn." Sighing, Amendal turned his cisthyrn toward where Fench had disappeared. "Lead the way."

————•———

Scialas abruptly opened her eyes as pain spread through her entire body. She lay in a strange place, somewhere she didn't recognize. Before she could focus her eyes, she gasped for breath, but that only made the pain worse. *What happened?* she wondered. *Where am I…?* The pain clouded her thoughts as she tried recalling her most recent memory.

She had been on the tower, with Fendar.

A sharp pain radiated through her side. She had broken several bones.

I… I fell…?

A terrifying image came to her, the face of that horrendous creature—a dull ache permeated her back, and she suddenly felt cold.

Have… have to heal…

Closing her eyes, Scialas focused on accessing the Arpran Channel. She struggled to say the words, but only managed to mouth them. That wasn't enough. Starting over, she slowly exhaled the words to the incantation.

She felt the rejuvenating particles appear around her hands, and she willed them to her chest. Through her magic she sensed a shattered rib. She struggled to say the words to the incantation as the fragments of bone aligned. As they re-knit, she ran out of breath, and the magic faded.

Scialas fought against the pain and struggled to focus. As an arpranist she had been trained to muster her magic amid anguish, but she had never experienced it to this extent.

After a time, she once again reached for the Arpran Channel and exhaled the words. The arpran particles appeared, more abundantly than before. They penetrated her broken chest, where more ribs had been cracked and snapped. Luckily for her, none had pierced her lungs, or her heart.

Unfortunately, the magic faded before she could complete the spell. But she managed to recast the incantation.

Eventually, she mended the bones in her chest and the surrounding tissues. Now that she could breathe, Scialas glanced about the strange room. It was a maroon color with smooth walls and a rounded ceiling. The floor too felt curved. From what she could tell, it was the size of a large bed-room, but it was nothing of the sort. Strange-looking bowls—looking al-most like seats—protruded from the wall. Were those perches for Fench's people?

Perhaps I'm in one of those tree-things.

She tried to sit upright, but her back refused. A sudden surge of alertness swam through her, and she mustered more of her magic. Now that she could breathe, Scialas could maintain her incantations for much longer. The rejuvenating particles fused the bones of her back and mended the fleshy parts along her spine. Feeling returned throughout the lower parts of her body, and she screamed as sharp pains surged up her legs. Shattered bones dug through muscle, though none pierced her skin.

Breathing heavily, she pressed her head into the floor, gasping. Tears filled her eyes and soon trickled to her ears.

I must focus, she told herself and struggled to control her breathing. Con-centrating on accessing the Arpran Channel once again, she whispered the words to the rejuvenating incantation. The green light surged to her legs. She managed to repair the bones before succumbing to the pain.

She closed her eyes and tried focusing on the magic again, but her mind wandered. What had happened to Fendar? And what about the others? She strained her hearing, but all was silent. Had the Orath-monster killed them all?

Through her mind's eye she envisioned the dead sprawled across the clearing outside the Tuladines' tower.

No! she chided herself. *You can't think that way.*

Once again, she mustered her magic. After repeating the incantation sev-eral times she was made whole.

Scialas pushed herself upright and studied the room once again. A round opening was on the wall opposite those strange bowls, leading to the Roost. *I must have fallen through that,* she thought and wobbled to the opening. Though she had mended her body, her limbs felt as if they were asleep.

The opening was the same size as a door, large enough for her to fall in-side it. She braced herself upon the opening's edge and peered through it. Those strange tree-like buildings stood all around, and the Tuladine Tower rose in the distance. She looked down, gauging the distance to the Roost's grassy ground. *Over three stories,* she thought, swallowing hard. *Probably four...*

Scialas turned around, studying the room. Another hole, half the size of the opening where she stood, was along the far wall and led to a cylindrical tunnel. *A hallway?* She hurried toward it and peered inside. Other tunnels branched off it.

Hopefully, she could find a way down.

Unfortunately, she found that the tunnel-like hall led only to other rooms and halls. None descended, but several rooms had openings to the outside.

Standing at another opening, she stared at the ground below her. *I'll have to jump.* It was not the first time she had leapt from a staggering height. During her middle years at the Sorothian Magical Order, the arpranist masters had tasked Scialas and her cohorts with a peculiar exercise: jump off the roof of the Order's Record Hall while maintaining an arpran aura.

"This is almost twice that height," she whispered. Sucking in her breath, Scialas mustered her rejuvenating magic. She concentrated it on her legs, but left some lingering through her torso. After finishing the incantation, she stepped through the opening.

She gasped as wind rushed past her. The bones in her legs cracked as she landed, but mended as she fell forward. Her face met the teal blades as the arpran magic re-knit her bones and flesh. The aura faded as the pain vanished.

"Master Igasan would be proud," she said with a chuckle, pushing herself to her feet.

A familiar voice hailed her, and she spun to see an illusion of Ildin descend beside her, settling a phineal off the ground. "You're alive! We thought the worst…" Ildin's illusion set its jaw, his lips contorting with worry.

Had the battle been that bad? She turned from the illusion and looked about. "You haven't seen Fendar, have you?"

"No," Ildin said. "I've been looking for Faelinia. The monster hurled her away."

Scialas sucked in her breath and turned, looking back to the Tuladine Tower. *He was too my left*, she thought, recalling Fendar's position on the bridge. From where she stood now, he would be to her left somewhere.

"Can you help me find him?" she asked, hurrying around the building she had come from. "I think he's over here."

Ildin's illusion sped past Scialas, and she struggled to keep up with it. After rounding several of the tree-like buildings she stopped to reorient herself. It all looked the same. *It's like searching a maze*, she thought. "Where are you, Fendar…?"

The illusion disappeared around a building, but soon returned. "If only the monster hadn't destroyed the map," Ildin said, and his illusion sped upward.

Is that why it attacked the tower? She swallowed hard as the illusion descended, pointing over her shoulder.

"I think I see something over there."

Heart pounding, Scialas twirled and followed the illusion, zigzagging around the strange structures. Several buildings away lay a black-haired man in a gray robe, his face buried in the grass. Her eyes widened as she ran, screaming Fendar's name repeatedly.

But the man didn't move.

Though his face was buried in the grass, she knew it was Fendar. She fell to her knees beside him and turned him over. His eyes were frozen, his mouth agape. "No… oh, Fendar." She cried the words to an arpran incantation as tears streamed down her face. The green light formed and wisped into Fendar. But nothing happened.

The illusion settled beside her. "I'm sorry, Scialas." There was a long pause before Ildin spoke again. "The others are moving toward the pit. They're almost there, and Calimir is of no mind to wait for anyone."

Scialas wrapped her arms around Fendar's lifeless body, sobbing.

"I'm going to continue searching for Faelinia." The illusion rose, but Scialas could barely see him through her tears. "Hopefully I'll see you with the others."

Sobbing, Scialas held tight to the man who had long been her friend, and more recently, her lover. He was no Amendal Aramien, but he would have been a great partner in life.

Grass crunched nearby.

Startled, Scialas jerked her head toward the noise and gasped as Faelinia stumbled around a nearby building, her left hand attempting to steady herself against the bark-like wall. She called for Scialas in a strangled voice and wobbled, her left leg buckling.

Blinking her tears away, Scialas stood and hurried toward Faelinia. She couldn't lose another friend. Green light surged around Scialas as she uttered an arpran incantation.

Faelinia stepped away from the building and fell forward, clutching her abdomen. She landed face-first with a groan.

Panic struck Scialas's heart, and she ran faster. She finished her incantation as she knelt beside Faelinia, and the green light surged into her friend.

———◆———

Amendal's cisthyrn galloped along one of the rivers flowing toward the pit. When his conjurations had spotted it, he insisted that Ildin send his illusion to continue searching for Faelinia. The illusionist was reluctant, but after some persuasion, he complied.

The river wound around several tree-like buildings and then flowed into the large clearing with the pit at its heart. Many of the expedition's packs were still along the river's bank, but no one was there except Ildin and the three conjurations.

The illusionist stood two hundred phineals away, on the stone walkway that divided the pit from the river's perfectly shaped overflow. An earthen ramp spanned the two-dozen-phineal-wide ring of water, probably made by Dugal or some other transmuter.

Faster, Amendal urged the cisthyrn, and the beast sprinted. It was no yidoth, but riding it was better than running. Now that the battle was over, his feet were beginning to throb. *If only I had someone to rub my toes...*

The cisthyrn darted up the earthen ramp, but Amendal slowed it once it reached the walkway. The surface was barely wide enough for three men to walk abreast, and Amendal didn't want to fall.

"Fendar is dead," Ildin said as Amendal approached. The illusionist looked solemn, and tears brimmed in his sapphire eyes. He lifted the pack beside him and handed it to Amendal.

"And Scialas?" Amendal asked, slinging the pack over his shoulders.

"She's fine... I think she's still with Fendar's body. And I haven't found Faelinia..."

Amendal frowned and glanced to the pit, searching for the others. If the pit were a hole in the wall it would be at least eight stories tall. Its depth, however, was staggering. By his estimation, its floor was probably over a hundred and thirty stories below the Roost.

Well, not really below. From what he remembered of Tardalim's three-dimensional map the pit actually ascended. Directions like up and down could not be trusted while in Tardalim.

"We should go," Ildin said with a sigh. "I'll keep the illusions searching until we're ready to step outside. We have till the sailors arrive. They should be out of the treasury soon." He turned, walking toward a ramp along the pit's walls. It descended in a corkscrew, but Amendal couldn't see where it met the bottom. The others were across the pit, only a few stories below him and Ildin.

Best I dismount, he thought, and slid off the cisthyrn. The beast looked too big to descend the ramp. The other conjurations wouldn't fit, either. *Well, their barsions are still active.*

While hurrying after Ildin, Amendal willed the conjurations to the stone walkway. They were about to jump when Fench flew across the pit. The winged creature fluttered beside Amendal, keeping pace with him. He wore the oversized helmet and held a strange gray bag that was stuffed to over-flowing. It was partly closed, the disintegrating rod sticking out of it.

"You have to hurry!" Fench said, pushing his oversized helm above his eyes.

Amendal raised an eyebrow. "And you should stay close," he said, and sent one of the earthen giants over the edge. The rocky behemoth plummeted through the pit. When it reached the bottom, its barsion shattered, and so did its legs.

Amendal winced, but there was no pain, as there would be with bestial conjurations. "Well, that's not going to work..."

"Do you need more barsion?" Ildin asked.

"Probably several layers. Tell Morgi to be a good boy and protect my pretties."

The descent to the bottom of the pit took almost half an hour. Morgidian had covered the cisthyrn, the yaeltis, and the last remaining earthen giant in ten layers of barsion. Not wanting to succumb to any pain in case Morgidian's efforts failed, Amendal hurled the elemental into the pit to test the barsion. Each layer shattered, but the conjuration held together.

Still, Amendal thought it prudent that Morgidian cast a few more layers on the yaeltis and the cisthyrn. All but one of the yaeltis's barriers shattered while three held true around the ice-wolf.

"Seems you were right," Morgidian said as Amendal stepped off the ramp. "When did you become an expert in barsions?"

Amendal chuckled and patted his friend on the shoulder.

Old Cali was shouting orders for everyone to continue through a wide corridor. It was almost twice the width of Tardalim's other halls, and was barely longer than it was wide. The squat hall ended at a pair of doors identical to those in the room where they had sought refuge after fleeing the crystal halls.

Hopefully we won't need Vaem to open it... During their descent, Ildin had said they couldn't find her or Kydol at the camp. And Old Cali wasn't of a mind to chase after her.

Once the survivors neared the doors, the symbols upon them began to glow. Fench fluttered to the massive slabs, and they swung open, as if reacting to his presence.

If Amendal hadn't known any better, he would have thought he was looking at Tardalim's entrance. The exit chamber rose four stories and was as wide as it was tall, lined with ornate pillars. Two hundred phineals from the doors, a shallow but wide staircase led up to a semicircular space slightly wider than the room. Part of the semi-circle's floor was sunken, a perfect circle about the size of Tardalim's halls.

Once inside the exit chamber, the soldiers and mercenaries dropped the packs and sat against the walls while Fench flitted to Calimir. The old soldier marched up the shallow staircase and stopped short of the sunken floor. Amendal was quick to follow. He was not about to let anyone leave, not with Faelinia still missing. From what he could tell, that sunken floor was engraved with glowing symbols, all arrayed in a spiraling pattern. His friends followed after him, chatting about the chamber.

"Is that how we escape?" Dugal asked.

"Well, we did come in through the floor," Morgidian said. "It only makes sense, since going *up* takes us to the sphere's center."

Jaekim groaned and wobbled from Amendal and the others. "All these jumbled directions make my head hurt." The necromancer groaned again. "I need a drink."

Dugal gave Jaekim a sidelong glance. "When don't you need a drink?"

"When I'm sleeping..."

A faint hum filled the room as Fench touched the center of the sunken floor. Amendal ascended the steps just in time to see the etched symbols glow with myriad hues. Their colors shifted until all became white.

Amendal stopped beside the old soldier, but the man didn't look at him. "I want my crystal back."

Old Cali sighed and looked over his shoulder to the survivors. "I suppose that's not an unreasonable request." He tugged at the armor padding around his neck and pulled at a golden chain. "Here."

Amendal snatched the necklace as the sunken floor separated along the spiral patterns, quickly receding into what was now the walls of a deep shaft.

"It's open," Fench said, and fluttered toward Amendal and the old soldier.

"Good." Calimir spun to face the others and shouted orders for them to stand and leave.

"What about the sailors?" Ildin shouted. "Shouldn't we wait for them? They're just leaving the campsite."

"And Scialas is still out there," Morgidian said. "Are you going to leave her behind?"

Calimir studied the mages and set his jaw. With a scowl, he turned to Fench. "Do you have to open anything else?"

Fench nodded and pointed into the shaft. "We all have to move down there. But once we do, we can't come back."

Calimir grumbled and stepped to the edge. "You have until the sailors arrive. Then we're leaving this place." He sighed and stomped back down the shallows steps, moving toward Hevasir and another soldier from squad one.

Amendal, however, moved to the edge of the shaft. It was longer than the one connecting the crystal halls to Tardalim. Most of it was transparent, like glass. A white stone walkway, perhaps ten phineals wide, circled the shaft in a corkscrew pattern. Faint, pale-blue light ebbed and flowed outside the glass-like sections. His friends gathered around him, each peering into the shaft.

"I think I'm going to vomit..." Jaekim muttered and spun away.

Morgidian knelt beside the shaft's edge. "It's like a bridge. An odd one, though."

"Why do you think the path is a corkscrew?" Dugal asked.

The transmuter and barsionist speculated about the shaft while Amendal turned to Ildin. "Any sign of Faelinia?" The illusionist shook his head.

As Amendal turned back to the shaft a faint shout echoed into the exit chamber. He focused through the yaeltis and directed the beast's gaze upward. Two figures hurried along the edge of the pit, but he couldn't tell who they were. More shouts echoed down the pit as the figures darted to the ramp.

The other survivors stirred as Amendal descended the steps. "Do you hear that?" he asked Ildin. The illusion nodded and began uttering an incantation.

"Who is that?" Calimir demanded.

A small brown bird flew from Ildin and sped past the conjurations at the bottom of the pit. Amendal watched it climb, but before it reached the top Ildin shouted, "It's Scialas and Faelinia!"

"I do not suggest conjuring more than one gangolin at a time. The mental exertion necessary to maintain sufficient control is quite taxing. Couple this with other conjurations and you might find yourself fainting."

- From *Colvinar Vrium's Bestiary for Conjurers*, page 258

The women ran from the ramp and past Amendal's conjurations. Scialas's face was flushed, and her eyes were red. *Mourning Fendar*, Amendal thought. *Poor girl.* Once through the doors leading to Tardalim's exit, Scialas dropped to her knees. Faelinia, however, continued toward Amendal, grinning. But the expression wasn't one of longing or yearning... it was more of triumph.

Furrowing his brow, Amendal studied the valiant woman who had fought tirelessly against Orath'issian. Her clothing was unsoiled. Not one hair was out of place. *Maybe an illusion?* Amendal thought, then glanced to a pack slung over her left shoulder. It was rather small, not like the one she had brought with her. Then again, Faelinia hadn't had her pack when Amendal and Miraden had rescued her and the others.

"Why the solemn face?" Faelinia asked, stopping at the shallow steps. "Don't you want to kiss me?" She raised her chin and gave him a small smile. Her left hand rested on her hip, causing the pack to shift.

She's in a good mood.

"Where were you?" Ildin asked Faelinia. "I couldn't find you anywhere."

"In one of those trees," she said. "It seems the monster had perfect aim. He knocked Scialas into one as well."

He? Amendal raised an eyebrow. He hadn't recalled Faelinia referring to Orath'issian by anything other than "it."

Morgidian, now standing a few steps below Amendal, folded his arms.

"You sound rather chipper."

"Arpran magic has that effect," Faelinia said, then waved in dismissal. "I'm just glad to be leaving this wretched place."

Old Cali stepped around Faelinia, eyeing her up and down. "Where are the sailors?" he asked Ildin.

"They're almost to the ramp."

The old soldier nodded, then pushed past Amendal and the others. "Let's start heading down. You mages can stay and wait. Let's move!"

Amendal and his friends made way for the other survivors. One by one, soldier and mercenary followed Calimir to the shaft that was Tardalim's exit.

"How about that kiss?" Faelinia asked. She ascended the steps until she stood in front of Amendal. "Well?"

Amendal chuckled. "You're awfully eager."

Faelinia's eyes lost their vivacious gleam. She leaned close, raising her left hand to Amendal's face. By the look in her eye it seemed as if she were getting ready to slap him. "Just kiss me," she whispered. "Before I change my mind about you."

"Feisty," Amendal said, but quickly leaned toward her. Their lips met and locked in a passionate kiss. Faelinia ran her left hand through Amendal's hair, then left it beside his ear while easing back.

"I suppose that'll do." She studied Amendal, then stepped past him. Her hand trailed from his face, down his chest, and around his arm. "Don't keep me waiting," she said over her shoulder.

Amendal turned, watching her approach the shaft. The other survivors had already filed onto the stone path and looked as if they were walking on the shaft's walls. *What a bizarre sight—*

A faint roar echoed from the doors leading to the pit. Amendal spun, settling into a wide stance. Ildin, Morgidian, and Dugal looked at each other with worry. Scialas rose from the floor and stumbled toward them, her hand to her mouth.

"It can't be alive," Dugal said, shaking his head. "It died!"

Morgidian turned toward Amendal, but glanced past him. Was he looking at Faelinia? Amendal followed the barsionist's gaze. Faelinia stood at the edge of the shaft, looking back toward the doors. Her face was stern, almost stony. Perhaps she didn't fear Orath'issian. Fench fluttered beside her, his trunk and tail stiff.

"It's coming," Ildin said.

"We need to get out of here!" Jaekim screamed and stumbled past Amendal. He wobbled and bumped into Faelinia, but twirled around her and onto the stone path.

"Can the sailors make it?" Dugal asked.

Ildin sucked in his breath and faced the transmuter. "I... I don't know."

"A pity a barsion won't stop it," Faelinia said.

It...? Amendal furrowed his brow, and she shot him an expression that said, "What's wrong?"

"It has passed the tower," Ildin said. "I don't think we should wait here."

Scialas backed into the steps. She stumbled and began to fall but Morgidian caught her. Once on her feet, the arpranist hurried up the steps and past Faelinia.

"I'm not waiting," Dugal said, following Scialas.

Morgidian was the next up the steps. "We should move into the shaft. If the Orath-monster gets past the sailors, then we can at least get to safety."

"That's a good plan," Ildin said. "I doubt they'll make it." He hurried to Morgidian and they began moving down the stone path. Now, only Amendal, Fench, and Faelinia remained in the exit chamber. The roars grew louder.

Tiny hands grabbed Amendal's shoulder. "We can't wait," Fench squeaked. "We have to leave. *You* have to leave. Or bad things will happen."

LISTEN TO HIM, the codger's voice boomed in Amendal's mind. TAKE YOUR CONJURATIONS, AND LET THE SAILORS DIE.

Amendal frowned and turned back to the doors. He didn't like the idea of leaving them behind. What had they done to deserve such a fate? But if he stayed to help, the three conjurations couldn't fend off Orath'issian, not even if they were enhanced or protected by magic. *I could wait for them, at least.* If he stayed that would give them a chance. If he ran, he would certainly doom them.

He glanced to the shaft, recalling how he entered Tardalim's entrance. The center of the shaft was too far away, but a galloping cisthyrn could make that jump...

Another roar echoed through the doors, much louder than the last.

Fench gripped Amendal's robe and tried pulling him. His efforts barely made Amendal lean sideways.

"Don't want me to die, huh?"

The winged creature shook his head, his helmet wobbling while his trunk flailed.

"Come on, Amendal," Faelinia urged, turning to the corkscrew path. "We can't help them."

Sighing, Amendal glanced back through the doors. His friends called for him as he sent a command to his conjurations to come to him.

"It's near the clearing!" Ildin shouted, and an enraged scream echoed down the pit.

The earthen giant was the first through the doors, then the yaeltis. The cisthyrn galloped around them and up the stairs, stopping in front of Amendal. He mounted the beast and gripped its fur with one hand.

"Ildin, Morgi, you better make some room." His friends hurried down the corkscrew path as the earthen giant ascended the steps. The path wasn't wide enough for the hunk of rock, so Amendal made it shuffle sideways. He felt the strange reorientation of *down* as the conjuration followed the others along the corkscrew path.

Fench began to shake and grabbed Amendal's sleeve.

"Don't worry," Amendal said, reaching for Fench's helmet. He patted the strange headgear, causing it to shift on Fench's head. "I won't let him get you."

The yaeltis was next. Once it stepped onto the path, Ildin shouted frantically for Amendal to hurry.

"Hold on to me," Amendal told Fench, and the winged creature hugged his arm.

Both conjurations were safely inside the shaft when a flash of black appeared beyond the doors. Orath'issian crashed into the floor of the pit and rose to his feet, shaking as he steadied himself. He turned toward the doors, baring his obsidian teeth.

Go! Amendal commanded the cisthyrn. The beast leapt into the shaft's center, and as they fell, a low hum whirred above them as the sunken floor closed. They soon tumbled to the right and Fench fluttered away while Amendal rolled away from the cisthyrn. *Catch me,* he commanded the other conjurations, but he fell sideways onto the stone pathway before either could reach him. Sharp pain radiated across his arm, as well as the cisthyrn's side. But the pain through the conjuration was faint... recognizable but not debilitating.

Great, he thought. *Seems we both broke something...*

His friends called to him, and Amendal struggled to move. He willed the cisthyrn upright and felt something crack in its right forepaw.

"Are you hurt?" Scialas asked, kneeling beside Amendal. Morgidian and Ildin stood behind the arpranist, their faces worried.

"Probably the arm again," he said, gritting his teeth. "And my cisthyrn needs help."

While green light flowed around him, Amendal closed his eyes for a moment. *We made it,* he thought. Orath'issian was trapped... but so were the sailors.

Once the rejuvenating surge faded, Ildin helped Amendal to stand.

"You are mad," Morgidian said. "No sane person would have waited that long."

Ildin sucked in his breath. "You don't fear anything, do you?"

Amendal chuckled and pushed past his friends. From where he stood, the shaft was now a tunnel. The corkscrew path continued through it for quite a way, how far he couldn't tell. Soldiers ahead of him looked as if they were upside down while Faelinia and Dugal looked as if they were standing sideways.

"It's strange, isn't it?" Ildin asked.

Amendal grunted. "What about Tardalim isn't strange?" He glanced to the transparent parts of the tunnel. An enormous cavern lay beyond the glass-like substance; one side jagged rock the other smooth and curved. Blue light surged around the smooth part, occasionally bursting to the jagged side.

"So, that's what Tardalim looks like," Ildin said. "A white sphere…"

"Mm-hmm," Morgidian hummed in agreement. "A white sphere suspended in a cavern by barsion. Very impressive."

Eventually, the tunnel's transparent sides were swallowed up in the jagged rocks. The corkscrew path continued for another grand phineal, ending at another stone slab identical to the floor of the exit chamber. Amendal was among the last to join the others, many of whom were sitting on the tunnel's transparent sides.

Now that Amendal had arrived, Fench fluttered near the stone slab. Its etchings glowed with shifting hues until only white light shone from it. It receded like the other slab, but its opening was accompanied by a gust of frigid air.

Despite the cold, almost everyone ran through Tardalim's final threshold. They hurried along the path, which continued through the opening and became an abrupt curve downward. Everyone who darted down the curve looked as if they were falling flat on their faces.

Amendal soon followed and felt the strange reorientation of *down* as he descended that curve. The floor soon leveled, and he stepped onto a plain dais made of charcoal stone. *Such a bizarre feeling…* He stepped aside and turned around. The tunnel he had traversed was now a deep shaft, a large hole in the plain dais.

Shivering, Amendal dropped his pack and removed his sloglien coat from it. He welcomed its warmth as he shrugged it on and looked about. The dais sat within a large cavern, three—maybe even four—stories tall. Pale-blue crystal stalactites of varying sizes studded the cavern's ceiling. *No stalagmites on the floor. How odd…*

Shaking the thought aside, Amendal turned to his conjurations. It was time he returned them. He swiftly opened a portal to the Aldinal Plane, the words rolling off his tongue as quickly as the reclaiming incantation he'd uttered before the battle.

Golden light surged from his hands, coalescing nearby and erupting into an oval portal. It grew quickly, becoming fully formed in less than a quarter of the time it *should* have taken.

"Go back, my pretties." He patted the cisthyrn as it passed and watched it lope into the portal. The yaeltis followed, then the earthen giant. He dismissed the portal and turned to watch as the others exited the tunnel-turned-shaft and gathered not far from the dais.

Fench flew from the hole, and the receded door shut beneath him. Its surface was smooth on this side. In fact, Amendal couldn't tell where the door ended and the dais began. It was one solid chunk of stone. The dais's surface rippled, and then transformed into a mound of snow and ice.

The transformation drew hushed speculations, but they were soon cut short by Old Cali. "Everyone grab onto one another. Mister Aramien, take us home."

While the others linked arms and grabbed shoulders, Amendal searched for Fench. The winged creature fluttered around the cavern, intrigued by the stalactites. "Fench, come here!"

Turning in the air, Fench cocked his head. He dove toward the crowd and hovered beside one of the soldiers. "What?"

"Hold on to someone," Amendal said.

Fench blinked. "Why?"

"So we don't leave you behind," Miraden said. "We're returning home."

Fench stroked his trunk and looked around. "How?"

"Will someone grab him!" a soldier shouted.

Scialas waved for Fench to come near. He flew toward her and settled on her shoulder.

Now that everyone was touching, Amendal uttered the teleporting incantation. Golden light shone from beneath his robe. It grew in intensity and washed from him, engulfing his vision. He felt the magic surround everyone and then snap back toward the crystal in a rush.

The golden light subsided and Amendal felt himself falling. He blinked and hit something cold. But what would be so cold back in Soroth? A soldier landed on top of him, followed by another. Men and women vomited around him. The stench of their bile mingled with a peculiar scent, a blend of rotten eggs and citrus juice. *That smells like rogulin...* But how was that possible? That scent never followed a conjurer through a portal.

Confused, Amendal glanced to the ground. It was covered in dense ice. The soldier atop him rolled away, and Amendal pushed himself upright.

To his surprise, they were still in the cavern outside Tardalim's exit. In fact, they were standing exactly where they had been when the portal opened. *But the crystal was bound to Father—*

He glanced to his pack, then to the floor. They had fallen a comparable height. He unslung his pack and reached inside, shuffling the contents until he touched the black, domed. Amendal lifted it from the pack and held it close to his face. "It can't be..."

Was this a tevisral that could bind rogulin? If so, how had the binding happened? The tales of those strange anchors never told how they worked, only that they did. If his crystal was now bound to this anchor, then there was no way for them to return home.

"Only one way to know for sure." He tossed the shan'ak beyond the vomiting soldiers and mercenaries. Amendal began his teleporting incantation as the domed disk hit the frigid ground. It bounced once, then skidded to a halt.

"Mister Aramien!" Calimir shouted, wobbling to his feet. "What are you doing?"

Giving the old soldier a sidelong glance, Amendal finished his incantation. Old Cali swore vehemently as golden light engulfed Amendal's vision. The brilliance soon faded and Amendal found himself standing across the cavern, facing the rest of the survivors.

The cursing abruptly ceased, and Calimir turned to Amendal, his jaw slack. Horror spread across his wrinkled face and he wobbled backward, collapsing among the others still disoriented from the teleportation.

"Well, it looks like we're stranded," Amendal said and looked down. The black dome was resting perfectly between his boots. "And here I thought I'd be home in time to have my toes rubbed before bed."

"There are several tactics to employ when using a gangolin on the battlefield. The most obvious is to crush your foes, but the creature's horns are also valuable weapons. Their many tines are large enough to skewer several men back to back."

- From *Colvinar Vrium's Bestiary for Conjurers*, page 261

Only some of the expedition lamented their predicament. Amendal's friends took the news in stride. Ildin was still hopeful that the council would send a ship. And Fench was too busy admiring the icy cavern to care one way or the other. Amendal supposed he hadn't the faintest idea what their dilemma implied. After all, the winged creature had never left Tardalim.

Old Cali held a meeting with Fench, Miraden, and Bilanus; the latter two were the only squad leaders to survive the battle with Orath'issian.

While they discussed their course of action, Amendal and his friends surveyed the rest of the cave. *There has to be a way out,* he thought, stroking the anchoring tevisral inside his coat pocket. Fench claimed his kind had fled Tardalim through these caves. Surely, there was a way to the surface.

Three other chambers branched off from the one housing Tardalim's exit. Each was frozen over, its ground uneven. One, however, had a shallow slope along its far wall that wrapped behind several low-hanging stalactites.

Amendal peered up the shallow slope, but the ramp wrapped around a bend in the cavern.

"Why don't you take a look?" Dugal said to Ildin.

Faelinia snickered at the suggestion. "Afraid of a little adventure, Dugal?"

The transmuter rolled his eyes. "I've had enough adventure for one day."

Gray illusory particles gathered around Ildin, taking the form of a bird. Soon a gosset took shape and flew up the shallow grade, disappearing behind the stalactites.

"Why don't you search, too?" Dugal pointedly asked Faelinia.

She shook her head. "I think Ildin can manage. Besides, it's only one tunnel."

Her reply struck Amendal as odd. He resisted the urge to furrow his brow and followed after Ildin's illusion. Morgidian hurried beside him, and they climbed the shallow grade.

Once they were near the bend, Morgidian leaned close to Amendal. "Do you think Faelinia is acting strange?"

Amendal shrugged. "There are some... peculiar things she's said."

The barsionist glanced over his shoulder, undoubtedly gauging the distance between him and Faelinia. "I just hope we didn't let *it* out..."

"I was the last one through the floor..." But no sooner had those words left Amendal's lips than he begun to reconsider. *It can't be...* he thought. But Ildin had seen the monster darting through the Roost. And Orath'issian had plummeted through the pit.

Unless that wasn't Orath'issian...

"I see you're wondering now, too," Morgidian said.

The path narrowed after the bend and was barely wide enough for them to squeeze through. Morgidian was almost too burly to continue. Luckily, the path wasn't narrow for long. It opened into a two-story chamber overlooking an expansive cavern. Both spaces were covered in large crystallized plants that looked very much like those outside Tardalim's gatehouse. If either cavern had been warm, the warmth had been lost long ago.

The floor of the smaller chamber—what wasn't covered in crystal—was veiled in thin ice. An occasional spot of dark gray stone, flecked with dull brown specks, dotted the walls, the ceiling, and the floor.

"Doesn't seem as cold in here," Morgidian said.

Amendal nodded and stepped toward the larger cavern. The smaller chamber was the size of a large home, but it paled in comparison to the cavern it overlooked. Larger than four Soroth city blocks, it rose at least three stories above the smaller chamber while its floor was too far below to gauge. Enormous flowery plants—now crystallized—hung along the cavern's walls. Many had long vines that interconnected them.

Well, we're not going that way...

He searched for Ildin's illusion, but it wasn't anywhere in the enormous cavern.

"Over here," Morgidian called, and Amendal turned to find the barsionist beside a large crystallized plant. "I found another tunnel. And it looks like this one is wider than the last."

Amendal was almost to Morgidian when Fench flew from the narrow path. "They want to sleep," Fench said. "And eat."

Morgidian eased from the opening. "I suppose we should head back."

Fench shook his head, trunk flailing and helmet bobbing. "Ildin told Wrinkly Face about this place. They want to rest here."

Wrinkly—ah, Old Cali… Amendal grinned, nodding in approval.

⎯⎯⎯⎯▷•◁⎯⎯⎯⎯

Before long, the survivors erected what few tents they had brought with them. Several of the soldiers began preparing a cold meal while Dugal transmuted a large pot from the icy ground. His magic, however, didn't affect any of the crystal. *This substance really is impervious,* Amendal thought. *Now if only I could find a crysillac…*

Soldiers hacked at the ice surrounding the camp while Amendal and Fench investigated the tunnel Morgidian had found. Amendal had conjured a cisthyrn and was using the beast's nose to sniff for any creatures that might be lurking ahead of them. The tunnel's path meandered from right to left, but always ascended.

"This has to be the way," Amendal said. *IT IS,* the codger's voice boomed in his mind. *KEEP GOING.*

Fench began to tremble, and his trunk stiffened.

"Did you hear him, too?" Amendal asked.

The winged creature nodded, and Amendal stroked his beard. *He really wants us to leave—*

"Amendal," Ildin shouted, and Amendal turned to face his friend. "The food is ready, and Faelinia is making everyone some tea."

DON'T GO BACK, the voice warned. *LEAVE, NOW!*

Amendal shot a perturbed glance to the tunnel's ceiling and followed Ildin back to camp. All his friends, except for Faelinia, were between the tunnel and the ledge, sitting on crude benches transmuted by Dugal. Their seats gave them a view of the enormous cavern.

"…do you really think so?" Jaekim asked.

Morgidian gave the necromancer a sullen glare. "Why else would it attack the tower? That thing was smarter than we gave it credit for."

Amendal commanded his cisthyrn to rest while he sat down beside Scialas. Of all his friends, she looked the most despondent. She lifted her eyes to Amendal and attempted a weak smile, but she only managed to contort her lips in an awkward expression. Fench settled on her shoulder and moved his face to hers. The gesture drew a tear and a chuckle from the arpranist.

"I found the way out," Amendal said. "And the codger wants us to leave—"

YOU NEED TO LEAVE, the voice said with a tone of annoyance.

Amendal clenched his teeth. "I'm not leaving without my friends."

"He really is mad…" Dugal muttered, and Scialas kicked his boot. "What?!" Everyone looked at the transmuter. Dugal shook his head and stood. "Anyone else want tea?"

Morgidian nodded.

Jaekim jumped to his feet. "I'll come with you!" the necromancer said, stumbling after Dugal.

Once they left, Amendal cleared his throat. "As I was saying... the codg-er says we should leave."

"Did he say why?" Scialas asked. Morgidian set his jaw and glanced back to the camp.

Amendal shook his head. "He never does... He's frustrating like that. Crazy old man probably doesn't have *his* wits aright."

"I should scout ahead then," Ildin said and began uttering an incantation.

Morgidian rose from his bench and approached Amendal. Once near he leaned close. "What about Faelinia?"

Amendal folded his arms and reared back. *She's not the monster,* he thought. But what if she was? *No, it can't be.* If Orath'issian had somehow become Faelinia, then there would have been an orange flash somewhere in the Roost. At no time had Amendal seen a burst like that. Besides, hadn't Scialas used her magic on Faelinia? He abruptly turned toward the arpranist. "What was wrong with Faelinia when you healed her?"

Scialas squinted and looked about, as if puzzled. "I... I can't remember."

Morgidian stepped back, his eyes widening as if he had realized some-thing.

Another gosset soon formed beside Ildin, and it took to flight through the ascending tunnel.

"What do you mean?" Amendal asked.

Scialas parted her lips and brought a hand to her forehead. At that mo-ment, Dugal returned with Jaekim, each holding simple mugs. The old codger began yelling in Amendal's mind but he ignored the fool.

Faelinia rounded the nearby tent, moving straight for Amendal. "I saved the hottest for you," she said, parting her lips in a flirtatious manner. "Here you are." She handed the mug to Amendal.

But he didn't grab it. He was too busy debating the possibility that the woman in front of him was not Faelinia. Amid his thoughts, the codger's voice continued badgering him to leave.

Faelinia's expression hardened, and she turned from Amendal. "Fine, if you don't want it, I have a better idea of how to warm you." She extended the mug to Fench. "Here, why don't you have it?"

The winged creature took the mug in both hands and his trunk twitched. Was he sniffing it?

Jaekim handed Ildin a mug while Dugal held one out to Morgidian. But the barsionist didn't take it.

"Are you coming?" Faelinia asked, reaching for Amendal's gloved hand. Her touch was firm. *She must really want me...* he thought. *Or something from me.*

Jaekim snorted with mirth. "Now this is something I thought I'd never see." He burst into raucous laughter. "Who thought Amendal Aramien would ever hesitate to bed a beautiful woman!"

Dugal joined the jovial outburst while Ildin chuckled. Amendal cocked his head at his friends and rose to his feet. All but Morgidian were drinking the tea, though the barsionist finally accepted his mug. Fench, however, was still sniffing it. "It stinks," he said and dumped the mug's contents onto the ice.

"Come on," Faelinia urged, pulling Amendal from his friends. While she led him toward the nearest tent, he continued debating with himself. *She only held one mug,* he thought. *And that was with her left hand.* Since rejoining the survivors, she had done *everything* with her left hand.

Faelinia backed into the tent's door, cracking it enough for her hand to slip inside—her right hand.

Amendal blinked in disbelief and fought the urge to widen his eyes. He glanced back to Morgidian as Faelinia pulled him inside. The barsionist put the mug to his lips as Amendal stumbled into the tent. He tripped and landed on his side with Faelinia still holding him. Her grip lessened and Amendal shook his hand free.

"And here I thought you'd be more eager," Faelinia said with disappointment. "Perhaps I misjudged you…"

Pushing himself upright, Amendal chuckled and reached for her right hand, but his fingers passed through it, as if it were an illusion.

Orath'issian! A surge of fury exploded within Amendal. Had Orath'issian killed Faelinia, like he had Edara and that necromancer—?

Strangled gasps erupted outside the tent, followed by a hurried commotion.

"My… aren't you clever," Orath'issian said in Faelinia's voice.

Amendal jerked to his feet and sent a command to the cisthyrn. *Attack!*

The woman before him grinned and shook her head. "You should have taken the tea. Your death would have been far less painful." Her flirtatious grin became a snarl, and she reached into the pocket of her coat, removing a pale-blue knife—no, a translucent shard. Was it the tip of a fang? *Or a tusk…!*

She swung its tip at Amendal, but he threw himself sideways, and the cisthyrn lunged into the tent. The beast collided with the imposter, knocking her through the tent wall.

They tussled, and the fake woman tried to get away, but Amendal held tight with the conjuration's paws and rolled them across the ground. All the while, Orath'issian stabbed the beast repeatedly, but Amendal did not even flinch at the wounds. His fury doused the conjuration's pain, and he willed the cisthyrn to clamp its teeth upon her forearm. With little effort he managed to keep the beast's grip firm.

The strangled noises grew louder, and Amendal hurried out of the tent. He stumbled to a halt as his friends, all but Morgidian, held their stomachs. Their faces contorted in sickened expressions. *No…!*

Fench fluttered between each of them, looking confused and scared. Ildin dropped his mug and fell off the bench, his arms shaking. The others tumbled to the icy floor except Morgidian. The barsionist steadied himself, struggling to stay upright.

A pale-blue tusk. Strangled noises. Convulsing.

Yaeltis venom, Amendal thought. *In the tea...* But how had Orath'issian come by a yaeltis's tusk—? Ideas rushed to his mind, accompanied by flashes of memory. One image stood out among the others, of Edara in the crystal halls with his pack raised above the flood. *He didn't want the tusk to get wet...*

"That bastard captain," Amendal muttered and hurried to Ildin. The illusionist shook all over, more violently than before. He tried to speak, but only made strangled noises. Amendal grabbed his friend's quivering hand. Ildin's sapphire eyes struggled to focus, and his head wobbled.

Amendal would not let his friend die, not here. Not after all they had survived thus far. Amendal clenched his teeth. "Ildin, hang on—"

An enraged cry echoed throughout the camp, and Amendal felt his conjuration tumble over the edge. The imposter was still in its clutches.

"Wh-wha-what's ha-hap—" Morgidian dropped to his knees beside Amendal.

"Yaeltis poisoning," Amendal said, putting his other hand on Morgidian's shoulder. The barsionist trembled, but not as bad as the others.

THIS IS WHY YOU WERE SUPPOSED TO LEAVE, the codger's voice boomed in Amendal's head. THEIR DEATHS WERE INEVITABLE.

"I won't let them die," Amendal said with determination. But he had no tevisrals that could heal them, and Scialas was also succumbing to the venom. *The Visirm!*

Uttering the incantation to open a portal to the Visirm Expanse, Amendal leapt to his feet. An orange flash erupted within the larger cavern. His cisthyrn's vision was blinded, and it hit the ground, breaking its neck before the light faded.

"YOU TRY MY PATIENCE, AMENDAL!" Orath'issian shouted, his voice echoing off the crystal walls. But his voice was slightly different than before, with a deeper and a more guttural intonation.

Golden light surged from Amendal, gathering behind Morgidian. The forming portal reached halfway to the chamber's ceiling and burst with a flash.

"Get yourself through the portal," Amendal said to the barsionist. "I promise, I'll find a way to save you." Morgidian tried to nod, and crawled away. He fell beside Dugal and grabbed the transmuter with shaking hands.

A loud swooshing reverberated through the adjoining cavern, repeating over and over.

Ignoring the noise, Amendal turned back to Ildin and uttered another incantation. If he were to save his friends, he would need help. Besides, if he were touching his friends when they met the portal, he too would be sucked into the Visirm Expanse. Golden light swirled from his hands as he dragged Ildin across the frigid ground. A portal soon formed near Scialas, and a humanoid form appeared within the light.

An earthen elemental emerged just as Amendal brought Ildin to the portal. Morgidian dragged both Jaekim and Dugal, but stumbled and fell forward. The barsionist pushed himself upright and reached for his friends, pulling them once again. *He really is heroic,* Amendal thought, and then commanded the elemental to grab Scialas.

Uttering another incantation, Amendal hurried around the tents. The soldiers and mercenaries were convulsing on the icy ground, some foaming at the mouth. Those nearest him were Miraden and Hevasir.

Another portal formed beside him as the swooshing ceased. An orange flash erupted beyond the tents and vibrant lightning surged from the larger cavern. It demolished tents and struck the ground between convulsing soldiers, exploding in another flash. Within the light was the silhouette of a brawny man pushing himself off the ground.

The second earthen elemental emerged as the orange light faded.

Grab them, Amendal commanded the conjuration, glancing to Miraden and Hevasir. At that moment he sensed Scialas enter the Visirm Expanse, and then Morgidian, Dugal, and Jaekim.

Sucking in his breath, Amendal turned back to the now-human Orath'issian. He looked as he had during the battle, and wore a face that did not belong to anyone from the expedition: he had a chiseled chin, thin lips, and a short nose, all framed by blonde hair. The monster-turned-man knelt beside Calimir, reaching across the old soldier.

Amendal backed away and reached out to the first elemental. It was lifting Ildin to the portal.

"This will end you…" Orath'issian stood, and flame burst from an ornate hilt in his left hand, his eyes alight with unquenchable hatred. "I will enjoy gutting you!" he shouted, charging across the convulsing men and women—

A purple beam shot from above Amendal, striking the ground in front of Orath'issian. It was followed by another and another, forcing the monster-turned-man to evade. But the blasts also killed a mercenary and maimed a soldier.

"I'm not scared of you!" Fench cried. "Not anymore!"

Amendal spun. The winged creature hovered in the air, firing his rod-like weapon.

Ildin entered the Visirm Expanse, and Amendal shifted his focus to the first conjuration, willing it toward Orath'issian. The monster-turned-man dashed around the convulsing soldiers, skirting the camp's edge. More of Fench's blasts maimed and killed those in Orath'issian's wake.

The first elemental bounded through a broken tent, moving directly toward Orath'issian. *Grab him,* Amendal commanded, and then uttered another incantation. Golden light swirled in front of him. It coalesced as the monster and elemental clashed. Orath'issian lunged, swinging his stolen blade. The flame sliced through the earthen body. Amendal tried to grab the monster-turned-man, but the elemental fell in three pieces.

Orath'issian spun, evading more of Fench's disintegrating blasts.

The portal in front of Amendal formed and another normal-sized earth-en elemental emerged. Amendal willed the conjuration into a run, charging it toward Orath'issian. *I'll get you this time.*

"It's futile, Amendal!" Orath'issian lunged, raising the flaming blade.

Amendal made the conjuration crouch, just managing to grab his foe's sword arm at the wrist. Before Orath'issian could pull back, the elemental reached for the creature's neck, lifting him off the ground. It held Orath'issian in the air and bounded over the broken elemental, running toward the ledge.

Enraged, Orath'issian yelled and kicked the elemental with unnatural strength. The blow sent them spinning. They tumbled across the ground, stopping short of the ledge. Fench fired a blast that skimmed Orath'issian's foot.

In that moment, Miraden entered the Visirm Expanse, followed by Hevasir.

Amendal turned the conjuration from the portal and sent it charging. *Hurl him over the ledge!* While it ran, Amendal began another incantation.

The elemental grappling with Orath'issian was kicked repeatedly. One of its arms cracked. The earthen limb came lose as the second conjuration tackled Orath'issian. The blow ripped him from the now-maimed conjuration and sent both elemental and monster over the ledge. All the while, Fench chased after them, firing his weapon.

Monster and conjuration tussled in the air as another portal formed and a fourth earthen elemental emerged. Amendal commanded the new creature to grab those still alive, then willed the maimed conjuration to do the same. But those two would not be enough. While Amendal summoned another elemental, a burst of orange light washed from the adjoining cavern.

Amendal no longer felt Orath'issian through his conjuration. The elemental hit the crystallized ground, but was soon pinned by a tremendous weight.

"PERHAPS I SHOULD COLLAPSE THIS CAVERN UPON YOU," Orath'issian bellowed, pressing harder on the conjuration's back. The force cracked the elemental. Orath'issian pressed harder and the conjuration shattered.

Fluttering at the ledge, Fench began yelling and firing his rod. An enraged cry echoed from the massive cavern, and an orange flash reflected off the crystal walls.

Another elemental emerged from a portal as Old Cali entered the Visirm Expanse. Two others were thrown in after the old soldier. *That's ten,* Amendal thought, surveying the camp. Four soldiers that had been foaming at the mouth lay still. Seven were partially disintegrated and would not survive their wounds. That left only thirteen he could save. At least his friends were safe... well, as safe as he was now. But if Orath'issian managed to kill him, then his friends would be banished to the Visirm Expanse for eternity.

And then, there was Faelinia.

Thinking of what Orath'issian had done to her evoked a rage like he had never felt before. *I'll kill him. Rip him limb from limb...* He played out the act with his hands. But he had killed Orath'issian before... Would he stay dead this time? *I'll give him a fate worse than death,* he thought with a smile, recalling the punishment for breaking his family's Oath: banishment to the Visirm Expanse.

While the conjurations grabbed five more of Orath'issian's victims, Fench ceased firing. "He's gone!"

"Where?"

"Down a toon-nel."

Amendal glanced back to the tunnel he had searched. But he didn't recall seeing any other passageways connecting to it.

"What do we do now?" Fench asked.

"We get out of here," Amendal said. "And when Orath'issian follows, I'll have a surprise waiting for him." He *would* tear Orath'issian limb from limb, and he knew exactly how to do it. Even in that monstrous form, Orath'issian could not withstand the might of a gangolin.

"I discovered the most bizarre tactic in a fictional tale: In The Legacy of Asirum Tandir, a conjurer unleashed four gangolins amid a battle. But she severed her bond to the beasts, allowing them to tear through friend and foe alike. Releasing the gangolins freed her mind to conjure other creatures. I can only recommend this tactic if you follow the Taidactin Code, as your gangolins could become lost forever."

- From *Colvinar Vrium's Bestiary for Conjurers*, page 262

Now riding atop a cisthyrn, Amendal hurried through the winding tunnel leading to the surface. Fench flew beside him, keeping pace with the conjuration. Patches of glowing crystal lined the tunnel, giving off just enough light to navigate by. Other passageways branched off, the farther they went, but Amendal held his course. The codger had said it was the correct way, after all.

During their ascent, Amendal secured the last convulsing survivor inside the Visirm Expanse. But he did not close the portal. *We're going to need supplies,* he thought, and commanded the three earthen elementals to gather what provisions had not been destroyed, as well as Amendal's pack and Fench's belongings.

"Mother's helmet!" Fench cried, and began to turn back. But Amendal grabbed the creature's tiny arm and held tight.

"There's no time. My conjurations can get it."

Fench blinked several times before nodding and resuming his flight ahead.

Once the conjurations gathered everything, they pulled a large piece of canvas from a broken tent. They bundled the supplies and belongings inside it, tied its end, and threw it into the portal.

Now the tevisrals... Amendal was not returning home empty-handed. Besides, perhaps something had been found that could save his friends.

The conjurations turned from the portal as a flash of orange burst within the large cavern. Orange lightning arced up, curving toward the ledge. Orath'issian appeared from a ball of light, falling toward the ruined camp. He tumbled onto the frigid ground, recovered the flaming weapon, and charged.

Grab the packs, Amendal commanded a conjuration, holding tight to his mount's white fur. The others he willed toward Orath'issian. They struggled to subdue their foe, and the monster-turned-man cut one to pieces.

The other did not survive for long, soon shattered by a kick from Orath'issian. How had he that much strength as a man? He had never seen anyone, even enhanced by magic, exude such strength, let alone shatter an earthen elemental.

He redirected his focus to the last conjuration. It was only a dozen phineals from the portal when it was thrust sideways. The conjuration hit the crystallized wall and dropped one of the packs. Before it could recover, Orath'issian impaled the conjuration with his sword through its chest.

"You underestimate me, Amendal. I am no stranger to this form. As a man, many have fallen to me. And so will you." He crushed the conjuration's head, severing Amendal's bond with it.

I hope the surface is close… Amendal dismissed his portal and focused ahead.

They rounded the next bend, and the tunnel dimmed. The crystal patches eventually vanished, and Amendal's eyes struggled to adjust to the darkness.

"Can you see?" he asked Fench, slowing the cisthyrn to a trot.

"Yes… Can't you?"

Sighing, Amendal closed his eyes and focused through the cisthyrn. Though it was dark, Amendal could make out the tunnel walls with the conjuration's eyes. "That's better," he said, spurring the cisthyrn to a pace equal with a horse's canter. He glanced over his shoulder, but there was no way to tell if Orath'issian was near.

The lack of light gave him an idea. He uttered an incantation, and the golden light lit the cave. He guided the magic to form a tiny portal near the tunnel's ceiling, and a seracius lepidor flittered from the mystical doorway. He made it hang from the tunnel's ceiling and uttered another incantation.

Amendal repeated the process over and over, spacing the conjurations three dozen phineals apart. While uttering his seventeenth incantation they rounded a bend and the tunnel brightened.

He cut the incantation short and opened his eyes. Faint sunlight reflected off the tunnel's gray walls. "We're almost there!"

"How can you tell…?"

Amendal raised an eyebrow at Fench. *That's right; he's never seen the sun.*

The tunnel turned once more, then straightened. A brilliant clear blue sky lay beyond the tunnel's mouth.

He whooped and uttered an incantation, invoking the Taidactin Code so that he could open a portal to both the Aldinal Plane and the Visirm Expanse.

The cisthyrn bounded through the tunnel's opening and tumbled onto a steep slope covered in fresh snow. To Amendal's surprise, they were high up the mountainside. But how far he did not know. He continued uttering his incantation but the cisthyrn lost its footing. The beast fell forward, hurling Amendal from its back.

He hit a layer of fresh powder and tumbled over his shoulder, rolling on his side. Fench fluttered overhead, squealing for Amendal.

Struggling to maintain his incantation, Amendal rolled down the mountainside. He sensed the cisthyrn nearing, and he redirected his focus to the conjuration.

Dig! he commanded, slamming the cisthyrn's claws through the powder in hopes of grabbing packed snow—

The conjuration hit him, completely interrupting the incantation. The magic faded as they tumbled together. The cisthyrn's weight forced Amendal face-first into the powder. He struggled to break free, but continued rolling with the conjuration. All the while, Fench continued shouting after him. He was panicked, unsure how to help.

He can blast a hole, Amendal thought. "Fench, fire at the slope"—snow flew into his mouth and jumbled his words—"Ahead of me!"

"What's a *slope?*"

Amendal grumbled, then shouted once he rolled from the snow. "Just aim at the"—his face hit snow again—"the ground ahead of me!"

Flashes of purple surged by, and Amendal tumbled past a large hole in the slope. *What bad aim...* he thought, and something rumbled beneath the snow. His face was forced into the slope again, but as he rolled over the cisthyrn he was abruptly separated from the conjuration.

The jolt sent him into the air, and the cisthyrn became lodged in the hole Fench had made. Amendal fell sideways and jerked at the waist before hitting the powder. He landed on his back and slid at an angle with his feet *mostly* pointed down.

"That's better!" He leaned to straighten himself. Now that he wasn't tumbling anymore, he gauged his speed. It felt slightly faster than a jog but not quite a sprint. *Perhaps it's not as steep as I thought...*

"You're free!" Fench shouted, zipping beside Amendal. "Now what?"

"We continue setting the trap," Amendal said, and took in his surroundings with a sweeping glance. They were quite high up the mountain. Snowy plains spread in each direction as far as he could see. To his right, a wide gorge cut through the icy lands. He fixed its location in his mind, then looked down the mountainside.

The slope's bottom was at least two, maybe even three, grand phineals away, leveling off at a plateau surrounded by rocky protrusions. Another slope continued beyond the plateau, but Amendal couldn't tell how far it descended nor what lay beyond it. He glanced back up the mountainside, but the cave was no longer visible. He reached out to the seracius lepidors, but Orath'issian was not near any of them.

I hope I have time, he thought. If not, he would have to find some cover. He called to Fench, eased onto his hip, and reached into his pocket. With shan'ak in hand he reeled onto his back. "Take it! Find a flat spot below—"

Rhythmic pounding echoed in Amendal's mind, through his bond with the first seracius lepidor.

"Far below!" he pointed down the slope. "He's coming!"

Fench zipped away and Amendal began the incantation to summon a gangolin. Golden light surged down the slope, gathering at the snowy plateau. The portal began to coalesce as Amendal sensed a blurred figure passing beneath his tiny conjuration.

The portal grew at an incredible rate, forming before Amendal reached the slope and Orath'issian escaped the tunnel. It rose eight stories and was two-thirds that height wide. *Hurry!* he commanded. A towering reptilian silhouette nearly filled the golden doorway. Gleaming white talons emerged from the portal, heralding a beige, scaled claw sparsely covered in off-white hairs. The claw barely touched the frozen ground and the off-white hairs stood on end while pain surged up the massive forelimb.

"Hurry, damn it!" Amendal shouted and willed the conjuration from the portal. It resisted, but he easily overpowered it. He had thought the struggle would be more intense, as well as the stinging from the cold. But neither affected him as they should...

As Amendal steadied the gangolin's first claw, the snowpack around the colossal limb cracked. The slope shook and a deep thud resonated up the mountainside. Behind Amendal, Orath'issian darted past the last conjuration in the tunnel.

A second claw emerged, followed by the gangolin's massive serpentine muzzle. The gangolin's snout was covered in the same beige scales as its claws. In contrast to the draconic reliefs Amendal had seen—and every other depiction of a dragon he was aware of—its snout was much wider. He supposed the gangolin's snout was half as long as a dragon's and twice as wide. Its eyes were a light tan, with diamond-shaped pupils.

Two white horns protruded from the gangolin's skull, curving behind the creature's head and curling back toward its lower jaw. Glistening tines—the length of a man's leg—lined both horns and reflected the sun. Between the horns stood a maroon mane with hairs taller than a man; it ran down the gangolin's emerging neck and continued down the conjuration's back. Its body was broad and muscular with a torso as thick as four stories were tall.

The slope shook again as the gangolin lumbered from the portal. More deep thuds resonated within the mountain while the snow across the plateau broke apart under the gangolin's immense weight. The slope also cracked and a thunderous roar surrounded Amendal, drowning out every other noise. He began to slide much faster. Slabs of snow and ice heaved upward around him while loose powder was thrown into the air. He felt the cisthyrn come loose and tumble down the mountainside. It too was surrounded by an upheaval of snow.

"Fench better have found a spot…" The gangolin's hind legs and stubby tail emerged, and Amendal shut the portal, swiftly uttering his teleporting incantation.

He was almost finished when a burst of orange flashed from behind. Clouds of powder began to cover the sky, but they did not hide the orange lightning streaking overhead.

The lightning exploded with a blinding burst more brilliant than any other time Orath'issian had transformed.

A wall of snow fell upon Amendal as the teleporting light engulfed him. Within a heartbeat, he found himself sitting upon solid ground. He fought back a wave of nausea while sensing the torrent of snow descending upon the gangolin. It swept the conjuration off its feet as Amendal's vision returned.

Far overhead, the enormous ball of orange light lessened, revealing the silhouette of Orath'issian's new form. He now had an enormous sinuous body held aloft by two gigantic beating wings. He stretched four legs wide while his tail whipped about. His neck reared back, pointing his thin but elegant snout skyward.

Amendal blinked in disbelief. "It can't be—"

Orath'issian unleashed an immense roar that shook the ground. The light around him vanished, and he dove toward the plain. He was covered in vibrant orange scales with an underbelly and wing-membranes that were dull amber. The black horns behind his skull were made of a substance that seemed to absorb light. Each of the talons upon his feet and the tips of his wings looked the same as the horns. Three pointed fins protruded from his tail, each tipped with similar talons. And as with every other form he had taken, his entire right forefoot was missing.

Shocked, Amendal struggled to stand. "A… a… dragon… an *actual* dragon!" Was that really Orath'issian's true nature? His debilitating gaze and his ability to change shape were both traits many legends attributed to dragons.

Orath'issian twirled before hitting the ground, redirecting his flight no more than one hundred phineals from the plain. He flew away from the mountain in a wide arc, his beating wings kicking up a trail of snow in his wake. "WHERE ARE YOU, AMENDAL?!"

Hearing his name dispelled his shock. Amendal hurried toward a large rock between him and the dragon, barely managing to take cover as a shadow veiled the ground. A gust of wind forced him to his knees while the rapid beating of wings roared overhead. Orath'issian soared past, his winged shape stark against the blue sky.

Amendal blinked and took in his surroundings. Ahead of him lay the shan'ak atop a slanted rock. That rock was surrounded by rough boulders and icy mounds. The mountain towered to his right, partly obscured by the massive cloud of upended snow.

Fench, however, was not around.

Pain filled Amendal's mind, a debilitating hurt shared through the bond with the gangolin. His conjuration tumbled down the mountainside within a dense cloud of snow and ice. He also felt the cisthyrn beneath the torrential avalanche, but most of the beast's body had been broken.

Amendal focused completely on the gangolin and struggled to regain its footing. He managed to rear its head from the cloud. Orath'issian soared over the gorge, approaching the mountain at an incredible speed.

"I SEE YOU'VE CONJURED ME A PLAYTHING!" Orath'issian flapped his wings and dove toward the mountain. The frigid torrent from his passage swept the gangolin under, but Amendal felt a tremendous force strike the conjuration's side. The gangolin tumbled from the avalanche as a five-taloned foot grabbed its neck. Orath'issian appeared from the snowy cloud, his violet eyes glaring at the gangolin with vehemence.

Amendal willed the gangolin to grab Orath'issian's left forefoot, and together they tumbled across the mountainside. As their tussle disturbed more packed snow, Amendal moved back toward the slanted rock and watched in awe as the colossal creatures started more avalanches in their wake. He glanced to the rock and picked up the shan'ak. "I should probably move you."

—————⊃•⊂—————

Fench pressed himself against a large gray rock. It was a little cool to the touch, as was the white stuff his tail was coiled upon. Amendal had called it snow. *Weird stuff—*

Loud honking noises, deafening growls, and constant rumbles echoed from the mountain. Fench flinched, pressing harder against the rock. Though he was scared, he glanced toward the noises, but he couldn't see anything through the white clouds. *So scary—*

A white bird flew past Fench's hiding place, holding something round and black in its beak. He turned to follow it, and then a weighty sigh carried around the rock, followed by Amendal muttering, "... but I suppose I'll sacrifice them if I have to..."

What did he mean?

Curious, Fench slid his way around the rock while the two-legs said those strange words to make his magic flow. Amendal stood upon slanted ground, golden light swirling from his hands and gathering atop the nearby snow. It formed an oval shape that stretched and pulled sideways and upwards. What had Amendal called it? "Poor...taahl," he whispered. He mouthed the strange word again, watching a streak of gray magic mingle with the golden light. It grew really big and a huge two-legged shape appeared within it.

One of those tall white furry things stepped out of the light. "Yell... tisk?" he muttered. It thumped loudly as it walked away, kicking up snow. A loud honk echoed from the mountain, this time closer than before.

Fench blinked, watching another big two-legged shape appear in the light. Amendal said weird words so fast Fench couldn't understand them. A second surge of gray magic mixed with the portal. Green hands with six fingers tipped in black were the first things to leave the light.

Fench squealed and reeled behind the rock, his trunk stiffening. More deafening roars and honking noises made Fench shudder.

Amendal called for him, but Fench didn't answer. "Is that you, Fench?"

He didn't reply, but stroked his trunk in hopes of soothing himself. All the while, Amendal continued repeating those strange words. Crunching noises mingled with footsteps, but Fench didn't dare look to see who they belonged to, at least not until his trunk was limp.

Once calm, Fench peered back around the rock. Three of those cis-somethings Amendal had ridden stood beside the giant two-legged monsters. The big green one had loose skin on its stomach. *Yucky*... Fench shuddered. A fourth cis-something lumbered from the portal while Amendal crept around the rock.

"Ah! There you are, Fench!" The two-legs smiled and held a hand out. "Come with me."

Reluctant, Fench fluttered over the rock and perched atop Amendal's shoulder.

"I have something important for you to do," Amendal said. "But first, let me free the rest of these conjurations." Another honking noise filled the air, and Amendal turned toward the mountain. "Seems I'll need more than one gangolin."

Though he did not relish the idea of losing his precious creatures, Amendal knew it was the only way to ensure victory. With their Aldinal copies trapped in Tardalim, there was no other alternative to conjuring them.

The last of the quinta'shals emerged from the portal, and Amendal shut the mystical doorway. He sensed the cisthyrn upon the mountainside in a precarious situation: buried in snow and suffocating. The gangolin was also in an unfortunate state. Orath'issian had pummeled it repeatedly and had driven the conjuration toward the plain.

He would rescue the cisthyrn first. If he let it die, his bond with it would be severed, and then sending it back to the Aldinal Plane would prove difficult.

He mustered his magic, and it wove around the nearby rocks and up the various slopes. Orath'issian would undoubtedly see the magic if Amendal arced it through the air. And that would give away his position.

The gangolin tumbled off a small rise in the foothills and rolled onto the plain. Orath'issian took to flight, then rammed the conjuration.

Why isn't he using magic? Dragons were supposed to be the masters of magic. Before he could think on it further, his portal began to form near the wounded cisthyrn. The conjuration gasped, and Amendal felt a faint burning in his lungs from its bond. But unexpectedly, he didn't stagger from the pain. As he marveled, the portal formed. The burning vanished as the cisthyrn was sucked through the portal.

Orath'issian rammed the gangolin again, but Amendal willed the conjuration to grab the dragon's hind legs, and its weight made the dragon falter. They soon crashed into the foothills, and Orath'issian retaliated with a flurry of blows that pushed the gangolin back onto the snowy plain.

Amendal commanded the gangolin to fight back while he uttered another incantation. A portal soon formed, and the other yaeltis emerged. With another incantation, the cisthyrn he had just rescued stepped from the portal. The wolf-like creature was renewed, as the damage done to its copied body was erased upon returning to the Aldinal Plane.

Steadying himself on the rock, Amendal pointed to the quinta'shals. "Fench, I want you to shoot them with your rod until they're glowing."

Fench blinked several times. "Won't it kill them?"

Amendal shook his head.

"What about the others?" asked Fench.

Good point... He willed the other conjurations to take defensive positions around him. The yaeltis flanked him, and the cisthyrn surrounded them. "There," he said, pointing once again to the quinta'shals. "Now you don't have to worry. The quinta'shals will absorb and store the magic."

While Fench fired at the enthralled creatures, Amendal opened another portal to conjure a gangolin. The magic surged behind him, its golden light reflecting off the snow and rocks.

Soon, a massive off-white claw moved overhead. As with the first conjuration, the second gangolin did not want to step onto the snow. Amendal willed it from the portal, and the creature begrudgingly complied. It was more stubborn about the snow than the first.

Just move!

The gangolin soon emerged, stepping over Amendal and his small army, who all easily fit beneath the gangolin's belly. The ground shook as it lumbered across the plain to the battle. Orath'issian had knocked off many of the first gangolin's scales, but he hadn't managed to crack any bones.

"Let's see if two will be enough," Amendal muttered. He sent the second gangolin charging to the battle. The ground shook violently while thunderous rumbling echoed across the plain. The noises alerted Orath'issian and he spun from the conjuration.

"SO, THAT'S WHERE YOU'VE BEEN HIDING." The dragon kicked the gangolin away and soared into the sky.

Pull back! Amendal commanded, then urged the first gangolin to hurry to him. Both gangolins complied as Orath'issian sped across the plain, a wall of snow trailing behind him. The dragon neared the protecting gangolin, but abruptly flew skyward. He arced in a tight corkscrew pattern, then plummeted straight for Amendal and the enthralled creatures.

Fench squealed and flew away. Amendal, however, held his ground, watching Orath'issian descend while focusing his will through the nearby gangolin.

"TIME TO DIE, BEASTCALLER—!"

The gangolin leapt overhead, tackling Orath'issian. They tumbled across the rocky ground, demolishing boulders and mounds. Fountains of snow flew into the air, partly obscuring the colossal creatures. They rolled across the rocky ground toward the gorge.

Amendal recalled Ildin's observations that the black layer had dispelled his magic. Would it do the same to the conjuration? *Best not let it fall,* he thought and struggled to stop the tumbling. The first gangolin charged past Amendal, shaking the ground. It soon neared the scuffle as both dragon and conjuration halted. They wrestled on the ground, and Amendal clawed at Orath'issian while grabbing the dragon's maimed arm.

The first gangolin lunged, landing atop Orath'issian. The conjuration's body pushed one of the wings toward the dragon's head, preventing it from flapping. Amendal wrapped the second gangolin's arms around Orath'issian's torso, but that didn't stop the dragon from moving. Orath'issian reared back and smacked the conjuration with his tail. The movement jolted the gangolin grabbing his arm, but Amendal willed the conjuration to hold tight.

Two is not enough, he thought and closed his eyes. *Hold him,* he commanded. *Whatever you do, do not let go!*

The gangolins howled as Amendal began the incantation to summon a third. He wondered if his concentration would wane. But despite all the creatures and conjurations he controlled, he barely felt any mental strain.

Orath'issian had nearly dragged his foes to the gorge's edge when the third gangolin emerged.

To Amendal's surprise, he could focus through all three gangolins without too much strain. He sent the third gangolin running, with the quinta'shals and the cisthyrns as escorts. The ground shook, and the enthralled creatures stumbled.

The third gangolin neared the melee as Orath'issian swung himself and the conjuration toward the gorge. Amendal dug both gangolins' hind legs into the rocky ledge. They all stopped short of falling, but a talon of the gangolin at the ledge hung over the precipice.

"IT'S FUTILE, AMENDAL." Orath'issian leaned toward the gorge. Another talon slid off the edge and the ledge began to crack. "JUST GIVE UP—"

The third gangolin grabbed Orath'issian's tail and pulled with all its might.

"YOU INSOLENT MEN'THAK!"

While Orath'issian's tail was held, Amendal focused on grabbing the wing closest to the first gangolin. They slowly pulled the dragon from the ledge, but Orath'issian burst with orange light.

No! He no longer felt the dragon through the conjurations, and the gangolin at the ledge stumbled toward the gorge.

Orange lightning surged past the advancing quinta'shals and cisthyrns, while the gangolin at the ledge stumbled. The lightning struck the snowy plain half a grand phineal from Amendal, and Orath'issian's monstrous silhouette appeared within a ball of light.

Orath'issian—now that black monster—charged from the fading light while Amendal willed the two gangolins to grab their falling sibling. But neither gangolin was fast enough.

The colossal beast fell into the gorge.

Amendal blinked once but swiftly uttered his teleporting incantation. His heart pounded as Orath'issian neared, misting that orange haze. The dragon-turned-monster came within arm's reach as the golden light enveloped Amendal. That mist also surrounded him, and some of it seeped into the teleporting magic.

The light faded and Amendal gasped. Flecks of orange floated in front of him, gently falling to the rocky ground. He stepped back, bumping into a jagged rock wall. The gosset had dropped the anchoring tevisral into a shallow crevice between the halves of a large rock about four grand phineals up the mountainside.

He was drawn back to the battle as he felt Orath'issian attack both yaeltis and the troll. The maddening mist engulfed all three.

Meanwhile, he sensed the gangolin plummeting through the gorge. The colossal conjuration fell into abysmal blackness, then hit something hard and began to break apart. In less than a heartbeat, the gangolin was reduced to nothing.

When such a disintegrating blast struck a conjuration, Amendal should have been brought to his knees. Instead, he merely shuddered and commanded the gangolins to attack while focusing on the three conjurations near Orath'issian. The troll and both yaeltis succumbed to the mist. Orath'issian impaled the troll with his tail while grabbing the nearest yaeltis. The monster ripped the tusk from the beast.

Faster! He spurred the gangolins, then aimed the quinta'shals hands at Orath'issian. Amendal unleashed their stored magic while focusing on the other yaeltis. He willed it to attack, and though its response was not effortless, making it move was still easier than when the beast had succumbed to the mist in Tardalim.

The yaeltis threw a punch, but Orath'issian deflected the furry wrist with one of his rear arms.

"IT'S POINTLESS," Orath'issian bellowed. "YOU CANNOT DEFEAT A GOD."

The yaeltis swung again, and the violet beams struck Orath'issian's back. Yelling, the monster spun and kicked the yaeltis away, only to face the two charging gangolins.

Amendal redirected his focus through his colossal conjurations. In his monstrous form, Orath'issian was only half their size. *Now I can tear him apart,* he thought, eyeing the monster's middle and rear arms. If he ripped them off, would Orath'issian lack wings as a dragon?

Orath'issian reared onto his hind legs, partly surrounded by that orange mist. He barely reached the gangolin's snouts.

One gangolin collided with Orath'issian, knocking him into the rocks. The other rounded the tussle. That orange haze wisped up to the gangolin's snout, but no terror accompanied it. The mist simply tingled the colossal creature's nostrils.

Well then, he thought, *weak against cold but immune to insanity!* He cackled while grabbing Orath'issian's rearmost left arm, squeezing with all the gangolin's might. The dragon-turned-monster thrashed but couldn't break free.

With his foe subdued, Amendal raced the other gangolin forward. It grabbed both of the middle and rear right arms and pulled. Both gangolin's reared back, lifting Orath'issian into the air. Loud cracks and pops were accented by a bellowing scream and a resounding snap. Amendal felt the break along Orath'issian's middle right forearm.

The dragon-turned-monster began to glow with that transforming light as his bent forearm was ripped from its elbow.

Lightning zipped above the gangolins, bursting high above them. But the severed arm remained in the gangolin's grasp.

Amendal tossed the limb aside as Orath'issian transformed in the air. The winged silhouette was misshapen, missing part of the right wing while the left was bent awkwardly.

The light faded and Orath'issian tried flapping his wings, but he floundered in the air. He bellowed words Amendal did not understand, except one he had said before, "men'thak." The dragon managed to hold out his wings and glide in a circle over the snowy battlefield.

"So that's the draconic tongue, huh?" Amendal took in a deep breath, glancing to the gosset resting beside him. "Go take that somewhere else." He pointed to the anchoring tevisral. The bird obeyed, and Amendal willed it to fly low.

He looked back to the sky, watching Orath'issian circle over the distant plains. The dragon shouted for Amendal, but he ignored the taunt.

Now where is Fench...?

A disappointed sigh carried over his shoulder and Amendal spun, snow crunching beneath him. The old codger sat on a squat boulder, his wrinkled face twisted in annoyance. "You're pushing your luck, Amendal."

He narrowed his eyes at the codger and snorted. "I doubt he'll be able to fly after that. Even if I have to teleport a few more times, it won't matter. I'll rip him apart, and then banish him forever!"

The codger raised an eyebrow. "Your little corner of the Visirm Expanse is not as secure as you think."

Amendal turned and walked away. The old fool obviously didn't know the workings of that plane. Only a conjurer knew exactly where he placed his things or creatures. One would have to—he flinched and his eyes went wide. "Read one's mind…"

"Yes," the codger said. "Do you think Orath'issian is the only dragon on this world? If another searched your mind, it could release him."

The comment made Amendal reconsider his plan. But how else was he going to defeat Orath'issian? And how would another dragon even know that Amendal had captured—? *Those powerful forces the codger had warned about…*

"Are they dragons?" he asked, glancing to the codger. "The forces you claimed are coming?"

The wrinkled lips twisted into an amused grin. "If you wish to survive, you need to fool Orath'issian into thinking you've been killed. That is the only way you can escape this wasteland. And you *must* escape. There are more important things for you to accomplish than exacting revenge for Faelinia and your friends. Find Fench and depart quickly. They'll be here soon." And then the codger vanished.

The mention of Faelinia made his entire body tremble with fury. Amid his rage he sensed Orath'issian landing upon the snowy plain.

"I'll make you pay dearly." Even if those *forces* were coming, he still had two gangolins left to conjure. They could tear Orath'issian apart, and then he would hurl the pieces of the wretched dragon into the Visirm Expanse.

Uttering an incantation to summon his next gangolin, Amendal climbed out of the crevice. The portal soon formed over the rocky foothills, and Amendal sent his enthralled creatures charging. Another melee broke out between Orath'issian and Amendal's forces. They soon subdued him, but the dragon transformed to free himself. He zipped between a gangolin's legs and became his human self, but not for long.

That's clever, Amendal thought and the fourth gangolin emerged. It hurried toward the battle as Orath'issian returned to his draconic form. The melee continued, and Fench popped up from a nearby rock.

"I'm glad you weren't too far away," Amendal said.

"The scary two-legs came back." Fench's voice was shaky, and his arms trembled. Amendal nodded but didn't speak until the portal formed.

"I know. He told me to leave. But I have to avenge *her* first."

Fench fluttered toward Amendal and perched upon his shoulder.

Before summoning the last gangolin, Amendal focused on the gosset. If he found a secluded spot—a cavity in the gorge wall, or a deep cleft in the mountain—he could retreat there once all his creatures were conjured. *And then I can send the gosset out again.* He nodded. Even if that "powerful force" appeared before he could finish, none would find him.

The fifth gangolin stepped from the portal, and Amendal felt a weight in his mind, but not so much that he became overwhelmed. *Perhaps I can conjure all five after all.* He sat, crossed his legs, and closed his eyes. He repeated the incantation, and the portal formed, but the gangolin he had lost did not emerge. *Perhaps the blackness wasn't a dispel*—

Orath'issian transformed, streaking between the legs of the advancing gangolin. Before Amendal could sense what form he had taken, Orath'issian transformed again. Amendal willed his conjurations toward him as the dragon charged up the foothills. They stopped Orath'issian less than a grand phineal away, repulsing him across the mountainside. The bout knocked several scales from the dragon's neck.

"Well, if I can't have all five, how about some gargantuans…"

A portal to the Aldinal Plane soon formed, but before the colossal conjuration emerged the gosset passed a narrow ledge leading to a small cave. It was large enough for two men to fit inside. *In there,* he commanded. As the bird circled, a shimmering white line appeared over the far horizon, on the other side of the mountain.

That can't be a cloud, Amendal thought, and willed the new elemental to the battle.

The gosset dropped the shan'ak inside the cave, and Amendal willed the bird to fly back across the gorge. That shimmering line was growing wider every passing moment. It was as if a string of white metal was waving through the air.

YOU'RE RUNNING OUT OF TIME, the codger boomed in Amendal's mind. THEY'RE COMING.

Orath'issian struck a blow that repulsed a gangolin. His tail swatted a cisthyrn, hurling it toward the gorge. The beast flew an incredible distance, landing near the ledge. Amendal tried stopping the cisthyrn, but it kept rolling until it fell into abysmal blackness and Amendal's bond to it vanished.

The gosset circled again as the shimmering line grew. Its top oscillated, rising and falling, but in no distinct pattern.

A gangolin grabbed Orath'issian's tail and another the maimed wing. They pulled while another grabbed Orath'issian's horns.

Orath'issian transformed again, breaking free. All the while, Amendal circled the gosset once more. The shimmering white line became individual shapes, each glistening.

Dragons… The thought of facing more dragons felt daunting. He was already struggling to kill one. How could he face—well, however many there were? Would they attack him as Orath'issian had? And what would they do to him if they didn't? Terrible scenarios whirled through his head. He saw no way to salvage his conjurations and escape unharmed. Besides, the yaeltis he had released from the Visirm Expanse had gone mad from Orath'issian's mist.

BRING THE FIGHT TO YOU, the codger urged. AND MOVE CLOSER TO THE GORGE.

Orath'issian returned to his draconic form as Amendal looked skyward. "Why?" Displeasure rumbled in his head. *You're so manipulative,* Amendal thought.

Fench flew from Amendal, zipping toward the gorge. Uttering another incantation, Amendal shook his head and ran after Fench. If he wanted to get Orath'issian's attention, it would be with a portal. As he finished the incantation, golden light coalesced above the rocky foothills, a few hundred phineals from the gorge.

Now to get there in time, Amendal thought. He ran toward the magic, still watching the battle.

Orath'issian soon caught sight of the magic and transformed once again. He became a man, then a dragon, and galloped toward the forming portal. "YOU CAN'T HOPE TO WIN!"

Amendal rounded the portal as the new gargantuan emerged. Within a heartbeat, Orath'issian darted past the portal, but the conjuration tackled the dragon, whirling him about. The blow sent Orath'issian's tail whipping through the air and toward Amendal.

He sucked in his breath as one of Orath'issian's tail fins struck him. The blow made him gasp, hurling him in a wide arc through the air. Fench fluttered after him, but Amendal plummeted to the gorge.

The snowy plains disappeared and Amendal struggled for breath. He fell into the gorge, struggling to utter the teleporting incantation. Fench caught his hand and reared back. But his attempt to halt Amendal's fall was futile.

Golden light surged around his hands as he fell into the blackness. No sooner had darkness consumed his vision than the teleporting light surged around him. He felt the magic surround Fench, then snap back to the crystal.

As the magic faded, Amendal landed upon hard ground. He blinked, finding himself in the cave. He immediately dismissed the bond to all but one of the gangolins. Through the last conjuration, he watched as the creatures roamed aimlessly across the mountainside while the gangolins succumbed to the cold.

"WHAT'S THIS...?" Orath'issian bellowed with amusement. "DID I KILL YOU, AMENDAL?"

Ignoring the question, Amendal willed the gangolin to mimic the others.

Fench fluttered from his shoulder and picked up the shan'ak. "I'm sorry..."

"For what?" Amendal asked, guiding the gosset to him. The bird flew inside the cave and opened its beak. "Put it in." He mustered a veil of invisibility as Fench dropped the shan'ak into the gosset's mouth. The bird flew away and disappeared.

"For... for breaking it," Fench said, and pointed out of the cave. "I was playing with them." Amendal raised an eyebrow, but jolted as Orath'issian cracked one of the gangolin's horns. Fench coiled on the ground. "You could have been home now if I hadn't broken it."

So Fench is responsible for pairing the shan'ak and the rogulin crystal. Drawing his lips to a line, Amendal knelt beside Fench. "Perhaps it's for the best. If you hadn't bound the crystal, then this battle would be occurring at my home.

And Orath'issian has destroyed enough homes today." He patted Fench's shoulder.

"You're not mad at me?" Fench asked.

Amendal shook his head. He focused through the gosset, which was already across the gorge. *I have to find a safe place.* But there hadn't been much on the plains besides snowdrifts. He considered the mouth of the crystal cavern, but quickly dismissed it as unsafe. If these dragons were indeed intent on entering Tardalim, they would do so through those caverns. "Perhaps the codger was right. We should have left sooner."

The faint beating of many wings carried into the cave.

Through the last conjuration, Amendal watched Orath'issian repulse an earthen gargantuan. The conjuration tumbled down the foothills, and Amendal turned his last remaining gangolin to look skyward. That line of dragons now stretched beyond either side of the towering mountain. Each was a glistening white. The noise of their wings reached the battlefield, and Orath'issian spun toward the mountain.

"WHAT IS THIS...?" He backed away from the gargantuan while swatting a cisthyrn with his tail. "SO," he growled at the oncoming horde, "YOU'RE NOT EXTINCT, AS THE HUMANS SUPPOSED."

The dragons cleared the mountain peak and erupted in brilliant white flashes. Their transformation blinded the last conjuration. If they descended as lightning, Amendal couldn't tell. A resounding crash, louder than thunder, shook the foothills, followed by a shocked cry of anguish. Amendal thought he saw the silhouette of Orath'issian tumbling backward.

He forced the gangolin to blink, and the light lessened.

Orath'issian had fallen.

The orange dragon lay on the rocky foothills, his head tilted toward the gangolin. The dragon must have rolled over, because his head was upright.

An armored man—clad in white form-fitting plates—drew a long, curved blade from Orath'issian's forehead. He flicked the blade free of the dragon's blood, then brought it to his waist. To Amendal's surprise, the blade transformed, becoming a simple wooden rod hovering alongside the armor.

Strange words—like incomplete incantations—roared across the foothills. Hundreds of armored men and women, each glowing with a wide array of colored light, surrounded the roaming conjurations and creatures.

"Those can't be incantations..."

He feigned confusion, and jerked the gangolin's head skyward. But the dragons were gone.

Magic formed all across the foothills. Waves of blue light shot to Orath'issian, completely enveloping him. *Inverted barsions,* Amendal thought. Golden light shot into the sky and portals formed parallel to the ground. Brilliant white tendrils shot from the portals, gripping each of the creatures and conjurations.

DISMISS YOUR BOND!

Amendal obeyed as the tendrils whisked the creatures and conjurations from the snowy ground. He shifted his focus to his gosset, and turned the bird. He could barely see the enormous portals hanging in the air. Soon, the vague shapes of gargantuans and gangolins rose in the air, then disappeared. Tiny figures fell from the portals, but were slowed from a fatal descent by gray light. Had those been the enthralled creatures?

White bursts flashed across the mountainside, obscuring the gosset's vision. The light also washed into the cave, and Amendal shielded his eyes. Wings beat outside, and he blinked against the light. His gosset's vision was blurred, so he moved to the cave's mouth, but could not see the foothills where the battle had taken place.

The beating of wings grew louder, and Amendal pulled back into the cave. Once his gosset's vision returned, he redirected it. The conjuration soon flew over a familiar valley between drifts. Amendal cocked the gosset's head but didn't alter its course as he had before. A large cave mouth was housed in the snowdrift behind the bird.

The entrance to the caverns... he thought, willing his gosset to continue flying. Sighing, he settled beside Fench. The winged creature clutched his rod to his chest while looking at the cave's floor. He sniffled and a tear trickled down his trunk.

"It'll be all right." Amendal caught the tear before it dripped to Fench's lips. "I'll make sure you're cared for."

Fench leaned close, burying his trunk in Amendal's coat.

"We'll make it home," Amendal said, wrapping his arm around Fench's wings. "And when we do, I'll have our chef serve every kind of cheese we own. Just for you."

Fench nodded and began to whimper. Amendal held the winged creature close and stroked the fins on the back of his head.

VEER IT TO THE RIGHT, the codger said.

Amendal complied without question.

The codger had been right all along. But if Amendal had listened to every instruction, his friends would truly be gone. *This is a better outcome,* he thought. *At least now they have a chance.*

More flashes burst outside the cave, followed by a tumultuous beating of wings. Amendal tightened his grip around Fench as dragon after dragon flew across the gorge at a tremendous speed.

Had that been all of them—?

DIVE!

Amendal immediately sent the command to the gosset. The bird plummeted into the snow, but not before Amendal glimpsed a small opening within the snowdrift. Best they teleport inside it.

He willed the gosset out of the snow and walked it to the opening. Hollowed with packed snow and ice, the opening was large enough for a man to crawl through. A narrow bend led to a small grotto made of ice. It had no adjoining tunnels or passageways. If it was a den, it had been abandoned long ago.

"Fench, hold on to me." Amendal uttered the teleporting incantation, and the golden light flowed from his hands. The magic soon enveloped the cave, whisking them from the lone mountain of Tardalim.

THE END OF
Part Four

Orath'issian awoke from death and struggled to move, but barsions pinned him in place. *Wretched pla'shas…* He growled, and the noise bounced off the barrier closest to him. *If only I were not cursed.* Had he been free to access the Channels of Power, he would not be in this predicament. Amendal would have fallen within Tardalim, at their first encounter.

Unfortunately, the only semblance of strength Orath'issian had retained was his immortality, and the supernal endowment he had received from his Master—the ability to become a dreaded qaun'tasiran and evoke irrational terror. But that had not been enough to subdue his foes. True, it had been a favorite form of his during the many battles against the rebellious pla'shas and their allies. He had been nigh unstoppable. But then, he'd also had the freedom to manifest the Channels of Power.

If only I can break this barsion, he thought, and attempted to transform. But something held him in his true form. If only he could free himself, he could utilize his divine gift and send these pla'shas into a delusional frenzy.

As he struggled, four of the wretched pla'shas—in the form of men—approached with determined gaits. Two had fanisars hoisted upon their backs, while the others bore no visible weapons. One of them had used Zinerath to deliver a deathblow. Though Orath'issian had felt the blade's sting only once before, its bite was unmistakable. But no, Zinerath's wielder could not be the same pla'sha he had once faced on the plains of Vesikar.

That wretch would have to be over eight thousand years old, if Heleron were correct. He'd had no opportunity to probe the minds of any Tuladine besides the child's, so he couldn't know for certain of time's true passing. The humans he encountered—even those who had freed him—had no recollection of the war to subdue the rebellious pla'shas and their allies.

We've slumbered into oblivion. He and the other divinities sealed within that miserable sphere had faded into nothing more than myth. Orath'issian supposed few men knew his name or the divine station appointed to him by his Master.

That enraged him. The world needed to know the powers that governed their existence. *The renown of Terror will spread once again—*

The four fools stepped close. One, who wore a metallic mask and was girded in the armor of an Aridian, removed a black sphere from a pack. The sphere was about the size of a man's head and filled with glistening specks that resembled the myriad of stars to which Kalda belonged.

Another, who wore the white, scaled armor of what the pla'shas called the Ulk'sha, took the sphere, and parts of his armor liquified. The scaled plating around his right hand and forearm receded, revealing the words of the Divine Tongue etched into his flesh. The words spiraled around his forearm, woven in seven strands—

An external will entered Orath'issian's mind, the probing of that wretched pla'sha. Images and memories flashed in his mind, extending from when he was freed from his cell to his battle with Amendal Aramien.

The probing faded, and the pla'sha held the black sphere aloft. It began to glow white, while the symbols etched into the pla'sha's flesh became glistening gold. But the words rose from his skin, reforming in the air.

That cannot be an incantation, Orath'issian thought. Perhaps the sphere was a tevisral of some kind.

The other three stepped away as the sphere began to glow. One burst with white light and took his true form, but the Aridian armored fellow and the other ran. Perhaps they were not sha'kalda.

Flakes of snow lifted from the ground as a shimmer washed from the pla'sha holding the black sphere. The white light surged skyward, as did the distortion. More snow shot upward, as if pulled by some powerful force. Soon, both Orath'issian and the armored pla'sha with the sphere rose from the snowy plain, but he could not feel the rising sensation—a true barsion negated such forces.

Once in the air Orath'issian spun, but not of his own volition. He glimpsed the frigid plain for a moment, and then everything changed.

The imprisoning barsion vanished, and scorching heat washed across his scales. In that same instant, the sky changed. What was once blue was now pale tan. A tremendous force pushed him downward, and he tried flapping his wings, but the force was too great and he soon hit unstable ground. Heat pierced his scales while—was that sand washing over him?

But how was that possible? He couldn't have traveled through a portal. And there were no deserts on Kalda. *At least not during Cheserith's reign...* He and the Master had changed the entire world, making it more habitable for mankind.

Orath'issian struggled to stand as a burning wind assailed him, pushing him downward. It howled past him, hurling sand across nearby dunes. "What is this place?!" The wind forced him into the sand, but his snout remained atop a dune.

"Another world," a deep voice said. "Your very own realm of exile."

Struggling to rise, Orath'issian managed to turn his head toward the voice. It came from that despicable pla'sha, who stood atop a dune's crest, holding the black sphere under one arm. The wind did not seem to affect him in the slightest. In his other hand he held an orange shard.

"Enjoy your new prison." The pla'sha-turned-human held up the shard and leapt skyward with ease.

The ground beneath Orath'issian gave way, and he tumbled sideways. The jolt turned him in a way that allowed him to watch the pla'sha speed through a shimmering sky and toward an enormous sphere rimmed in white light. The sphere spanned at least a grand phineal in diameter, and within it was a distorted view of a snowy plain and a lone mountain set against the backdrop of a clear blue sky.

Tardalim—?

The pla'sha hit the sphere, then appeared upon the landscape within it. The sphere's surface rippled, and then it collapsed upon itself. The oppressive force pinning Orath'issian vanished, and the wind lessened. But instead of blowing down it blew across the dunes.

Now able to stand, Orath'issian climbed atop the shifting dune and looked about. Winds howled across dunes that spread as far as he could see. A vibrant red sun hung above the distant horizon.

Another world…? Orath'issian knew such realms existed, but the means to traverse the stars was not something his Master had revealed, neither to him nor to the other gods. *So, how could those wretches accomplish such a feat?*

"They had help."

Orath'issian knew that voice. He spun, kicking up sand. Wind howled past a tall, masculine human figure in a red robe. His face was obscured by the blowing sand, but his white hair hung to his shoulders and he looked to have a full white beard. The Emblems of Divinity were woven into the robe, all seven. "It has been some time, Orath'issian." The wind settled, and the sand dropped.

Though the newcomer's face was wrinkled, Orath'issian recognized him. "Cheserith… is that you?"

The robed man chuckled, and his sapphire eyes flashed with amusement.

Had Cheserith been hurled to this desolate place as well? But why had he aged—?

Sand blew *through* the robed man.

"The Visage…" Orath'issian muttered. He bowed, lowering his arms so his neck and snout lay upon the sand. "Forgive me, my Master."

The Visage grinned and stepped soundlessly across the dune. "Your reverence is not necessary, Orath'issian. And no, Cheserith is not trapped on this desolate rock." He glanced back across the darkening horizon. "His prison is far from this world."

Curiosity crept into Orath'issian's mind as he lifted his snout. What could have toppled the Cheserithean Empire? Heleron hadn't said what he learned from the Tuladine. The men who had freed them had feared something called the Crimson Eye. But their interpretation of it baffled Orath'issian.

"That is not something that concerns you," the Visage said as he eyed the wounds Orath'issian had sustained. "It seems Amendal was quite formidable."

He knew of the conjurer—? *Of course he knew,* Orath'issian chided himself.

"And a good thing he was," said the Visage. "He is important."

Orath'issian raised his scaled brow. "But isn't he dead?"

The Visage laughed, his mirth becoming somehow ominous.

"Oh," Orath'issian said. "You intervened. But why did you not do so sooner? I nearly killed him, on several occasions. He and I could have escaped together, and I would not be trapped here!"

The Visage quelled his laughter. "You are where you need to be, Orath'issian. Besides, if you had relented, then Amendal would not be what he needs to be, and he would not be hidden from those platinum beasts. Any deviation from that would throw everything into disarray. The Unspoken One cannot rise without Amendal or his prowess, nor can Cheserith return."

"I do not understand," Orath'issian said.

Amused, the Visage related a prophecy given by Cheserith after Orath'issian's imprisonment. It told of a man who would wield his power without the use of incantation. Orath'issian was incredulous. Although many of the gods had been endowed with the ability to manifest the Channels of Power without words, could a man be blessed with such prowess?

That can only lead to folly...

"I assure you it won't," said the Visage. "This one, the Unspoken One, is the Harbinger of Hemran'na." Orath'issian shuddered at the mention of his Master's sacred name. "He will usher in the reign of Kalda's true God, and Amendal Aramien will be beside him. He is a boon companion to the Harbinger, upon whom he will rely during his most troubling trials."

Orath'issian turned away. The sun was setting, and the heat began to dissipate. Though he was immortal, the scorching heat was still irksome. *How long will I remain in this prison?*

"Until after the Advent of the Unspoken One," the Visage replied, sensing the thought. "You shall be among the first to return home to Kalda. But for now, you should come with me. Leave your body here, and travel with me to Vabenack."

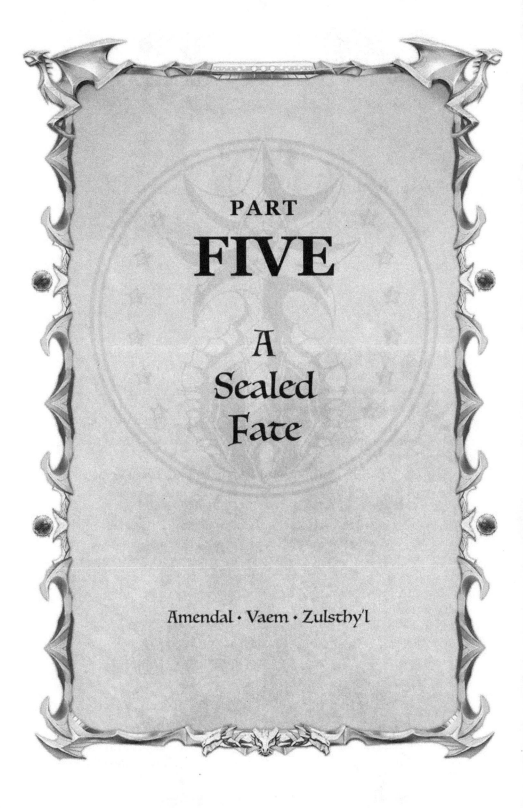

PART

FIVE

A
Sealed
Fate

Amendal · Vaem · Zulsthy'l

"In the ancient days, so I've read, Beastcallers were required to seek all these conjurations. Now, many of the creatures have fallen into obscurity."

- From *Colvinar Vrium's Bestiary for Conjurers*, Endnote

No sooner had the teleporting light faded than Amendal reached for the shan'ak. "I would wait," said the old codger, and Amendal turned toward the sound of his voice. Dressed in only that red robe, the codger sat against the icy wall of the grotto. He leaned forward and smiled.

Fench shook and his trunk bounced against Amendal's coat as the codger spoke. Pulling the trembling creature closer, Amendal narrowed his eyes. "Why?"

The codger chuckled. "You are fond of that question." He looked to the small tunnel leading to the snowy plains. "Those platinum beasts will fly by shortly, and the next Warder's Grotto is too far for your gosset to reach. The conjuration would freeze after several hours of flight, being forced to drop the shan'ak. So you would be teleporting to an exposed position, and the dragons will spot you."

That made sense to Amendal. Though the bird was a manifestation from the Aldinal Plane, it was still as susceptible as a regular gosset—perhaps even more, as Aldinal copies were not as resilient as their real-world counterparts.

"I guess we rest in this den," Amendal said and glanced to Fench, who still trembled.

"This isn't a den," the codger said. "The Esharian Warders use these as shelter when scouring the plains."

Warders? Amendal puzzled over the codger's words, but his thoughts uncontrollably shifted to Faelinia. Sorrow swelled in his heart, and his eyes filled with tears.

"She is only one woman, Amendal. There are so many others."

Though that idea was something Amendal had lived by, it no longer felt a part of him. He longed for *her* and only *her*. Of all the women he had romantically pursued, she was the only one who genuinely cared for him and his wellbeing. Her prowess in the magical arts made her all the more attractive, and her tenacity crowned her with an allure that eclipsed her beauty.

He recalled every moment with Faelinia until the end. But his final memory of her was defiled by Orath'issian. *How dare he wear her likeness*—his thoughts abruptly shifted to that illusory hand, then to the monster at the bottom of the pit. *Both were illusions.*

But Orath'issian hadn't used magic during their battle. Did that mean Faelinia was still alive? Had *she* cast those illusions? Many legends claimed dragons could manipulate the minds of those they gazed upon...

Amendal shot a glance to the codger, who shook his head. "Do you really believe Orath'issian would have spared her? Did he have even a speck of pity in him?" He took a deep breath. "She is gone, Amendal. Forget about her."

"But it doesn't make sense!" Amendal cried. "She has to be alive. There was no way Orath'issian could have killed her after we fled!"

"So stubborn..." The codger sighed. "But you wouldn't be you without that irritating trait."

Amendal shot to his feet, leaving Fench. "Answer me!"

The codger pursed his lips and his brow narrowed. "Forget about her, Amendal." He waved in a dismissal. "You could not have saved her."

Could not? he thought, wobbling back toward Fench. *Could not?*

"You should rest," the codger said, looking to the grotto's entrance.

I've really lost her, Amendal thought. Tears overflowed as the somber realization washed over him. He fell to his knees, crawling to the grotto's wall. Fench fluttered beside him, still shaking. Sniffling, the winged creature buried his face in Amendal's coat.

Besides those sorrowful noises, all was quiet in the tiny cave, except for an occasional strong breeze that whistled across the tunnel's mouth. The codger remained against the icy wall but kept his gaze directed toward the icy plain. As Amendal huddled with Fench, fatigue crept over him, but not enough to drive him to slumber.

After a short time, faint oscillations carried through the tunnel, growing louder and louder. Soon, the beating of wings rushed by then faded.

"You should try to sleep," the codger said. "Three more patrols will pass, and then you can continue your trek." He rose from the ground but stooped as he crossed the grotto. "There is no hurry, though. It will be some time before your Order's council sends a vessel."

Amendal started.

"Yes," the codger said. "Ildin's assumptions were correct. Now, rest. I will return once it's safe for you to leave."

With that, the codger vanished.

A GUARDIAN'S INQUEST

"But I believe it is our duty to cull the beasts of our world. We are the stewards of creation."

- From *Colvinar Vrium's Bestiary for Conjurers*, Endnote

Frigid gusts blew across Zulsthy'l's armor as he landed upon the frozen foothills. A deep whoosh filled the air, and the bits of snow and ice rising to the tethering-portal fell all around him. Large chunks shattered, their pieces tinkling as they rolled across the plain.

"So, you left only one survivor," he whispered, turning to the wide gorge. *If one could call it survival...* Then there was the matter of Amendal Aramien. But the chances of a man teleporting before striking the magical barrier in the abyss were slim. *We should search for him—*

The beating of wings carried overhead, and Zulsthy'l's son Dorith descended, riding his transmogrified drake, a winged serpentine creature one tenth the size of a dragon. The mount was the immortal essence of Eradas, once Dorith's loyal mount in the rebellion against the Karthar Empire.

Eradas settled upon the plain not far from Zulsthy'l, but Dorith did not dismount from the creature. "Ilnari is leading the others into the caves. But Grandfather has taken a few dozen to Tardalim's exit. They just entered the mountain."

As a leader of the Guardians of Kalda, Zu'mal'thisr'nsar and any others with him could enter Tardalim through its exit. But that privilege did not extend outside their tetrad of leadership.

"Best we follow my father," Zulsthy'l said, handing the shiz'nak to Dorith. His son took the black sphere, placed it within a satchel, and then removed folded clothes from the satchel—the tunic and pants Zulsthy'l had worn in Usazma'thirl.

Once his clothes were over his armor, Zulsthy'l slipped the orange shard

into the inner pocket of his tunic. He climbed atop Eradas's tail to sit behind Dorith, and the transmogrified drake took to flight. They soon
reached a small cave two-thirds up the mountainside. Eradas hovered beside it, as there was no place for him to land.

"I'll be right behind you," Dorith said. "Once Eradas is secured."

Zulsthy'l nodded and leapt into the cavern. He made his descent into the
tunnels, and though it was dark he could easily see the twists and turns
through his armor. He walked at a brisk pace until Dorith joined him, and
then they ran through the caves.

The tunnel eventually emptied into a two-story chamber littered with
broken tents, a mess of camping gear, and dead bodies. Bits of earthen conjurations were strewn about, and one near the cavern wall held full packs.

"I wonder what happened here," Dorith thought aloud.

"Orath'issian happened," Zulsthy'l said, recalling the massacre from his
probing of the wretched cafis'sha. "He poisoned them all, except a Tuladine
and that conjurer."

Dorith looked surprised. "Are you saying one Mindolarnian was controlling all those conjurations?"

Zulsthy'l shook his head. "A Sorothian."

"Even more surprising…" Dorith turned and scanned the ruined camp,
pointing to the many cups beside the dead. "I suppose the poison was distributed through some sort of drink?"

Zulsthy'l nodded, hurrying to the tunnel leading to the caverns housing
Tardalim's exit. Faint voices carried up a narrow path, but their conversation was too distorted to understand.

The voices became discernible as Zulsthy'l and his son descended a natural ramp lined with stalactites. "…they had ingested something," a female
Guardian said. "But I'm not well enough versed in Mindolarnian poisons to
know which."

"I don't think it was a poison," another voice responded. "There was an
amber residue in what was undoubtedly a transmuted fire pit."

Once off the ramp, Zulsthy'l hurried around a corner. The Guardians—
all in their human forms and clad in white-scaled armor—moved through a
large cavern, toward a shallow mound at the cavern's heart.

Zulsthy'l's father knelt at the edge of the shallow mound, pressing his
bare hand against its surface. The ice and snow covering the mound rippled
before vanishing completely, revealing Tardalim's exit. The metallic dais
spanned eighty phineals in diameter and was completely smooth.

Conversations ceased and were replaced by incantations as Zulsthy'l
reached the dais. A rim of golden light appeared at its heart, about half the
size of the dais, and then the area inside the light vanished.

Zu'mal'thisr'nsar rose and stepped to the opening, peering down into the
tubular shaft leading to Tardalim. "It's empty."

As the incantations ceased, Zulsthy'l joined his father. "We won't find
any others; the only other prisoner to escape fled during the second incur-

sion."

His declaration drew hushed murmurs from the others.

Zu'mal'thisr'nsar raised an eyebrow. "You probed the cafis'sha?"

As they descended toward Tardalim's exit, Zulsthy'l related the memories he received from Orath'issian: his roaming of the shifting halls, infiltrating the Sorothian expedition, the battle within Tardalim's core, and the partial destruction of the Tuladine Tower. Many of the others ran past, enhanced with magic. They gathered at another circular doorway adorned with symbols denoting the Channels of Power. The door also contained a brief history of Tardalim and how the prison used the Channels to fulfill its purpose.

Once at the door, Zulsthy'l knelt and touched its frame. "Es'umak." His armor receded while the floor depressed in front of him, becoming a squared hole slightly larger than his hand. He reached inside, and the space lit with pale-green light. A bond soon formed between him and Tardalim. *Open*, he commanded.

A faint hum filled the shaft, and the symbols upon the door glowed with shifting hues. But the various colors soon became white, and the circular door opened, compressing into the frame.

Dorith stepped toward his father, his fanisar in hand. "If that qui'sha is still alive, I'll find her."

"I'm sure you will," Zulsthy'l said, and stepped through the doorway. "But you'll have to find an alternative means to locate her—try the tower's fourth tier."

"I know where to look."

Zulsthy'l was the first to continue up the corkscrew path. The anteroom housing the exit was empty, and the four-story doors were wide open. Many of the Guardians hurried past him, running into a vast circular chamber which the Tuladine called the pit. It spanned from Tardalim's outermost layer to the Heart of the Sphere, or the Roost as the Tuladine called it.

Once in the pit, Zulsthy'l's eyes fell upon mangled corpses littering the floor and the ramp that circled its edge. Several were blown apart, as if they had been struck by some type of arcane blast. Many were surrounded by blood.

Though Orath'issian had not witnessed their deaths, Zulsthy'l knew the cafis'sha had caused their demise. *You poor fools…*

Telekinetic incantations sounded around Zulsthy'l. Several Guardians, including Dorith, shot upward, trailing gray particles. They soared through the pit and soon disappeared beyond its edge.

Nearly all had ascended the pit when Zulsthy'l's father approached from the anteroom. "What is this?"

"The result of an atrocity," Zulsthy'l said. "I'll meet you at the Tower. There's something that requires my immediate attention."

Zu'mal'thisr'nsar frowned at the bodies, then followed the others. Once his father began rising upward through the pit, Zulsthy'l turned back to the corpses. *We should bury them,* he thought, and then mustered his own burst of telekinetic magic.

He soared through the pit, and soon entered the Heart of the Sphere.

Tardalim's core was a bizarre sight, but then Tardalim was a bizarre place. There were not many structures on Kalda that rivaled its grandeur and ingenuity of architecture. *A true relic,* he thought, searching the tree-like buildings covering the Heart of the Sphere. Several other Guardians had transformed and were flying toward the four stairwells leading to Tardalim's labyrinth.

A seven-tiered tower covered in overgrowth rose above the brown buildings. *There,* he thought and mustered another telekinetic blast that sent him toward the tower. Its highest tier was marred with a crude hole where a balcony had once overlooked the Heart of the Sphere, but Orath'issian had since demolished it. What remained of the balcony was rubble scattered on the tier below.

A clever move, destroying the map, he thought, passing over the battered clearing surrounding the tower. Corpses littered the ground while large patches of grass were missing. Raw matter was strewn about, as were debris from the nearby buildings. Holes marred the ground, made by disintegration and transmutative magic.

Zulsthy'l redirected his blast, soaring toward the spot where Orath'issian had *died.* He dismissed the magic and landed upon the teal grass. Closing his eyes, he recalled the path the cafis'sha had taken after the battle. He followed that course, eventually arriving at an unmarred Tuladine structure. Mustering his telekinetic magic, he rose to the eighth floor.

He leaned forward, gliding inside a room fit only for a Tuladine. Perch-like chairs hung on a wall, but little else was in the space, except the sole survivor of Tardalim's third incursion, Faelinia Tusara.

She lay facing the far wall, her blond curls partially draping her naked back. She twitched and wheezed with each breath. The sight of her evoked dreadful memories of Dorith's mother, but Zulsthy'l pushed them from his mind before the sorrow overtook him. Even so, a tear trickled down his cheek.

He averted his gaze and held up a hand, eyeing his tunic and pants. *She looks about my height... Fortunate I am wearing my armor.* But even if he hadn't been, he could have transmuted clothing for her. Turning away, he quickly pulled off his tunic and pants.

With his clothes in hand he crossed the room. "You can put these on, if you'd like." He stopped within arm's reach and knelt beside her, but she neither moved nor spoke.

"I'm going to search your mind," he said, draping his clothes atop her. "I need to see the damage that wretch caused. I can't promise anything, but I'll do my best to restore you."

Another tear trickled down his cheek as he reached for her chin. Her face was damp and her jaw was slack. She didn't even resist as he turned her face toward his. Her sea-gray eyes darted back and forth, completely unfocused. Her lower lip drooped, and drool trickled off her chin.

Zulsthy'l's heart sank. Though he had known of Orath'issian's atrocious act, it was still hard to behold. Over the centuries he had seen many men and women lose their identity in a similar manner. Though he had the ability to perform such a feat, he had never tampered with a human mind in such a manner. Made some forget him, yes… but never had he shattered one's mind and stripped their identity.

He allowed his eyes to shift to their natural state. To Faelinia, or anyone else looking, the lines of his irises would appear to swirl around his pupils.

"I'm going to look into your eyes, and you'll feel my mind touching yours." She blinked, but did not respond to Zulsthy'l. He focused on her darting eyes, hoping to catch their erratic movement.

A heartbeat later she froze, and Zulsthy'l felt her mind opening to his. Her thoughts were a jumbled mess, mostly incoherent nonsense. Her memories were rearranged and spliced together from different parts of her life. Her inner monologue was not even intelligible. She knew neither her name nor her nativity.

That sickened Zulsthy'l.

But her ability to muster magic was well intact. From what Zulsthy'l could tell, she was quite proficient in harnessing the Xu and the Au Channels of Power. *At least you still have that,* he thought, focusing on her most recent memories.

The farthest coherent incident was only hours old and involved a man with many wounds. This fellow knelt over her, taking her clothes and altering his form to look identical to hers. He made the woman conceal him under an illusion, replacing a missing hand with illusory particles.

Faelinia then mustered arcane magic and concealed it within a monstrous illusion. She then sent it after a fleeing band; some were at Tardalim's exit with a very young Tuladine while others were descending through the pit. That conjurer—Amendal Aramien—grabbed the Tuladine and threw himself through Tardalim's exit. Then Faelinia attacked those in the pit, unleashing her magic in an explosive blast.

"That's what killed those men," Zulsthy'l muttered, but held his gaze.

Faelinia had remained alone after that, until he arrived.

"You poor thing," he whispered. "You do not deserve such a fate. I'll do my best to restore you…" He sighed, but kept his eyes locked on hers. Never before had he seen a mind as shattered as Faelinia Tusara's. Even with the knowledge he had received from Orath'issian, it would be hard to rebuild her identity. Though the practice of restoring a mind was known among the sha'kalda, it wasn't one readily used in Kalda's current era. The process would be an arduous one at best.

Even so, she would never be herself, not completely.

He bade her to dress and severed his probing gaze. Once she was clothed, he urged her to stand, but she did not move. "I suppose I'll carry you," he said, and knelt to lift her.

Once she was in his arms, Zulsthy'l walked to the opening. He mustered a barsion and leapt, making two deep impressions on the teal grass. The rapid flapping of wings carried overhead, and Eradas sped past the Tuladine homes with Dorith atop him. They soon disappeared and the beating wings faded. Dorith must have found that alternative means within the tower and spotted the qui'sha elsewhere in Tardalim—if she were dead, Dorith would have joined Zulsthy'l. *Well, that qui'sha will not live for long...*

"It is my hope that you seek as many of these creatures as possible.
Bring them to your menageries in no small number."

- From *Colvinar Vrium's Bestiary for Conjurers*, Endnote

Unfortunately, the arpranist had not healed all of Vaem's wounds. *If only Orath'issian hadn't killed*—Sharp pain shot through her left shin as she crawled onto Tardalim's thirty-first floor. Her shoulder had fallen back into place, but the joint was still sore.

Gritting her teeth, she dragged herself from the stairs. Her satchel lurched beside her, its contents rattling. She had been lucky to find it among the debris after Orath'issian destroyed the camp. She supposed Calimir must have taken it from the tower but hadn't had the time to transfer it with the supplies.

Retrieving it had been a struggle, as was her descent. But she could not fail her emperor.

I... wi—sharp pain surged through her leg—*will... fulfill*—

She screamed as another spike of pain spread up her thigh, and her toes became cold. Her breathing quickened, and she struggled to slow her breath. "Th... the..." She pressed her head against the cool floor. "Man... date!"

Then a wave of pain consumed her, and she closed her eyes against it.

Once the pain receded and became bearable, she looked down the hall. The closest door was open. It was enormous and reached to the ceiling, a circular opening almost as wide as Tardalim's shifting halls.

"Go..." She clenched her jaw and pulled herself across the floor. "Don't... gi—" The pain surged, and she screamed, but she forced herself forward.

Vaem felt as if an eternity had passed before she neared the door. The chamber beyond the opening was square, and at its heart stood an enormous cylindrical crystal wreathed in a golden framework. The crystal and its framing barely hovered above the floor and nearly touched the ceiling. Inside it was an oblong silhouette that had a hint of red to it.

If the crystal was like the others she had seen, then Vaem couldn't know for certain until she was closer.

She fought against the pain and continued through the vast door. A dark-red, sinuous shape wrapped around the silhouette while the outline of dark talons became visible near its bottom.

Once halfway across the chamber, the beating of wings carried into the room. Had Orath'issian triumphed over the others? But the halls were too small for a divine being to spread their wings.

Vaem pushed herself forward as the flapping grew louder. A gust pressed against her, and she screamed. Something brown circled the crystal while a flash of maroon and gold landed in front of her.

A man barred her path, wearing a maroon robe with golden armor melded into it. He held an intricate staff in one hand and planted it beside him. The staff struck the stone with a high-pitched clang.

That brown streak flew from the crystal and landed beside the man. It was a diam'sha... but its serpentine body was made of dirt, as if transmuted. O-or... *transmogrified*...

"Seems I arrived just in time," the man said. "I can't have you freeing any more of Tardalim's prisoners."

"Wh-who... ar-are—?" She winced, struggling to maintain her focus on the man amid her pain.

A disappointed grunt left the golden helmet. "And here I thought most Mindolarnians recognized me. Eradas, seize her!"

The strange diam'sha flew toward Vaem and ripped her from the floor. The jolt made her scream in anguish, and she felt her satchel fall. "No—!"

She gasped and glimpsed the man lifting the satchel. The diam'sha circled the room, soaring near the crystal. The divine being trapped inside *was* covered in crimson scales.

Vaem lamented her misfortune as the diam'sha swooped to the floor. A flash of maroon and gold sped upward. She searched the chamber, but the man was nowhere within it.

The diam'sha turned abruptly and flew into the hall with Vaem still in its clutches. The air whipped around her, and the extreme pressure made the pain intolerable. Vaem screamed, and the world became a blur. She glimpsed what she thought were stairs, then black figures, and then leafless trees.

Brown shapes against a teal background whirled around her, and Vaem felt herself falling. She hit something hard, and her leg cracked. Screaming, she buried her face in what could only be grass. *Th-the... R-ro-roost?*

Voices—masculine and feminine—spoke all around her, but she couldn't discern their words. They spoke the Divine Tongue, unlike that man who had barred her from glory.

The voices quieted, and Vaem managed to roll onto her side.

Figures in white stood all around her. But she couldn't make out any details.

Soon, one knelt beside her and pushed her onto her back. He grabbed her cheeks with his bare hands and—

Vivid images flashed in Vaem's mind, accompanied by an intruding force. Her vision became clear, and though she was reliving her past, she knew she was gazing into dark-brown eyes. *Such wonderful eyes...* The pain fled as joyous memories became present reality. Once more she shared the bed of a thousand lovers. The devotion they gave her was intoxicating! And then came the calling of her emperor, and his behest that she venture to Tardalim to free the gods. She reveled in the task once again, and found herself on Soroth. Surges of jealousy clouded memories of their journey. Intense passion flared in her soul as she entered Tardalim, and she yearned to kill that irksome coquette—

The visions ended, and the pain returned.

A deep and charming voice spoke above her, belonging to the owner of those brown eyes. "My, such hate you have for Faelinia."

Vaem blinked and reached a hand to activate the euphorinizer—

"Not so fast, Vaem." The owner of the charming voice caught her wrist. "Dorith, remove that glove."

The man in maroon grabbed her other hand, yanking the euphorinizer from her. The owner of the charming voice dropped her wrist and walked away, but he was replaced by others, all wearing white armor.

"What say you of her fate, Zulsthy'l?" asked one taller than the rest.

"We should wait for Ilnari," replied the charming voice. "But she *is* the architect of this third incursion."

"Then she is deserving of death," another said. "There are three of you here. If you are in agreement, then why wait?"

The tallest one nodded, then spoke an incantation in the Divine Tongue. Lightning surged around his white gauntlets, condensing and becoming a sword-like shaft. It pulsed and crackled. Its presence made Vaem's hair rise while tingling her skin.

"I am in agreement," said the man in maroon. He stood not far from Vaem, his arms folded.

"As am I," the charming one said, but with regret in his voice.

The tall man twirled the crackling blade. Its tip pointed down. "Then death it is."

Heart pounding, Vaem struggled. She had to get away, but the slightest movement sent pain up and down her leg. An armored boot struck her stomach, pinning her in place. She writhed in an attempt to break free, but the boot weighed too much, and her pain was too great.

I-I've... fa-failed—

Vaem wailed, watching in horror as the lightning blade raced toward her face.

———◦•◦———

In the hours since Zu'mal'thisr'nsar had slain Vaem Rudal, Zulsthy'l had studied Faelinia's mind. He had managed to repair some basic behaviors, including sitting and standing—but she still wobbled as she moved.

He had since taken Faelinia to the tower's fourth tier, to a chamber where one could observe Tardalim's past. Shelves lined the walls, but instead of books or scrolls it held tevisrals containing the living history of the prison. Those records could be viewed at the room's center, where two divots—perfectly aligned on the floor and ceiling—projected illusory particles. Such manifestations of magic were so refined that one might not think that the light in front of them were from the Channels of Power.

In addition to those records, the living map of Tardalim could be viewed. Dorith had ventured to this chamber upon arriving at the Roost to discover Vaem's location, since the main projection had been destroyed. *If the humans had known about this chamber, perhaps Orath'issian would not have escaped...*

While sifting through Faelinia's memories, Zulsthy'l had activated the map and observed Ilnari and the Kardorthians as they ascended to Tardalim's center. *Ascending to a center,* he thought, chuckling.

The Kardorthians had spread throughout the Roost when Dorith, Ilnari, and Zu'mal'thisr'nsar entered the observation chamber.

Ilnari inquired after Faelinia, and Zulsthy'l explained her predicament. "I propose she stays with us. Even if I can mend her mind, sending her away will arouse suspicion."

"Do you propose she become one of us?" Dorith asked.

Zulsthy'l nodded. "But if I fail, she is still our responsibility."

"We should keep her here," Ilnari said, glancing to Zulsthy'l's father. "She can help."

Sucking in his breath, Zulsthy'l began to pace around the room. "I suppose Tardalim's fate is a matter we need to discuss..."

"I think the three of us are in agreement," Dorith said. "Tardalim cannot remain in its current state, despite what you said."

Through his probing of Vaem, Zulsthy'l had discovered the Mindolarnians possessed four nullifiers. Three were here in Tardalim.

"Surely they'll send another wave," Dorith said. "If their actions thus far are anything to judge by. But, I don't understand why they would waste their forces."

"Their religion," said Zu'mal'thisr'nsar. "They were *commanded* to do so."

Ilnari nodded. "It goes against all strategic sense. Unless there is an ulterior purpose to these incursions..."

Zulsthy'l set his jaw.

"Do you think this entire situation an elaborate ruse, Father?" asked Dorith.

Zulsthy'l stopped pacing and eyed his son. "I don't know. But whatever we decide, we must consider that the Ma'lishas wanted us to act in such a manner."

"This is a simple matter, my son," said Zu'mal'thisr'nsar. "Tardalim's location is known, and our enemy has a means to free its captives. This place is no longer secure. I propose that we begin an evacuation of its inhabitants. One prisoner has already escaped—and a powerful one at that. We must seal off the mountain and use the caverns outside the exit as a staging area for sending the prisoners to a realm of exile."

Dorith raised a finger. "I know you think it an arduous task, Father, and it is. But it is necessary."

"Shem'rinal is willing to aid us," Ilnari said. "And we will enlist the Esharian Collective."

Dorith nodded in agreement. "Ilnari and I will regularly check on Tardalim. Exiling the prisoners will probably take fifty some odd years." He gestured to Faelinia. "Perhaps she can aid us in that regard."

If only I can mend her, Zulsthy'l thought.

"We should formalize this decision," said Zu'mal'thisr'nsar. "Are you in agreement with us, my son?"

Zulsthy'l considered the dilemma. Vaem had been determined to free Tardalim's prisoners, and her cohorts were no less zealous. The Mindolarnians would come again, and if the Ma'lisha had the means of replicating those nullifiers, they might come as well. Then there was the matter of Heleron... *But would he return to this prison after fleeing it?* Sighing, he pushed aside the thought. "You have my support. But we should return the shiz'nak to where it belongs and receive another from the Ril'sha."

"That is sound," Ilnari said. "With the proof we have, receiving a tethering stone from them will not be... painful."

Zu'mal'thisr'nsar folded his arms and took a deep breath. "Then it is settled. Tardalim will be purged and its prisoners exiled."

.

"Those that dedicate themselves to the gathering of these beasts will become unrivaled. None will prevail against them."

- From *Colvinar Vrium's Bestiary for Conjurers*, Endnote

Amendal could not rest after the codger disappeared from the grotto. His sorrow and anxiety over the dragons' arrival spurred his imagination. The roar of beating wings carried into the icy grotto, but soon faded. *That's three groups*, he thought. The codger claimed there would be four.

While he waited for the last set of dragons, the conjured gosset began to succumb to the frigid temperature. But Amendal ignored the pain. Ever since his waking from that dreaded nightmare, his conjurations' afflictions felt distant, almost like a faint buzz one could barely discern.

The gosset wobbled and then collapsed. It refused to move, and Amendal felt his bond with it fading. *Perhaps when I get home, I can find an incantation for ice birds in the family tomes...* But he hadn't recalled such an incantation while skimming *Greater Conjurations from the Aldinal Plane*.

Eventually, his thoughts turned to the codger's promise of a rescue. But when would that vessel arrive? From what he had gleaned throughout the expedition, the council planned on them traveling to Tardalim and then back to the shore, and finally sailing home.

"It'll be months before they come," he whispered. *But what of the Mindolarnians?* Surely, they would send a fourth expedition. They might even arrive before the council's rescue.

But all that was speculation.

Closing his eyes, Amendal thought of his journey across the wastes. With dragons roaming about he would have to stay hidden. *Perhaps I can hide in those mountains we came across...* But then there was the matter of reaching them. True, he could travel invisibly, but he would leave tracks in the snow. He pulled the anchoring tevisral from his pocket and studied the black disk.

"If only the gossets were not so feeble…"

But they were his best option. The birds could carry the anchoring tevisral to any crevasse or cave. Then he and Fench could teleport to the new hiding spot.

He turned the shan'ak in his fingers, studying its smooth surface. *Shan'ak is undoubtedly your draconic name… so what would you be called in Common?* He considered the object's nature, then smiled. *Conjuration anchor. That's what I'll name you…*

No sooner had the thought come to him than hunger pangs struck. So he opened a portal to the Visirm Expanse, and the makeshift bag the earthen conjurations had packed fell onto the icy floor, rattling as it landed. With the portal open, Amendal felt his friends' anguish. *I will save you all… I promise.* Their pain lingered until he shut the portal.

He woke Fench and together they ate a cold meal. Once they were finished, Amendal put the bag back in the Visirm Expanse. He left a few things out, though: a blanket for him and Fench, as well as some dried meat they could eat as snacks. *Hopefully Fench won't try to steal mine…*

Eventually, that third wave of dragons sped past the icy grotto. Amendal had begun conjuring another gosset from the Aldinal Plane when the codger returned. His presence made Fench tremble, and the winged creature dropped his dried meat.

"This time, you'll have to follow my every instruction," said the codger. "No deviations."

———◦•◦———

The next two days were uneventful—at least, what Amendal called days. For all he knew, three or four days could have passed since the sun hardly moved overhead. The mountain of Tardalim had since disappeared beyond the horizon. If the old codger hadn't led him, Amendal would have used the mountain to keep his heading true.

Even after the mountain vanished, he hadn't needed a compass. The old codger kept Amendal on course, guiding him to grottos identical to where he had taken shelter after fleeing Tardalim.

While he and Fench broke for their second meal of the supposed-third day, a sprawling mountain range rose ahead of the gosset. "I didn't think we were that close," he said, scratching his beard. It was growing too long. *I'll look like a wild man before I return home…*

They teleported twice before reaching the mountain's foothills. Fench complained of hunger, and Amendal decided to break once more, in a shallow cavity beside a boulder.

While they ate, the codger told Amendal that he would be staying in the mountains for a while. Their shelter would keep him safe from the dragons and a coming storm. It would also afford him opportunities to expand his menagerie. Once they finished, Amendal and Fench watched the sun. It moved farther through the sky now, but it never dipped below the horizon.

That night the codger led Amendal's gosset to a small cavern in the mountainside. There, they set up camp and slept.

For many days they meandered through the mountains, traveling through caves and high valleys. They encountered more of the moth-like viliasim in tunnels Amendal assumed belonged to a crysillac. He hoped to encounter one of those mythical beasts. But their dens were long abandoned—or so the codger claimed.

On his second week in the mountains, he and Fench stumbled across large footprints in the snow. *Belonging to a yaeltis?* he thought. The tracks led to a cave, and Amendal conjured an Aldinal copy of his only cisthyrn. Sure enough, two full-grown yaeltis were hibernating deep inside.

Careful not to repeat the mistake of charging into their den, Amendal set a trap and lured the beasts to him. Unfortunately for the yaeltis, two earthen gargantuans were too much for them. The colossal conjurations hurled the beasts into the Visirm Expanse.

Once the yaeltis den was cleared, Amendal and Fench settled in for several days. The codger hadn't bothered them, and the storm had finally arrived. With the storm raging, Amendal decided to rest.

It wasn't until a day after the storm that they began moving again. Fench had found a small crystallized passageway that led to a vast network of caves not unlike the caverns outside Tardalim. The passageway was too small for Amendal, so he sent Fench through with the conjuration anchor.

They spent several days exploring those tunnels and their adjoining caverns, searching for anything of value: beast and tevisral alike. Amendal hoped to come across a crysillac, but nothing lived in the tunnels. Eventually, the codger returned and guided them through winding paths that led deeper and deeper below ground. Amendal assumed they were still in the mountains, until a winding tunnel brought them to a frigid plain.

"You're nearly halfway to the shore," the codger said. "Those platinum beasts have stopped patrolling the skies, so you should be safe." He turned, pointing to what was Amendal's left. "Over there you'll find a pack of cisthyrns. Capture them, then make your way north." He pointed to the right of the tunnel. "There is another Warder's Grotto not far from here."

As the codger predicted, there was a pack of cisthyrn upon the snowy plains. But their number was greater than Amendal had expected. *Twenty-eight,* he thought, watching from atop the crest of a snowdrift. "So many pretties."

Fench wriggled his trunk. "They don't look pretty…"

"We're going to need a perch," Amendal said, stroking his unkempt beard. He decided upon an earthen giant, but no sooner had the conjuration emerged than the pack rounded on him. Luckily, the conjuration lifted him before the cisthyrns reached the snowdrift. Fench of course fluttered into the air.

Amendal captured the entire pack quickly. Once they reached the icy grotto they settled in for the night.

Another day passed, and no caves marked the plains beyond the mountains. The winds picked up, and Amendal conjured two earthen gargantuans to block out the frigid gusts. It was still cold, so he conjured a magma elemental to provide warmth. He thought he might need to dismiss the three conjurations before he and Fench teleported, but he managed to move them all.

Evening drew near as the sun dipped closer to the horizon in the east, but the western sky didn't darken completely.

Amendal began to grow tired, but still no shelter had been found. He studied the gargantuans and considered their dilemma. Fench would probably be fine, but sleeping on the plain would be too cold for Amendal. "I'll have to sacrifice one of you for shelter," he said to the gargantuans.

They teleported once more, and then he killed one of the colossal creatures. Once the bond with it was severed, he summoned two giants and five regular-sized earthen creatures and went to work building the shelter from the felled earthen gargantuan. The interior was the size of a small room, but shaped like a bean. His conjurations patched holes with snow and the results soon resembled a snow-covered mound. Fench marveled at Amendal's ingenuity, zipping in and out of their shelter.

But there was still the matter of keeping warm.

Amendal searched the remaining rubble and found several flat rocks that were partly bowed. "Take those inside," he commanded the small conjurations. Then he pointed to the magma elemental. "And kill that."

The small conjurations laid the flat pieces at both ends of the shelter and returned with chunks of molten magma. They set the molten chunks on a flat rock, which began to warm the shelter's interior. While the conjurations continued reinforcing the shelter with snow, Amendal arranged the interior, placing his bedding atop a flat slab. Once the inside was finished, Amendal had the conjurations roll a boulder in front of the entrance. He dismissed the still-living elementals and retrieved some belongings from the Visirm Expanse.

Fench fell asleep soon after they ate, but Amendal struggled to get comfortable. It was plenty warm, the pieces of the magma elemental still smoldering. But the journey was wearing on him.

He longed for Faelinia, and his friends. Tears filled his eyes as he imagined Faelinia succumbing to that wretched Orath'issian. *If only we hadn't come,* he thought. His frustration turned to Vaem. If it hadn't been for her, Faelinia and his friends would still be alive.

"Damned Mindolarnians…" He tossed, facing the blocked entrance. A faint wind howled through a crack. His anger simmered, and his thoughts returned to Faelinia. How he longed to run his hands through her golden curls and gaze into those incredible eyes.

Fatigue soon crept upon him, and he felt sleep drawing near. As he drifted into slumber, Faelinia's smiling face greeted him, and her beauty took his breath away.

"I miss you…" he murmured.

She bit her lower lip and reached for his face. Amendal thought he felt her long fingers upon his cheek. Her touch was so vivid! But it couldn't be real. Faelinia was gone, and Amendal was alone.

———◦•◦———

After waking from nightmares of perpetual death, Amendal dismissed the makeshift shelter, sending the bits and pieces back to the Aldinal Plane. Partway through the day, he and Fench discovered a shallow gorge, no more than three stories deep, lined with long icicles.

"Better than nothing," he said. *At least it'll shield us from the wind.* He sent another gosset flying as Fench fluttered along the icicles.

They found shelter in another icy grotto that evening, but the next two days Amendal had to summon more earthen gargantuans to make camp.

Faint trumpeting roused Amendal from his slumber. He looked about the makeshift shelter and strained his hearing. The trumpeting grew louder, its tones both joyous and playful.

Penguins?

He hurried from his bedding, shook Fench awake, and then darted to a crack at the shelter's blocked entrance. A line of black moved down a nearby snowdrift.

"What is that?" Fench asked.

Amendal smiled. "A waddle of penguins. And I think you'll enjoy them!" He summoned an earthen giant and removed the boulder barring the entrance.

As the black line drew near, the individual penguins became discernible. To Amendal's surprise, there were smaller creatures among them. *The chicks?* Faelinia had mentioned something of chicks upon their first encounter.

"You should follow them," the codger suggested.

Amendal spun around to find the old man standing atop the snow, but he made no footprints. "Are we close to the shore?"

The codger nodded, a sly grin spreading across his face as he disappeared. Amendal turned back to the entrance, watching the penguins approach. *Best we tear this down…*

The waddle of penguins didn't seem the least bit bothered by Amendal or the dismissal of the elemental remains. Many of the larger penguins trumpeted what Amendal thought was a greeting. Several of the chicks hurried toward Amendal and Fench, running awkwardly with their wings spread behind them.

"They're small," Fench said, fluttering toward the chicks now gathered around Amendal. "They have weird wings…"

"Their wings don't work," Amendal said. "Faelinia said they're flightless birds. They use those fins to swim in the water."

Fench shook his head, his trunk flapping back and forth. The gesture made the chicks trumpet an odd noise.

Deep trumpeting carried from the waddle, and the chicks hurried away.

"Well, let's follow them," Amendal said. "A pity Faelinia isn't here. She would have loved to see this."

------◦•◦------

The penguins were good company. Fench played with the smaller ones as they walked. Amendal, however, held a one-sided conversation with a trumpeting penguin. He supposed the bird probably thought its conversation was one-sided.

"Yes," Amendal said, patting the penguin on the head, "I quite agree." The bird seemed to enjoy that. "I find this patch of snow quite nice, too. It's probably the best on this icy rock." He raised his chin in mock appraisal.

Their path took them in a direction which Amendal supposed was northwest, but it veered to the north in the midafternoon. As the sun began to dip toward the east, the penguins kept walking.

Amendal had expected them to rest, but the birds kept marching through the night. They occasionally stopped for short durations but then resumed waddling across the snow.

Near noon the following day, the horizon began to change. A dark-blue line appeared, dividing the sky from the frozen ground. "The ocean!" Amendal cried, moving away from the penguins. "Fench, we made it!"

Feeling as if a weight had lifted from his shoulders, Amendal ran. His hasty flight startled the penguins, and several trumpeted in alarm. Fench fluttered beside him, and together they hurried across the snowy plain and toward the edge of a cliff—*No, the ice shelf.*

Jumbled shouts blew on the wind. To a normal man they would probably have sounded like nonsense. But Amendal parsed orders for adjusting a rigging. He quickened his pace, and more of the ocean became visible, as did a large four-masted vessel sailing half a grand phineal from the icy coastline. The vessel's white sails bore no emblem, but atop its tallest mast waved the green flag of the Principality of Soroth.

"Such are the great ones, fit to be acknowledged among ancient guardians and keepers of truth."

- From *Colvinar Vrium's Bestiary for Conjurers*, Endnote

Coming to a halt, Amendal peered over the edge of the ice shelf. The frigid water was maybe three or four stories below him. "What fortuitous timing," he said, glancing to Fench. *But what will they do when they see you?* Though he hadn't interacted with Vaem since entering Tardalim, he supposed she knew about Fench and the necessary role he had played in their escape. But had she told the council? Morgi claimed Vaem had detailed notes on the dreaded place.

As possible scenarios played in Amendal's mind, the old codger appeared. "I suggest you hide Fench in the Visirm Expanse. There are those within your Order that you cannot trust." He turned to Fench. "It's for your own good. Not to mention the council will want your weapon. You don't want to lose it, do you Fench?"

The winged creature fluttered behind Amendal, his shaking trunk brushing against Amendal's shoulder.

The old man turned back to Amendal. "And you should omit mention of your friends' predicament." The codger looked to the nearby vessel, clasping his hands behind his back. "This is where we part, my friend. Farewell, until the Crimson Eye is unearthed and Kalda's true God returns."

Confused, Amendal opened his mouth to speak, but the man vanished. Amendal turned to Fench, who was no longer shaking. "I'll fetch you once we return to my family's home."

Fench nodded and grasped Amendal's shoulder. "Be careful."

Once the portal to Visirm Expanse opened, Fench zipped into it. Thoughts of curiosity accompanied the winged creature, but it was soon drowned out by the pain of Amendal's friends. *I promise, I will save you. All of you.*

He closed the portal and pulled the conjuration anchor from his pocket. *Do I dare use you?* The council would undoubtedly confiscate the anchor… "Best I keep this safe, too."

The ship sailed parallel to him now, moving toward what he assumed was Crisyan Bay. If he didn't act quickly, the ship would sail past him.

I could always try shouting…

Cupping his hands to his mouth, Amendal yelled at the vessel, but his cries didn't seem to reach anyone on the ship.

Perhaps something more drastic, he thought, uttering an incantation to conjure an Aldinal copy of his dark-blue nactilious. Golden light soon surged from his hands, coalescing half a grand phineal ahead of the ship. A trail of magic connected him to the forming portal. Soon, that multi-limbed silhouette appeared in the light, and the vessel abruptly turned. He slowed his incantation to an exhale as the limbs reached from the golden light, waving above the water.

See me…

His thought made the portal flicker, but he regained his focus, slowly exhaling the rest of the incantation.

More tentacles reached from the portal as a bird flew from the ship. It was a gosset, not unlike the one he had used to traverse the wasteland. The bird landed on the ice shelf and held up its beak. In its mouth the gosset held a small rogulin crystal.

"Is that you, Father?" he asked and dismissed the portal. The nactilious's limbs rushed back into the golden light as the portal collapsed upon itself.

The bird nodded, then spat the crystal onto the ice. It stamped in the frozen ground, then pointed with its beak back to the ship.

"It'll teleport me there?" he asked, picking up the crystal. "I'll see you soon."

While watching the vessel turn westward, Amendal uttered the teleporting incantation. The crystal erupted with golden light, and then a hurried commotion whirled about him; the furling and flapping of canvas sails, the grunts of sailors, and water crashing against a hull.

Before the teleporting magic faded, Amendal felt firm hands clasping his arms. "Oh, Amendal! You're alive!"

Amendal turned to see his father beside him, dressed in his own sloglien coat. Arenil's eyes brimmed with tears as he pulled Amendal close.

"What happened? Where are the others?"

Amendal sucked in his breath and looked about. Besides the sailors, no one else was on the ship's main deck. "Unfortunately, I am the sole survivor of the third expedition to Tardalim."

His father's face paled, and his lips quivered. "What do you mean the *third expedition?*"

"That is a long story…" Amendal sighed. "Do you want me to tell it to you now, or before the council?"

Arenil's face continued contorting with uneasiness. "Just tell me the high points."

The rescuing vessel was still sailing toward Crisyan Bay when Amendal finished explaining the Mindolarnian's deceit. Furious, Arenil stomped off toward the quarterdeck. A faint exchange with the captain carried on the wind, and then Amendal's father returned.

"Best we teleport back to Soroth," Arenil said, removing a green necklace from an inner coat pocket. Like the one Amendal had received from his father, this necklace also had a rogulin crystal as its pendant. "Arintil should still be at the Order, so we can relay this matter promptly."

"Hopefully we won't land on one of his students!"

Arenil pursed his lips, not amused by the remark. "I'll gather the other council members. Once we return, go wait in our chambers."

⬥ ⬥ ⬥

Besides the sound of Amendal's steps, all was quiet in the Order's council chambers. None of the masters had arrived yet.

Deciding not to sit, he paced around the large room, admiring the opulent décor themed to represent each Channel of Power. Though it was only one story, the room occupied nearly one-quarter of the building's fourth floor.

At the center of the room sat a large ornate table. If it were meant for hosting meals it could sit at least fourteen, but that was not its purpose. Seven grand chairs surrounded it, three on either side and one at its head. Each chair was unique, covered with a colored lacquer matching the discipline of the master who sat upon it. The chairs were also carved with the Order's symbols, symbols that were commonly understood throughout the world for the various Channels of Power.

Six pillars held up the room, each equally spaced from the walls and one another. Upon each were floor-to-ceiling tapestries colored to match the chairs belonging to all but the grandmaster, with embroidered symbols of the corresponding disciplines woven throughout them. On the wall opposite the doors, the grandmaster's tapestries hung behind the head chair, along with long, unfurled scrolls telling the origins of the Sorothian Magical Order.

Amendal had heard that the council chambers of the Mages of Alath had similar pillars, except their symbols were etched into the stone and glowed with hues unique to the magics of each discipline.

The positions of the chairs and the tapestries changed as the council changed. Occasionally a council mage would retire, but most stayed until death. When the old head illusionist—Amendal couldn't remember his name—had passed, those occupying the seventh through fourth seats moved up to the sixth and third, leaving the seventh seat vacant for the new head illusionist—

Hurried footsteps echoed into the council chamber, and Amendal spun. He rounded the table and stood at the foot, opposite the grandmaster's seat. *Four pairs*, he thought, parsing the footsteps.

Their owners soon entered the council chambers: Amendal's father, Arenil Aramien; Grandmaster Brantis Secarin; Barsionist Master Emirna Trutim, one of three women on the council; and Ildin's father, Illusionist Master Ilyanin Cetarin.

Though Arenil, the grandmaster, and the barsionist looked troubled, Ilyanin was distraught. His long face was stained with tears. The other three took their seats at the table, but Ilyanin stepped toward Amendal. His lips quivered as he grabbed Amendal's shoulder. "My… my boy—?" Ilyanin's voice shook, and more tears streamed down his face.

Sympathetic tears brimmed in Amendal's own eyes. He'd opened his mouth to speak when more footsteps carried into the council room. "I… I'm sorry."

Ilyanin squeezed Amendal's shoulder, then took his seat at the table.

Soon the other women on the council arrived: Transmuter Master Silasia Vorcus and Arpranist Master Chorlia Igasan. Each wore the robes matching the colors of their chairs and tapestries. They took their seats as a youthful scribe crossed to the far corner of the room and took her place at a table behind the pillar nearest Arenil. Each of the masters looked anxious except for Ilyanin, who seemed to be doing his best to hold back more tears.

The last to enter was Master Cordis Rishan, the head of the necromancer discipline. Instead of a robe, he wore a regal-looking doublet of maroon and black with matching trousers. He took his seat on the grandmaster's left, between the arpranist and Ildin's father. "My apologies," Cordis said with a slight whine to his words. "I had an important meeting with a fellow setting sail tomorrow."

The grandmaster nodded and cleared his throat, but that did nothing to help his dry and cracking voice. "Seeing as this is an emergency meeting, we will not cover any prior business. You all know as much as I, that young Amendal Aramien here was the only survivor of the expedition to Tardalim. If you would please relate what occurred, Amendal, and would you like a seat?"

Amendal declined, then began. "Well, it all started when we were attacked by a pack of nactili in Crisyan Bay…" His father did his best not to smile when Amendal spoke of capturing the nactili, and then the yaeltis and the cisthyrns. The other masters listened intently. Besides Amendal's voice, the racing quill of the scribe was the only noise in the room.

When recounting their discovery of the Mindolarnian corpses, all but Cordis were surprised. Cordis tried to act that way, but Amendal noted the distinct lack of muscles tightening around his eyes. Amendal had often paid attention to details, but never so strongly. *Perhaps it is a boon*, he thought. *Madness for mastery…!*

While continuing the tale, he kept an eye on Cordis. Was he one of those in the Order whom Amendal could not trust? Though he was speaking about Tardalim and its bizarre structure, Amendal couldn't help but wonder about Cordis and that fellow he had met with. *Perhaps a Mindolarnian leading the fourth expedition?*

Amendal omitted the discovery of the conjuration anchor. *They'll try to take it,* he thought. After all, it was the only thing that had come from Tardalim.

Several of the masters gave him skeptical looks when he related the first encounter with Orath'issian. Their doubt became even more apparent when he retold the battle in the Roost. The only masters who hadn't given way to cynicism were his father and Master Cetarin.

He lied and said that Old Cali had lost the rogulin in the battle, and that was why they couldn't return home.

Amendal set his jaw and then recited a variation of what occurred outside Tardalim. "We had all taken the cups when choking noises filled the camp. The monster attacked the others as I rounded the tents and found Old Cali. I threw him and another into the Visirm Expanse until we were forced to flee through the tunnels."

The grandmaster raised an eyebrow. "So, the commander is alive?"

"I wouldn't quite say that." Amendal stroked his chin. "I'd say he is as good as dead, unless you know a way to stop the poison."

While reciting his and his friends' fictional flight from Tardalim, Amendal eyed Ilyanin. *I should embellish Ildin's role.*

"There I was"—Amendal held his hands out as if to balance himself—"sliding down the icy slopes with Fench fluttering beside me. I looked back to see if we were being pursued when a flash of orange lightning zipped across the sky." He swept an open finger above his head. "And then the monster became a dragon!"

Master Trutim held back a snicker, and Amendal cocked his head at her. "What? Don't you believe dragons are real?" He didn't wait for the answer and kept relating the tale of the battle. "I'd managed to unleash my first gangolin when Orath'issian swooped across the mountain side!"

His rendition of the battle was glorious, painting his friends in a light that could be sung about in taverns, or even written in tales. He almost believed it himself, until he recalled their cries of pain echoing from the Visirm Expanse.

"...I had ripped one of the dragon's wings when I saw a line of glistening metal beyond the horizon, shining as bright as the sun at high noon. And then they came. Hundreds of dragons covered in glistening white scales. They descended like a storm of lightning, shaking the mountain and killing Orath'issian. I knew I had to flee, so I took Fench and darted to a cave. They dismissed my conjurations"—he snapped his fingers—"in an instant. After hiding for a time, I emerged from my hiding spot, only to find nothing... No dragons, white or orange. They had vanished."

Master Trutim burst with laughter. "Can't all of you see he's mad?"

Master Cordis nodded, but there was something in his eyes that said he believed Amendal's tale to be true... *You know something, you sneaky bastard. Perhaps he had been in league with Vaem all along.*

"I'm sorry Master Aramien," said the head barsionist. "But your son's imagination is a bit much." Her lips twisted in a doubtful expression, seemingly on the edge of a chuckle.

Arenil sat back and folded his arms. "I believe every word of it. My son is no liar, and he does indeed have control over *five* gangolins."

The grandmaster held out his hands to quiet the others. "Is there more?"

Amendal nodded and told a sad variation of his trek across the wasteland, how Fench left with an Esharian Warder and how Amendal had wandered for many days.

Once he finished, the grandmaster spoke again. "I find your tale hard to believe, young Aramien. So I wish to request more witnesses." He looked to Master Igasan. "Do you feel confident enough to mend the commander?" The arpranist nodded. "Good, then we shall take a vote. All in favor of releasing Commander Calimir Sharn, please signify it."

All but Arenil and Ilyanin extended their right hands over the table.

Amendal's father shook his head. "Didn't any of you pay attention to the aftermath in the caves? The arpranists could not save those men."

"They were not masters," said Master Igasan. "I will call together every arpranist at my disposal. No poison nor venom will stop us from saving this man." She studied Arenil before speaking again. "You of all people should be invested in his survival, especially if he can verify your son's... tale."

Amendal snorted. *I bet she wanted to say outlandish.* He was annoyed at their reaction, but would he have acted any different if he had been in their seats? *Yes.*

Soon after the meeting, the council moved to the rear courtyard near the fountain. The sun had set completely. *Too late to take young Vargos to dinner...* he glanced across the Order's grounds. *I'll have to leave him a note.* Amid the thought, several arpranists arrived.

"You will give us the commander," Master Igasan said to Amendal. "And once we heal him, then we will retrieve the other man you mentioned."

Amendal only gave a slight incline of his head, and then uttered the incantation to open the portal to the Visirm Expanse. Gasps left the mouths of those around him. The masters were as shocked as his friends had been.

His father was the only one not surprised.

Old Cali soon fell from the portal, his entire body convulsing. The arpranists hurried their incantations, and the courtyard became lit with a green hue.

Amendal closed the portal and sauntered across the grounds. Two pairs of footsteps followed after him, and then his father and Master Cetarin arrived beside him.

"That was remarkably fast, son. I take it that's the side effect you mentioned?"

"Yes," Amendal said, then smiled. "Listen to this." Focused ahead, he opened a portal to summon a cisthyrn. Arenil and Ilyanin marveled at the speed of his incantation and the swiftness of the portal's formation. The cisthyrn leapt onto the grass, and Amendal willed the beast to howl.

His father clasped his shoulder. Arenil's voice was full of paternal joy as he spoke, "How incredible! Now I have no doubt you *are* one of the greatest conjurers to walk the face of Kalda."

"For a conjurer is only as strong as his menagerie."

- From *Colvinar Vrium's Bestiary for Conjurers*, Endnote

W hat a remarkable beast your cisthyrn is," Arenil said from atop his conjured yidoth. He too was fond of riding the great felines. "And its eyes are so… peculiar." Together, he and Amendal rode through the forest to the Aramien Estate. Autumn had long since settled upon the Isle of Soroth, and the leaves of the forest were near to falling. "It is a pity only one survived."

Amendal snickered. "Oh, I have plenty more! The old codger led me to a large pack on my way to the coast."

Arenil furrowed his brow. "I thought you didn't find anything on your return trek?"

"Do you think they would have believed me if I had told the truth?"

His father shook his head. Then Amendal related a truncated account of his trek across the wastes. They arrived at the gate to the Aramien Estate as Amendal mentioned the penguins.

"So, if there was no Esharian Warder, where is Fench now?"

Amendal gave his father a sidelong grin. "Hiding…"

Arenil shook his head and sighed. "I'd say your tendency for theatrics has increased." Chuckling, he guided his yidoth toward the estate's coach gateway and dismounted. Amendal did the same and patted the cisthyrn's coarse coat. Though they began opening their portals together, Amendal finished much faster than his father.

Once his yidoth vanished, Arenil beamed with excitement. "Remarkable!" He led Amendal through the coach gateway and to the estate's side entrance.

Arenil called for a servant with a name Amendal didn't recognize. A plump man hurried around a corner and snapped to attention. "Will you send for Bilia and Arintil? I know it's late, but we would like to eat." He gestured to Amendal, and the servant hurried away.

"And bring a platter of cheese," Amendal called after the man. "Some of everything we have."

They walked down the hall, and then turned a corner, entering the estate's two-story dining hall. An opulent table for twenty-four spanned the room, surrounded by high-backed chairs most people would consider thrones. Arenil sauntered to the room's far side, stopping at the oversized mantel near the table's head.

Amendal, however, moved to the towering windows. Moonlight lit the clearing behind the estate and the trees at the forest's edge. "Fench is going to find this a shock…"

"So, you are hiding him," Arenil said, then sighed. "Let me guess, in the Visirm Expanse. Tell me, Amendal, what else are you concealing?"

Amendal turned to his father. *Should I tell him?* Arenil stood beside his seat at the table's head, holding a decorative tin of lavin root.

Stroking his unkempt beard, Amendal considered the request. He would have to swear him to secrecy, but such a secret might drive a wedge between Arenil and the other council members… *But they* did *call me mad.* If anything, that alone would create such a divide. He glanced to the ceiling, but no reply came from the old codger. *Well, he did say his goodbyes…*

Sucking in his breath, Amendal walked to the table. "The full truth." That made his father tense. "My friends are still alive… in a manner of speaking. They're like Old Cali, poisoned by that damned dragon." Arenil looked taken aback, but he didn't speak. "I intend to save them, even if that means I scour this world for the rest of my days. I'll become an adventurer, if I must. But I will save them."

Deliberate applause filled the dining hall, and Amendal turned toward the clapping. His mother walked from the dining room's doors, but she was not the source of the applause. Behind her walked Uncle Krudin, his grin widening with each clap. The lanky man stood as tall as Bilia, his wavy blonde hair accented by a streak of gray. But unlike his sister, Krudin was quite ugly—especially with that hook-shaped nose. He continued clapping as he rounded the table. "Said like a true adventurer! It seems that expedition made you a *real* man!"

Amendal snorted and glanced to his mother. Bilia sighed and pursed her lips. Uncle Krudin had claimed only *real* men ventured out into the world.

Krudin pulled out a chair, sat, and propped his feet atop the table. "It's about time I had another Aramien in my band. What's it been?" He poked his chin at Arenil. "Fifteen years? Sixteen?"

Amendal's father smiled, set down his decorative tin, and removed its lid. "Seventeen," he said, taking a pinch of the pale-purple mulch and placing it in his long pipe.

Uncle Krudin grunted. "Figures you'd remember the day you stopped being a man…"

"Behave yourself," Bilia scolded her brother, stopping one chair from Arenil. Her mood lightened as she eyed Amendal. "I'm glad you're safe. And what did I tell you? It wouldn't be *that* bad?"

"Don't jump to conclusions," Arenil said. "Amendal was the sole survivor."

Bilia paled and brought a hand to her mouth. A tear trickled down her cheek, followed by another. She gazed past Amendal to the windows, most likely imagining everyone who had attended the festivities before their departure. "But… but all those people."

Heavy footsteps carried into the dining hall, and then Arintil appeared. "How was the meeting?" His jaw tensed as he looked between Amendal and their father.

"Not well," Arenil said. He had since lit his pipe, most likely by a basic elemental incantation.

Arintil frowned and took the seat beside Bilia.

"Why don't you tell us *everything*," Arenil said. "But first, why don't you release Fench."

Bilia turned to her husband, confused, but Arenil simply pointed to Amendal.

The incantation rolled off Amendal's tongue so swiftly that Arintil nearly fell out of his chair. Krudin choked and his eyes bulged. Once the portal to the Visirm Expanse opened, Fench zipped from it. He floated above the table, twirling around.

"Where are we?" asked the winged creature.

Amendal smiled. "Home. And I'd like to introduce you to your new family—" Thick-soled footsteps carried into the dining room, and the servant arrived, carrying a platter of cheese. Upon seeing Fench, he nearly dropped it. "Ah, Fench, just in time. As promised, here is your cheese. Now… where should I start?"

Unlike his report to the council, Amendal gave a very detailed retelling of the expedition to Tardalim. While he devoured the cheese, Fench made so many strange noises that Bilia turned away in disgust. She held a hand to her mouth and gave Arenil a look that said, "Do something." Of course, he didn't.

The meal had come and gone before Amendal finished with his tale. He had begun relating his and Fench's trek across the wastes when the chef brought out individual ramekins of a fruit-filled pudding. As the chef served the dessert, he studied Fench with interest rather than alarm. *The server must have warned him about our peculiar guest.*

Everyone was nearly finished with dessert when Amendal finished talking about the penguins. "And when I spotted *The Farling*, the codger said I should hide him." He nodded toward Fench, who was slurping up the dregs of his pudding. "So I put him in the Visirm Expanse."

Uncle Krudin laughed. "That's one way to do it."

He looked around the table, gauging his family's reaction to what they'd heard. None were disbelieving. They didn't even question anything about the old codger.

The he showed his family the conjuration anchor and gave a demonstration. His father and brother marveled at it, and each took their turn inspecting the tevisral.

Bilia was the first to mention Fench. "He can stay with us," she said, struggling to smile. She had cried as he retold the tragedy. "You're part of our family now, Fench."

"We'll have to keep him a secret," Arintil said. "No one can ever know he's a Tuladine."

"A fairy," Bilia said, thoughtfully. "A deranged creature Krudin brought back from one of his adventures. And Amendal named him after the Tuladine that had saved his life."

Fench looked up from his bowl and blinked innocently, pudding staining his trunk. "A faa-ree?"

"Fairy," Krudin said with a grunt. He cocked his head toward Amendal. "Well, if you're determined to find a mystical tevisral that will cure your friends, you might as well join my band."

"Now that we're on that topic," Amendal said. "There's a young barsionist that wants to work with you. Before I left, he wanted to take me to lunch at the Sea Vistonia so I could put in a good word with you. Anyway, I left a message for him that I had returned."

"The Sea Vistonia," Krudin chortled. "What a wise choice! Why don't I join you, and I'll bring my head thief along. Cedath will undoubtedly want to meet the boy."

⸺⊂●⊃⸺

A week had passed since Amendal's return. On the night after Amendal's report to the council, Arenil relayed some news of Old Cali. Though he hadn't died, Calimir was not himself. He could neither talk nor move. His meals had to be fed to him, and he wet himself like a baby.

The council had taken a vote and decided against Amendal releasing the other soldier. *It seems arpran magic is not enough,* he thought. Whatever tevisral he was to find, it would have to do more than harness that Channel of Power.

And as Amendal had hoped, his father did not say a word about his friends, Fench, or the conjuration anchor. Those were secrets he planned to take to his grave, and he encouraged Amendal to do the same. In fact, he had forbidden Amendal from ever speaking of the matter to the Cetarins. Arenil thought it best for them to grieve their son and move past his death. Why dangle such a faint glimmer of hope for what might never come to pass?

If a means to *truly* cure the yaeltis venom were found, then they could deal with the ramifications of falsifying so many deaths.

Arintil had also vowed himself to silence over the matter, as had Bilia. Krudin had not said so much, but Bilia believed he would stay silent. If anything, he would only spin tales about the expedition that no one would actually believe.

That left only Fench.

Before retiring to bed, Amendal took the winged creature to the family library. "You understand how important it is that the survivors remain a secret, don't you Fench?"

The winged creature fluttered about, inspecting each of the tomes.

"Fench?"

"Yes, Master," he said in a monotone, but then giggled. The past week, Amendal had been schooling Fench on a new demeanor, meant to suggest that the winged creature was a servant to Amendal.

"Yes, Master, I understand? Or..."

Fench flew from the bookshelves in a wide arc. "I won't say a word." He rolled up his trunk so his lips touched his forehead.

"Well, you can't go flying about like that."

Laughing, Fench released his trunk, and it flopped against his chest. The clicking of heels echoed into the library, then Bilia crossed the room. "And what am I reading tonight?"

Fench flew across the library and pulled a small book from the shelf. He handed it to Amendal's mother, who sat down in one of the oversized chairs. Fench coiled his tail on the floor while resting his trunk across her lap. As she began reading, Bilia stroked Fench's trunk. She had grown fond of the winged creature these last few days, and she had come to accept him as if he were one of her own children.

⊂•⊃

The following day, Amendal received a note from Vargos. The youth had taken a trip to the Isle of Sorti after becoming a full-fledged barsionist and had returned to Soroth the prior evening, narrowly missing Arenil as he finished his council duties at the Order and left for home.

Amendal sent a messenger for Uncle Krudin to meet him at the Sea Vistonia, then made his way to the Sorothian Magical Order to fetch Vargos.

Once on the Order's grounds, he found the young barsionist reading a book under the same tree where Dugal and Fendar had pulled their prank. Only part of the book's title was visible: *The Disk of Eternity, The Mind of...* Vargos's hand covered the rest of it.

The youth didn't seem to notice Amendal, not even when he cleared his throat. "Is that any good?"

Vargos jumped, fumbling the book. "Oh, you scared—oh, you!" He pushed himself up, dusted off his robe, and ran a hand through his hair.

"How do I look, Mister Amendal?"

He certainly didn't look as disheveled as the day Amendal had first met him. "Fine. The book?"

"Oh!" Vargos held it out and examined it. "Uh, well, it's good. But it sort of reads like *Master of the Orbs*. People say the story gets different in later books. It has a dragon in it I think?"

Amendal raised an eyebrow at the mention of dragons. "The author probably got it wrong. I'll have to see if it's right. Come, let's meet my uncle."

The Sea Vistonia hummed with noisy conversations. Krudin sat at the L-shaped bar with a short fellow wearing a fancy green doublet. *Cedath?* Whoever it was twirled the ends of a long mustache.

Vargos gasped. "Oh, it's them!"

Must be him, Amendal thought, and Vargos hurried toward the bar. The dining hall was full, and only the bar had vacant seats, though they were sparse. Vargos took the empty spot beside Uncle Krudin, leaving no room for Amendal.

After some brief introductions, young Vargos gushed over Krudin and his band's accomplishments. Some of the things he mentioned Amendal had never heard.

"You know, I have two openings." Krudin leaned back, rubbing his hands together. "We could use another barsionist. You can't be too careful while out in the world."

"And the other spot?" Vargos asked. "I have a friend—"

Krudin pointed to Amendal. "My nephew will be joining us. He's quite formidable, what with being a dragon slayer."

Vargos's eyes went wide. "Dragonslayer?"

"Oh yes," Krudin said, and recited a much-embellished rendering of the battle with Orath'issian, one in which the dragon breathed fire.

As his uncle continued the far-fetched tale, Amendal moved farther down the bar, near the windows overlooking the ocean. Having recognized him, the bartender approached with a glass of brandleberry wine. "Here you are, Mister Aramien."

Taking a sip, Amendal looked about the room, recalling his last visit. The thought of it pained his soul, and he ached for his friends. Eyes on the door, Amendal imagined Ildin walking inside and asking the host for Amendal, then waving as he crossed the room. *Will I ever see him like that again?*

He had to. No matter the cost, he *would* save them. *I'll find that tevisral... whatever it is.*

After he finished his wine, a woman took the seat beside him. He probably would have thought her pretty, even beautiful. But he had no desire to even speak to her. Never had he *not* tried to seduce such a woman. In all truth, he had barely paid attention to her. She had received a brief glance, but that was all. Now, if he had seen her two months prior, he would probably have attempted to bed her, but not now.

Not after Faelinia. She had molded him into the man he was now. It was she who had made him reconsider the expedition. Their exploring together had evoked a curiosity that could only be satisfied while exploring the world. And she had revealed his bravery in the direst of circumstances.

The thought of the qurasiphage crept into his mind, but no, it wasn't Orath'issian's curse that had changed him. *I was already a different man when that mist engulfed me. It was her… it was* always *her.*

Of all the women in the world, none could rival Faelinia Tusara; for there was no woman who shared her beauty, her bravery, her tenacity, her tenderness, or her magical prowess. She was perfect. But she was gone, and never would Amendal Aramien love another woman.

THE END OF

The Prisoner of Tardalim
A TALES OF THE AMULET NOVEL

GLOSSARY

A glossary of names, people, places, objects, and terms found in *The Prisoner of Tardalim*. Pronunciations and brief descriptions or definitions included. Spoilers contained within many descriptions.

Pronunciation Key:

ə .... banana, collide, abut
ər.... further, merger, bird
a .... mat, map, mad, gag, snap, patch
ā .... day, fade, date, aorta, drape, cape
ä .... bother, cot
är .... car, heart, bazaar, bizarre
aů .... now, loud, out
e .... bet, bed, peck
er .... bare, fair, wear, millionaire
ē .... easy, mealy
i .... tip, banish, active
ir .... near, deer, mere, pier
ī .... site, side, buy, tripe
j .... job, gem, edge, join, judge
k .... kin, cook, ache

k̲ ....German ich, Buch; loch
ŋ .... sing\'siŋ\, singer\siŋ-ər\, finger\'fiŋ-gər\, ink\iŋk\
ō .... bone, know, beau
ȯ .... saw, all, gnaw, caught
ȯi .... coin, destroy
ȯr .... boar, port, door, shore
th .... thin, ether
t̲h̲ .... then, either, this
ü .... rule, youth, union, few
ů .... pull, wood, boo
ůr .... boor, tour, insure
zh .... vision, azure\'a-zher
’ .... marks preceding syllable with primary stress
- .... marks syllable division

Abodal (ab’-ō-dal): the Elvish name for the Abodine Wasteland.

Abodine Wasteland (ab’-ō–dīn): the Common name for the southernmost continent of Kalda, located on the planet's southern pole.

Adrin (ad’-rin): a grand mage from Alath, slayer of Emperor Mentas. He is married to Gwenyth Cetarin, and is the father of Iltar and Almar. He is also known as the "Hero of the West."

Aes’shivar (ae-shi’-vär): a female Eshari Warder.

Alath (ə’-lath): the city of mages, located in the northern regions of the Kingdom of Los.

Alberous Kenard, (ȯl’-bər-aus | ken-ärd): the first mate aboard the *White Duchess* and son of the vessel's captain.

Aldinal Plane (ȯl’-din-ȯl): another plane of reality where all matter is a broken down to its base form. Conjurers access the Aldinal Plane to manifest objects and creatures.

Alnese (ȯl-nēs): the granddaughter of Dorith.

Amendal Aramien (ōmen’-dal | ‘ə-rā-mē-en): the youngest son of Arenil and Bilia Aramien. He is a conjurer from Soroth well versed in the magical arts of his discipline.

annihilation magic: a sub-branch of the Decay Channel of Magic. Red in color, it instantly turns living tissue to dried husks.

apprentice: the highest rank for fledgling mages in the Sorothian Magical Order.

Aramien Estate (ˈə-rā-mē-en): the sprawling woodland mansion owned by the Aramien family, situated in the forests an hour's horse ride from the city of Soroth.

Aramien Test of Valor (ˈə-rā-mē-en): a test administered to members of the Aramien Family to embark on a quest to traverse the Melar Forest in the Kingdom of Los. The primary goal of the test is to find a gangolin and capture it.

Arbath (är'-bath): a major port city in the Kingdom of Los, well known for setting trends in fashion and furniture.

Arcane Channel: one of the primary Channels of Power.

arcane magic: forms of magic manifested from the Arcane Channel.

arcanist: a subclass of the wizardry discipline, primarily focused on using incantations to manifest the Arcane Channel of Power.

Arenil Aramien (är-in-ˈil | ˈə-rā-mē-en): a powerful conjurer from Soroth, and the head conjurer of the Sorothian Magical Order. Husband to Bilia, and father to Amendal and Arintil.

Aridian (ä'-ri-dē-ən): a group of humans from the now destroyed continent of Aridia. The first human magic wielders on Kalda.

Arintil Aramien (är-in-ˈil | ˈə-rā-mē-en): the eldest son of Arenil and Bilia Aramien, the elder brother of Amendal.

arpran magic (är-prən'): a type, or channel, or magic that can heal, regenerate, and prolong life.

arpranist (är-prən'-ist): a mage who specializes in utilizing arpran magic.

Au: the draconic name for the Manipulation Channel of Power.

barsion (bär'-zhən): a type, or channel, of protective magic used primarily to create defensive barriers, but it can also restrain.

barsion shield (bär'-zhən): a barrier of barsion magic, often a partial sphere.

barsionist (bär'-zhən-ist): a mage who uses the Barsion Channel of Power.

Battle Tactics of the Beastcallers: one of four books held by the Aramien conjurers detailing the strategies used by ancient conjurers throughout Kalda's history, particularly during the Dragon Wars.

Beastcaller: an early name for conjurers and one of the twenty orders for the Keepers of Truth and Might.

Bilanus (bil-ə-nus'): a burly squad leader in Calimir's expedition to Tardalim.

Bilia Aramien (bil-ē-a' | ˈə-rā-mē-en): the wife of Arenil Aramien and mother to Amendal and Arintil.

Black Mountains: the vast range of mountains spanning the Mainland continent. They are located roughly sixty degrees north of Kalda's equator. The southern foothills of the range run along the northern reaches of the Elven Realm and the human nations of Cordath and Comdolith. Beyond its northern foothills lie the Carda Wastes.

Brantis Secarin (bran-tis' | sec-är'-in): the grandmaster of the Sorothian Magical Order, a wizard.

Braynar (brāy'-när): a squad leader in Calimir's expedition to Tardalim.

Burlai (bůr'-laī): a pet cisthyrn belonging to Aes'shivar.

cafis'sha (cä-fēs'-shȯ): a draconic breed of chromatic orange.

Calimir Sharn (kal'-ē-mīr | shärn): a retired naval commander who was well decorated in his military service. He is a thick built man of average height, with a broad face and a bulbous nose.

Carda Wastes (kär-də'): an arctic wasteland on the Mainland, located north of the Black Mountains.

Cedath (cē'-dəth): an expert thief who possesses several unique tevisrals, and a member of Krudin's adventuring band.

Channels of Magic: the system by which magic is categorized on the world of Kalda. It consists of seven distinct channels, or types of magic: arcane, arpran, barsion, conjuration, elemental, manipulation, transmutation.

Channels of Power: the true name for the Channels of Magic, see Channels of Magic.

Cheserith (chez'-ər-ith): the god of Cherisium, worshiped by the Mindolarnians.

Cheserithean Empire (chez'-ər-ith-ē-en): an ancient empire that once ruled all of Kalda, lead by Cheserith.

Cherisium (chər-is-ē–'əm): an ancient religion dating back to the reign of Cheserith.

Chorlia Igasan (chor-lia' | ī'-ga-san): a powerful arpranist from Soroth, head of the arpran school at the Sorothian Magical Order.

cisthyrn(s) (cis-<u>th</u>ůrn'): wolf-like creatures that inhabits the Abodine Wasteland. Cisthyrns are twice the size of the average wolf, with pale-blue crystalline horns and claws. The whites of their eyes are blue while their irises are white.

Cluvis (clů-vīs'): a sailor aboard the *Giboran*, first mate to Captain Edara.

colina(s) (cō-li-nə'): snake-like creatures native to the Abodine Wasteland.

Colvinar Vrium (cōl'-vin-när | vrīüm): a conjurer from a past era, author of *Colvinar Vrium's Bestiary for Conjurers*.

Colvinar Vrium's Bestiary for Conjurers (cōl-vin-när | vrīüm): an ancient tome containing knowledge about various creatures found across Kalda and how they pertain to the conjurers. One of four tomes kept sacred by the Aramien conjurers.

Common Tongue: the primary language spoken by the humans of Kalda.

communications rod: a tevisral designed by Vaem Rudal to enable verbal communication across great distances. Its proposed design would use a sub-branch of illusory magic to enable communication between linked devices.

conjuration anchor: the name Amendal Aramien has given to a tevisral capable of binding rogulin.

Conjuration Channel: the Channel of Power that enables access to the Aldinal Plane, the Visirm Expanse, as well as enable teleportation through portals.

conjuration magic: the magic wielded by conjurers to manifest creatures from the Aldinal Plane and the Visirm Expanse, golden in color.

conjurer: a mage who accesses the Conjuration Channel of Power to access the Aldinal Plane and the Visirm Expanse. The Aldinal Plane contains raw matter while the Visirm Expanse is a timeless void.

conjurer's stone: the layman's term for rogulin crystals.

conjurer's void: the laymen's term for the Visirm Expanse.

Corasian (ʻkòr-a-sean*):* a soldier from the third squad of Calimir's expedition to Tardalim.

Cordis Rishan (ʻkòr-dis | ri'-shòn*):* a powerful necromancer and the head of that discipline at the Sorothian Magical Order.

Coridician (ʻkòr-i-di-cian*):* a scholar from the Hilinard.

corusilist (ʻkòr-ů-sil-ist*):* a type of mage specializing in corrosive magic. They are similar to necromancers but do not apply the practice of reanimation. Few schools in the human realm train mages to become Corusilists. They're mostly found among the elves of Kalda.

Crimson Eye: the name given by devouts of Cherisium to the Amulet of Draconic Control, the Au'misha'k.

Crisyan Bay (crĩ'-sē-an*):* a small bay locked by ice on the continent of Abodal.

crysillac (cry'-sil-lak*):* subterranean behemoths attributed with the ability to turn anything they touch to crystal. They have dozens of legs and tentacles.

Desert of Ash: a desert on the Forsaken Lands, the continent of Azrin'il. Known for its greenish-gray sand. Gangolins are rumored to roam parts of the desert.

Desidan (de-sī-dan'*):* a god who once walked Kalda alongside Cheserith.

diam'sha (diam-shò'*):* draconic for drake. See drake.

Disk of Eternity: a series of fictional novels on Kalda.

disintegrating barsion (bär'-zhən*):* a mixture of barsion and disintegrating magic.

disintegrating magic: a sub-branch of the Arcane Channel of Power, manifesting with purple light.

dispel: a type of arcane magic that negates magic.

Divine Tongue: an ancient language spoken by the gods of Kalda, sharp and guttural.

Dohaliem (dō-ʻha-lēm*):* the headquarters of the usa'zin'sha within the underground city of Usazma'thirl. Also the elvish word for "grand training hall."

Dorith (dòr'-ith): the son of Zulsthy'l, and one of four leaders of the Guardians of Kalda.

dorin (dòr'-in): a coin from the Kingdom of Los.

Dragon Wars: a mythical war rumored to have occurred thousands of years ago, waged between the factions of dragonkind.

drake: winged serpentine creatures, though not as large as dragons. By comparison, most drakes are about one tenth the size of a dragon. Though they are intelligent, drakes do not speak nor manifest magic. They have four limbs: two legs and a pair of wings.

dualist mage: a mage specializing in two channels of magic.

Dugal Vintris (dü-gal' | vīn-tris'): a transmuter from Soroth, friend to Amendal Aramien. He is known for his pragmatic attitude.

Dusel Nadim (dü-sl | nə-dēm): the first and last Guardian of Kalda, the founder of the Keepers of Truth and Might.

earthen conjuration: humanoid creatures manifested from the Aldinal Plane and made of dirt, rocks and vegetation.

earthen giant(s): humanoid creatures manifested from the Aldinal Plane and made of dirt, rocks and vegetation, standing the equivalent of three stories, thirty feet or twenty and a half phineals.

Edara, Sauron (ē-'där-ə | saû-rōn): the captain of the *Giboran*.

Dardel Draile (där'-del | dräy-lē): a retired naval officer, and the right hand man of Calimir Sharn.

Edicts of the Mage-King: the supreme law of the Kingdom of Los. Its primary decree was the confiscation of all tevisrals within the human realm.

Elara (ē'-lär-ə): one of Amendal Aramien's lovers.

Elarin (ē'-lär-in): the true name for the Common Tongue.

elemental [creature]: beings manifested from the Aldinal Plane by conjurers. Supposed to have once existed long ago on Kalda. They exist in various forms; magma, earth, air, water, fire, etc.

Elemental Channel: the channel of magic capable of manifesting naturally occurring forces, including: wind, water, fire, earth, ice, acid, magma, etc.

elemental giant(s): mid-sized creatures composed of elemental matter from the Aldinal Plane, standing the equivalent of three stories, thirty feet or twenty and a half phineals. Supposed to have once existed long ago on Kalda. They exist in various forms; magma, earth, air, water, fire, etc.

elemental gargantuan(s): the largest creatures composed of elemental matter from the Aldinal Plane, standing the equivalent of six stories, sixty feet or forty-one phineals. Supposed to have once existed long ago on Kalda. They exist in various forms; magma, earth, air, water, fire, etc.

elementalist: a subclass within the wizardly discipline, specializing in manifesting the Elemental Channel of magic.

Emblems of Divinity: the seven symbols of Cherisium.

Emirna Trutim *(ē'-mirn-ə | trŭ-tim'):* a powerful barsionist. She is the head of the barsion discipline at the Sorothian Magical Order.

enhancement magic: a sub-branch of the Manipulation Channel of Power, manifesting as white light.

enthralling component: part of an incantation conjurer's use to trap creatures in the Visirm Expanse. It is akin to enthralling magic.

enthralling magic: a sub-branch of the Manipulation Channel of Power, manifesting as gray light.

Eradas *(ər'-ad-as):* a faithful drake who belonged to Dorith but is now a baelnarn.

es'umak *(ē'-sŭ-mak'):* a draconic command for removing parts of an Ulk'sha's armor.

Eshari *(ē'-shär-ī):* an ancient humanoid race who inhabited the Abodine Wasteland, capable of thriving in the extreme cold. Their features resemble the elves of Kalda, but their skin is a pale-blue.

Esharian *(ē'-shär-īən):* a member of the Eshari race.

Esharian Collective *(ē'-shär-īən):* the name of the Eshari nation.

Esharian Warder *(ē'-shär-īən):* see Warder of the Plains.

euphorinizer *(eüphor-in-i-zər):* a tevisral designed by Vaem Rudal, the only one of its kind. Capable of creating an enthralling-like bond by manipulating sexual urges.

Faelinia Tusara *(fae'-lin-iə | tu-sar-a'):* a powerful dualist mage from Soroth. She specializes as a dualist wizard and an illusionist.

fanisar *(fən-ē-sär):* a bladed staff weapon. Variants exist throughout Kalda among both humans and elves. Typical fanisars in the human realm consist of a single shaft, between three and four feet in length, a curving blade at one end, and a weight at the other end; often sphere-shaped. The elven variation is a double-bladed staff. The staff can break apart into three sections and is bound together by a chain.

Farling: a large four mast vessel often charted for private voyages.

Fate of Mirdrys *(mŭr-dris'):* a legend of the nation of Mirdrys who used powerful tevisrals to protect themselves and their cities, veiling them in impenetrable barriers that made them disappeared from the rest of the world.

Faziac *(fā'-zhi-ak):* a soldier turned adventurer and member of Calimir's expedition to Tardalim.

Fen'chalim'nidam *(fen-cha'-lim-nī'-dām):* a young Tuladine, the last of his kind in Tardalim.

Fench *(fench):* see Fen'chalim'nidam. A nick name given to Fen'chalim'nidam by Amendal Aramien.

Fendar Callis *(fen'-där | kāl'-lis):* an illusionist from Soroth. He is Scialas's lover, and a friend to Amendal Aramien.

flaming barsion *(bär'-zhən):* a barrier of barsion infused with fiery magic.

flaming orb: a condensed palm-sized sphere of fiery magic.

Forcu'sia (for-'cŭ'-siə): an ancient god who once walked Kalda with Cheserith.

Forsaken Lands: one of Kalda's continents, situated in the northeastern hemisphere of the world. Also known as Azrin'il.

galstra (gal'-strə): a stone variant of granite native to Soroth, often gray.

gangolin (gāŋ-gòl-in'): a mythical creature akin to a dragon, but without wings. Rumored extinct, but some claim gangolins roam the Melar Forest.

Giboran (gī-bor'-an): a private vessel owned by Sauron Edara, comparable to the Sarin-class warships of the Sorothian Navy: it has six masts and six decks, three below the main.

gosset(s) (gäs-set'): a white long-necked bird. Black tips mark the edges of their wings. Pale yellow feathers cover their crowns and run partway down their necks. When hunting for food they dive into the water.

grand mage: a magic wielder who specializes in accessing each of the seven Channels of Power.

grand phineal (phin-e'-al): a thousand phineals, a length used for denoting large distances and often abbreviated in the Elarin characters of G.P. on road signs and in conversations.

Greater Conjurations from the Aldinal Plane (òl'-din-òl): an ancient tome containing knowledge and incantations to summon powerful and unique creatures from the Aldinal Plane, particularly elemental conjurations. One of four tomes kept sacred by the Aramien conjurers.

Guardians of Kalda (kòl-də): an ancient order of protectors, consisting of humans, elves, dragons, and qui'sha. They are led by Ilnari, Dorith, Zulsthy'l, and Zu'mal'thisr'nsar. The last three are separate generations of the same family.

Guardians of Soroth (sòr'-òth): an elite guard responsible for protecting the Principality's state officials. They wear brown plate armor and wield fanisars.

Gwenyth Cetarin (gwen-yth | ce-tär'-in): an illusionist from Soroth, Ildin's older sister and wife of Adrin.

Haedral Scurn (hae'-dral | skərn): a necromancer originally from the Island of Sarn.

Halisium (hal-is'-īum): a type of beer.

Halls of the Damned: see Tardalim.

Halls of Damnation: see Tardalim.

Harbinger of Hemran'na (hem-ren-nò'): see Unspoken One.

Heart of the Sphere: see Roost, the. The true name of Tardalim's core.

Hedgetrancer: an early name for barsionists and one of the twenty orders for the Keepers of Truth and Might.

Heleron (hel-ər'-òn): the god of the ocean, worshiped primarily by sailors and some Sorothians.

Hemran'na (hem-ròn-na'): God of gods. Often referred to as Master by the other gods of Kalda.

Hero of the West: a title given to Adrin by the citizens of Tor and the rebels of the Western Soverignty.

Hevanisa (he'-van-ī-sò): a type of cheese.

Hevasir (he'-vā-sir): a soldier turned adventurer.

Hilinard (hil'-in-ärd): an institution of higher learning in Mindolarn, responsible for curating knowledge and creating tevisrals.

ice flyer: see Seracius Lepidor.

ice moth: see Viliasim.

Ildin Cetarin ('il-dīn | . ce-tär'-in): an illusionist from Soroth, the son of Ilyanin Cetarin, the younger brother of Gwenyth, and the closest friend of Amendal Aramien.

illusionist: a mage who specializes in the Manipulation Channel of Power, creating illusions, enhancements, and manipulations of the mind.

Illusory Channel: a sub-branch of the Manipulation Channel of Power.

illusory magic: the type of magic manifested from the Illusory sub-branch of the Manipulation Channel of Power.

Ilnari (il-när-ē'): the mentor of Zulsthy'l, one of four leaders of the Guardians of Kalda.

Iltar ('il-tär): the newborn nephew of Ildin, son of Gwenyth and Adrin.

Ilyanin Cetarin ('il-yān-in | ce-tär'-in): a powerful illusionist, the head of that discipline, and member of the Sorothian Magical Order's council. Father of Ildin.

imbuing, magical: the process of placing an enhancement upon an object.

Isle of Merdan (mər-dan'): an island in the southwest ocean of Kalda, the Kalishir Ocean.

Isle of Sarn (sərn): the second largest island in the Principality of Soroth.

Isle of Soroth (sòr'-òth): the largest island in the Principality of Soroth, home to the nation's capitol sharing the same name.

Isle of Sorti (sòr'-ti): a minor island in the Principality of Soroth.

Irum'mak'sha (ir-üm-'mäk-shò): draconic title for the twelve dragons holding the highest knowledge for each Channel of Power.

Jaekim Nordim (jā-kim' | nòr-dīm'): a necromancer from Soroth, friend to Amendal Aramien. He is known for his drunken demeanor and raucous laughter.

Kaelyrn (kā-lē-ûrn'): one of Kalda's moons which shines with speckled light.

Kaerune (kā'-rŭn): a squad leader in Calimir's expedition to Tardalim.

Kaladorn Frontier (kal'-ə-dòrn): the western plains in the nation of Kaladorn, near the borders of the Elven Realm.

Kalda (kòl-də'): the name of the World.

Kaldean Alliance (kòl-dē'-en): a union between a small faction of humans, the entirety of elvenkind and several metallic breeds of dragons, including the platinum, gold and copper breeds. They fought against the

Cheserithean Empire.

Kaldean Common Tongue (Common Tongue): the primary language spoken by the humans of Kalda.

Kardorth (kär'-dòrth): one of the oldest elven cities and capitol of the elven realm.

Kardorthian (kär'-dòrth-en): the name for elves living in Kardorth.

Karthar (k'ər-thär): a region along the northeastern continent of the Mainland. Much of it is uninhabited by humans and is a forbidden land decreed by the early kings of Los. The neighboring nations enforce the borders, barring travelers or adventurers from entering the Karthar region.

Karthar Empire (k'ər-thär): an empire which rose to power over eleven hundred years before Amendal Aramien's adventure to Tardalim. The empire reigned over the entire continent known as the Mainland until it was overthrown by rebels based in Alath.

Kenard (ken'-ärd): a family of seafarers who have owned the *White Duchess* for several generations.

Kildath (kil'-dath): a large city-nation located on the Kaldean Mainland. It is one of three powerful human nations on Kalda.

Kingdom of Los: the largest of three powerful human nations on Kalda; the others being Kildath and the Western Sovereignty. After the fall of the Karthar Empire, the Kingdom ruled all the Kaldean Mainland until the ninth king divided the borders, establishing a new Kildath and the Western Sovereignty. Since then, many other nations have sprung from each of the three countries. Established by Dorin, the Mage-King, Los has been a peaceful realm devoted to protecting all humanity.

kisalic (ki'-sä-lic): a Tuladine fruit used for putting one to sleep.

Kistern (kis-tŭrn'): one of Kalda's moons who shines the brightest.

Klath (k'lath): a port city off the Aglin Gulf, located on the Mainland in the Kingdom of Los.

Ko'delish (ko-də-lish): a type of magic capable of dissolving all it touches, manifesting as a black mist.

Krudin (krŭ'-dĭn): the leader of an adventuring band based out of Soroth, uncle to Amendal Aramien.

Ku'tharn (kü'-thärn): the daughter of Cheserith, and the acknowledged God-Empress of the Order of the Red and the fractured Cheserithean Empire.

Kydol Virain (kī-dòl' | vir-ain'): a Mindolarnian lieutenant under General Vidaer's command, sent to accompany Calimir's expedition to Tardalim.

lavin root (lā-vin): a sweet root often smoked in a pipe. It is a "cheap" substance used by the lower castes of the human realm.

Laws of the Visirm (vis-ər'-m): a book held by the Aramien conjurers detailing the specifics of the Visirm expand, a definitive volume on the subject.

Legacy of Asirum Tandir (ə'-sir-um | tan-dir'): a fictional novel.

life-draining magic: a sub-branch of the Decay Channel of Power.

lightstone: a stone capable of emitting magic in the form of light. Lightstones are considered magical in nature. Some believe their light a result of tevisrals—magical objects—while others believe they are tevisrals.

*lish'qui'sha (*lish-kē-shò'*):* draconic for "half-breed" particularly those that are half-red dragon and half-human.

*lish'sha (*lish-shə'*):* a draconic breed of chromatic dragons, red.

*Losian (*los'-en*):* the term for citizens of the Kingdom of Los.

magma elemental(s): humanoid elemental beings composed of magma, typically the size of a man or elf.

mage: any person who is trained to access the Channels of Power.

Mage-King: a title held by the first monarch of the Kingdom of Los, Dorin the son of Lith Luzdom.

mages' parasite: layman's term for quinta'shal. See quinta'shal.

magnifier: a tevisral capable of magnifying vision similar in size to a monocle, but has the appearance of a solid black dome.

Mainland: the largest continent on Kalda, located in the northwestern hemisphere of the world.

*Makivir's Lounge (*mä'-ki-vir*):* a nightlife establishment located on Soroth, with a bar, tavern, and dance hall.

*ma'lisha (*mä'-lish-ò*):* draconic for "immortal demon," beings who came into existence during the Thousand Years War. They were created by Cheserith.

Master of the Orbs: a fictional series of novels.

*Medis Midivar (*med'-is | mid-i-'vär*):* the third ruler of the Mindolarn Empire, and a brother of Mindolarn.

*Melar Forest (*mel-är'*):* a sprawling woodland in the Kingdom of Los. It was decreed forbidden by the early monarchs of the kingdom.

*men'thak (*men-thak*):* a vulgar draconic curse word

*Mentas Midivar (*men'-tas | mid-i-'vär*):* the second ruler of the Mindolarn Empire, and a brother of Mindolarn. Assassinated by the Hero of the West and the rebels of Tor during Amendal's Aramien Test of Valor.

*Mentil (*men'-til*):* a soldier turned adventurer from the second squad of Calimir's expedition to Tardalim.

*Meradis (*mər'-a-dis*):* a scholar from the Hilinard.

*Merath (*mər'-ath*):* an elven city on the eastern coast of the Kaldean Mainland, one of two remaining elven cities from Kalda's ancient era.

*Merdan (*mər'-dan*):* see, Isle of Merdan.

*messel (*mes-sel'*):* a popular tea made from the inner bark of a tree of the same name.

mind-circlet: an ancient tevisral capable of permanently altering one's mind. When used by another person it can be used as a permanent solution to mind-control. The effect leaves no magical trace.

*Mindolarn Empire (*mīn-dō'-lärn*):* a nation on the Kaldean Mainland also known as Mindolarn.

Mindolarnian (mīn-dō'-lärn-ē-en): a term for citizens of the Mindolarn Empire.

Miraden (mir-ä'-den): a retired soldier turned mercenary-adventurer, and a squad leader in Calimir's expedition to Tardalim.

Morgidian Shival (môr'-gī-di-an | shi-vòl'): a barsionist from Soroth, and a friend to Amendal Aramien. He is of a burly stature.

nactilious (näc-til-ē'-ûs): an enormous aquatic sea creature with thirty-two tentacles. Each tentacle ranges from twenty phineals to thirty-three phineals in length. The creature's overall length ranges between fifty and seventy phineals, with a head around seventeen phineals long. An incredibly hard carapace protects most of its head, with openings for its four eyes. A beak sits at the base of its head with small white antennae lining the beak's interior. Like other cephalopods of Kalda, the nactilious secretes ink that is black-red. Most nactili are various shades of blue and greens with silver or gray accents, with earthen toned carapaces and beaks.

nactili (näc-til-ē'): the pural for Nactilious.

Naedra (nä-drä'): a soldier turned adventurer and squad leader from Calimir's expedition to Tardalim.

Nai'ul (näi-ül'): the daughter of Zulsthy'l, half-sister to Dorith.

necromancer: a mage class specializing in the darker arts of the various Channels of Power. They are capable of reanimating the dead, siphoning the life of the living, and mustering corrosive magics.

Never-ending Labyrinth: see Tardalim.

Niza Hiram (nē-zò' | hir'-am): author of the *Realm of Sorrow*.

Nordis (nòr-dis'): a former naval officer and squad leader in Calimiar's expedition to Tardalim.

nullifier: an ancient tevisral capable of dissolving the bonds of the Eldari power.

Orath'issian (ôr'-ath-iss'-ē-an): the god of terror. Cafis'sha breed (a draconic breed of chromatic orange), captured and held in Tardalim in his divine form of a quan'tasiran—the name of this form is unknown to the Kaldean Alliance. He is capable of emitting a mist that causes irreparable mental debilitation, qurasiphage.

Orchin's Tavern (ôr-chin'): a middle class tavern on the Isle of Soroth, known for their spherical gambling chips.

Order of Histories: an organization of scholars from Soroth dedicated to keeping records, cataloging knowledge, and maintaining museums.

Orin (ôrin): a soldier turned adventurer and squad leader in Calimir's expedition to Tardalim.

Os'icasa'nidas (ôs-i'-casə-nidäs'): an adult Tuladine, one of four adult survivors of Tardalim's second incursion.

phantasmal essence: a creature capable of mimicking the appearance of other beings. They are often the true culprits behind ghost stories on

Kalda.

phedan (fed'-an): the standard measurement for plots of land on Kalda, the equivalent of three hundred square phineals.

phineal (fen-ē'-al): the standard length of measurement on Kalda; the equivalent of seventeen and a half inches or forty-three centimeters.

pla'sha (pòl-shò'): a draconic breed of metallic dragon, platinum.

Plains of Vesikar (ves-ē-kär'): a now desolate plain located on the Desolate Lands.

potential: a rank of aspiring usa'zin'sha.

Principality of Soroth (sòr'-òth): a nation in the southwestern waters of the Kalishir Ocean, consisting of seventeen islands: Soroth, Sereth, Sarn, Silgarn, Seriel, Sorgil, Scagarn, Sogil, Sorti, Sangarn, Scain, Seril, Sargon, Seron, Spilath, Scon, Scagil. Each island has their own democratic system. Representatives from each island sit on a national council arbitrated by the Governor of Soroth.

qaun'tasiran (kaùn-'tās'-ir-ən): a mythical creature of terror. They are rumored to have eight limbs, four arms and four legs, and stand three stories when on all eights. Their tails are tipped with pincers, and their hides are incredibly thick. Orange gills line their heads that mist a substance called qurasiphage.

qurasiphage (kùra-zi'-fāge): an orange haze emitted by a qaun'tasiran's gills. If inhaled, it will drive one mad. Its effects have permanence similar to solistum.

quinta'shal (kēn-'ta'-shòl): humanoid creatures whose primary form of sustenance comes from magic. They are gray-skinned with large pores, several inches in diameter, lining their bodies. Long forked tongues absorb the magic and are the primary digestive organ.

qui'sha (kē-shò'): draconic for "half breed."

Ran'disan (ran-dis'-ən): a pet cisthyrn to the Eshari Warder, Aes'shivar.

Realm of Sorrow: a fictional tale about Tardalim.

Redogan (re'-dō-gan): a soldier from the second squad of Calimir's expedition to Tardalim.

rejuvenating magic: a type of arpran magic.

Ril'sha (ril-shò'): draconic name for, council. Anciently, the Ril'sha was the ruling body of all dragonkind, with representatives from each draconic breed. After the Thousand Years War, the Ril'Sha consisted of seven to twelve platinum dragons.

Rogulin (ròg-ü'-lin): a type of blue crystal with golden flecks, native to Kalda with transporting capabilities. It is exotic matter. The crystal's mass determines the size of the portal it can form and the matter it can transport.

Rogulin Crystal (ròg-ü'-lin): typically a small chunk of rogulin.

Rogulin Sphere (ròg-ü'-lin): refined rogulin usually twice the size of a man's head. Such spheres are capable of teleporting large forces.

Roost: the heart of Tardalim, the residence of the Tuladine. It is covered in bizarre vegetation not commonly found on Kalda: teal grass, multi-colored florescent vines, and buildings similar to massive tree-trunks.

saniuri *(*sani-ůrĭ'*):* weapons consisting of a forearm length handle with a curved blade on one end and a long chain at the other. Their chains vary in length, but can be up to twenty phineals. At the end of the chain is a spiked tetrahedron, whose spikes are about the length of a finger.

sarin-class warship *(*sär'-in*):* the largest class of warship in the Sorothian Navy. The vessels have five masts, sixty two canons, two of which are long-range artillery canons. They have eight decks; three above the main deck, and four below. They measure one hundred and forty phineals from stem to stern, with a beam of twenty seven and a half phineals. Each vessel has a crew compliment of three hundred and twenty eight.

Sarn *(*sarn*):* an island-state in the Principality of Soroth. The second largest in geographical size but third in population.

Scialas Jeroid *(*scĭ'-las | jůr-ȯid'*):* an arpranist from Soroth, and friend to Amendal Aramien.

Scurn House *(*skərn*):* a minor house in Sarn's aristocracy.

Sea Vistonia *(*vis-ton-ia*):* a notorious restaurant in the northeastern corner of Soroth, the city.

Selicas *(*sel-ē'-cas*):* a squad leader from Calimir's expedition to Tardalim.

Seracai(s) *(*ser-a-kaĭ'*):* six-winged serpentines, twice the size of an average man. They are capable of naturally producing certain types of magic.

seracius lepidor *(*ser-a-cĭus' | lep'-ē-dȯr*):* a tiny ice conjuration from the Aldinal Plane, representative of an insect.

sha'kalda *(*shȯ'-kȯl-də'*):* draconic for, dragon.

shan'ak *(*shan-äk'*):* draconic for conjuration anchor, see conjuration anchor.

Sharzen *(*shär'-zhen*):* a game of chance played with a card deck consisting of seven suits of twelve cards.

Shem'rinal *(*shem'-rin-ȯl*):* a magical essence, a being composed of life and magic inseparably connected.

Shift: a mechanical and magical process within Tardalim that causes its halls to change.

Shiz'nak *(*shiz-nək'*):* draconic for, "tethering stone." A magical object capable of opening a spherical portal to another world, created by the Irum'mak'sha during the Dragon Wars. Various texts claim it was made from rogulin crystals and imbued with draconic magic. The portals are one-way, encased by barsion magic on the tethered world's side. In order to cross back and forth one must possess a Tel'k'shak, or Key of the Stars.

Silasia Vorcus *(*sil-ȯ-sēȧ' | vȯr'-cus *):* a powerful transmuter from Soroth. She is the head of that discipline and a council member of the Sorothian Magical Order.

Sildina *(*sil'-dinə*):* one of Amendal Aramien's former lovers.

sini'sha (sin-ē-shō'): a draconic breed of chromatic dragons, blue.

sloglien (slŏg'-lēn): a large mammal native to the Carda Wastes and the Black Mountains, whose brown fur is extremely tough. Their fur is often woven into sacks and bags meant to carry sharp objects.

solistum (sŏl'-ist-um): a mystical rock, often ground to powder, that inhibits magical effects, particularly healing. A wound caused by solistum cannot be restored by arpran magic.

Soroth (sòr'-ŏth): the capitol city of the island and nation sharing that same name. One of the larger ports in the Kalishir Ocean.

Sorothian (sòr'-ŏth-ē-en): a term for citizens of Soroth, the island, and the Principality of Soroth.

Sorothian Magical Order (sòr'-ŏth-ē-en): the original magical society established on Soroth, where all forms of magic were taught. It differed from many other orders because of its acceptance of necromancy.

Sortie of Hectilis (hec-til-ēs): a fictional military tale.

spiked xileran(s) (xil-ûr'-ən): snakes with rows of retractable spikes lining their backs. Their spikes are sharp enough that a mere prick can draw blood. Unlike most snakes, xilerans don't coil on top of themselves. They often rest around boulders or tree trunks.

Taidactin Code (tai-dak'-tin): an ancient methodology that combines the Aldinal Plane and the Visirm Expanse. The ideals of the Taidactin Code overcome the inherent weaknesses of both planes. They enable conjurers to access the creatures and objects they had trapped within the Visirm Expanse by using the replicating power of the Aldinal Plane.

Tardalim (tär-dò-lim): in myth, Tardalim is the eternal prison of damned souls, the Hell of Kalda. But in actuality it is a gigantic spherical prison created during the Dragon Wars. See "Tardalim's Structure" for a detailed description.

telekinetic magic: a sub-branch of the Manipulation Channel of Power that manipulates physical forces.

tevisral (tev'-is-rəl): any device capable of manifesting or channeling magic.

Teyvarn (tāy-värn'): a mercenary and member of Calimir's expedition to Tardalim.

Thousand Years War: a series of conflicts spanning over a millennium. It began when Cheserith, a red dragon, rebelled against his fellow Ril'Sha, seeking to lay claim to his right to rule all Kalda. It brought about a permanent schism between dragonkind. Among men it is commonly known as the "Dragon Wars" and is generally believed to be myth.

tirlatium (tir-latē'-um): a pale-blue transparent metal the Eshari elders claim is only found on Abodal. Possibly a byproduct of a crysillac transforming certain alloys.

tirlatium armor (tir-latē'-um): thin plate armor made of tirlatium. Transformative in nature, the armor can condense upon itself and rematerialize with a flash of pale-blue light.

Tor, City of: a large port city on the Kaldean Mainland, and former capitol of the Western Sovereignty. Recently independent from Mindolarn's annexing of the Western Sovereignty.

transmutative magic: a type, or Channel, of magic that changes the composition of physical matter from one state to another.

transmuter: a mage specializing in transforming matter through transmutive magic.

transportium (trans-port-i-um)**:** a tevisral capable of instantaneous teleportation to another transportium. It consists of a platform or dais, and four to seven focus orbs that project the magic. They are activated by key-words and not incantations, then lastly stating the destination.

trans-tube line: a type of underground transportation network used throughout Kalda before the reign of Karthar. Trans-tube lines connected to every major city and allowed the humans and elves of Kalda to travel cross continent in a matter of hours. All trans-tube lines in the human realm were sealed by Dorin, the Mage-King during his reign after the Karthar Empire fell.

troll(s): large creatures that inhabits the high mountains of Kalda. Although humanoid, they are more reptilian than mammal. Dark green scales cover their body, except for their underbellies which are a stretchy yet tough pale green skin. Their heads uniformly flow from their neck, like a snake. Four nostrils line their snouts. Their eyes are oval with curved hexagon-shaped pupils. Both arms are un-proportionally long, similar to an ape, with six claws tipped with sharp gray talons.

Tuladine (tū-la'-dīn)**:** a winged race of beings who are mostly gray in color. About half the size of a human, Tuladines have a humanoid torso, a tail, four wings—which are translucent—and a face with a trunk reminiscent of a sea horse. They are some of the longest living creatures on Kalda, some living as long as ten thousand years old.

Tuladine Tower (tū-la'-dīn)**:** a seven tiered structure within the Roost.

Ul'thirl (ūl'-thīr)**:** draconic for a seer's stone. An ancient tevisral for communication.

Uldric (ūl'-dric)**:** a necromancer from Soroth, a member of Calimir's expedition to Tardalim.

Ulk'sha (ūlk-shô')**:** the highest rank of warrior among the dragons of Kalda, particularly the pla'sha breed.

Umardin (ū-mär'-din)**:** a soldier turned adventurer in Calimir's expedition to Tardalim.

Umvilium (ūm-vil'-ē-üm')**:** a Tuladine fruit capable of keeping one awake for a considerable amount of time.

Unspoken One: a title for a prophesied man who has the power to wield magic without incantation. Throughout Kalda's history, no one but Cheserith could muster magic without incantation unless gifted an Orb of Power. Not even the most powerful of the dragons could perform such a feat. The prophecy tells of a man who would herald Cheserith's return, and to him would his power be given, particularly the ability to muster the Ko'delish without incantation.

usa'zin'sha *(û-sa'-zhin-shö'): draconic, one who infiltrates or spies.*

Usazma'thirl *(û-saz'-mə-thīr'): the draconic name for the city of the usa'zin'sha.*

Vabenack *(və-ben'-ök): an alternative dimension linked to Kalda, capable of showing one the past, the present, and the future.*

Vaem Rudal *(vām | rü'-dal): a Mindolarnian scholar well versed in her craft.*

Vaerym(s) *(vā-rim'): a ferocious breed of amphibious horned serpents. Vaeryms are large creatures, sometimes growing as long as eighty phineals. They often keep below ice sheets, only breaking through if a creature dares traverse the frozen surface. Their bodies are covered in dark blue scales and their heads are shielded by black shells ending in a glistening black beak.*

Vai'kassia *(vəi-kas-siə'): a female usa'zin'sha.*

Vargos *(vär'-gōs): a young barsionist aspiring to become an adventurer.*

Varquilus *(vär'-kē-laüs): the capitol of the Esharian Collective.*

Vasliran, Lake *(vas-lir'-an): a frozen lake on the Abodine Wasteland.*

Verdian *(ver'-diən): a mercenary from the twenty-fourth squad of Calimir's expedition to Tardalim.*

Verdin *(ver'-din): a fledgling necromancer from Soroth. She is a close friend to Vargos.*

Vesikar *(ves-ē-kär'): a region located in the Desolate Lands.*

Vidaer *(vi-daer'): a general from Mindolarn.*

Vigarian *(vīg-ə'-rian): an illusionist master at the Sorothian Magical Order. Ildin assisted him with his acolyte students.*

vik'sha *(vīk-shö'): draconic for "exile."*

Viliasim(s) *(vil-ē'-ə-sim): moth-like creatures native to the Abodine Wasteland. They feed off the crystal created by the crysillac and cause whatever crystal they touch to become luminescent. Their wings are white, sometimes pale-blue patterns adorn them. They also have four light blue tentacles protruding from the rear of their abdomen, about the length of a small finger.*

vis'ack *(vīs-ək'): a draconic curse word. A more vulgar word for bastard.*

Visage: *another name for the Messenger of the Promise, the Herald of Cheserith.*

Visalisan *(viz'-əl-ī'-san): a god who once walked Kalda.*

Visirm Expanse *(vis-ər'-m): another plane of reality, a timeless void used by conjurers to trap creatures and objects they wish to summon at a future time.*

Vorsim *(vör'-sim): a mercenary from the eleventh squad of Calimir's expedition to Tardalim.*

Warder of the Plains: *an Esharian who has devoted their life to the protection of Abodal (the Abodine Wasteland) and ensuring that no non-*

Esharian enters the frozen lands.

Warder's Grotto: a small den in the icy plains of Abodal (the Abodine Wasteland) used as places of resort by the Eshari Warders.

warming tevisral *(*tev'-is-rəl*):* a magical device capable of keeping objects warm.

Weldar *(*wel-där'*):* a soldier turned adventurer, and a member of Calimir's expedition to Tardalim.

Weslis *(*wes'-lis*):* a crewman aboard the *Giboran* and loyal companion to Captain Edara.

Western Sovereignty: a formerly powerful nation on the western side of the Mainland. Its capital was the coastal city, Tor.

White Duchess: Captain Kenard's sea vessel, made of a material that cannot rot nor rust. It has six decks, two above the main deck, and three masts.

Will: a manifestation of the Cherisium God. The divine guidance claimed by devouts of Cherisium. A direct communication with their god, Cheserith by either; hearing his voice, experiencing a vision, or a visitation from the Messenger of the Promise.

wizard: a mage specializing in destructive elemental and arcane magics.

World's Frown: a strip of ocean also known as the "Anomalous Corridor" where storms are said to be ever persistent.

wyvern: a winged serpentine creature, larger than a drake but still smaller than a dragon. They are also more burly than most of their dragon-like cousins.

Xu: the draconic name for the Arcane Channel of Power.

yaeltis *(*yel'-tis*):* burly creatures native to the colder parts of Kalda. They are cousins to trolls, but have thick white coats of fur. They also possess curved tusks that jut out from their lower jaws that are covered in lethal venom.

yaeltis venom *(*yel'-tis*):* an amber substance encrusting on a yaeltis's tusks and capable of killing a man in a quarter of an hour.

yidoth(s) *(*yid-ōth'*):* large feral felines native to the southern forests of the Mainland. The beasts are as long as a man is tall, their backs rising to a man's stomach. They are covered in green fur, and several breeds have dark brown spots or are lined with stripes.

Yvenna *(*ee-ven-nò'*):* one of Amendal Aramien's former lovers.

Zinerath *(*zin-ər'-ath*):* an ancient sword passed down from the leaders of the Kaldean Alliance. According to legend, it amplifies the soul of whoever wields it and can produce magic without incantation. Also known as the "Eon Blade."

Zulsthy'l *(*zül'-thil*):* an usa'zin'sha, and one of four leaders of the Guardians of Kalda. He is an Ulk'sha and the wielder of Zinerath.

Zu'mal'thisr'nsar *(*zü'-mal-thesr'-nsär*):* Zulsthy'l's father and one of four leaders of the Guardians of Kalda.

AUTHOR'S AFTERWORD

ROBERT ZANGARI

The tragedy of Amendal Aramien is a story that has lingered in the back of my mind for years. In fact, the earliest imagery for what would become the end of Part One and most of Part Two came to me in a dream before I ever started writing fantasy fiction, sometime between 2007 and 2009. I can still recall those images as if I had lived them myself.

The expedition's voyage along the icy shores of Abodal was exceptionally vivid, particularly the sailing through a tunnel of ice. Although I didn't dream of any nactili, the frozen bay left a distinct impression on me. I then saw a large band of adventurers move through icy caves, only to be halted at an impassable gorge, one that appeared bottomless. And then came the band's descent into a crystal labyrinth once inhabited by dragons but now abandoned.

When I started working with my father, I recalled those images but didn't put them to paper until I started coming up with Amendal's backstory, sometime in 2013. We needed an explanation for Amendal's madness, so I thought, "Why not be the sole survivor of an expedition gone wrong?"

In the first novel we ever published (*The Dark Necromancer/The Dragons' Legacy*), Iltar and his band came across three platinum dragons. As they prepared to attack, Amendal made a comment to the effect that he and Iltar could take on one of the three dragons all by themselves. That got me thinking about Amendal's capabilities.

From there I came up with several iterations of Amendal's tale. They were mostly the same: a sole survivor who battles a dragon and barely survives to tell the tale—except no one believes him.

While working on the companion novella, *Guardians of Kalda,* we gave a speculated origin of Amendal's madness, citing the substance solistum as a possible culprit. The context of the conversation dealt with the Ma'lisha, Nethon and why his voice was raspy. Solistum prevents arpran magic from working. Any living tissue that comes in contact with solistum, even immortalized tissue, cannot be healed by magic. But after careful consideration, we decided we wanted solistum to merely solidify his predicament, not cause it.

Ultimately, we knew Amendal needed to be cursed—as Cornar mentions in *A Prince's Errand* after Kaescis negotiates safe passage with the Wildmen. So, we went back to the drawing board.

Eventually, while designing aspects of Orath'issian's monster form, we happened upon our solution... partially. Cheserith had endowed many of his followers with certain abilities, making them gods over a particular element or an aspect of reality. "A god of terror," I remember saying to my father. "And instead of manipulating water or something like that, he makes people go insane—not by magic, but by a substance that physically alters one's mind. An orange haze."

But others would also be affected by the maddening mist. We were part-way through the novel when we came up with the Tuladine fruits: umviliums and kisalics. The Tuladine are otherworldly, and the vegetation within the Roost is different from what is currently spread across Kalda.

Much of Amendal's behavior in the original iteration of our series re-minded me of someone hyped up on caffeine. That inspired much of the umviliums' properties. They're essentially all-natural Tuladine caffeine pills.

Yet Amendal's situation still needed to be unique. So, we decided to combine the two substances. Amendal was the only person who ate the umviliums and succumbed to Orath'issian's innate ability.

Tardalim the prison has its own story, and you can read about it in the next section. But to boil it down, Tardalim's structure was inspired by com-bining a Rubik's Cube and multiple Dyson spheres in the form of shells nested inside each other to make a constantly shifting spherical puzzle, with each level adjusting at intervals that, when plotted, resembled an asymptotic curve. I know that's a mouthful... but that's what you get when two engi-neers design a fantasy setting.

Of all the novels we've worked on, *The Prisoner of Tardalim* has been the most challenging. But I'm glad we persevered. It was a tale that needed to be written, and the aspects of Kalda we've learned from it will make TA-LES OF THE AMULET all the better.

–Robert Zangari
Salt Lake City, 2018

Tardalim's Structural Analysis

This section contains spoilers for *The Prisoner of Tardalim*. Use your own discretion.

In several of our works published before *A Prince's Errand*, the characters have mentioned Tardalim. It was a place where Cheserith's allies were imprisoned prior to the use of the Amulet of Draconic Control. We had written about a couple of prisons on Kalda, one of which holds criminal mages. But for this novel I wanted to make something grander. One of the prisons we had designed was a cube, but Tardalim needed to be different. Unique.

I thought about different structures and liked the idea of a sphere with a type of artificial gravity pushing from its center. A person who stumbled into such a prison would wander forever through a never-ending, always-changing labyrinth.

Dyson spheres have always intrigued me particularly the shell concept when used as the habitat for an enormous civilization. So many people can fit on a sphere's (or shell's) interior—if some sort of artificial gravity can be maintained. The shell concept became the basis for Tardalim's structure.

But Tardalim needed to be smaller than a Dyson shell, small enough that it could be hidden on a planet, yet large enough to hold millions of prisoners. So, we came up with multiple layers, as if Dyson shell were nested within Dyson shell, like a set of Russian nesting dolls, matryoshka.

The idea for the Shift came about while I watched my wife play with her Rubik's Cube. I immediately saw Tardalim's labyrinth as a spherical puzzle. That made my head hurt at first.

Since it is hard for Amendal and the others to explain Tardalim's dimensions throughout the story, here are a few specifics that should help readers visualize the fabled prison.

Tardalim is one mile in diameter, with thirty-three levels/floors. The Roost, or Heart of the Sphere, is the thirty-fourth floor and is half a mile in diameter. The floors are eighty feet apart, despite the hallways being only forty feet tall (or four stories). That other forty feet is divided between five feet of floor, five feet of ceiling, and thirty feet of mechanisms that facilitate the Shift. There are eight stairwells on floors two through thirty-two: four ascending, four descending. The stairwells of Tardalim seem fixed, but they are also affected by the Shift, moving only when both floors' Shifts are harmonized. However, the stairs leading from the thirty-second floor to the thirty-third do not move. They are fixed, as Fench says, so one can always find their way to the Roost.

We wanted to increase the complexity of the structure to thwart anyone attempting to free the prisoners, so we decided to make the Shift occur at different intervals on each floor, starting with a twenty-four-hour interval on the first floor and progressing to a one-minute interval on the thirty-second floor. The thirty-third floor is stationary.

Now let's talk about size on the various floors. If the Shift aligned the halls on the first level so one could walk a straight line, the circumference would be 3.14 miles. There would be a slight curve to the floor, almost unnoticeable, with a one-degree change every forty-six feet. On the thirty-third floor the circumference is 1.57 miles, with a degree change in the floor every twenty-three feet. This is why Amendal notices the curve right before they enter the Roost, as the curve is more pronounced the higher one climbs (or the closer one gets to the center). You can get a good simulation of this by standing between two mirrors that face each other, then slightly angling the mirrors toward the floor. The reflection within the mirrors will look bowed.

So, we've covered distance and curvature of the floor. Now for the area. The total square footage of the first floor is 3.14 square miles, which translates into 87,538,176 square feet. That's just the first floor. There is a gradual decrease, but even on the thirty-third floor the total square footage is 22,023,936.

As Amendal and the others note, all levels of Tardalim look the same. When the prison was constructed, it was built in identical sections. Each section is 120 feet by 120 feet. Each section contains one corridor and one large room (or multiple small rooms within the same space as a larger room). Each section is the same size, like the individual squares of a Rubik's Cube. As with the floors and ceiling, the walls in these sections are five feet thick.

Tardalim's first floor has around 6,000 of these sections, and the thirty-second floor has 1,529 sections. Each of these sections, except on the first floor, contains cells for Tardalim's prisoners. A large room contains roughly 700 prisoners. By a rough calculation, Tardalim's second floor contains 4,356,000 humanoid prisoners. Floors two through twenty-four contain the humans and the qui'sha (and some of the other humanoid variants). Floors twenty-five through thirty-one contain the larger prisoners, dragons in their various forms. The most dangerous dragons are placed on the thirty-first floor, along with some Ma'lisha and the so-called gods of Cheserith's pantheon. No cells are located within the thirty-second or thirty-third floors.

Potentially, Tardalim can hold around 75,000,000 humanoid prisoners and 10,000 dragons. Exiling that many prisoners would be an arduous task—at best, requiring around fifty years, give or take a year or two.

Acknowledgements

We owe much of this novel's completion to David Farland (aka Dave Wolverton), *The New York Times* bestselling author of The Runelords saga. This novel would still be an idea floating around in Robert's head if it were not for Dave. Robert hadn't intended to write this story for quite some time, but after attending Dave's Master Plotting Workshop in Provo, Utah, in 2019, he realized that the novel *needed* to be written, and written *now*. Of the fifty scenes created from exercises in that workshop, thirty-five were included in the final draft.

Later in 2019, Robert attended Dave's renowned week-long "Death Camp" retreat in St. George, Utah, and took the first two parts of the novel for critiquing. He returned with some valuable insights that helped refine the story. Dave, your mentorship has been invaluable, and we truly appreciate you and your insights.

A heartfelt thank-you to our wives: Belinda and Tamila. Tamila, we appreciate your patience and encouragement, especially for allowing Robert to write some scenes while vacationing at Disneyland.

To our alpha and beta readers, Ginger, Chris, Arthur, and Joel: We love your feedback and enthusiasm! Thank you for all your suggestions.

Once again we're grateful for the wonderful team who has helped us bring *The Prisoner of Tardalim* to life. Kerem Beyit has captured our imagined story world and characters perfectly with his art. Kerem, your depiction of Fench perfectly matches the picture we've held in our heads for nearly a decade. We could not have asked for a better artist.

Linda, your guidance has been invaluable, and we truly appreciate your diligence in editing our work. You keep us on our toes.

We wish to give a special thanks to Michael Kramer, who has produced the audiobook edition of this novel and provided narration for the Kickstarter video. Michael, your voice has legitimized us in the fantasy genre. Thank you so much for making time to work with us. And a special thank-you to Kate Reading, who has worked behind the scenes with us during the entire production process.

Kickstarter Backers

And now we would like to acknowledge and give thanks to the following people who helped bring *The Prisoner of Tardalim* to life by contributing to our Kickstarter campaign. First and foremost we want to give a special thanks to those contributors who backed the project and our previous campaigns at the "Patron-for-Life" tier: Patricia Johnson, John Johnson, Devon Nelson, Becca Summers.

Abdul Hadi Sid Ahmed • /amqueue • Aaron M. Grieger • Adam D.J. Thompson • Alan • Ser Alexander of house Ourique • Amber Walsh • Andrew Council • Andromeda Taylor-Wallace • Anthony (Tony) Hernandez • Arthur "NightScribe" Fortune • Bartimaeus • Ben Nichols • Ben Bertolero • Bob Jacobs • Brandon Dickson • Brian Patton • Caleb Heuer • Catherine Holmes • Dr. Charles E. Norton III • Charles Spivey • Chau Huh • Christopher Heuer • Christopher J. Richard • Christian Meyer • Christopher Kranz • Cody Allen • Dain Eaton • Dale A. Russell • Danielle Riggs • Danny Soares • Dena Duff • Derek Duff • David Quist • Derek J. Bush • D.T. Read • Diane Kitevski • Doni Savvides • Doug Triplett • Duane Eisele • Dyrk Ashton • Edward Benitez • Elizabeth Davis of Dead Fish Books • Emilia Marjaana Pulliainen • Eric Travoli • Eva Hernandez • Frank Lee • Gary McGinnis • Gary Phillips • Gareth Burton • Gemini • Gerald Mistal • Gerald P. McDaniel • Gianna Pratten • Ginger Heuer • Gordon Milligan • Gordon Pfeil • Gordon Sturgeon • Hilary Anderson • Ian T. Rankine • Ivan Torres • Jacob White • Jake Odell • James Heuer • James McGinnis • Jay Smith • Jeff Heuer • Jennifer L. Pierce • Jennifer Poole • Jeremiah Crouch • Joann K. • Joel Baumgart • Joel Harris • Joel Norden • Joel Silvey • Johana Cheshire • John Idlor • John Morrissey • Jonathan Torres • Jonathon Whitington • John Jordan Schreck • Joseph Fleischman • Josette Gentile • Joshua Hardy • Joshua Preece • Kevin (BigO) Daniels • Kimberly Heuer • Larry Couch • Larry Lonsby Jr. • Lauri Ciani • Lee Phelan • Lily Heuer • Lyssa Spurgeon • maileguy • Marvin W. Weddle • Matthew Sonshine Moore • Mark C. • Matt Armstrong • Matthea Ross • Matthew Steinhaus • Matt Wolf • Michael Bakker • Michael Brooker • Michael Pulsipher • Michał Kabza • Mikael Monnier • Mortimer C. Spongenuts III • N. Scott Pearson • Nathan Memmott • Nicholas Liffert • P. Morin • Pedro Silva • Peter Hong • Phillip Huff • Phil Johnson • Pieter Willems • Pookie • René Schultze • Dr. Rich Williams • Robert C Flipse • Robert Felden Zimmerman • Robin Heuer • Robin Mayenfels • Robson • RtG Gary • Priotar • Russell Nohelty • Russell Ventimeglia • Ryan Buell • Ryan Coe • Ryan T. Drake • Scot Busby • Scott Maynard • Sean Caballero • Shannon Tusler • Simona Kao • Stacy Shuda • Steffen Nyeland • Stefke Leuhery • Stephanie Meier • Steven A. Guglich • Steve Locke • John Chattaway • Stuart Renz • Susan J. Voss • Teri Quigg • Troy Osgood • Vickie Smith • Wilhelm Rahn • Win Grawe • Wolfgang Steinmaurer • Zach Sallese • Zeb Berryman

ABOUT THE AUTHORS

Dan Zangari is the creator of the Legends of Kalda fantasy universe, a work-in-development since the early 1990's. He received a Bachelor's of Science in Aerospace Engineering from the University of Southern California and a Masters Degree in Systems Management. His love for science fiction and fantasy prompted the creation of this fantasy universe. When he's not writing he enjoys reading, watching movies, spending quality time with family and serving in his local church congregation.

Robert Zangari is the creator of the Legends of Kalda fantasy universe, a work in development since the early 1990s. He received a Bachelor of Science in Aerospace Engineering from the University of Southern California and a Master's Degree in Systems Management. His love for science fiction and fantasy prompted the creation of this fantasy universe. When he's not writing he enjoys reading, watching movies, spending quality time with family, and serving in his local church congregation.

Together, Dan and Robert have won multiple awards for their novel *A*

Prince's Errand: the 2019 Chanticleer International Book Awards in the OZMA (Fantasy) division, the 2020 Global Ebook Awards for Fantasy, the 2020 International Book Awards for Fantasy, the 2020 American Fiction Awards for Fantasy, the 2020 Best Book Awards for Fantasy, and the 2020 Royal Dragonfly Book Awards for Science Fiction/Fantasy.

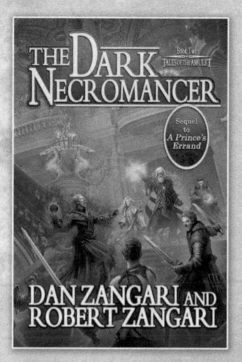